NO ONE RETURNS from the ENCHANTED FOREST

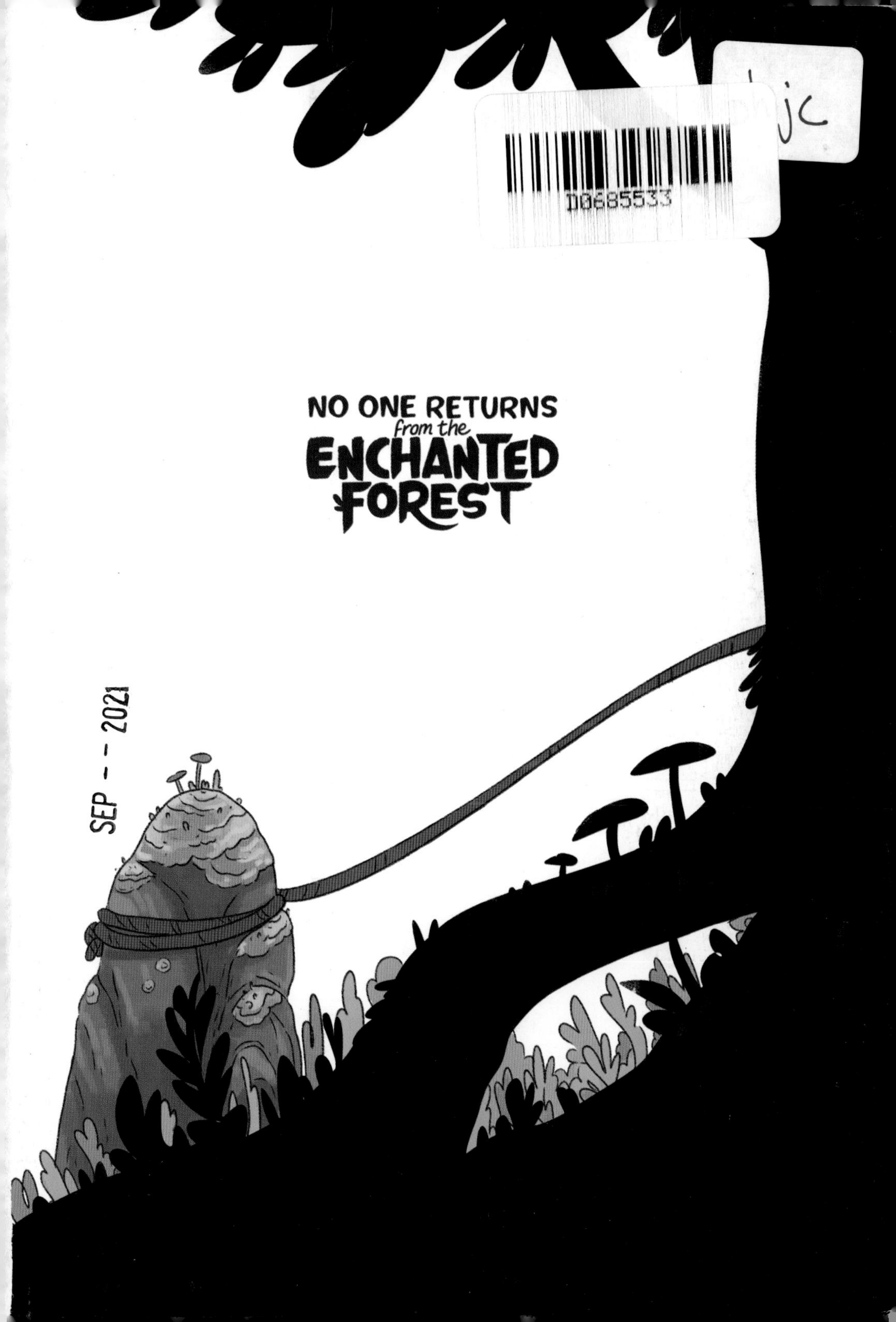

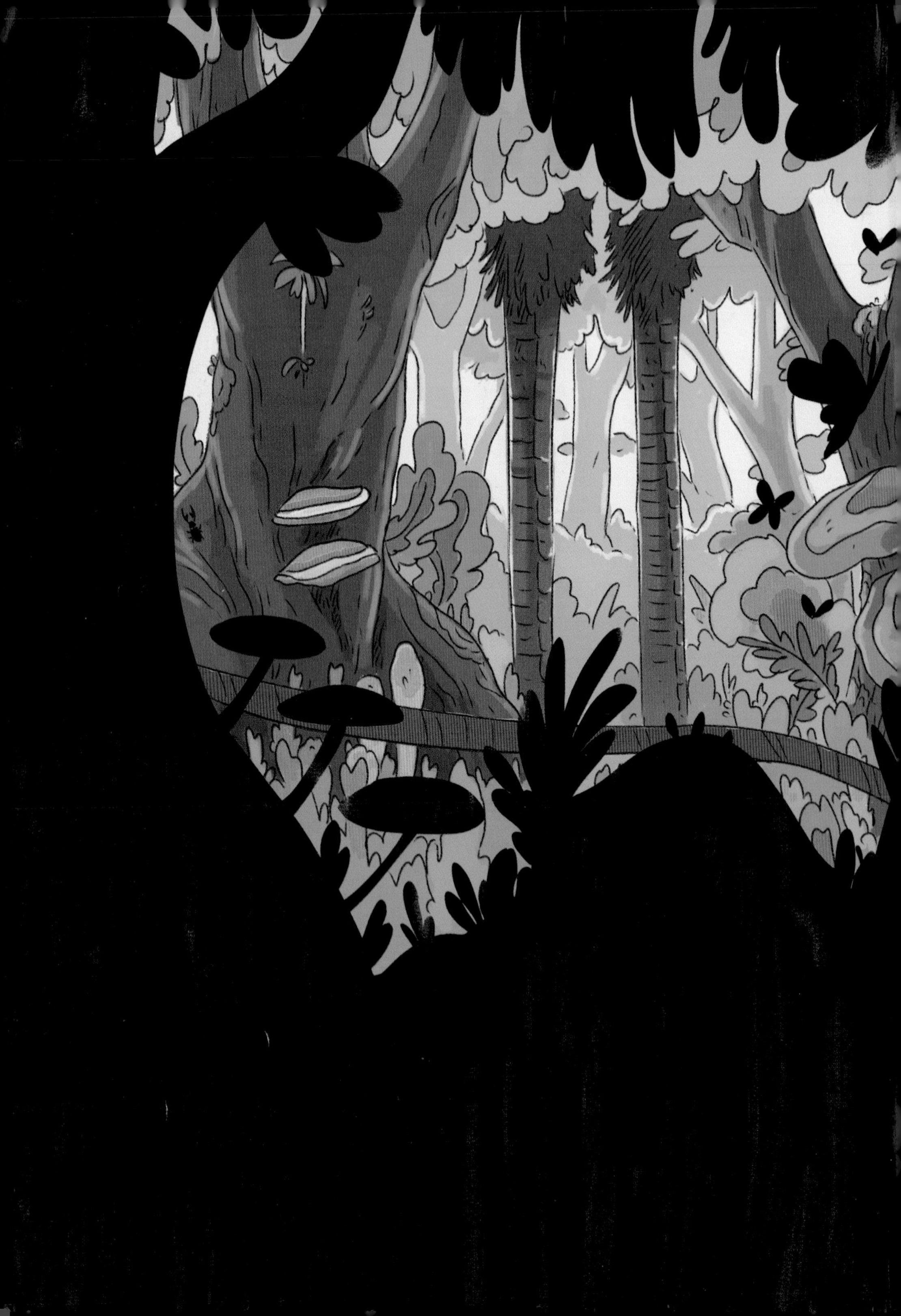

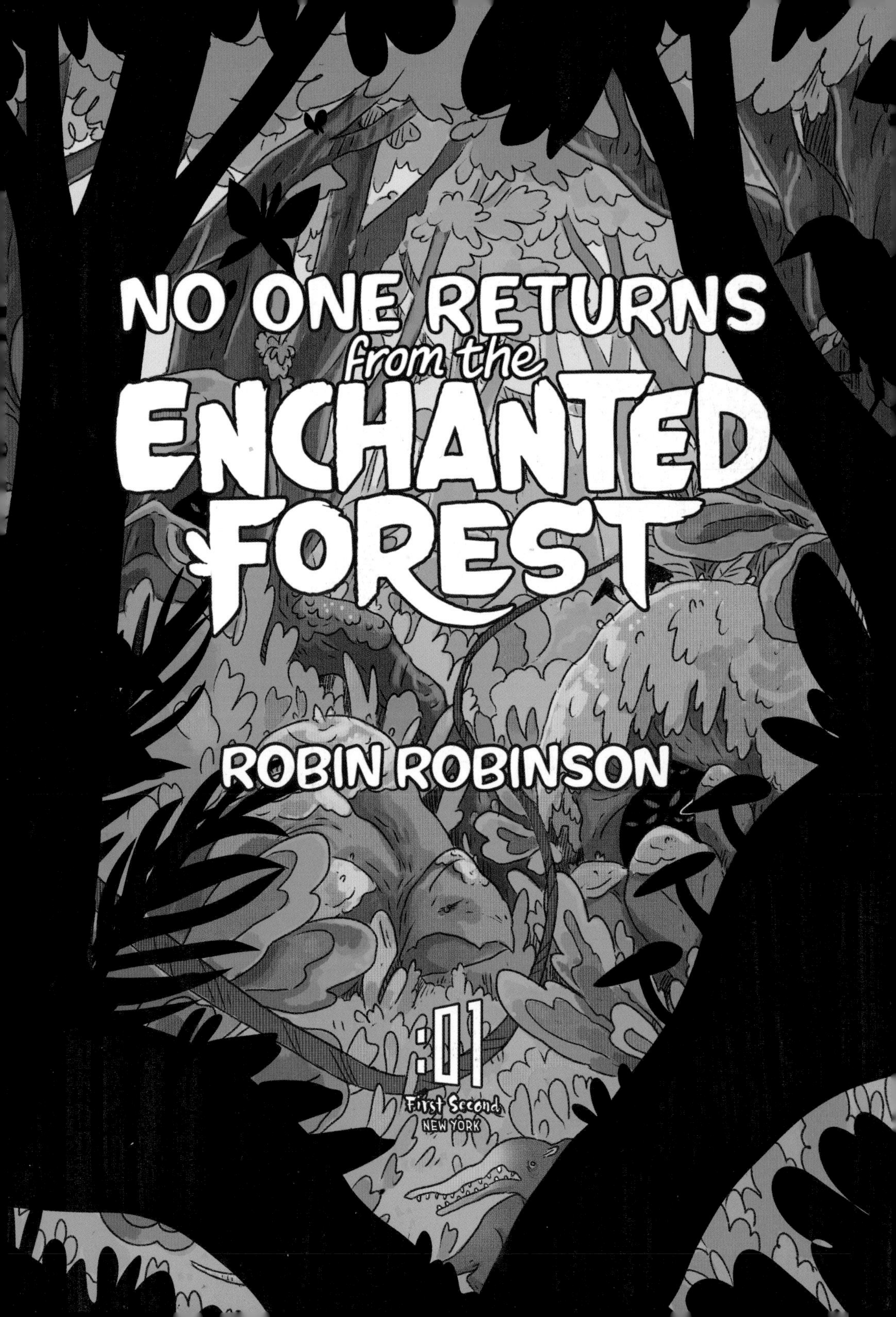

NO ONE RETURNS from the ENCHANTED FOREST

ROBIN ROBINSON

:01
First Second
NEW YORK

:01

First Second

Published by First Second
First Second is an imprint of Roaring Brook Press,
a division of Holtzbrinck Publishing Holdings Limited Partnership
120 Broadway, New York, NY 10271
firstsecondbooks.com
mackids.com

Library of Congress Control Number: 2020919818

Our books may be purchased in bulk for promotional, educational, or business use.
Please contact your local bookseller or the Macmillan Corporate and Premium Sales Department
at (800) 221-7945 ext. 5442 or by email at MacmillanSpecialMarkets@macmillan.com.

FIRST

EDITION

First edition, 2021
Edited by Robyn Chapman and Bethany Bryan
Cover design by Kirk Benshoff
Title design by A. L. Kaplan
Interior book design by Molly Johanson and Robin Robinson
Color assistance by Nathan Robison
Printed in China by 1010 Printing International Limited, North Point, Hong Kong

ISBN 978-1-250-21153-8 (paperback)
1 3 5 7 9 10 8 6 4 2

ISBN 978-1-250-21152-1 (hardcover)
1 3 5 7 9 10 8 6 4 2

Digitally penciled and inked in Clip Studio. Colored in Photoshop with custom brushes.

Don't miss your next favorite book from First Second!
For the latest updates go to firstsecondnewsletter.com and sign up for our enewsletter.

THIS BOOK IS FOR MY LITTLE BROTHERS, ALK AND JAK.
I WOULD DEFINITELY VENTURE INTO THE ENCHANTED FOREST FOR YOU.
(BUT PLEASE DON'T MAKE ME--I'M NOT THAT GOOD AT KNITTING!)

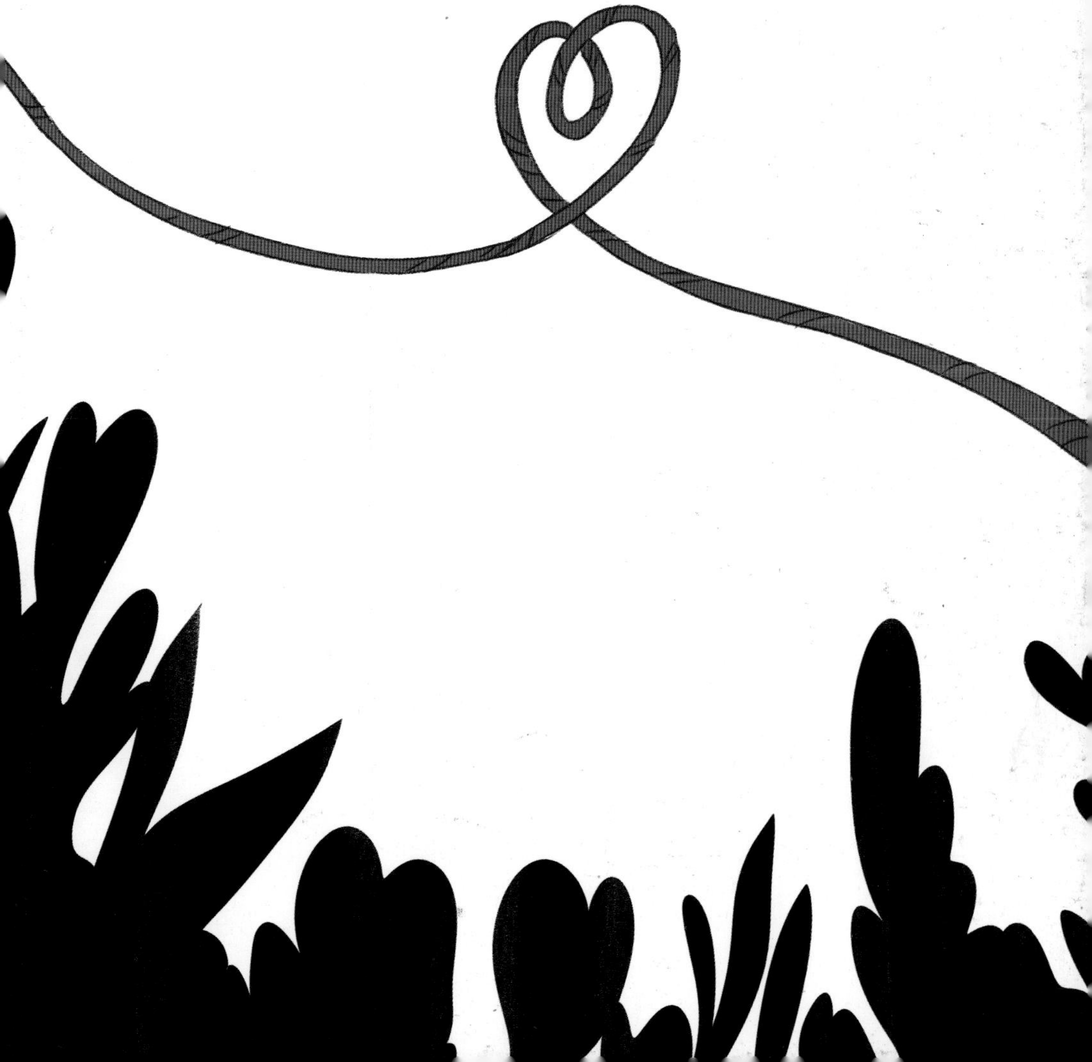

CHAPTER
ONE
PELLA

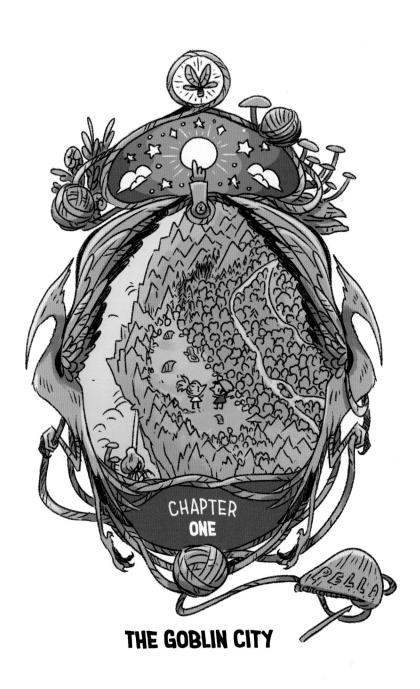

THE GOBLIN CITY

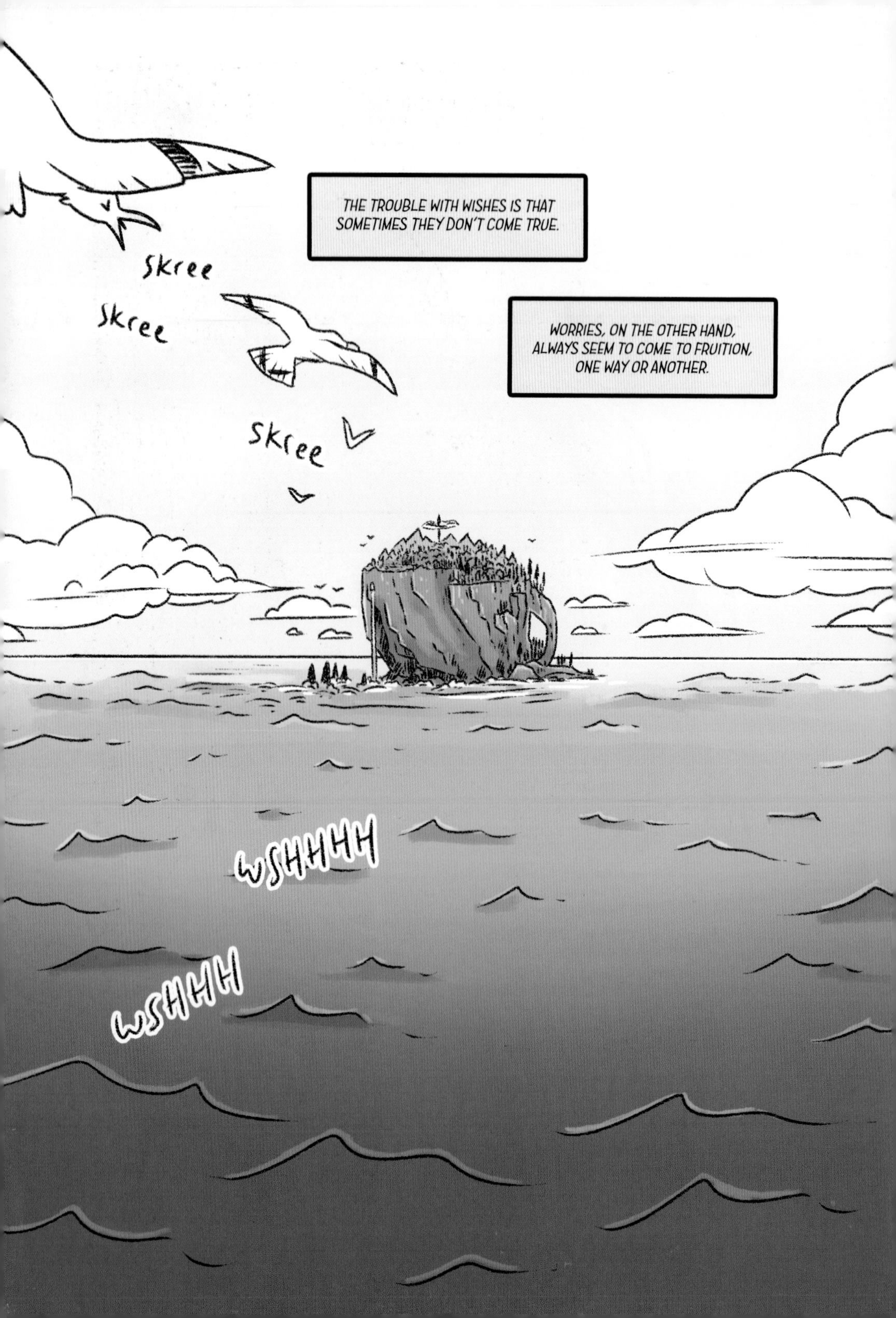
THE TROUBLE WITH WISHES IS THAT SOMETIMES THEY DON'T COME TRUE.
WORRIES, ON THE OTHER HAND, ALWAYS SEEM TO COME TO FRUITION, ONE WAY OR ANOTHER.
SKREE
SKREE
SKREE
WSHHHH
WSHHH

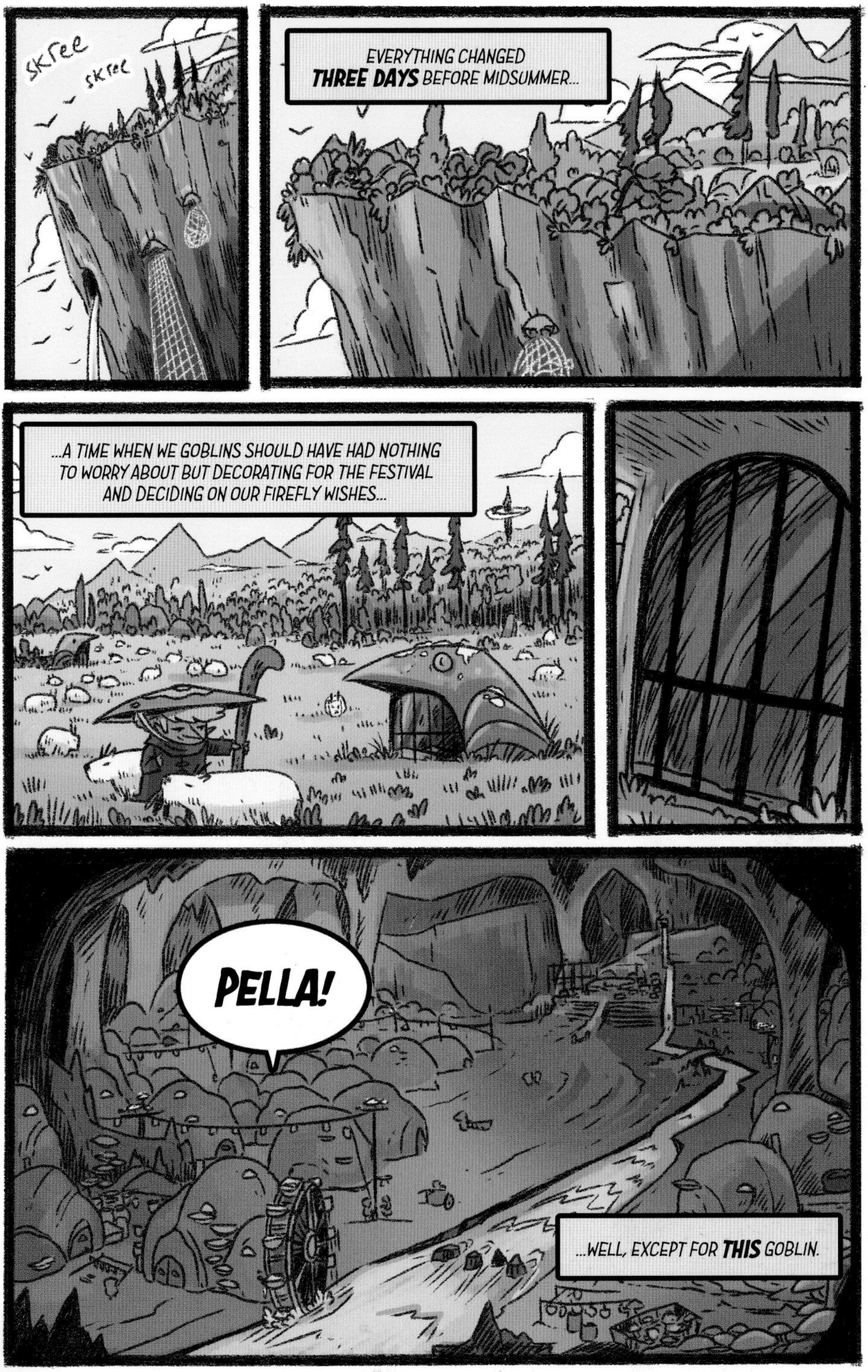
skree
skree
EVERYTHING CHANGED **THREE DAYS** BEFORE MIDSUMMER...
...A TIME WHEN WE GOBLINS SHOULD HAVE HAD NOTHING TO WORRY ABOUT BUT DECORATING FOR THE FESTIVAL AND DECIDING ON OUR FIREFLY WISHES...
PELLA!
...WELL, EXCEPT FOR **THIS** GOBLIN.

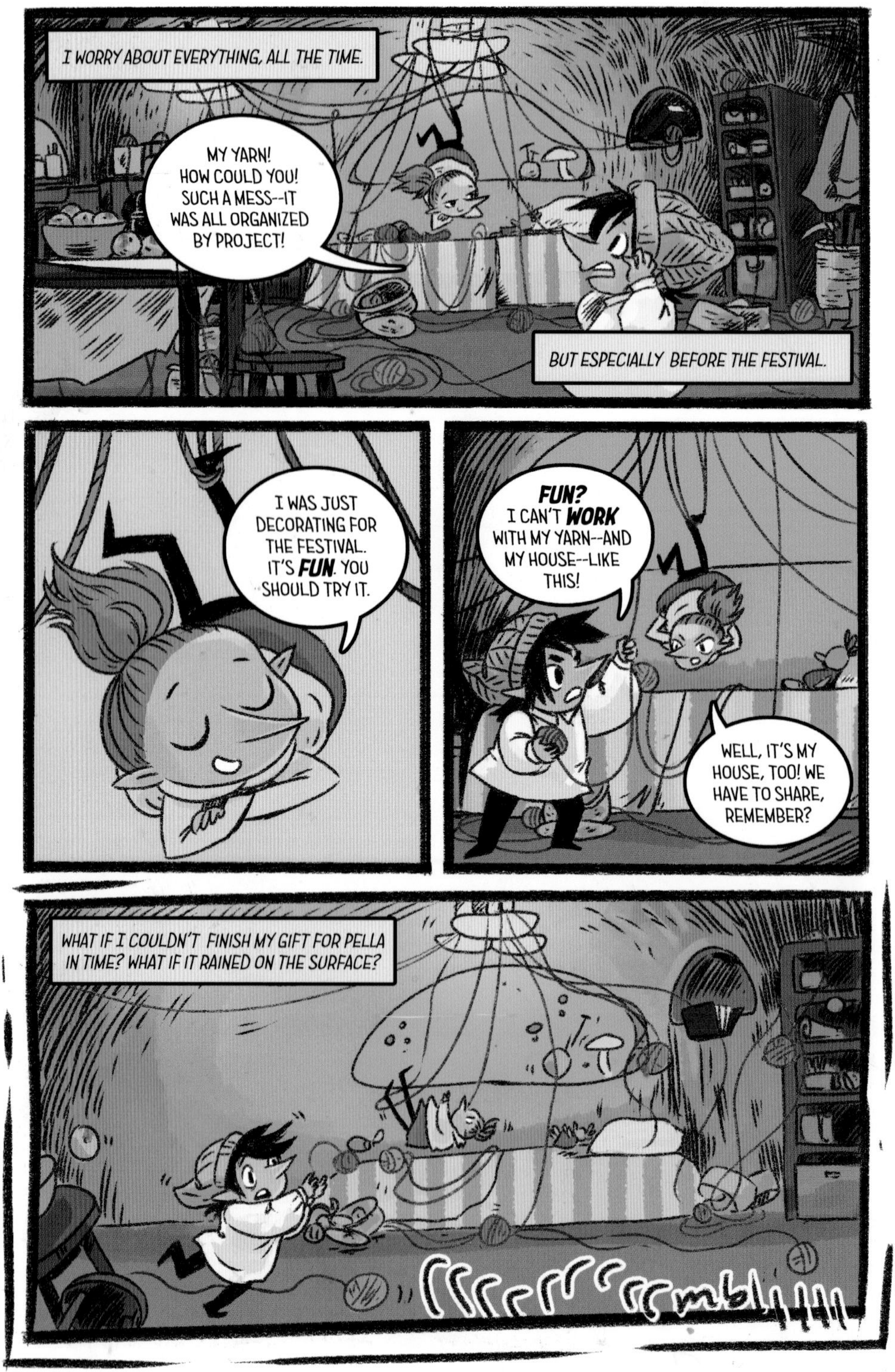
I WORRY ABOUT EVERYTHING, ALL THE TIME.
MY YARN! HOW COULD YOU! SUCH A MESS--IT WAS ALL ORGANIZED BY PROJECT!
BUT ESPECIALLY BEFORE THE FESTIVAL.
I WAS JUST DECORATING FOR THE FESTIVAL. IT'S **FUN**. YOU SHOULD TRY IT.
FUN? I CAN'T **WORK** WITH MY YARN--AND MY HOUSE--LIKE THIS!
WELL, IT'S MY HOUSE, TOO! WE HAVE TO SHARE, REMEMBER?
WHAT IF I COULDN'T FINISH MY GIFT FOR PELLA IN TIME? WHAT IF IT RAINED ON THE SURFACE?

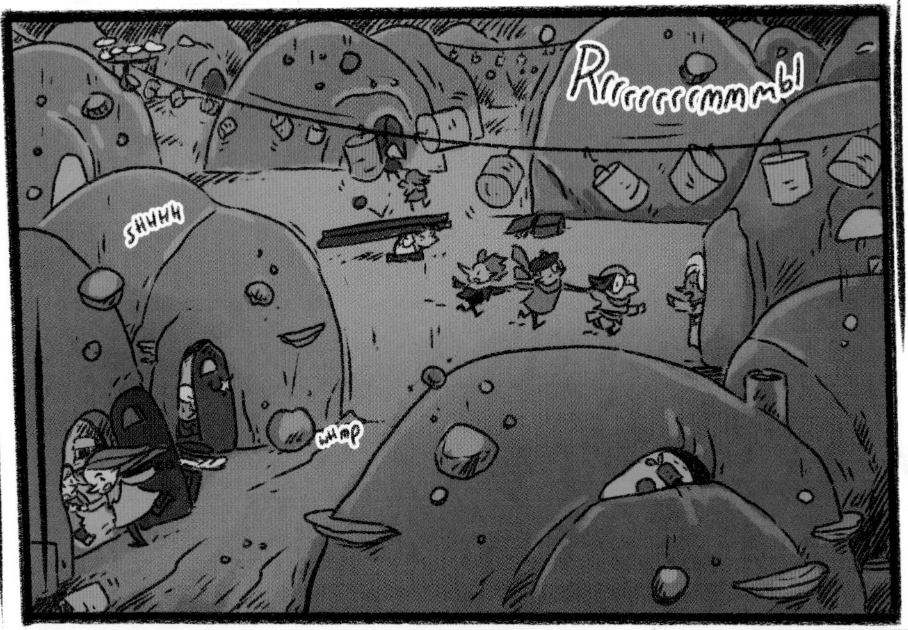
Rrrrrrrrmmmmbl
SHHHH
WHMP

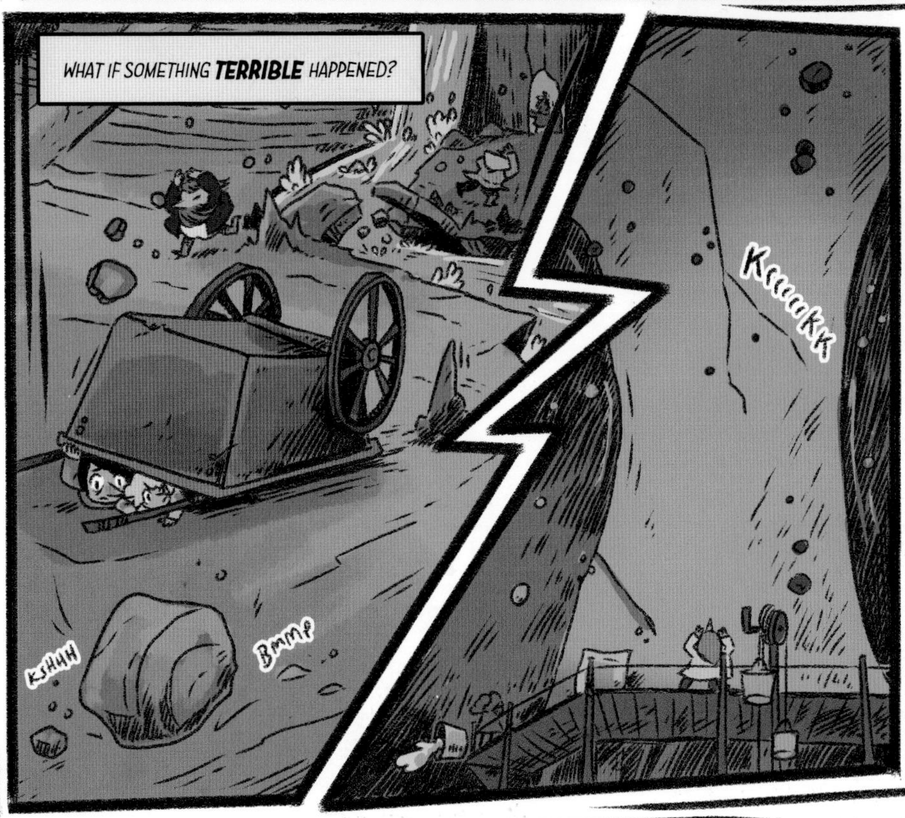
WHAT IF SOMETHING **TERRIBLE** HAPPENED?
KRRRRRKK
KSHHH
BMMP

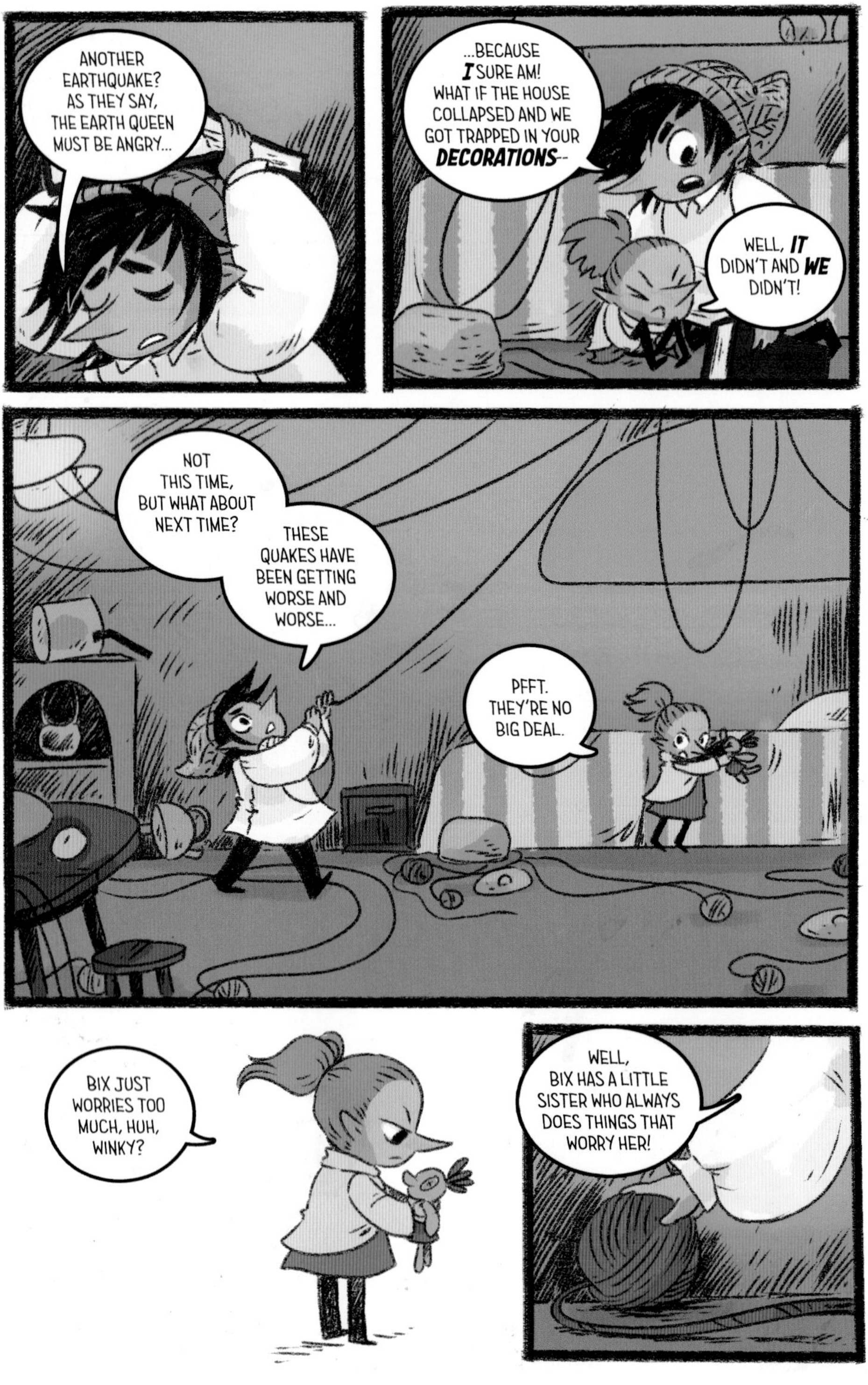
ANOTHER EARTHQUAKE? AS THEY SAY, THE EARTH QUEEN MUST BE ANGRY...
...BECAUSE ***I*** SURE AM! WHAT IF THE HOUSE COLLAPSED AND WE GOT TRAPPED IN YOUR ***DECORATIONS***--
WELL, ***IT*** DIDN'T AND ***WE*** DIDN'T!
NOT THIS TIME, BUT WHAT ABOUT NEXT TIME?
THESE QUAKES HAVE BEEN GETTING WORSE AND WORSE...
PFFT. THEY'RE NO BIG DEAL.
BIX JUST WORRIES TOO MUCH, HUH, WINKY?
WELL, BIX HAS A LITTLE SISTER WHO ALWAYS DOES THINGS THAT WORRY HER!

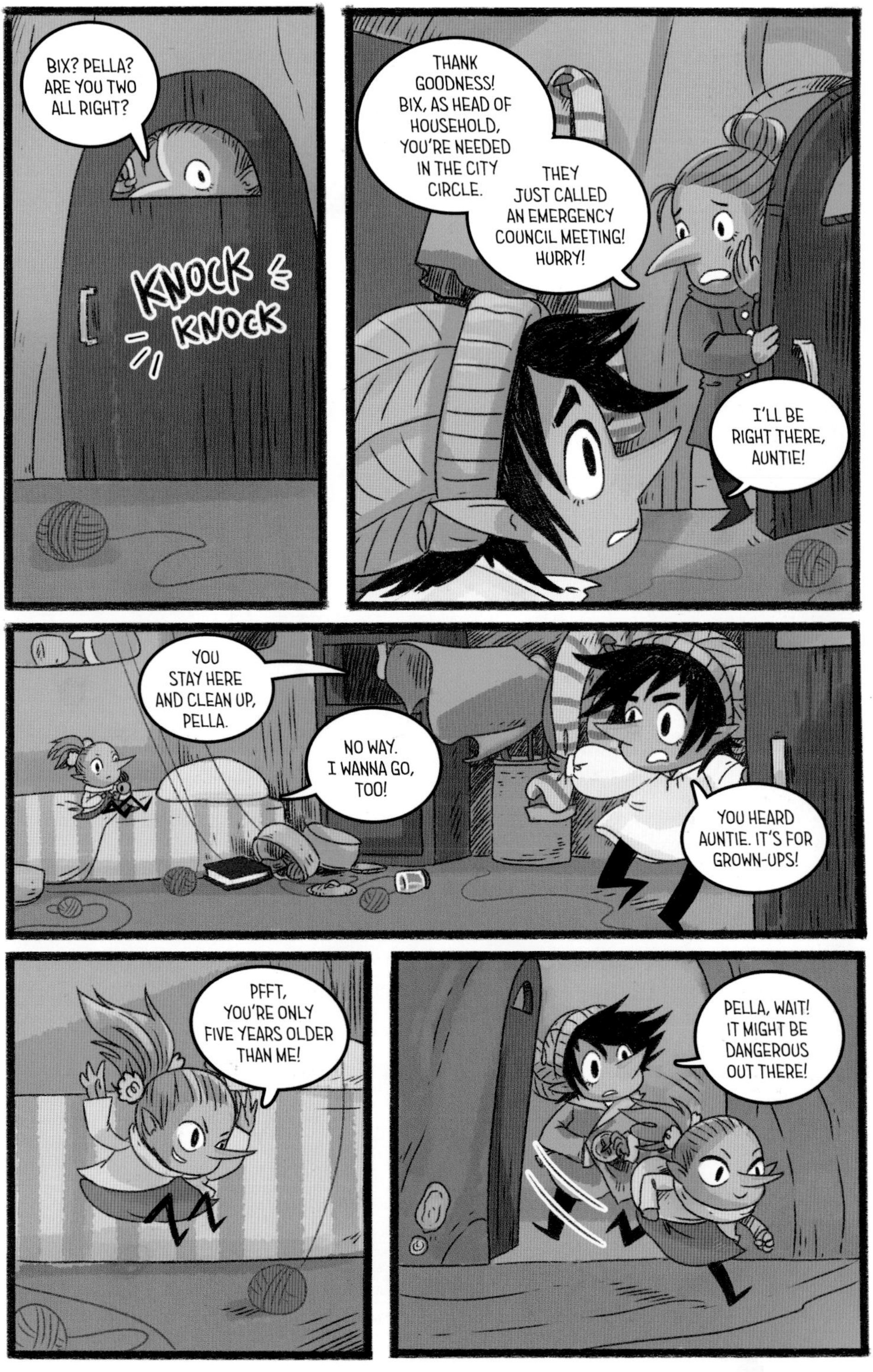
BIX? PELLA? ARE YOU TWO ALL RIGHT?
KNOCK KNOCK
THANK GOODNESS! BIX, AS HEAD OF HOUSEHOLD, YOU'RE NEEDED IN THE CITY CIRCLE.
THEY JUST CALLED AN EMERGENCY COUNCIL MEETING! HURRY!
I'LL BE RIGHT THERE, AUNTIE!
YOU STAY HERE AND CLEAN UP, PELLA.
NO WAY. I WANNA GO, TOO!
YOU HEARD AUNTIE. IT'S FOR GROWN-UPS!
PFFT, YOU'RE ONLY FIVE YEARS OLDER THAN ME!
PELLA, WAIT! IT MIGHT BE DANGEROUS OUT THERE!

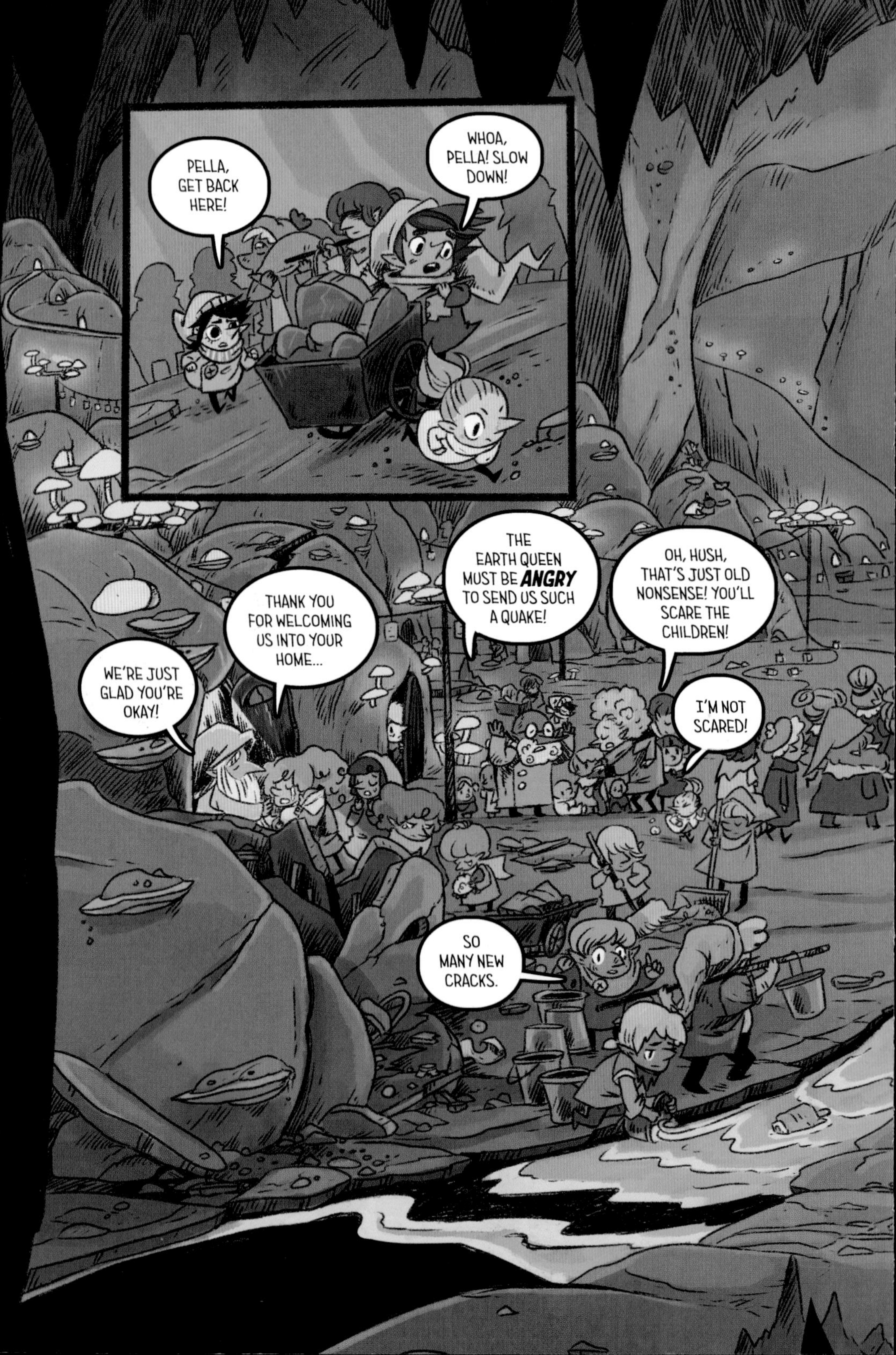
PELLA, GET BACK HERE!
WHOA, PELLA! SLOW DOWN!
WE'RE JUST GLAD YOU'RE OKAY!
THANK YOU FOR WELCOMING US INTO YOUR HOME...
THE EARTH QUEEN MUST BE ANGRY TO SEND US SUCH A QUAKE!
OH, HUSH, THAT'S JUST OLD NONSENSE! YOU'LL SCARE THE CHILDREN!
I'M NOT SCARED!
SO MANY NEW CRACKS.

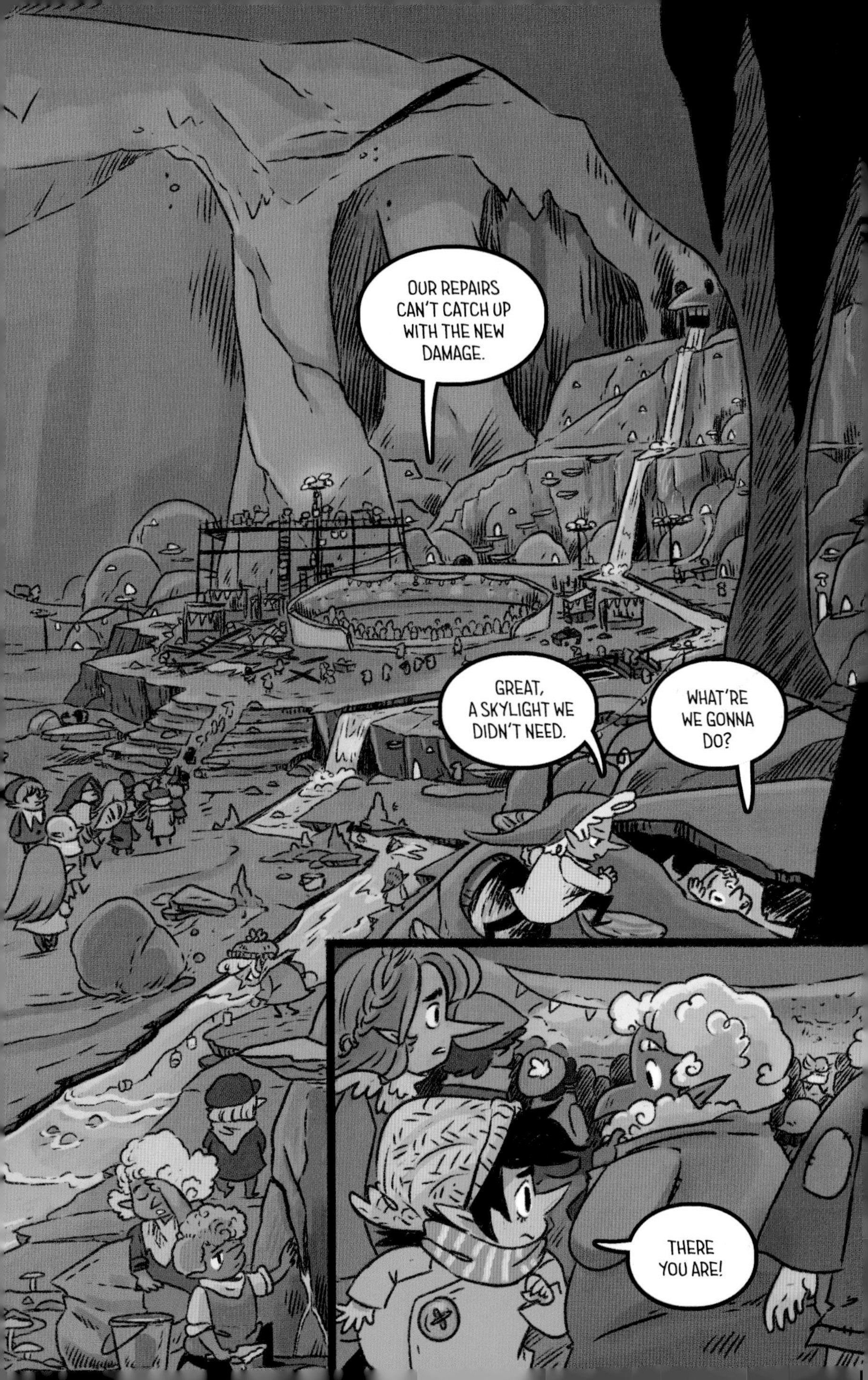
OUR REPAIRS CAN'T CATCH UP WITH THE NEW DAMAGE.
GREAT, A SKYLIGHT WE DIDN'T NEED.
WHAT'RE WE GONNA DO?
THERE YOU ARE!

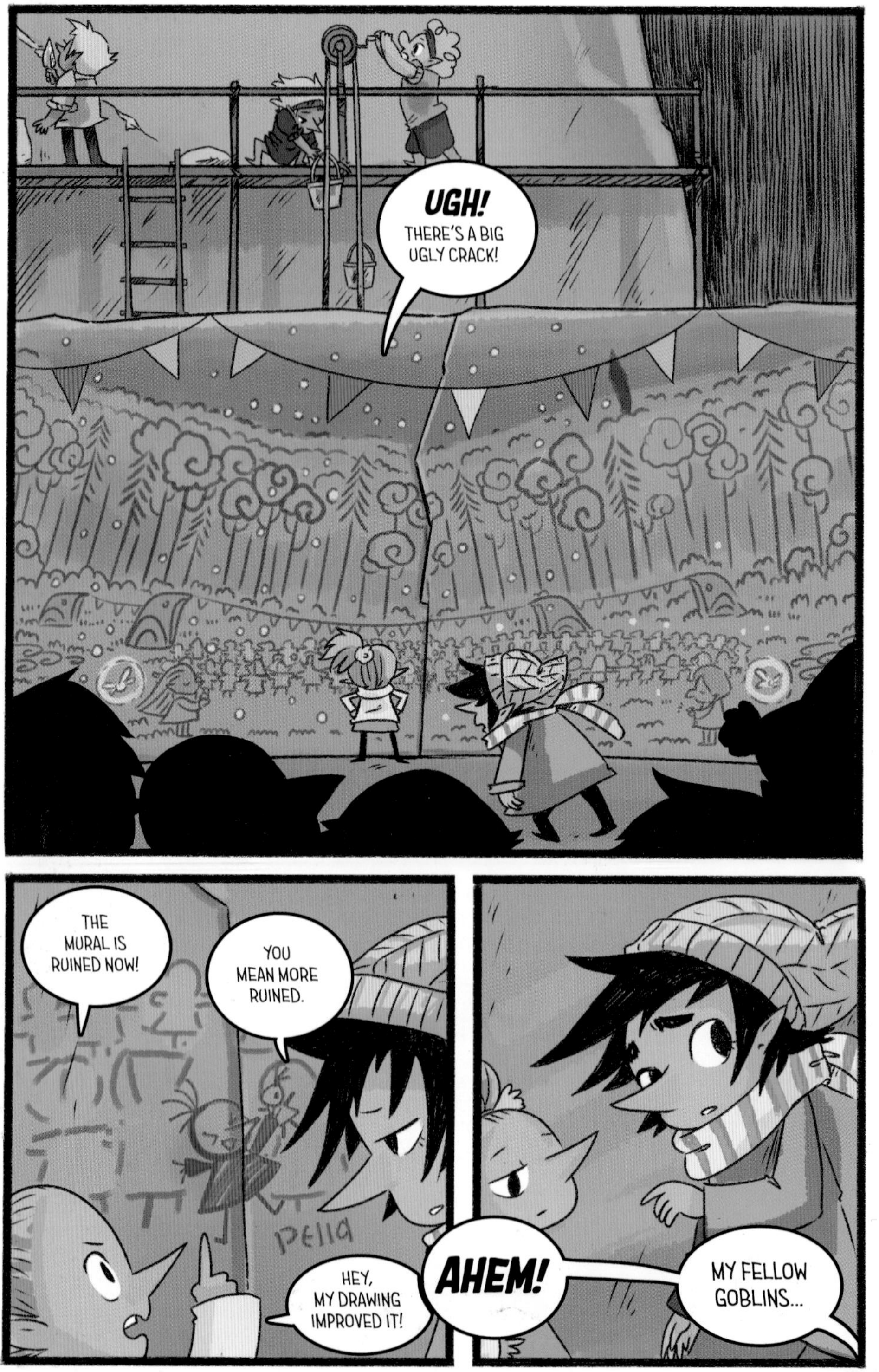
UGH!
THERE'S A BIG UGLY CRACK!
THE MURAL IS RUINED NOW!
YOU MEAN MORE RUINED.
Pella
HEY, MY DRAWING IMPROVED IT!
AHEM!
MY FELLOW GOBLINS...

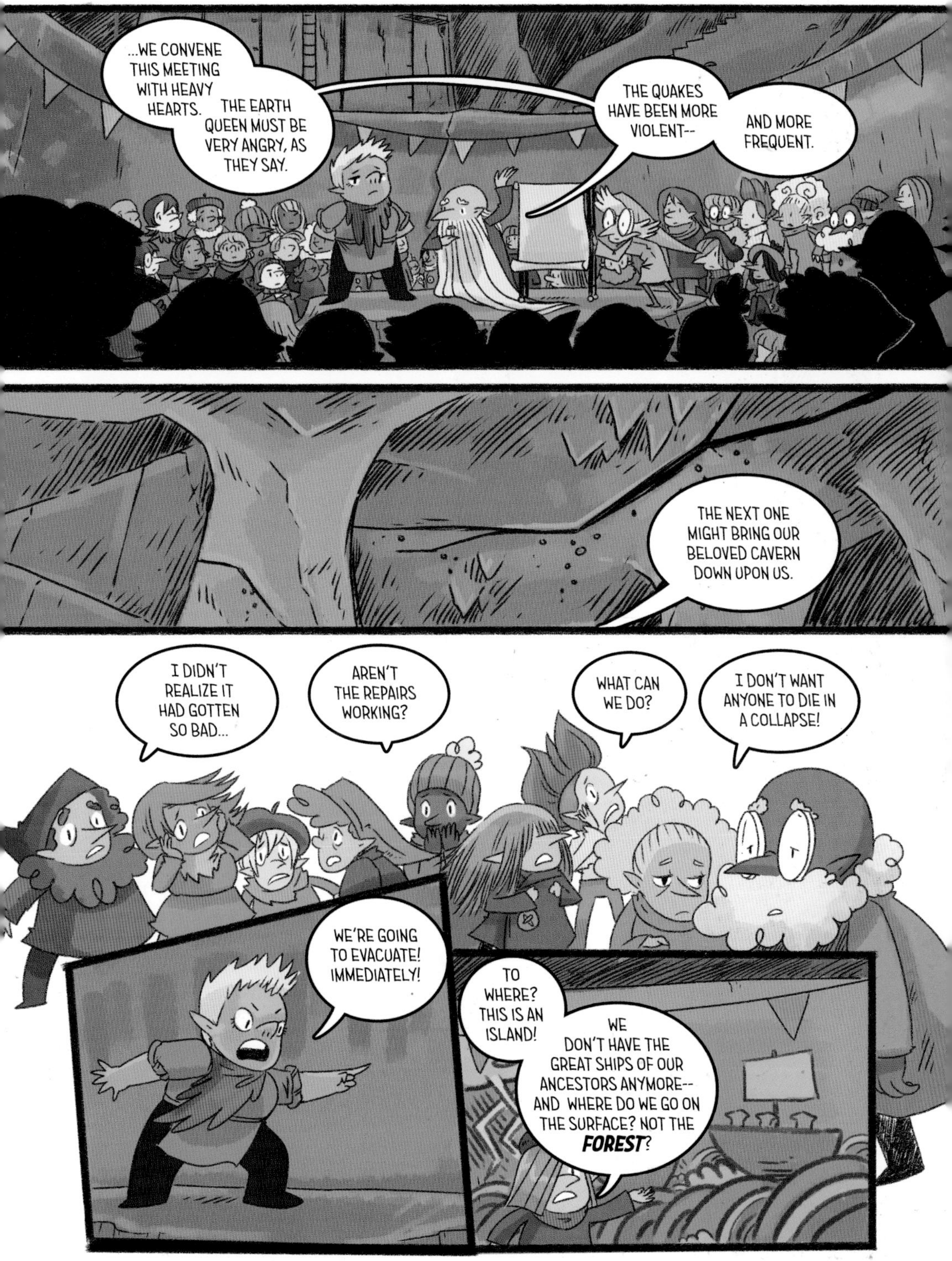

...WE CONVENE THIS MEETING WITH HEAVY HEARTS.
THE EARTH QUEEN MUST BE VERY ANGRY, AS THEY SAY.
THE QUAKES HAVE BEEN MORE VIOLENT--
AND MORE FREQUENT.
THE NEXT ONE MIGHT BRING OUR BELOVED CAVERN DOWN UPON US.
I DIDN'T REALIZE IT HAD GOTTEN SO BAD...
AREN'T THE REPAIRS WORKING?
WHAT CAN WE DO?
I DON'T WANT ANYONE TO DIE IN A COLLAPSE!
WE'RE GOING TO EVACUATE! IMMEDIATELY!
TO WHERE? THIS IS AN ISLAND!
WE DON'T HAVE THE GREAT SHIPS OF OUR ANCESTORS ANYMORE-- AND WHERE DO WE GO ON THE SURFACE? NOT THE FOREST?

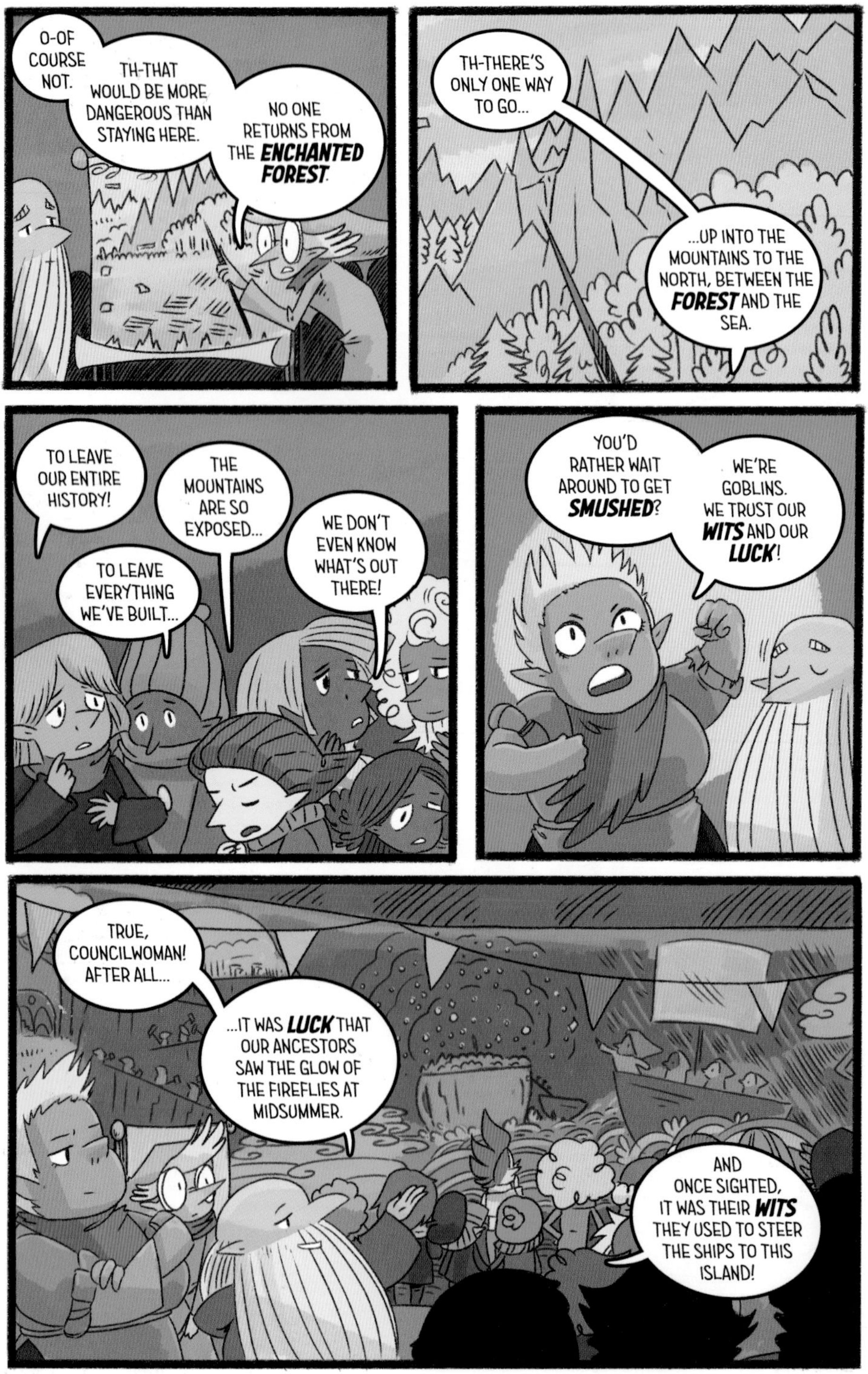
O-OF COURSE NOT.
TH-THAT WOULD BE MORE DANGEROUS THAN STAYING HERE.
NO ONE RETURNS FROM THE **ENCHANTED FOREST**.
TH-THERE'S ONLY ONE WAY TO GO...
...UP INTO THE MOUNTAINS TO THE NORTH, BETWEEN THE **FOREST** AND THE SEA.
TO LEAVE OUR ENTIRE HISTORY!
TO LEAVE EVERYTHING WE'VE BUILT...
THE MOUNTAINS ARE SO EXPOSED...
WE DON'T EVEN KNOW WHAT'S OUT THERE!
YOU'D RATHER WAIT AROUND TO GET **SMUSHED**?
WE'RE GOBLINS. WE TRUST OUR **WITS** AND OUR **LUCK**!
TRUE, COUNCILWOMAN! AFTER ALL...
...IT WAS **LUCK** THAT OUR ANCESTORS SAW THE GLOW OF THE FIREFLIES AT MIDSUMMER.
AND ONCE SIGHTED, IT WAS THEIR **WITS** THEY USED TO STEER THE SHIPS TO THIS ISLAND!

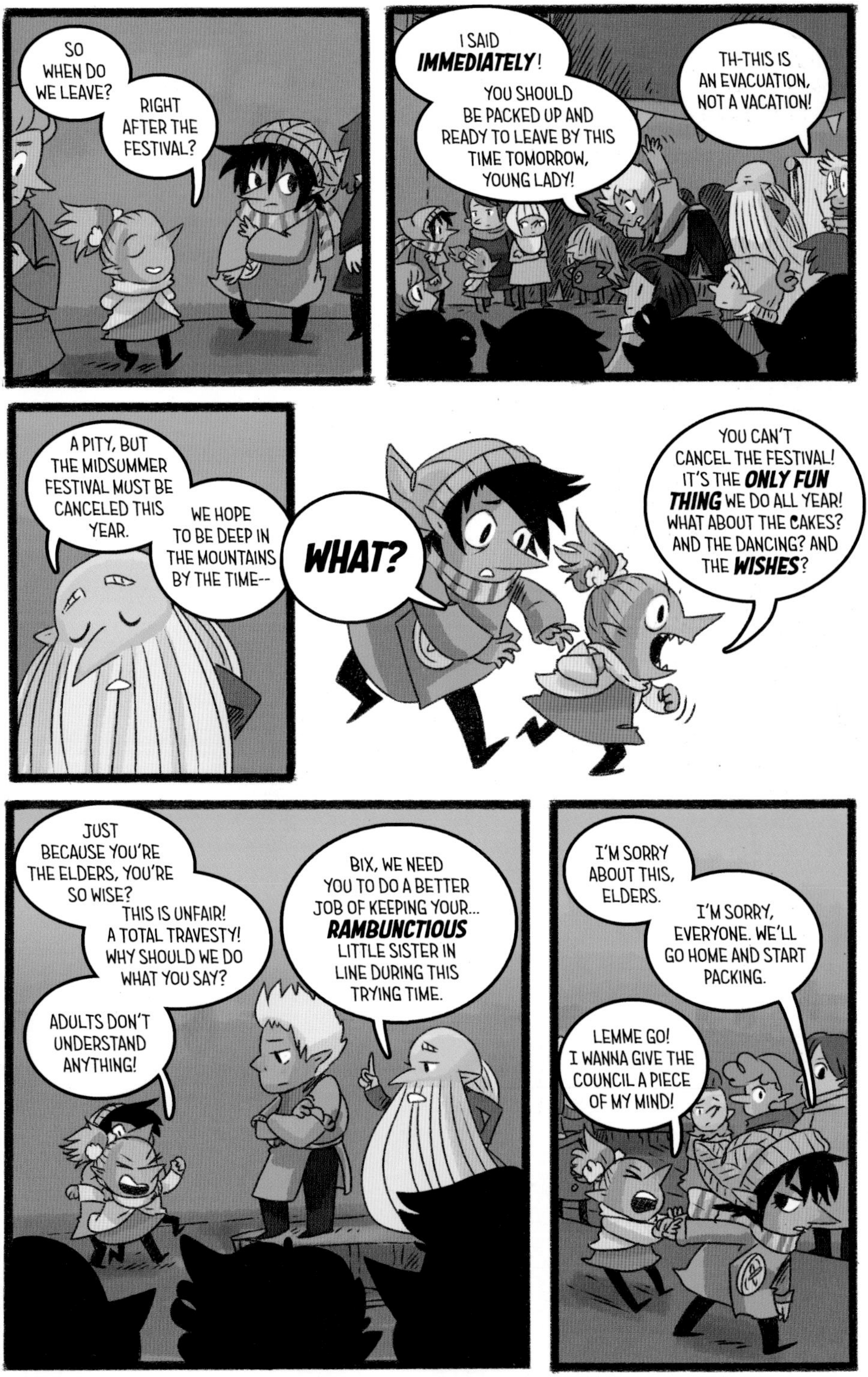
SO WHEN DO WE LEAVE?
RIGHT AFTER THE FESTIVAL?
I SAID IMMEDIATELY!
YOU SHOULD BE PACKED UP AND READY TO LEAVE BY THIS TIME TOMORROW, YOUNG LADY!
TH-THIS IS AN EVACUATION, NOT A VACATION!
A PITY, BUT THE MIDSUMMER FESTIVAL MUST BE CANCELED THIS YEAR.
WE HOPE TO BE DEEP IN THE MOUNTAINS BY THE TIME--
WHAT?
YOU CAN'T CANCEL THE FESTIVAL! IT'S THE ONLY FUN THING WE DO ALL YEAR! WHAT ABOUT THE CAKES? AND THE DANCING? AND THE WISHES?
JUST BECAUSE YOU'RE THE ELDERS, YOU'RE SO WISE?
THIS IS UNFAIR! A TOTAL TRAVESTY! WHY SHOULD WE DO WHAT YOU SAY?
ADULTS DON'T UNDERSTAND ANYTHING!
BIX, WE NEED YOU TO DO A BETTER JOB OF KEEPING YOUR... RAMBUNCTIOUS LITTLE SISTER IN LINE DURING THIS TRYING TIME.
I'M SORRY ABOUT THIS, ELDERS.
I'M SORRY, EVERYONE. WE'LL GO HOME AND START PACKING.
LEMME GO! I WANNA GIVE THE COUNCIL A PIECE OF MY MIND!

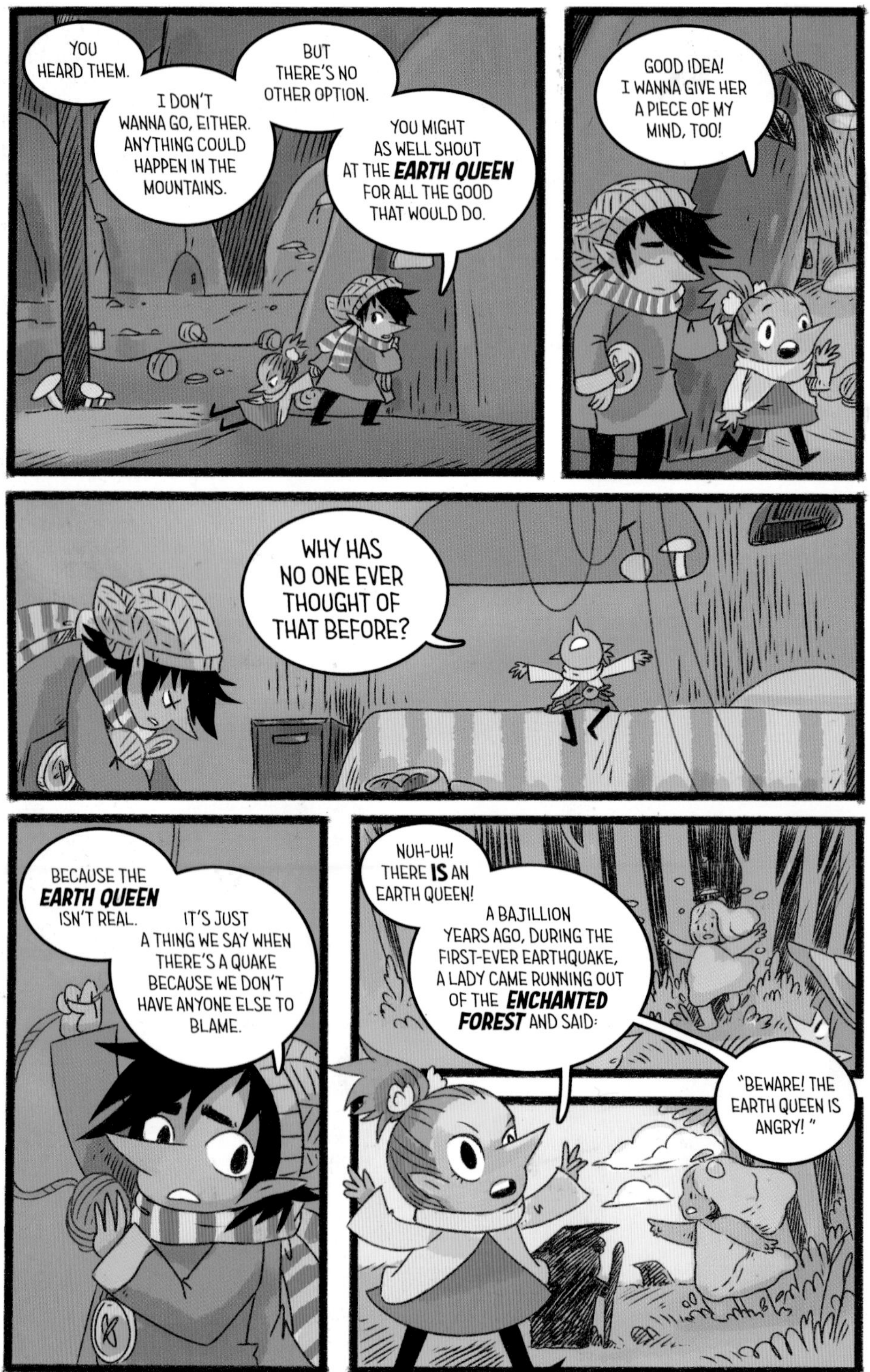
YOU HEARD THEM.
I DON'T WANNA GO, EITHER. ANYTHING COULD HAPPEN IN THE MOUNTAINS.
BUT THERE'S NO OTHER OPTION.
YOU MIGHT AS WELL SHOUT AT THE EARTH QUEEN FOR ALL THE GOOD THAT WOULD DO.
GOOD IDEA! I WANNA GIVE HER A PIECE OF MY MIND, TOO!
WHY HAS NO ONE EVER THOUGHT OF THAT BEFORE?
BECAUSE THE EARTH QUEEN ISN'T REAL.
IT'S JUST A THING WE SAY WHEN THERE'S A QUAKE BECAUSE WE DON'T HAVE ANYONE ELSE TO BLAME.
NUH-UH! THERE IS AN EARTH QUEEN!
A BAJILLION YEARS AGO, DURING THE FIRST-EVER EARTHQUAKE, A LADY CAME RUNNING OUT OF THE ENCHANTED FOREST AND SAID:
"BEWARE! THE EARTH QUEEN IS ANGRY!"

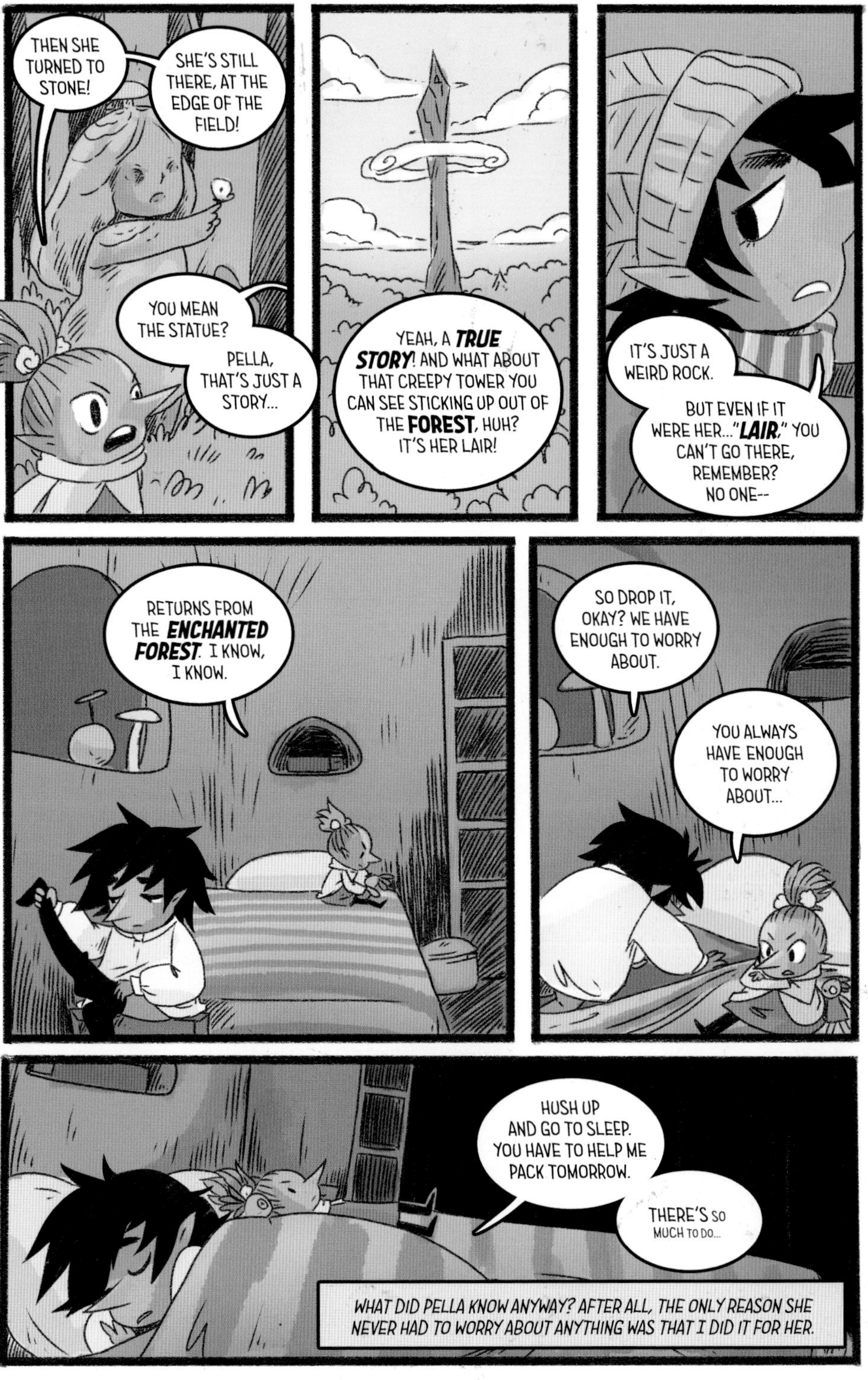

THEN SHE TURNED TO STONE!
SHE'S STILL THERE, AT THE EDGE OF THE FIELD!
YOU MEAN THE STATUE?
PELLA, THAT'S JUST A STORY...
YEAH, A **TRUE STORY**! AND WHAT ABOUT THAT CREEPY TOWER YOU CAN SEE STICKING UP OUT OF THE **FOREST**, HUH? IT'S HER LAIR!
IT'S JUST A WEIRD ROCK.
BUT EVEN IF IT WERE HER..."**LAIR**," YOU CAN'T GO THERE, REMEMBER? NO ONE--
RETURNS FROM THE **ENCHANTED FOREST**. I KNOW, I KNOW.
SO DROP IT, OKAY? WE HAVE ENOUGH TO WORRY ABOUT.
YOU ALWAYS HAVE ENOUGH TO WORRY ABOUT...
HUSH UP AND GO TO SLEEP. YOU HAVE TO HELP ME PACK TOMORROW.
THERE'S SO MUCH TO DO...
WHAT DID PELLA KNOW ANYWAY? AFTER ALL, THE ONLY REASON SHE NEVER HAD TO WORRY ABOUT ANYTHING WAS THAT I DID IT FOR HER.

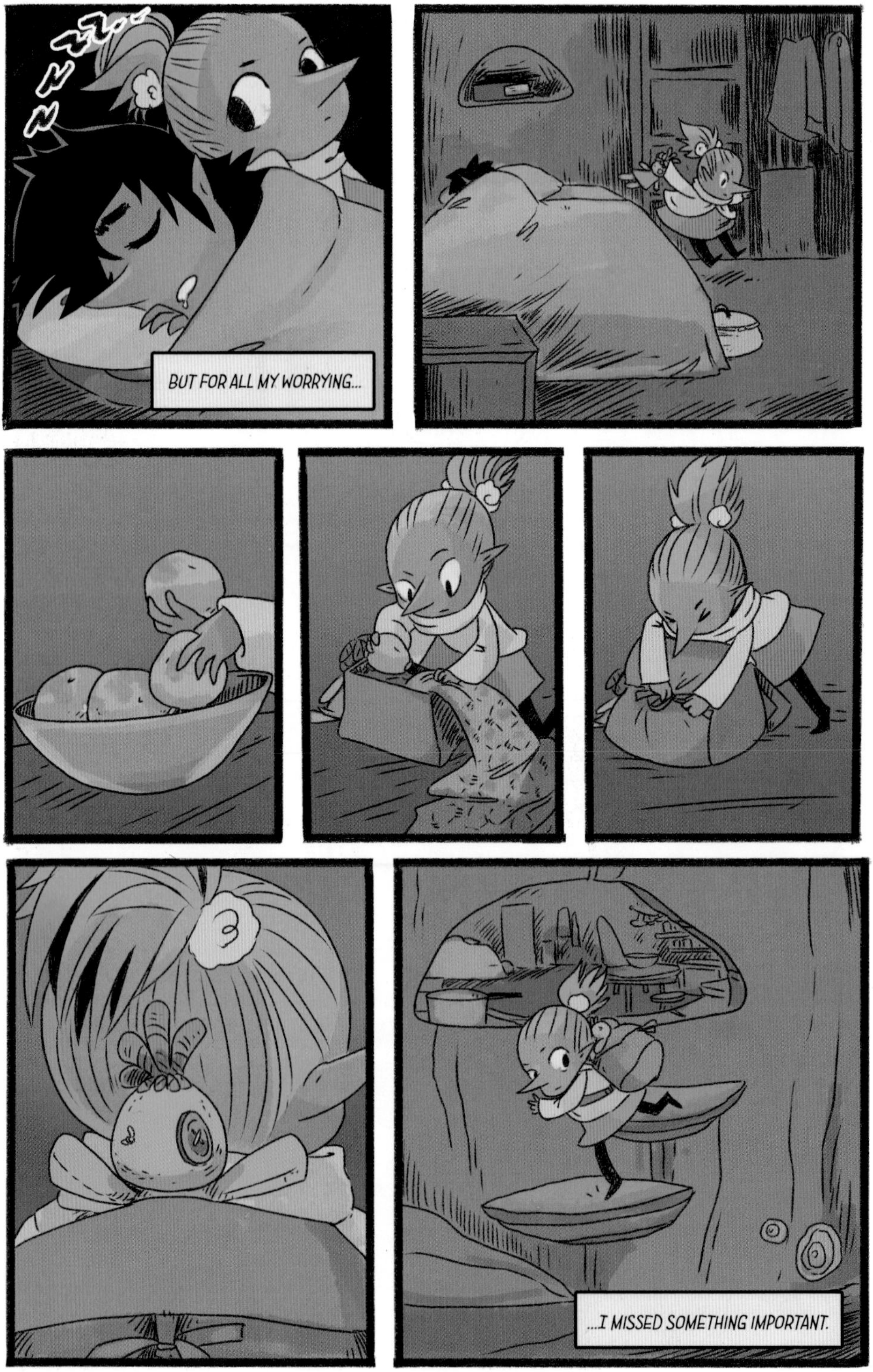

ZZZ...
BUT FOR ALL MY WORRYING...
...I MISSED SOMETHING IMPORTANT.

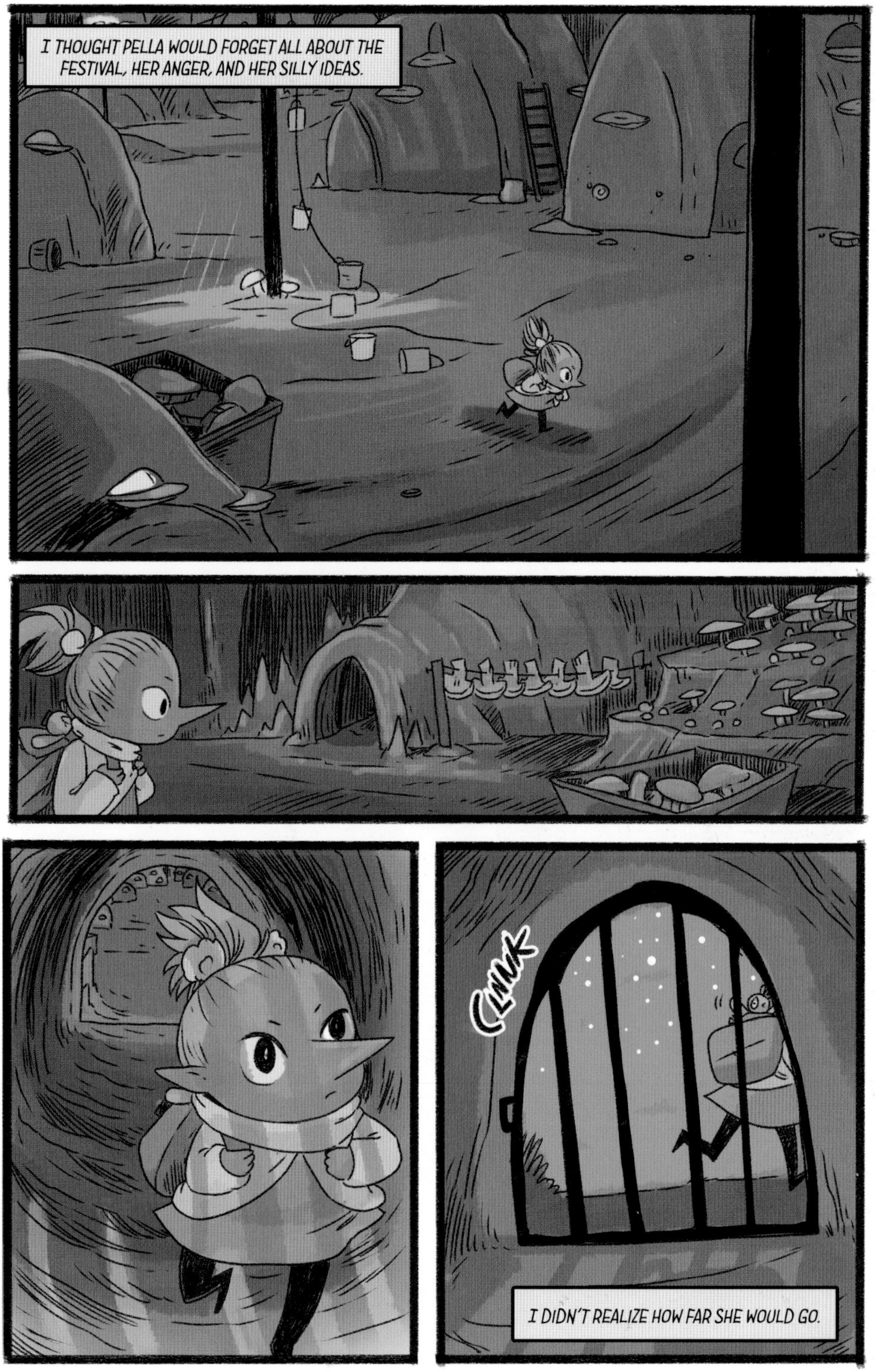
I THOUGHT PELLA WOULD FORGET ALL ABOUT THE FESTIVAL, HER ANGER, AND HER SILLY IDEAS.
CLUNK
I DIDN'T REALIZE HOW FAR SHE WOULD GO.

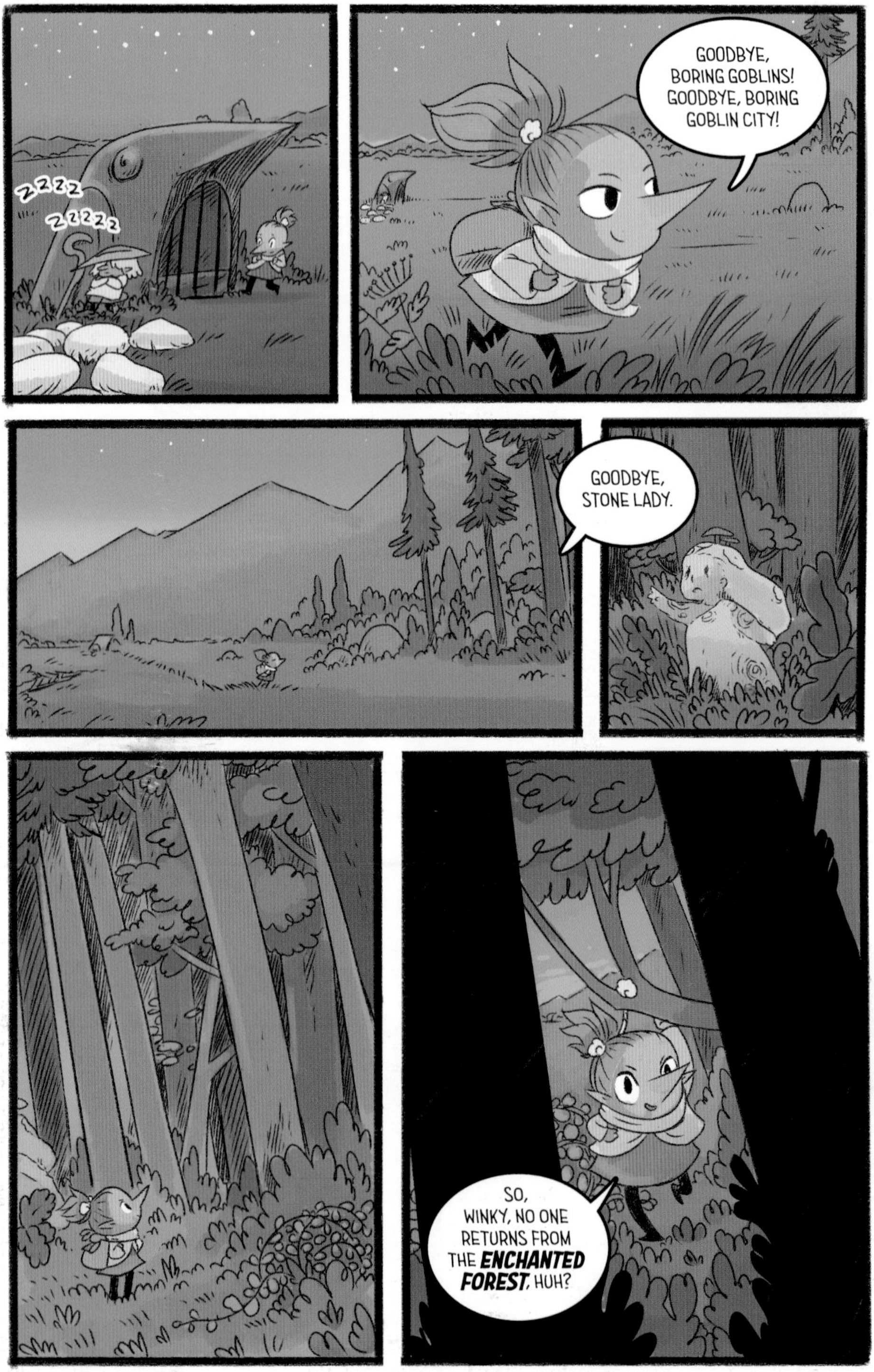
ZZZZ
ZZZZZ
GOODBYE, BORING GOBLINS! GOODBYE, BORING GOBLIN CITY!
GOODBYE, STONE LADY.
SO, WINKY, NO ONE RETURNS FROM THE **ENCHANTED FOREST**, HUH?

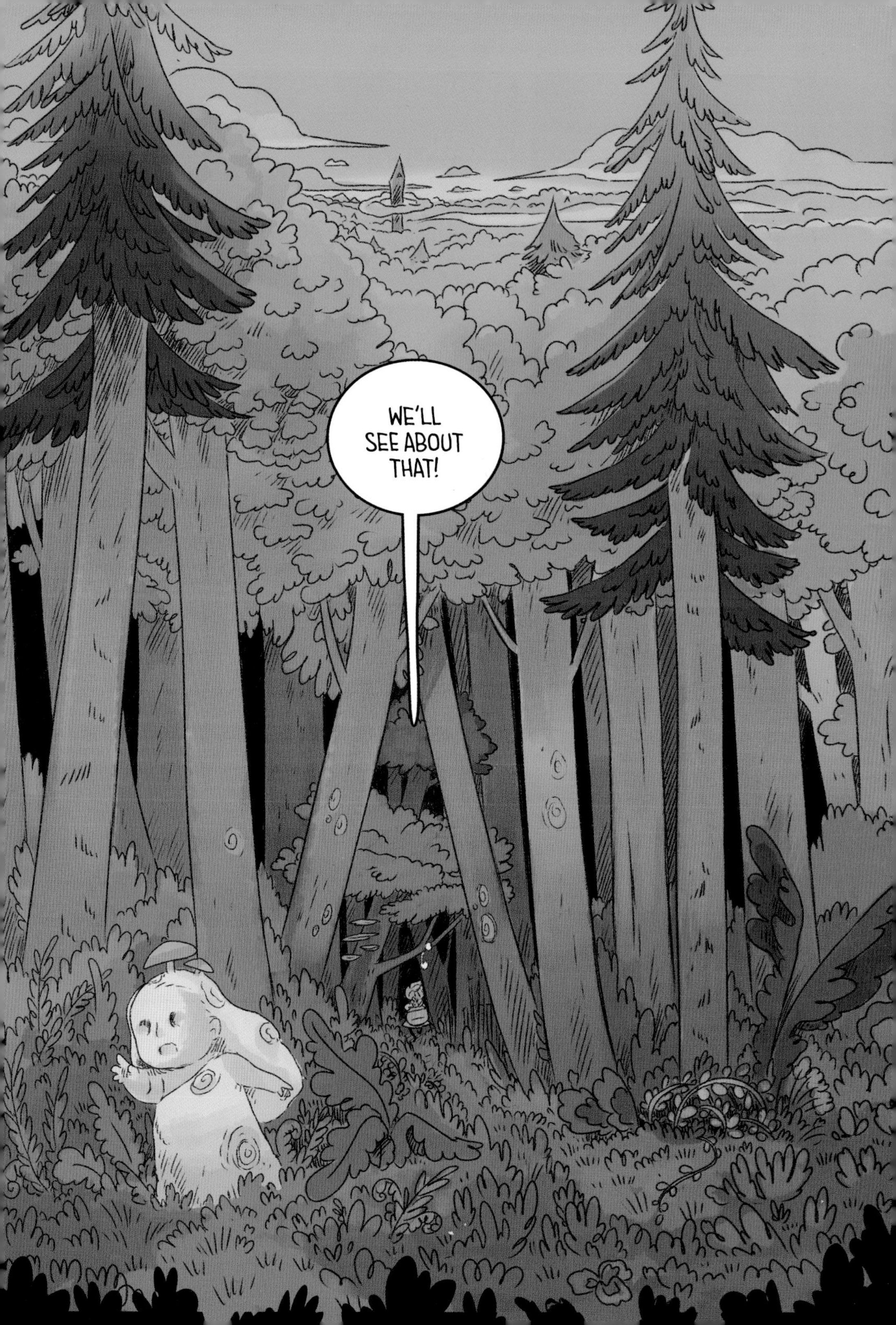
WE'LL SEE ABOUT THAT!

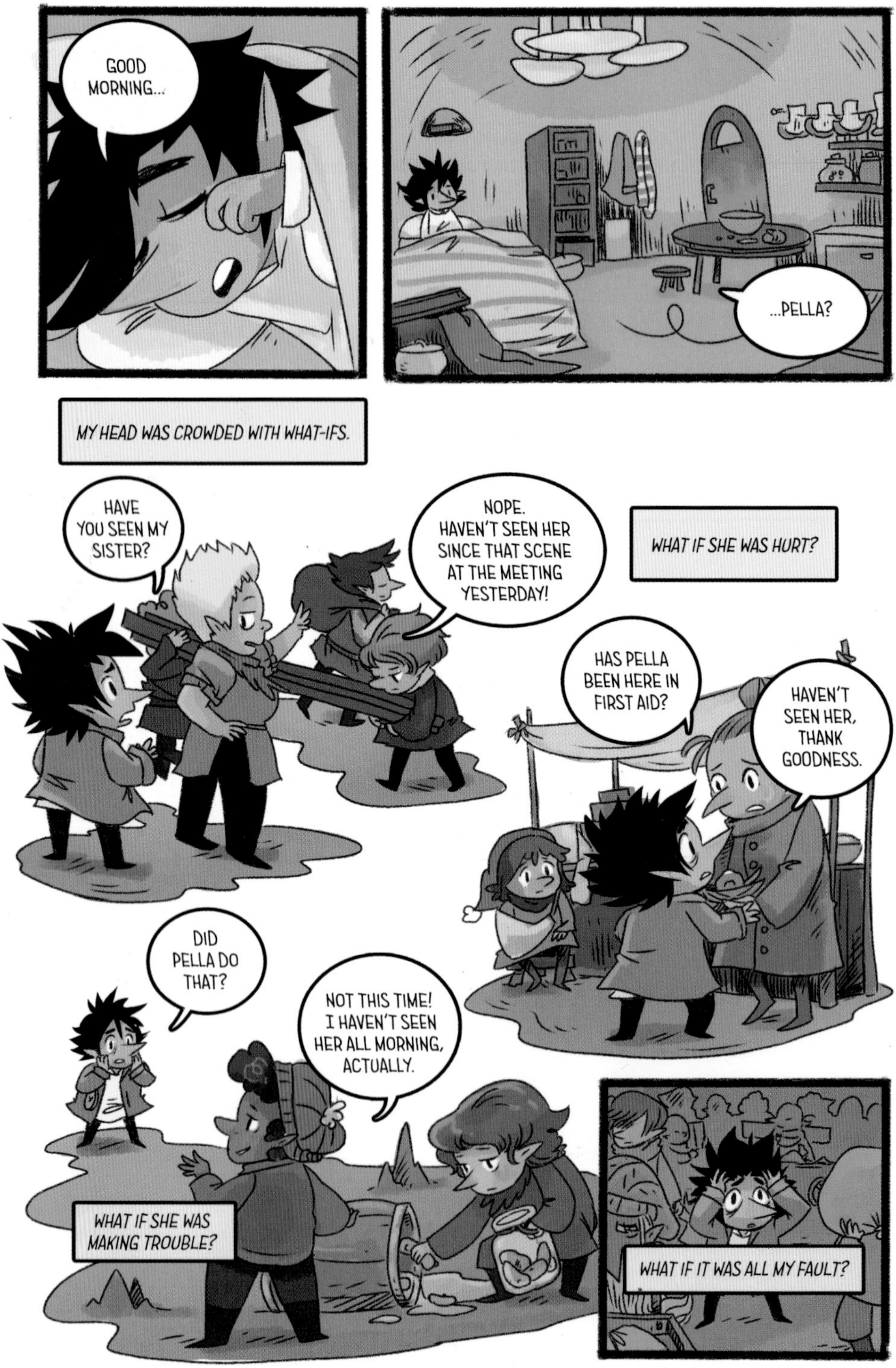
GOOD MORNING...
...PELLA?
MY HEAD WAS CROWDED WITH WHAT-IFS.
HAVE YOU SEEN MY SISTER?
NOPE. HAVEN'T SEEN HER SINCE THAT SCENE AT THE MEETING YESTERDAY!
WHAT IF SHE WAS HURT?
HAS PELLA BEEN HERE IN FIRST AID?
HAVEN'T SEEN HER, THANK GOODNESS.
DID PELLA DO THAT?
NOT THIS TIME! I HAVEN'T SEEN HER ALL MORNING, ACTUALLY.
WHAT IF SHE WAS MAKING TROUBLE?
WHAT IF IT WAS ALL MY FAULT?

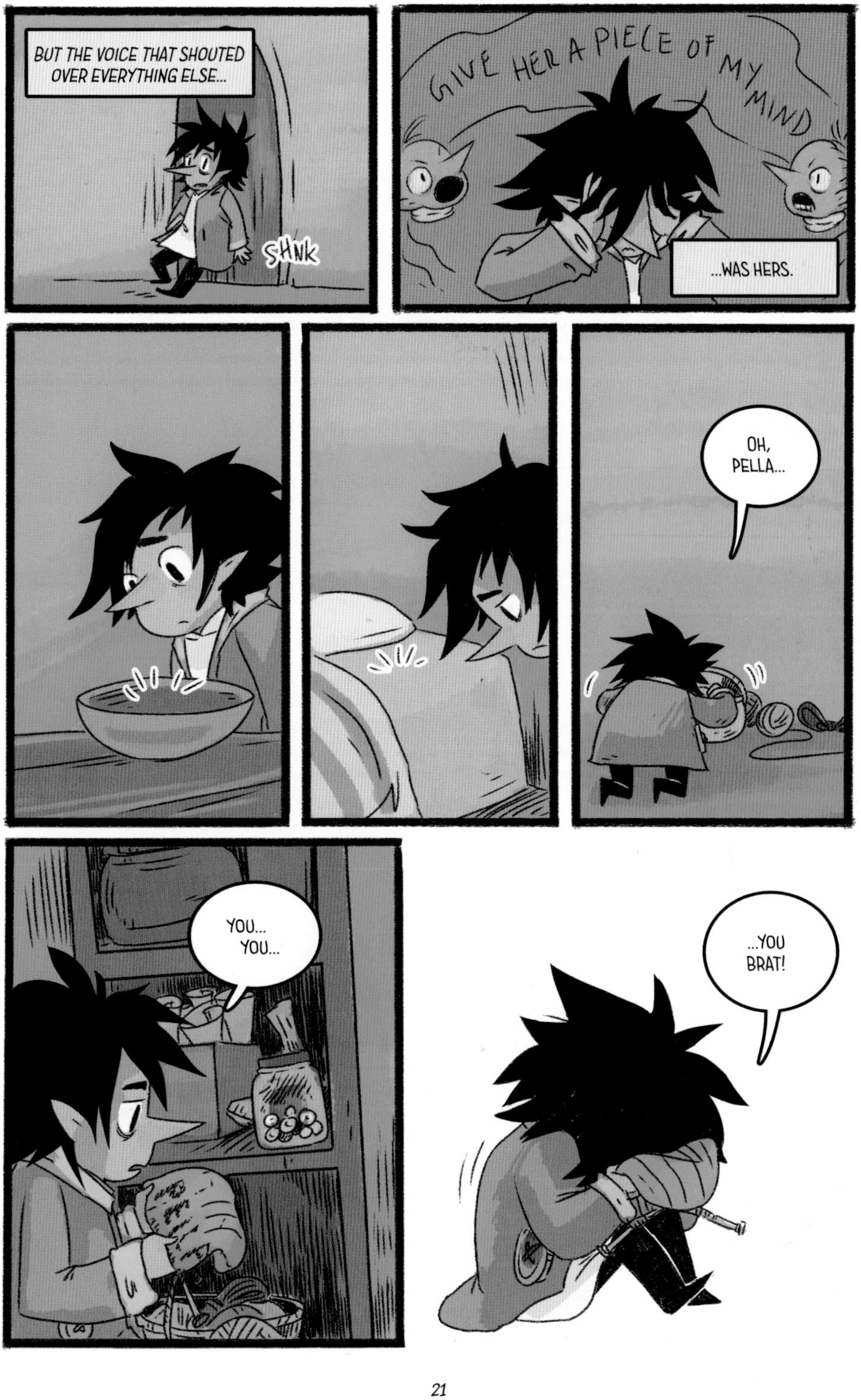

BUT THE VOICE THAT SHOUTED OVER EVERYTHING ELSE...
SHNK
GIVE HER A PIECE OF MY MIND
...WAS HERS.
OH, PELLA...
YOU... YOU...
...YOU BRAT!

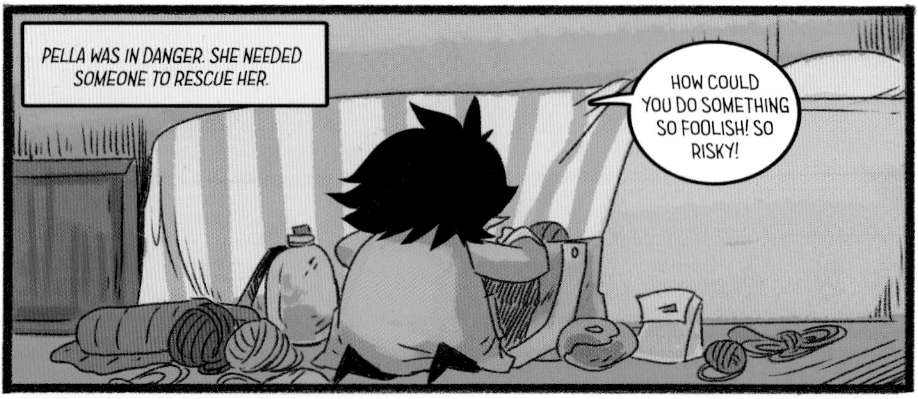
PELLA WAS IN DANGER. SHE NEEDED SOMEONE TO RESCUE HER.
HOW COULD YOU DO SOMETHING SO FOOLISH! SO RISKY!

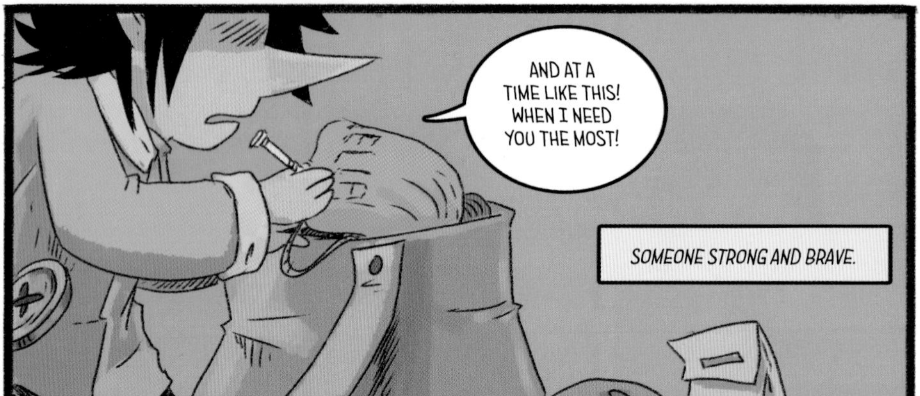
AND AT A TIME LIKE THIS! WHEN I NEED YOU THE MOST!
SOMEONE STRONG AND BRAVE.

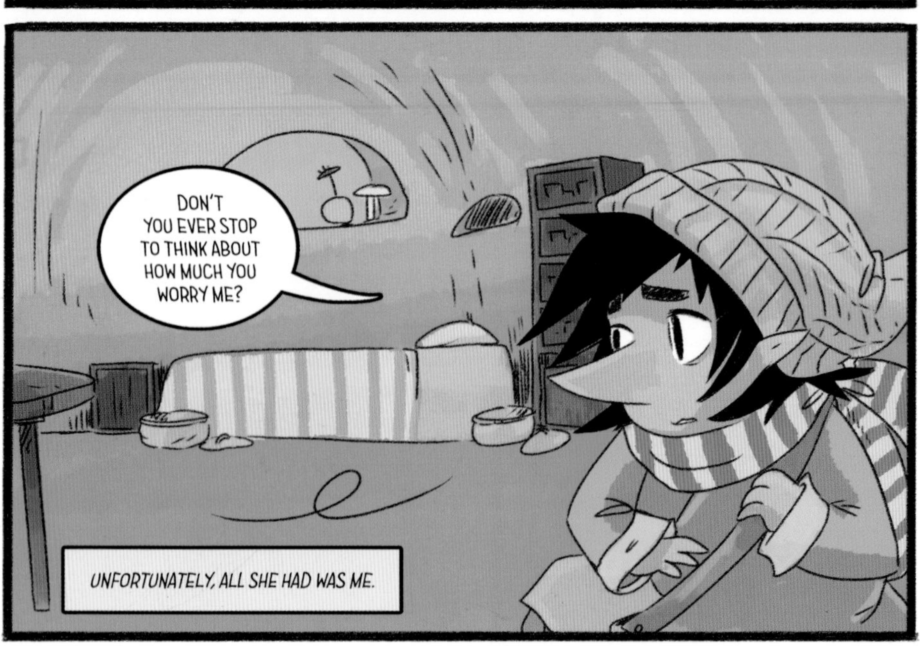
DON'T YOU EVER STOP TO THINK ABOUT HOW MUCH YOU WORRY ME?
UNFORTUNATELY, ALL SHE HAD WAS ME.

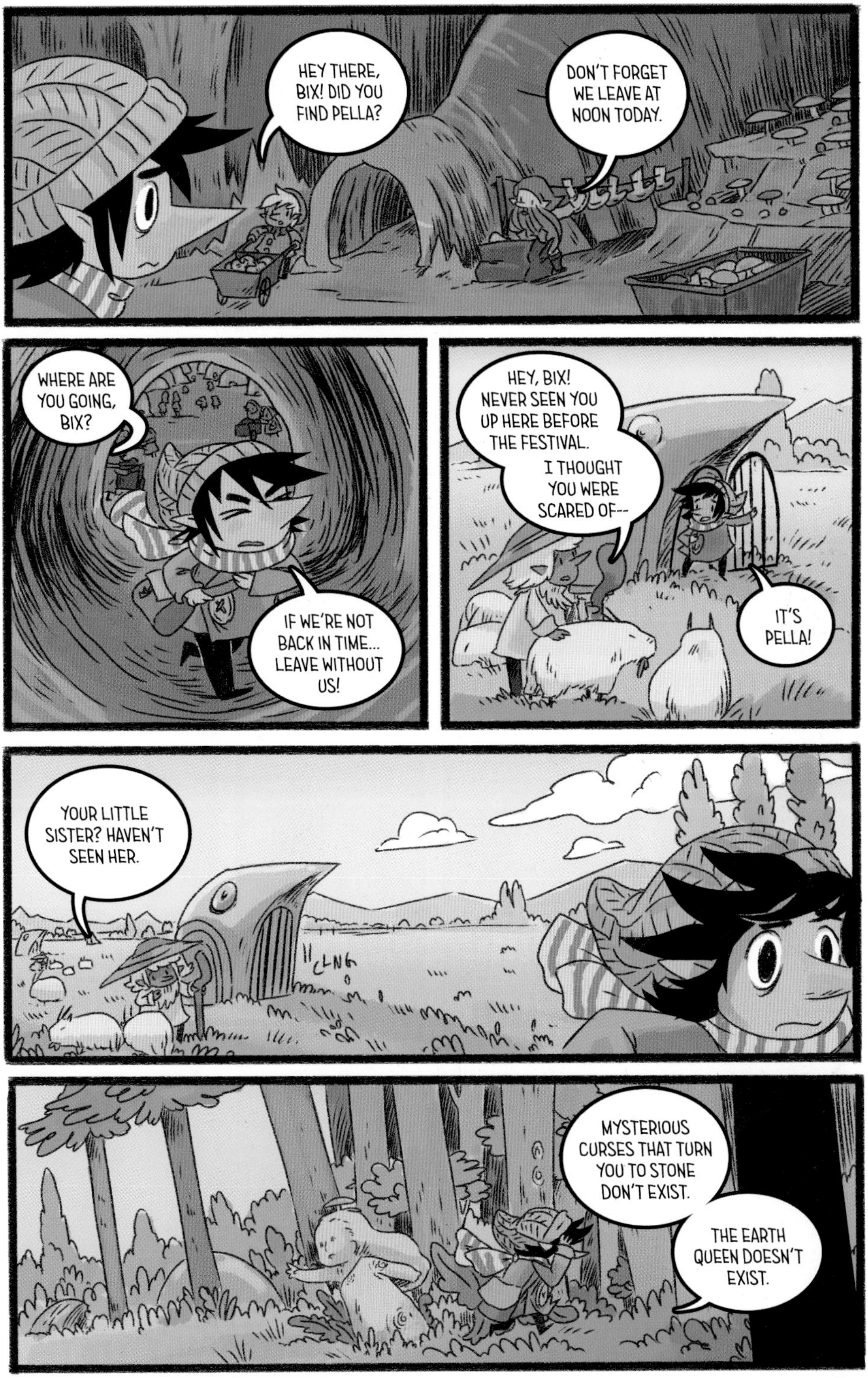
HEY THERE, BIX! DID YOU FIND PELLA?
DON'T FORGET WE LEAVE AT NOON TODAY.
WHERE ARE YOU GOING, BIX?
IF WE'RE NOT BACK IN TIME... LEAVE WITHOUT US!
HEY, BIX! NEVER SEEN YOU UP HERE BEFORE THE FESTIVAL.
I THOUGHT YOU WERE SCARED OF--
IT'S PELLA!
YOUR LITTLE SISTER? HAVEN'T SEEN HER.
CLNG
MYSTERIOUS CURSES THAT TURN YOU TO STONE DON'T EXIST.
THE EARTH QUEEN DOESN'T EXIST.

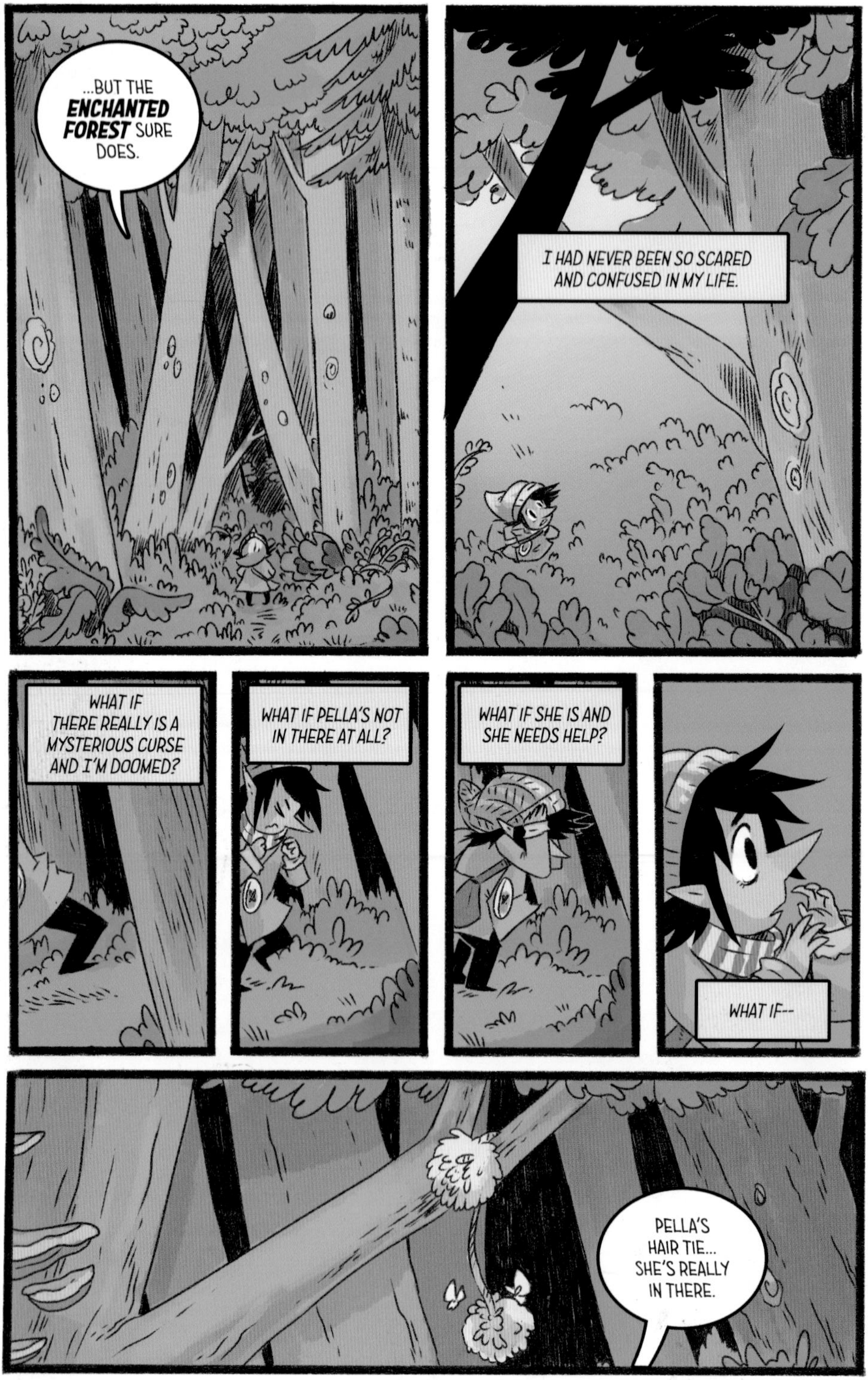
...BUT THE ENCHANTED FOREST SURE DOES.
I HAD NEVER BEEN SO SCARED AND CONFUSED IN MY LIFE.
WHAT IF THERE REALLY IS A MYSTERIOUS CURSE AND I'M DOOMED?
WHAT IF PELLA'S NOT IN THERE AT ALL?
WHAT IF SHE IS AND SHE NEEDS HELP?
WHAT IF--
PELLA'S HAIR TIE... SHE'S REALLY IN THERE.

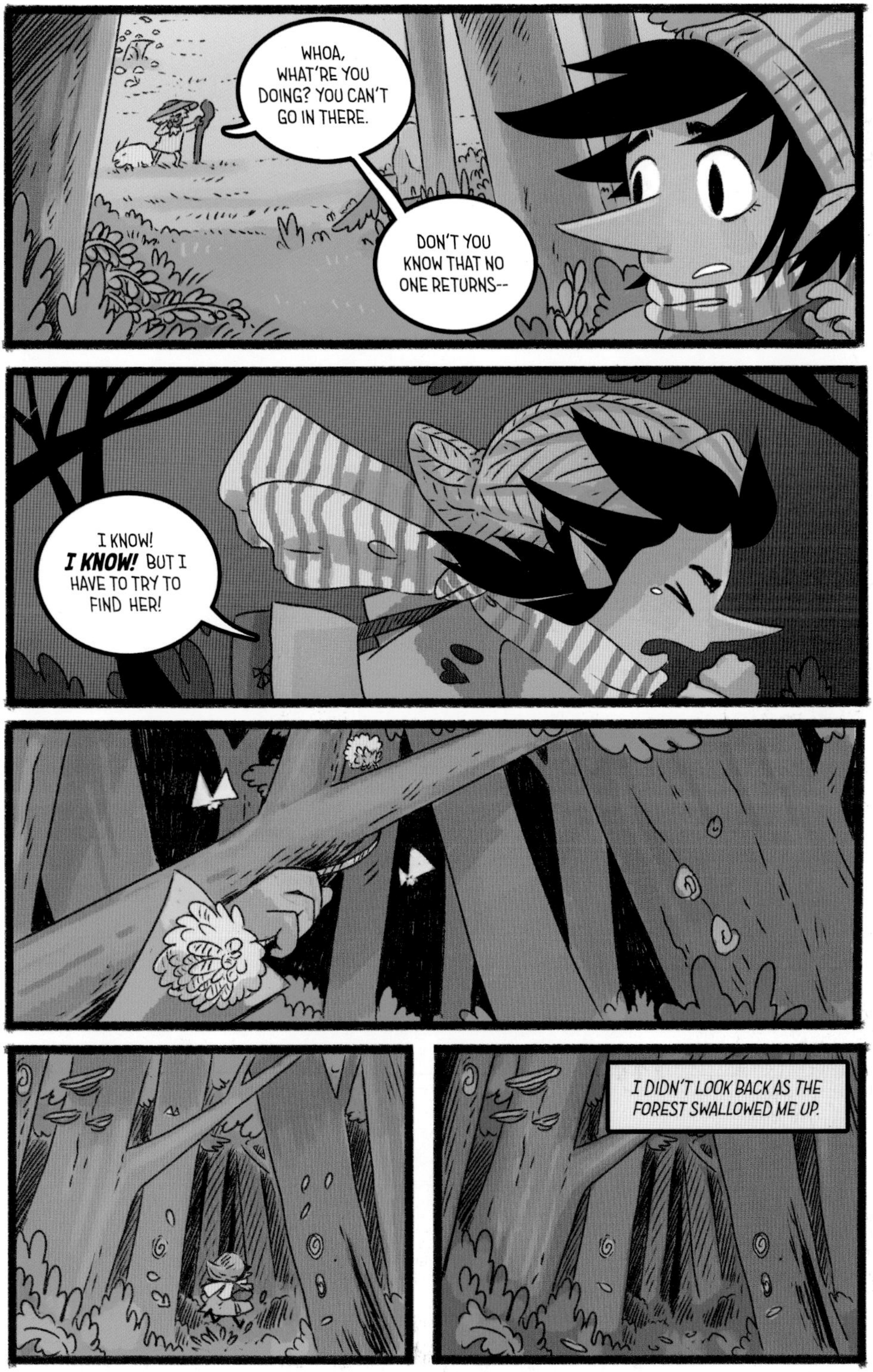
WHOA, WHAT'RE YOU DOING? YOU CAN'T GO IN THERE.
DON'T YOU KNOW THAT NO ONE RETURNS--
I KNOW! I KNOW! BUT I HAVE TO TRY TO FIND HER!
I DIDN'T LOOK BACK AS THE FOREST SWALLOWED ME UP.

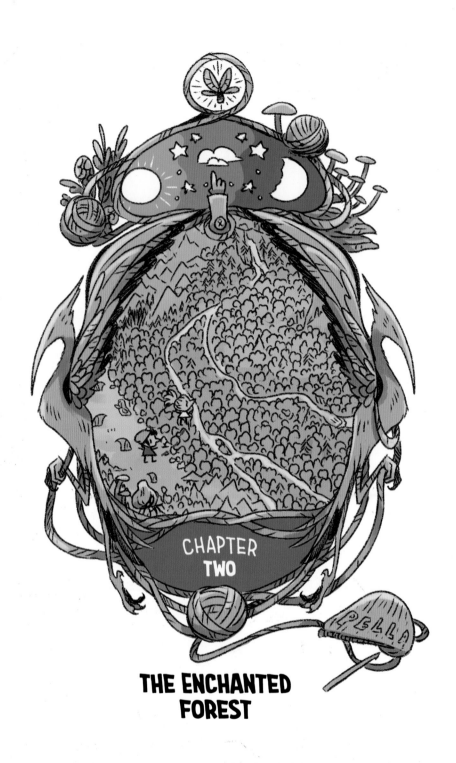

CHAPTER TWO

THE ENCHANTED FOREST

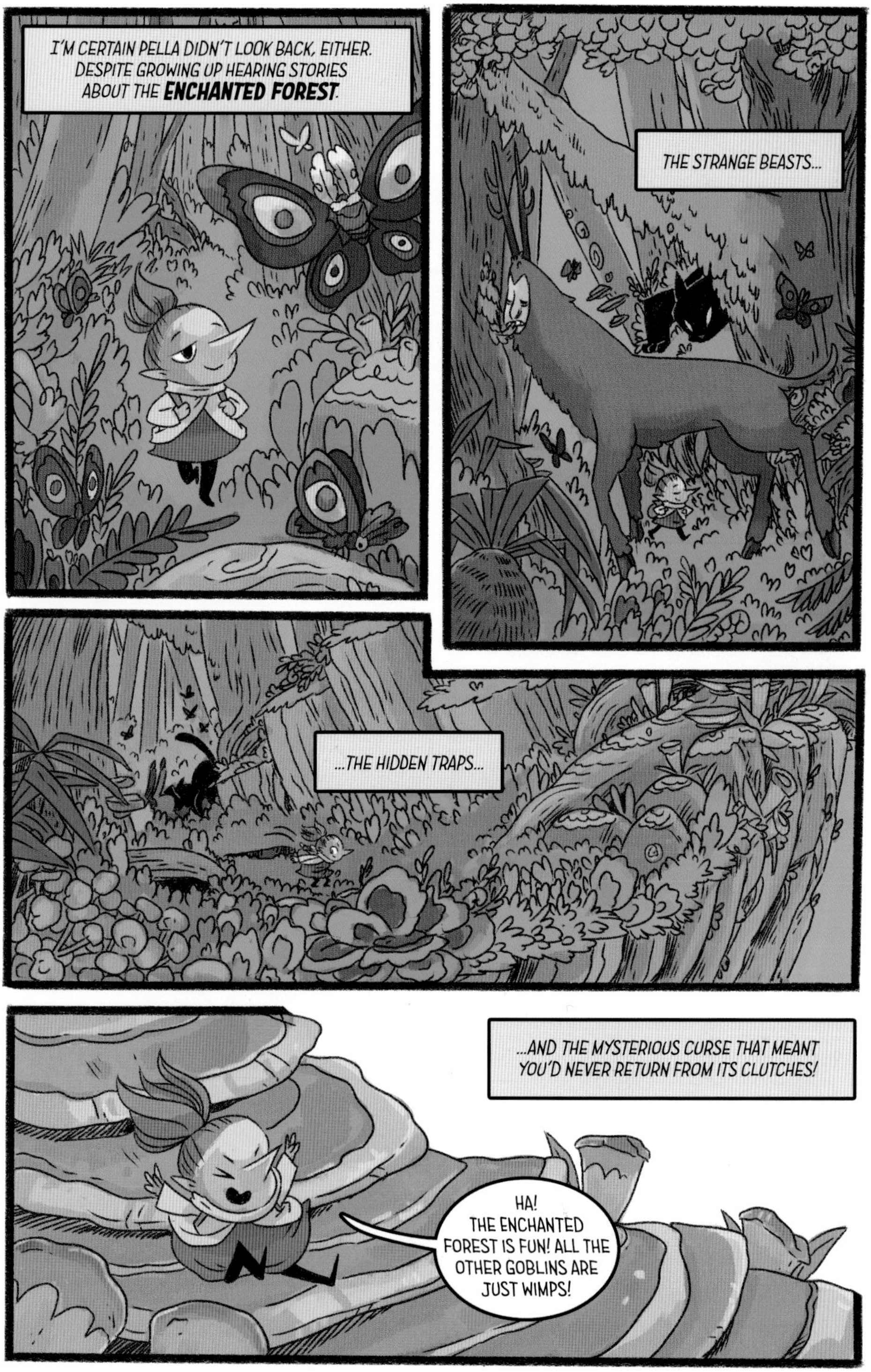
I'M CERTAIN PELLA DIDN'T LOOK BACK, EITHER. DESPITE GROWING UP HEARING STORIES ABOUT THE ENCHANTED FOREST.
THE STRANGE BEASTS...
...THE HIDDEN TRAPS...
...AND THE MYSTERIOUS CURSE THAT MEANT YOU'D NEVER RETURN FROM ITS CLUTCHES!
HA! THE ENCHANTED FOREST IS FUN! ALL THE OTHER GOBLINS ARE JUST WIMPS!

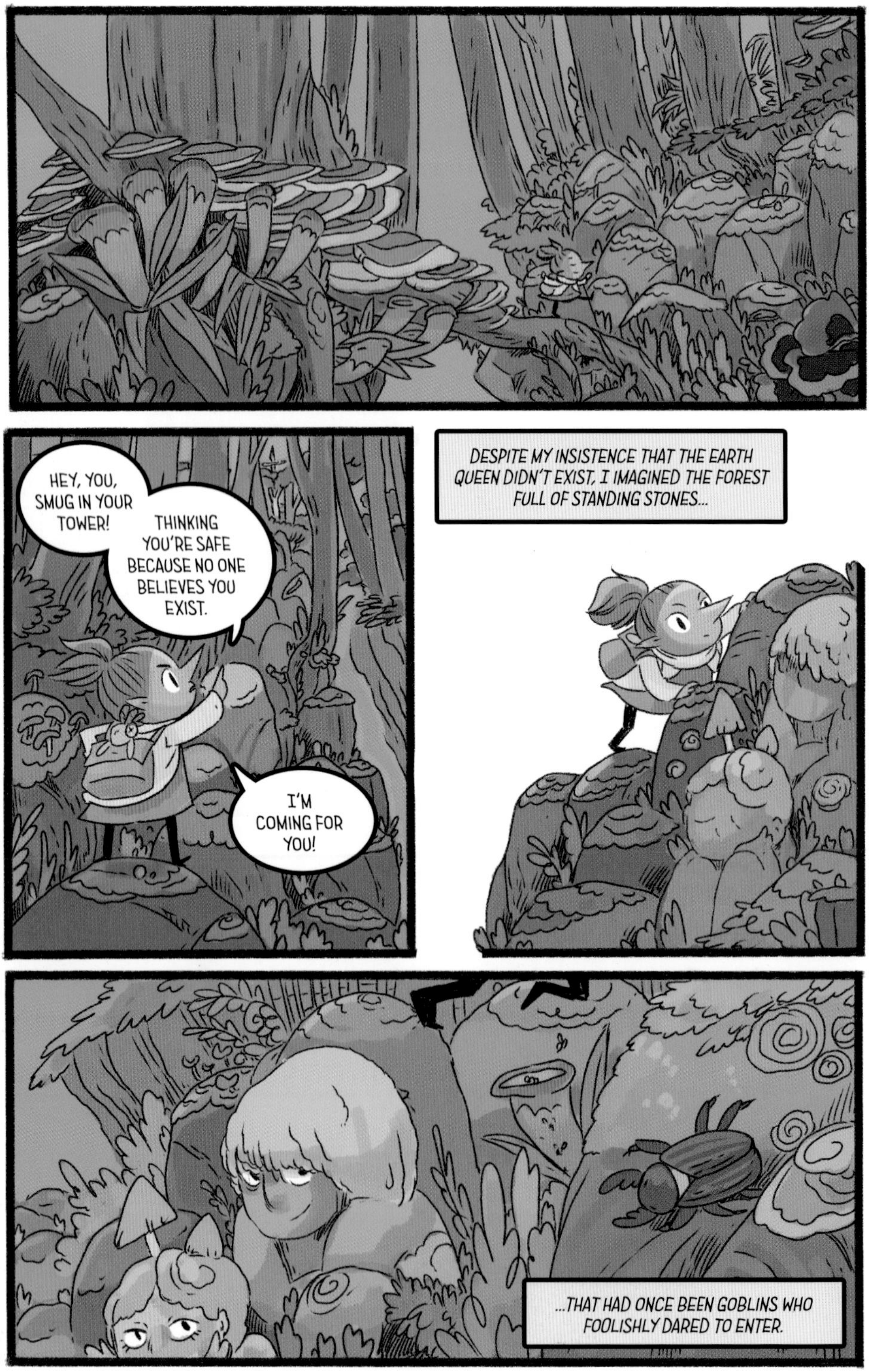
HEY, YOU, SMUG IN YOUR TOWER!
THINKING YOU'RE SAFE BECAUSE NO ONE BELIEVES YOU EXIST.
I'M COMING FOR YOU!
DESPITE MY INSISTENCE THAT THE EARTH QUEEN DIDN'T EXIST, I IMAGINED THE FOREST FULL OF STANDING STONES...
...THAT HAD ONCE BEEN GOBLINS WHO FOOLISHLY DARED TO ENTER.

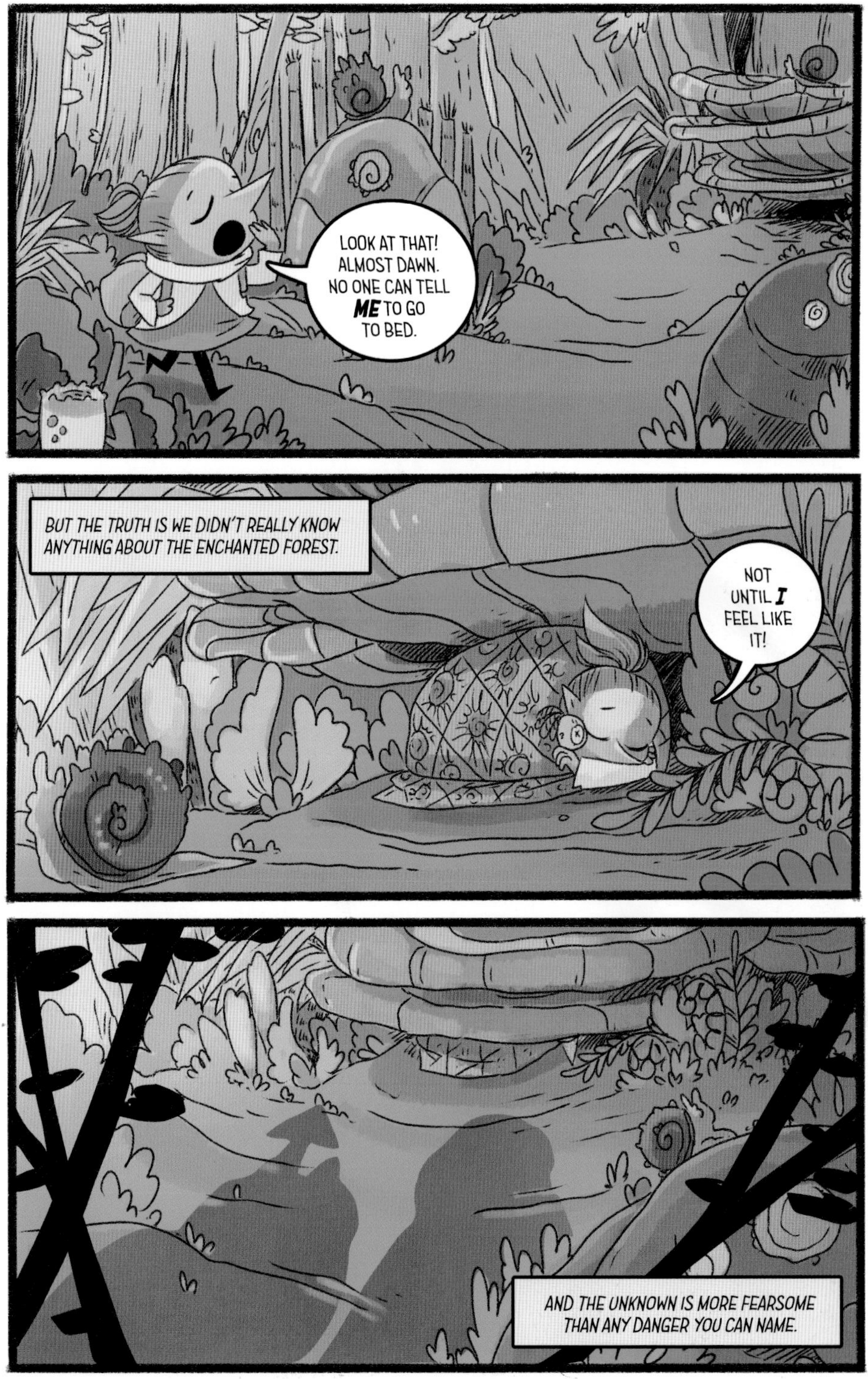
LOOK AT THAT! ALMOST DAWN. NO ONE CAN TELL ME TO GO TO BED.
BUT THE TRUTH IS WE DIDN'T REALLY KNOW ANYTHING ABOUT THE ENCHANTED FOREST.
NOT UNTIL I FEEL LIKE IT!
AND THE UNKNOWN IS MORE FEARSOME THAN ANY DANGER YOU CAN NAME.

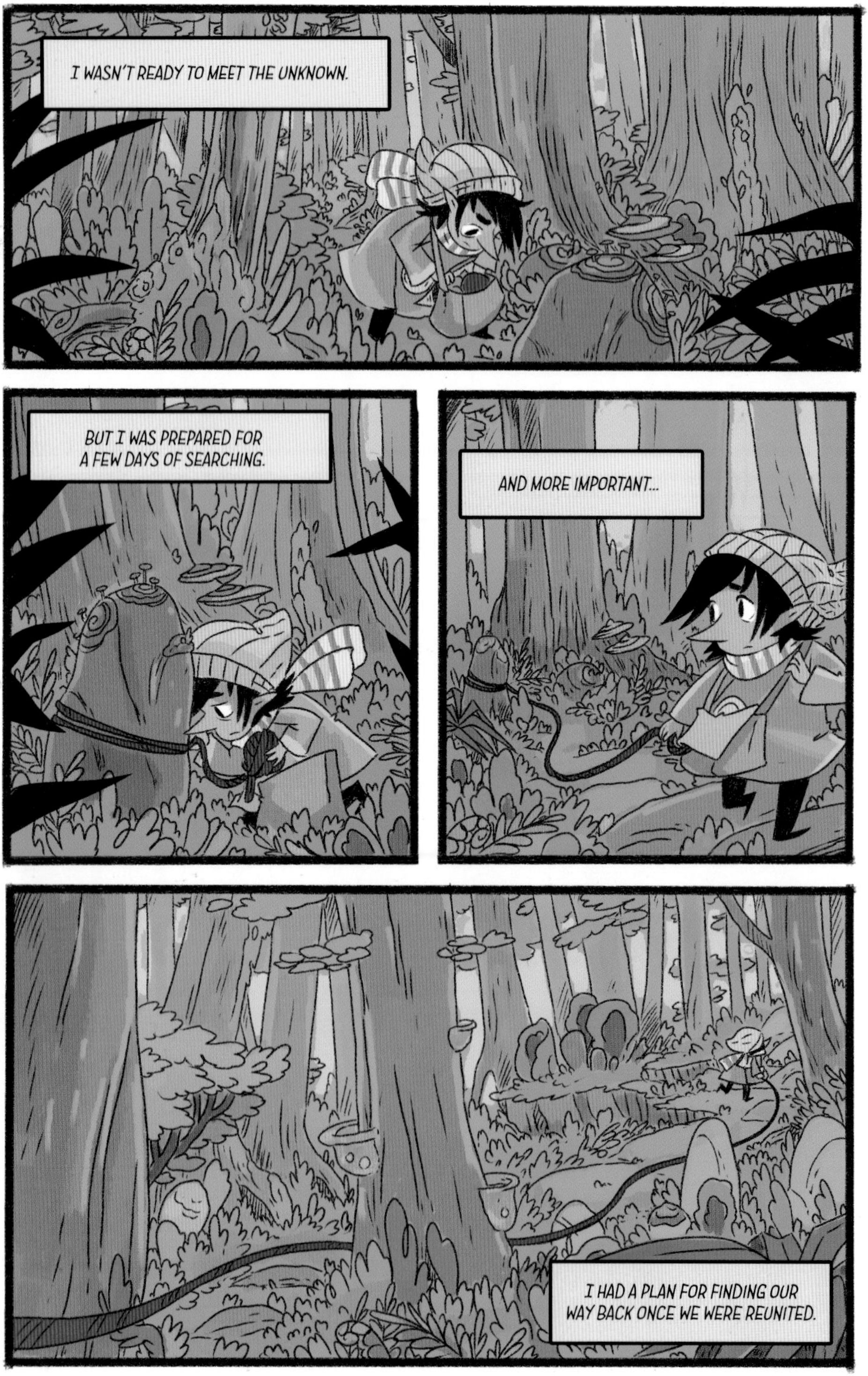
I WASN'T READY TO MEET THE UNKNOWN.
BUT I WAS PREPARED FOR A FEW DAYS OF SEARCHING.
AND MORE IMPORTANT...
I HAD A PLAN FOR FINDING OUR WAY BACK ONCE WE WERE REUNITED.

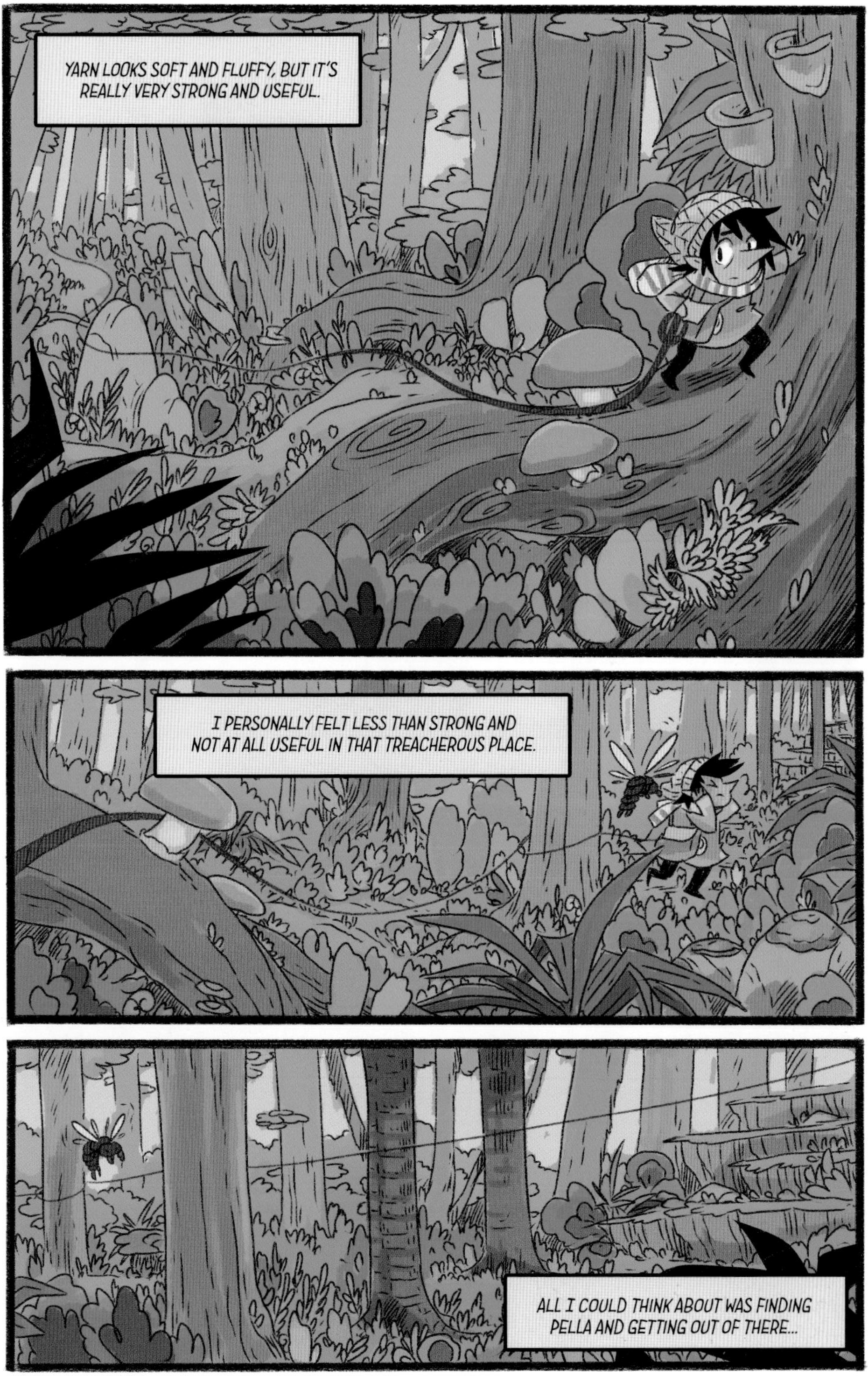
YARN LOOKS SOFT AND FLUFFY, BUT IT'S REALLY VERY STRONG AND USEFUL.
I PERSONALLY FELT LESS THAN STRONG AND NOT AT ALL USEFUL IN THAT TREACHEROUS PLACE.
ALL I COULD THINK ABOUT WAS FINDING PELLA AND GETTING OUT OF THERE...

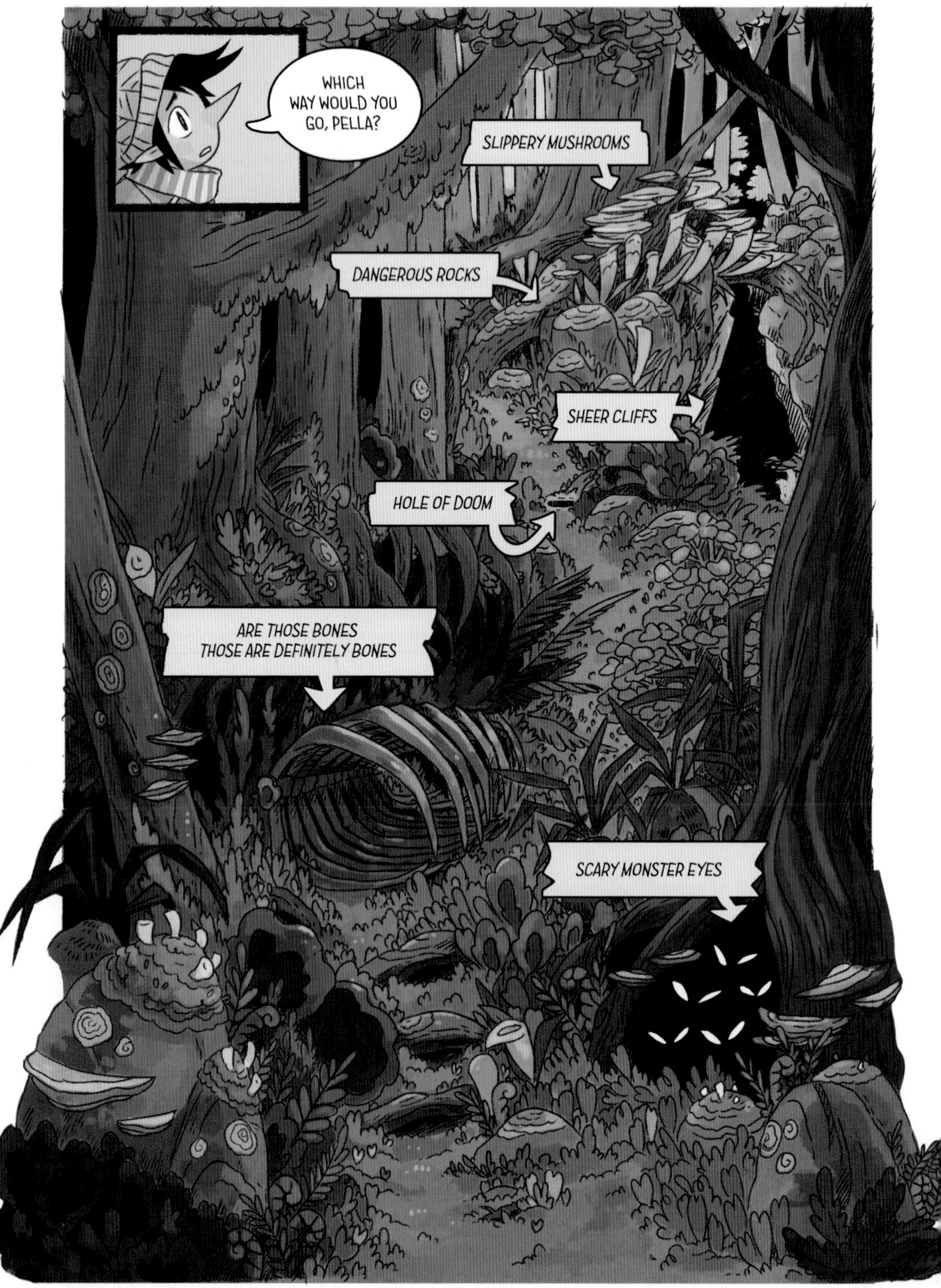
WHICH WAY WOULD YOU GO, PELLA?
SLIPPERY MUSHROOMS
DANGEROUS ROCKS
SHEER CLIFFS
HOLE OF DOOM
ARE THOSE BONES
THOSE ARE DEFINITELY BONES
SCARY MONSTER EYES

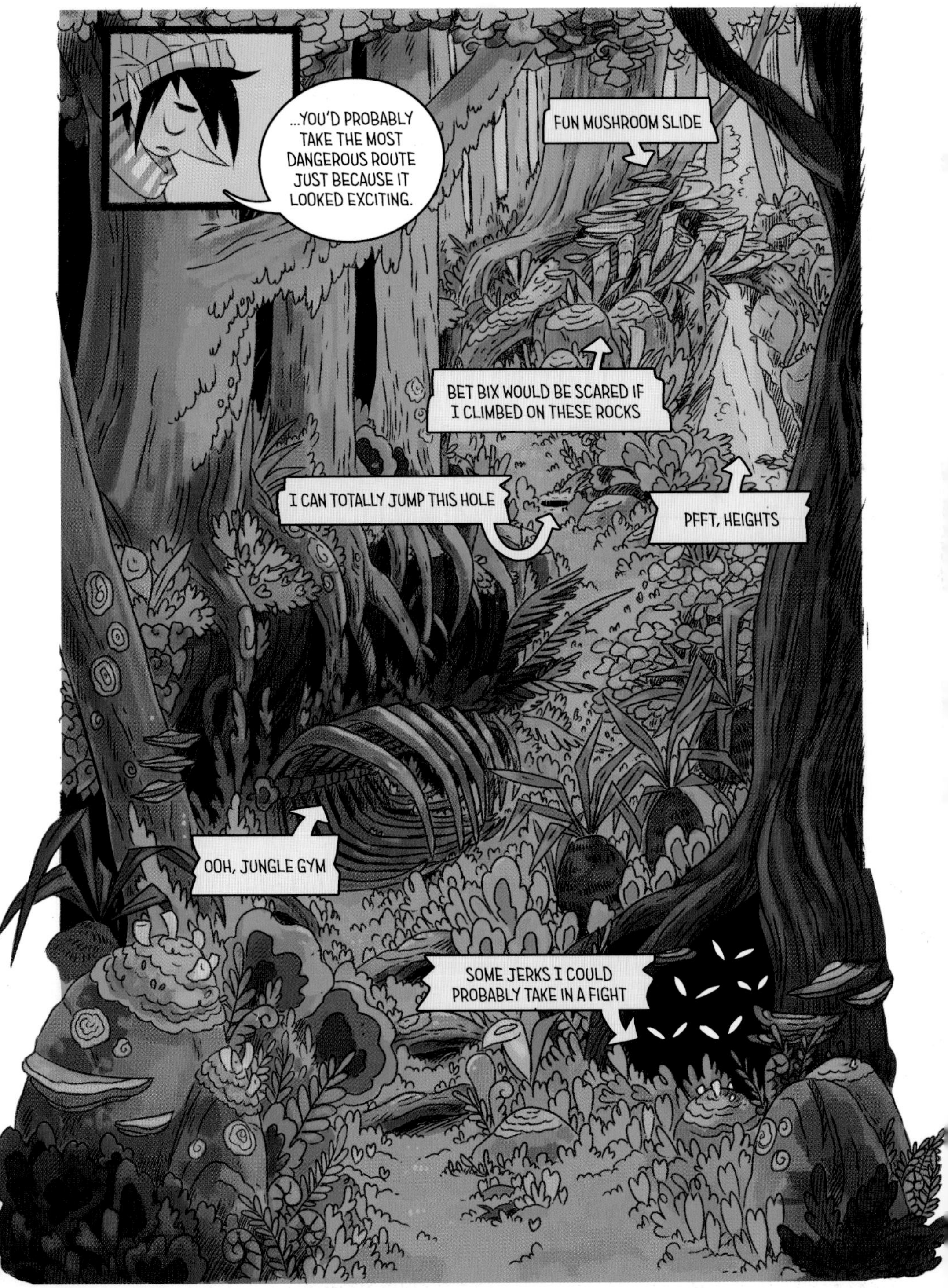
...YOU'D PROBABLY TAKE THE MOST DANGEROUS ROUTE JUST BECAUSE IT LOOKED EXCITING.
FUN MUSHROOM SLIDE
BET BIX WOULD BE SCARED IF I CLIMBED ON THESE ROCKS
I CAN TOTALLY JUMP THIS HOLE
PFFT, HEIGHTS
OOH, JUNGLE GYM
SOME JERKS I COULD PROBABLY TAKE IN A FIGHT

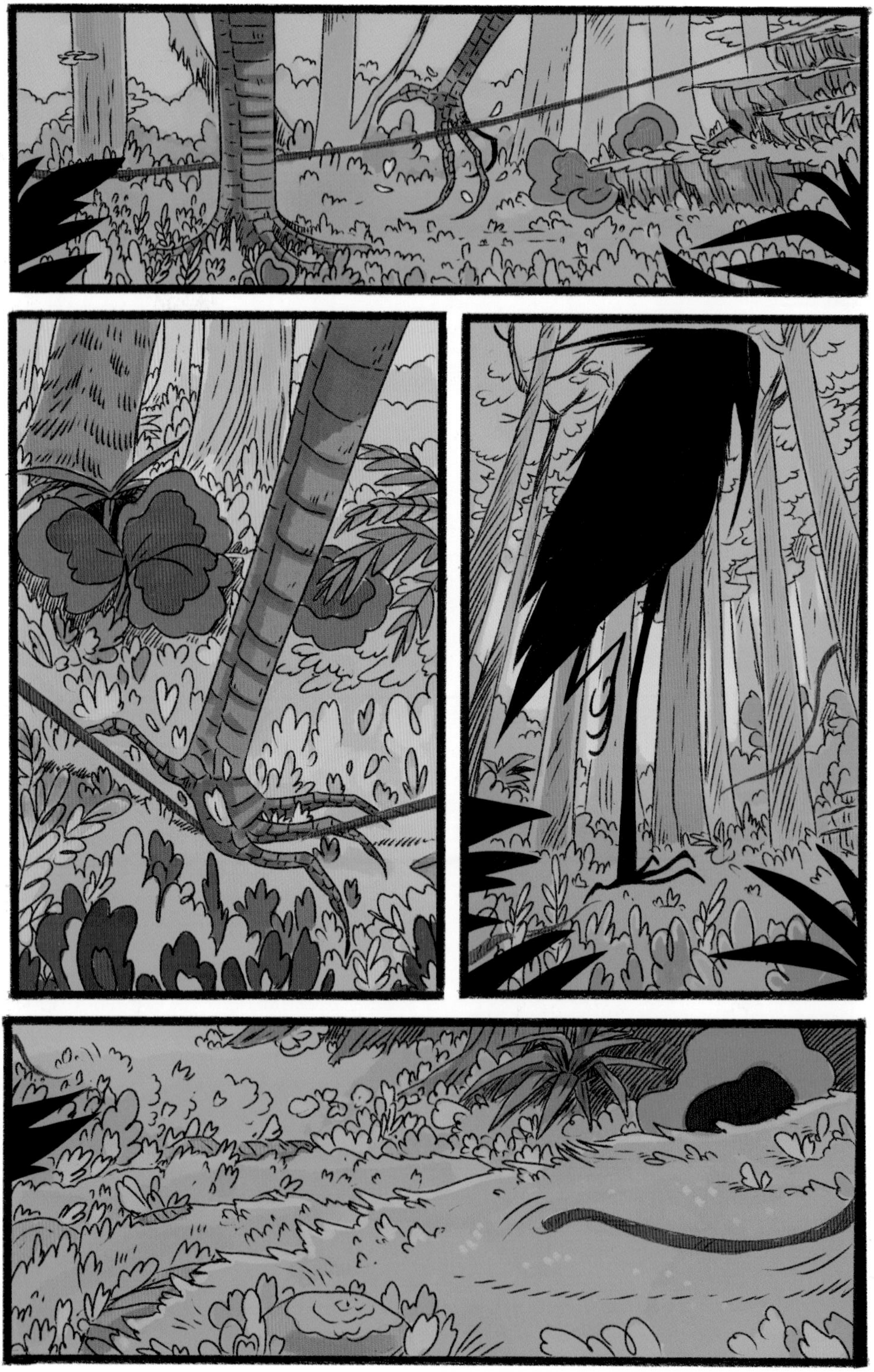

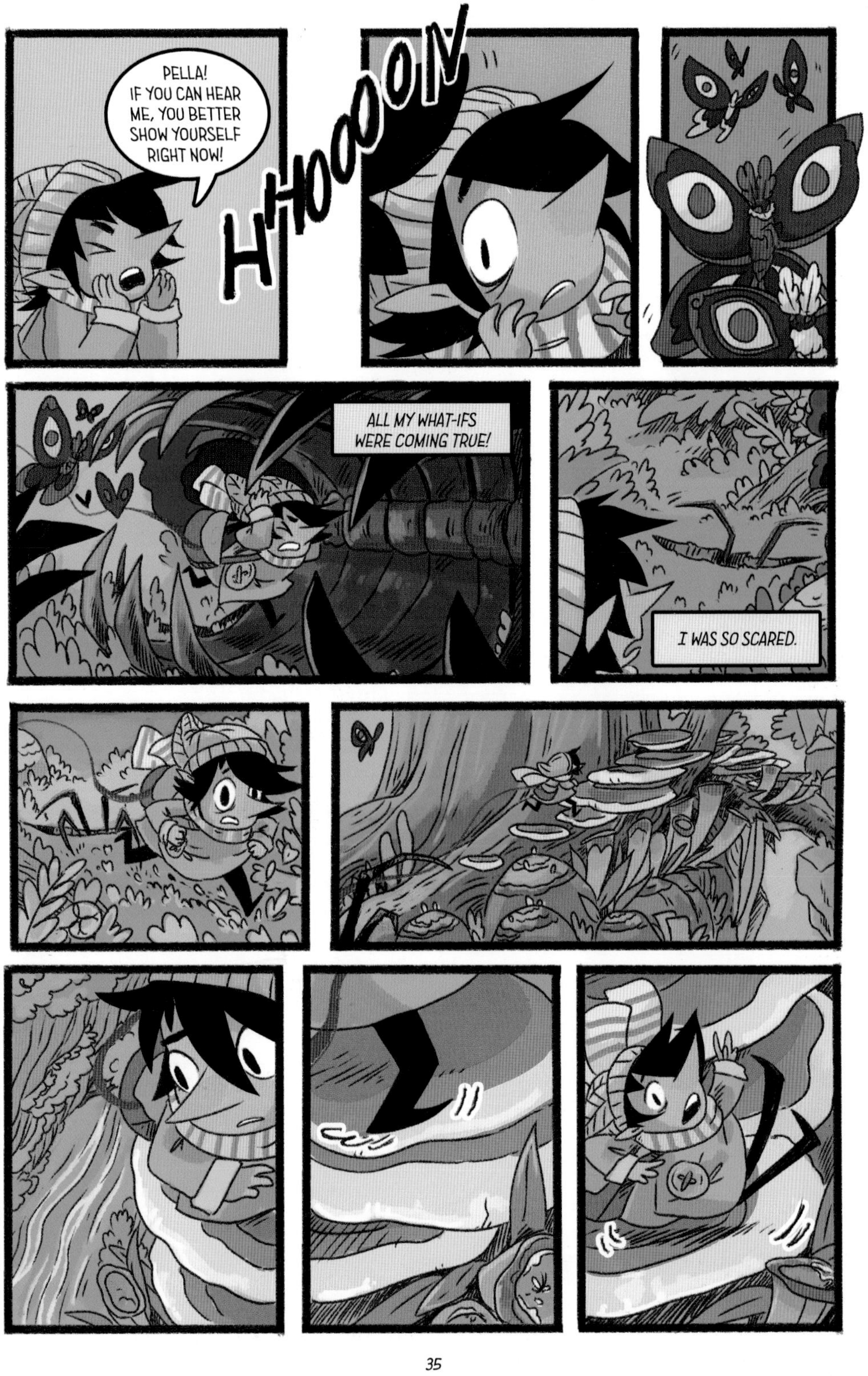
PELLA! IF YOU CAN HEAR ME, YOU BETTER SHOW YOURSELF RIGHT NOW!
HHOOOOON
ALL MY WHAT-IFS WERE COMING TRUE!
I WAS SO SCARED.

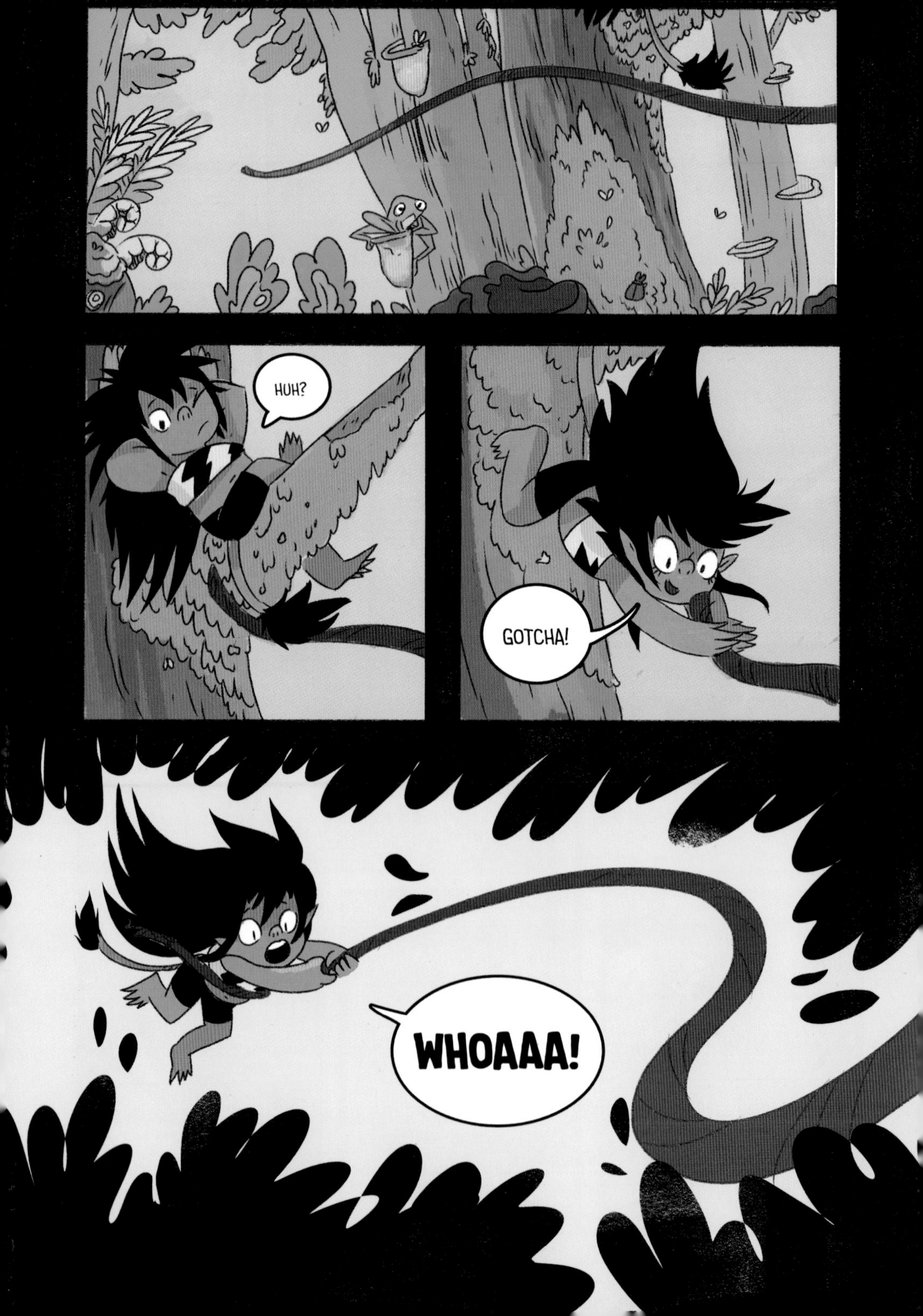
HUH?
GOTCHA!
WHOAAA!

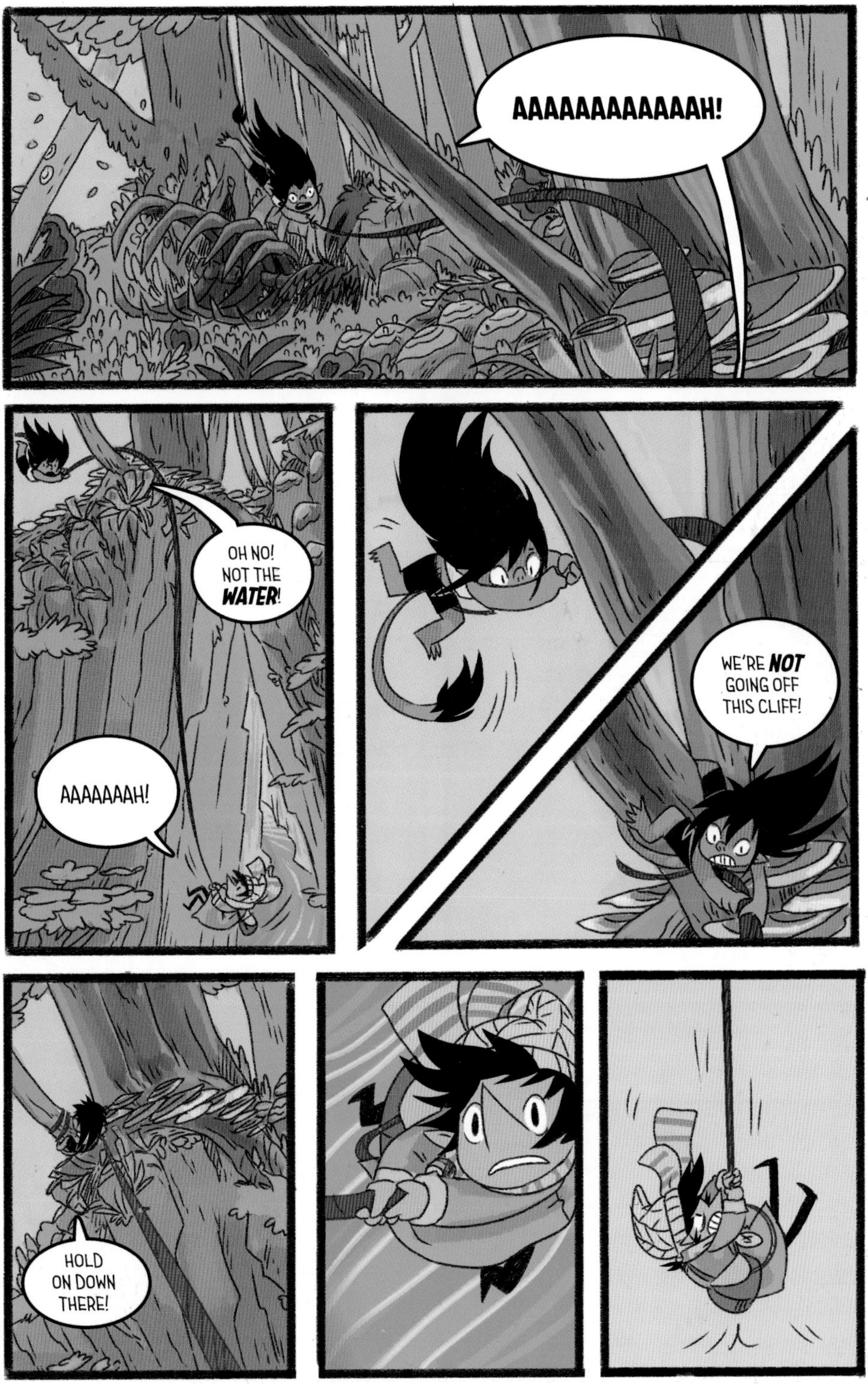
AAAAAAAAAAAAH!
OH NO! NOT THE **WATER**!
AAAAAAAH!
WE'RE **NOT** GOING OFF THIS CLIFF!
HOLD ON DOWN THERE!

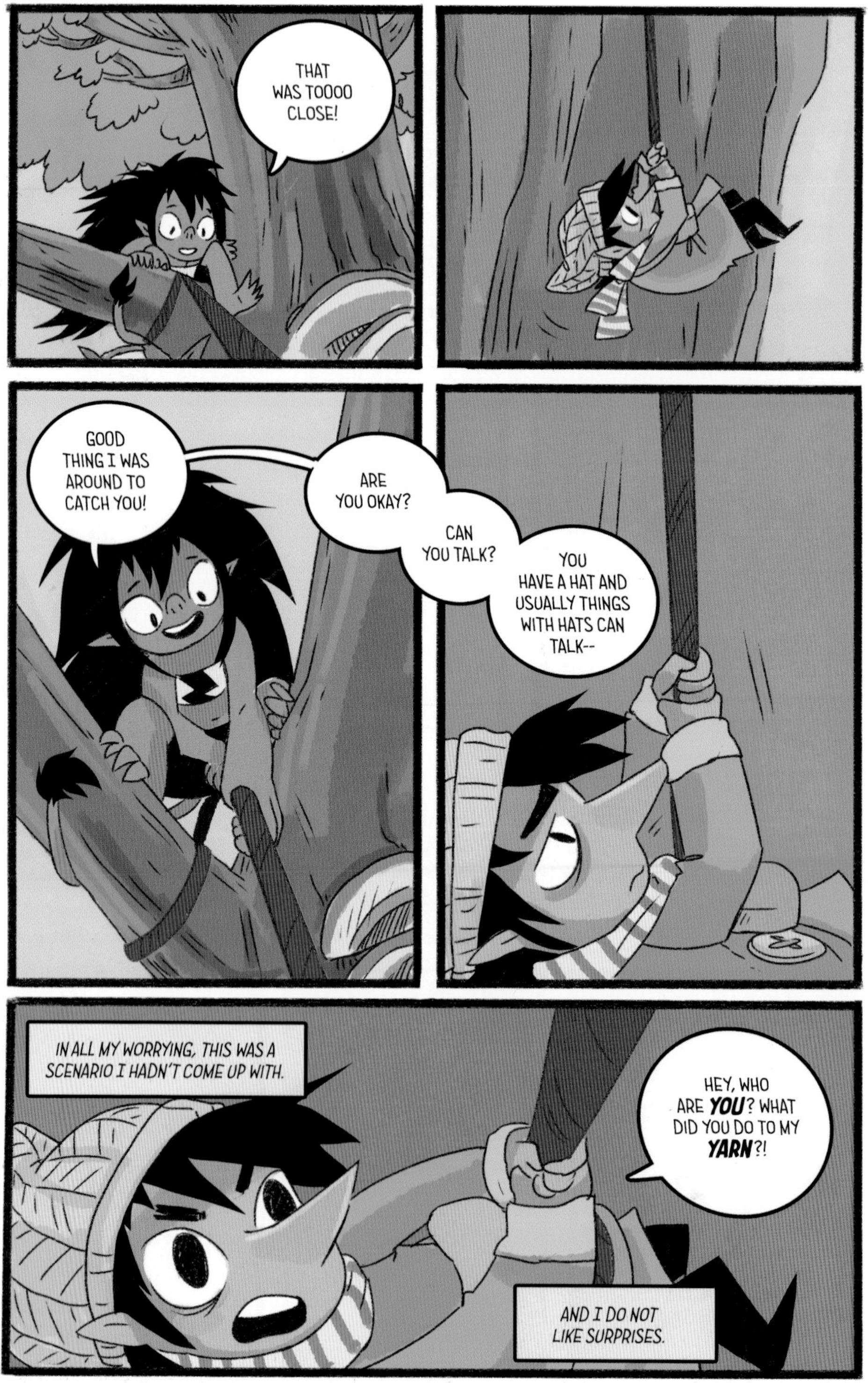
THAT WAS TOOOO CLOSE!
GOOD THING I WAS AROUND TO CATCH YOU!
ARE YOU OKAY?
CAN YOU TALK?
YOU HAVE A HAT AND USUALLY THINGS WITH HATS CAN TALK--
IN ALL MY WORRYING, THIS WAS A SCENARIO I HADN'T COME UP WITH.
HEY, WHO ARE **YOU**? WHAT DID YOU DO TO MY **YARN**?!
AND I DO NOT LIKE SURPRISES.

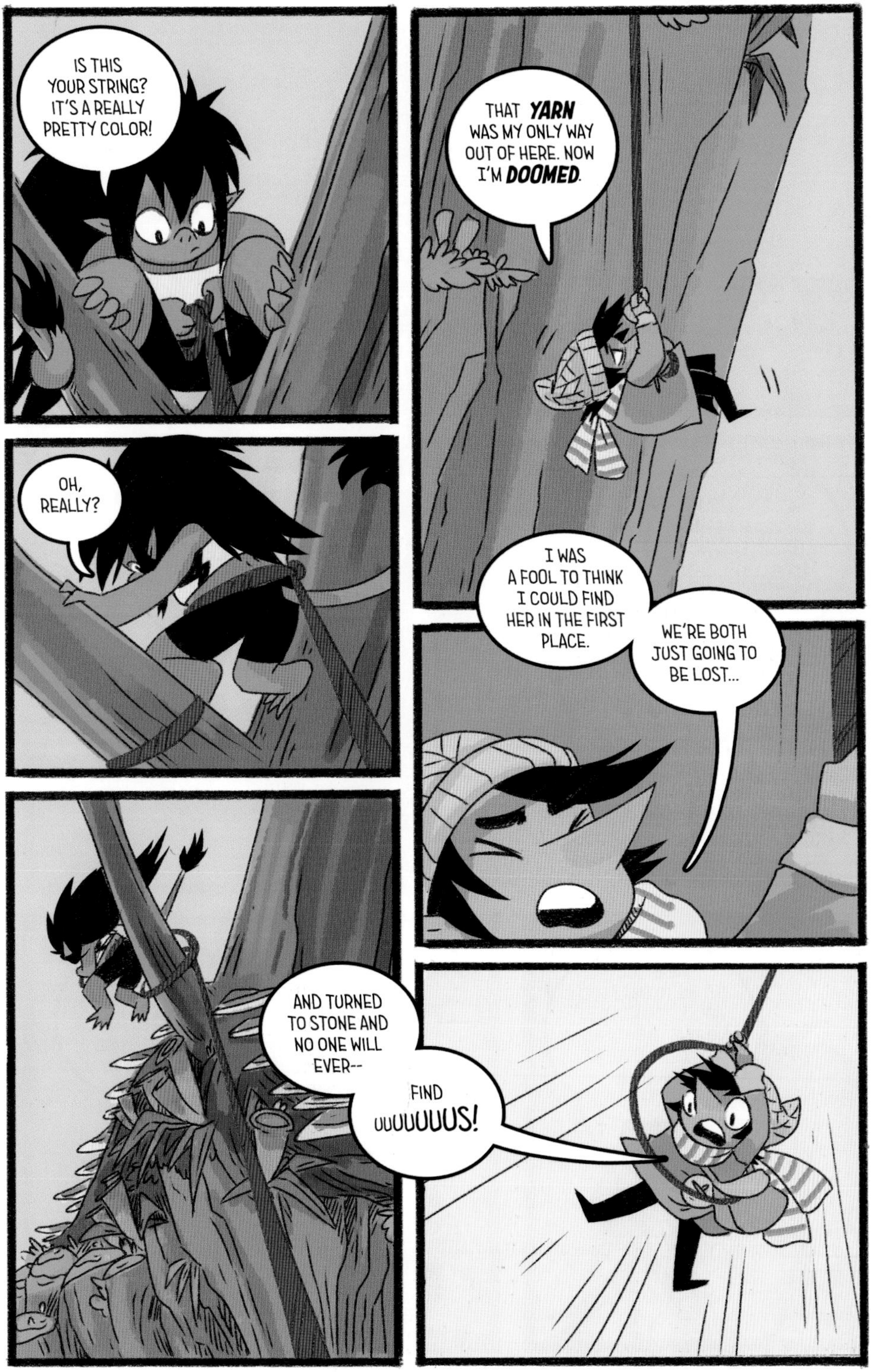
IS THIS YOUR STRING? IT'S A REALLY PRETTY COLOR!
THAT **YARN** WAS MY ONLY WAY OUT OF HERE. NOW I'M **DOOMED**.
OH, REALLY?
I WAS A FOOL TO THINK I COULD FIND HER IN THE FIRST PLACE.
WE'RE BOTH JUST GOING TO BE LOST...
AND TURNED TO STONE AND NO ONE WILL EVER--
FIND UUUUUUUS!

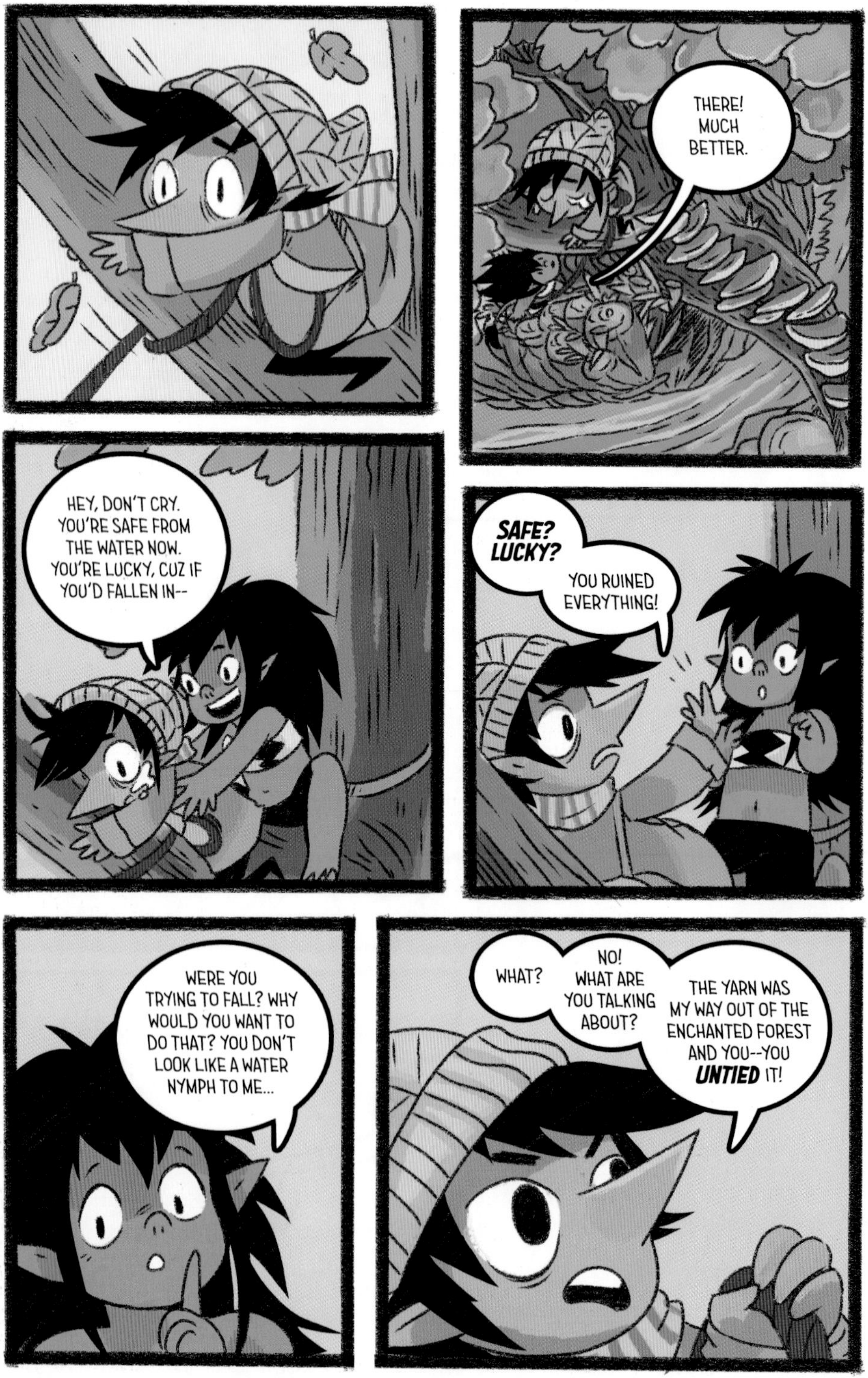
THERE! MUCH BETTER.
HEY, DON'T CRY. YOU'RE SAFE FROM THE WATER NOW. YOU'RE LUCKY, CUZ IF YOU'D FALLEN IN--
SAFE? LUCKY?
YOU RUINED EVERYTHING!
WERE YOU TRYING TO FALL? WHY WOULD YOU WANT TO DO THAT? YOU DON'T LOOK LIKE A WATER NYMPH TO ME...
WHAT?
NO! WHAT ARE YOU TALKING ABOUT?
THE YARN WAS MY WAY OUT OF THE ENCHANTED FOREST AND YOU--YOU UNTIED IT!

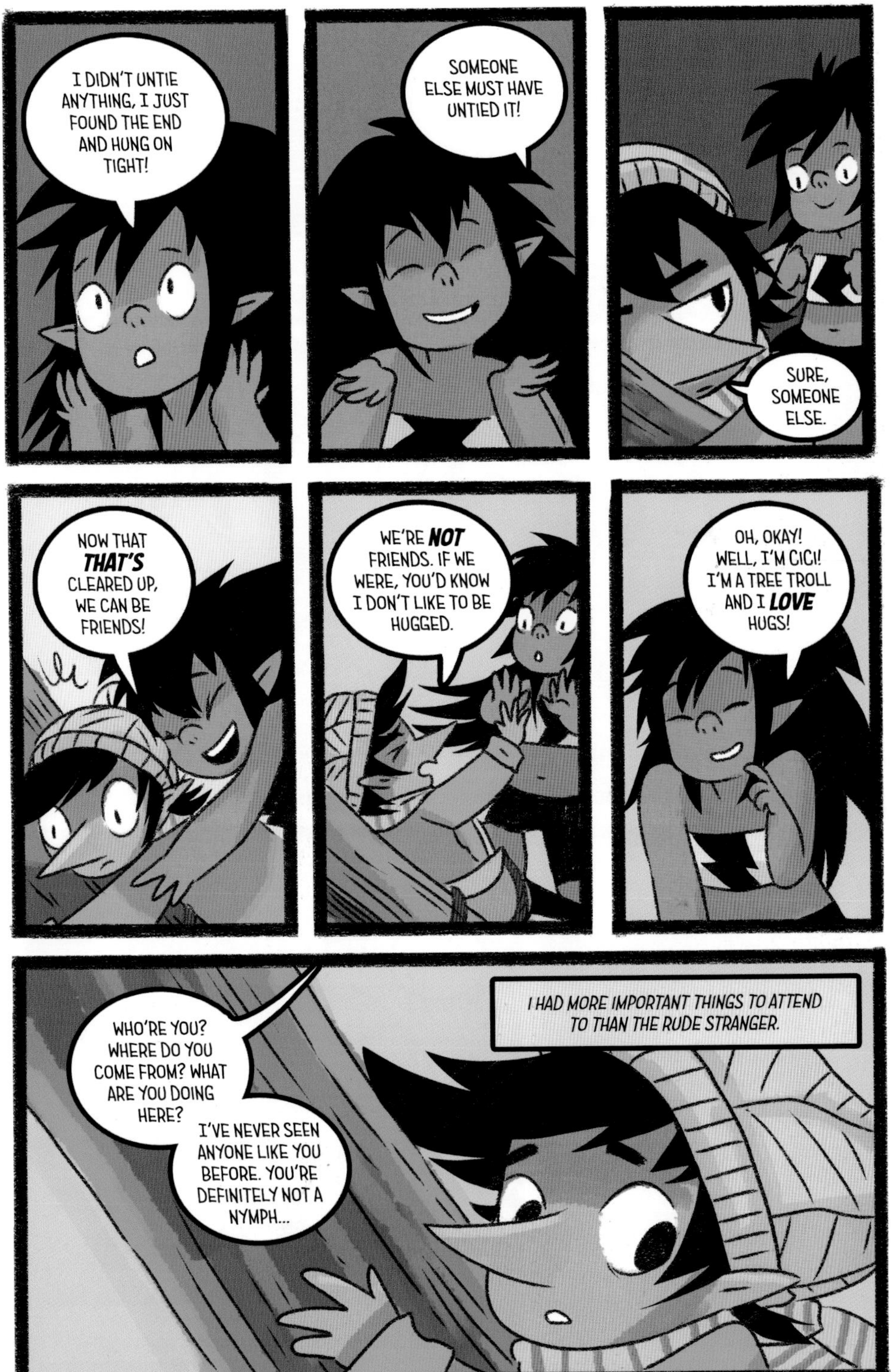
I DIDN'T UNTIE ANYTHING, I JUST FOUND THE END AND HUNG ON TIGHT!
SOMEONE ELSE MUST HAVE UNTIED IT!
SURE, SOMEONE ELSE.
NOW THAT **THAT'S** CLEARED UP, WE CAN BE FRIENDS!
WE'RE **NOT** FRIENDS. IF WE WERE, YOU'D KNOW I DON'T LIKE TO BE HUGGED.
OH, OKAY! WELL, I'M CICI! I'M A TREE TROLL AND I **LOVE** HUGS!
I HAD MORE IMPORTANT THINGS TO ATTEND TO THAN THE RUDE STRANGER.
WHO'RE YOU? WHERE DO YOU COME FROM? WHAT ARE YOU DOING HERE?
I'VE NEVER SEEN ANYONE LIKE YOU BEFORE. YOU'RE DEFINITELY NOT A NYMPH...

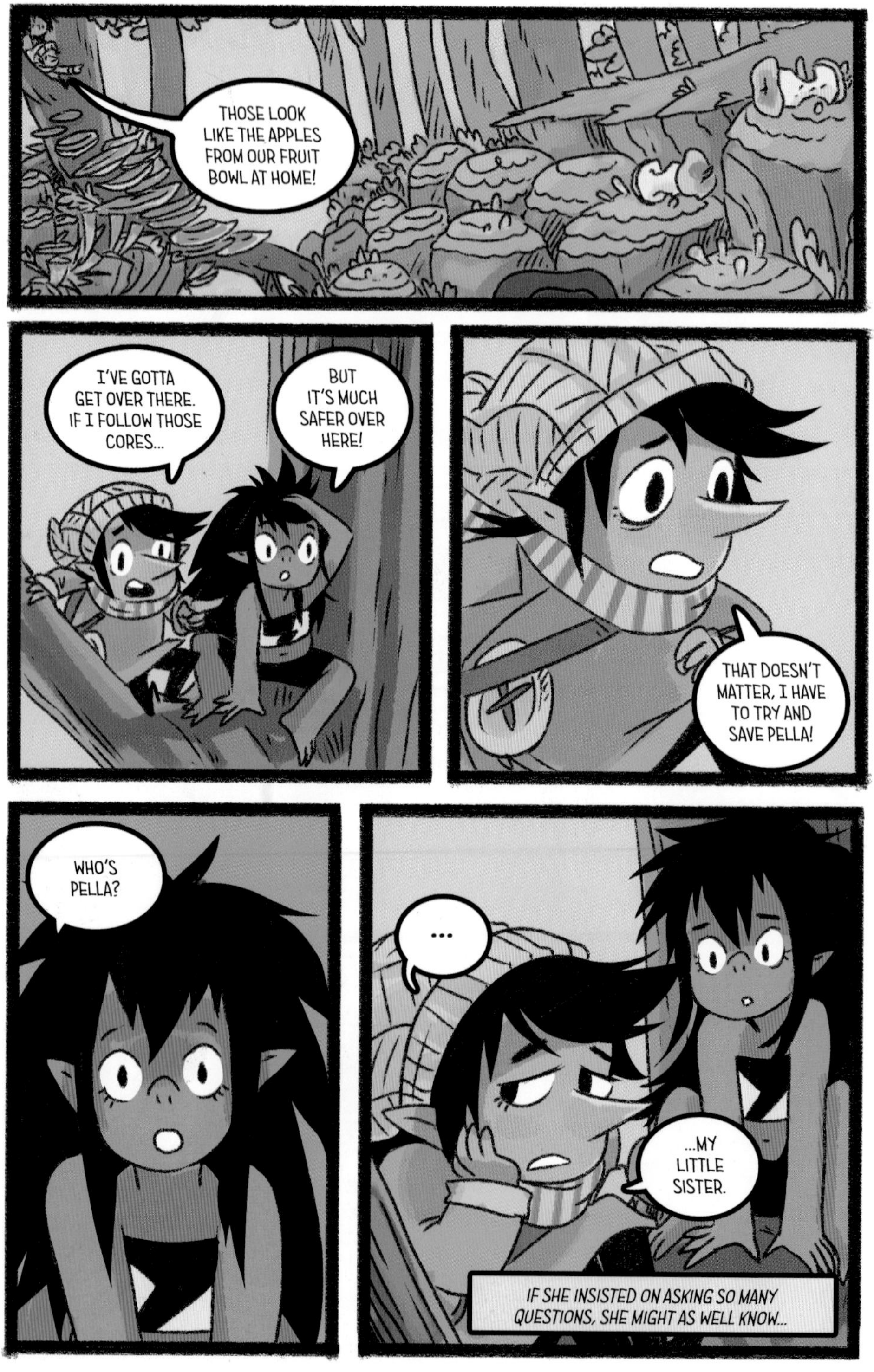
THOSE LOOK LIKE THE APPLES FROM OUR FRUIT BOWL AT HOME!
I'VE GOTTA GET OVER THERE. IF I FOLLOW THOSE CORES...
BUT IT'S MUCH SAFER OVER HERE!
THAT DOESN'T MATTER, I HAVE TO TRY AND SAVE PELLA!
WHO'S PELLA?
...
...MY LITTLE SISTER.
IF SHE INSISTED ON ASKING SO MANY QUESTIONS, SHE MIGHT AS WELL KNOW...

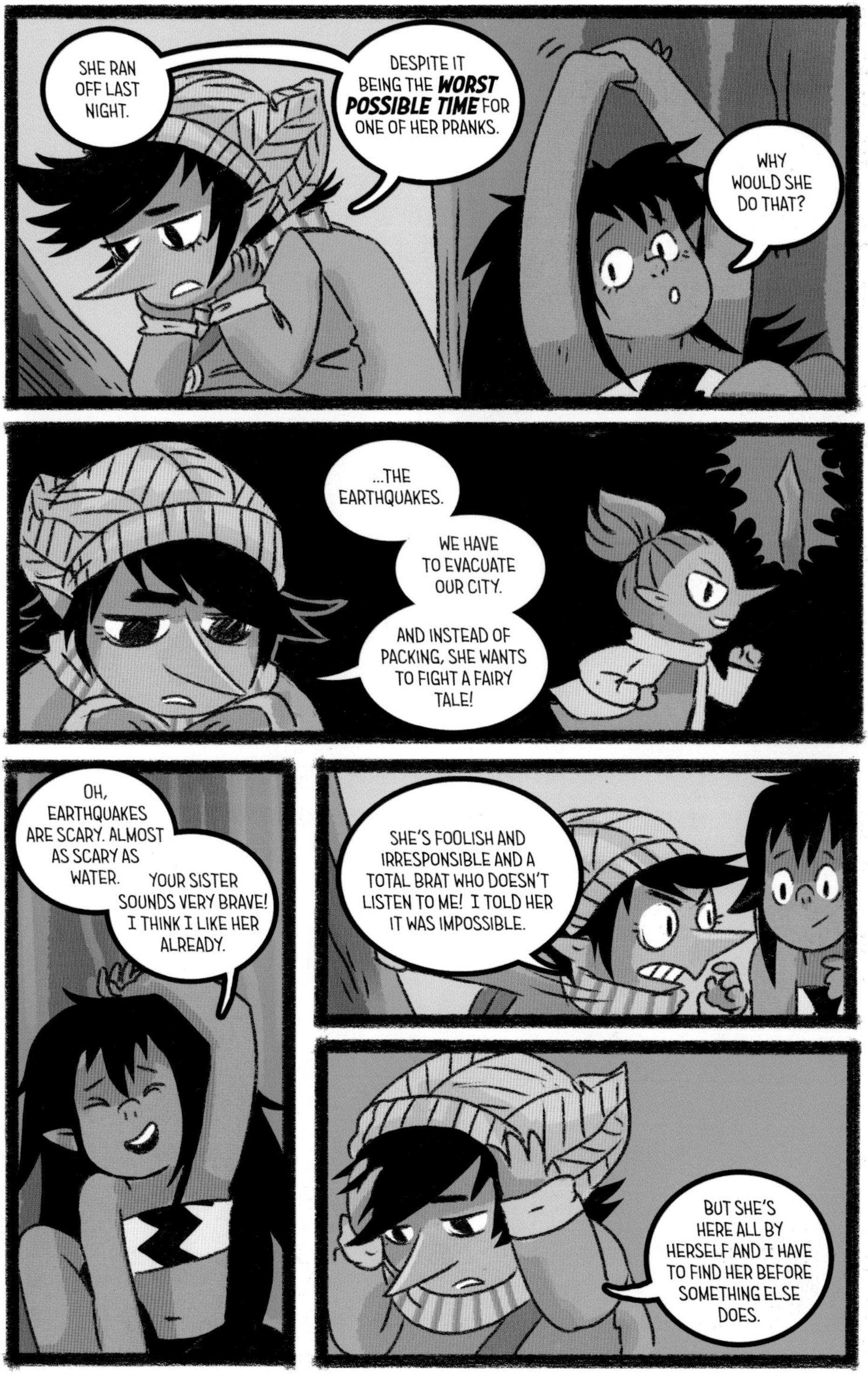
SHE RAN OFF LAST NIGHT.
DESPITE IT BEING THE **WORST POSSIBLE TIME** FOR ONE OF HER PRANKS.
WHY WOULD SHE DO THAT?
...THE EARTHQUAKES.
WE HAVE TO EVACUATE OUR CITY.
AND INSTEAD OF PACKING, SHE WANTS TO FIGHT A FAIRY TALE!
OH, EARTHQUAKES ARE SCARY. ALMOST AS SCARY AS WATER.
YOUR SISTER SOUNDS VERY BRAVE! I THINK I LIKE HER ALREADY.
SHE'S FOOLISH AND IRRESPONSIBLE AND A TOTAL BRAT WHO DOESN'T LISTEN TO ME! I TOLD HER IT WAS IMPOSSIBLE.
BUT SHE'S HERE ALL BY HERSELF AND I HAVE TO FIND HER BEFORE SOMETHING ELSE DOES.

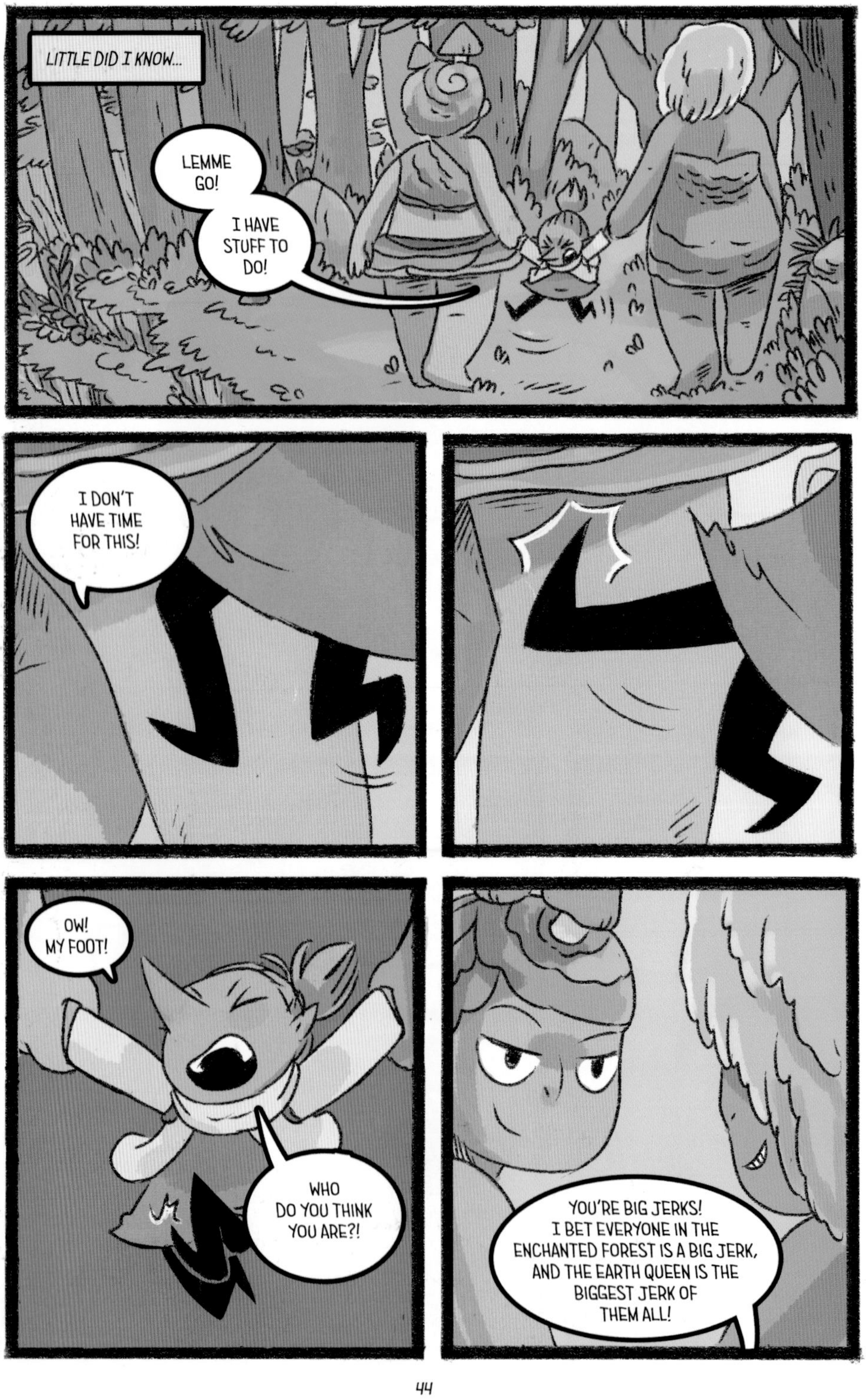

LITTLE DID I KNOW...
LEMME GO!
I HAVE STUFF TO DO!
I DON'T HAVE TIME FOR THIS!
OW! MY FOOT!
WHO DO YOU THINK YOU ARE?!
YOU'RE BIG JERKS! I BET EVERYONE IN THE ENCHANTED FOREST IS A BIG JERK, AND THE EARTH QUEEN IS THE BIGGEST JERK OF THEM ALL!

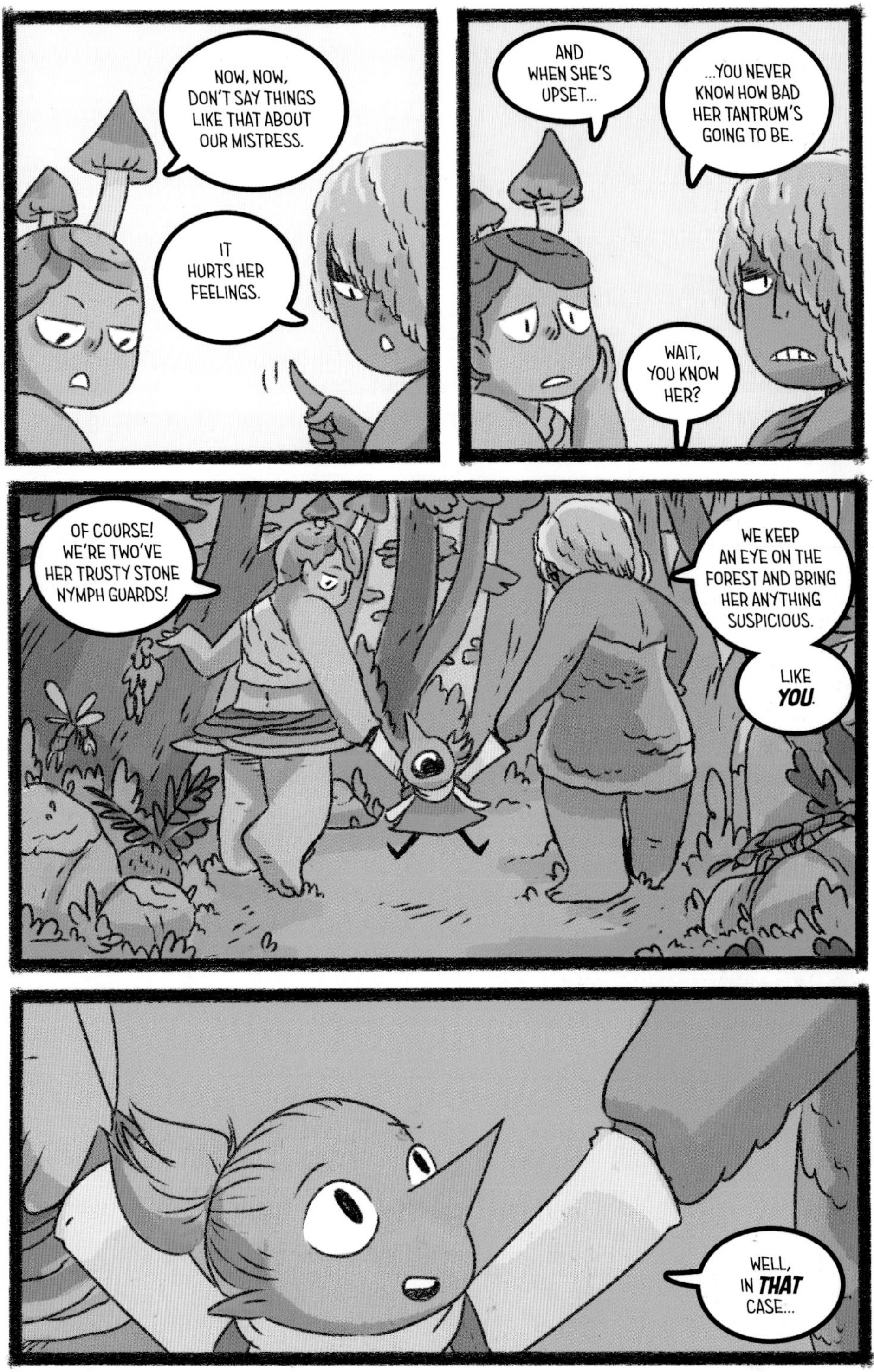
NOW, NOW, DON'T SAY THINGS LIKE THAT ABOUT OUR MISTRESS.
IT HURTS HER FEELINGS.
AND WHEN SHE'S UPSET...
...YOU NEVER KNOW HOW BAD HER TANTRUM'S GOING TO BE.
WAIT, YOU KNOW HER?
OF COURSE! WE'RE TWO'VE HER TRUSTY STONE NYMPH GUARDS!
WE KEEP AN EYE ON THE FOREST AND BRING HER ANYTHING SUSPICIOUS.
LIKE ***YOU***.
WELL, IN ***THAT*** CASE...

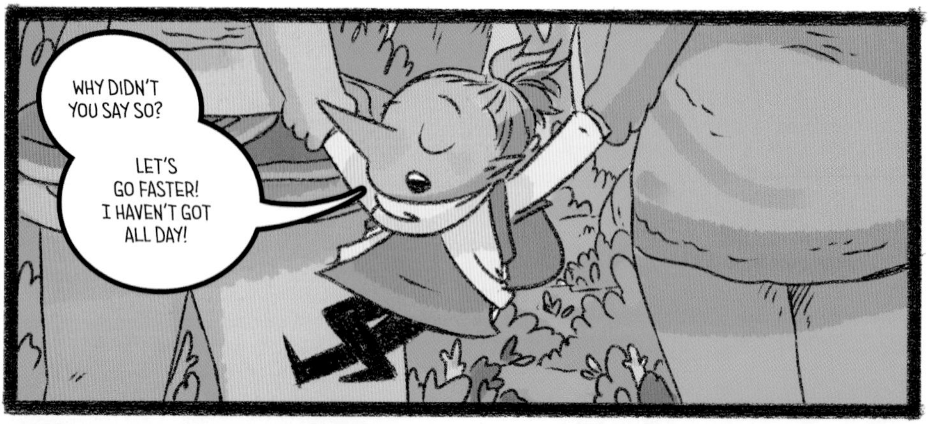
WHY DIDN'T YOU SAY SO?
LET'S GO FASTER! I HAVEN'T GOT ALL DAY!

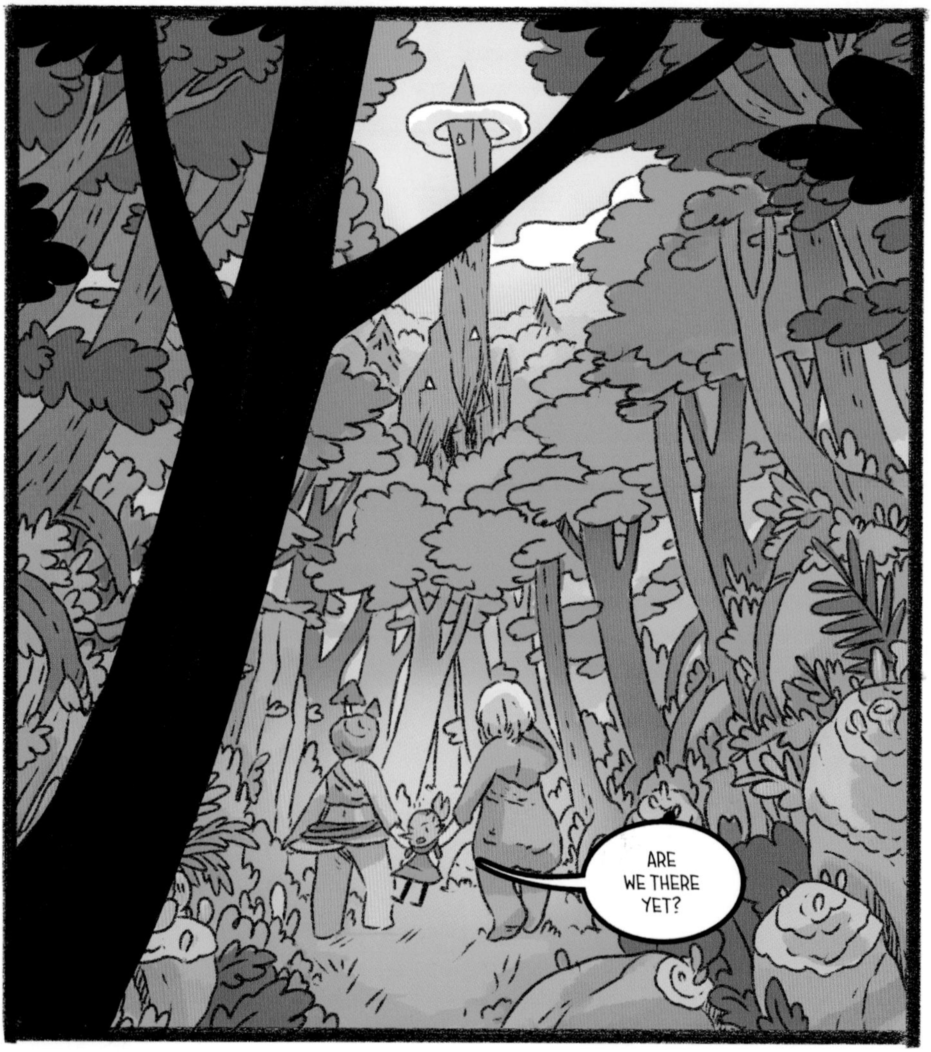
ARE WE THERE YET?

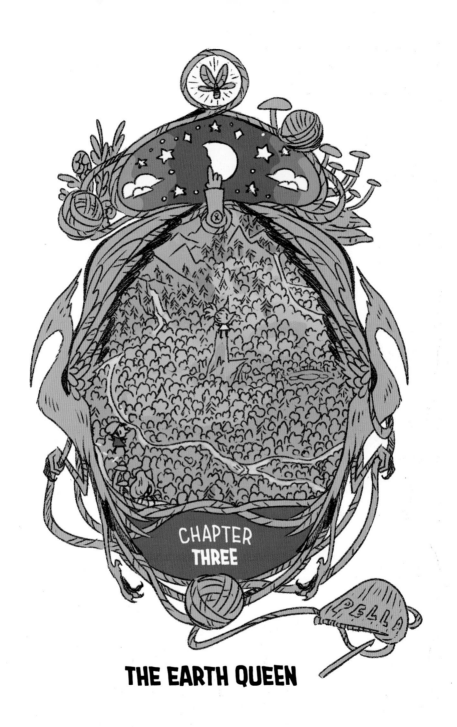

CHAPTER
THREE

THE EARTH QUEEN

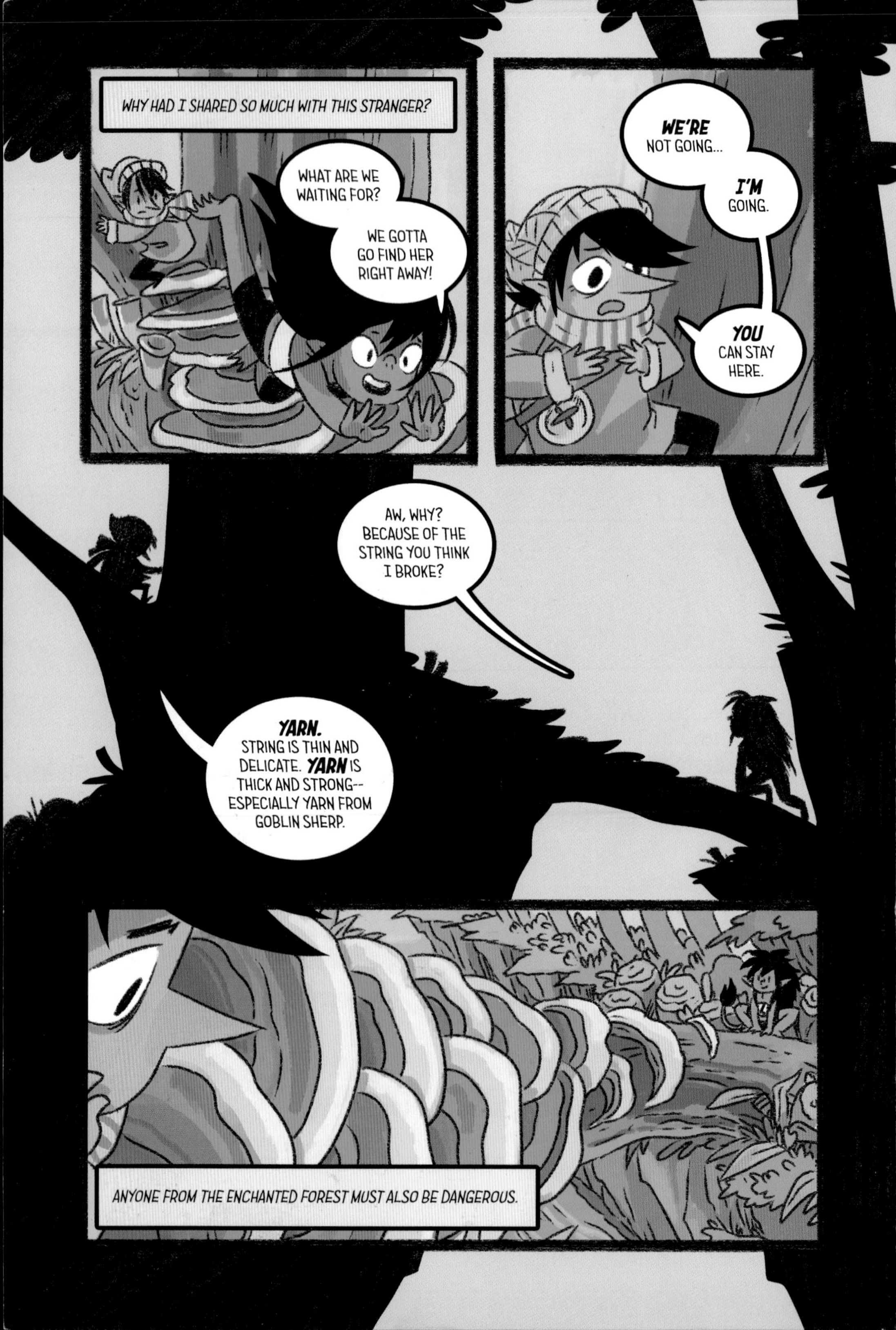
WHY HAD I SHARED SO MUCH WITH THIS STRANGER?
WHAT ARE WE WAITING FOR?
WE GOTTA GO FIND HER RIGHT AWAY!
WE'RE NOT GOING...
I'M GOING.
YOU CAN STAY HERE.
AW, WHY? BECAUSE OF THE STRING YOU THINK I BROKE?
YARN. STRING IS THIN AND DELICATE. YARN IS THICK AND STRONG--ESPECIALLY YARN FROM GOBLIN SHERP.
ANYONE FROM THE ENCHANTED FOREST MUST ALSO BE DANGEROUS.

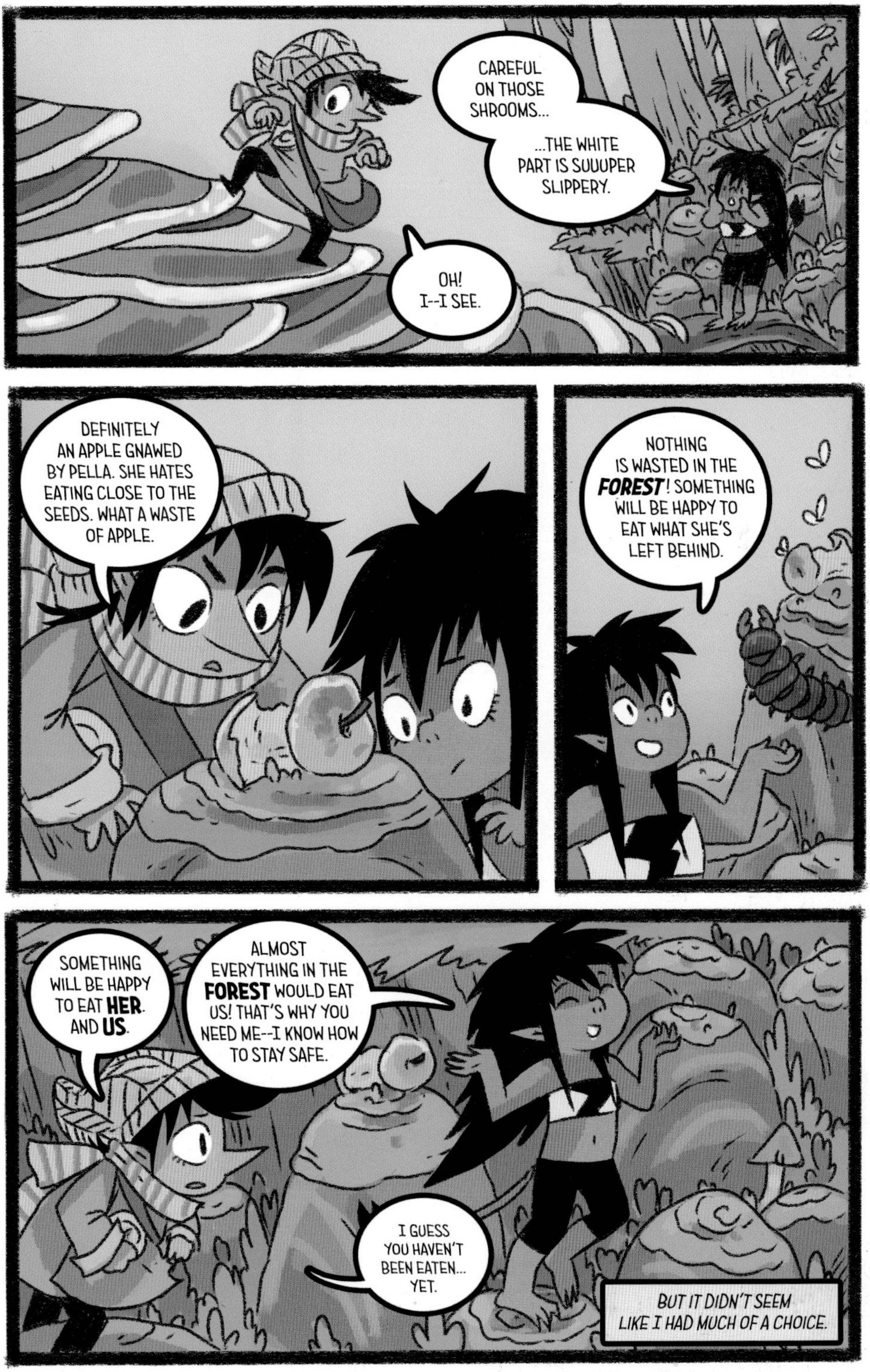
CAREFUL ON THOSE SHROOMS...
...THE WHITE PART IS SUUUPER SLIPPERY.
OH! I--I SEE.
DEFINITELY AN APPLE GNAWED BY PELLA. SHE HATES EATING CLOSE TO THE SEEDS. WHAT A WASTE OF APPLE.
NOTHING IS WASTED IN THE FOREST! SOMETHING WILL BE HAPPY TO EAT WHAT SHE'S LEFT BEHIND.
SOMETHING WILL BE HAPPY TO EAT HER. AND US.
ALMOST EVERYTHING IN THE FOREST WOULD EAT US! THAT'S WHY YOU NEED ME--I KNOW HOW TO STAY SAFE.
I GUESS YOU HAVEN'T BEEN EATEN... YET.
BUT IT DIDN'T SEEM LIKE I HAD MUCH OF A CHOICE.

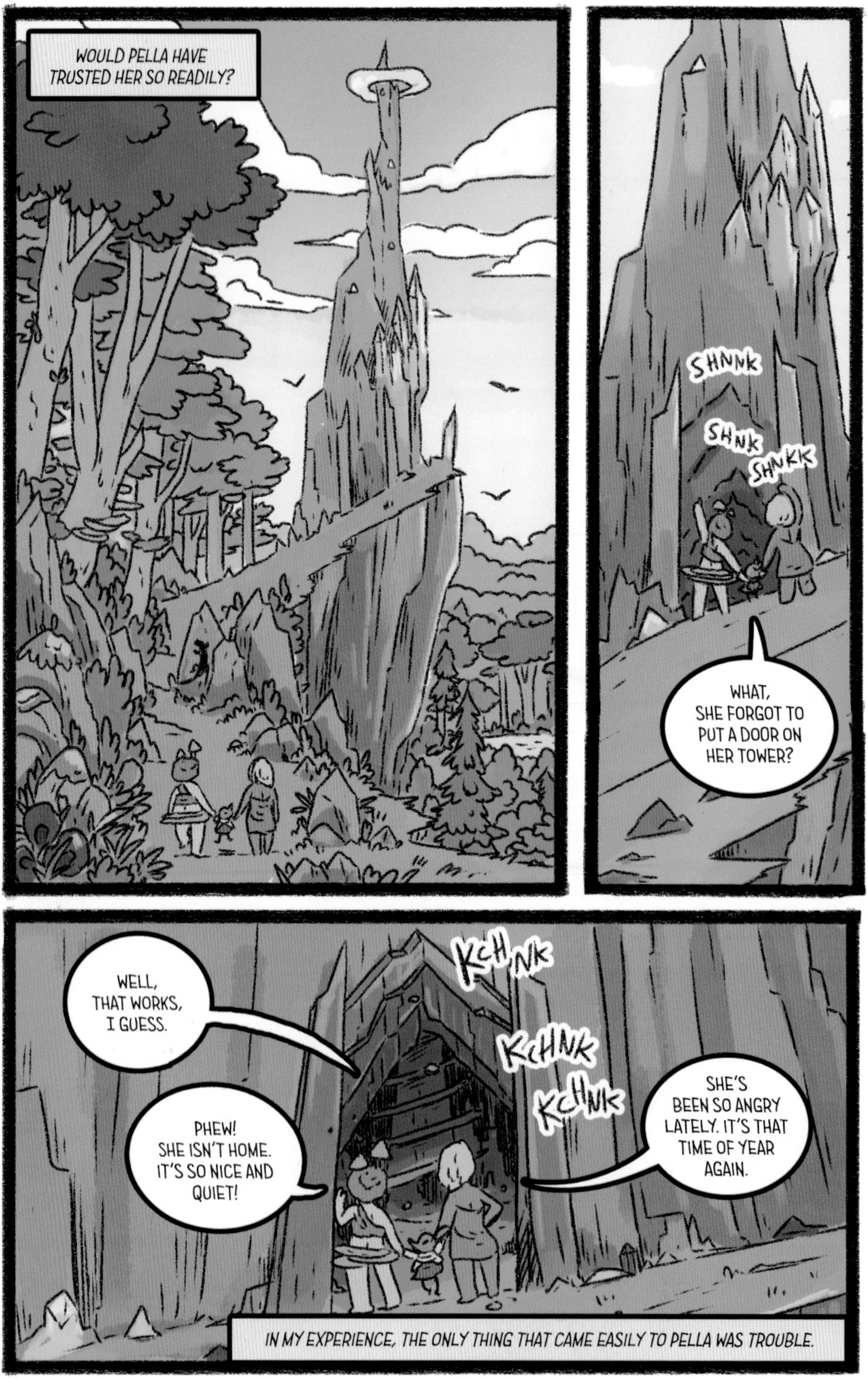
WOULD PELLA HAVE TRUSTED HER SO READILY?
SHNNK
SHNK
SHNKK
WHAT, SHE FORGOT TO PUT A DOOR ON HER TOWER?
KCHNK
KCHNK
KCHNK
WELL, THAT WORKS, I GUESS.
PHEW! SHE ISN'T HOME. IT'S SO NICE AND QUIET!
SHE'S BEEN SO ANGRY LATELY. IT'S THAT TIME OF YEAR AGAIN.
IN MY EXPERIENCE, THE ONLY THING THAT CAME EASILY TO PELLA WAS TROUBLE.

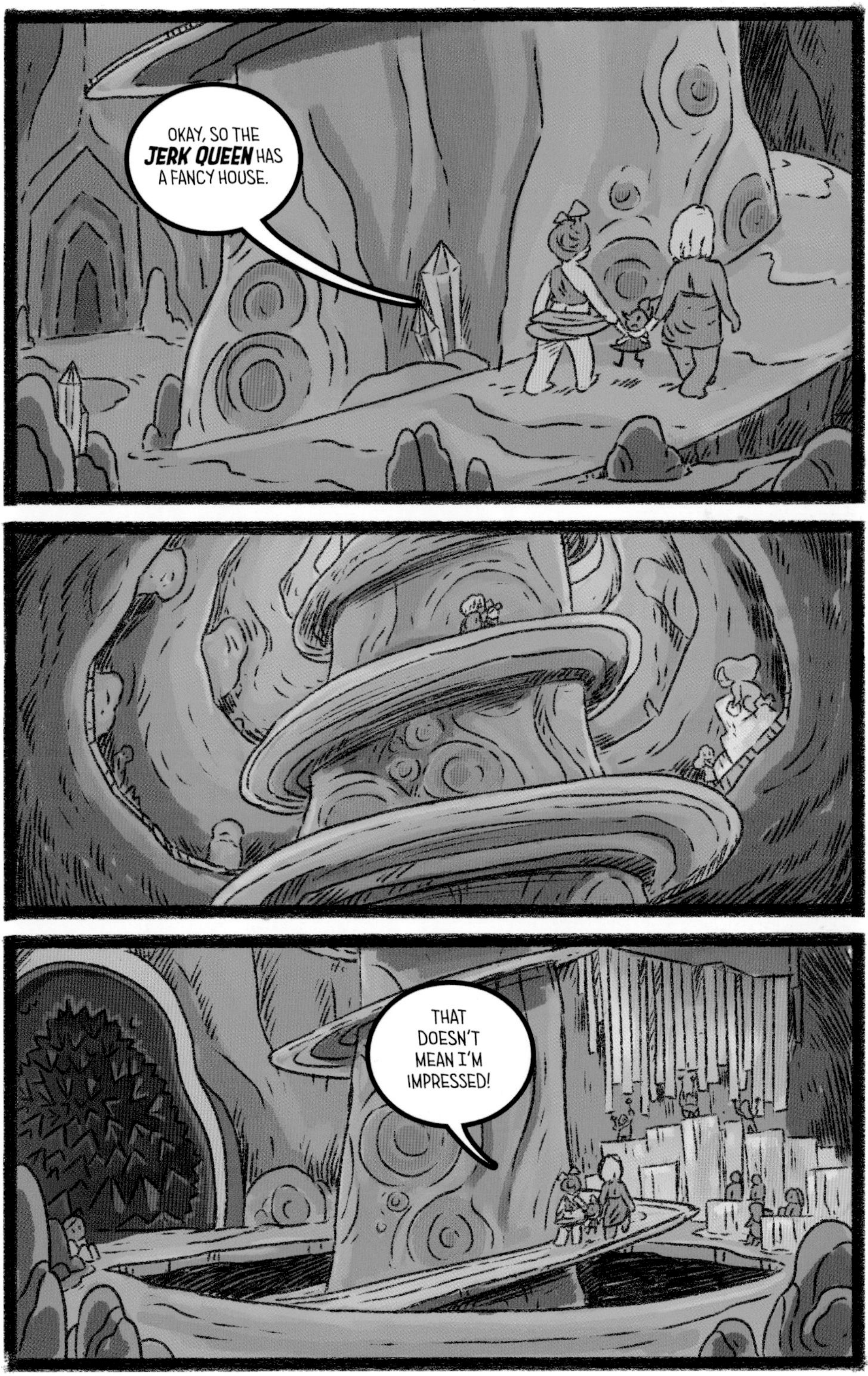
OKAY, SO THE JERK QUEEN HAS A FANCY HOUSE.
THAT DOESN'T MEAN I'M IMPRESSED!

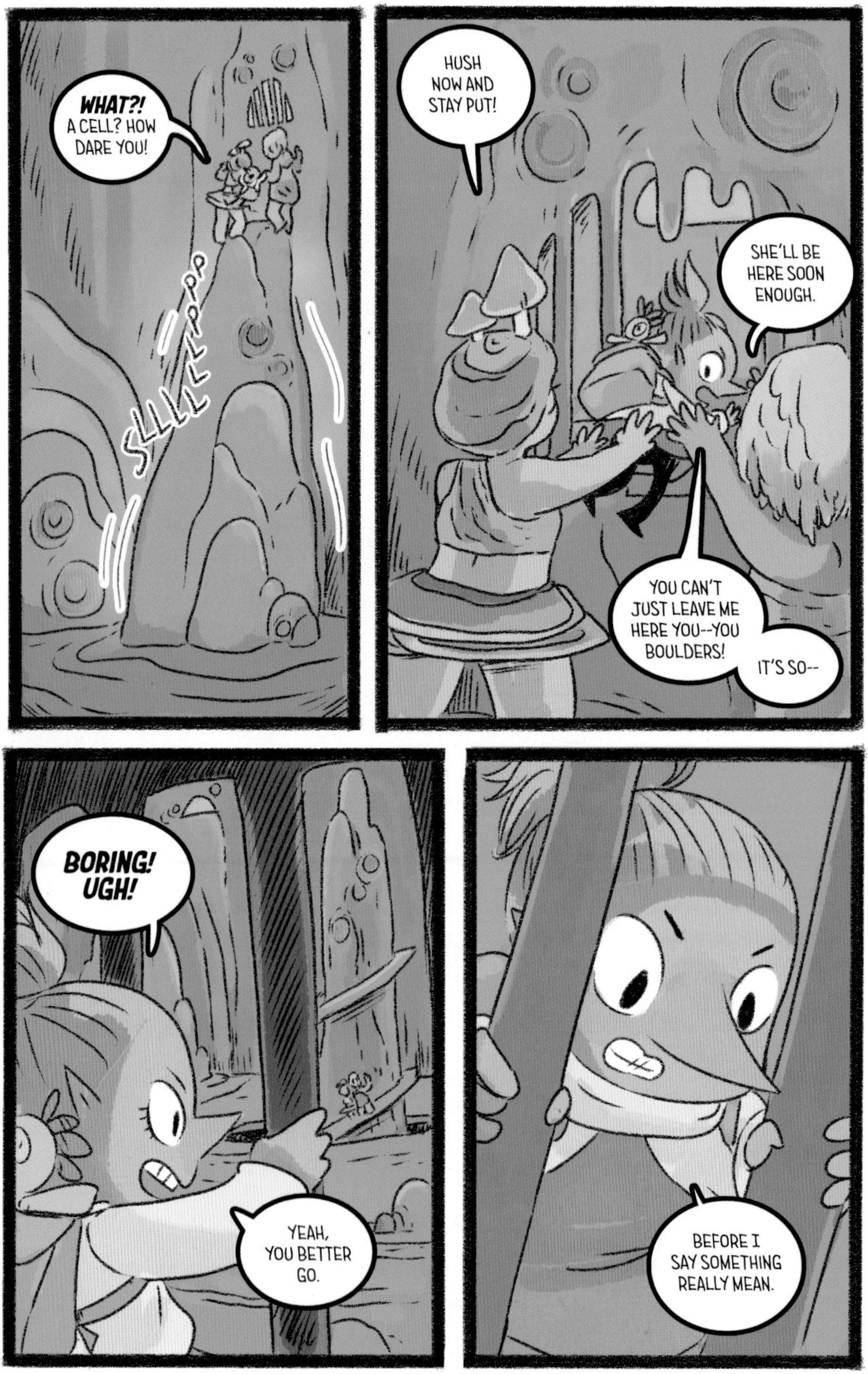
WHAT?! A CELL? HOW DARE YOU!
SLLLLPPPP
HUSH NOW AND STAY PUT!
SHE'LL BE HERE SOON ENOUGH.
YOU CAN'T JUST LEAVE ME HERE YOU--YOU BOULDERS!
IT'S SO--
BORING! UGH!
YEAH, YOU BETTER GO.
BEFORE I SAY SOMETHING REALLY MEAN.

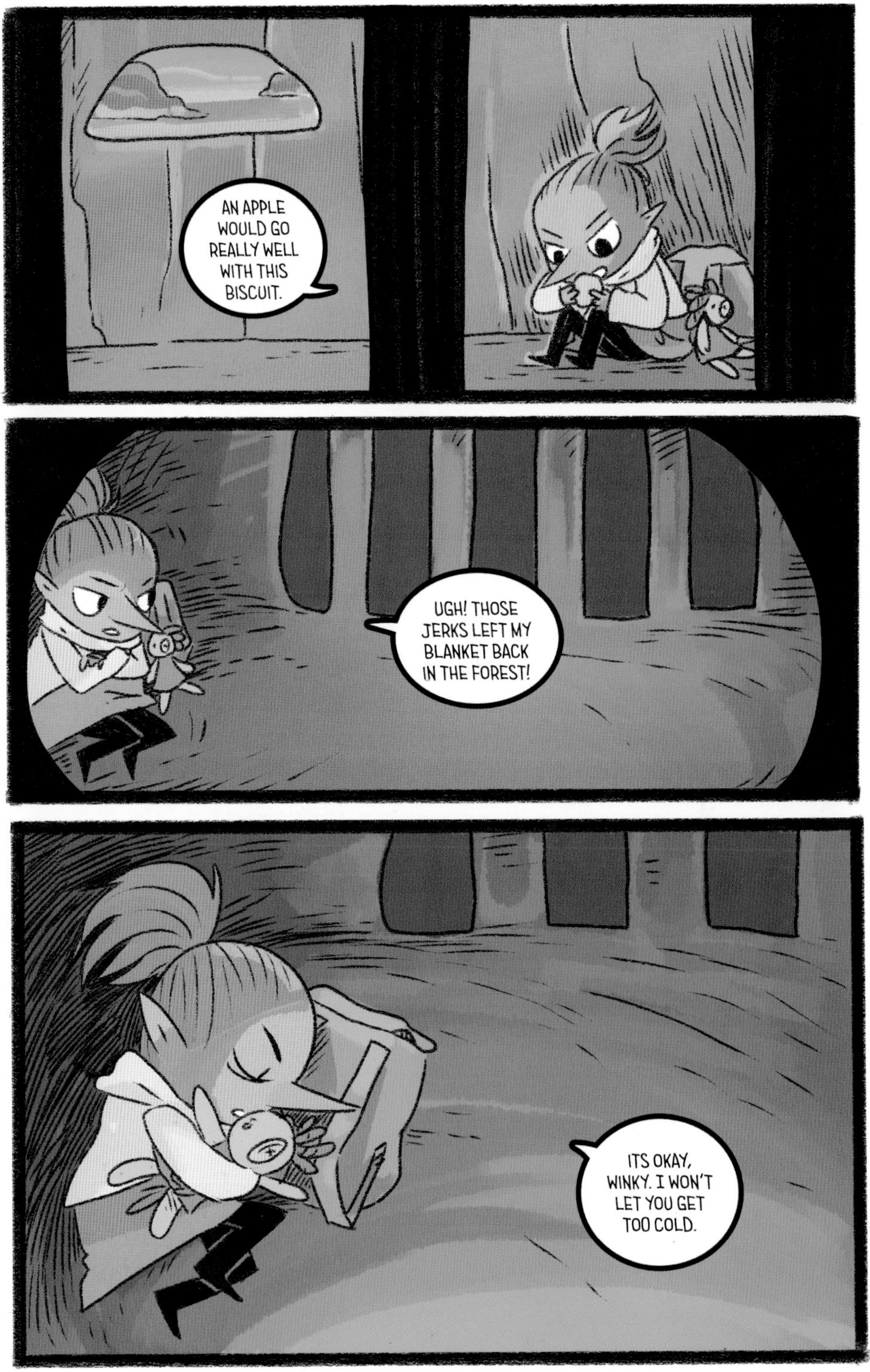
AN APPLE WOULD GO REALLY WELL WITH THIS BISCUIT.
UGH! THOSE JERKS LEFT MY BLANKET BACK IN THE FOREST!
ITS OKAY, WINKY. I WON'T LET YOU GET TOO COLD.

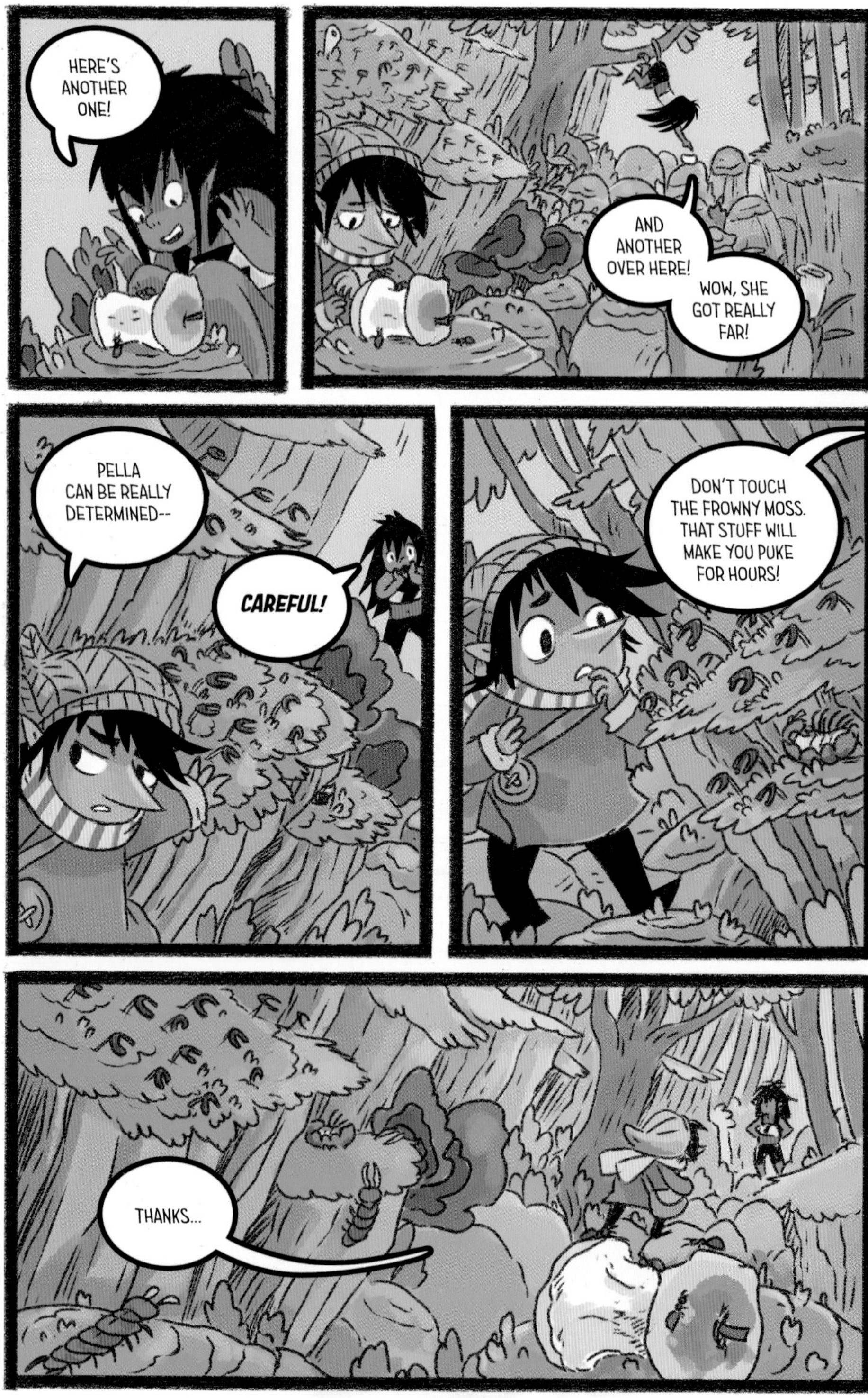
HERE'S ANOTHER ONE!
AND ANOTHER OVER HERE!
WOW, SHE GOT REALLY FAR!
PELLA CAN BE REALLY DETERMINED--
CAREFUL!
DON'T TOUCH THE FROWNY MOSS. THAT STUFF WILL MAKE YOU PUKE FOR HOURS!
THANKS...

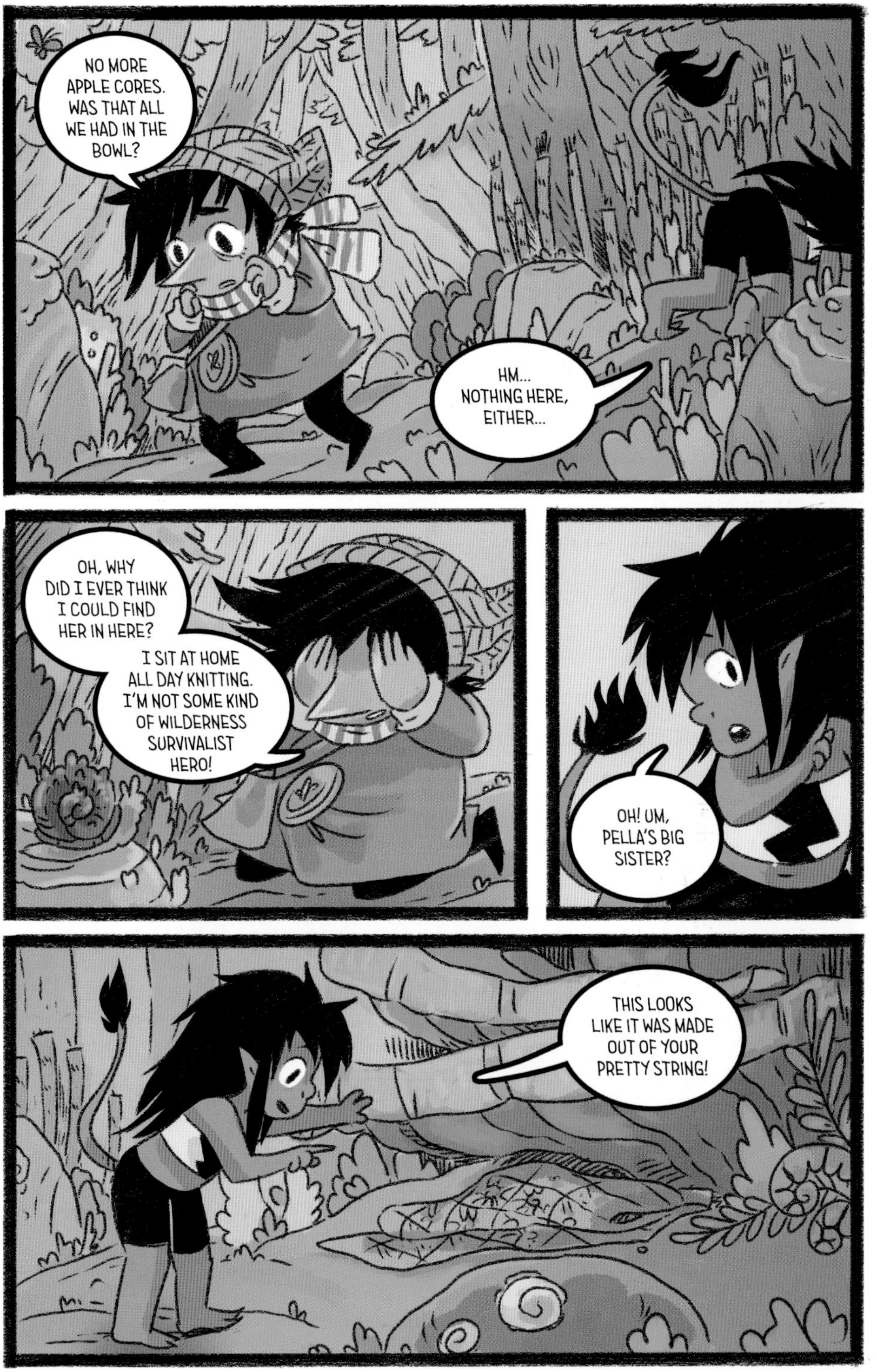
NO MORE APPLE CORES. WAS THAT ALL WE HAD IN THE BOWL?
HM... NOTHING HERE, EITHER...
OH, WHY DID I EVER THINK I COULD FIND HER IN HERE?
I SIT AT HOME ALL DAY KNITTING. I'M NOT SOME KIND OF WILDERNESS SURVIVALIST HERO!
OH! UM, PELLA'S BIG SISTER?
THIS LOOKS LIKE IT WAS MADE OUT OF YOUR PRETTY STRING!

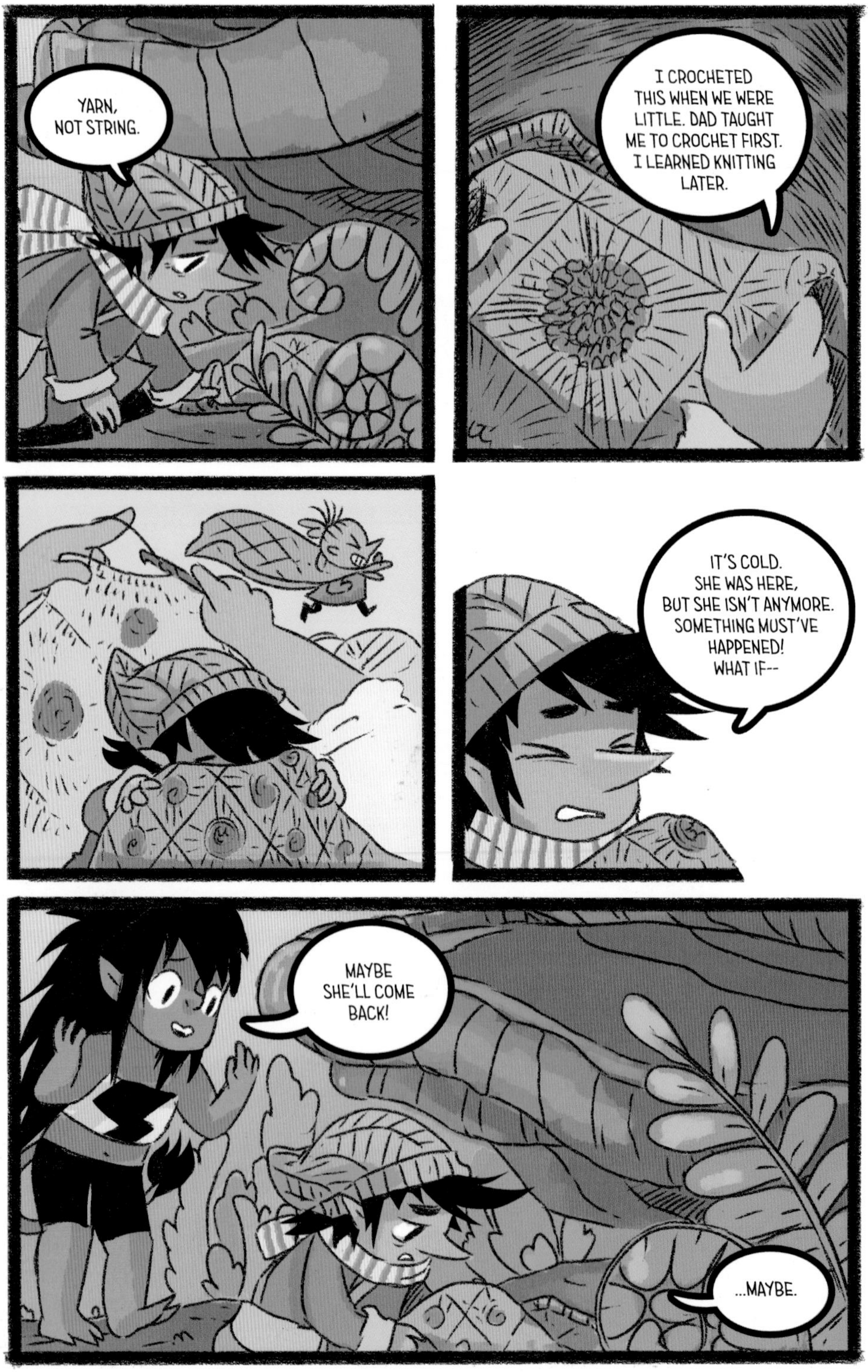
YARN, NOT STRING.
I CROCHETED THIS WHEN WE WERE LITTLE. DAD TAUGHT ME TO CROCHET FIRST. I LEARNED KNITTING LATER.
IT'S COLD. SHE WAS HERE, BUT SHE ISN'T ANYMORE. SOMETHING MUST'VE HAPPENED! WHAT IF--
MAYBE SHE'LL COME BACK!
...MAYBE.

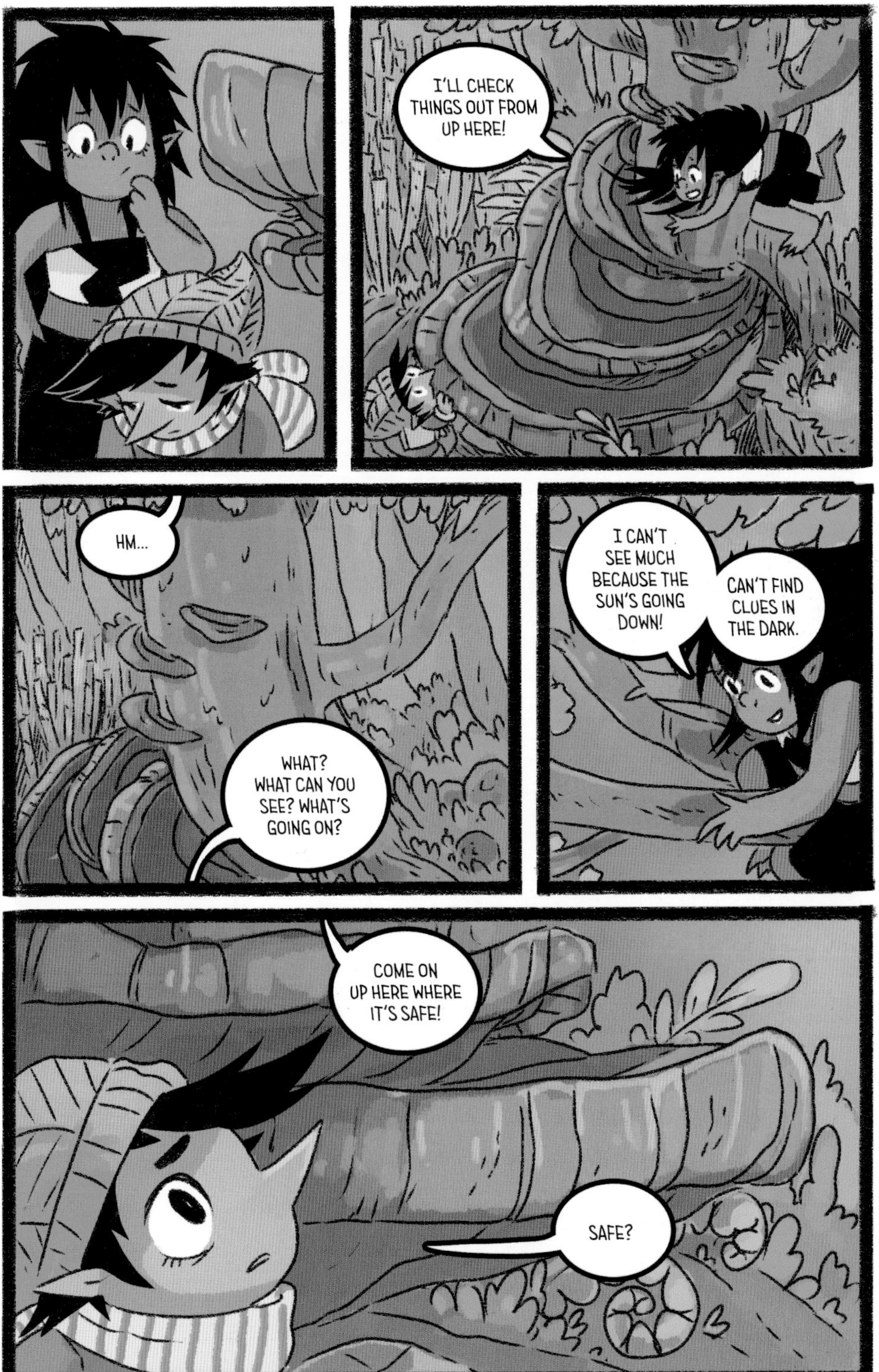
I'LL CHECK THINGS OUT FROM UP HERE!
HM...
WHAT? WHAT CAN YOU SEE? WHAT'S GOING ON?
I CAN'T SEE MUCH BECAUSE THE SUN'S GOING DOWN!
CAN'T FIND CLUES IN THE DARK.
COME ON UP HERE WHERE IT'S SAFE!
SAFE?

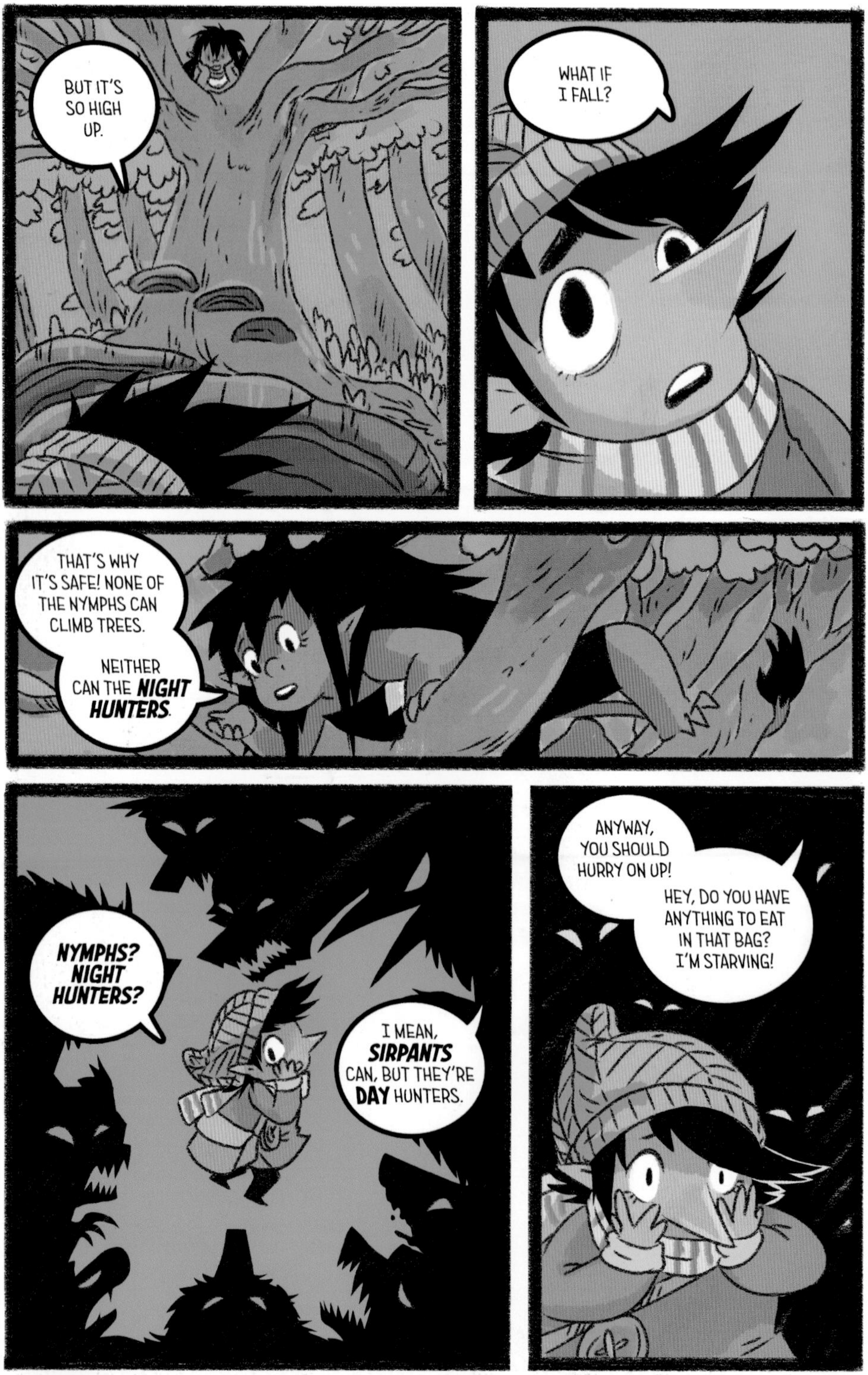
BUT IT'S SO HIGH UP.
WHAT IF I FALL?
THAT'S WHY IT'S SAFE! NONE OF THE NYMPHS CAN CLIMB TREES.
NEITHER CAN THE **NIGHT HUNTERS**.
NYMPHS? NIGHT HUNTERS?
I MEAN, **SIRPANTS** CAN, BUT THEY'RE **DAY** HUNTERS.
ANYWAY, YOU SHOULD HURRY ON UP!
HEY, DO YOU HAVE ANYTHING TO EAT IN THAT BAG? I'M STARVING!

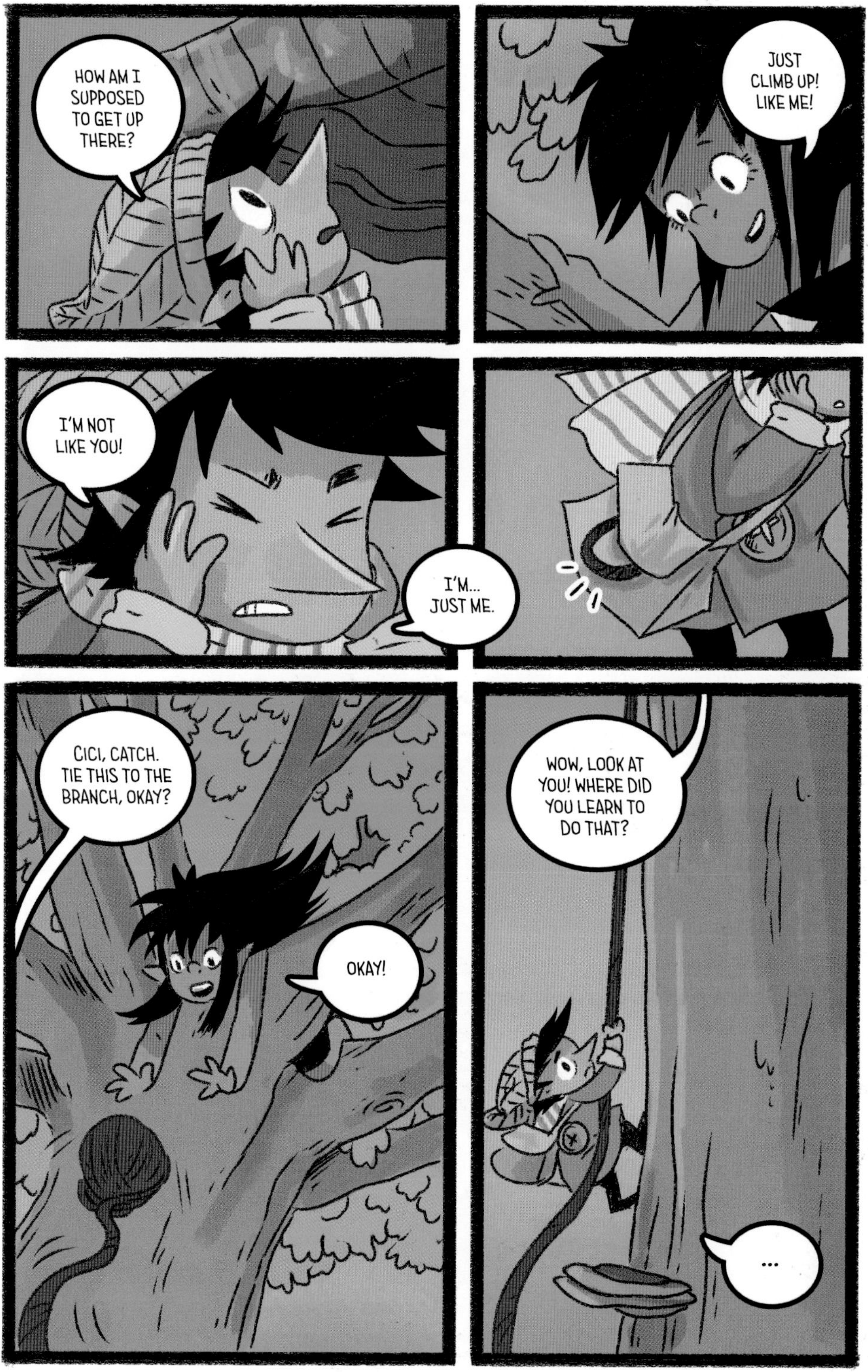
HOW AM I SUPPOSED TO GET UP THERE?
JUST CLIMB UP! LIKE ME!
I'M NOT LIKE YOU!
I'M... JUST ME.
CICI, CATCH. TIE THIS TO THE BRANCH, OKAY?
OKAY!
WOW, LOOK AT YOU! WHERE DID YOU LEARN TO DO THAT?
...

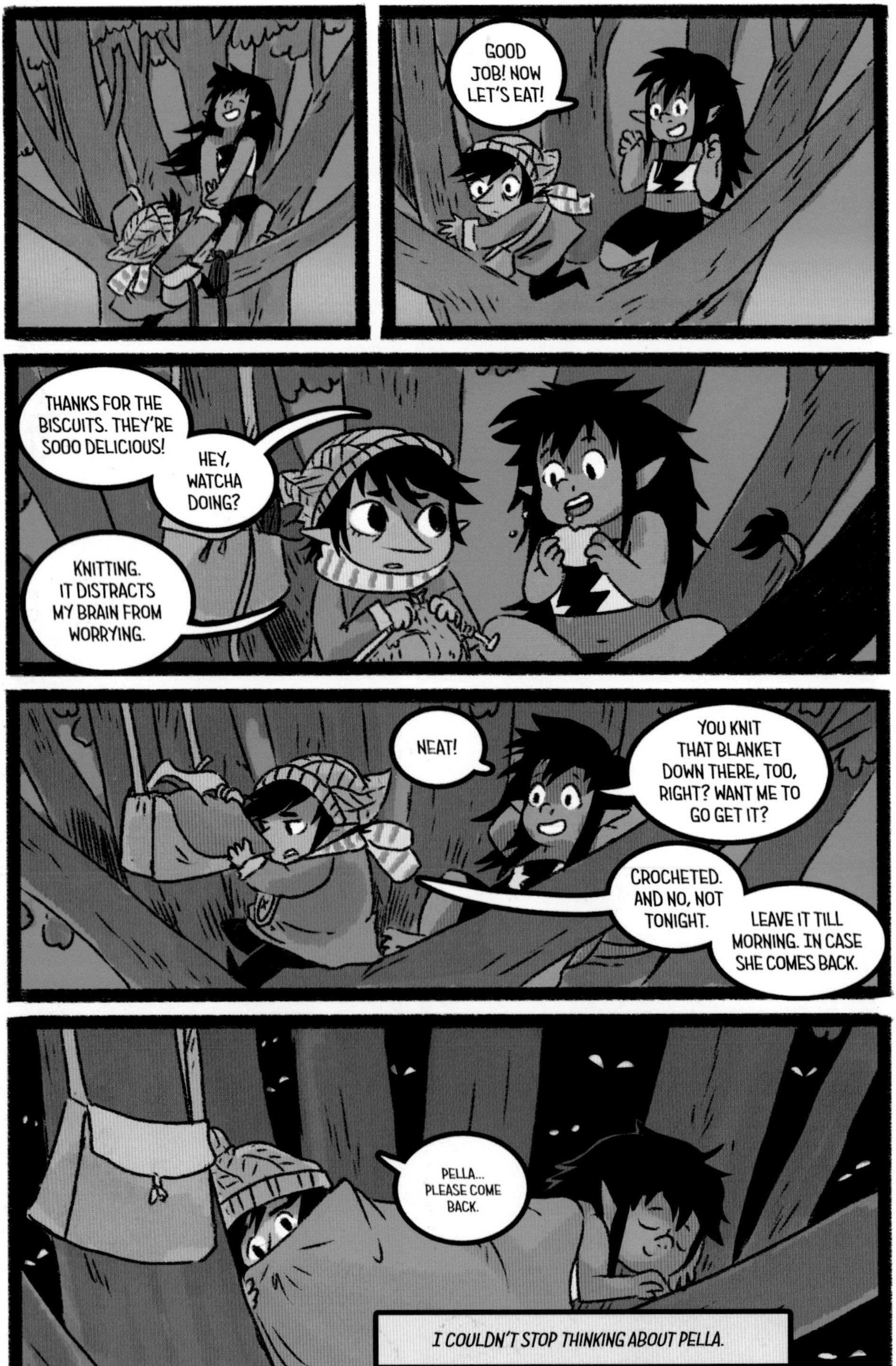
GOOD JOB! NOW LET'S EAT!
THANKS FOR THE BISCUITS. THEY'RE SOOO DELICIOUS!
HEY, WATCHA DOING?
KNITTING. IT DISTRACTS MY BRAIN FROM WORRYING.
NEAT!
YOU KNIT THAT BLANKET DOWN THERE, TOO, RIGHT? WANT ME TO GO GET IT?
CROCHETED. AND NO, NOT TONIGHT.
LEAVE IT TILL MORNING. IN CASE SHE COMES BACK.
PELLA... PLEASE COME BACK.
I COULDN'T STOP THINKING ABOUT PELLA.

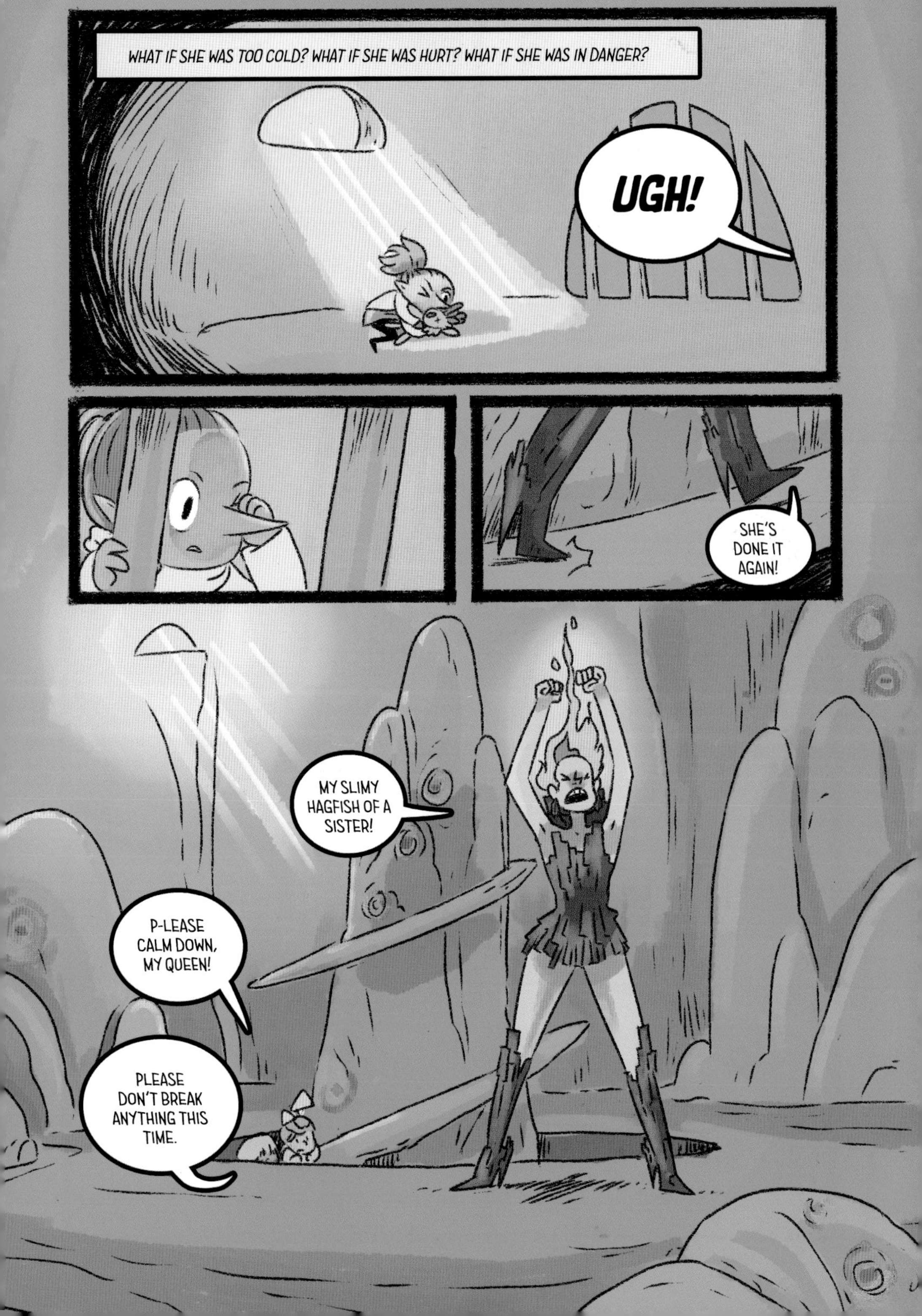
WHAT IF SHE WAS TOO COLD? WHAT IF SHE WAS HURT? WHAT IF SHE WAS IN DANGER?
UGH!
SHE'S DONE IT AGAIN!
MY SLIMY HAGFISH OF A SISTER!
P-LEASE CALM DOWN, MY QUEEN!
PLEASE DON'T BREAK ANYTHING THIS TIME.

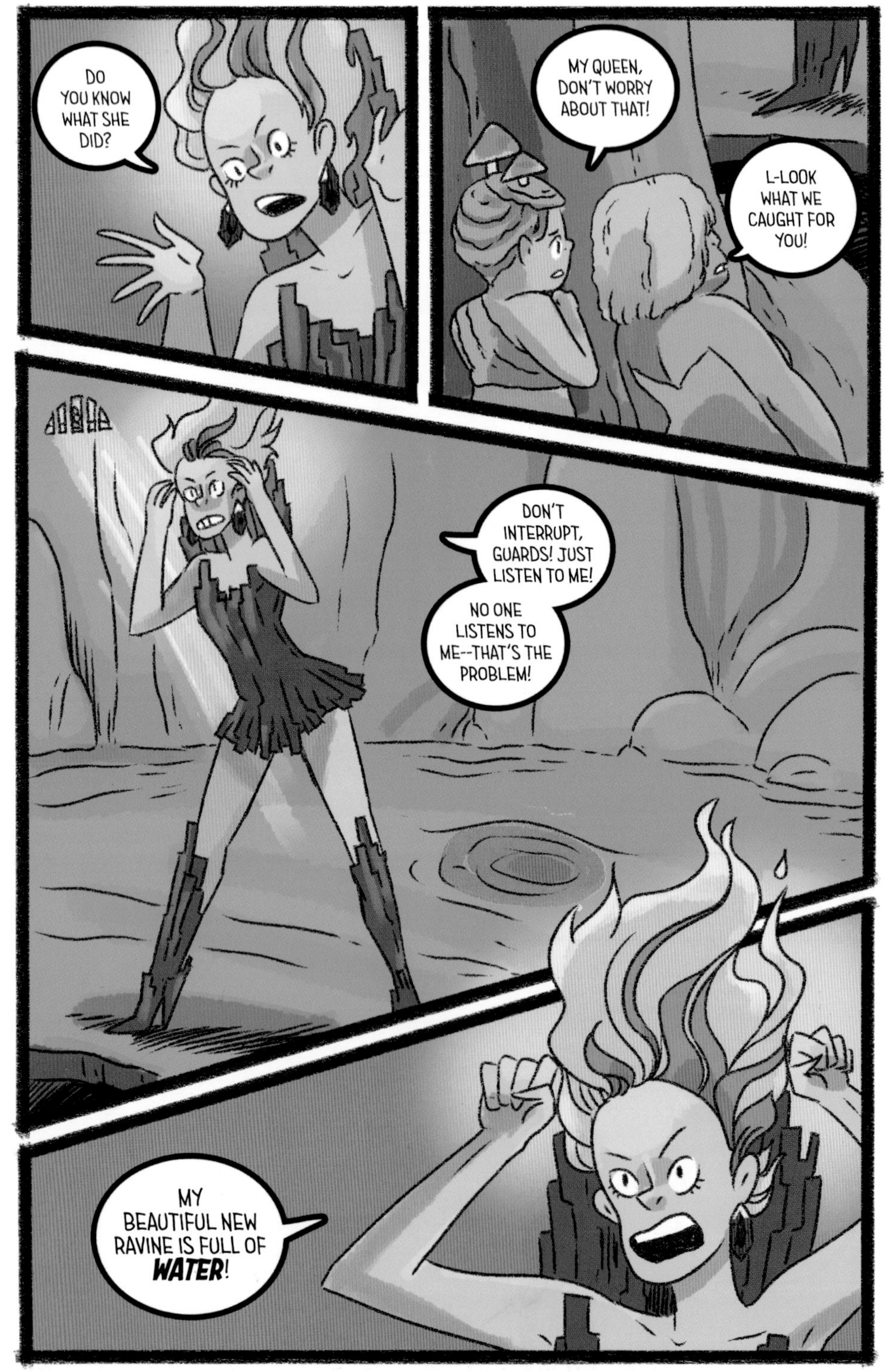
DO YOU KNOW WHAT SHE DID?
MY QUEEN, DON'T WORRY ABOUT THAT!
L-LOOK WHAT WE CAUGHT FOR YOU!
DON'T INTERRUPT, GUARDS! JUST LISTEN TO ME!
NO ONE LISTENS TO ME--THAT'S THE PROBLEM!
MY BEAUTIFUL NEW RAVINE IS FULL OF WATER!

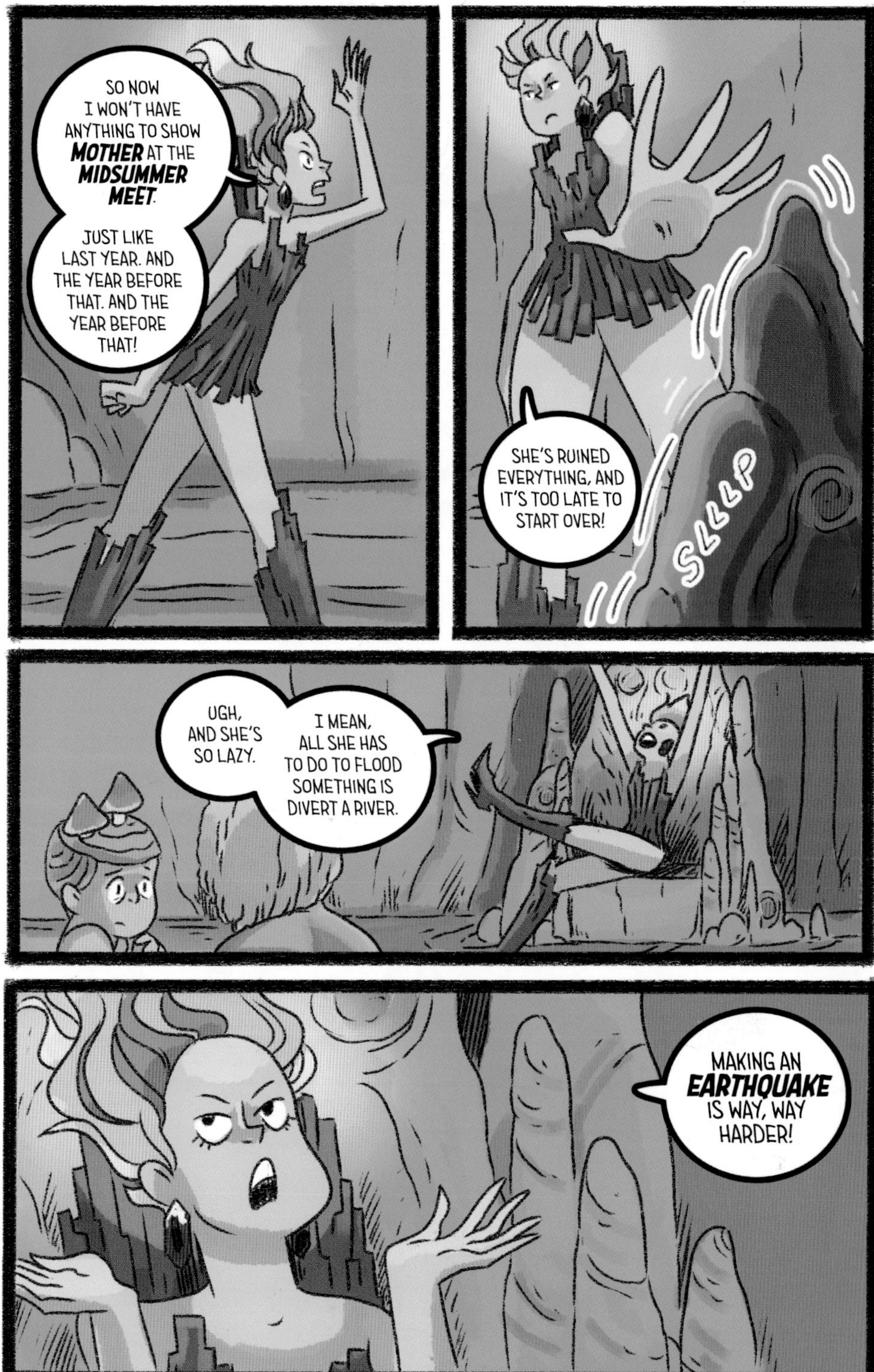
SO NOW I WON'T HAVE ANYTHING TO SHOW **MOTHER** AT THE **MIDSUMMER MEET**.
JUST LIKE LAST YEAR. AND THE YEAR BEFORE THAT. AND THE YEAR BEFORE THAT!
SHE'S RUINED EVERYTHING, AND IT'S TOO LATE TO START OVER!
SLLLP
UGH, AND SHE'S SO LAZY.
I MEAN, ALL SHE HAS TO DO TO FLOOD SOMETHING IS DIVERT A RIVER.
MAKING AN **EARTHQUAKE** IS WAY, WAY HARDER!

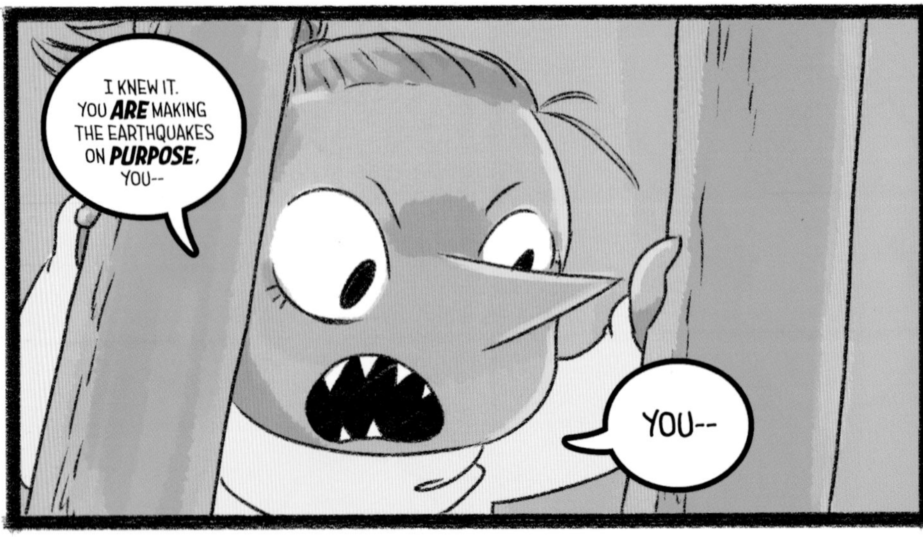
I KNEW IT. YOU ARE MAKING THE EARTHQUAKES ON PURPOSE, YOU--
YOU--

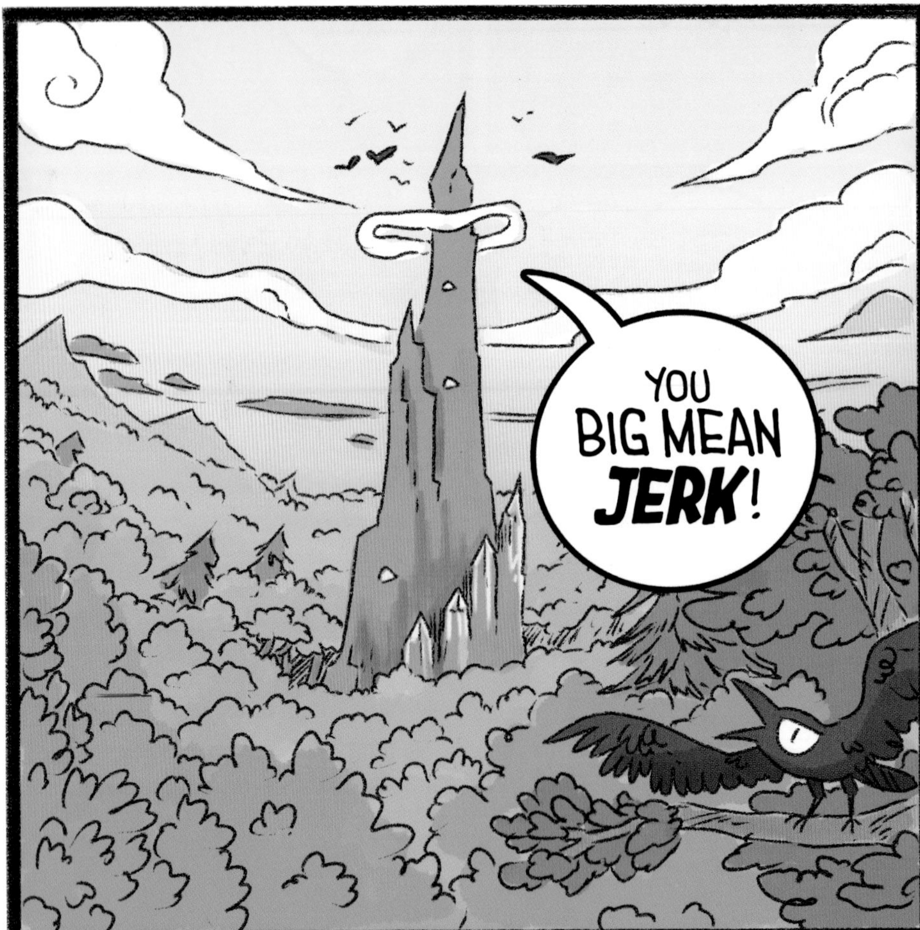
YOU BIG MEAN JERK!

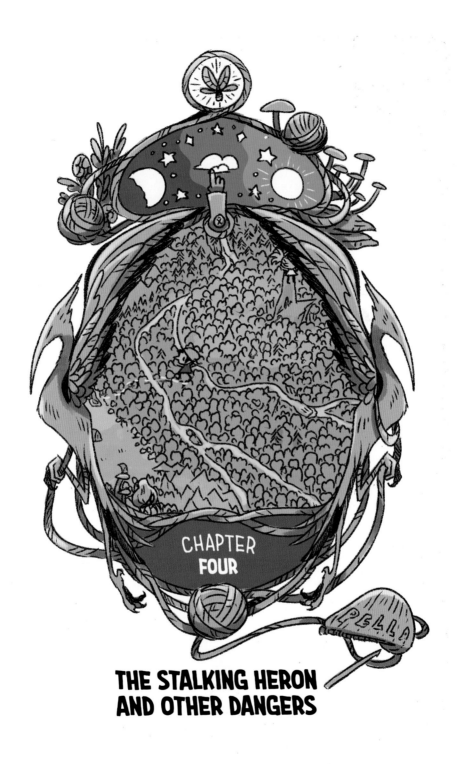

CHAPTER
FOUR

THE STALKING HERON
AND OTHER DANGERS

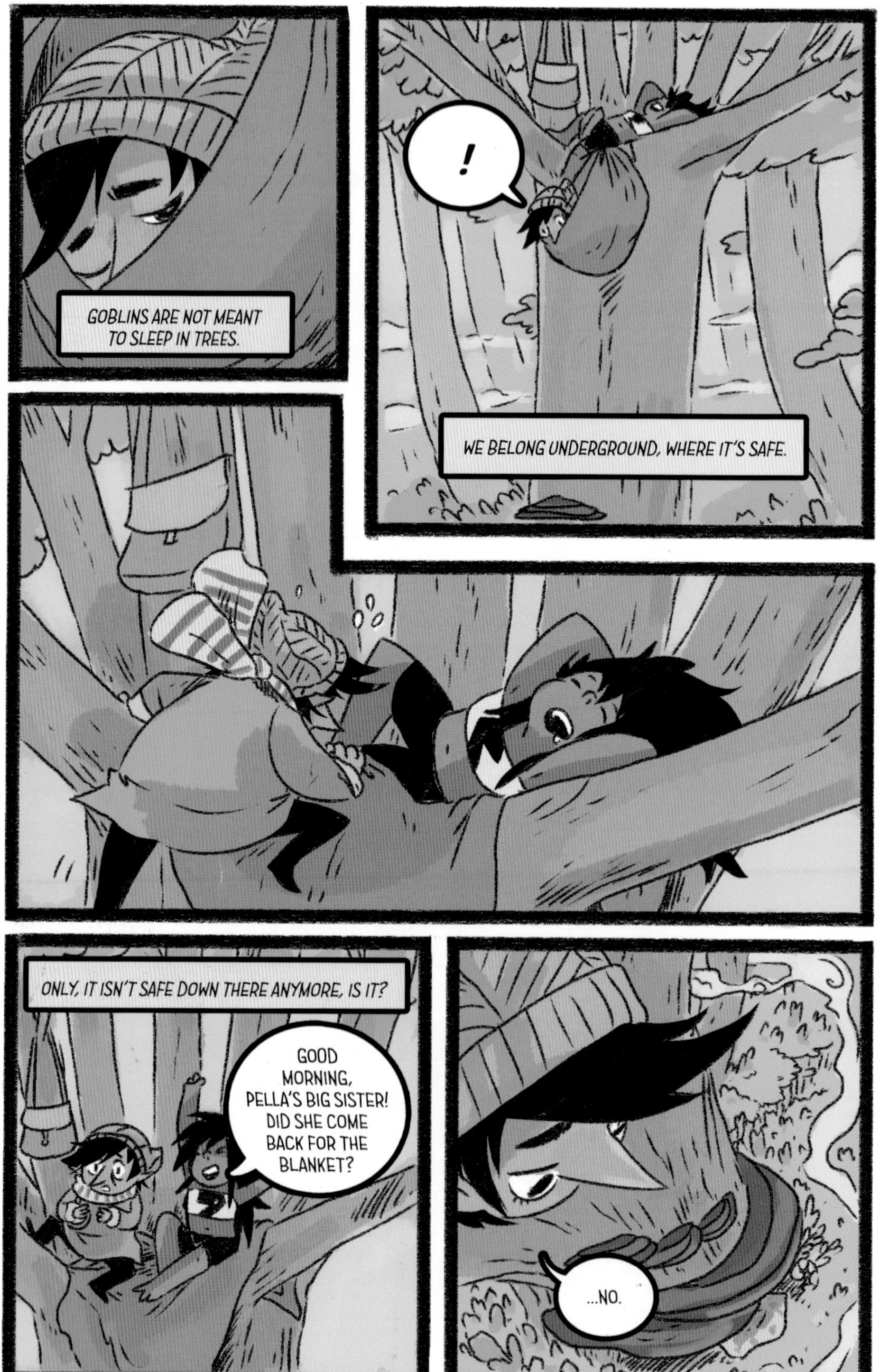
GOBLINS ARE NOT MEANT TO SLEEP IN TREES.
!
WE BELONG UNDERGROUND, WHERE IT'S SAFE.
ONLY, IT ISN'T SAFE DOWN THERE ANYMORE, IS IT?
GOOD MORNING, PELLA'S BIG SISTER! DID SHE COME BACK FOR THE BLANKET?
...NO.

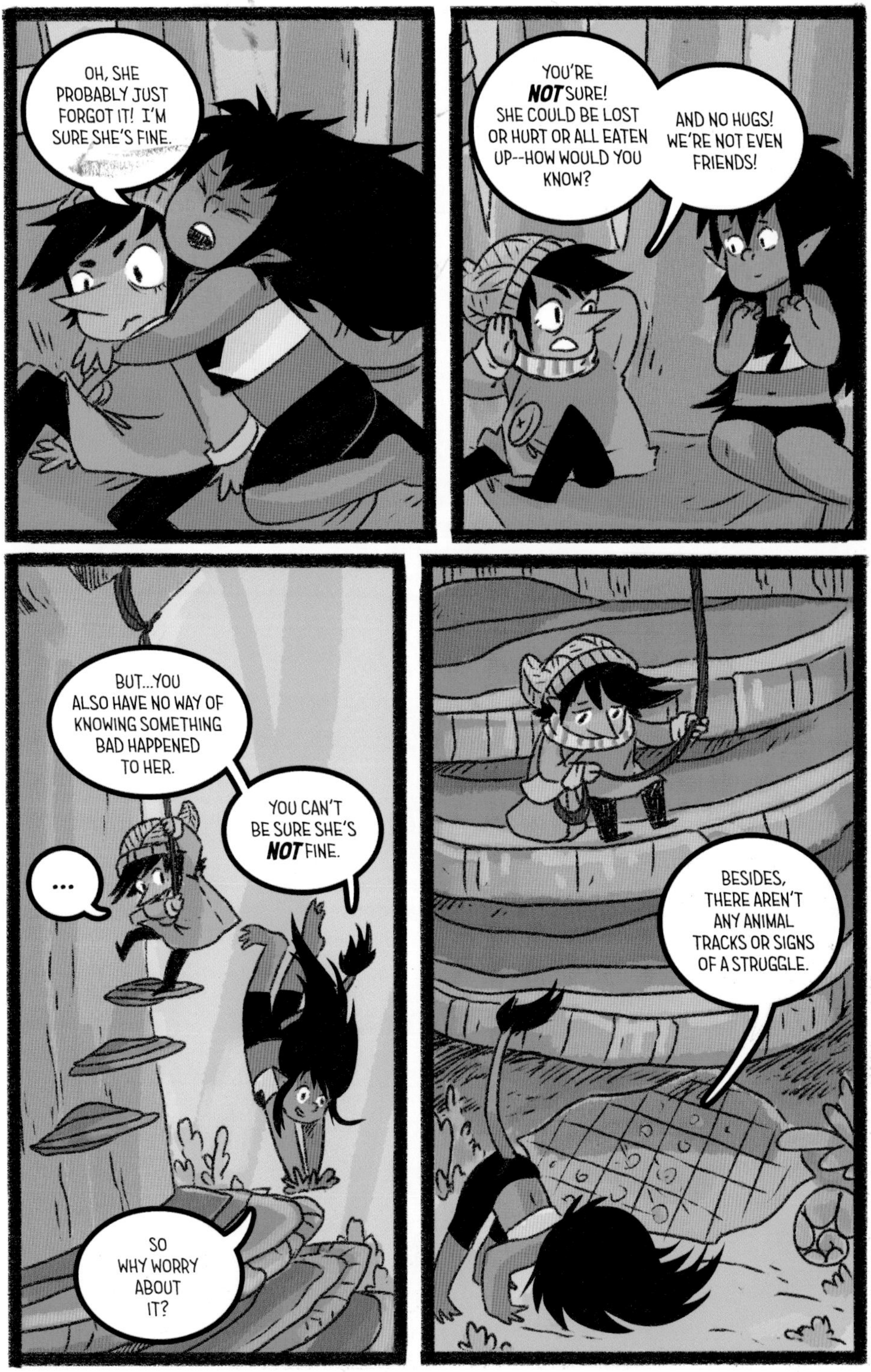
OH, SHE PROBABLY JUST FORGOT IT! I'M SURE SHE'S FINE.
YOU'RE **NOT** SURE! SHE COULD BE LOST OR HURT OR ALL EATEN UP--HOW WOULD YOU KNOW?
AND NO HUGS! WE'RE NOT EVEN FRIENDS!
BUT...YOU ALSO HAVE NO WAY OF KNOWING SOMETHING BAD HAPPENED TO HER.
YOU CAN'T BE SURE SHE'S **NOT** FINE.
...
SO WHY WORRY ABOUT IT?
BESIDES, THERE AREN'T ANY ANIMAL TRACKS OR SIGNS OF A STRUGGLE.

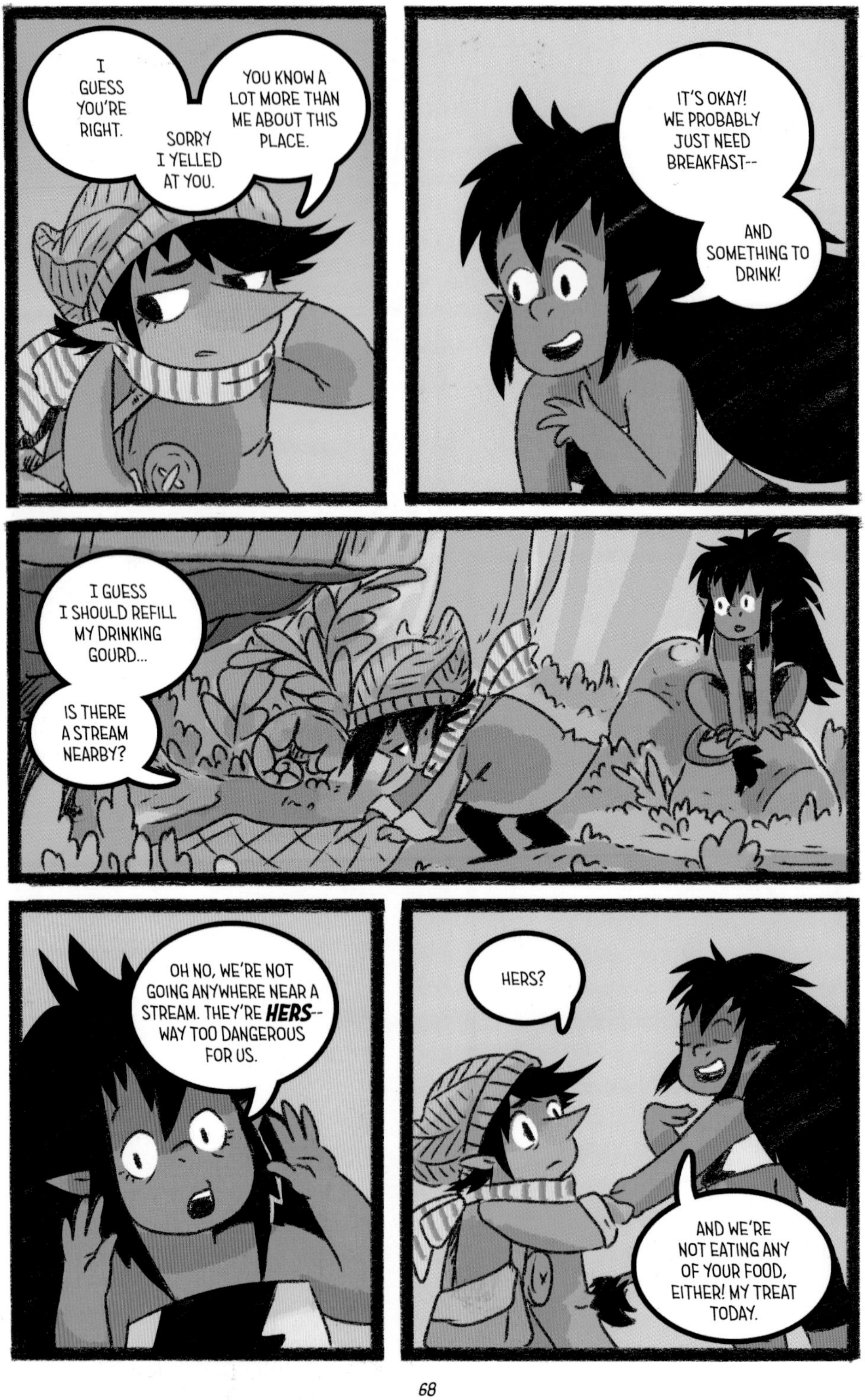
I GUESS YOU'RE RIGHT.
SORRY I YELLED AT YOU.
YOU KNOW A LOT MORE THAN ME ABOUT THIS PLACE.
IT'S OKAY! WE PROBABLY JUST NEED BREAKFAST--
AND SOMETHING TO DRINK!
I GUESS I SHOULD REFILL MY DRINKING GOURD...
IS THERE A STREAM NEARBY?
OH NO, WE'RE NOT GOING ANYWHERE NEAR A STREAM. THEY'RE **HERS**-- WAY TOO DANGEROUS FOR US.
HERS?
AND WE'RE NOT EATING ANY OF YOUR FOOD, EITHER! MY TREAT TODAY.

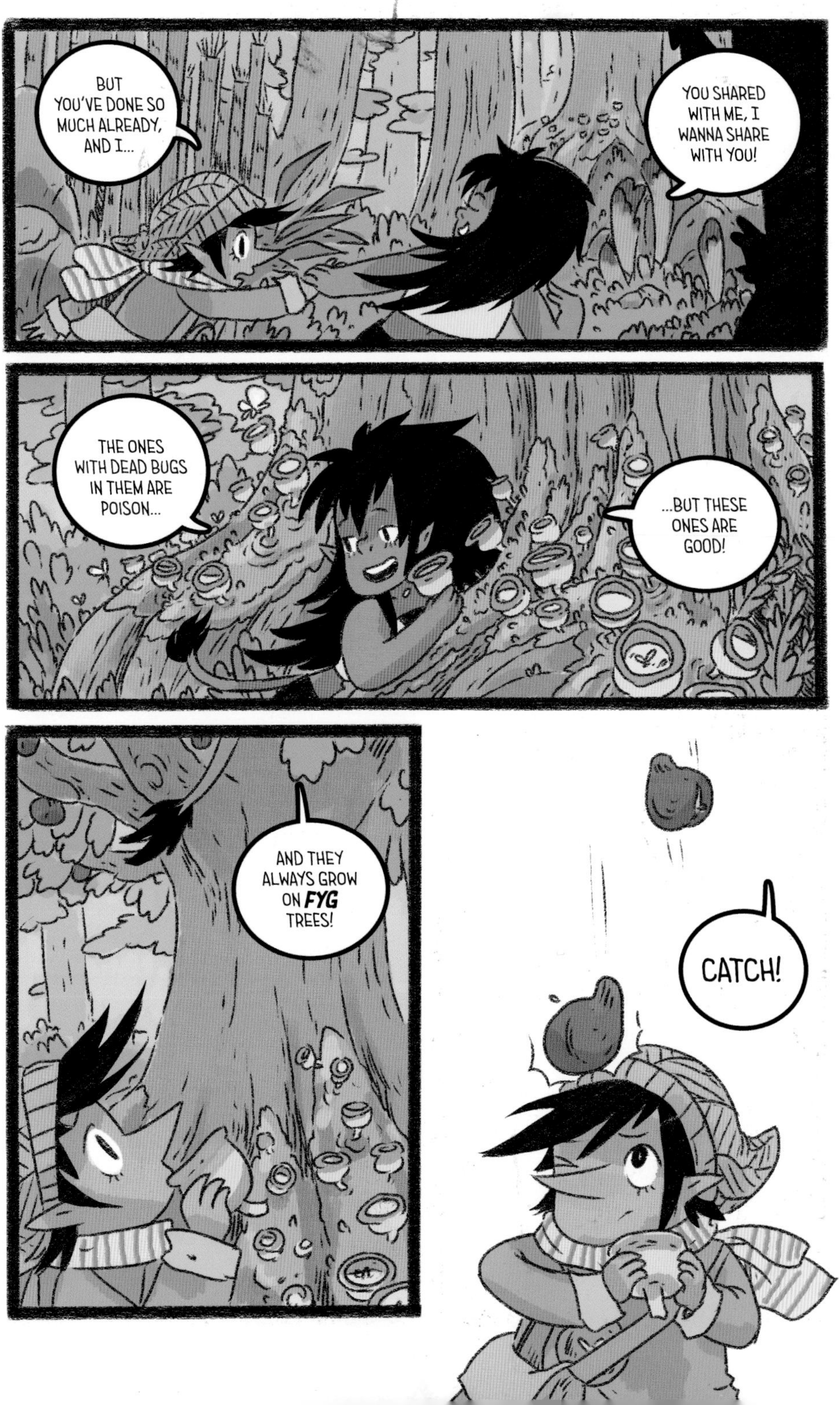
BUT YOU'VE DONE SO MUCH ALREADY, AND I...
YOU SHARED WITH ME, I WANNA SHARE WITH YOU!
THE ONES WITH DEAD BUGS IN THEM ARE POISON...
...BUT THESE ONES ARE GOOD!
AND THEY ALWAYS GROW ON FYG TREES!
CATCH!

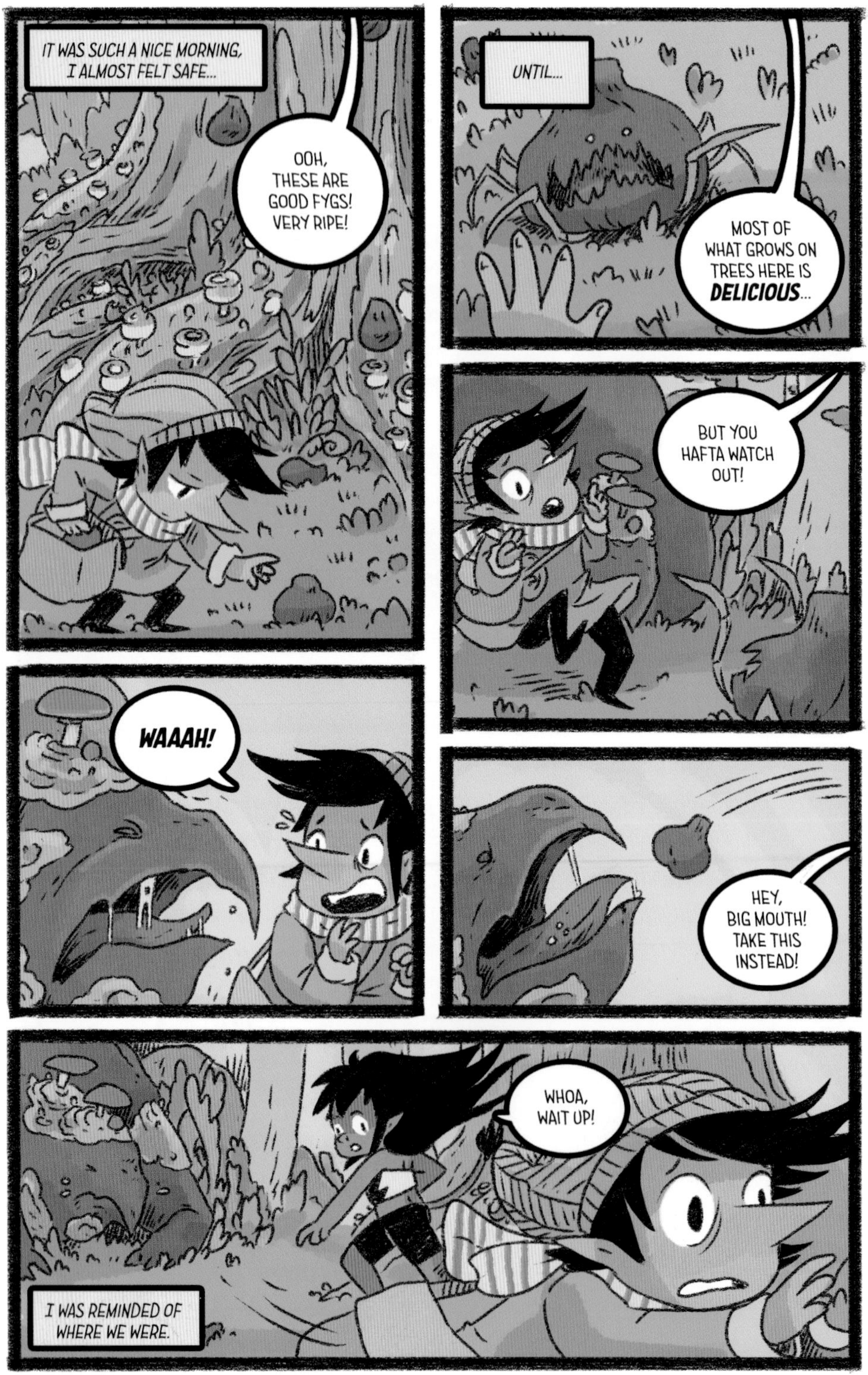
IT WAS SUCH A NICE MORNING, I ALMOST FELT SAFE...
OOH, THESE ARE GOOD FYGS! VERY RIPE!
UNTIL...
MOST OF WHAT GROWS ON TREES HERE IS **DELICIOUS**...
BUT YOU HAFTA WATCH OUT!
WAAAH!
HEY, BIG MOUTH! TAKE THIS INSTEAD!
WHOA, WAIT UP!
I WAS REMINDED OF WHERE WE WERE.

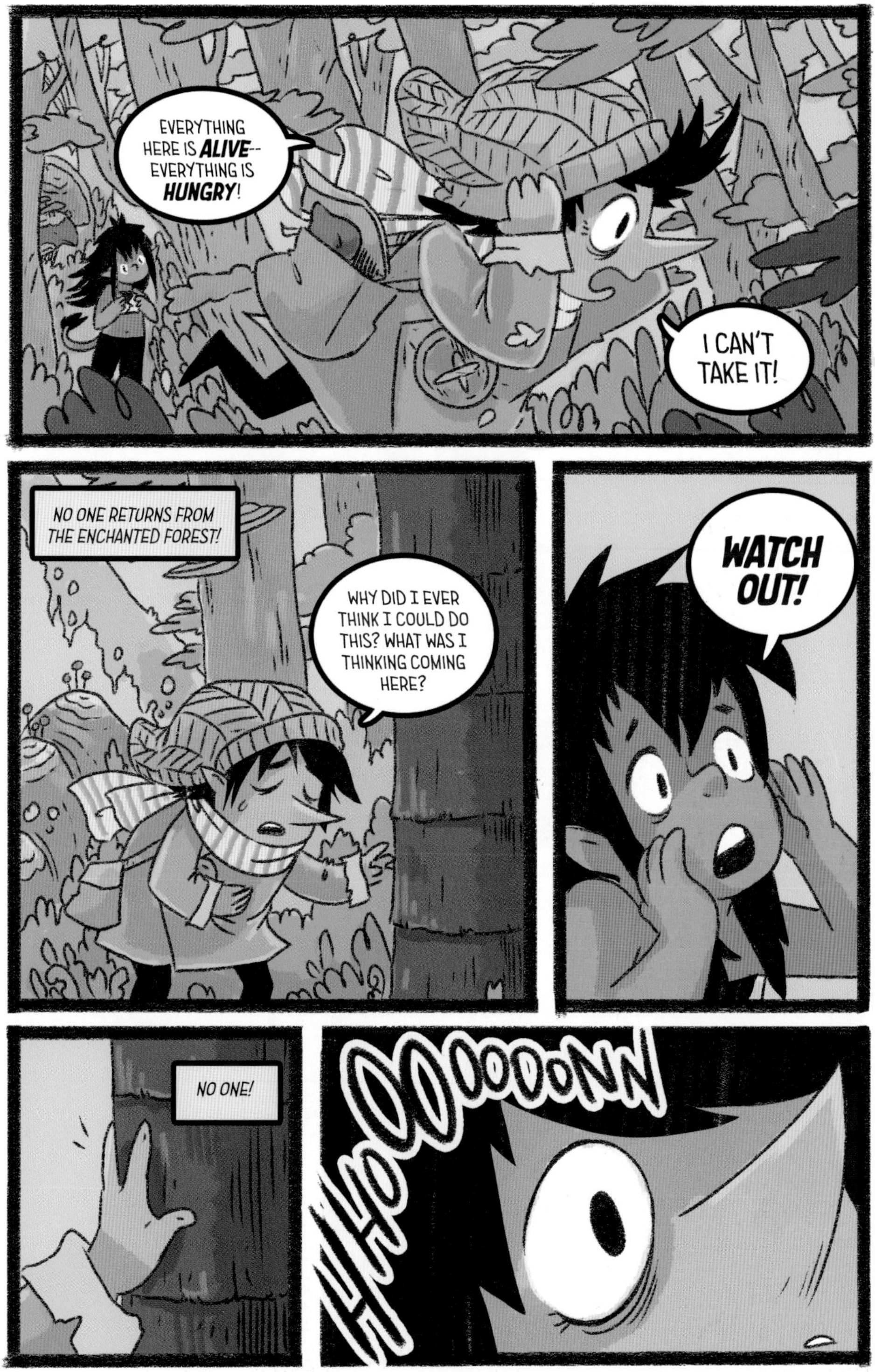
EVERYTHING HERE IS **ALIVE**-- EVERYTHING IS **HUNGRY**!
I CAN'T TAKE IT!
NO ONE RETURNS FROM THE ENCHANTED FOREST!
WHY DID I EVER THINK I COULD DO THIS? WHAT WAS I THINKING COMING HERE?
WATCH OUT!
NO ONE!
WHOOOOOOOOONN

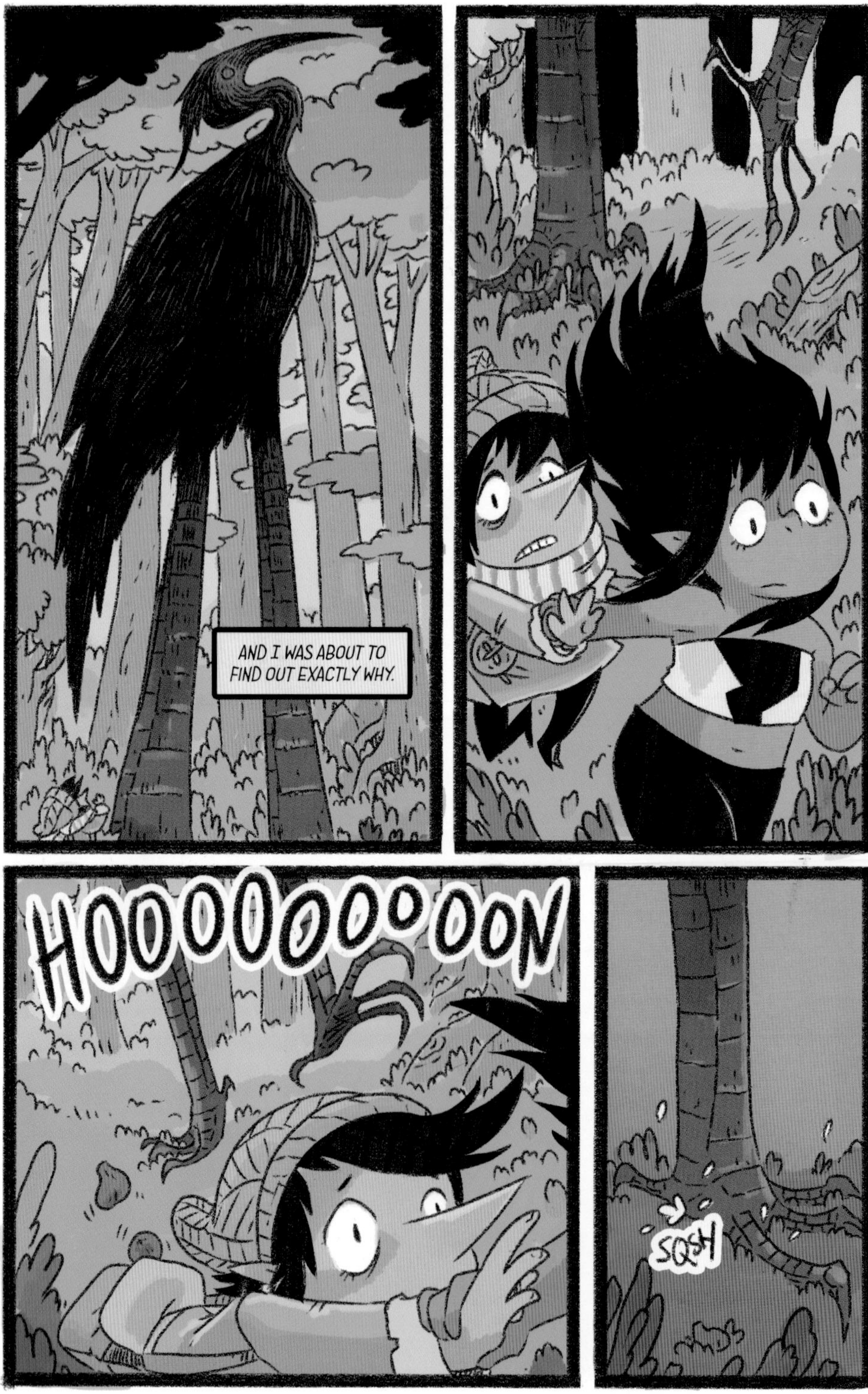
AND I WAS ABOUT TO FIND OUT EXACTLY WHY.
HOOOOOOOOON
SQSH

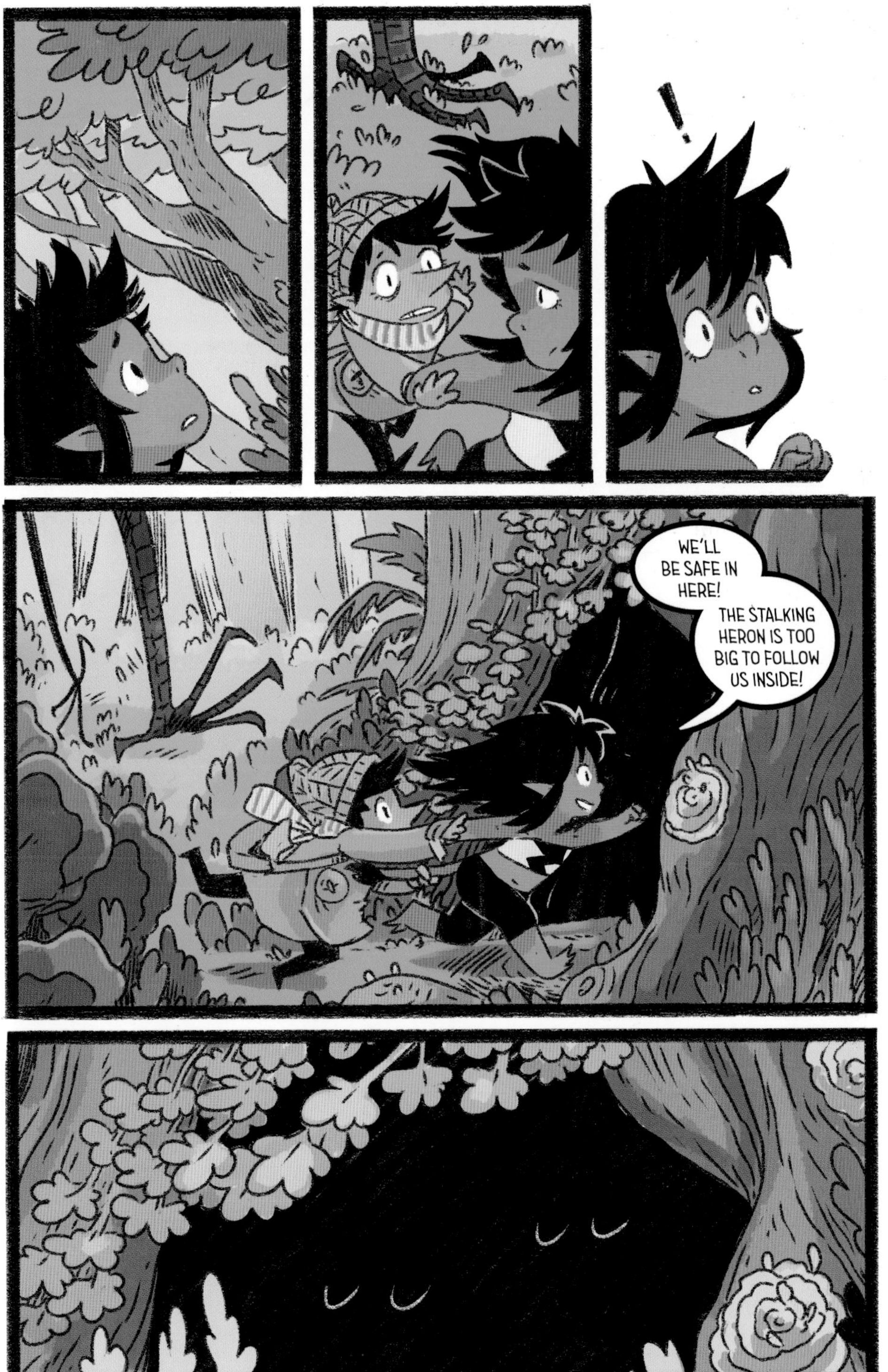
!
WE'LL BE SAFE IN HERE!
THE STALKING HERON IS TOO BIG TO FOLLOW US INSIDE!

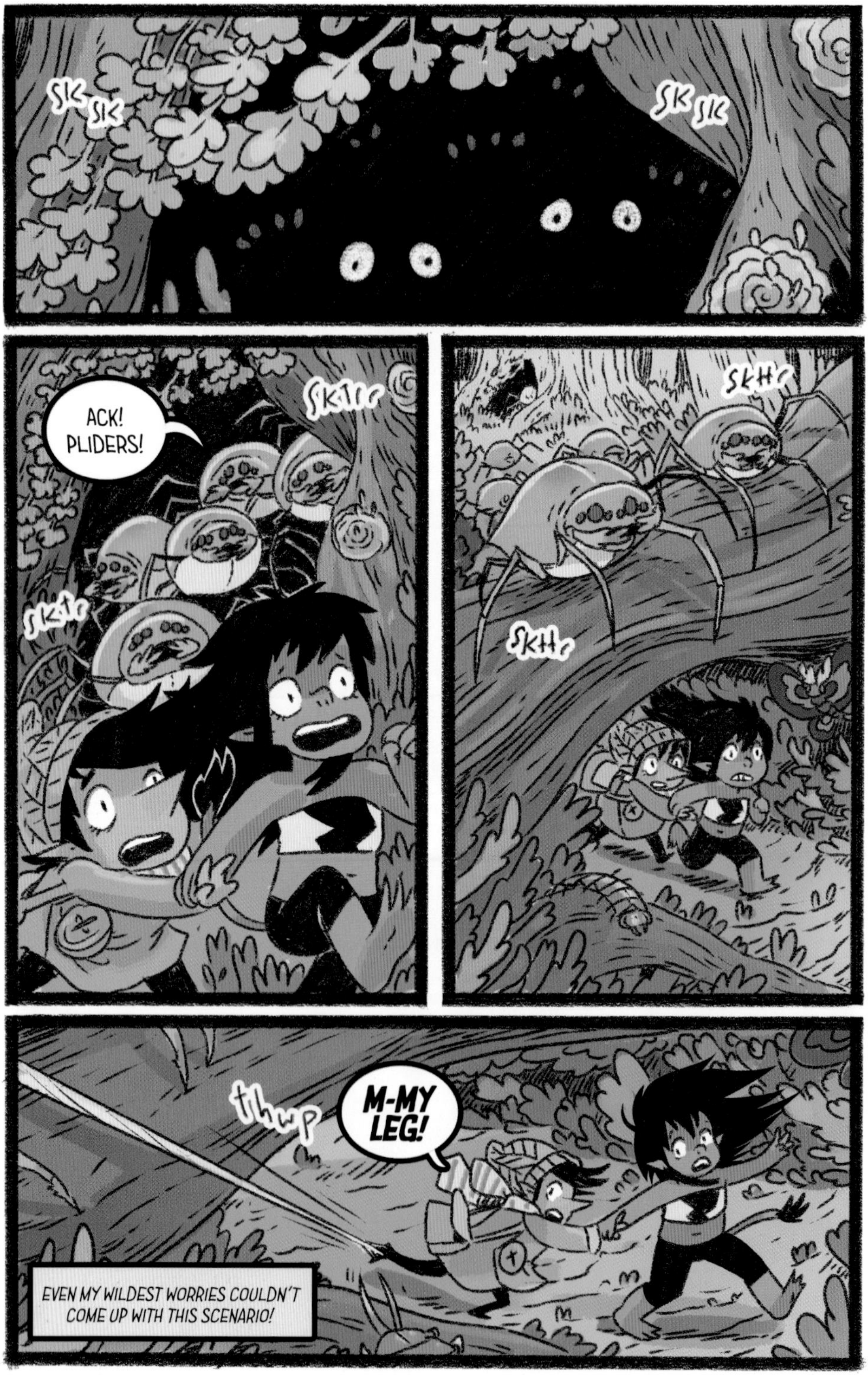
SK SK
SK SK
ACK! PLIDERS!
SKTTR
SKTTR
SKHR
SKHR
THWP
M-MY LEG!
EVEN MY WILDEST WORRIES COULDN'T COME UP WITH THIS SCENARIO!

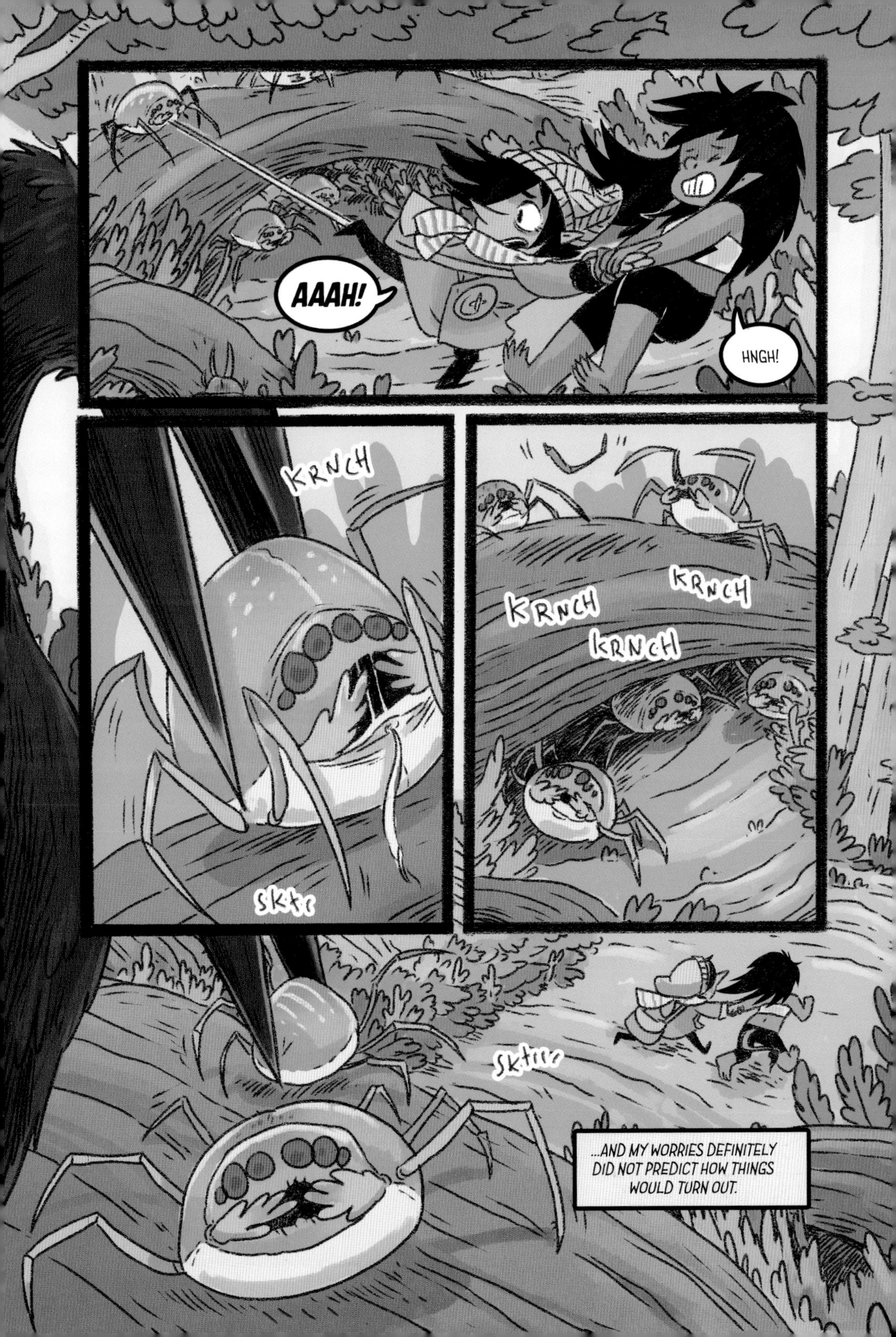
AAAH!
HNGH!
KRNCH
sktr
KRNCH
KRNCH
KRNCH
sktrr!
...AND MY WORRIES DEFINITELY DID NOT PREDICT HOW THINGS WOULD TURN OUT.

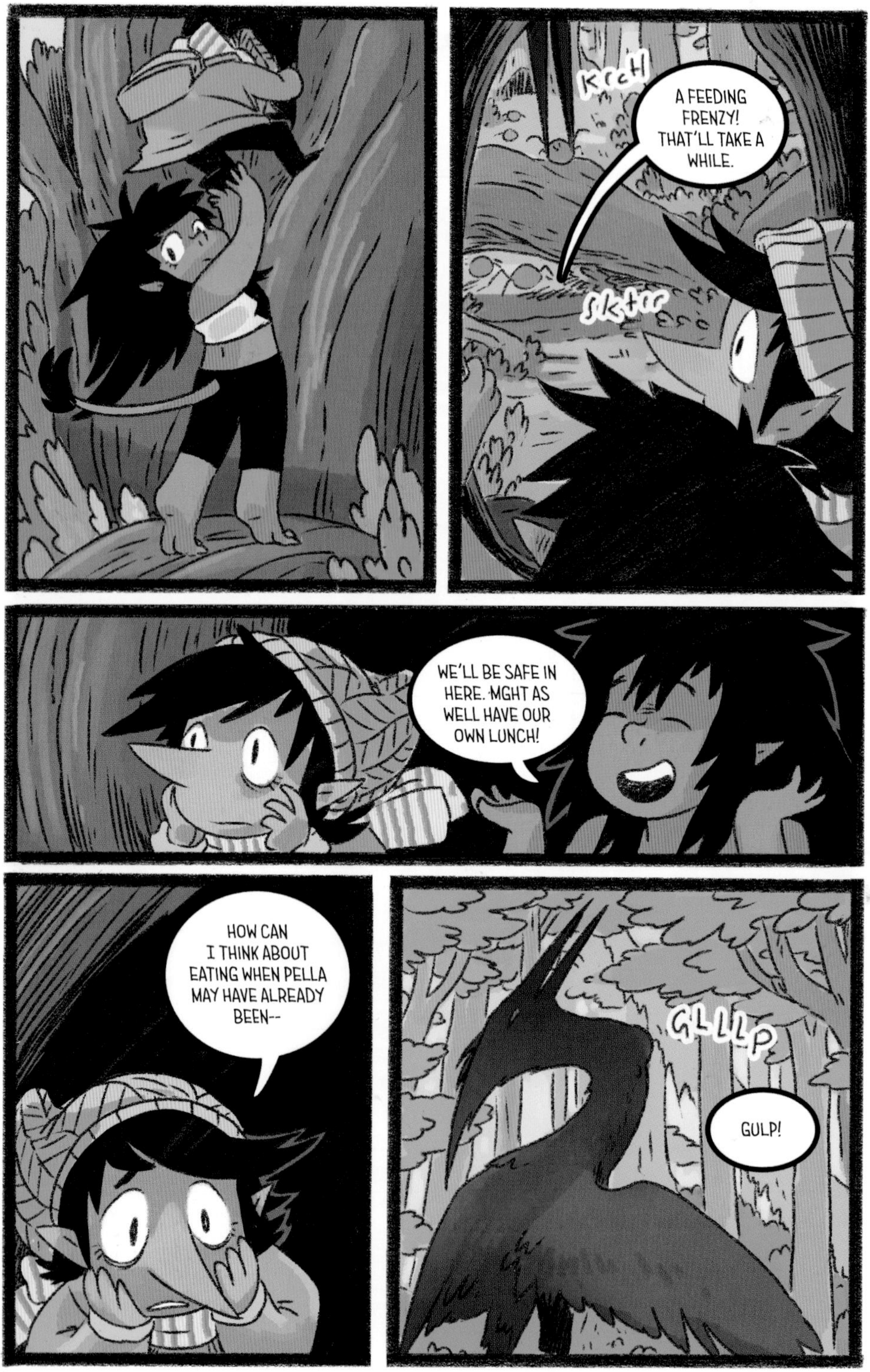
KRCH
A FEEDING FRENZY! THAT'LL TAKE A WHILE.
SKTER
WE'LL BE SAFE IN HERE. MGHT AS WELL HAVE OUR OWN LUNCH!
HOW CAN I THINK ABOUT EATING WHEN PELLA MAY HAVE ALREADY BEEN--
GLLLP
GULP!

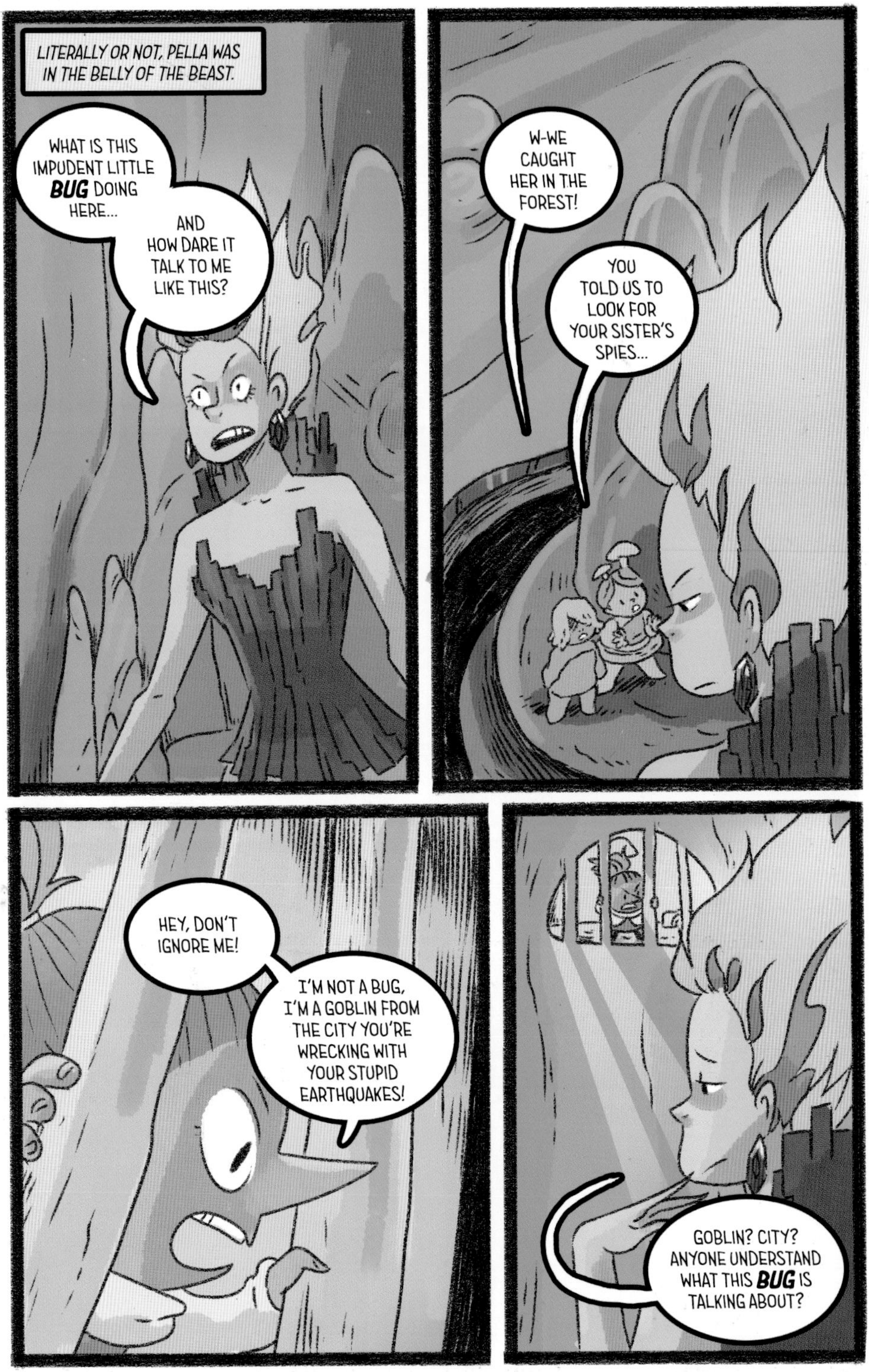
LITERALLY OR NOT, PELLA WAS IN THE BELLY OF THE BEAST.
WHAT IS THIS IMPUDENT LITTLE **BUG** DOING HERE...
AND HOW DARE IT TALK TO ME LIKE THIS?
W-WE CAUGHT HER IN THE FOREST!
YOU TOLD US TO LOOK FOR YOUR SISTER'S SPIES...
HEY, DON'T IGNORE ME!
I'M NOT A BUG, I'M A GOBLIN FROM THE CITY YOU'RE WRECKING WITH YOUR STUPID EARTHQUAKES!
GOBLIN? CITY? ANYONE UNDERSTAND WHAT THIS **BUG** IS TALKING ABOUT?

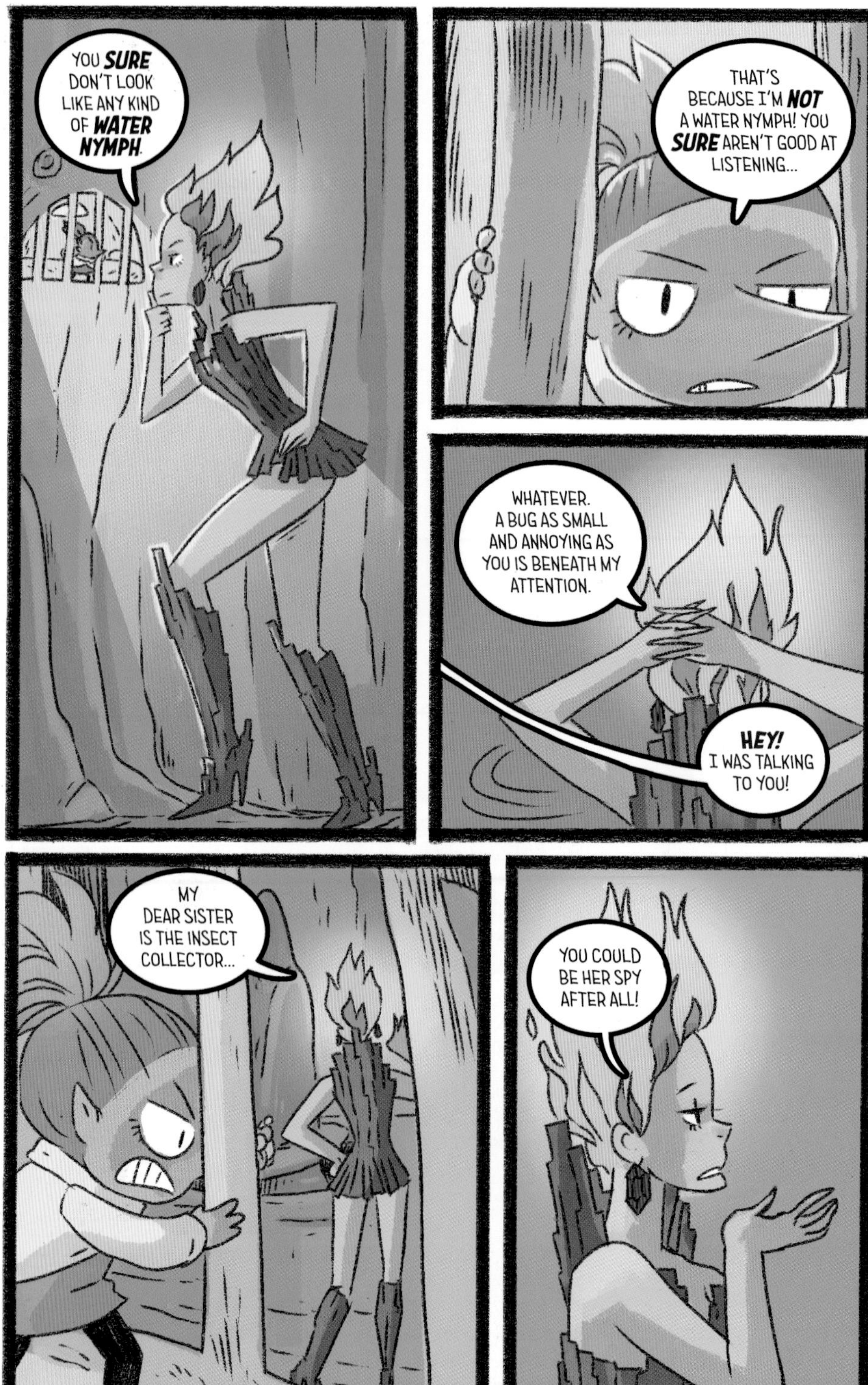
YOU SURE DON'T LOOK LIKE ANY KIND OF WATER NYMPH.
THAT'S BECAUSE I'M NOT A WATER NYMPH! YOU SURE AREN'T GOOD AT LISTENING...
WHATEVER. A BUG AS SMALL AND ANNOYING AS YOU IS BENEATH MY ATTENTION.
HEY! I WAS TALKING TO YOU!
MY DEAR SISTER IS THE INSECT COLLECTOR...
YOU COULD BE HER SPY AFTER ALL!

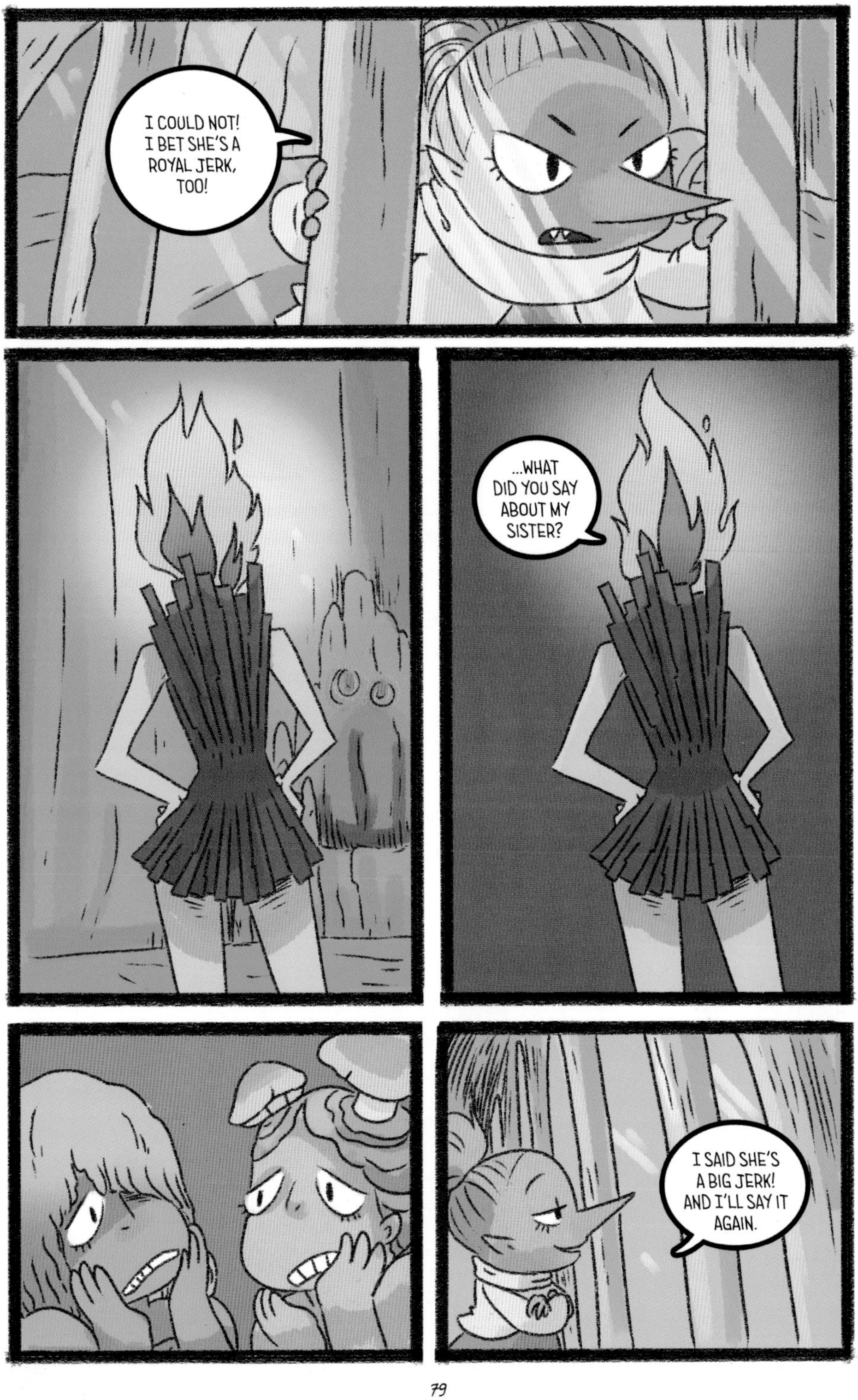
I COULD NOT! I BET SHE'S A ROYAL JERK, TOO!
...WHAT DID YOU SAY ABOUT MY SISTER?
I SAID SHE'S A BIG JERK! AND I'LL SAY IT AGAIN.

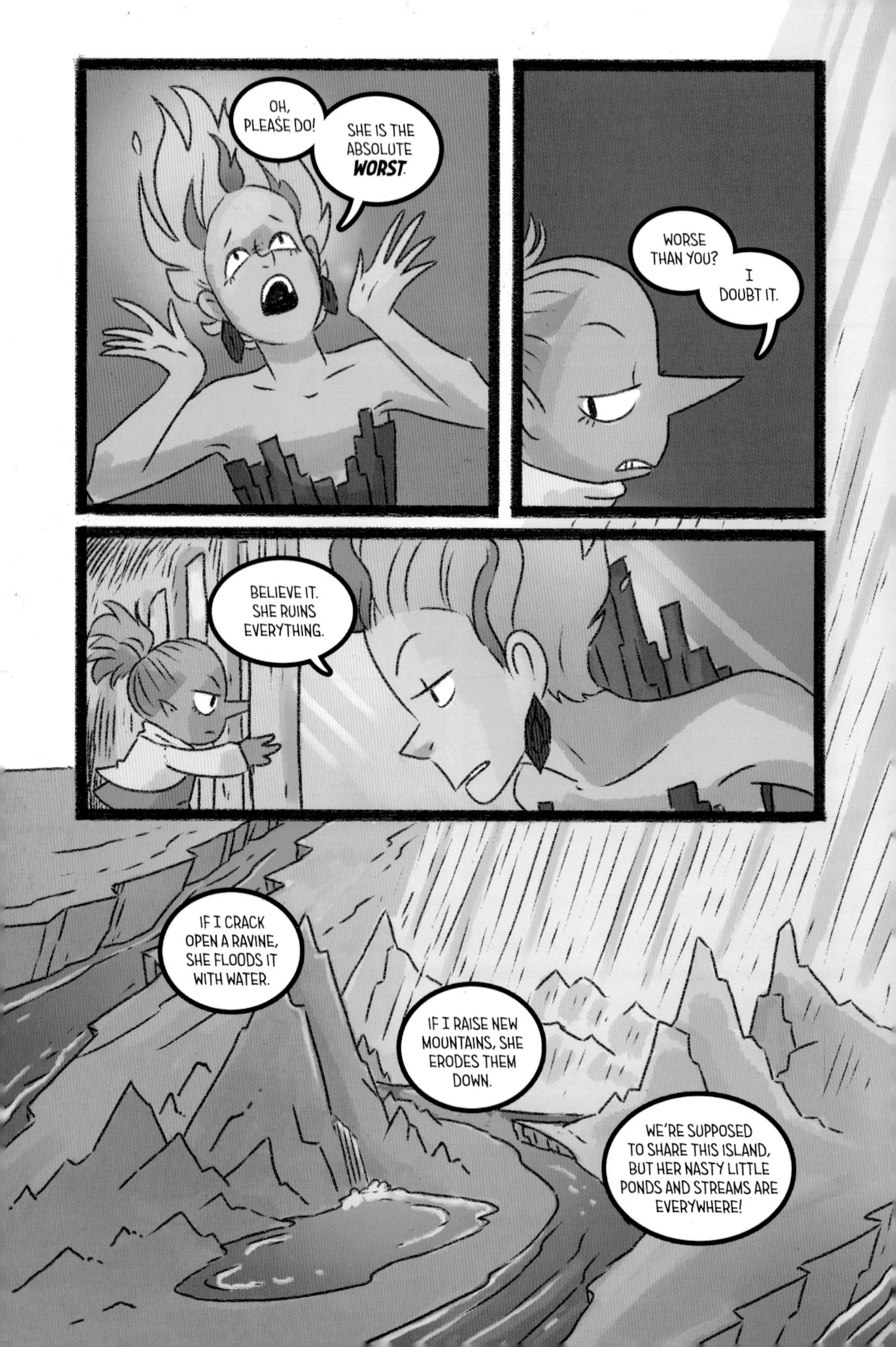
OH, PLEASE DO!
SHE IS THE ABSOLUTE **WORST**.
WORSE THAN YOU?
I DOUBT IT.
BELIEVE IT. SHE RUINS EVERYTHING.
IF I CRACK OPEN A RAVINE, SHE FLOODS IT WITH WATER.
IF I RAISE NEW MOUNTAINS, SHE ERODES THEM DOWN.
WE'RE SUPPOSED TO SHARE THIS ISLAND, BUT HER NASTY LITTLE PONDS AND STREAMS ARE EVERYWHERE!

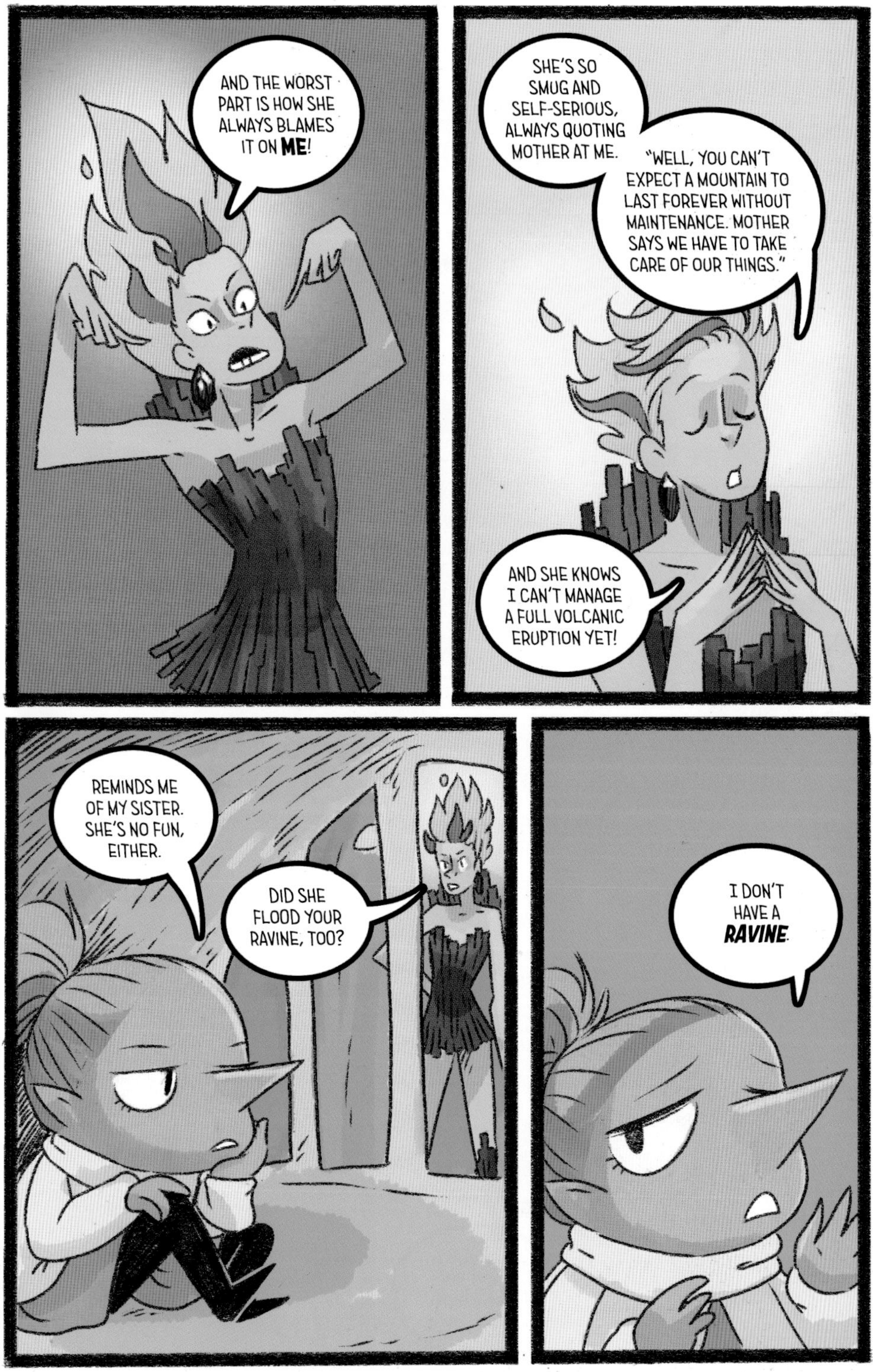
AND THE WORST PART IS HOW SHE ALWAYS BLAMES IT ON **ME**!
SHE'S SO SMUG AND SELF-SERIOUS, ALWAYS QUOTING MOTHER AT ME.
"WELL, YOU CAN'T EXPECT A MOUNTAIN TO LAST FOREVER WITHOUT MAINTENANCE. MOTHER SAYS WE HAVE TO TAKE CARE OF OUR THINGS."
AND SHE KNOWS I CAN'T MANAGE A FULL VOLCANIC ERUPTION YET!
REMINDS ME OF MY SISTER. SHE'S NO FUN, EITHER.
DID SHE FLOOD YOUR RAVINE, TOO?
I DON'T HAVE A ***RAVINE***.

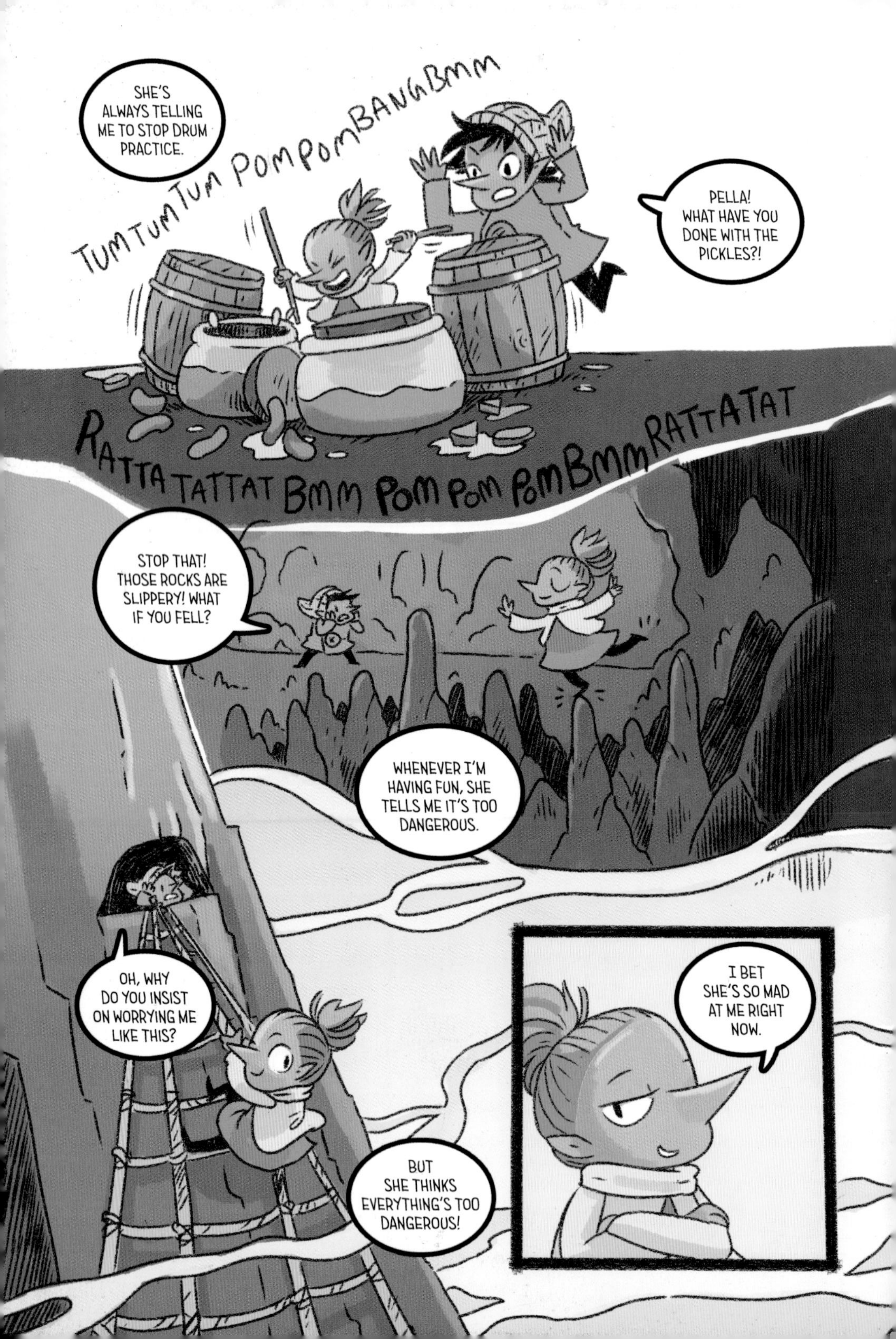

SHE'S ALWAYS TELLING ME TO STOP DRUM PRACTICE.
TUMTUMTUM POMPOMBANGBMM
PELLA! WHAT HAVE YOU DONE WITH THE PICKLES?!
RATTATATTAT BMM POM POM POMBMMRATTATAT
STOP THAT! THOSE ROCKS ARE SLIPPERY! WHAT IF YOU FELL?
WHENEVER I'M HAVING FUN, SHE TELLS ME IT'S TOO DANGEROUS.
OH, WHY DO YOU INSIST ON WORRYING ME LIKE THIS?
I BET SHE'S SO MAD AT ME RIGHT NOW.
BUT SHE THINKS EVERYTHING'S TOO DANGEROUS!

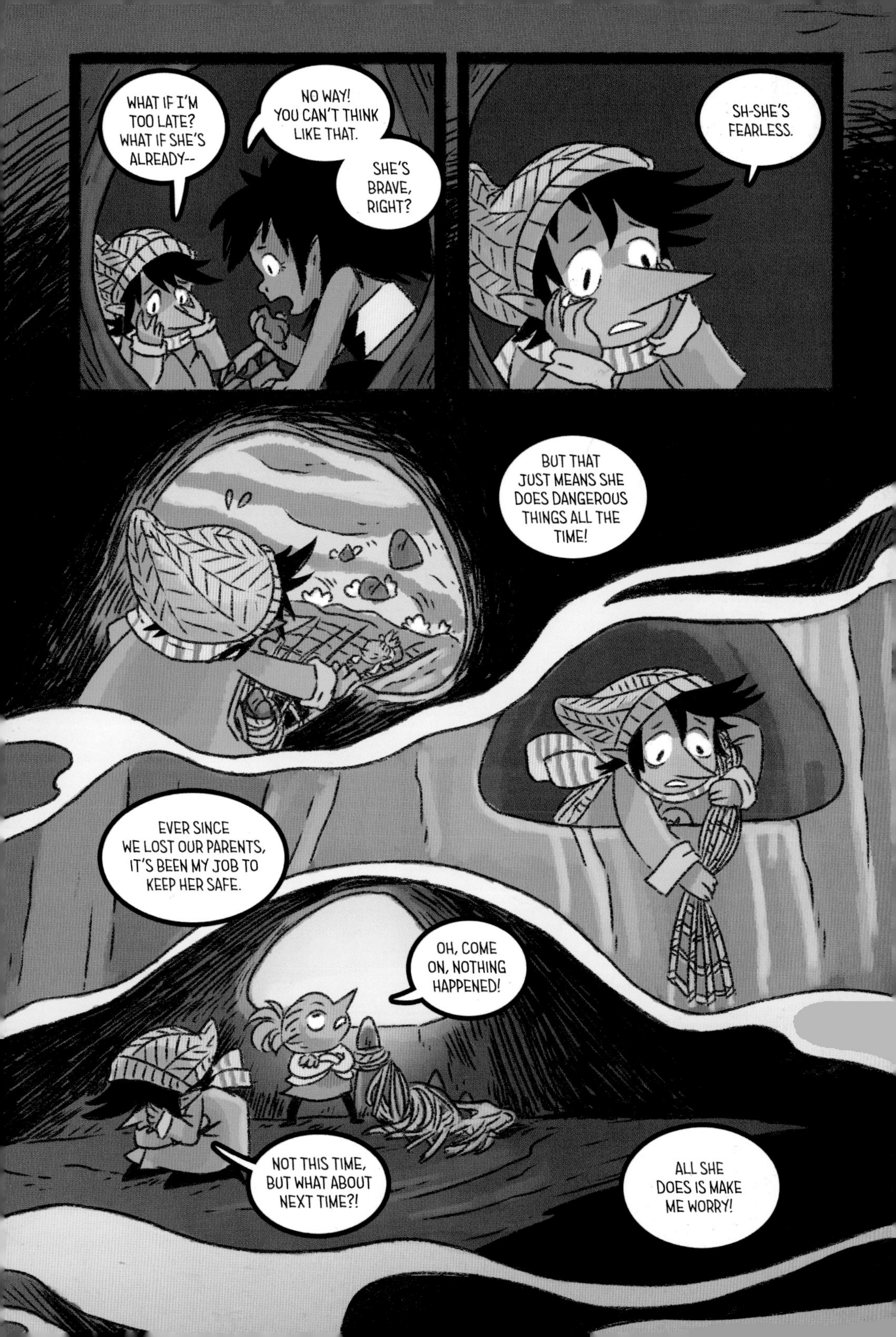
WHAT IF I'M TOO LATE? WHAT IF SHE'S ALREADY--
NO WAY! YOU CAN'T THINK LIKE THAT.
SHE'S BRAVE, RIGHT?
SH-SHE'S FEARLESS.
BUT THAT JUST MEANS SHE DOES DANGEROUS THINGS ALL THE TIME!
EVER SINCE WE LOST OUR PARENTS, IT'S BEEN MY JOB TO KEEP HER SAFE.
OH, COME ON, NOTHING HAPPENED!
NOT THIS TIME, BUT WHAT ABOUT NEXT TIME?!
ALL SHE DOES IS MAKE ME WORRY!

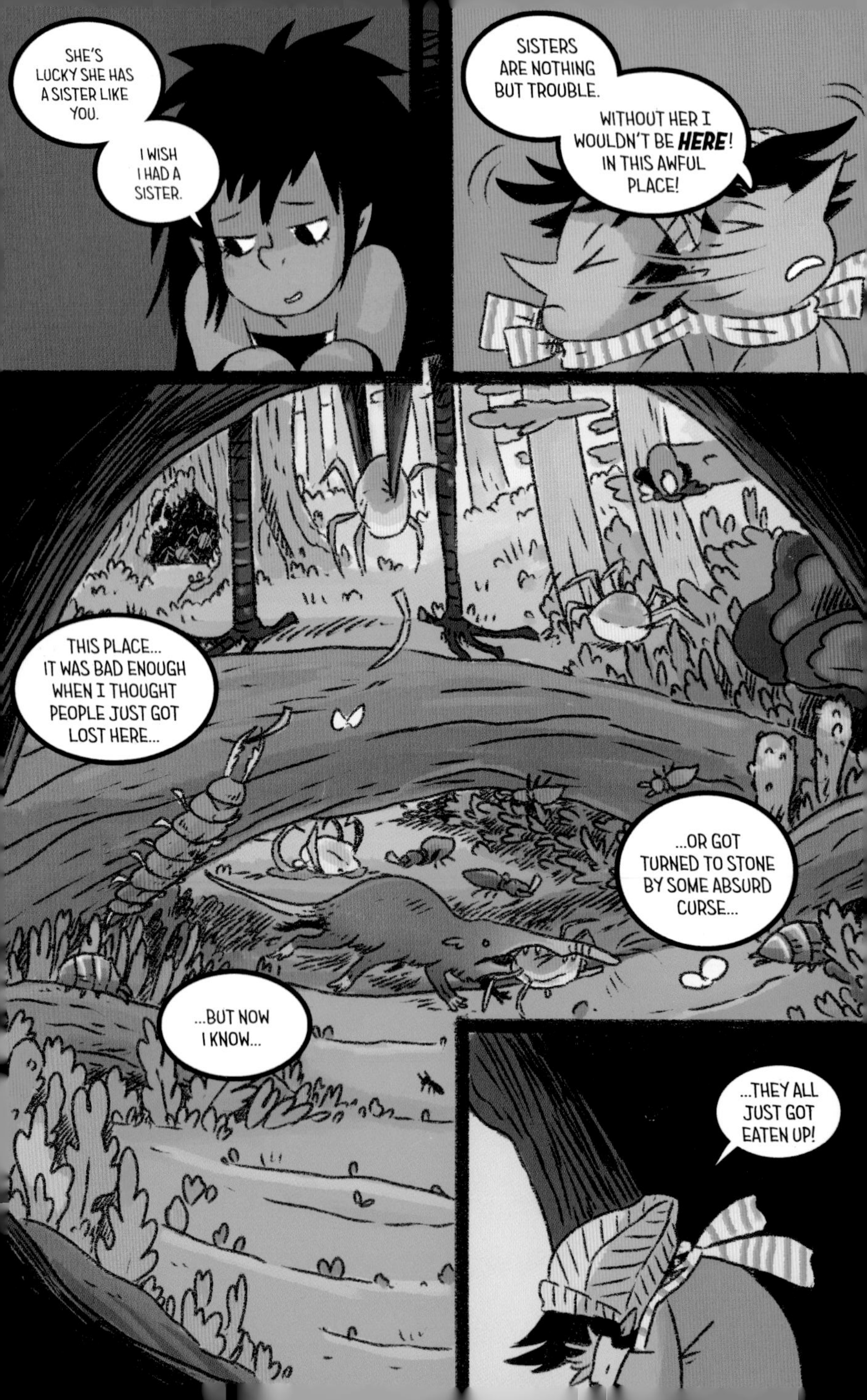
SHE'S LUCKY SHE HAS A SISTER LIKE YOU.
I WISH I HAD A SISTER.
SISTERS ARE NOTHING BUT TROUBLE.
WITHOUT HER I WOULDN'T BE **HERE**! IN THIS AWFUL PLACE!
THIS PLACE... IT WAS BAD ENOUGH WHEN I THOUGHT PEOPLE JUST GOT LOST HERE...
...OR GOT TURNED TO STONE BY SOME ABSURD CURSE...
...BUT NOW I KNOW...
...THEY ALL JUST GOT EATEN UP!

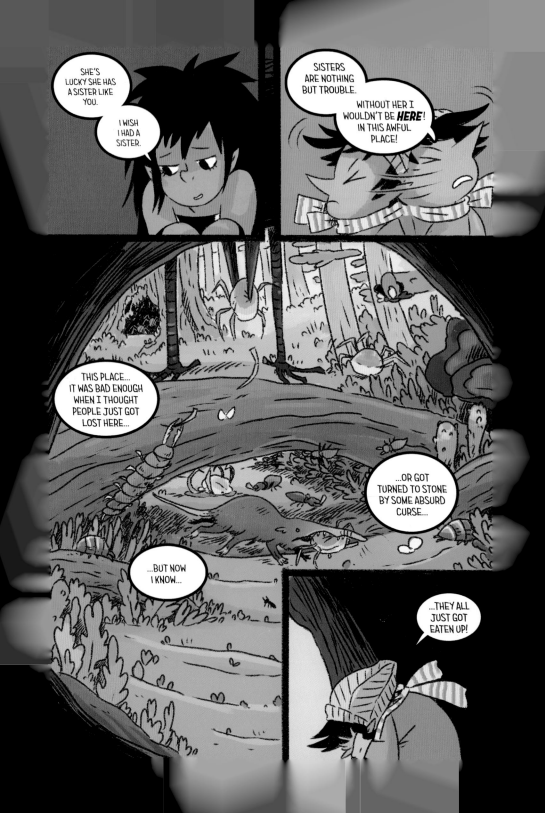

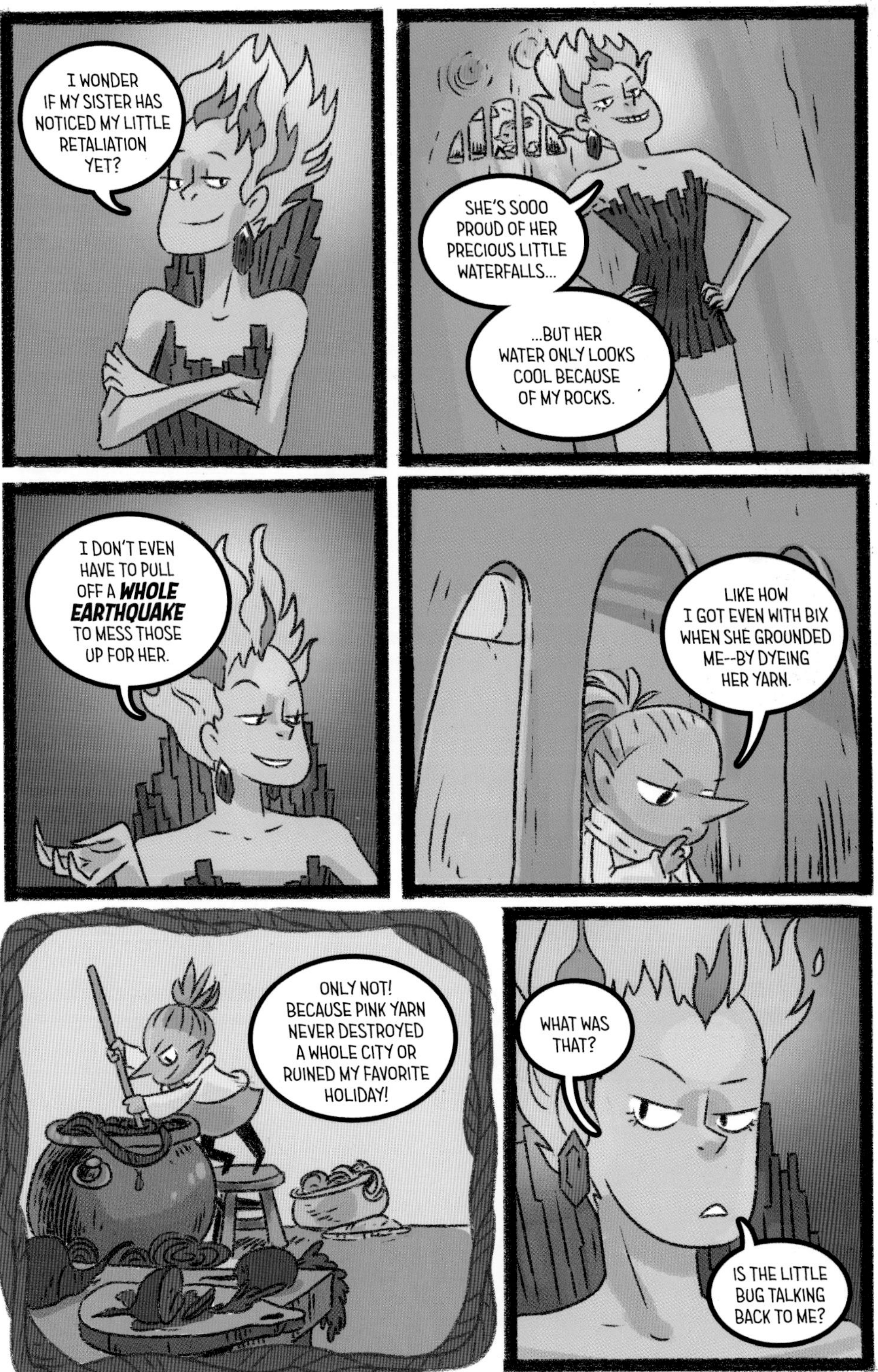
I WONDER IF MY SISTER HAS NOTICED MY LITTLE RETALIATION YET?
SHE'S SOOO PROUD OF HER PRECIOUS LITTLE WATERFALLS...
...BUT HER WATER ONLY LOOKS COOL BECAUSE OF MY ROCKS.
I DON'T EVEN HAVE TO PULL OFF A ***WHOLE EARTHQUAKE*** TO MESS THOSE UP FOR HER.
LIKE HOW I GOT EVEN WITH BIX WHEN SHE GROUNDED ME--BY DYEING HER YARN.
ONLY NOT! BECAUSE PINK YARN NEVER DESTROYED A WHOLE CITY OR RUINED MY FAVORITE HOLIDAY!
WHAT WAS THAT?
IS THE LITTLE BUG TALKING BACK TO ME?

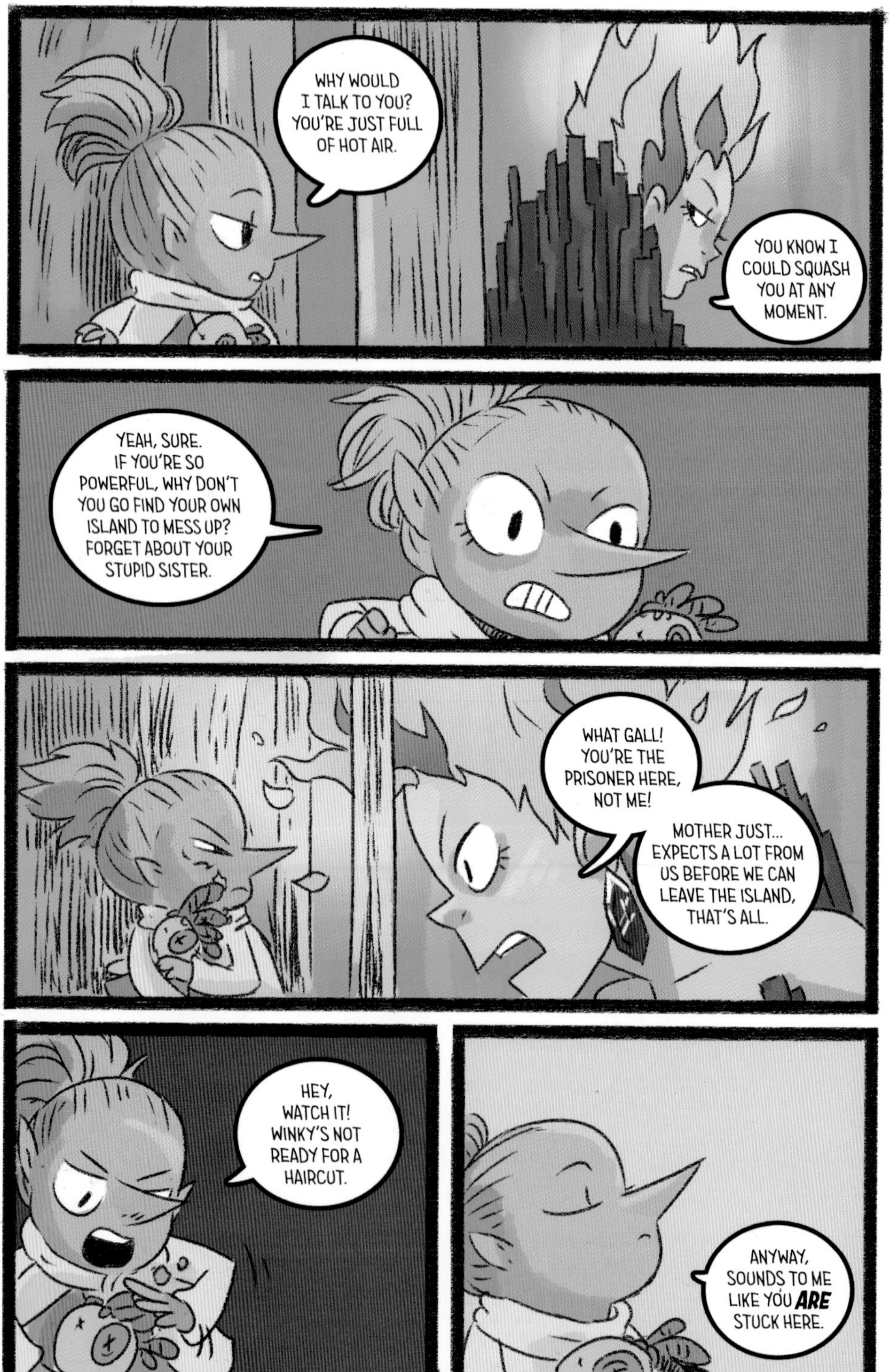
WHY WOULD I TALK TO YOU? YOU'RE JUST FULL OF HOT AIR.
YOU KNOW I COULD SQUASH YOU AT ANY MOMENT.
YEAH, SURE. IF YOU'RE SO POWERFUL, WHY DON'T YOU GO FIND YOUR OWN ISLAND TO MESS UP? FORGET ABOUT YOUR STUPID SISTER.
WHAT GALL! YOU'RE THE PRISONER HERE, NOT ME!
MOTHER JUST... EXPECTS A LOT FROM US BEFORE WE CAN LEAVE THE ISLAND, THAT'S ALL.
HEY, WATCH IT! WINKY'S NOT READY FOR A HAIRCUT.
ANYWAY, SOUNDS TO ME LIKE YOU **ARE** STUCK HERE.

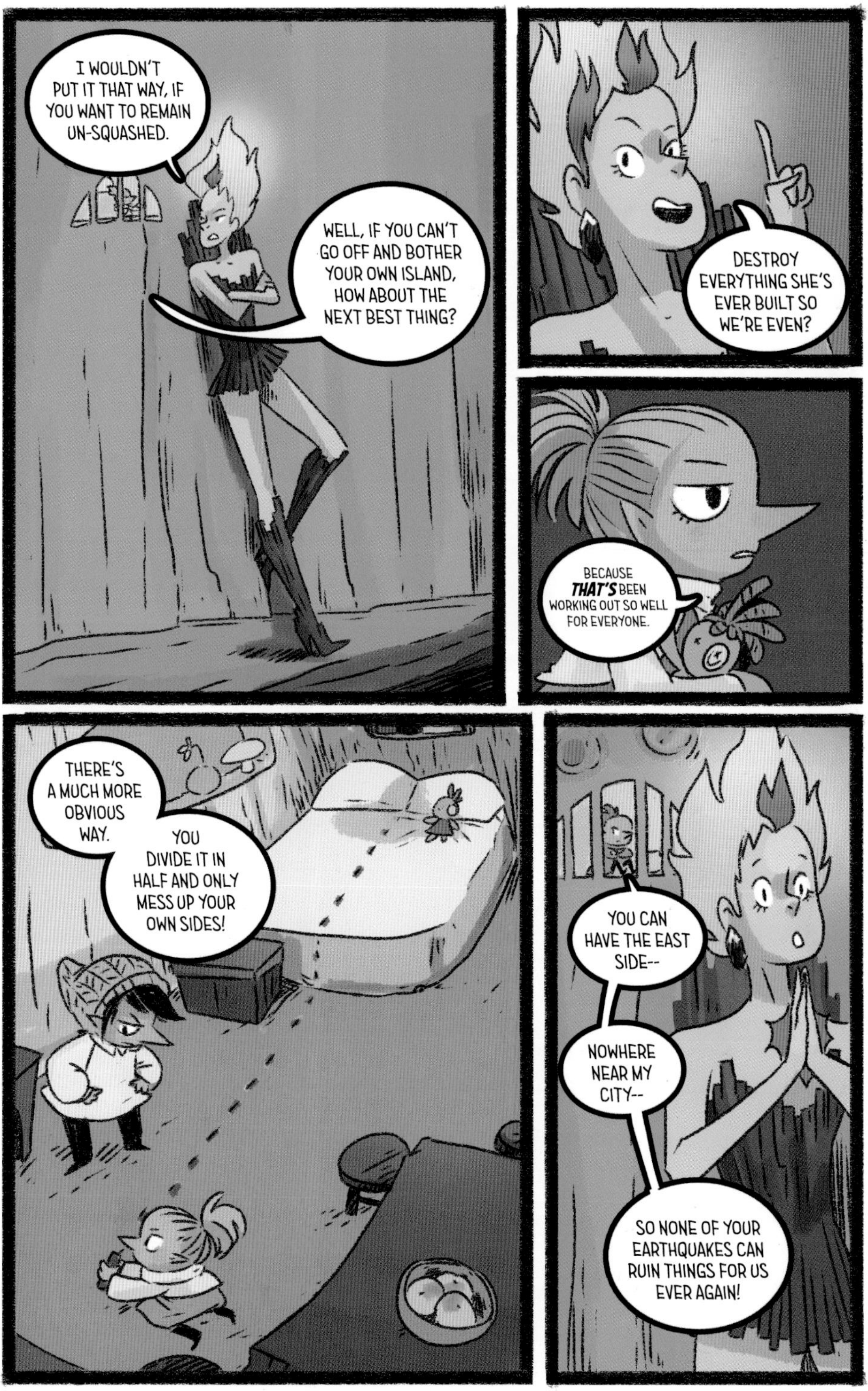
I WOULDN'T PUT IT THAT WAY, IF YOU WANT TO REMAIN UN-SQUASHED.
WELL, IF YOU CAN'T GO OFF AND BOTHER YOUR OWN ISLAND, HOW ABOUT THE NEXT BEST THING?
DESTROY EVERYTHING SHE'S EVER BUILT SO WE'RE EVEN?
BECAUSE **THAT'S** BEEN WORKING OUT SO WELL FOR EVERYONE.
THERE'S A MUCH MORE OBVIOUS WAY.
YOU DIVIDE IT IN HALF AND ONLY MESS UP YOUR OWN SIDES!
YOU CAN HAVE THE EAST SIDE--
NOWHERE NEAR MY CITY--
SO NONE OF YOUR EARTHQUAKES CAN RUIN THINGS FOR US EVER AGAIN!

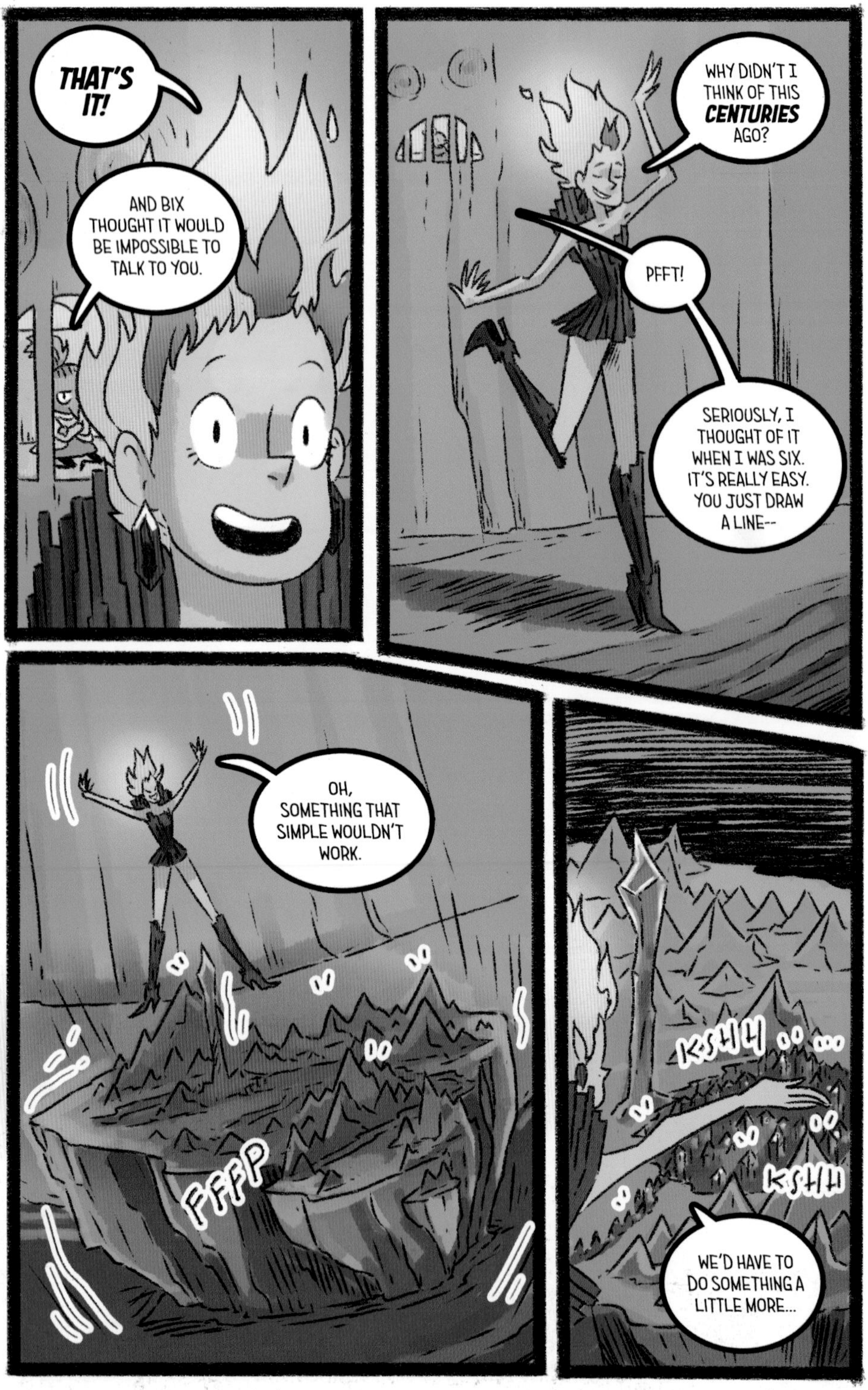
THAT'S IT!
AND BIX THOUGHT IT WOULD BE IMPOSSIBLE TO TALK TO YOU.
WHY DIDN'T I THINK OF THIS CENTURIES AGO?
PFFT!
SERIOUSLY, I THOUGHT OF IT WHEN I WAS SIX. IT'S REALLY EASY. YOU JUST DRAW A LINE--
OH, SOMETHING THAT SIMPLE WOULDN'T WORK.
FFFP
KSHH
KSHH
WE'D HAVE TO DO SOMETHING A LITTLE MORE...

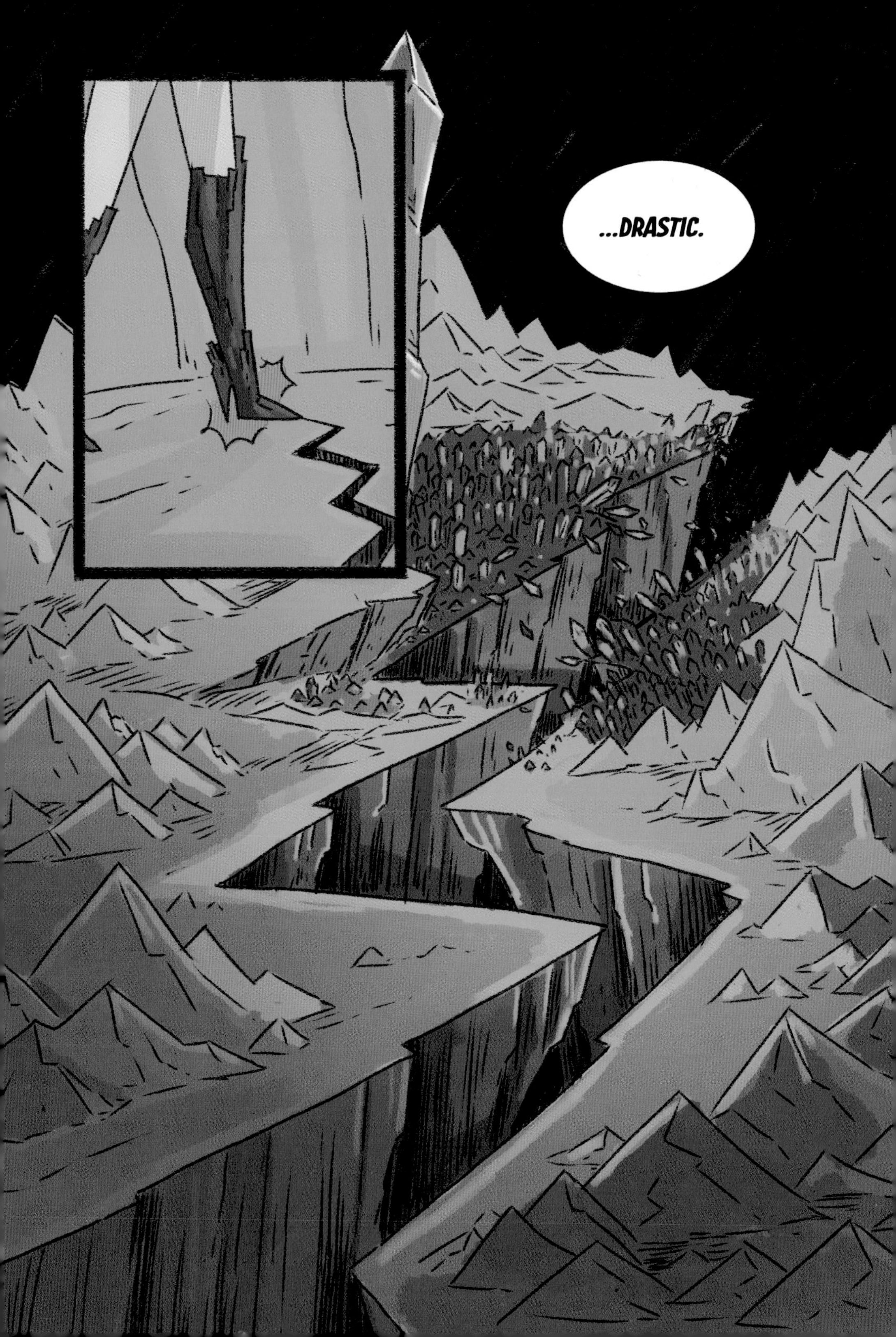
...DRASTIC.

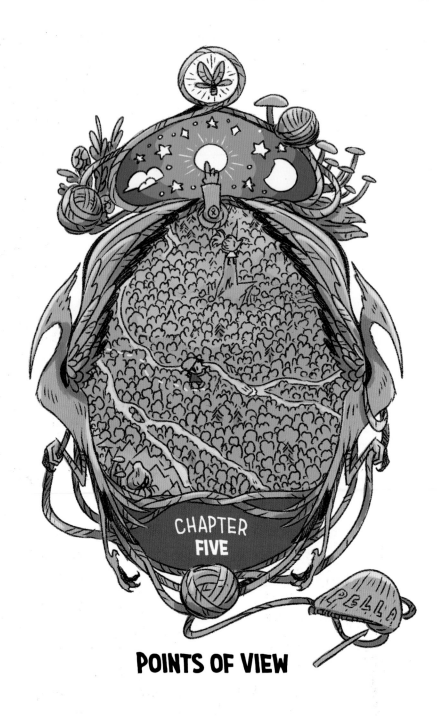

CHAPTER
FIVE

POINTS OF VIEW

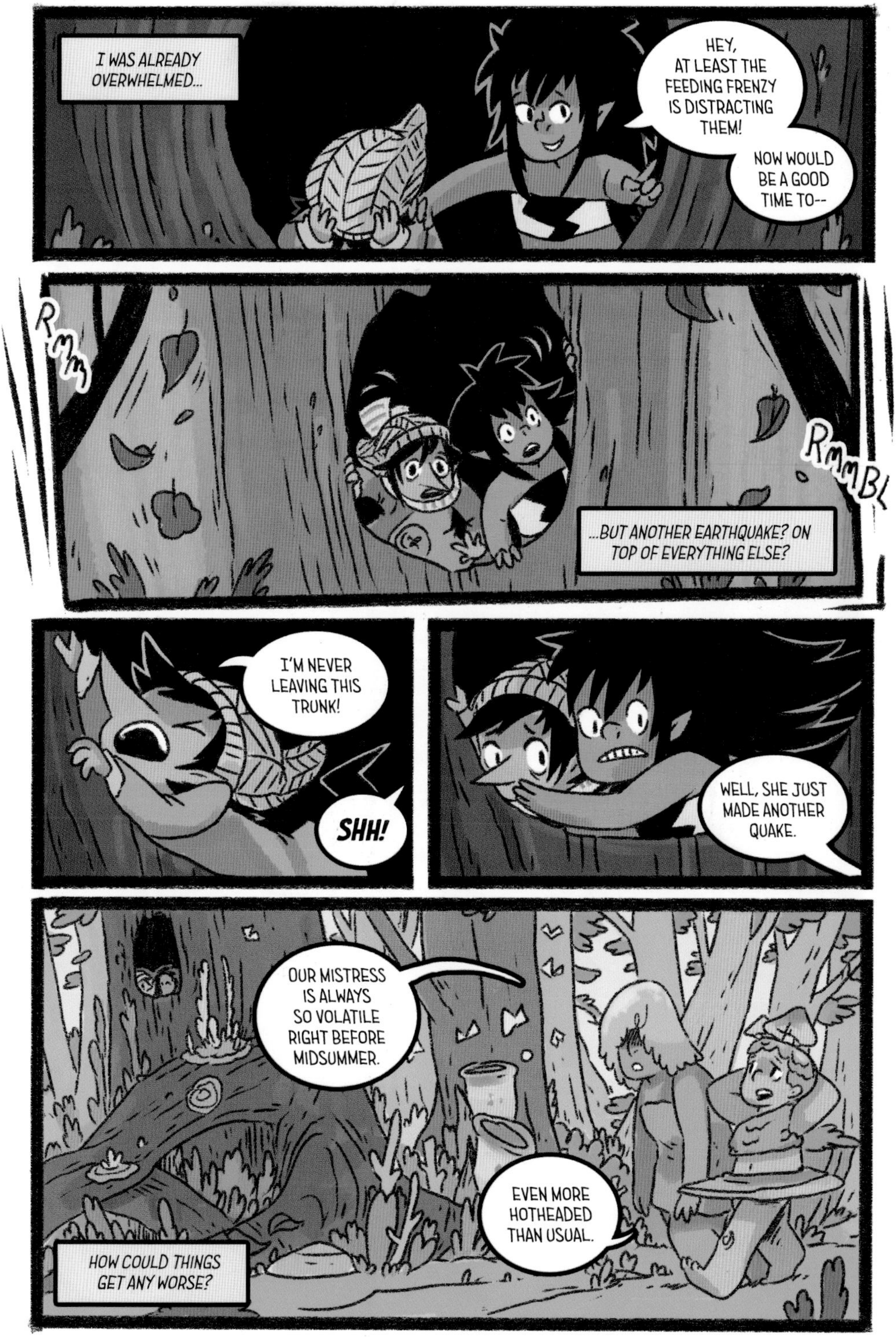

I WAS ALREADY OVERWHELMED...
HEY, AT LEAST THE FEEDING FRENZY IS DISTRACTING THEM!
NOW WOULD BE A GOOD TIME TO--
RMM
RMMBL
...BUT ANOTHER EARTHQUAKE? ON TOP OF EVERYTHING ELSE?
I'M NEVER LEAVING THIS TRUNK!
SHH!
WELL, SHE JUST MADE ANOTHER QUAKE.
OUR MISTRESS IS ALWAYS SO VOLATILE RIGHT BEFORE MIDSUMMER.
EVEN MORE HOTHEADED THAN USUAL.
HOW COULD THINGS GET ANY WORSE?

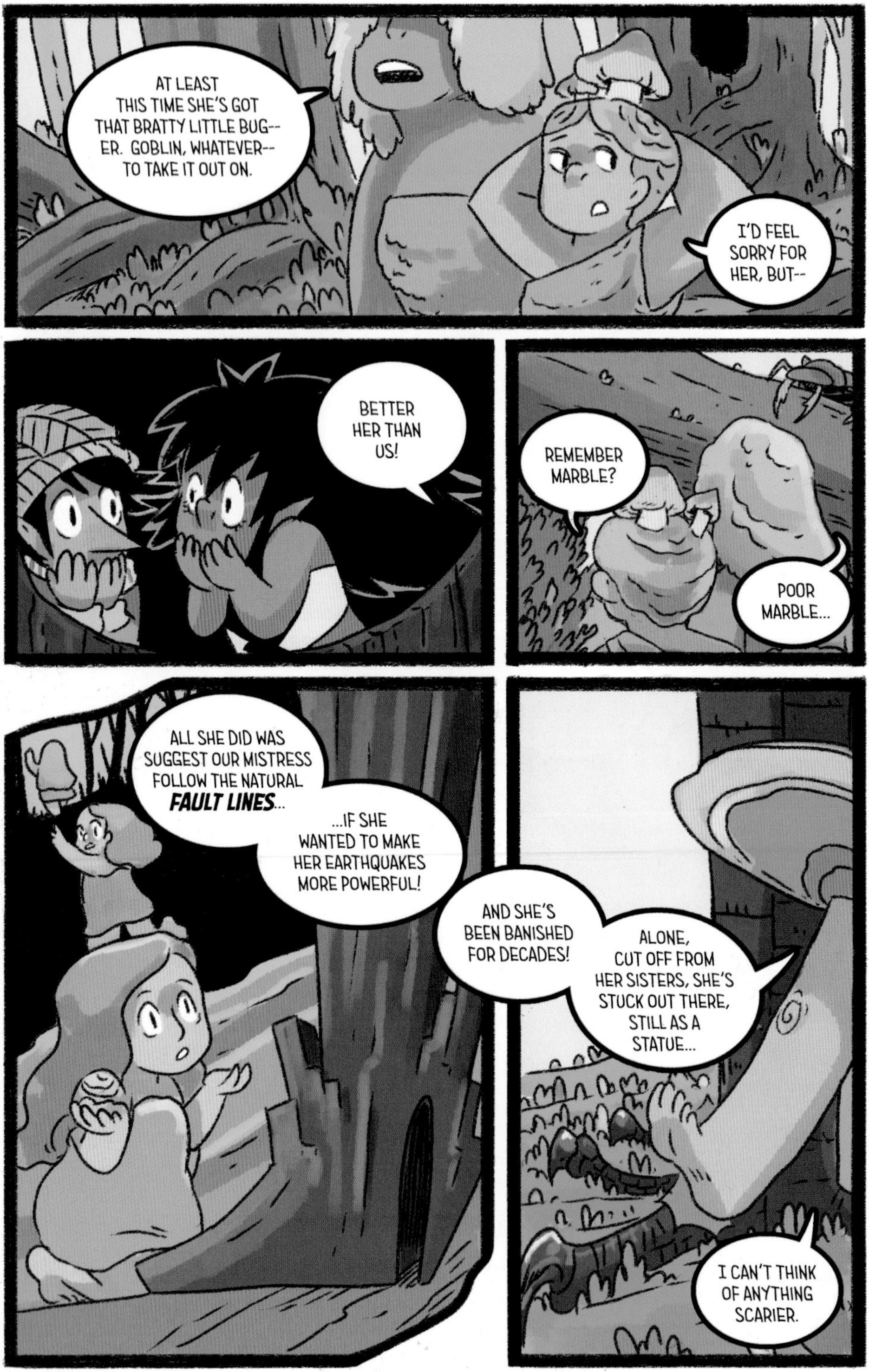
AT LEAST THIS TIME SHE'S GOT THAT BRATTY LITTLE BUG-- ER. GOBLIN, WHATEVER-- TO TAKE IT OUT ON.
I'D FEEL SORRY FOR HER, BUT--
BETTER HER THAN US!
REMEMBER MARBLE?
POOR MARBLE...
ALL SHE DID WAS SUGGEST OUR MISTRESS FOLLOW THE NATURAL **FAULT LINES**...
...IF SHE WANTED TO MAKE HER EARTHQUAKES MORE POWERFUL!
AND SHE'S BEEN BANISHED FOR DECADES!
ALONE, CUT OFF FROM HER SISTERS, SHE'S STUCK OUT THERE, STILL AS A STATUE...
I CAN'T THINK OF ANYTHING SCARIER.

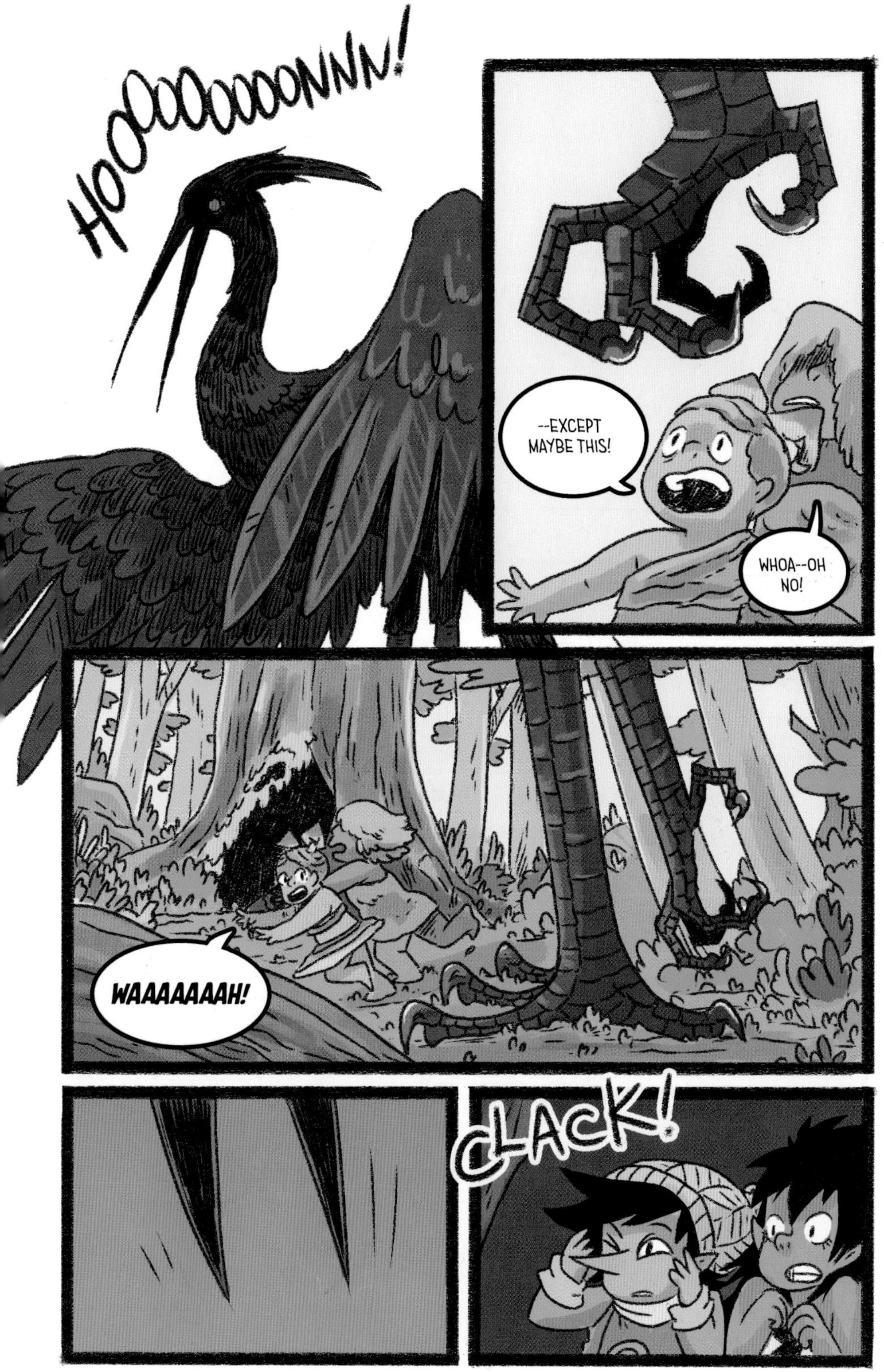
HOOOOOOOONNN!
--EXCEPT MAYBE THIS!
WHOA--OH NO!
WAAAAAAAH!
CLACK!

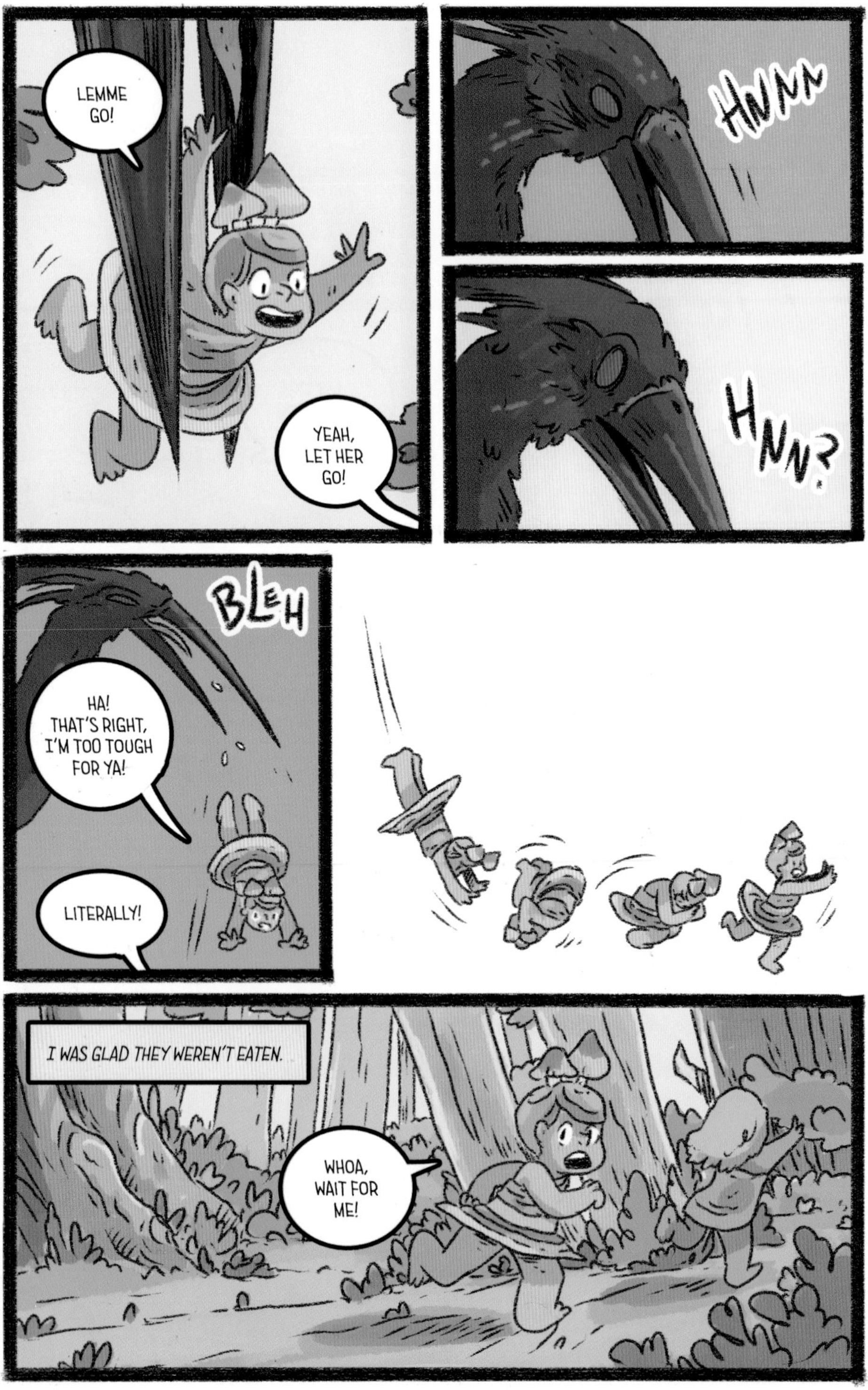
LEMME GO!
YEAH, LET HER GO!
HNNN
HNN?
BLEH
HA! THAT'S RIGHT, I'M TOO TOUGH FOR YA!
LITERALLY!
I WAS GLAD THEY WEREN'T EATEN.
WHOA, WAIT FOR ME!

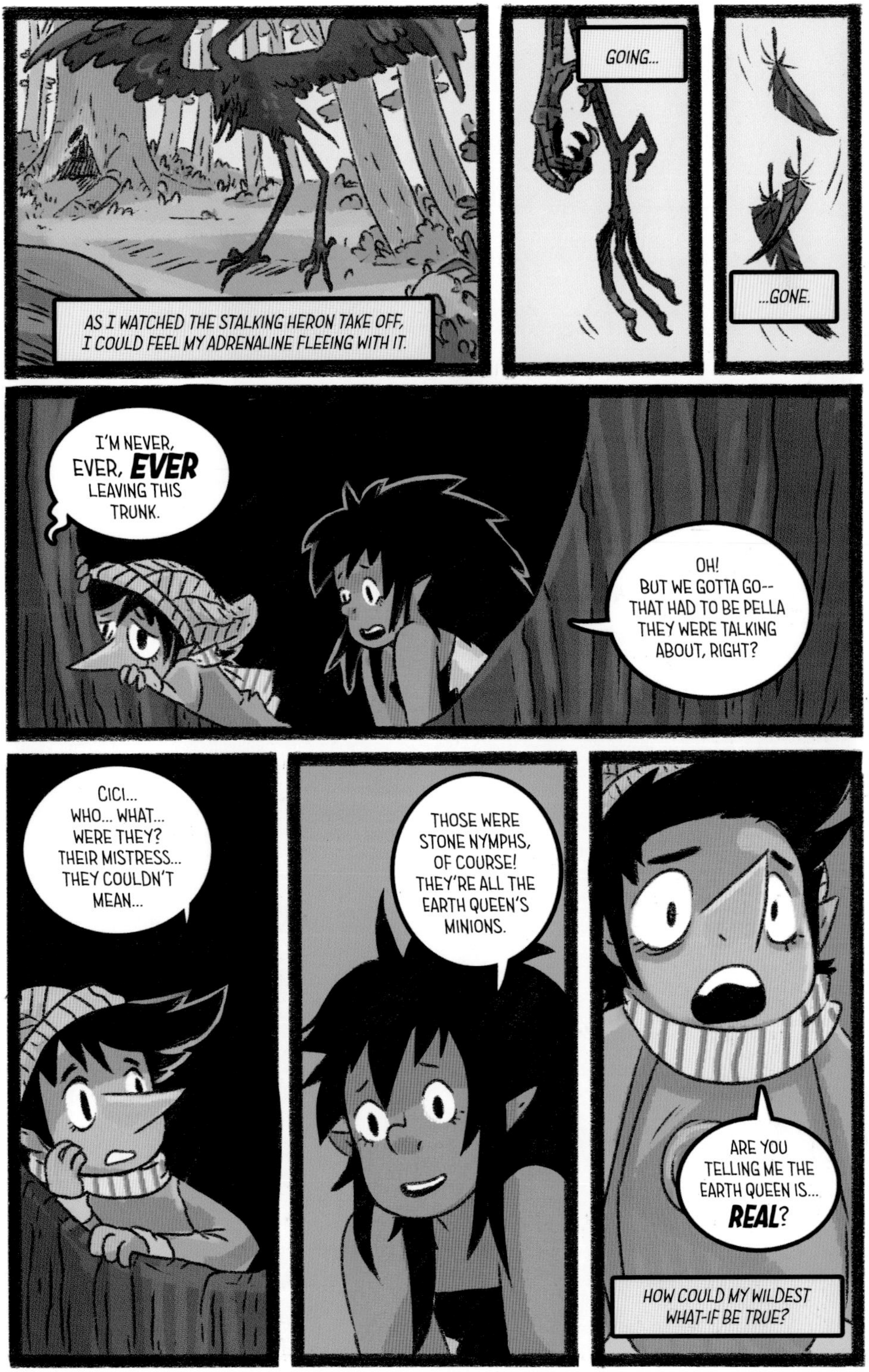

AS I WATCHED THE STALKING HERON TAKE OFF, I COULD FEEL MY ADRENALINE FLEEING WITH IT.
GOING...
...GONE.
I'M NEVER, EVER, **EVER** LEAVING THIS TRUNK.
OH! BUT WE GOTTA GO-- THAT HAD TO BE PELLA THEY WERE TALKING ABOUT, RIGHT?
CICI... WHO... WHAT... WERE THEY? THEIR MISTRESS... THEY COULDN'T MEAN...
THOSE WERE STONE NYMPHS, OF COURSE! THEY'RE ALL THE EARTH QUEEN'S MINIONS.
ARE YOU TELLING ME THE EARTH QUEEN IS... **REAL**?
HOW COULD MY WILDEST WHAT-IF BE TRUE?

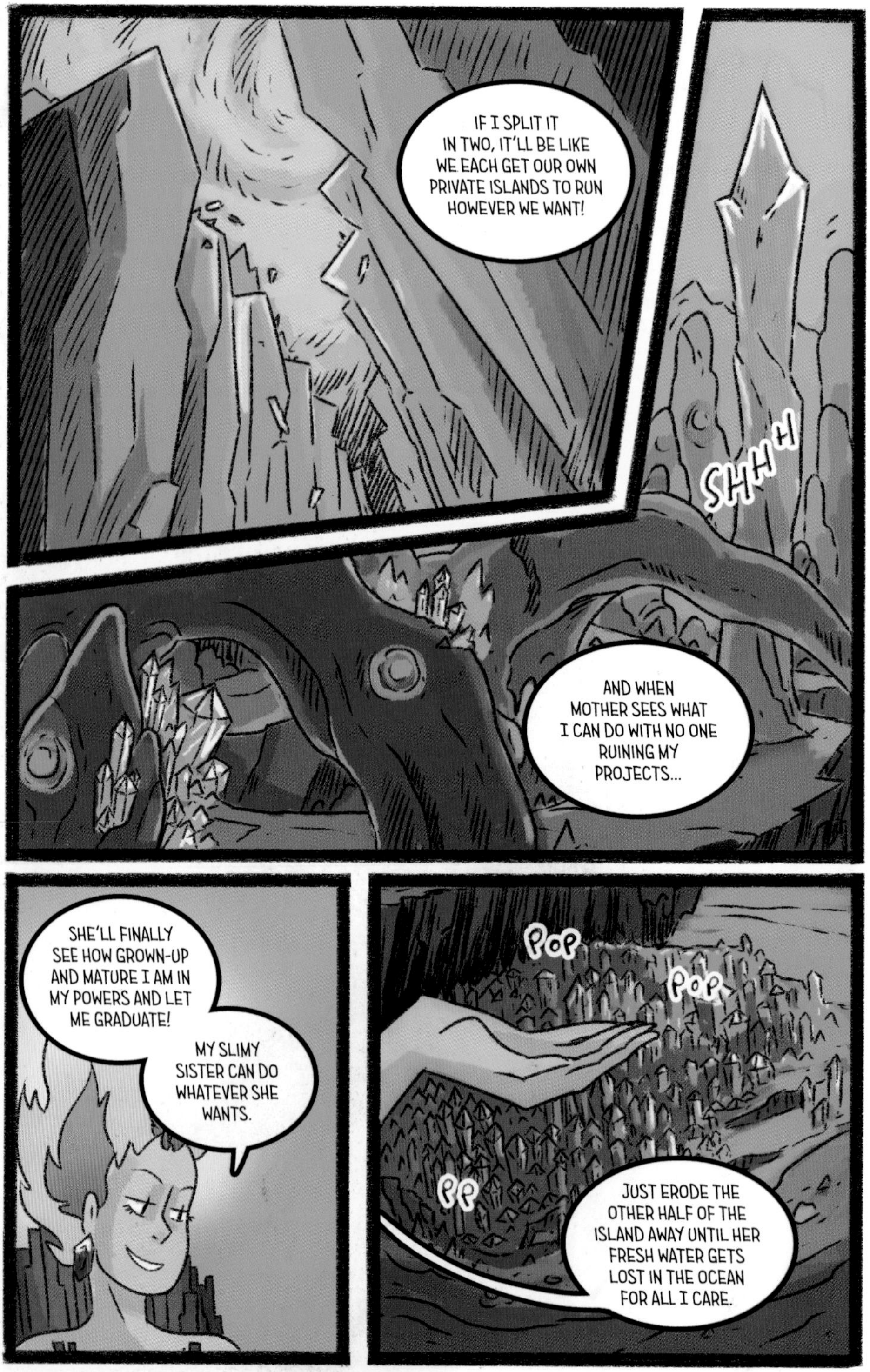
IF I SPLIT IT IN TWO, IT'LL BE LIKE WE EACH GET OUR OWN PRIVATE ISLANDS TO RUN HOWEVER WE WANT!
SHHHH
AND WHEN MOTHER SEES WHAT I CAN DO WITH NO ONE RUINING MY PROJECTS...
SHE'LL FINALLY SEE HOW GROWN-UP AND MATURE I AM IN MY POWERS AND LET ME GRADUATE!
MY SLIMY SISTER CAN DO WHATEVER SHE WANTS.
POP
POP
PP
JUST ERODE THE OTHER HALF OF THE ISLAND AWAY UNTIL HER FRESH WATER GETS LOST IN THE OCEAN FOR ALL I CARE.

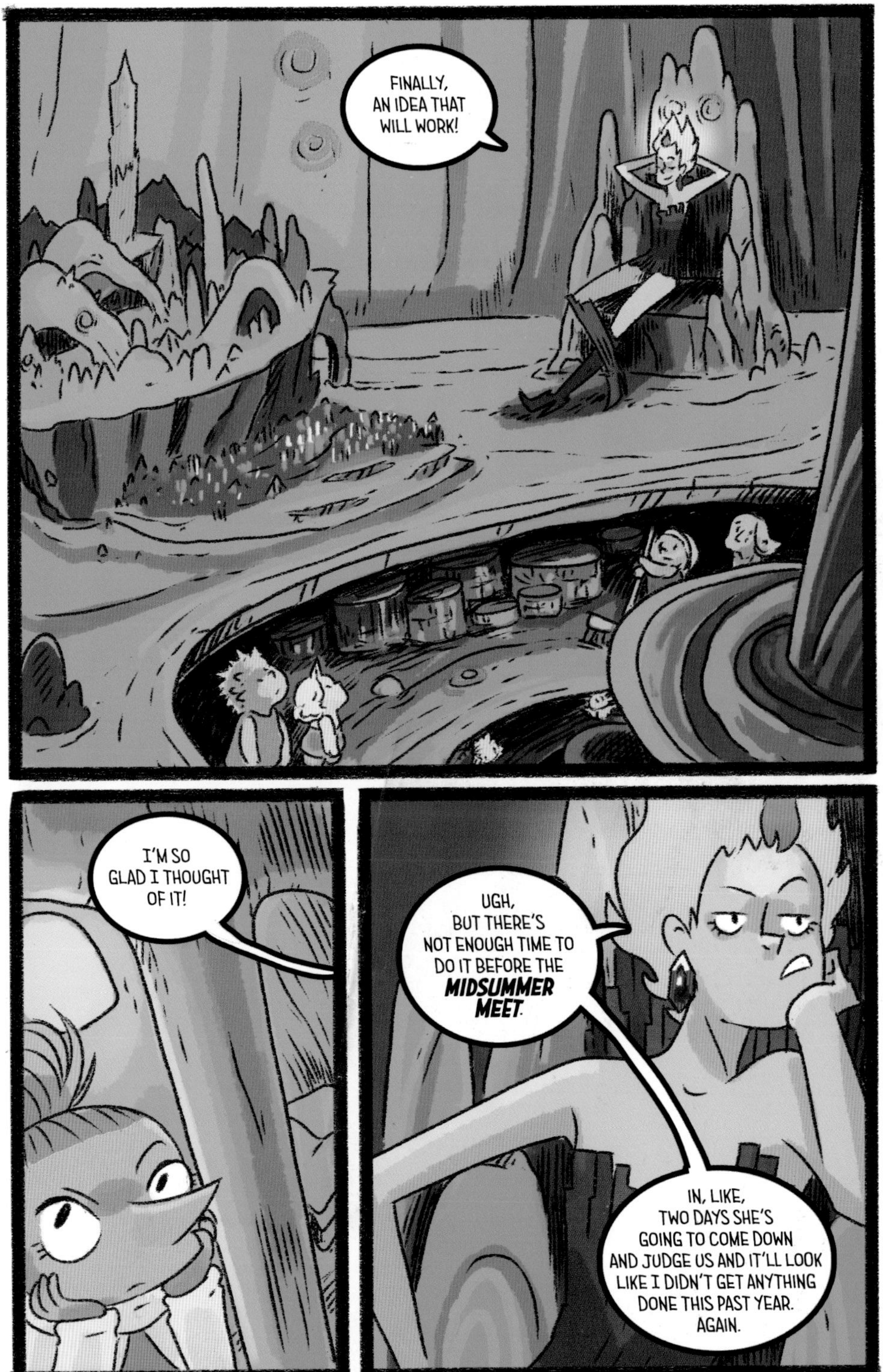
FINALLY, AN IDEA THAT WILL WORK!
I'M SO GLAD I THOUGHT OF IT!
UGH, BUT THERE'S NOT ENOUGH TIME TO DO IT BEFORE THE MIDSUMMER MEET.
IN, LIKE, TWO DAYS SHE'S GOING TO COME DOWN AND JUDGE US AND IT'LL LOOK LIKE I DIDN'T GET ANYTHING DONE THIS PAST YEAR. AGAIN.

UNLESS...
A BIG TALKER LIKE YOU CAME ALONG TO HELP EXPLAIN THE PLAN.

ARE YOU SERIOUS?

YOU'RE ASKING ME FOR HELP...

...WHEN YOU'RE THE REASON MY FIREFLY WISHES WON'T COME TRUE THIS YEAR!

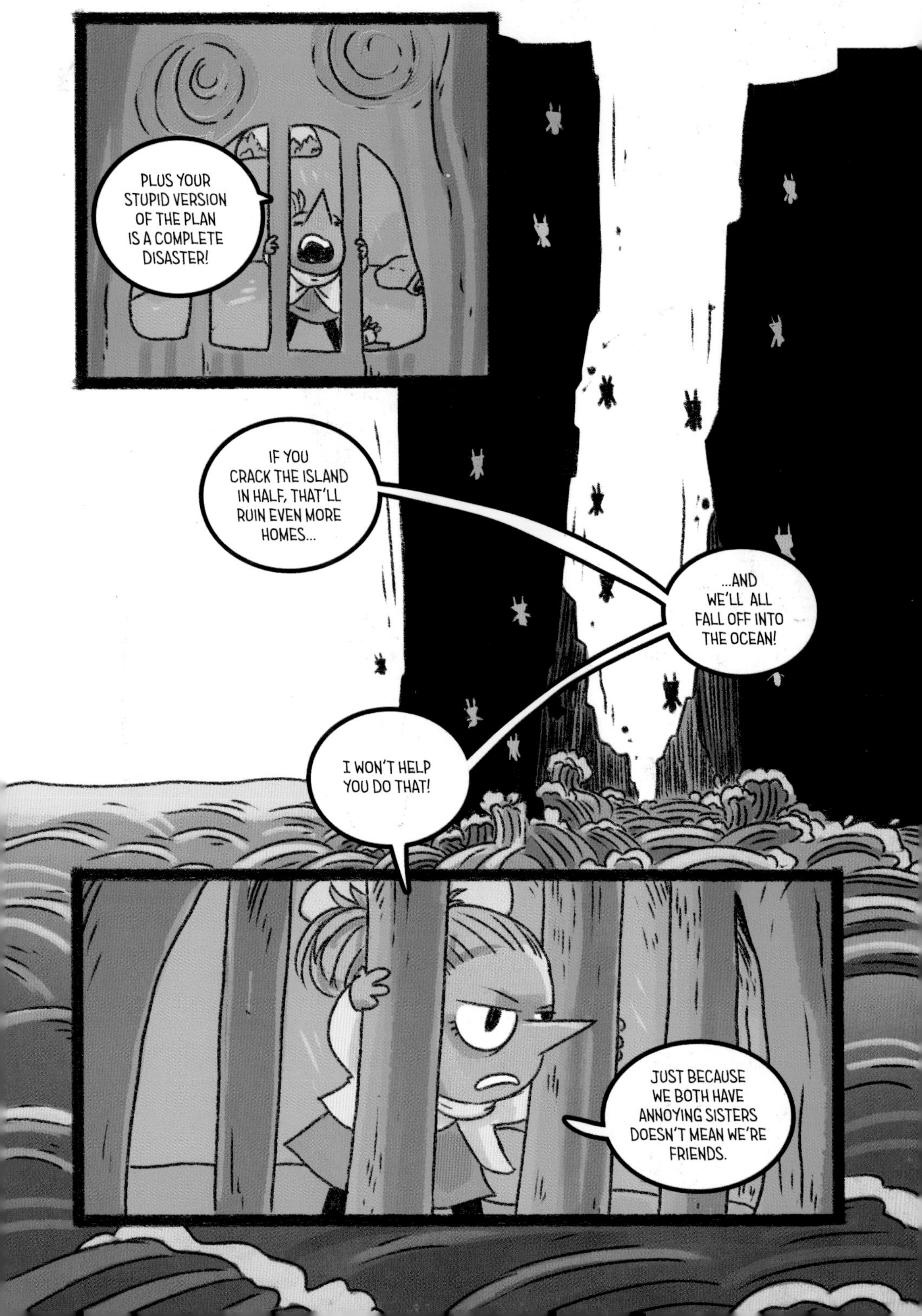
PLUS YOUR STUPID VERSION OF THE PLAN IS A COMPLETE DISASTER!
IF YOU CRACK THE ISLAND IN HALF, THAT'LL RUIN EVEN MORE HOMES...
...AND WE'LL ALL FALL OFF INTO THE OCEAN!
I WON'T HELP YOU DO THAT!
JUST BECAUSE WE BOTH HAVE ANNOYING SISTERS DOESN'T MEAN WE'RE FRIENDS.

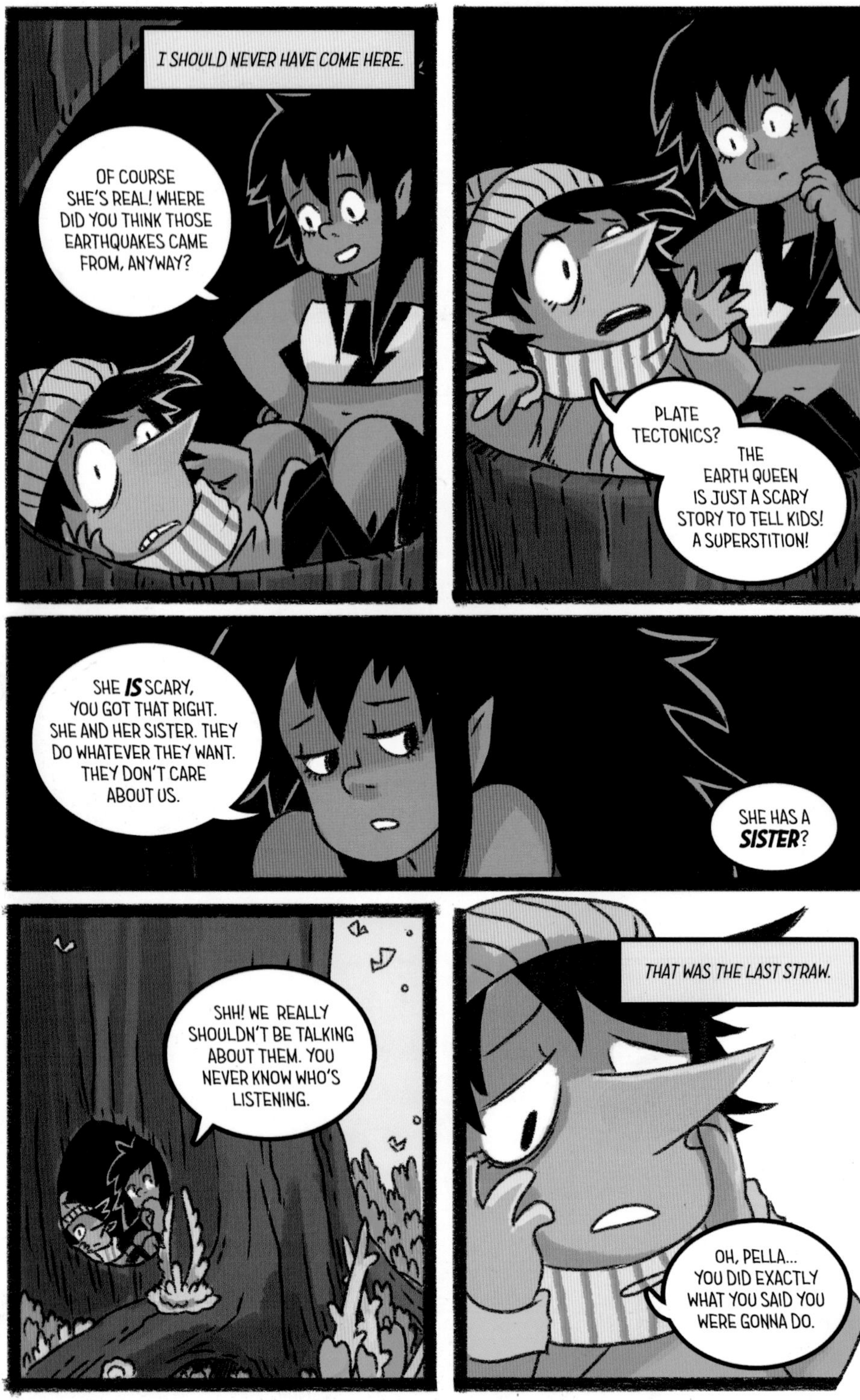
I SHOULD NEVER HAVE COME HERE.
OF COURSE SHE'S REAL! WHERE DID YOU THINK THOSE EARTHQUAKES CAME FROM, ANYWAY?
PLATE TECTONICS?
THE EARTH QUEEN IS JUST A SCARY STORY TO TELL KIDS! A SUPERSTITION!
SHE IS SCARY, YOU GOT THAT RIGHT. SHE AND HER SISTER. THEY DO WHATEVER THEY WANT. THEY DON'T CARE ABOUT US.
SHE HAS A SISTER?
SHH! WE REALLY SHOULDN'T BE TALKING ABOUT THEM. YOU NEVER KNOW WHO'S LISTENING.
THAT WAS THE LAST STRAW.
OH, PELLA... YOU DID EXACTLY WHAT YOU SAID YOU WERE GONNA DO.

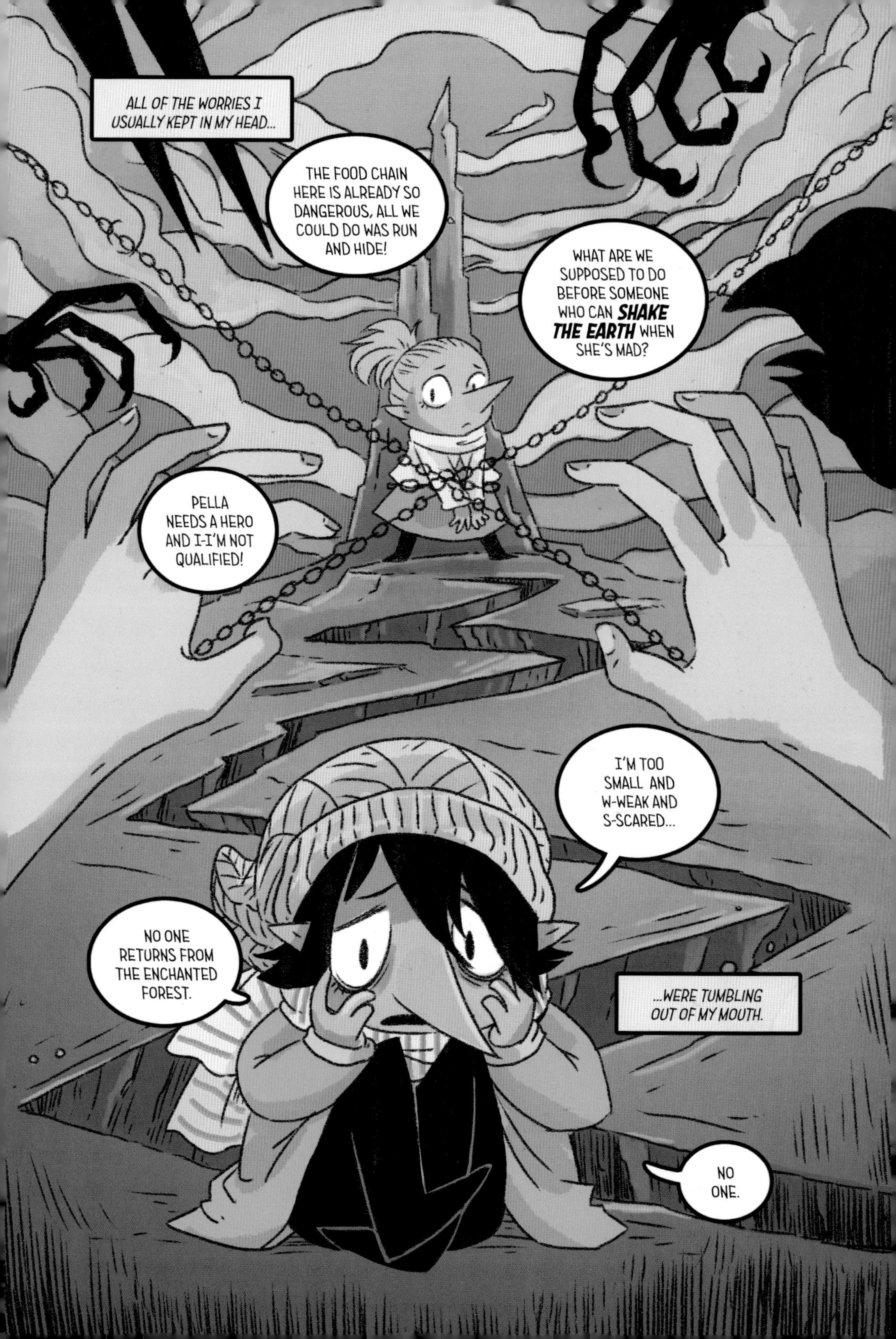
ALL OF THE WORRIES I USUALLY KEPT IN MY HEAD...
THE FOOD CHAIN HERE IS ALREADY SO DANGEROUS, ALL WE COULD DO WAS RUN AND HIDE!
WHAT ARE WE SUPPOSED TO DO BEFORE SOMEONE WHO CAN SHAKE THE EARTH WHEN SHE'S MAD?
PELLA NEEDS A HERO AND I-I'M NOT QUALIFIED!
I'M TOO SMALL AND W-WEAK AND S-SCARED...
NO ONE RETURNS FROM THE ENCHANTED FOREST.
...WERE TUMBLING OUT OF MY MOUTH.
NO ONE.

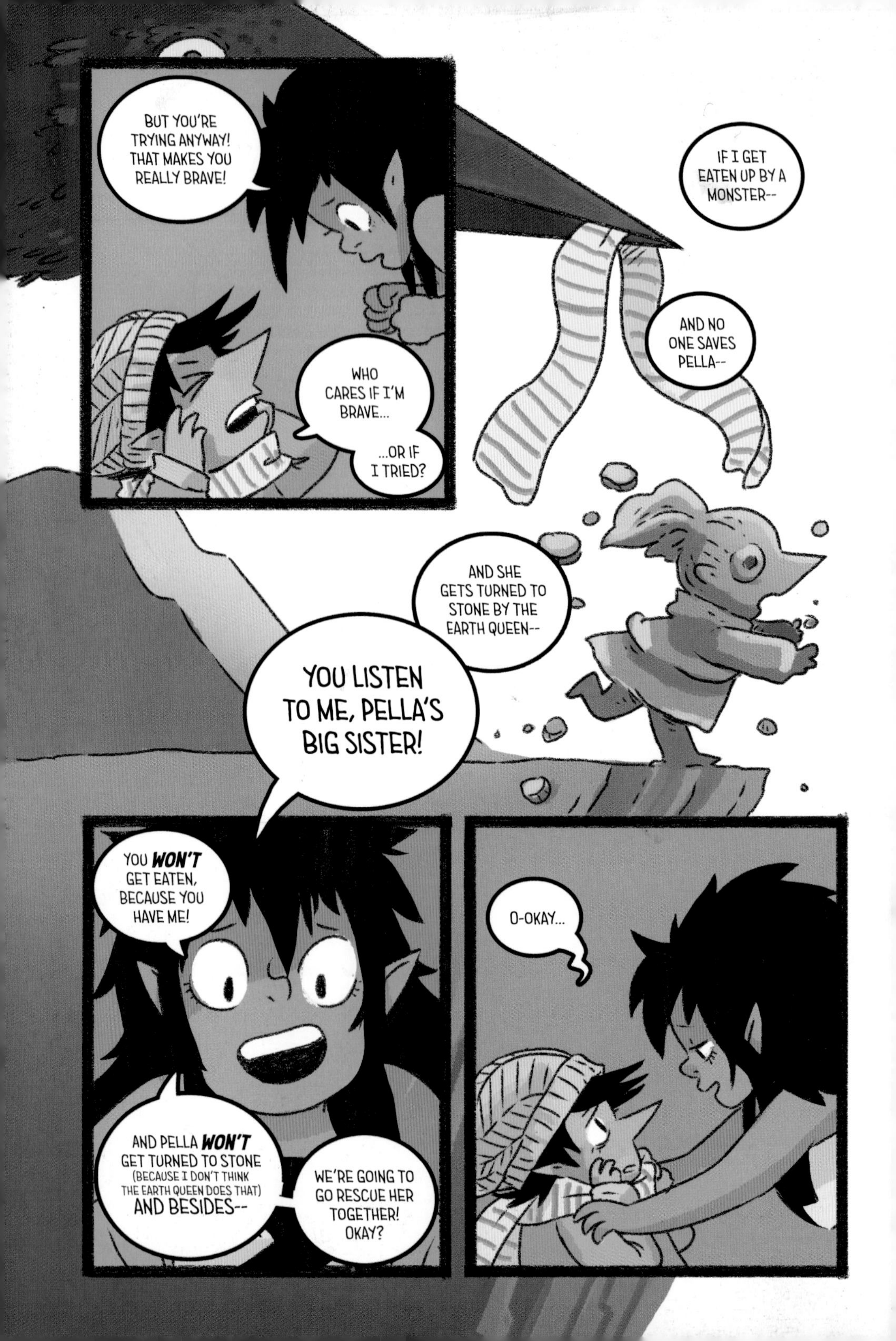
BUT YOU'RE TRYING ANYWAY! THAT MAKES YOU REALLY BRAVE!
WHO CARES IF I'M BRAVE...
...OR IF I TRIED?
IF I GET EATEN UP BY A MONSTER--
AND NO ONE SAVES PELLA--
AND SHE GETS TURNED TO STONE BY THE EARTH QUEEN--
YOU LISTEN TO ME, PELLA'S BIG SISTER!
YOU WON'T GET EATEN, BECAUSE YOU HAVE ME!
AND PELLA WON'T GET TURNED TO STONE (BECAUSE I DON'T THINK THE EARTH QUEEN DOES THAT) AND BESIDES--
WE'RE GOING TO GO RESCUE HER TOGETHER! OKAY?
O-OKAY...

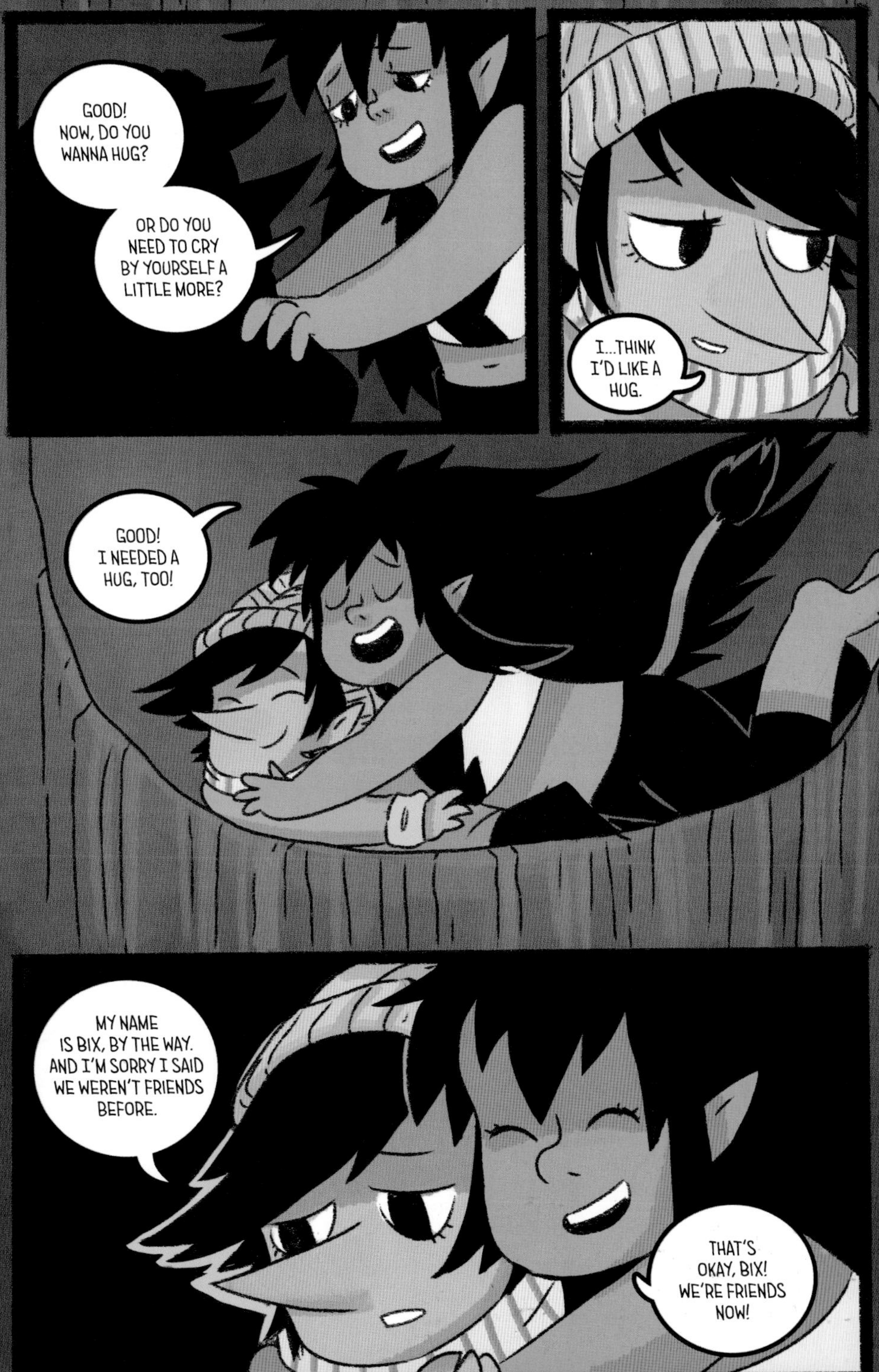
GOOD! NOW, DO YOU WANNA HUG?
OR DO YOU NEED TO CRY BY YOURSELF A LITTLE MORE?
I...THINK I'D LIKE A HUG.
GOOD! I NEEDED A HUG, TOO!
MY NAME IS BIX, BY THE WAY. AND I'M SORRY I SAID WE WEREN'T FRIENDS BEFORE.
THAT'S OKAY, BIX! WE'RE FRIENDS NOW!

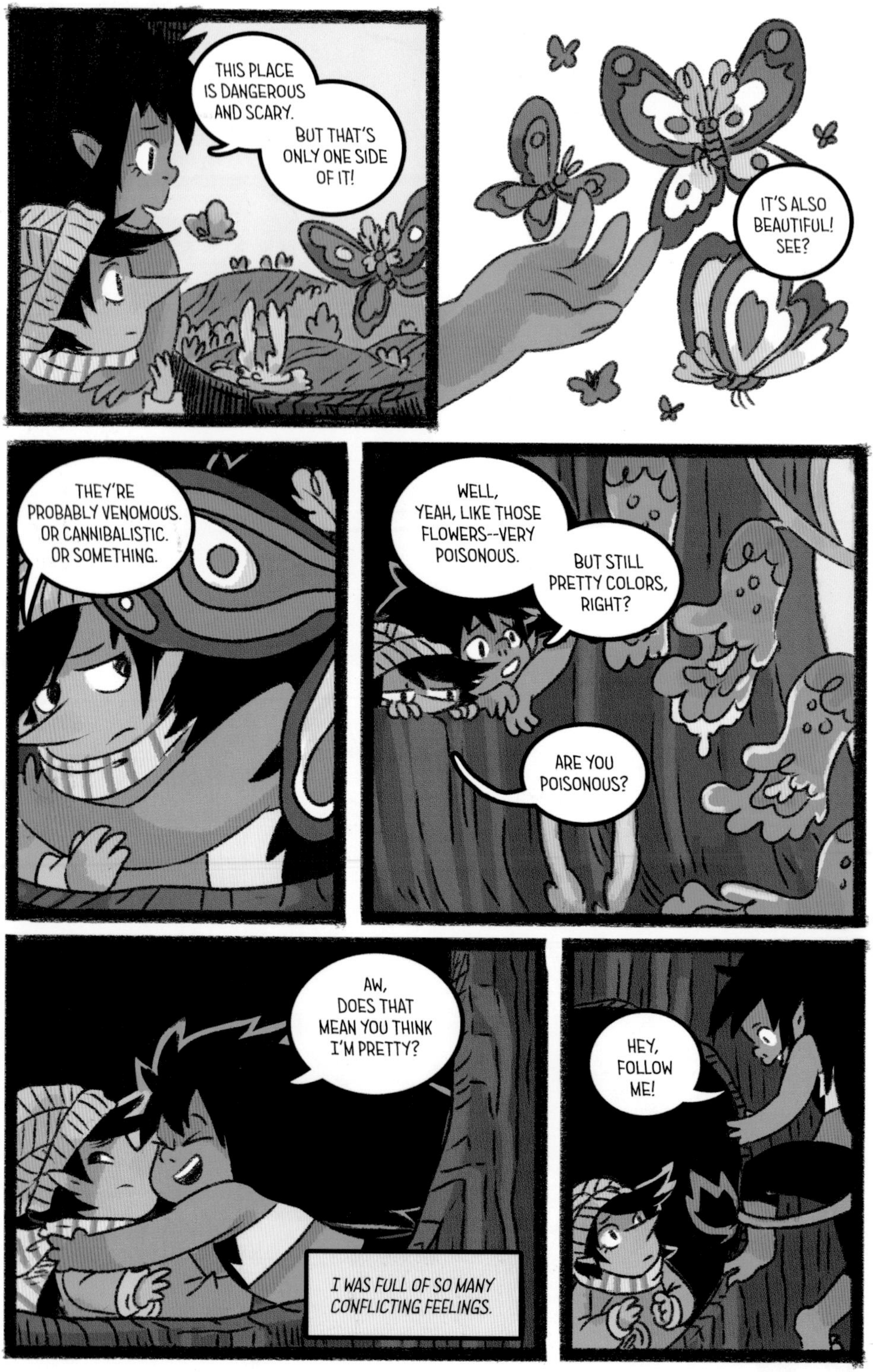
THIS PLACE IS DANGEROUS AND SCARY.
BUT THAT'S ONLY ONE SIDE OF IT!
IT'S ALSO BEAUTIFUL! SEE?
THEY'RE PROBABLY VENOMOUS. OR CANNIBALISTIC. OR SOMETHING.
WELL, YEAH, LIKE THOSE FLOWERS--VERY POISONOUS.
BUT STILL PRETTY COLORS, RIGHT?
ARE YOU POISONOUS?
AW, DOES THAT MEAN YOU THINK I'M PRETTY?
I WAS FULL OF SO MANY CONFLICTING FEELINGS.
HEY, FOLLOW ME!

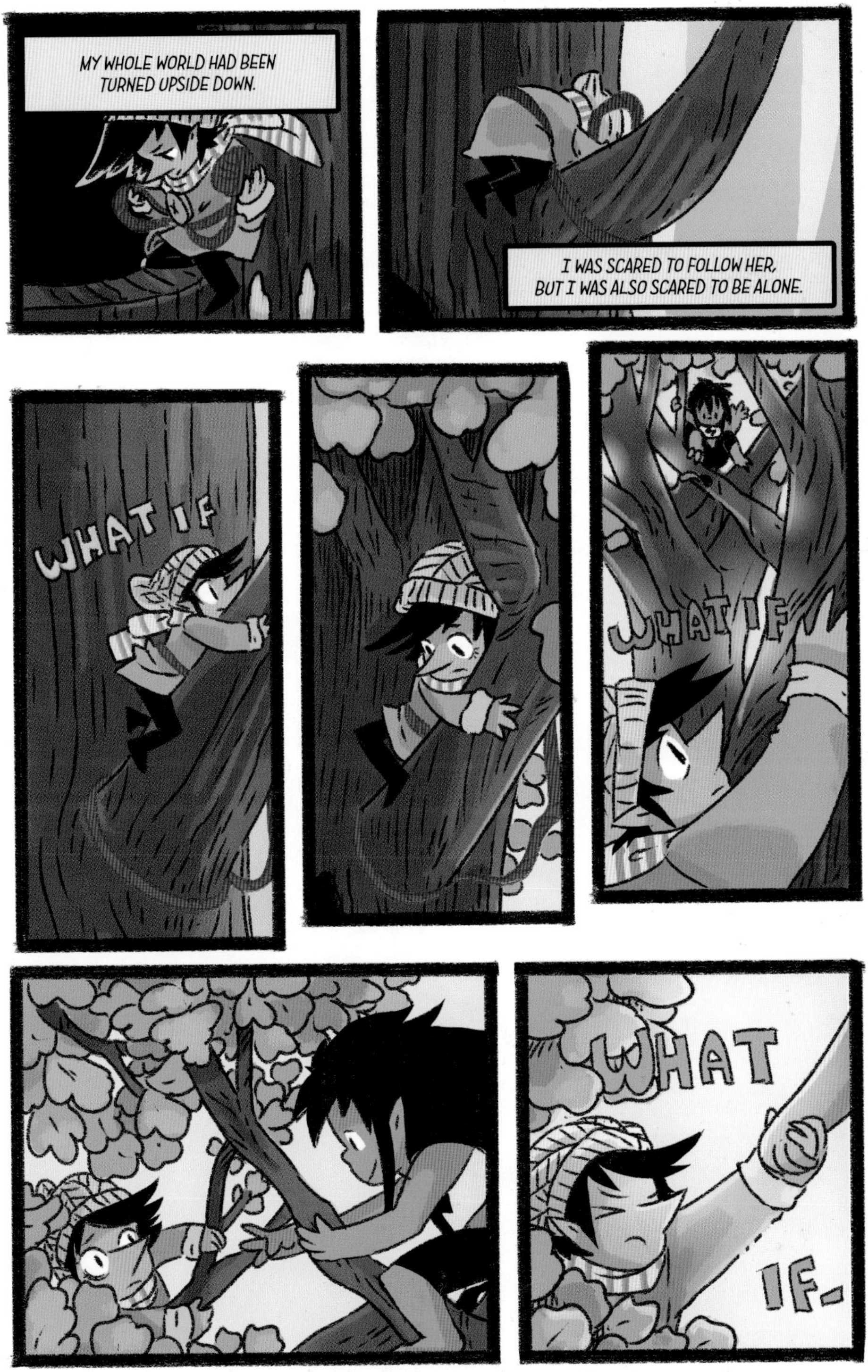

MY WHOLE WORLD HAD BEEN TURNED UPSIDE DOWN.
I WAS SCARED TO FOLLOW HER, BUT I WAS ALSO SCARED TO BE ALONE.
WHAT IF
WHAT IF
WHAT
IF-

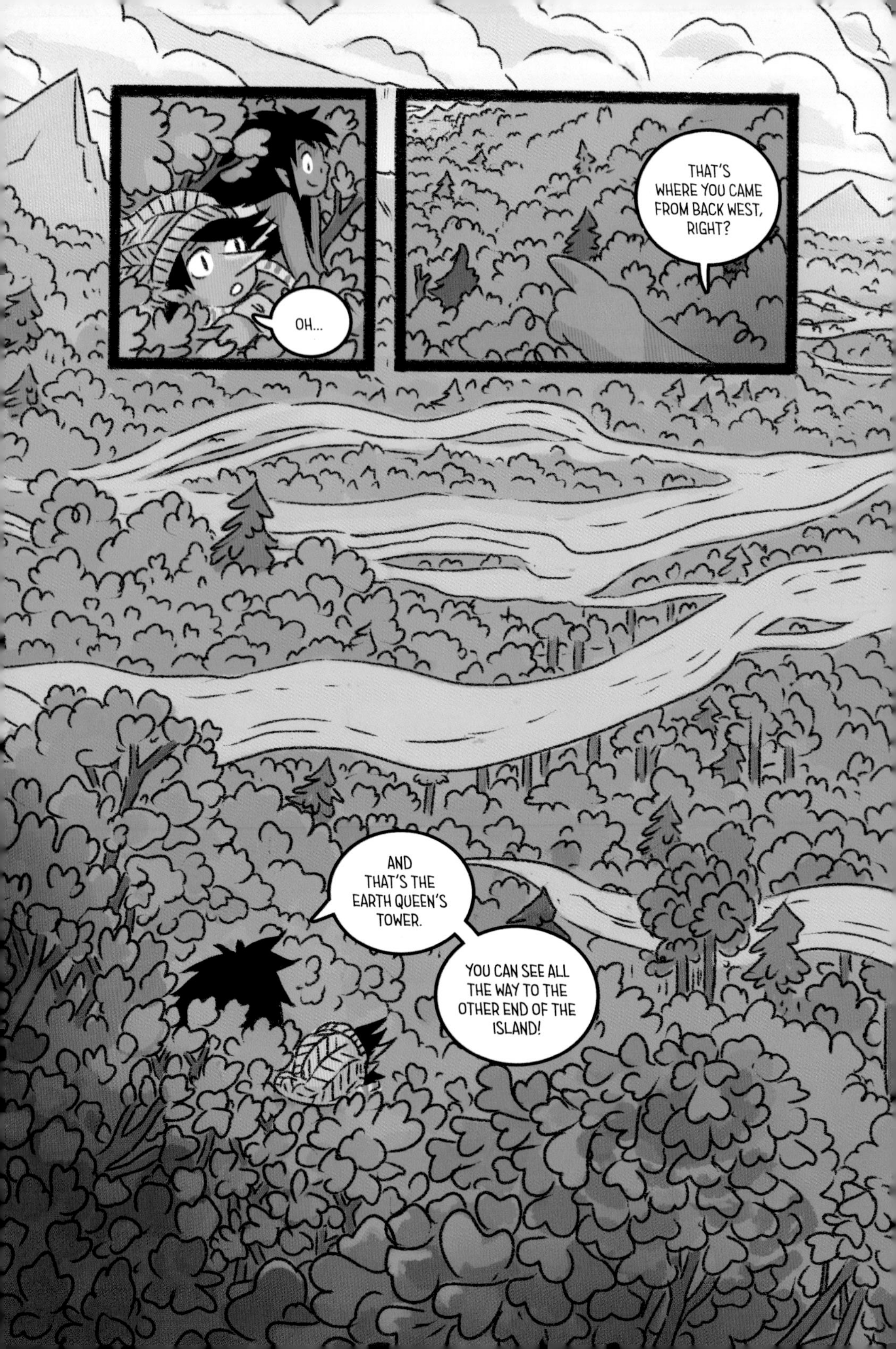
OH...
THAT'S WHERE YOU CAME FROM BACK WEST, RIGHT?
AND THAT'S THE EARTH QUEEN'S TOWER.
YOU CAN SEE ALL THE WAY TO THE OTHER END OF THE ISLAND!

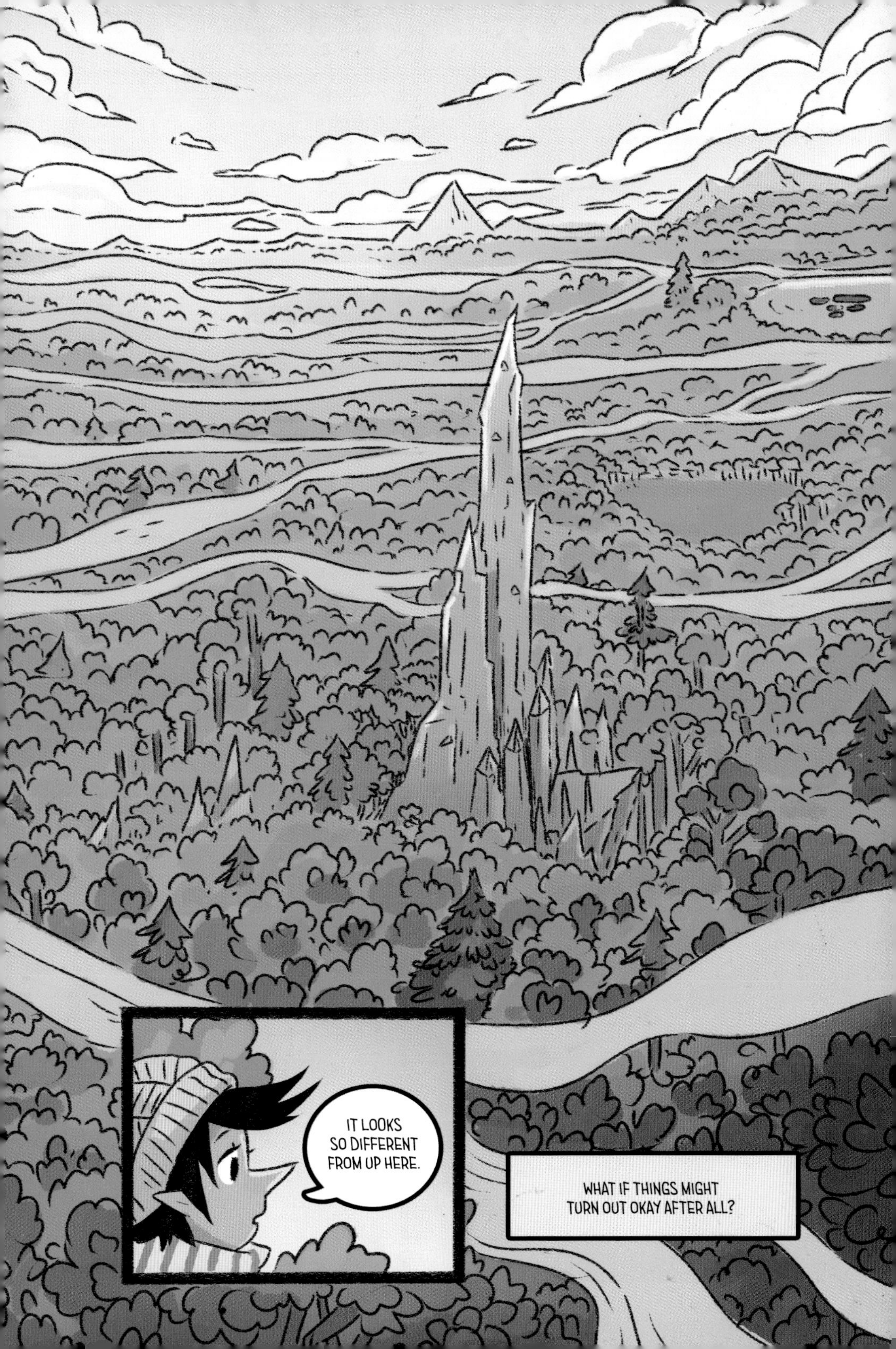
IT LOOKS SO DIFFERENT FROM UP HERE.
WHAT IF THINGS MIGHT TURN OUT OKAY AFTER ALL?

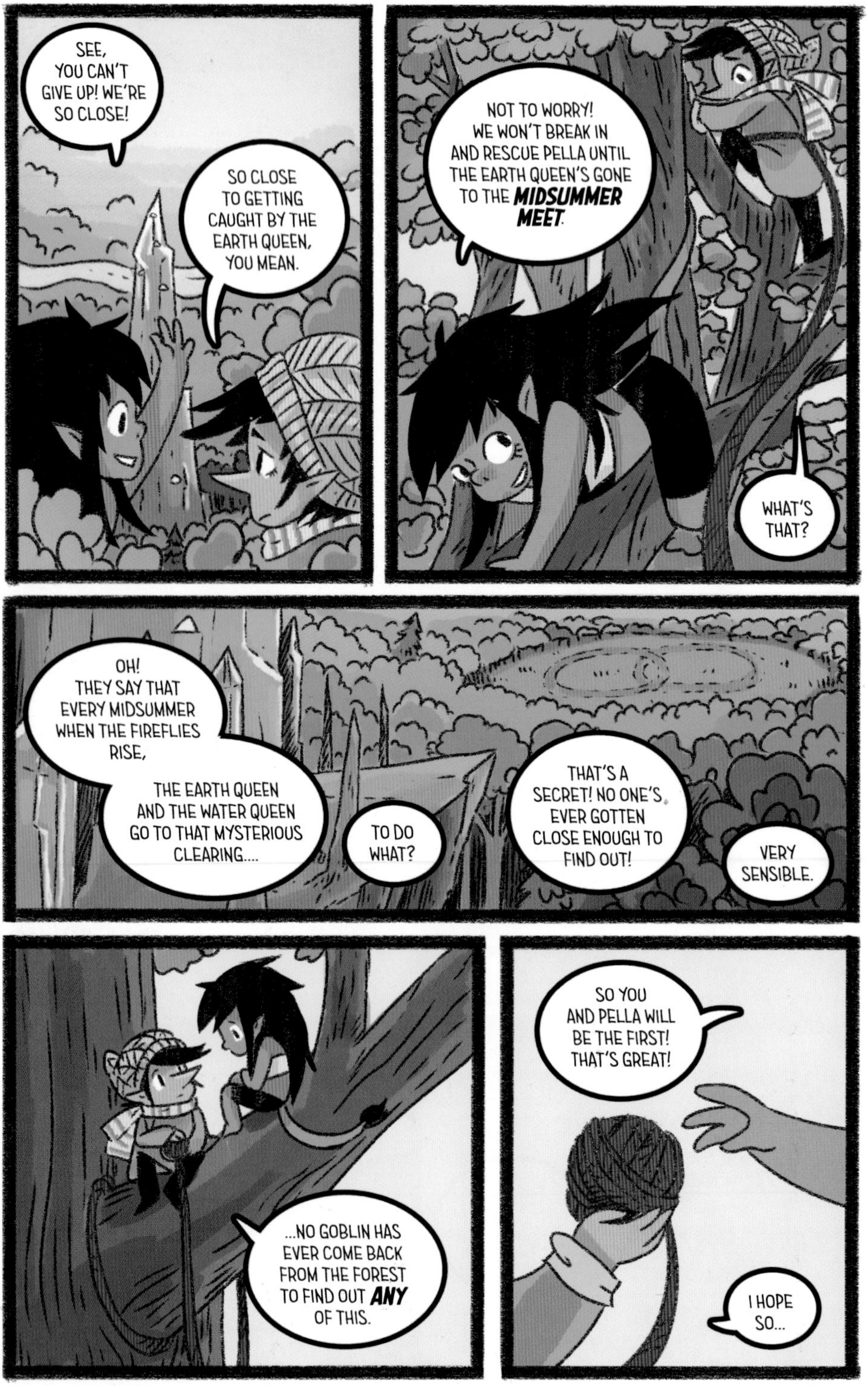
SEE, YOU CAN'T GIVE UP! WE'RE SO CLOSE!
SO CLOSE TO GETTING CAUGHT BY THE EARTH QUEEN, YOU MEAN.
NOT TO WORRY! WE WON'T BREAK IN AND RESCUE PELLA UNTIL THE EARTH QUEEN'S GONE TO THE MIDSUMMER MEET.
WHAT'S THAT?
OH! THEY SAY THAT EVERY MIDSUMMER WHEN THE FIREFLIES RISE,
THE EARTH QUEEN AND THE WATER QUEEN GO TO THAT MYSTERIOUS CLEARING....
TO DO WHAT?
THAT'S A SECRET! NO ONE'S EVER GOTTEN CLOSE ENOUGH TO FIND OUT!
VERY SENSIBLE.
...NO GOBLIN HAS EVER COME BACK FROM THE FOREST TO FIND OUT ANY OF THIS.
SO YOU AND PELLA WILL BE THE FIRST! THAT'S GREAT!
I HOPE SO...

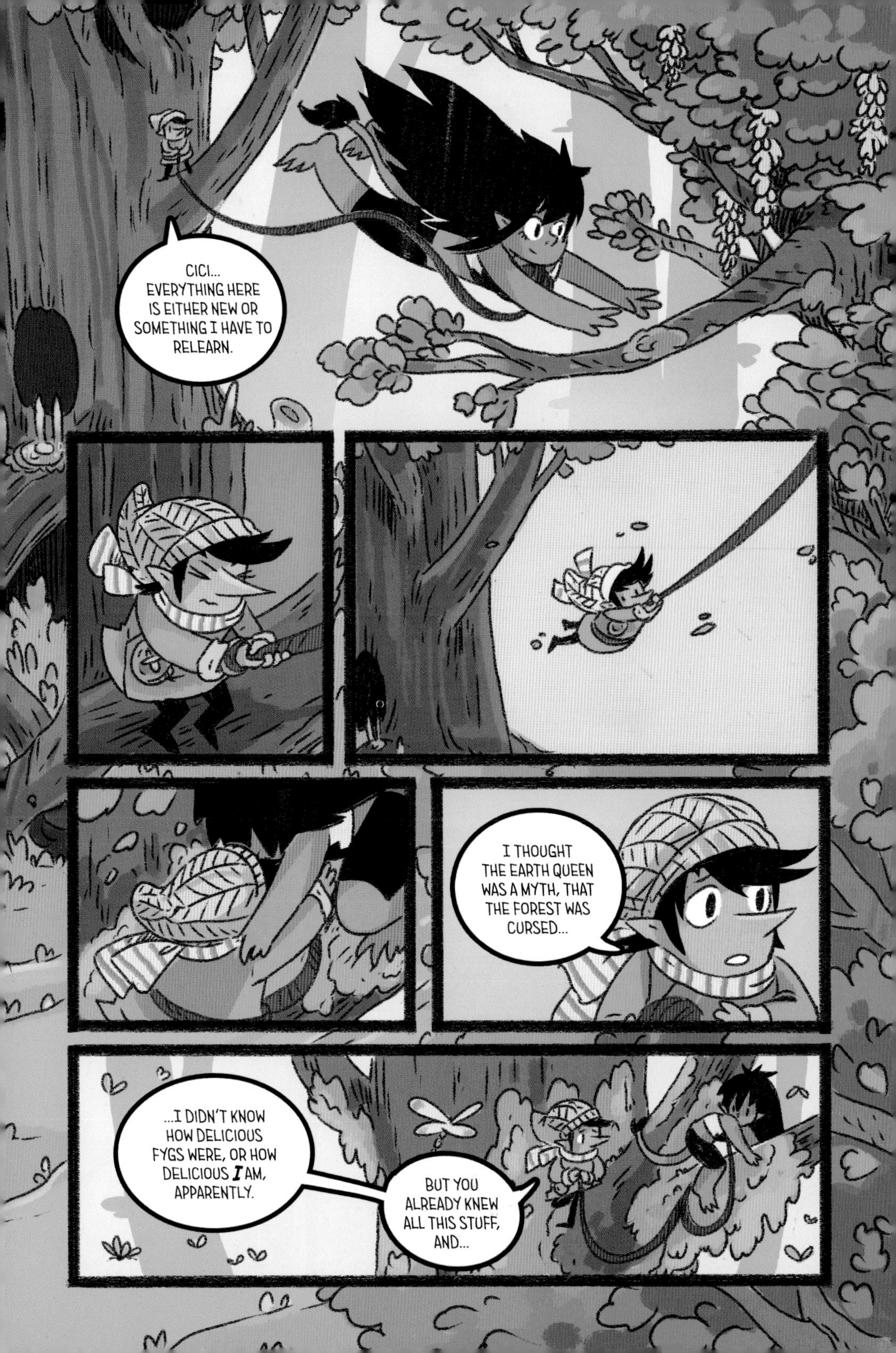
CICI... EVERYTHING HERE IS EITHER NEW OR SOMETHING I HAVE TO RELEARN.
I THOUGHT THE EARTH QUEEN WAS A MYTH, THAT THE FOREST WAS CURSED...
...I DIDN'T KNOW HOW DELICIOUS FYGS WERE, OR HOW DELICIOUS *I* AM, APPARENTLY.
BUT YOU ALREADY KNEW ALL THIS STUFF, AND...

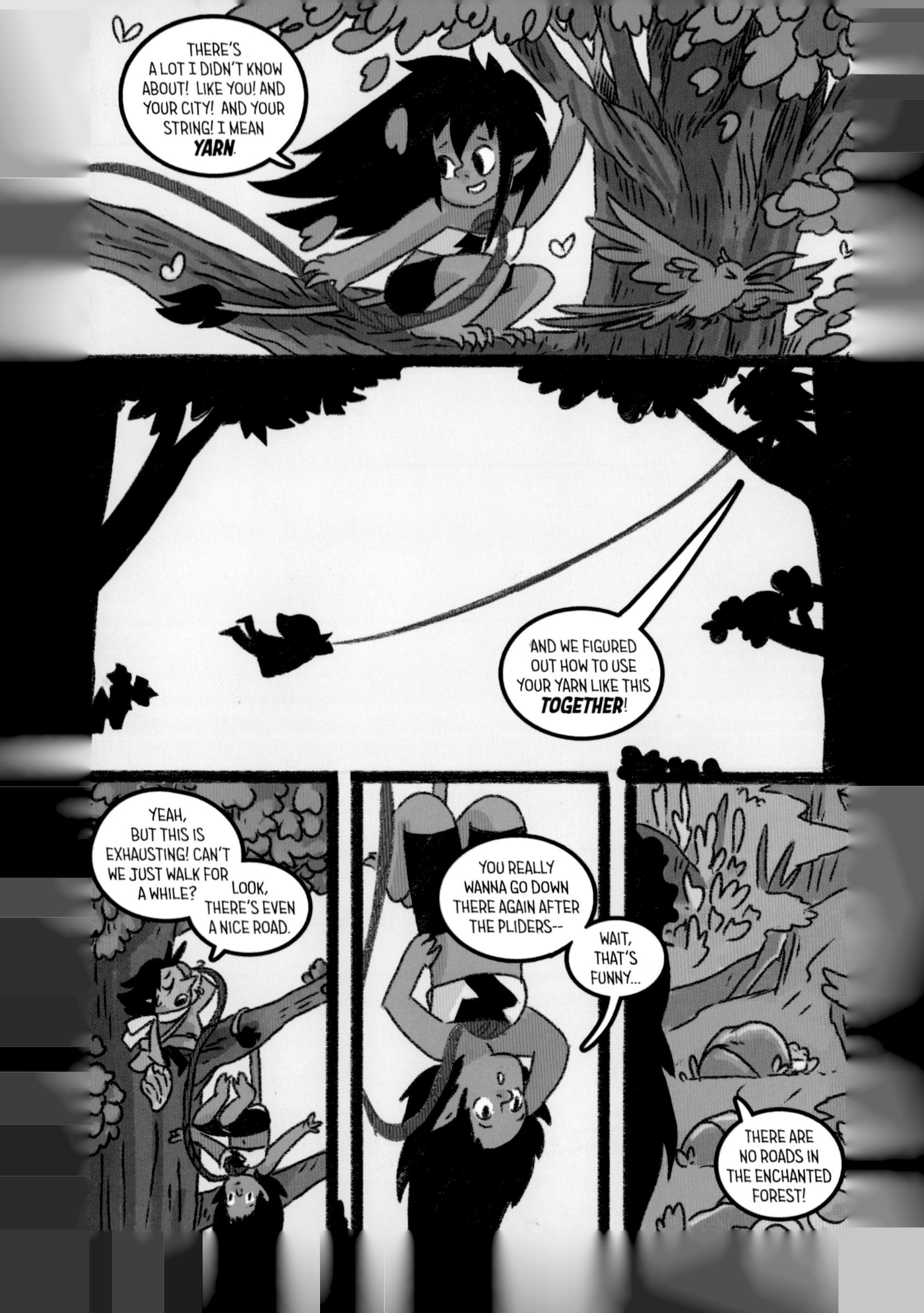
THERE'S A LOT I DIDN'T KNOW ABOUT! LIKE YOU! AND YOUR CITY! AND YOUR STRING! I MEAN **YARN**.
AND WE FIGURED OUT HOW TO USE YOUR YARN LIKE THIS ***TOGETHER***!
YEAH, BUT THIS IS EXHAUSTING! CAN'T WE JUST WALK FOR A WHILE?
LOOK, THERE'S EVEN A NICE ROAD.
YOU REALLY WANNA GO DOWN THERE AGAIN AFTER THE PLIDERS--
WAIT, THAT'S FUNNY...
THERE ARE NO ROADS IN THE ENCHANTED FOREST!

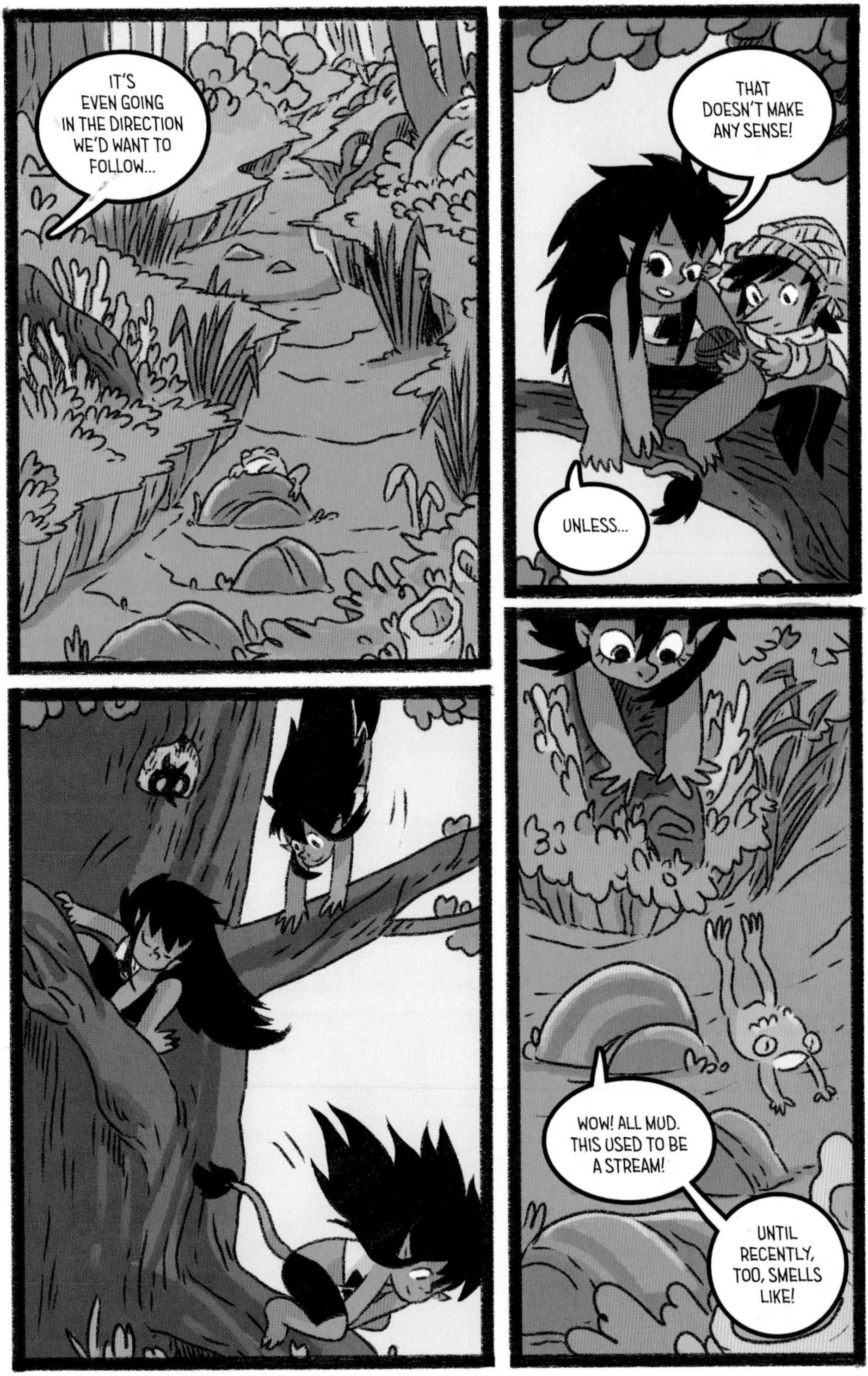
IT'S EVEN GOING IN THE DIRECTION WE'D WANT TO FOLLOW...
THAT DOESN'T MAKE ANY SENSE!
UNLESS...
WOW! ALL MUD. THIS USED TO BE A STREAM!
UNTIL RECENTLY, TOO, SMELLS LIKE!

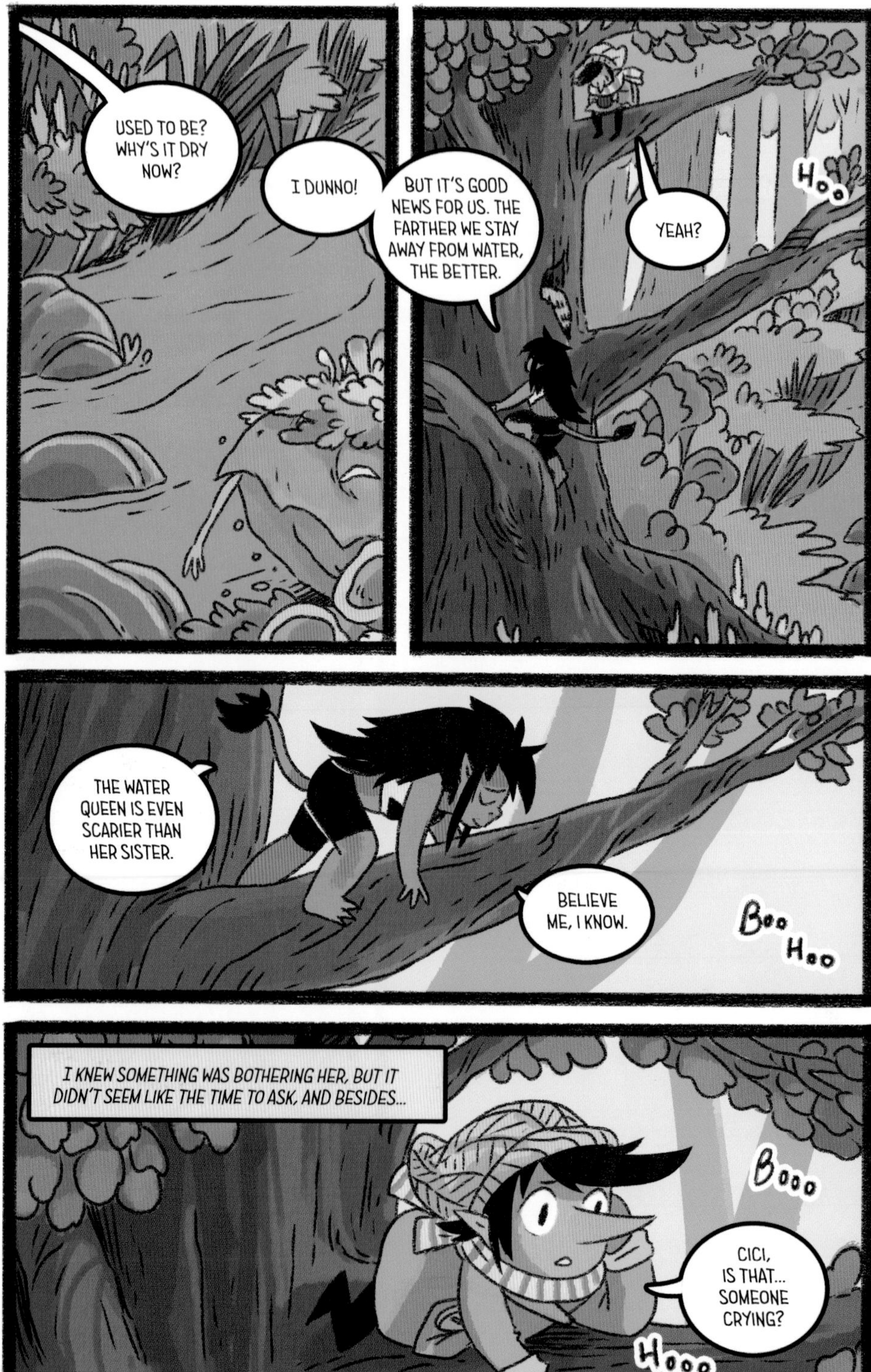
USED TO BE? WHY'S IT DRY NOW?
I DUNNO!
BUT IT'S GOOD NEWS FOR US. THE FARTHER WE STAY AWAY FROM WATER, THE BETTER.
YEAH?
Hoo
THE WATER QUEEN IS EVEN SCARIER THAN HER SISTER.
BELIEVE ME, I KNOW.
Boo Hoo
I KNEW SOMETHING WAS BOTHERING HER, BUT IT DIDN'T SEEM LIKE THE TIME TO ASK, AND BESIDES...
Booo
CICI, IS THAT... SOMEONE CRYING?
Hooo

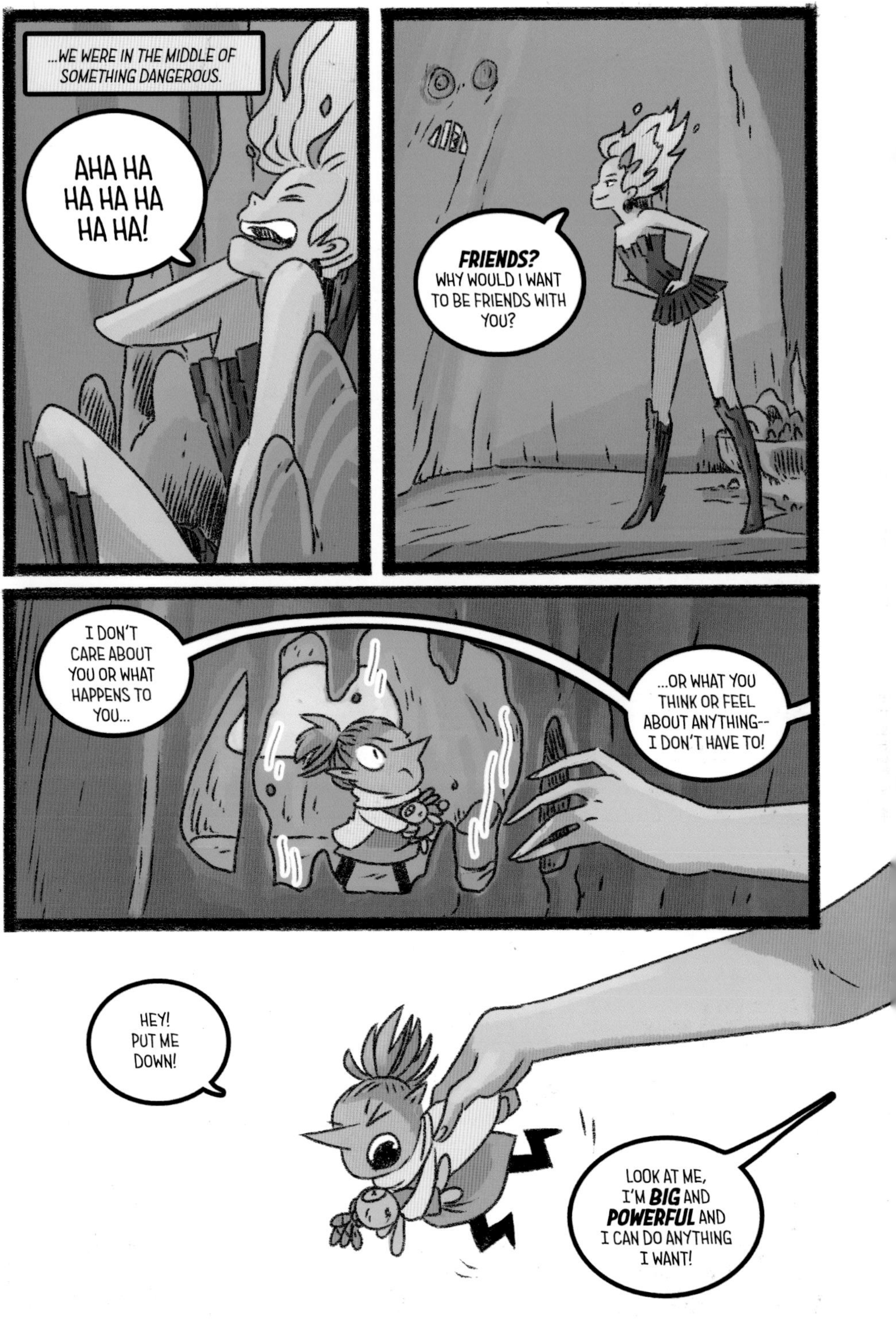
...WE WERE IN THE MIDDLE OF SOMETHING DANGEROUS.
AHA HA HA HA HA HA HA!
FRIENDS? WHY WOULD I WANT TO BE FRIENDS WITH YOU?
I DON'T CARE ABOUT YOU OR WHAT HAPPENS TO YOU...
...OR WHAT YOU THINK OR FEEL ABOUT ANYTHING-- I DON'T HAVE TO!
HEY! PUT ME DOWN!
LOOK AT ME, I'M BIG AND POWERFUL AND I CAN DO ANYTHING I WANT!

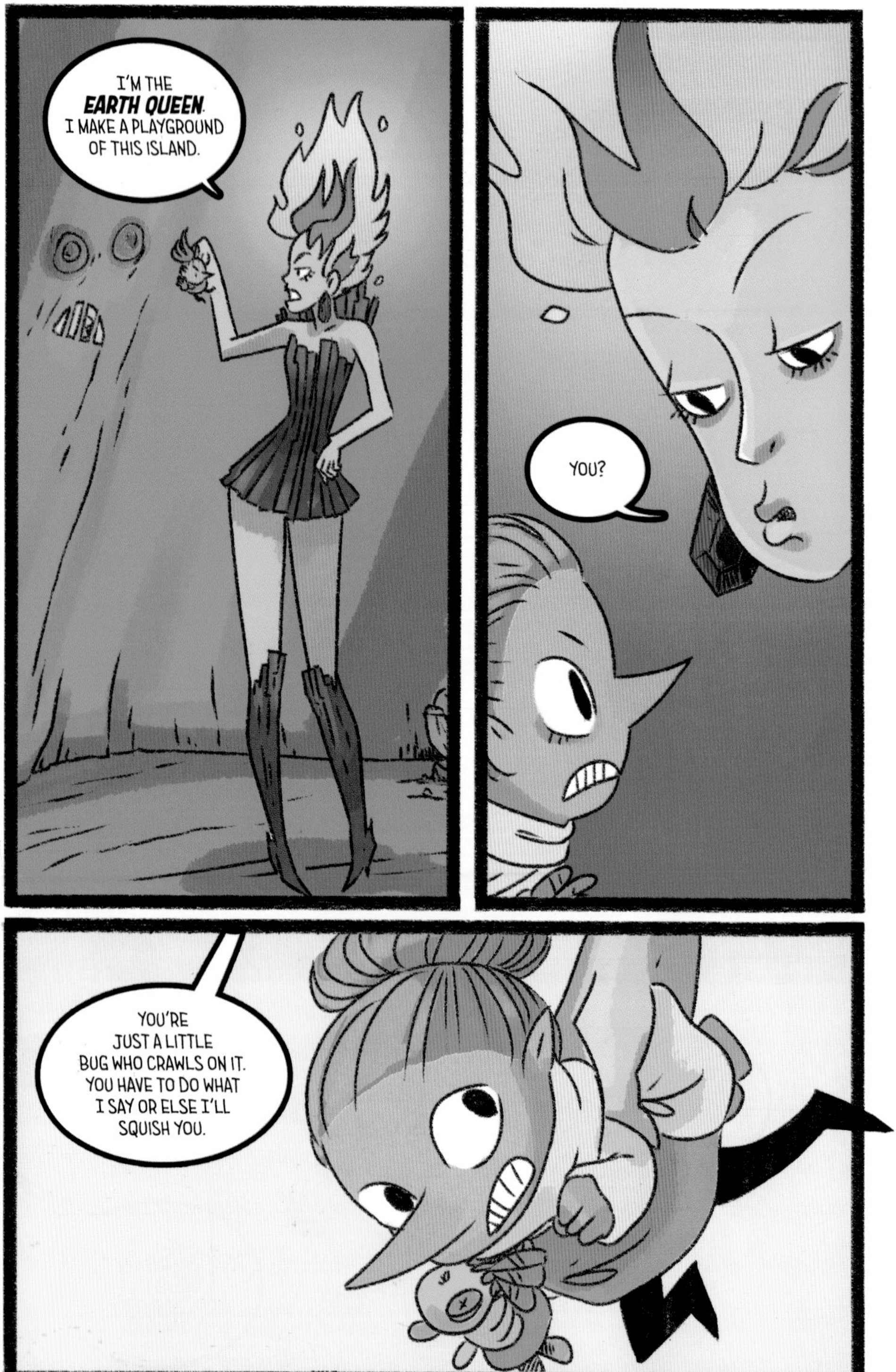
I'M THE **EARTH QUEEN**. I MAKE A PLAYGROUND OF THIS ISLAND.
YOU?
YOU'RE JUST A LITTLE BUG WHO CRAWLS ON IT. YOU HAVE TO DO WHAT I SAY OR ELSE I'LL SQUISH YOU.

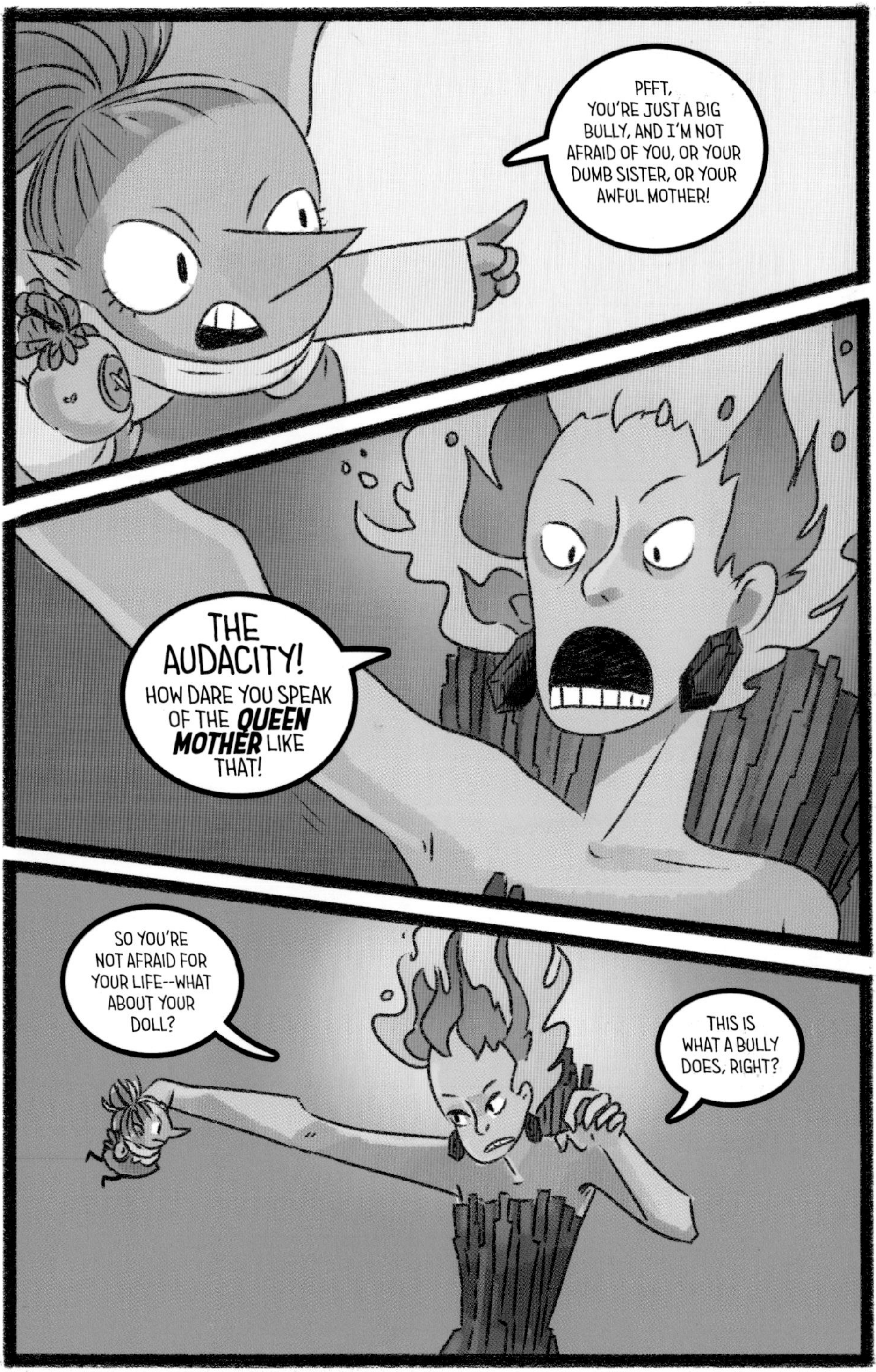
PFFT, YOU'RE JUST A BIG BULLY, AND I'M NOT AFRAID OF YOU, OR YOUR DUMB SISTER, OR YOUR AWFUL MOTHER!
THE AUDACITY! HOW DARE YOU SPEAK OF THE QUEEN MOTHER LIKE THAT!
SO YOU'RE NOT AFRAID FOR YOUR LIFE--WHAT ABOUT YOUR DOLL?
THIS IS WHAT A BULLY DOES, RIGHT?

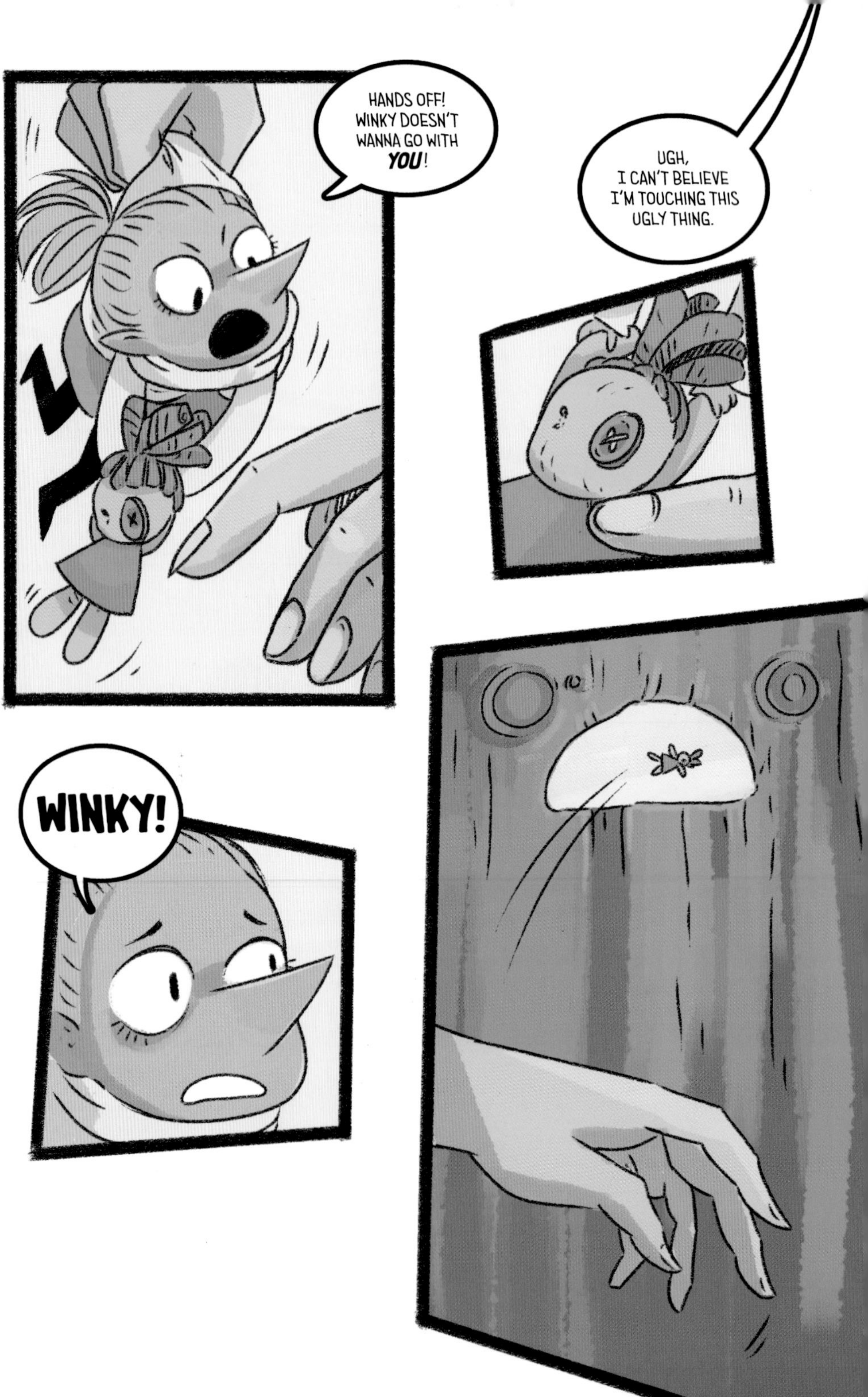
HANDS OFF! WINKY DOESN'T WANNA GO WITH ***YOU***!
UGH, I CAN'T BELIEVE I'M TOUCHING THIS UGLY THING.
WINKY!

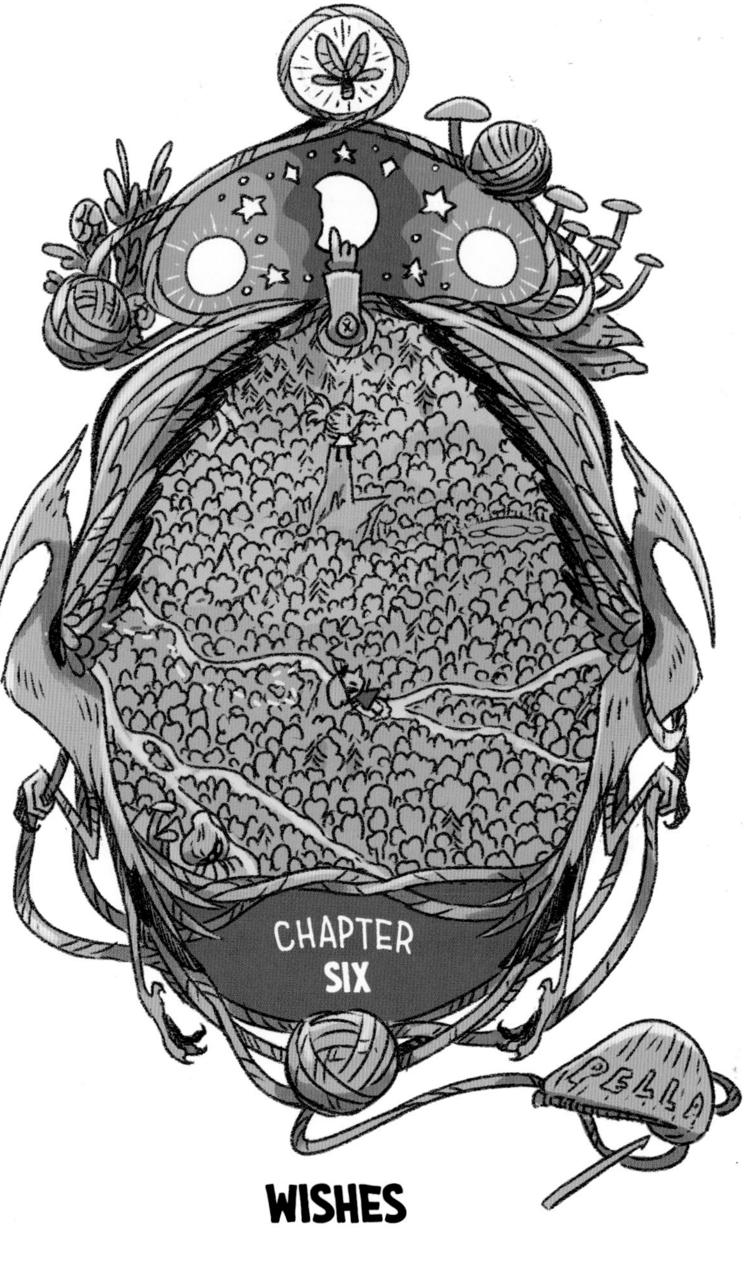
CHAPTER
SIX
PELLA

WISHES

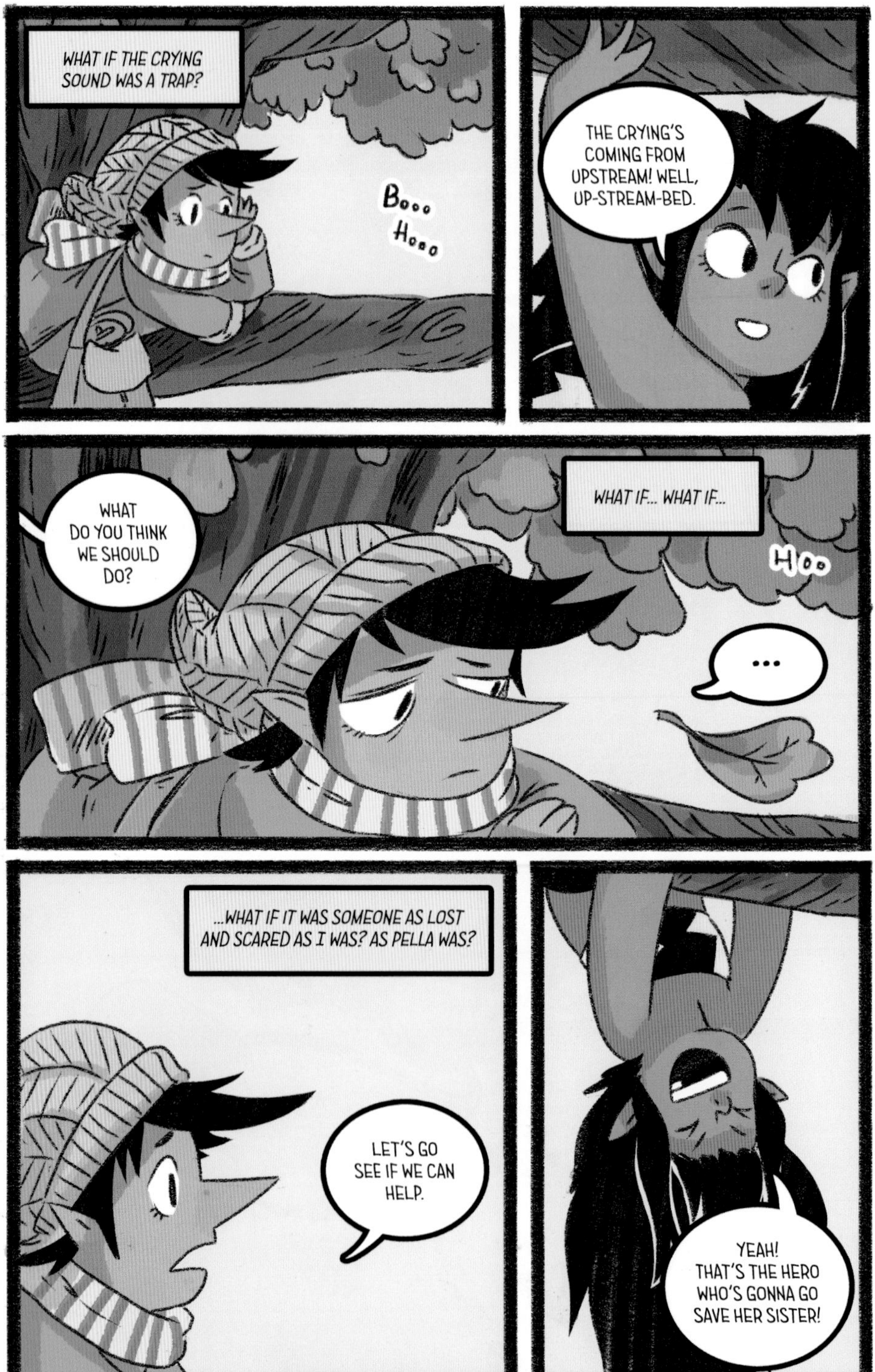
WHAT IF THE CRYING SOUND WAS A TRAP?
Booo Hooo
THE CRYING'S COMING FROM UPSTREAM! WELL, UP-STREAM-BED.
WHAT DO YOU THINK WE SHOULD DO?
WHAT IF... WHAT IF...
Hoo
...
...WHAT IF IT WAS SOMEONE AS LOST AND SCARED AS I WAS? AS PELLA WAS?
LET'S GO SEE IF WE CAN HELP.
YEAH! THAT'S THE HERO WHO'S GONNA GO SAVE HER SISTER!

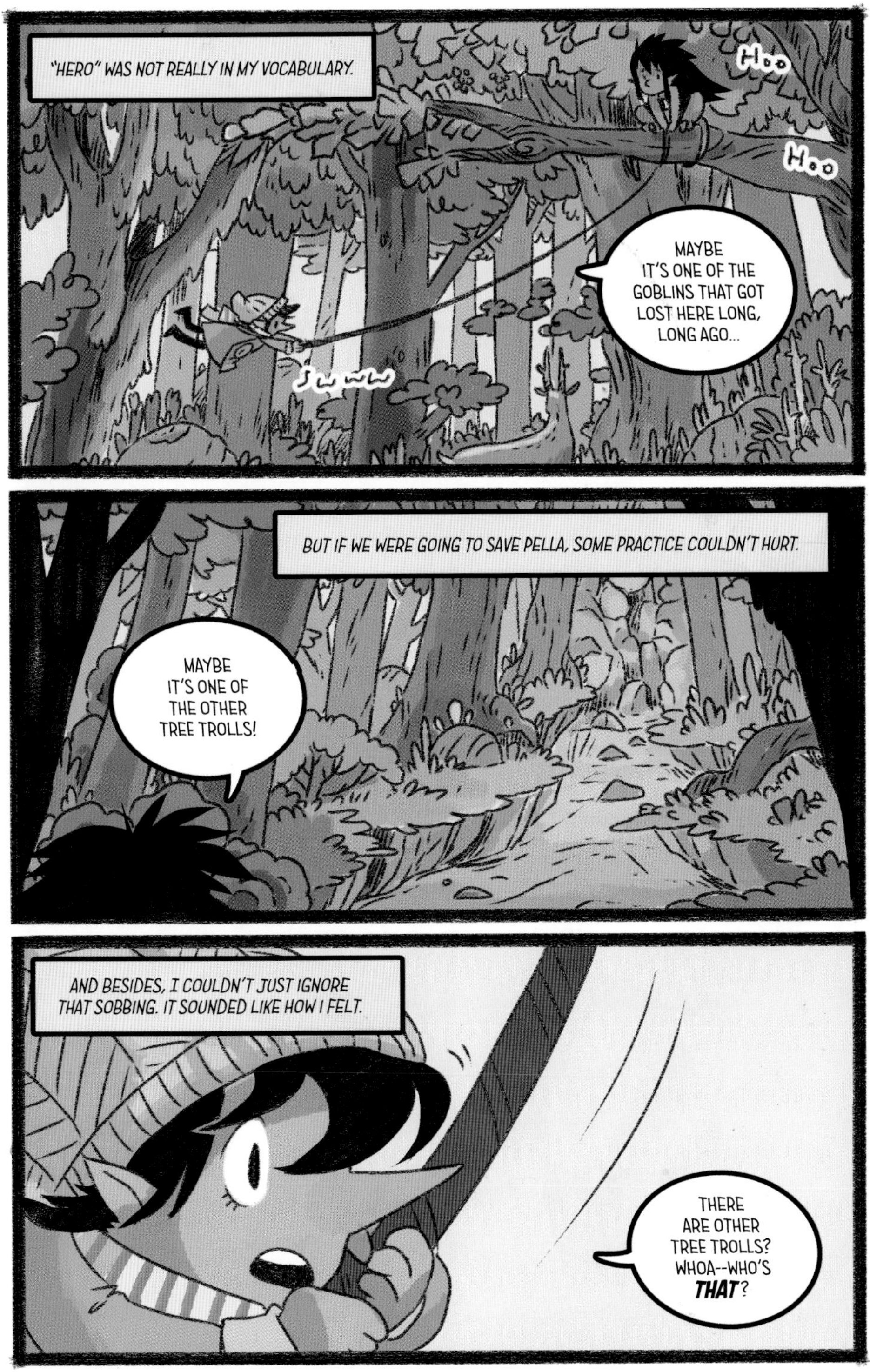
"HERO" WAS NOT REALLY IN MY VOCABULARY.
Hoo
Hoo
MAYBE IT'S ONE OF THE GOBLINS THAT GOT LOST HERE LONG, LONG AGO...
BUT IF WE WERE GOING TO SAVE PELLA, SOME PRACTICE COULDN'T HURT.
MAYBE IT'S ONE OF THE OTHER TREE TROLLS!
AND BESIDES, I COULDN'T JUST IGNORE THAT SOBBING. IT SOUNDED LIKE HOW I FELT.
THERE ARE OTHER TREE TROLLS? WHOA--WHO'S **THAT**?

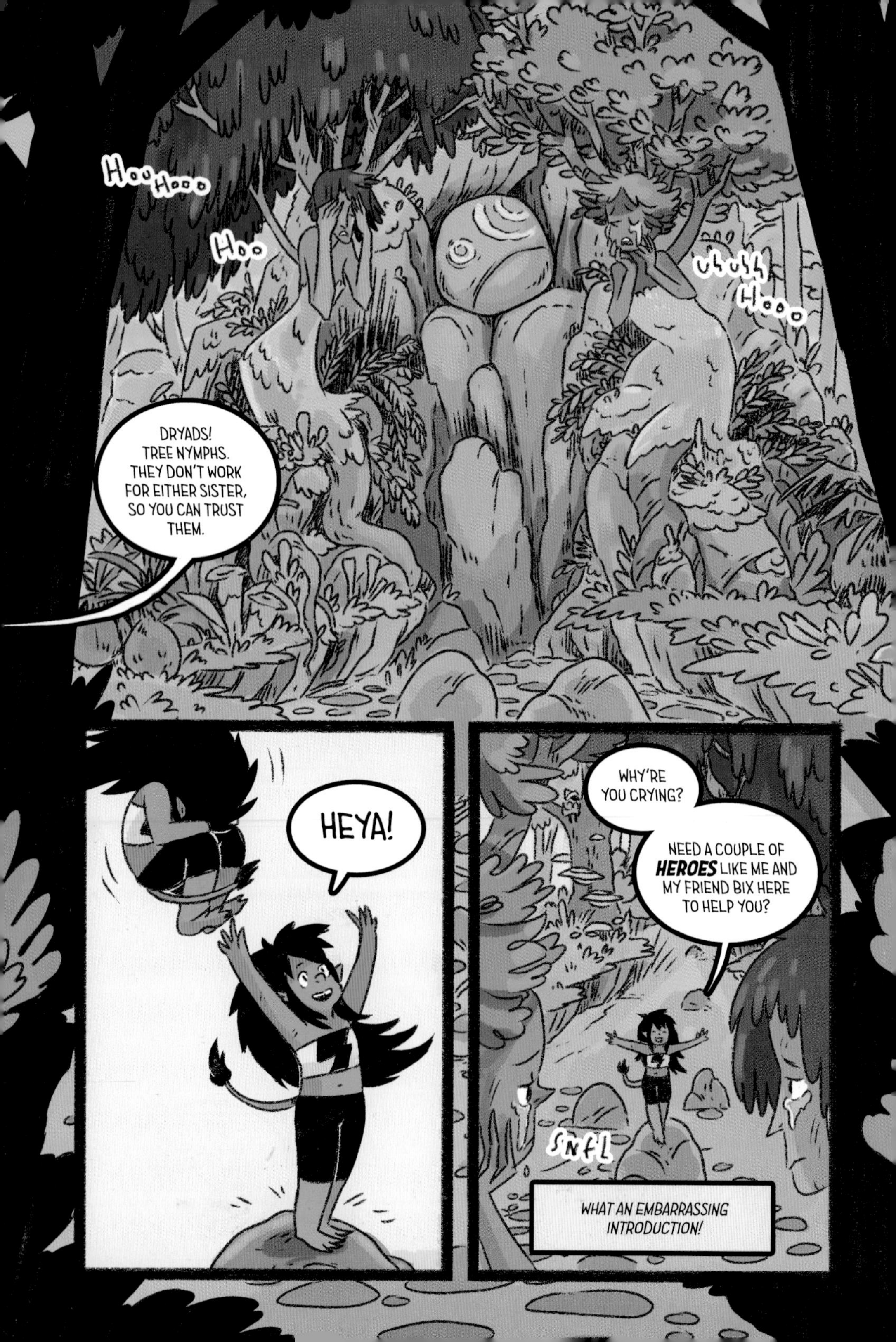
Hoo Hooo
Hoo
uhuhh Hooo
DRYADS! TREE NYMPHS. THEY DON'T WORK FOR EITHER SISTER, SO YOU CAN TRUST THEM.
HEYA!
WHY'RE YOU CRYING?
NEED A COUPLE OF **HEROES** LIKE ME AND MY FRIEND BIX HERE TO HELP YOU?
SNFL
WHAT AN EMBARRASSING INTRODUCTION!

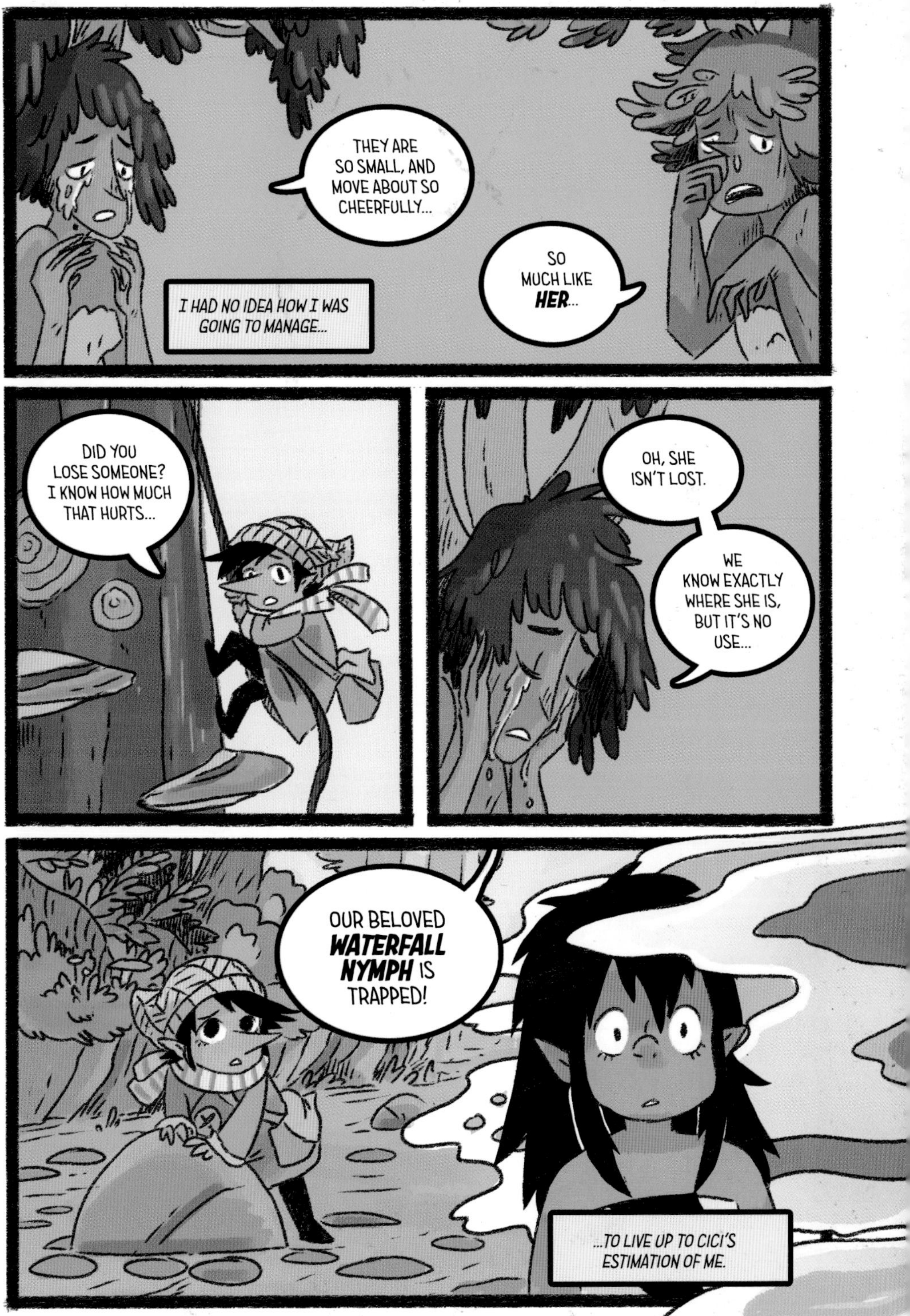
THEY ARE SO SMALL, AND MOVE ABOUT SO CHEERFULLY...
I HAD NO IDEA HOW I WAS GOING TO MANAGE...
SO MUCH LIKE HER...
DID YOU LOSE SOMEONE? I KNOW HOW MUCH THAT HURTS...
OH, SHE ISN'T LOST.
WE KNOW EXACTLY WHERE SHE IS, BUT IT'S NO USE...
OUR BELOVED WATERFALL NYMPH IS TRAPPED!
...TO LIVE UP TO CICI'S ESTIMATION OF ME.

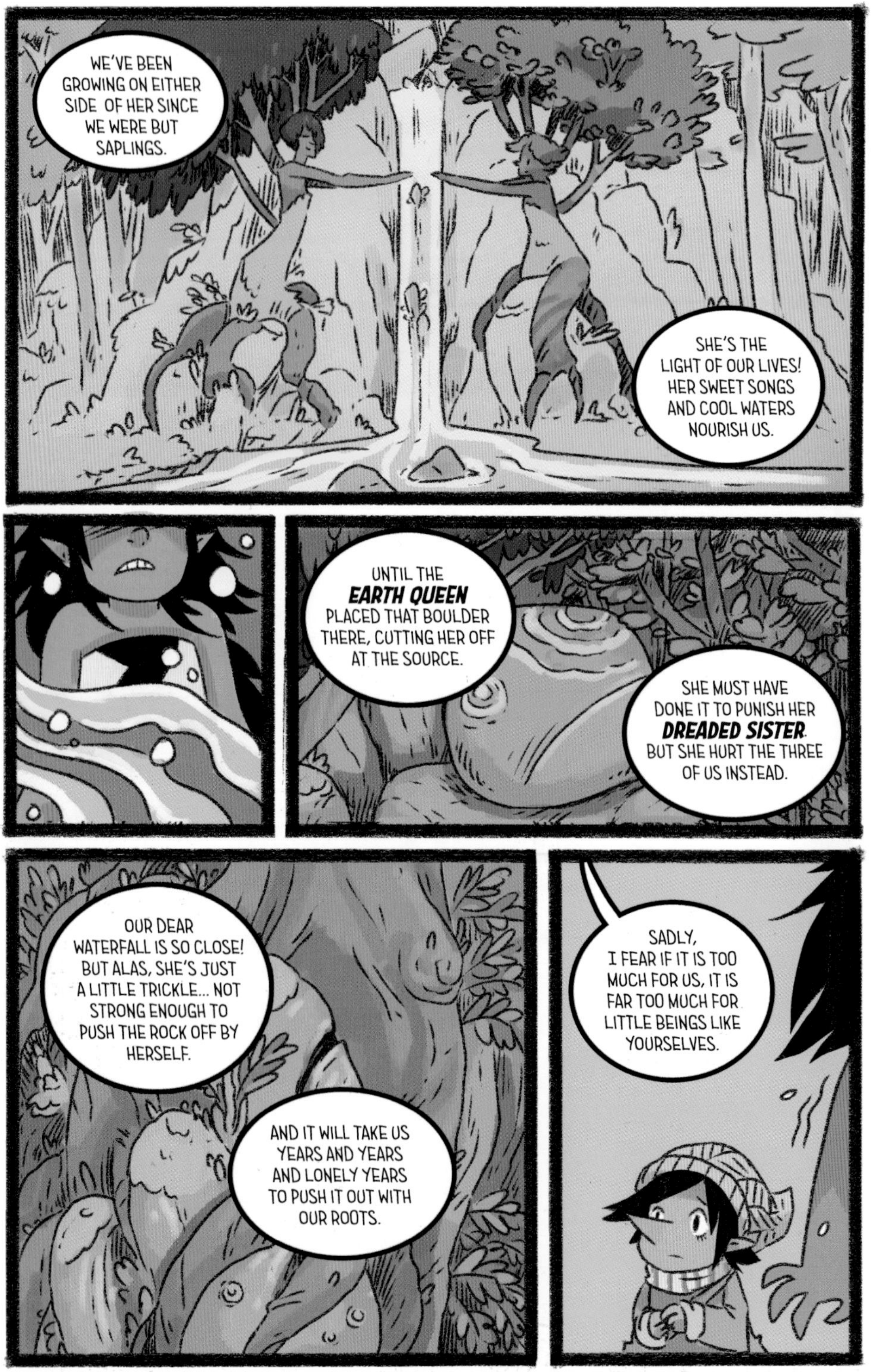
WE'VE BEEN GROWING ON EITHER SIDE OF HER SINCE WE WERE BUT SAPLINGS.
SHE'S THE LIGHT OF OUR LIVES! HER SWEET SONGS AND COOL WATERS NOURISH US.
UNTIL THE **EARTH QUEEN** PLACED THAT BOULDER THERE, CUTTING HER OFF AT THE SOURCE.
SHE MUST HAVE DONE IT TO PUNISH HER **DREADED SISTER**. BUT SHE HURT THE THREE OF US INSTEAD.
OUR DEAR WATERFALL IS SO CLOSE! BUT ALAS, SHE'S JUST A LITTLE TRICKLE... NOT STRONG ENOUGH TO PUSH THE ROCK OFF BY HERSELF.
AND IT WILL TAKE US YEARS AND YEARS AND LONELY YEARS TO PUSH IT OUT WITH OUR ROOTS.
SADLY, I FEAR IF IT IS TOO MUCH FOR US, IT IS FAR TOO MUCH FOR LITTLE BEINGS LIKE YOURSELVES.

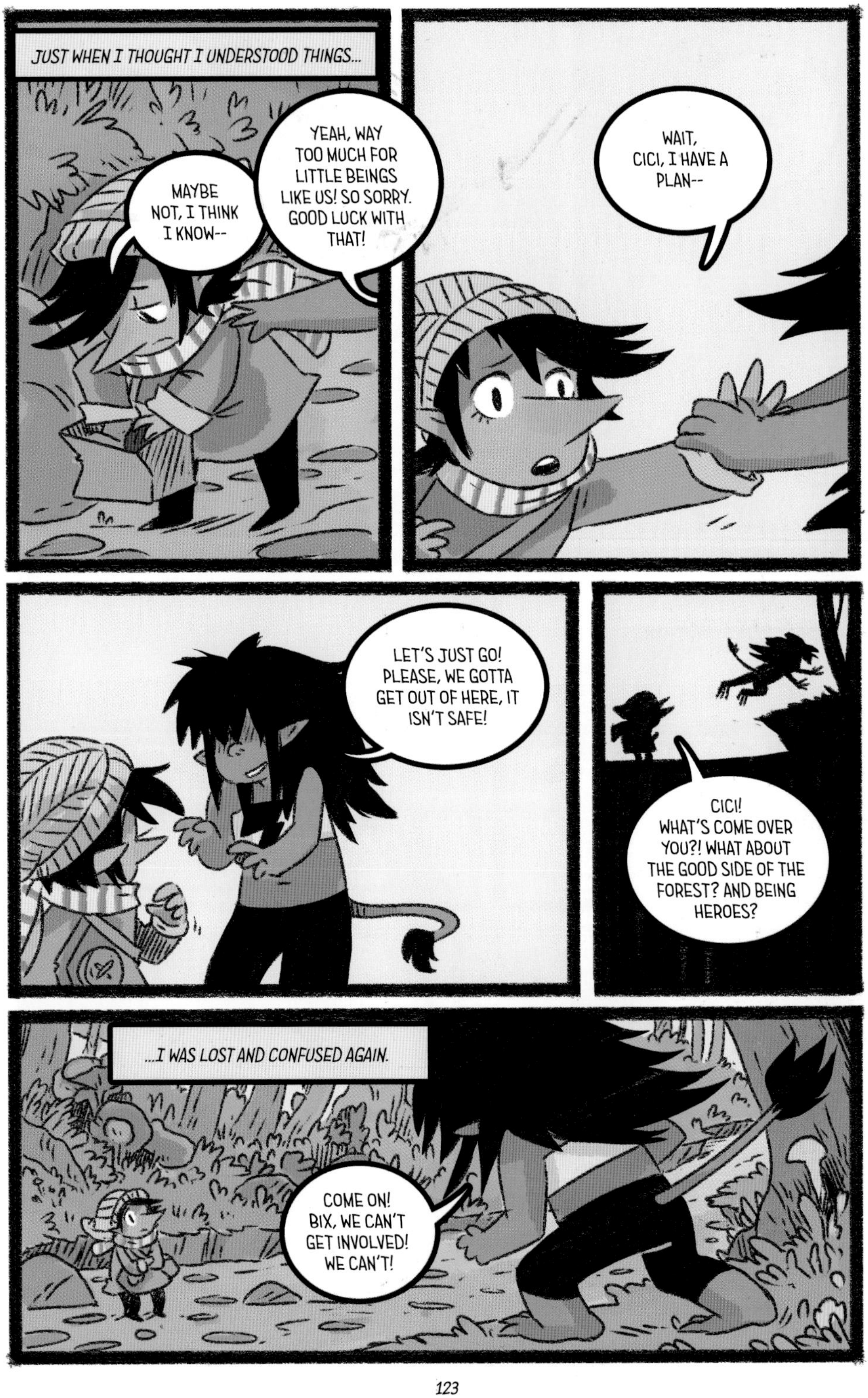
JUST WHEN I THOUGHT I UNDERSTOOD THINGS...
MAYBE NOT, I THINK I KNOW--
YEAH, WAY TOO MUCH FOR LITTLE BEINGS LIKE US! SO SORRY. GOOD LUCK WITH THAT!
WAIT, CICI, I HAVE A PLAN--
LET'S JUST GO! PLEASE, WE GOTTA GET OUT OF HERE, IT ISN'T SAFE!
CICI! WHAT'S COME OVER YOU?! WHAT ABOUT THE GOOD SIDE OF THE FOREST? AND BEING HEROES?
...I WAS LOST AND CONFUSED AGAIN.
COME ON! BIX, WE CAN'T GET INVOLVED! WE CAN'T!

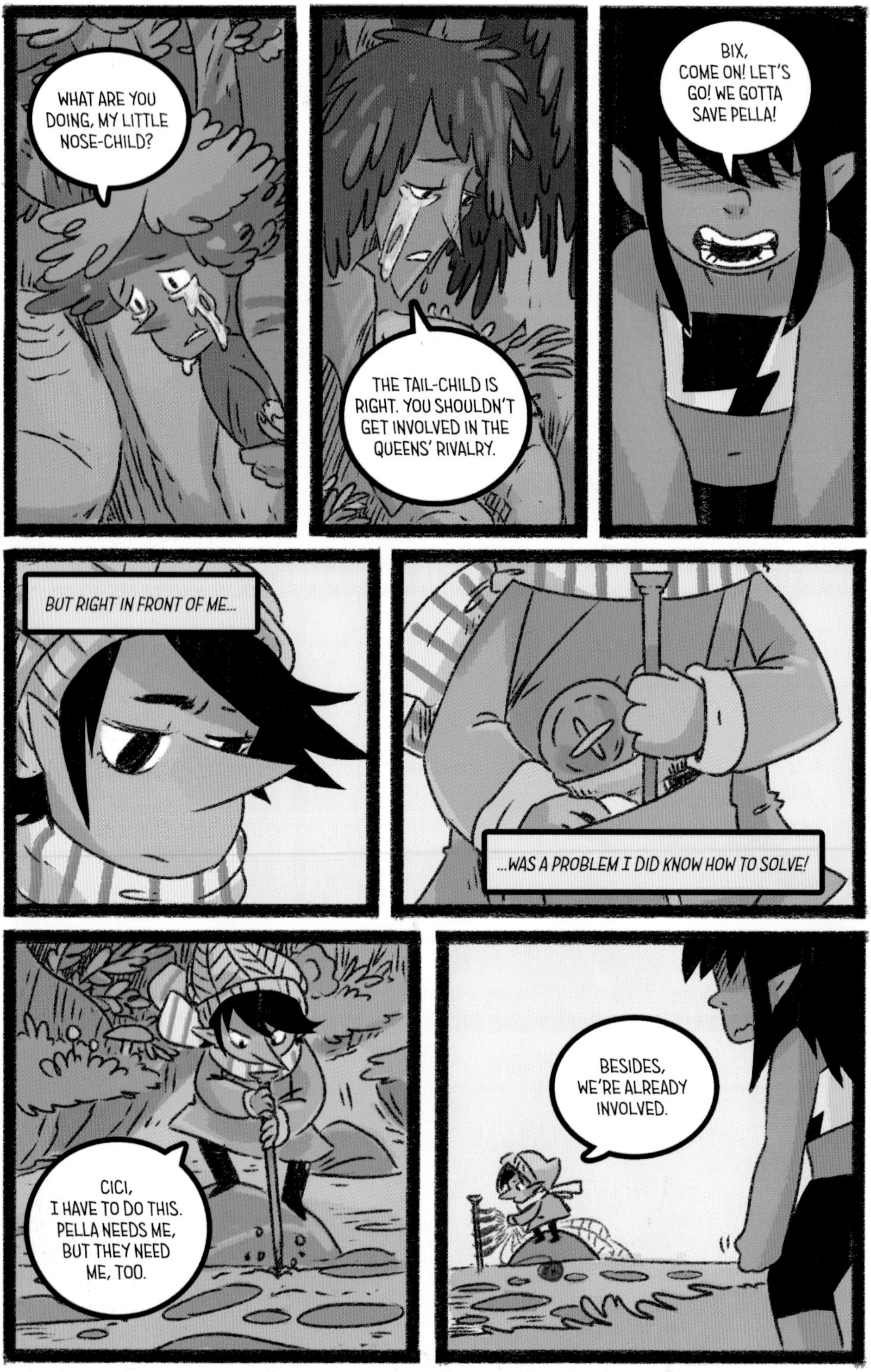
WHAT ARE YOU DOING, MY LITTLE NOSE-CHILD?
THE TAIL-CHILD IS RIGHT. YOU SHOULDN'T GET INVOLVED IN THE QUEENS' RIVALRY.
BIX, COME ON! LET'S GO! WE GOTTA SAVE PELLA!
BUT RIGHT IN FRONT OF ME...
...WAS A PROBLEM I DID KNOW HOW TO SOLVE!
CICI, I HAVE TO DO THIS. PELLA NEEDS ME, BUT THEY NEED ME, TOO.
BESIDES, WE'RE ALREADY INVOLVED.

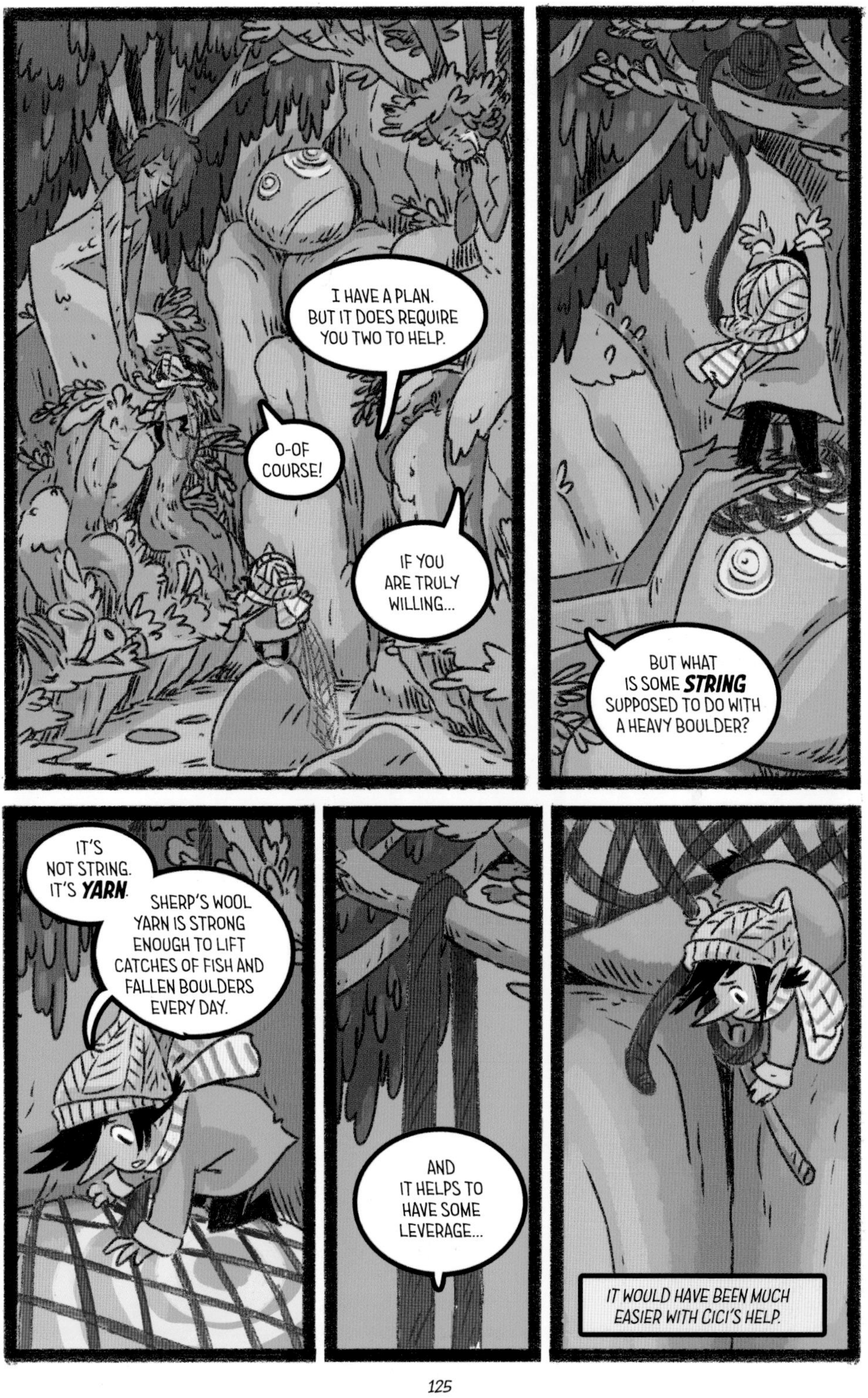
I HAVE A PLAN. BUT IT DOES REQUIRE YOU TWO TO HELP.
O-OF COURSE!
IF YOU ARE TRULY WILLING...
BUT WHAT IS SOME STRING SUPPOSED TO DO WITH A HEAVY BOULDER?
IT'S NOT STRING. IT'S YARN.
SHERP'S WOOL YARN IS STRONG ENOUGH TO LIFT CATCHES OF FISH AND FALLEN BOULDERS EVERY DAY.
AND IT HELPS TO HAVE SOME LEVERAGE...
IT WOULD HAVE BEEN MUCH EASIER WITH CICI'S HELP.

BUT IF I COULDN'T RELY ON HER, I WOULD HAVE TO RELY ON MYSELF.

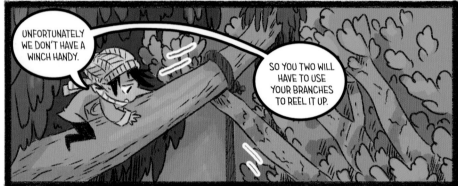

UNFORTUNATELY WE DON'T HAVE A WINCH HANDY.

SO YOU TWO WILL HAVE TO USE YOUR BRANCHES TO REEL IT UP.

OVER!

UNDER!

I-I THINK I FELT IT MOVE!

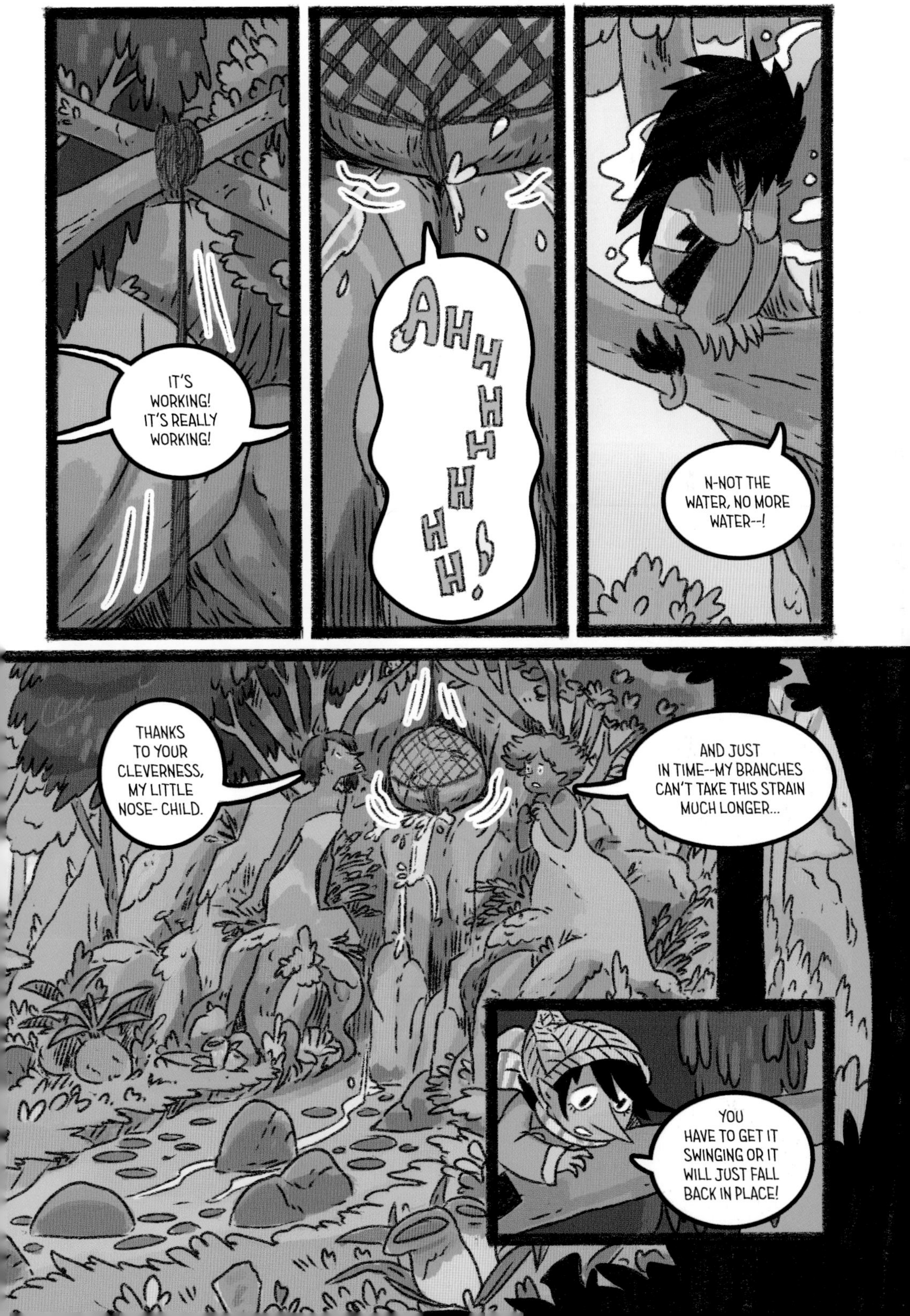
IT'S WORKING! IT'S REALLY WORKING!
AHHHHHHHHH!
N-NOT THE WATER, NO MORE WATER--!
THANKS TO YOUR CLEVERNESS, MY LITTLE NOSE- CHILD.
AND JUST IN TIME--MY BRANCHES CAN'T TAKE THIS STRAIN MUCH LONGER...
YOU HAVE TO GET IT SWINGING OR IT WILL JUST FALL BACK IN PLACE!

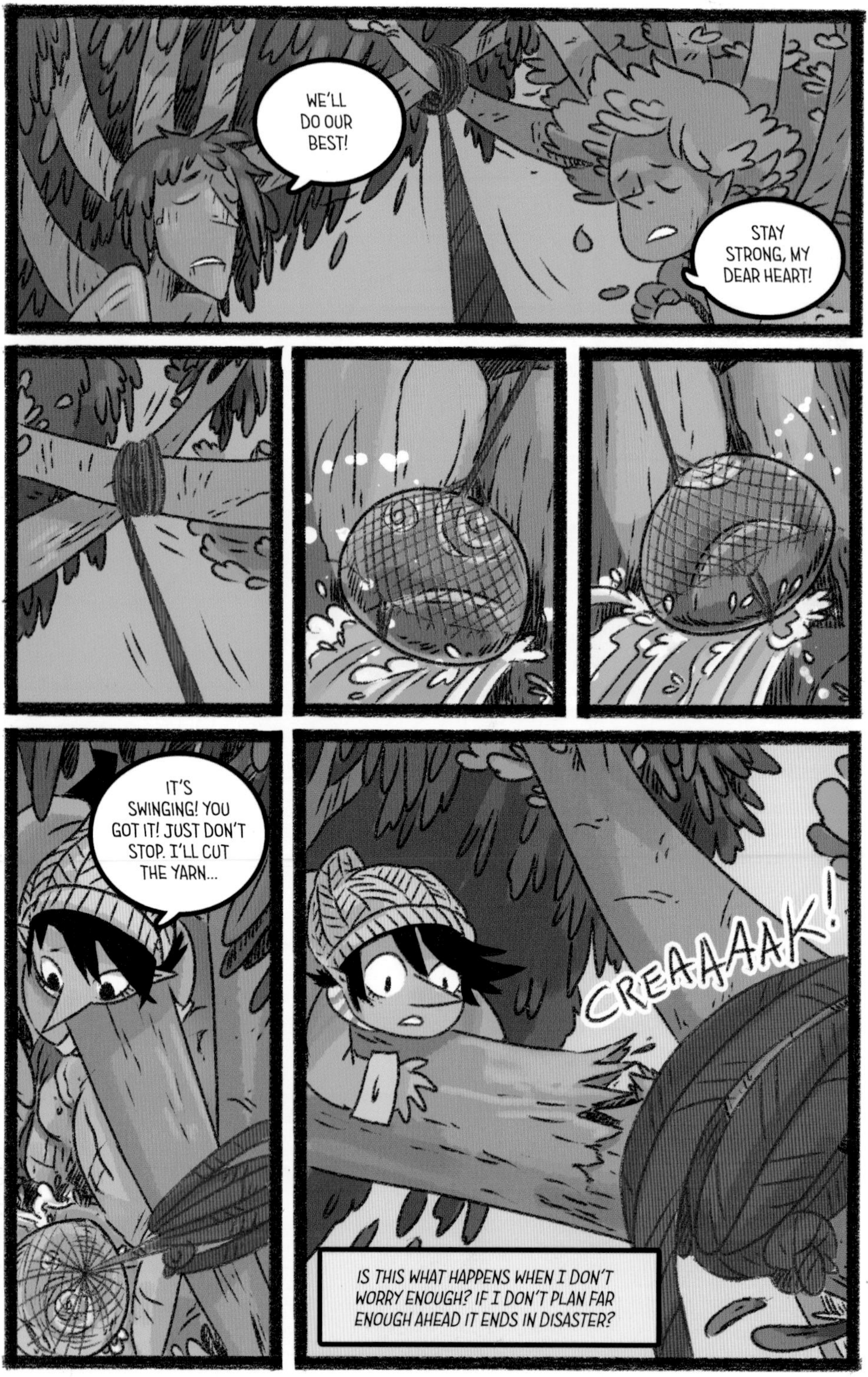
WE'LL DO OUR BEST!
STAY STRONG, MY DEAR HEART!
IT'S SWINGING! YOU GOT IT! JUST DON'T STOP. I'LL CUT THE YARN...
CREAAAAK!
IS THIS WHAT HAPPENS WHEN I DON'T WORRY ENOUGH? IF I DON'T PLAN FAR ENOUGH AHEAD IT ENDS IN DISASTER?

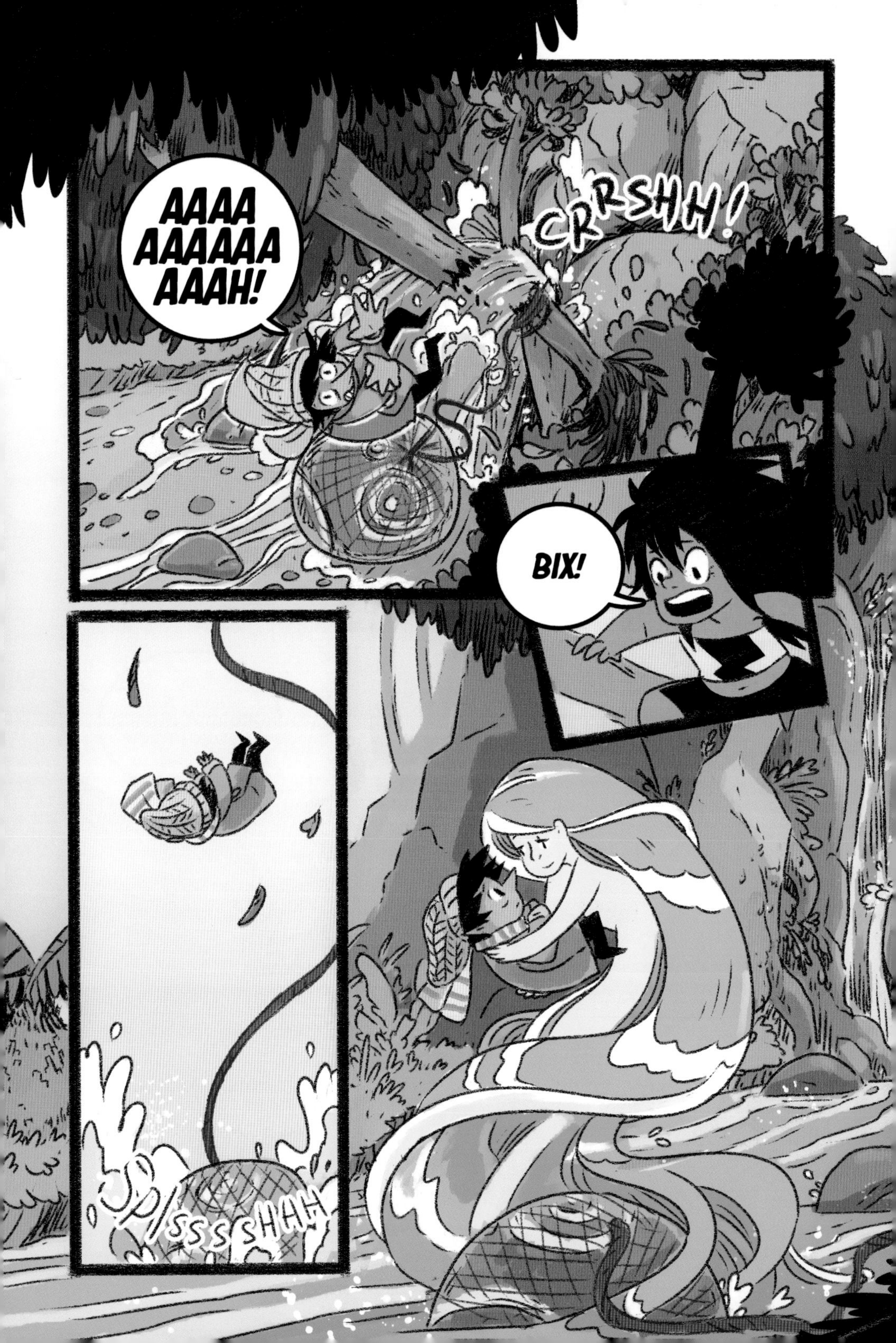
AAAA AAAAAA AAAH!
CRRSHH!
BIX!
SPLSSSSHH

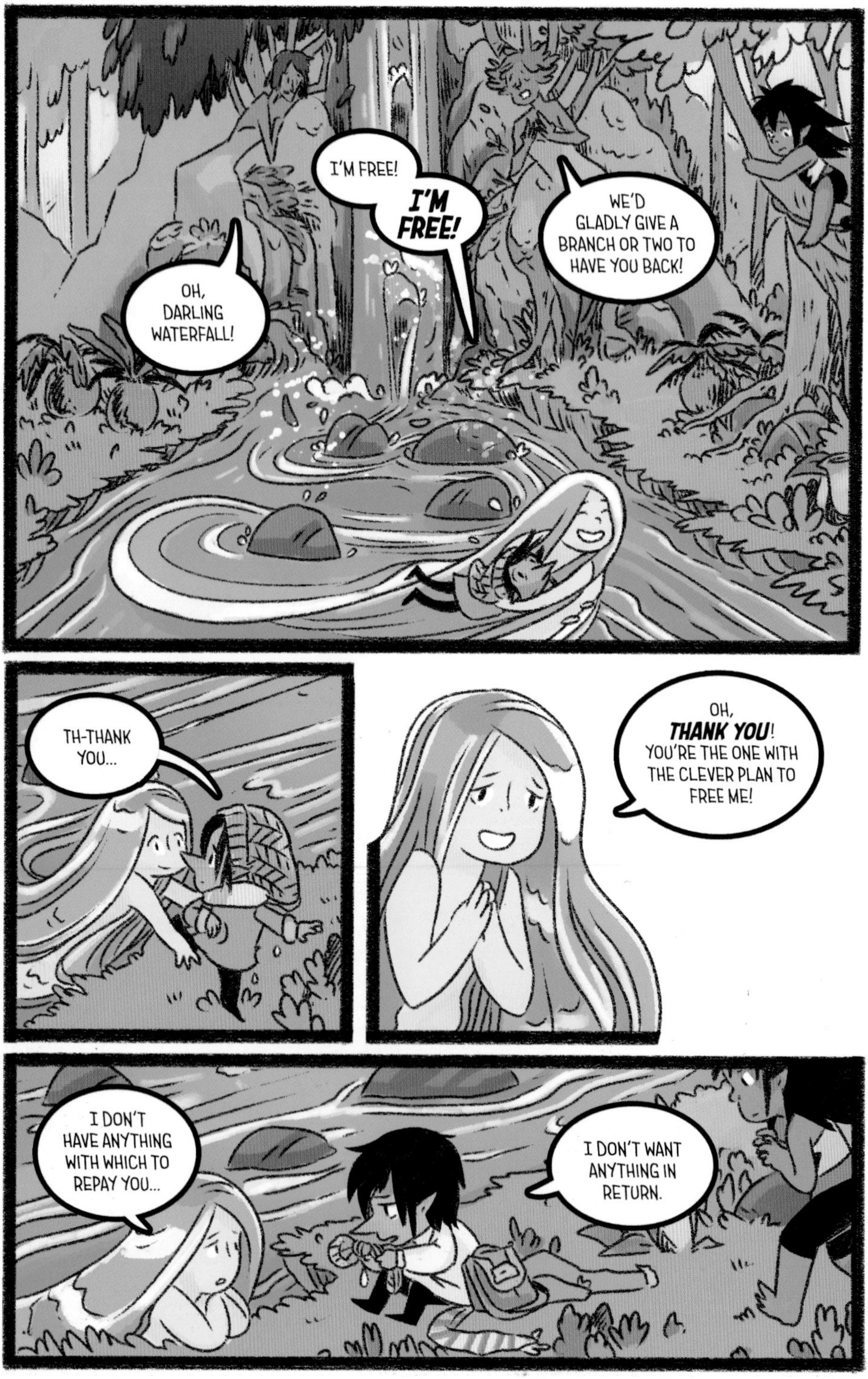
OH, DARLING WATERFALL!
I'M FREE!
I'M FREE!
WE'D GLADLY GIVE A BRANCH OR TWO TO HAVE YOU BACK!
TH-THANK YOU...
OH, THANK YOU! YOU'RE THE ONE WITH THE CLEVER PLAN TO FREE ME!
I DON'T HAVE ANYTHING WITH WHICH TO REPAY YOU...
I DON'T WANT ANYTHING IN RETURN.

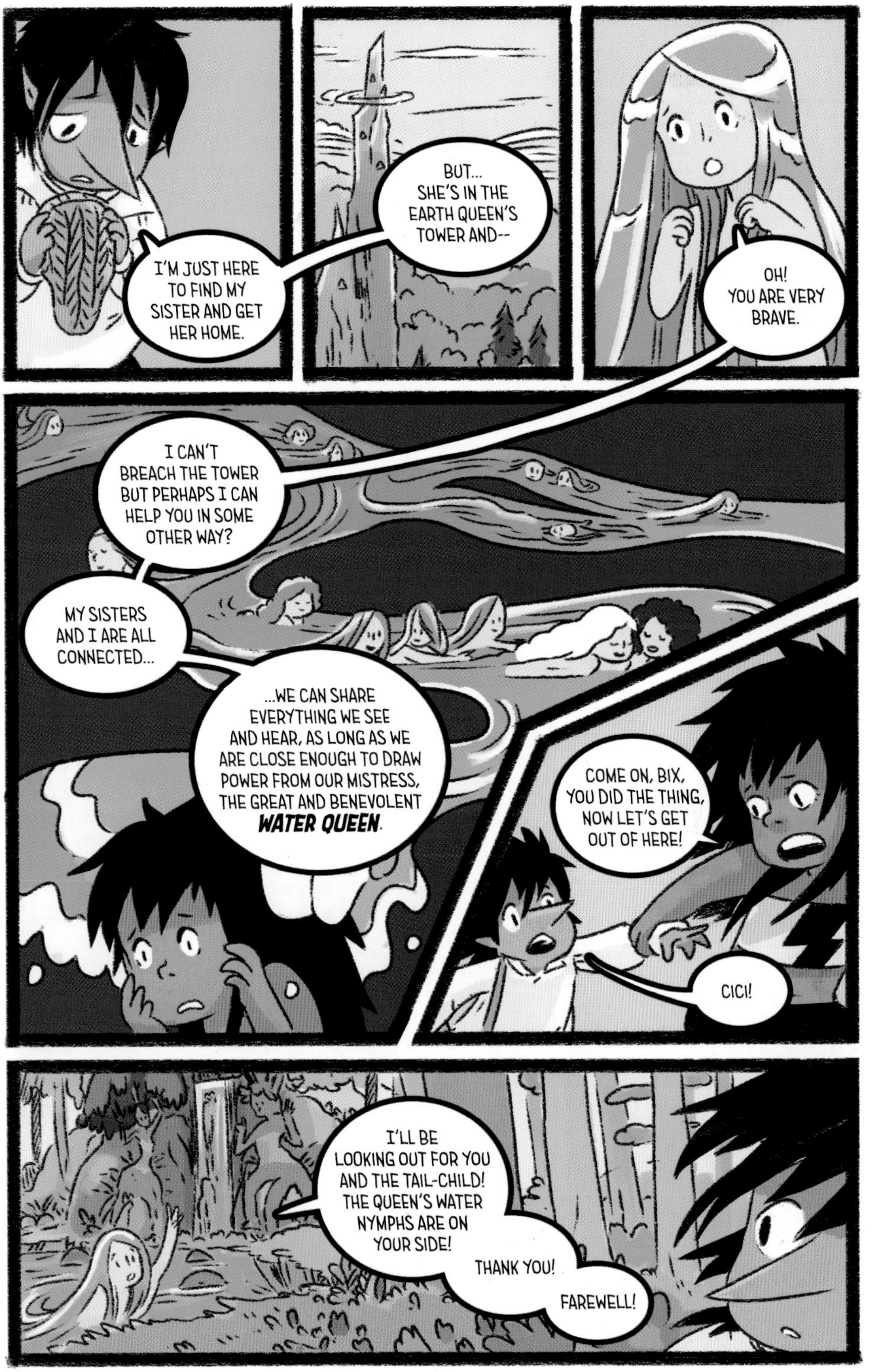
I'M JUST HERE TO FIND MY SISTER AND GET HER HOME.
BUT... SHE'S IN THE EARTH QUEEN'S TOWER AND--
OH! YOU ARE VERY BRAVE.
I CAN'T BREACH THE TOWER BUT PERHAPS I CAN HELP YOU IN SOME OTHER WAY?
MY SISTERS AND I ARE ALL CONNECTED...
...WE CAN SHARE EVERYTHING WE SEE AND HEAR, AS LONG AS WE ARE CLOSE ENOUGH TO DRAW POWER FROM OUR MISTRESS, THE GREAT AND BENEVOLENT **WATER QUEEN**.
COME ON, BIX, YOU DID THE THING, NOW LET'S GET OUT OF HERE!
CICI!
I'LL BE LOOKING OUT FOR YOU AND THE TAIL-CHILD! THE QUEEN'S WATER NYMPHS ARE ON YOUR SIDE!
THANK YOU!
FAREWELL!

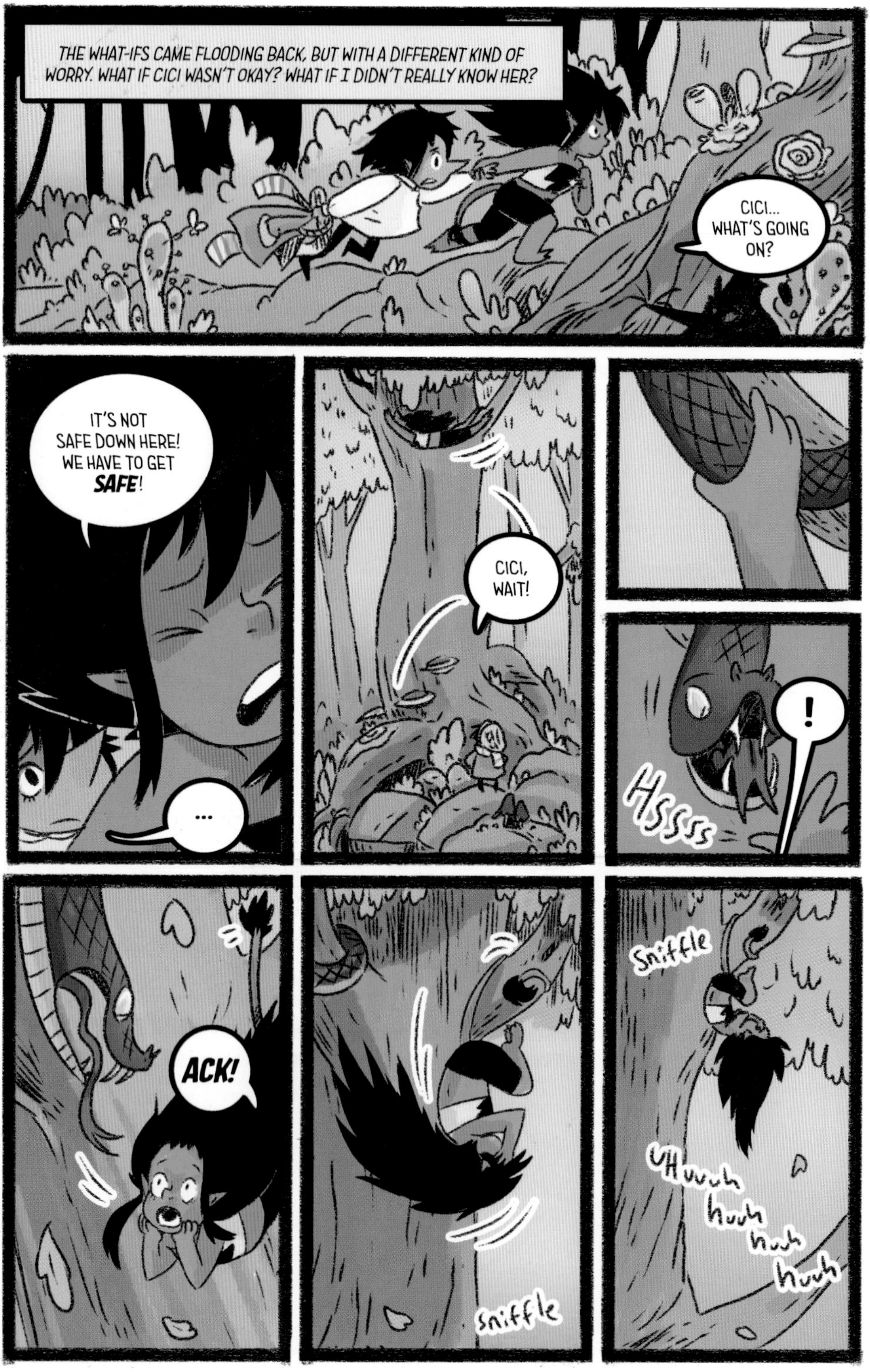
THE WHAT-IFS CAME FLOODING BACK, BUT WITH A DIFFERENT KIND OF WORRY. WHAT IF CICI WASN'T OKAY? WHAT IF I DIDN'T REALLY KNOW HER?
CICI... WHAT'S GOING ON?
IT'S NOT SAFE DOWN HERE! WE HAVE TO GET SAFE!
...
CICI, WAIT!
HSSSSS
!
ACK!
sniffle
sniffle
UHuuh huuh huuh huuh

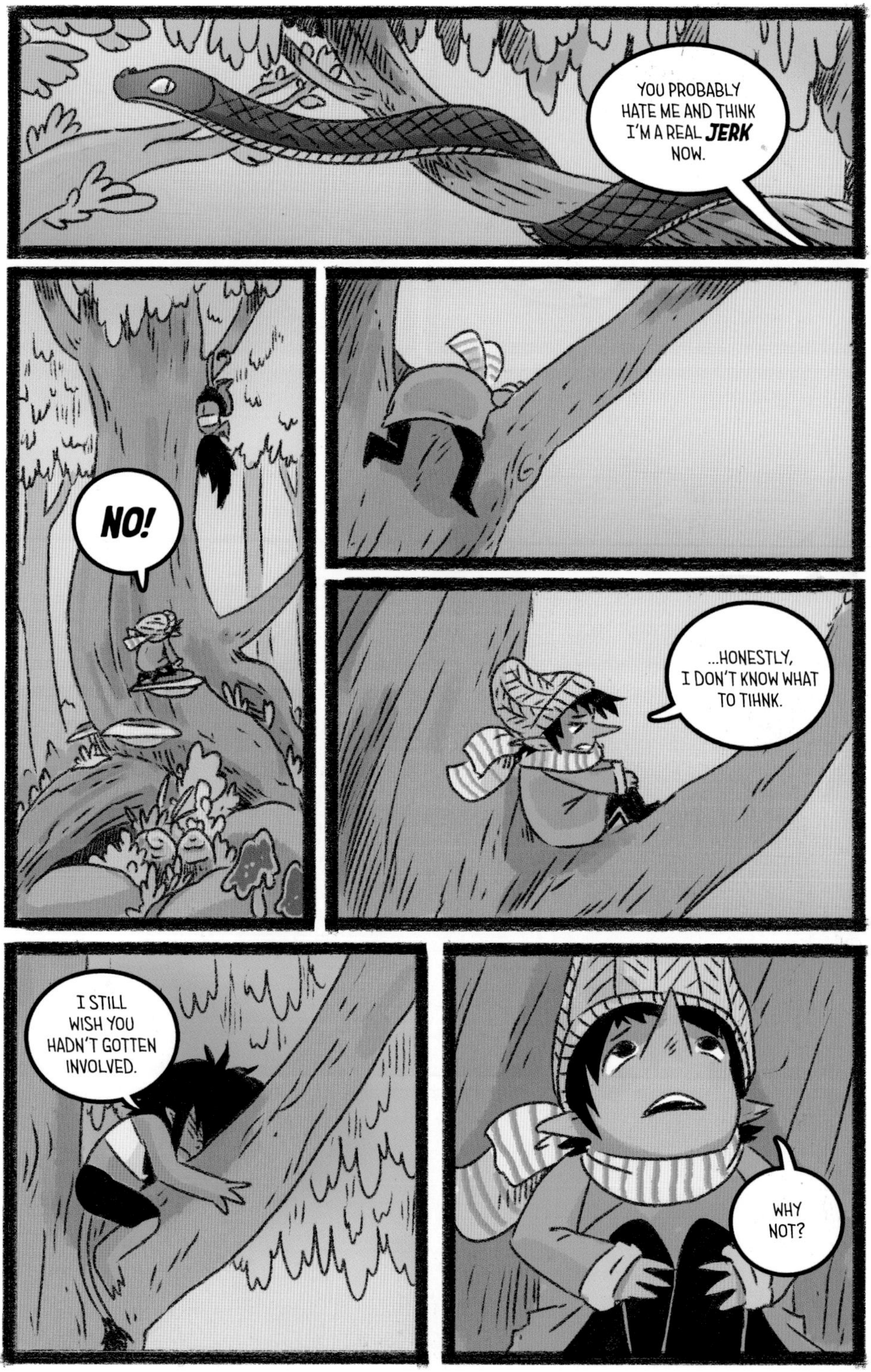
YOU PROBABLY HATE ME AND THINK I'M A REAL JERK NOW.
NO!
...HONESTLY, I DON'T KNOW WHAT TO TIHNK.
I STILL WISH YOU HADN'T GOTTEN INVOLVED.
WHY NOT?

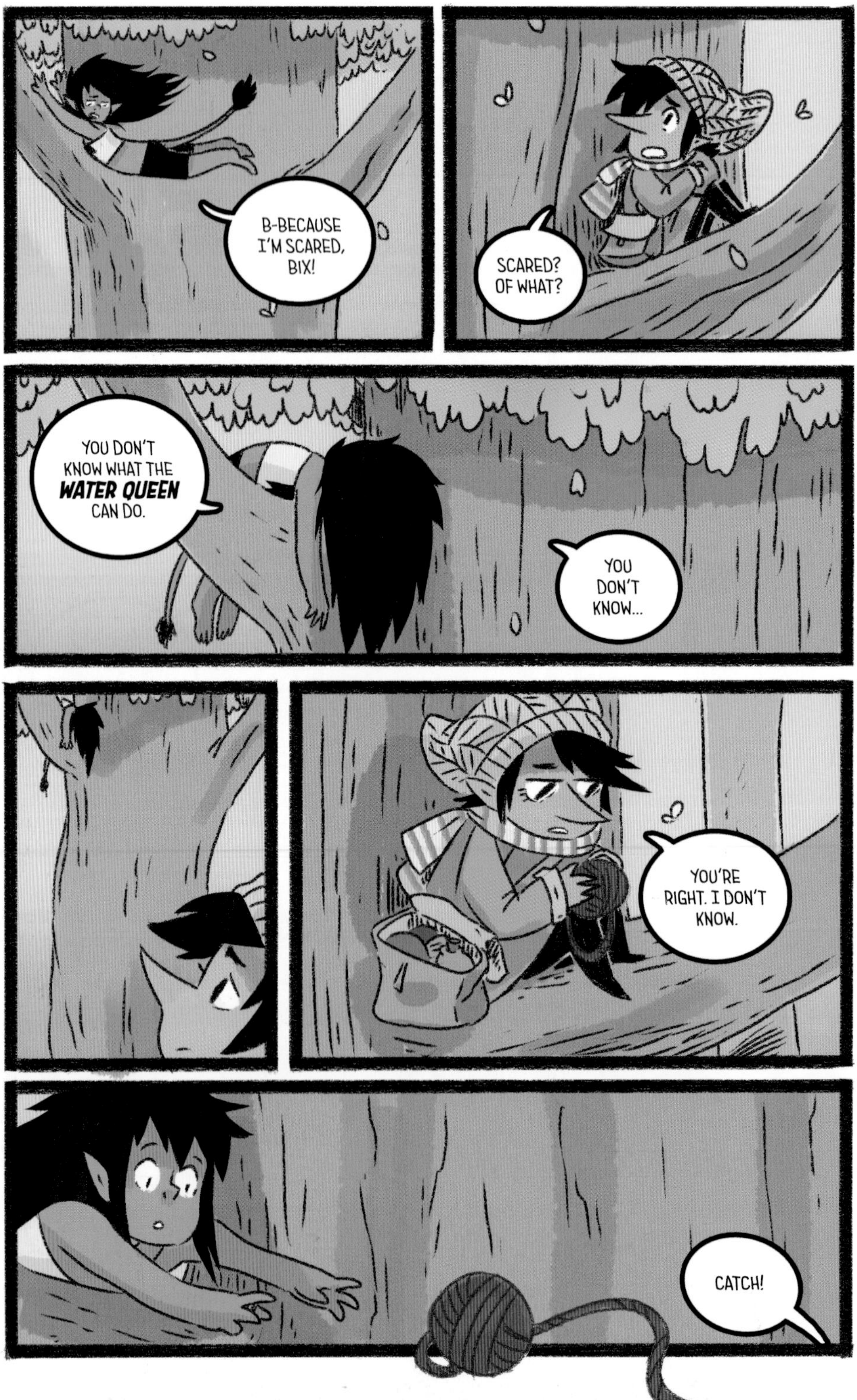
B-BECAUSE I'M SCARED, BIX!
SCARED? OF WHAT?
YOU DON'T KNOW WHAT THE **WATER QUEEN** CAN DO.
YOU DON'T KNOW...
YOU'RE RIGHT. I DON'T KNOW.
CATCH!

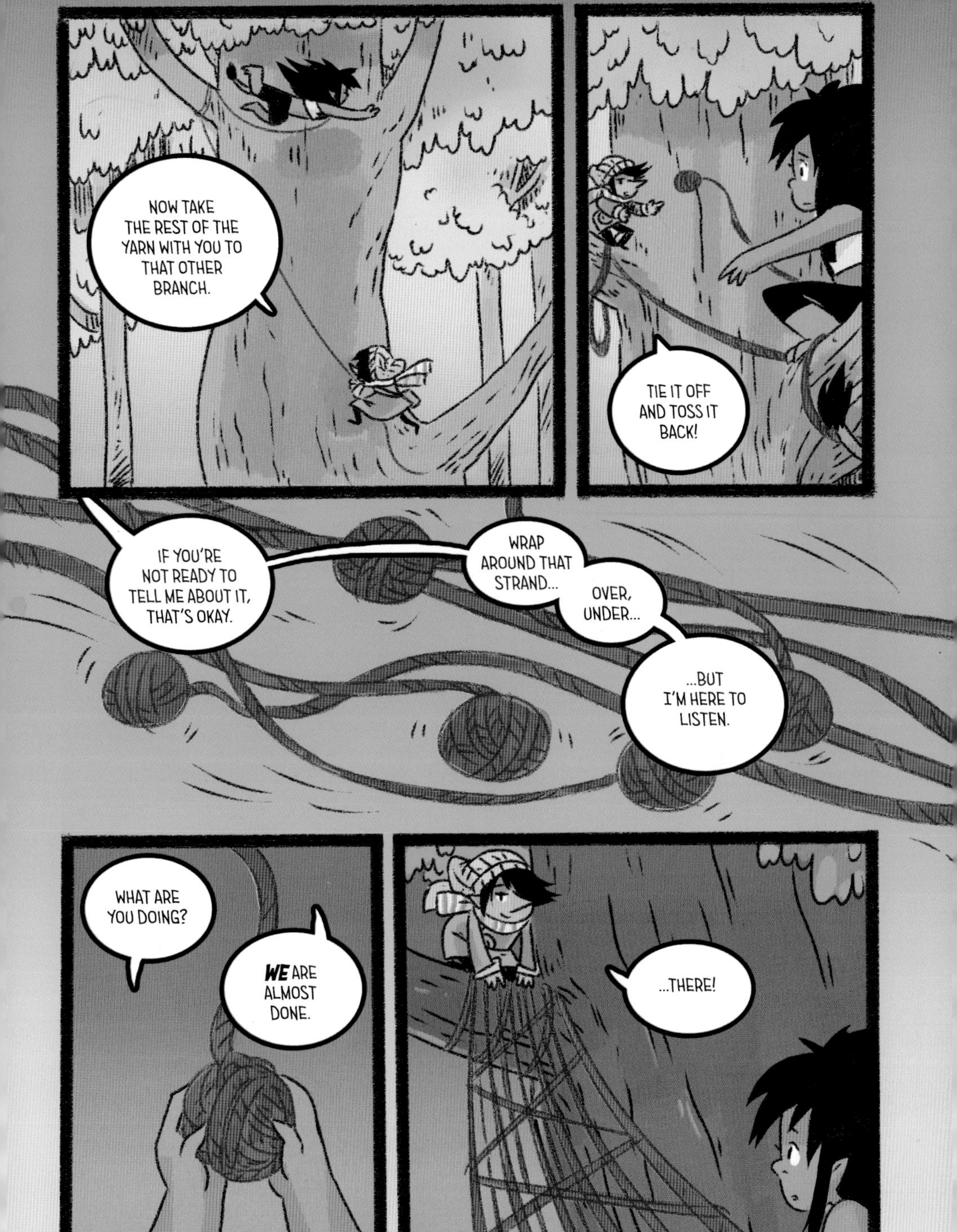
NOW TAKE THE REST OF THE YARN WITH YOU TO THAT OTHER BRANCH.
TIE IT OFF AND TOSS IT BACK!
IF YOU'RE NOT READY TO TELL ME ABOUT IT, THAT'S OKAY.
WRAP AROUND THAT STRAND...
OVER, UNDER...
...BUT I'M HERE TO LISTEN.
WHAT ARE YOU DOING?
WE ARE ALMOST DONE.
...THERE!

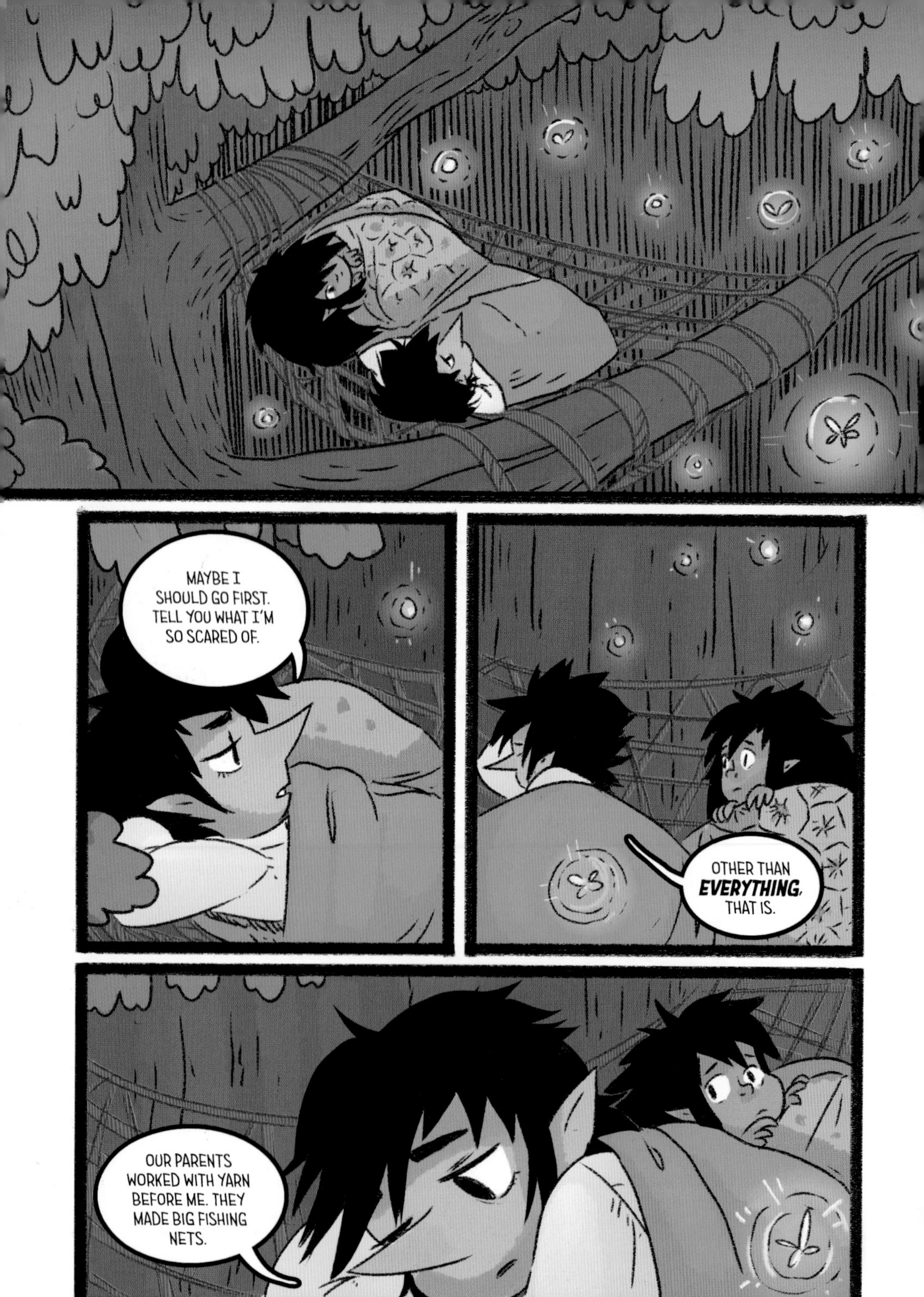
MAYBE I SHOULD GO FIRST. TELL YOU WHAT I'M SO SCARED OF.
OTHER THAN **EVERYTHING**, THAT IS.
OUR PARENTS WORKED WITH YARN BEFORE ME. THEY MADE BIG FISHING NETS.

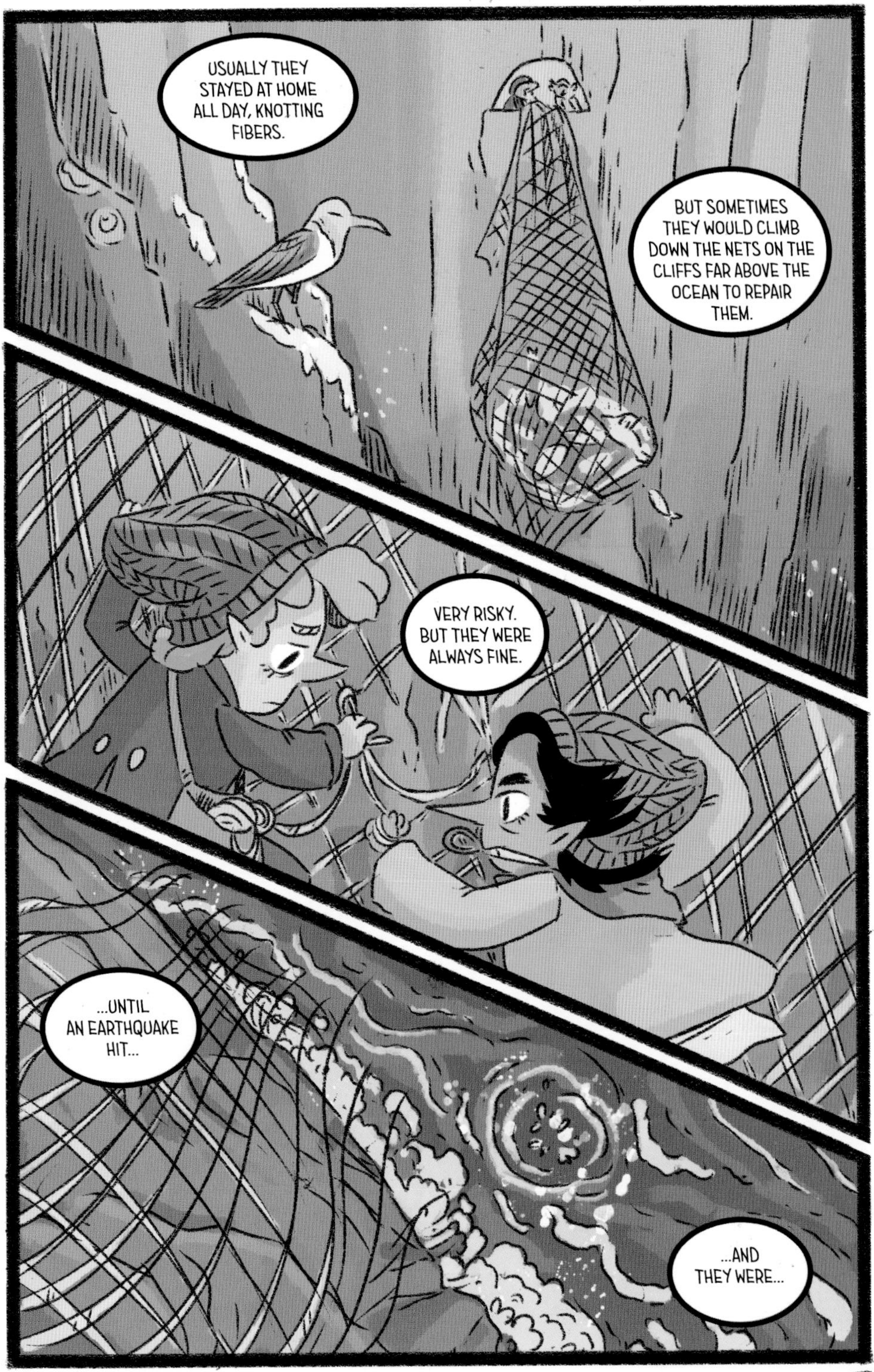
USUALLY THEY STAYED AT HOME ALL DAY, KNOTTING FIBERS.
BUT SOMETIMES THEY WOULD CLIMB DOWN THE NETS ON THE CLIFFS FAR ABOVE THE OCEAN TO REPAIR THEM.
VERY RISKY. BUT THEY WERE ALWAYS FINE.
...UNTIL AN EARTHQUAKE HIT...
...AND THEY WERE...

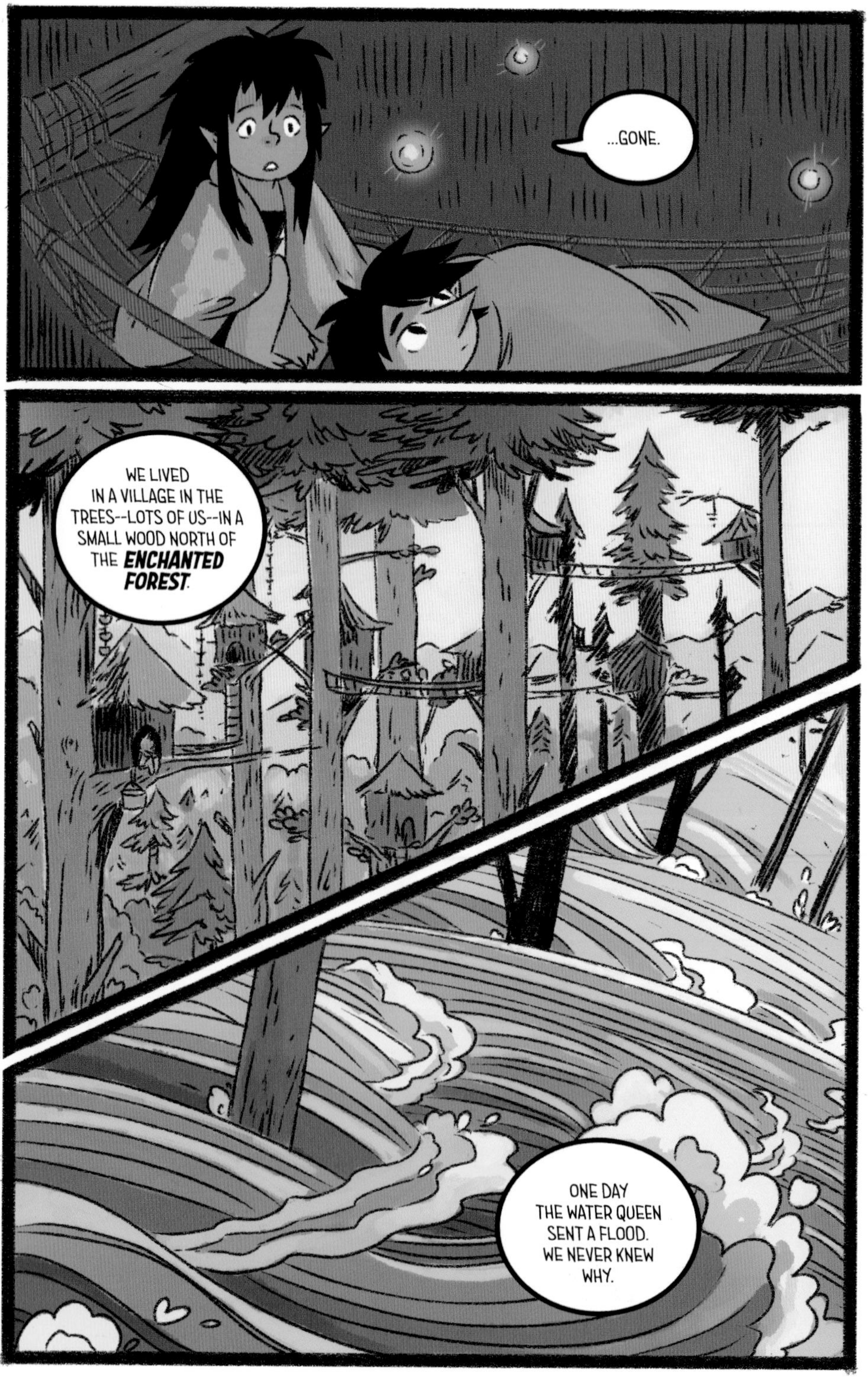
...GONE.
WE LIVED IN A VILLAGE IN THE TREES--LOTS OF US--IN A SMALL WOOD NORTH OF THE ENCHANTED FOREST.
ONE DAY THE WATER QUEEN SENT A FLOOD. WE NEVER KNEW WHY.

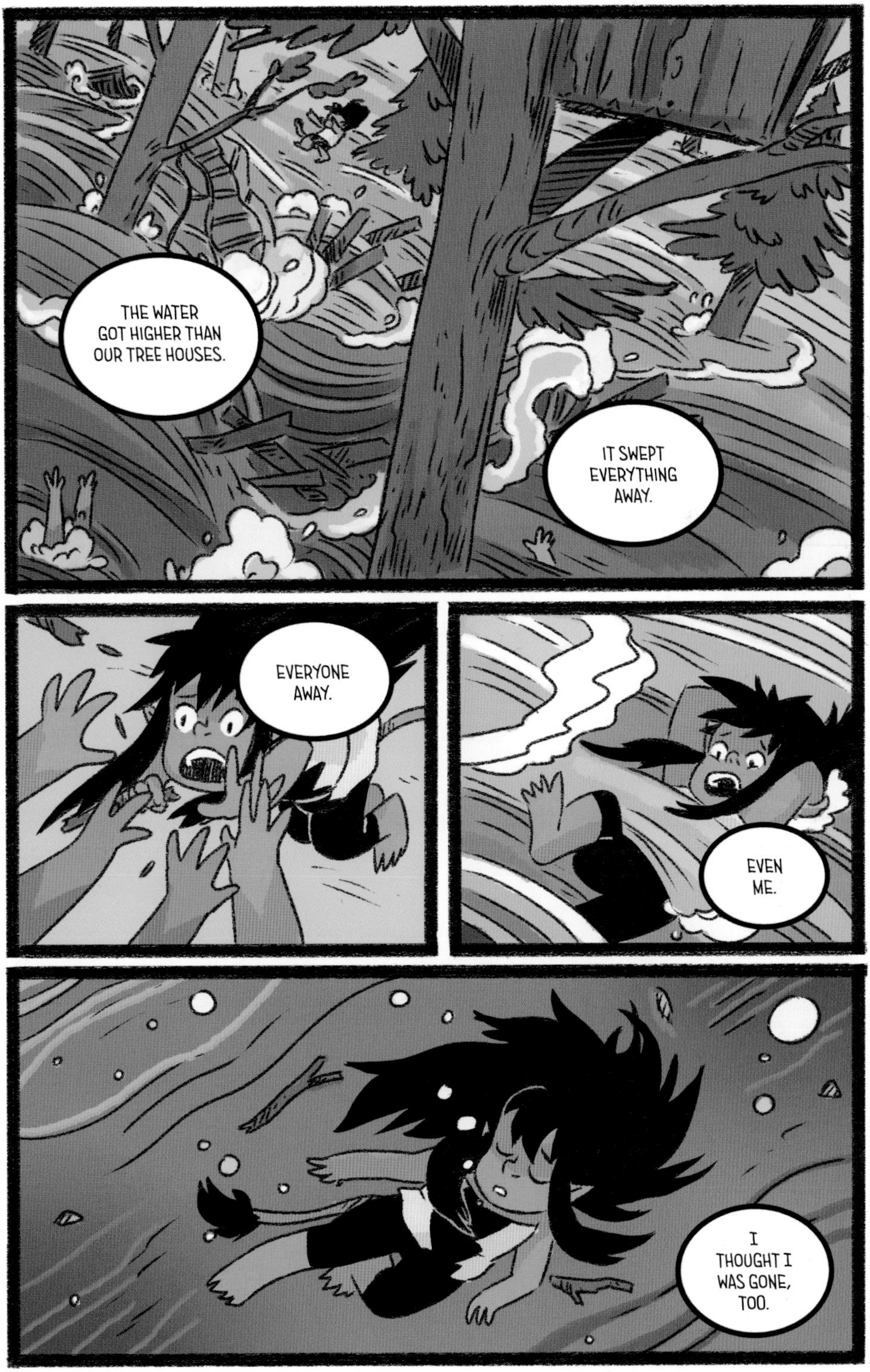
THE WATER GOT HIGHER THAN OUR TREE HOUSES.
IT SWEPT EVERYTHING AWAY.
EVERYONE AWAY.
EVEN ME.
I THOUGHT I WAS GONE, TOO.

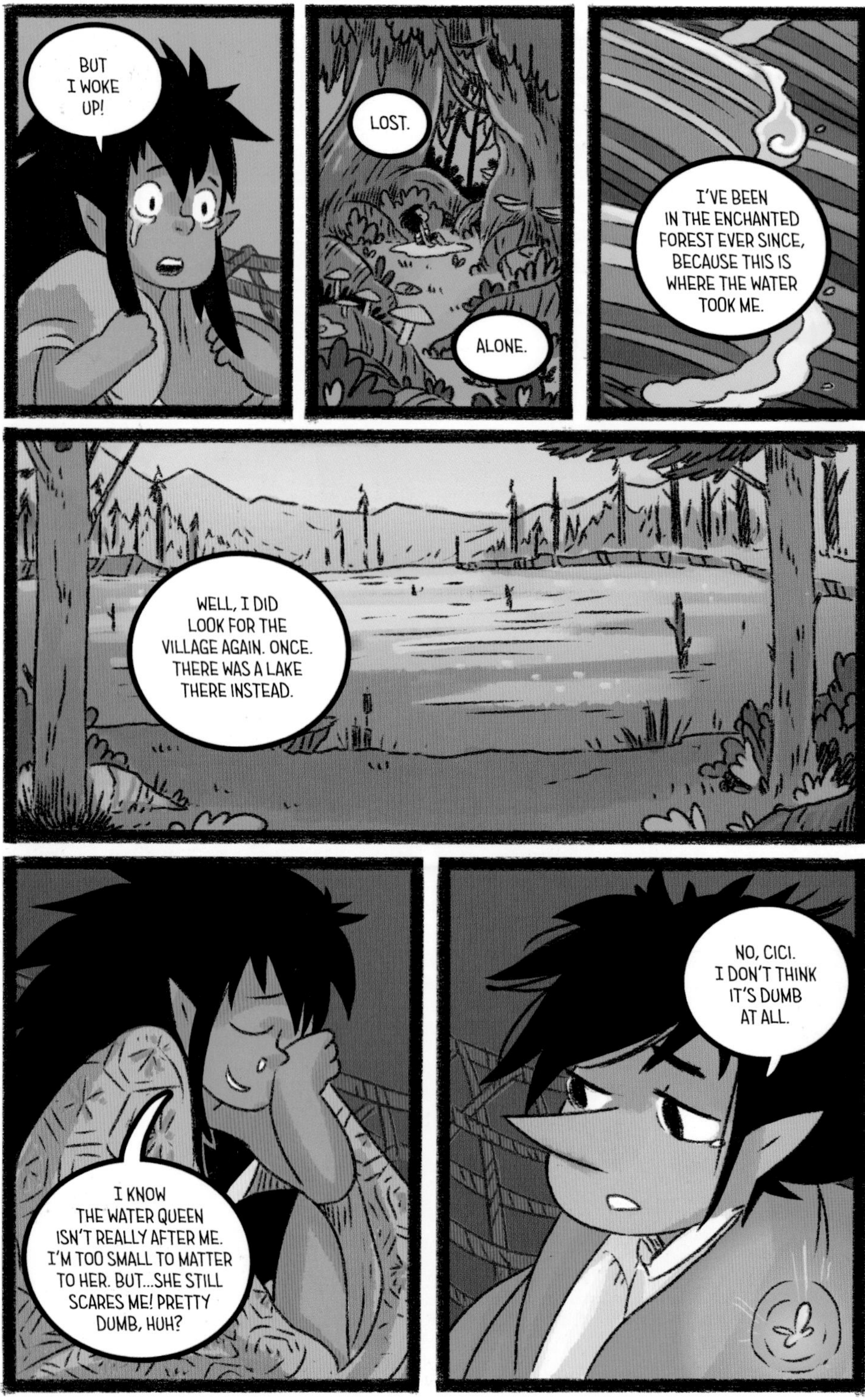

BUT I WOKE UP!
LOST.
ALONE.
I'VE BEEN IN THE ENCHANTED FOREST EVER SINCE, BECAUSE THIS IS WHERE THE WATER TOOK ME.
WELL, I DID LOOK FOR THE VILLAGE AGAIN. ONCE. THERE WAS A LAKE THERE INSTEAD.
I KNOW THE WATER QUEEN ISN'T REALLY AFTER ME. I'M TOO SMALL TO MATTER TO HER. BUT...SHE STILL SCARES ME! PRETTY DUMB, HUH?
NO, CICI. I DON'T THINK IT'S DUMB AT ALL.

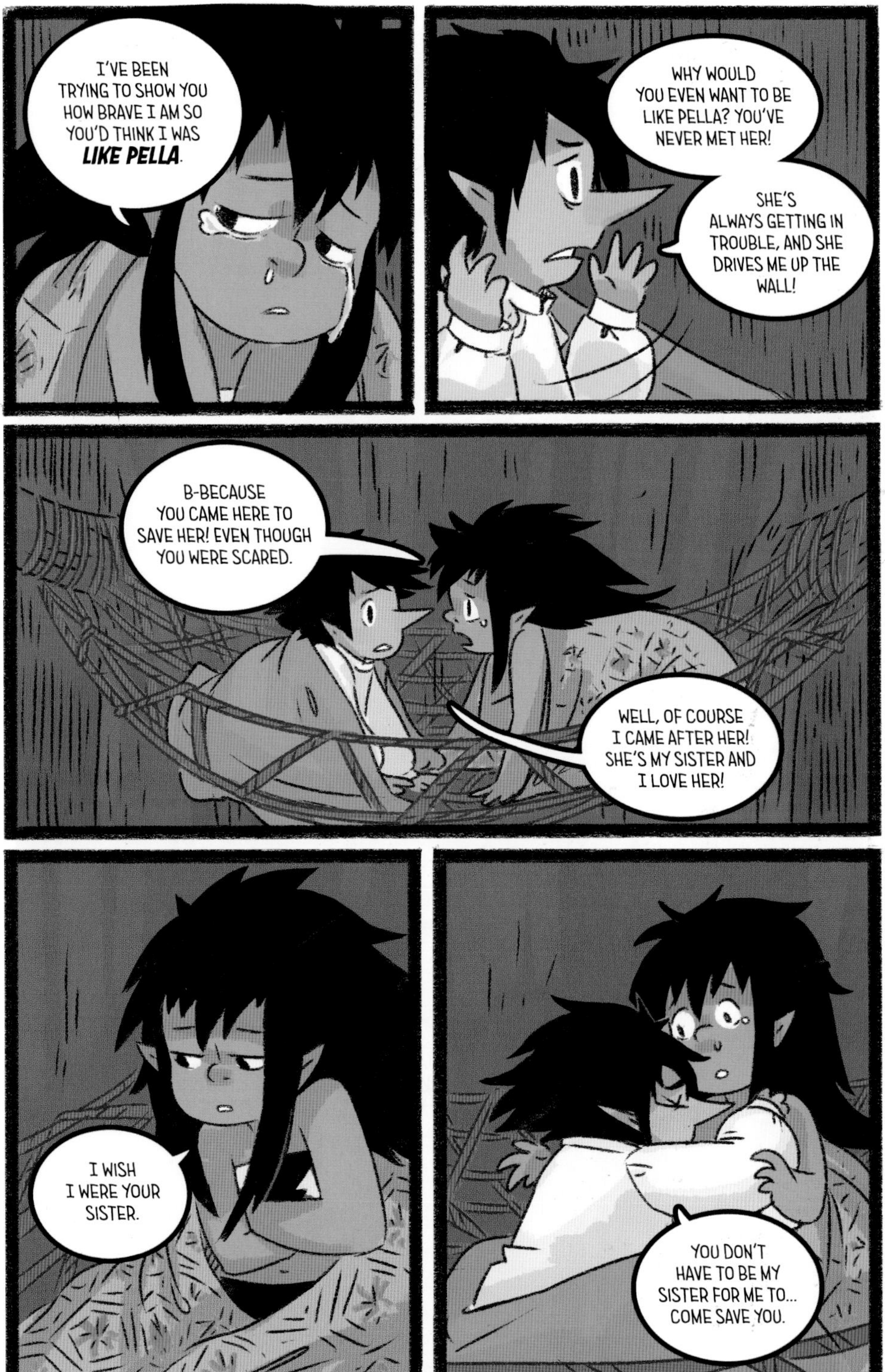
I'VE BEEN TRYING TO SHOW YOU HOW BRAVE I AM SO YOU'D THINK I WAS **LIKE PELLA**.
WHY WOULD YOU EVEN WANT TO BE LIKE PELLA? YOU'VE NEVER MET HER!
SHE'S ALWAYS GETTING IN TROUBLE, AND SHE DRIVES ME UP THE WALL!
B-BECAUSE YOU CAME HERE TO SAVE HER! EVEN THOUGH YOU WERE SCARED.
WELL, OF COURSE I CAME AFTER HER! SHE'S MY SISTER AND I LOVE HER!
I WISH I WERE YOUR SISTER.
YOU DON'T HAVE TO BE MY SISTER FOR ME TO... COME SAVE YOU.

WHAT A TOTAL WASTE OF TIME.

GUESS YOU REALLY CAN'T REASON...

...WITH THE WORLD'S BIGGEST, MOST SELFISH BRAT!

MAYBE THIS IS HOW BIX FEELS WHEN I EAT BOTH SHARES OF PUDDING WHILE SHE'S OUT DOING DELIVERIES.

EVEN AFTER SHE ASKED ME NOT TO.

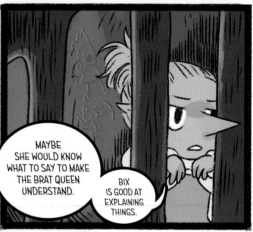

MAYBE SHE WOULD KNOW WHAT TO SAY TO MAKE THE BRAT QUEEN UNDERSTAND.

BIX IS GOOD AT EXPLAINING THINGS.

AND LISTENING WHEN YOU HAVE A PROBLEM.

AND MAKING THINGS.

LIKE BLANKETS.

AND DOLLS...

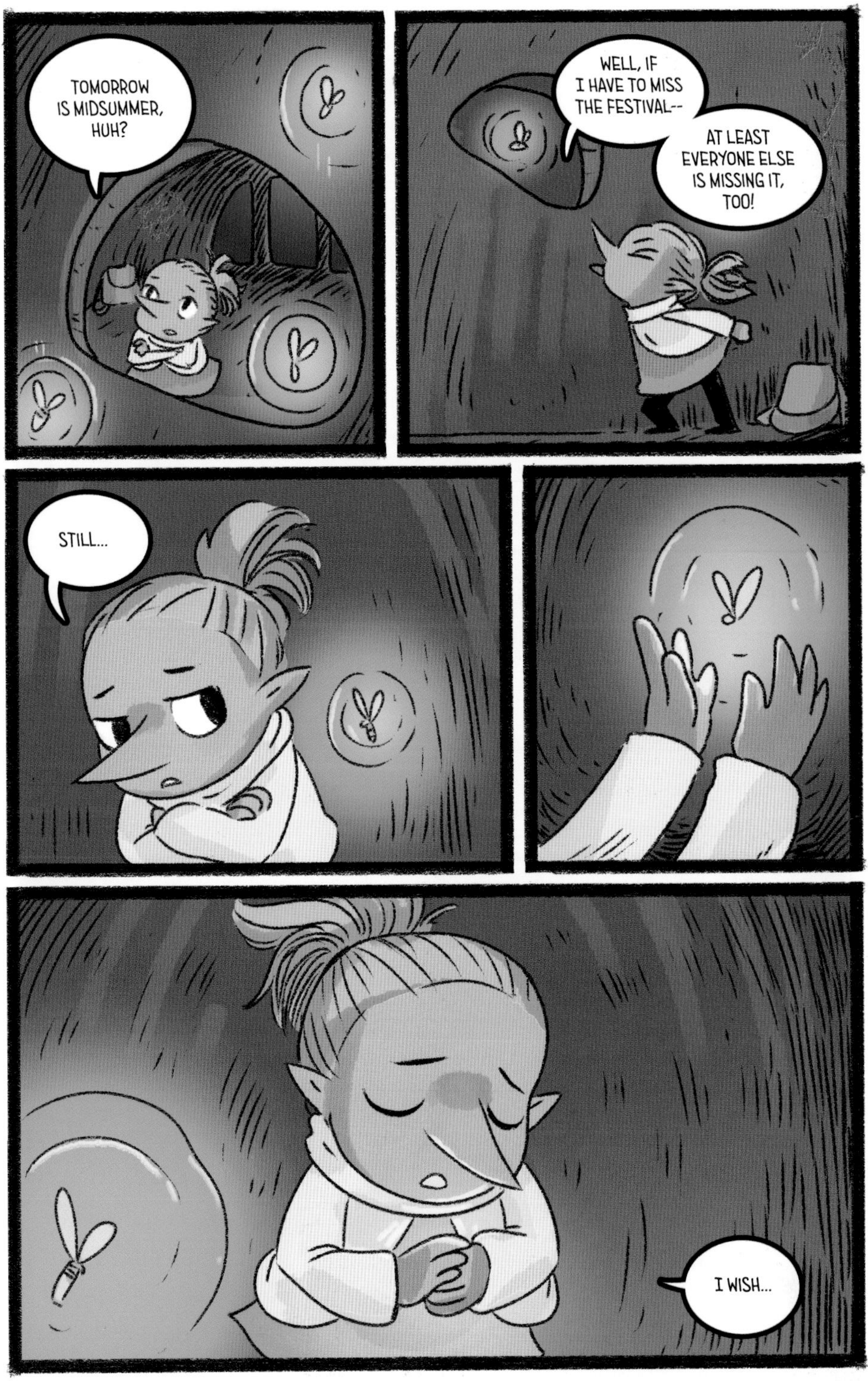
TOMORROW IS MIDSUMMER, HUH?
WELL, IF I HAVE TO MISS THE FESTIVAL--
AT LEAST EVERYONE ELSE IS MISSING IT, TOO!
STILL...
I WISH...

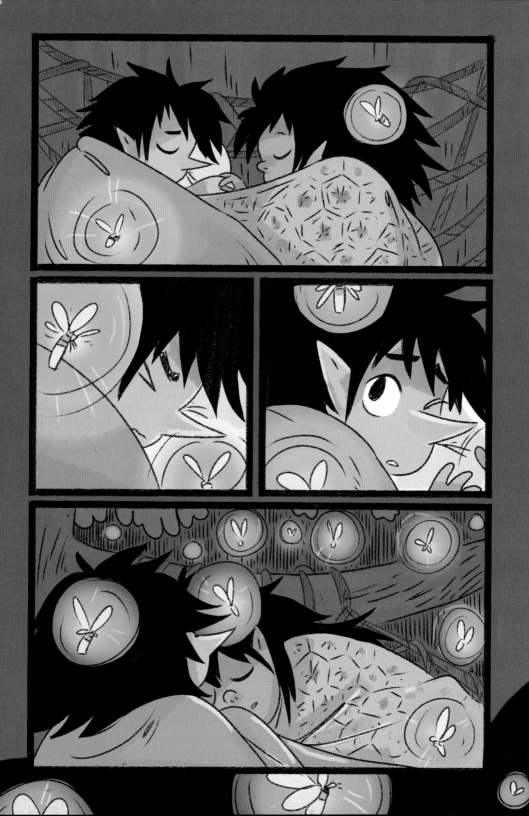

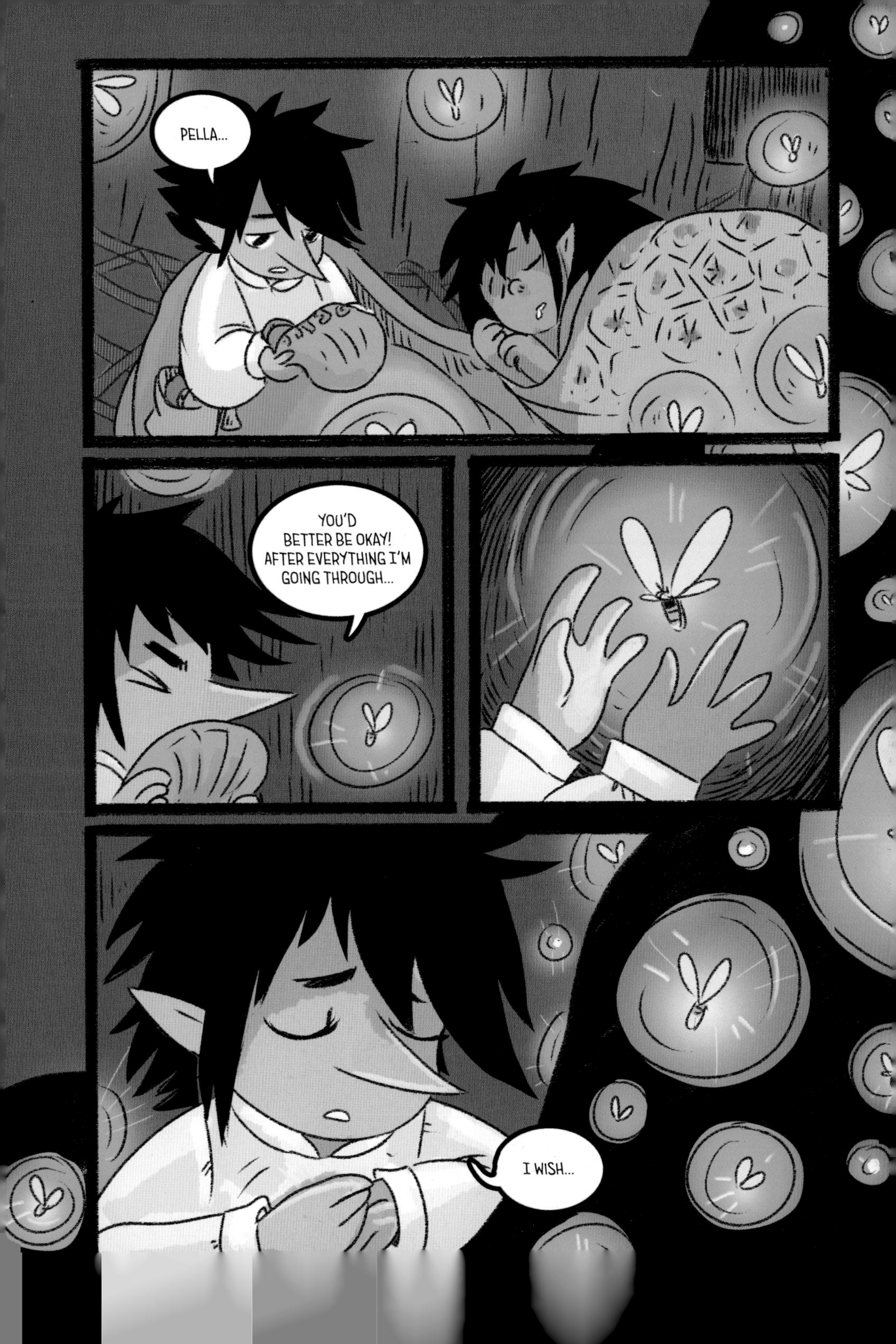
PELLA...
YOU'D BETTER BE OKAY! AFTER EVERYTHING I'M GOING THROUGH...
I WISH...

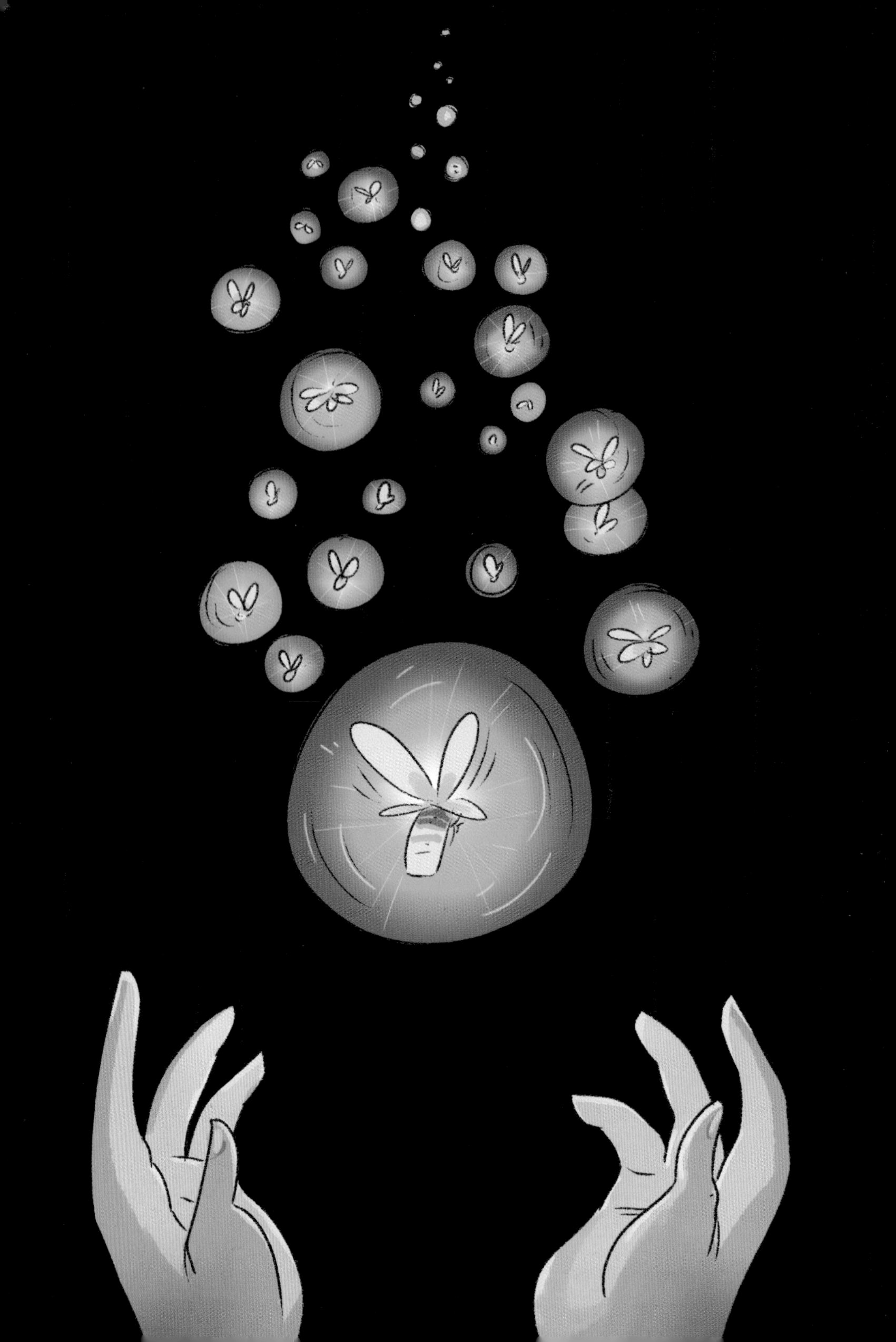

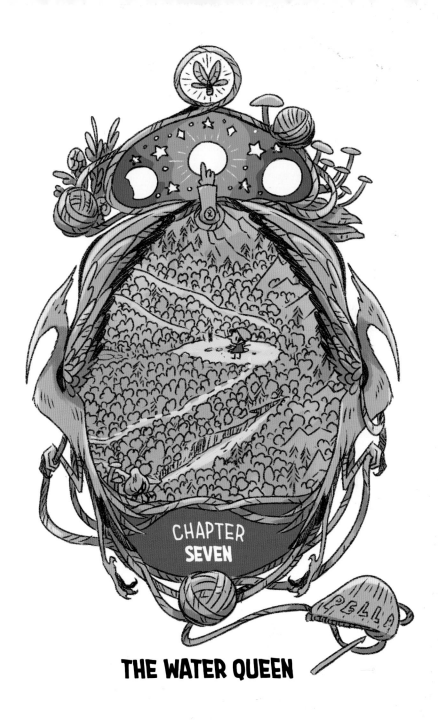

CHAPTER
SEVEN

THE WATER QUEEN

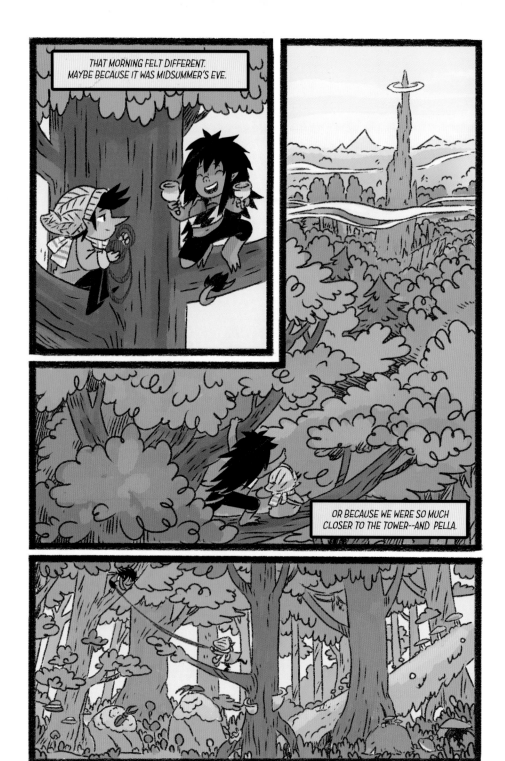

THAT MORNING FELT DIFFERENT.
MAYBE BECAUSE IT WAS MIDSUMMER'S EVE.

OR BECAUSE WE WERE SO MUCH
CLOSER TO THE TOWER--AND PELLA.

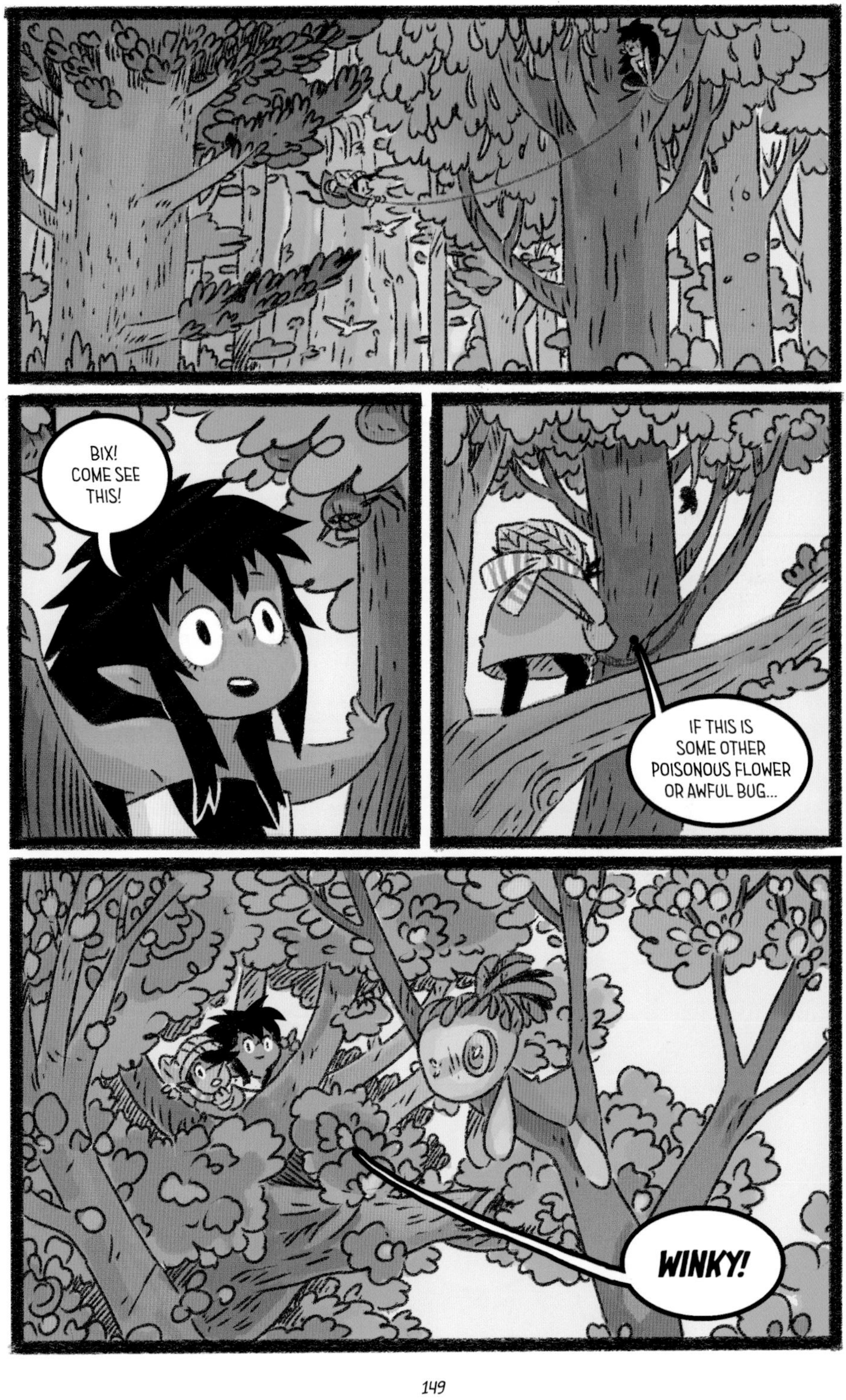
BIX! COME SEE THIS!
IF THIS IS SOME OTHER POISONOUS FLOWER OR AWFUL BUG...
WINKY!

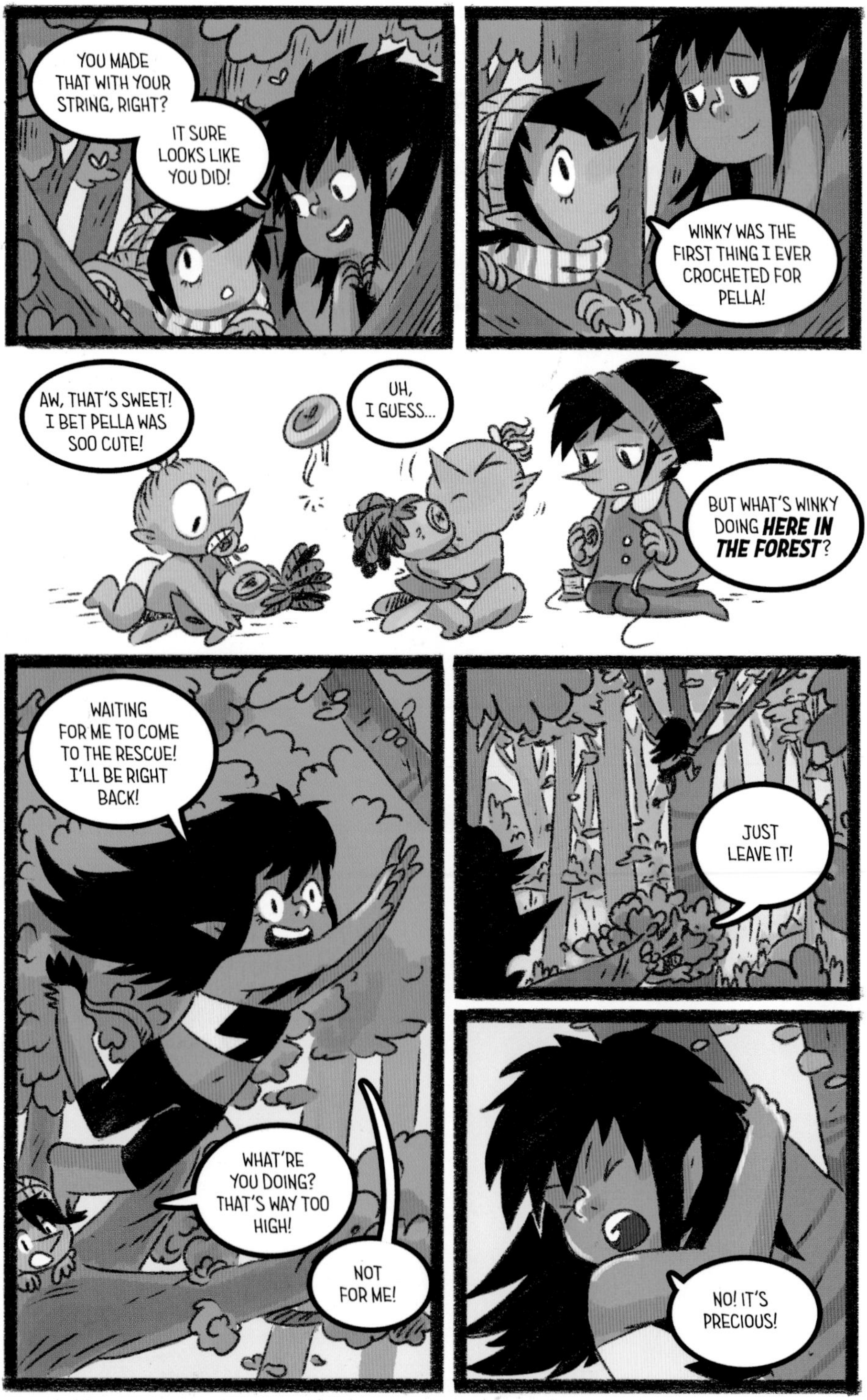
YOU MADE THAT WITH YOUR STRING, RIGHT?
IT SURE LOOKS LIKE YOU DID!
WINKY WAS THE FIRST THING I EVER CROCHETED FOR PELLA!
AW, THAT'S SWEET! I BET PELLA WAS SOO CUTE!
UH, I GUESS...
BUT WHAT'S WINKY DOING **HERE IN THE FOREST**?
WAITING FOR ME TO COME TO THE RESCUE! I'LL BE RIGHT BACK!
WHAT'RE YOU DOING? THAT'S WAY TOO HIGH!
NOT FOR ME!
JUST LEAVE IT!
NO! IT'S PRECIOUS!

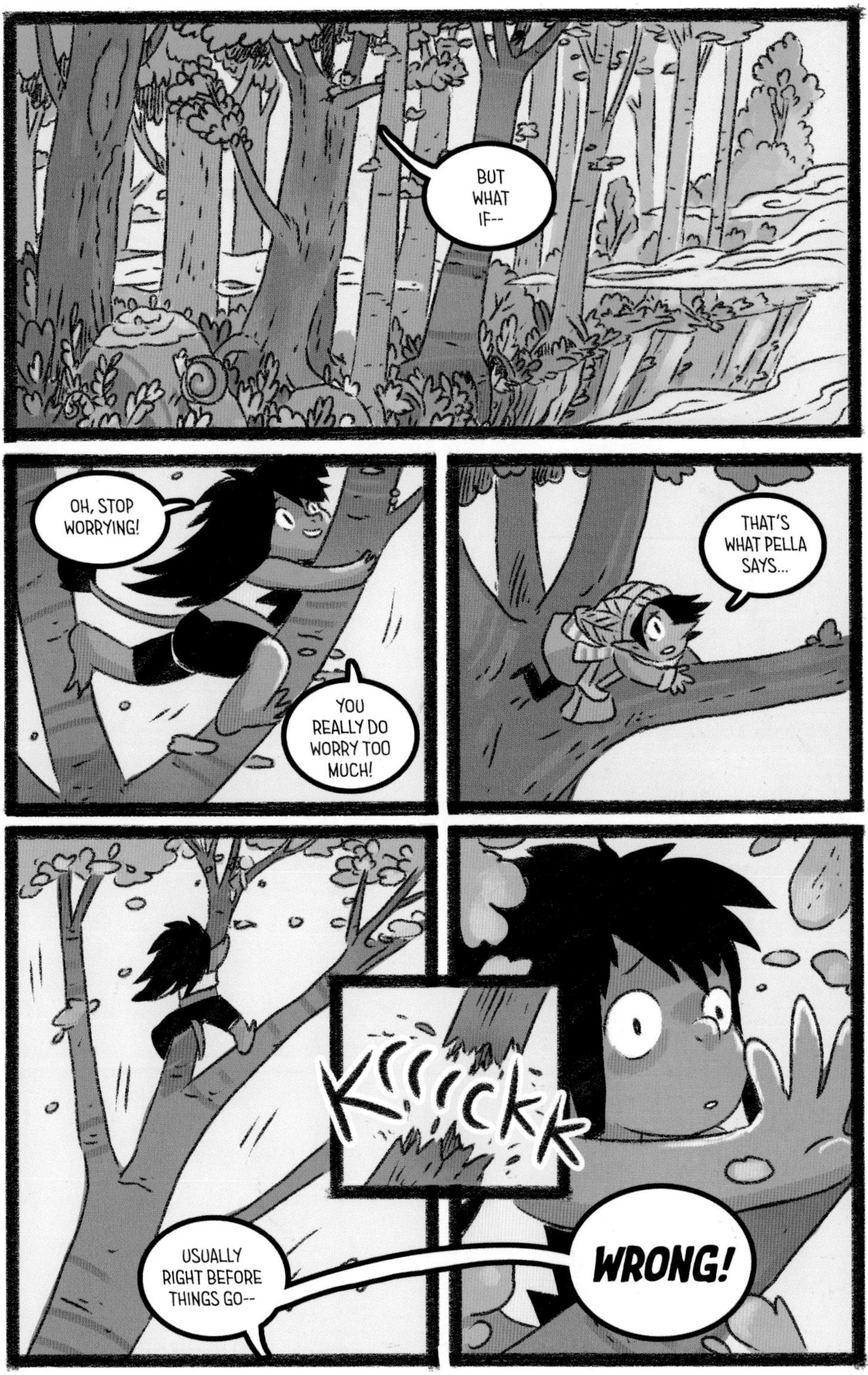
BUT WHAT IF--
OH, STOP WORRYING!
YOU REALLY DO WORRY TOO MUCH!
THAT'S WHAT PELLA SAYS...
USUALLY RIGHT BEFORE THINGS GO--
KRRRCKK
WRONG!

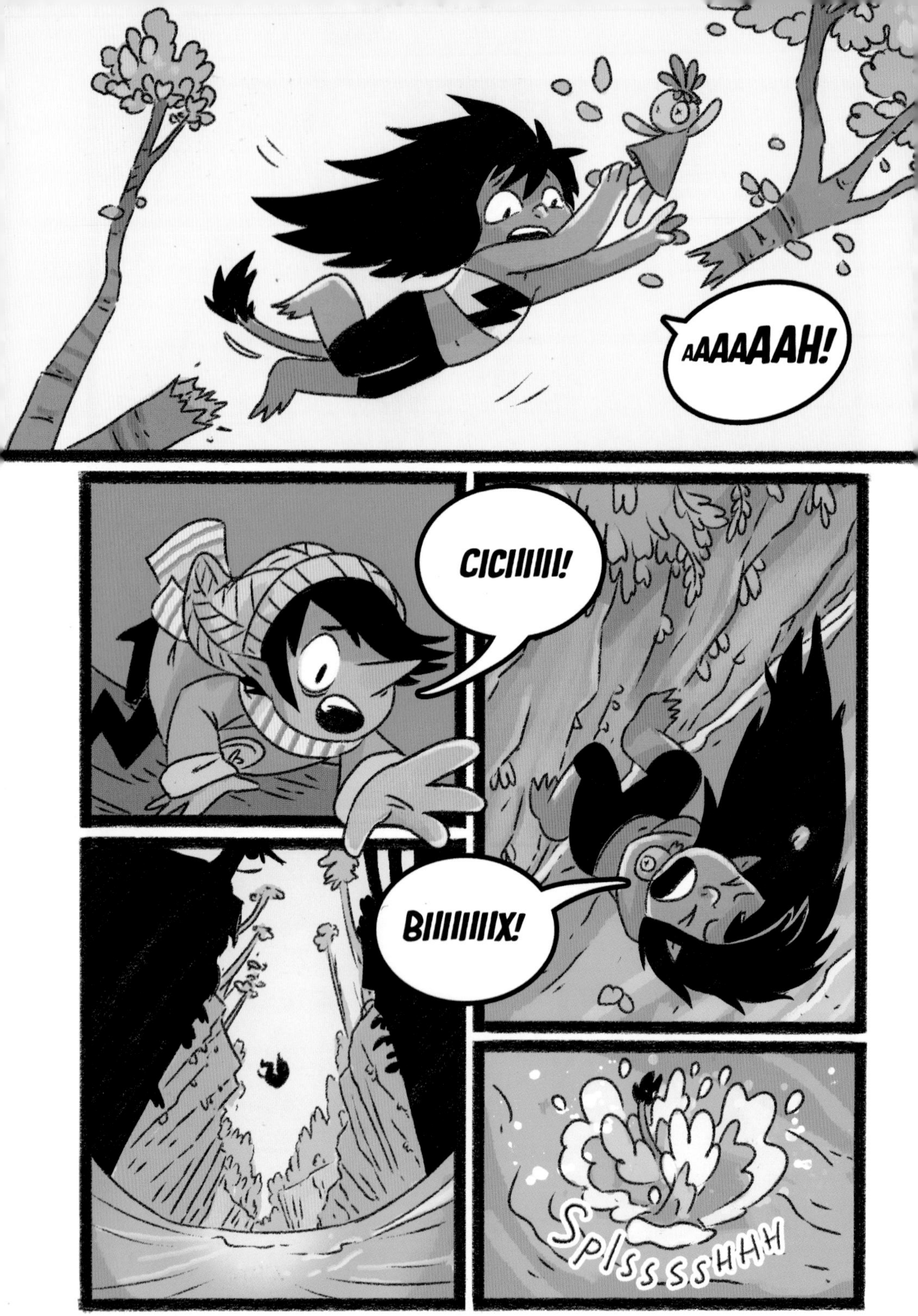
AAAAAAH!
CICIIIIII!
BIIIIIIIX!
Splssssshhh

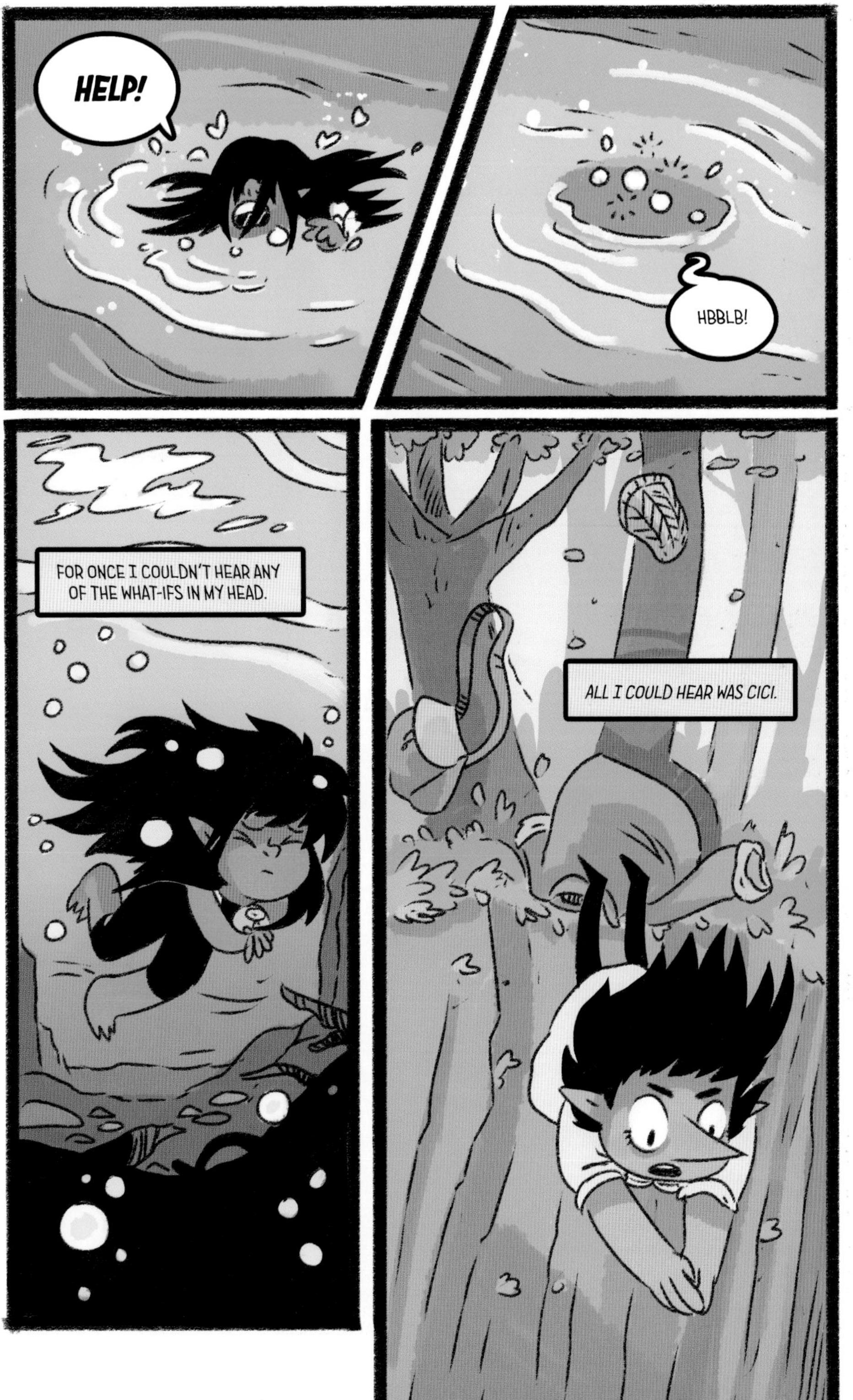
HELP!
HBBLB!
FOR ONCE I COULDN'T HEAR ANY OF THE WHAT-IFS IN MY HEAD.
ALL I COULD HEAR WAS CICI.

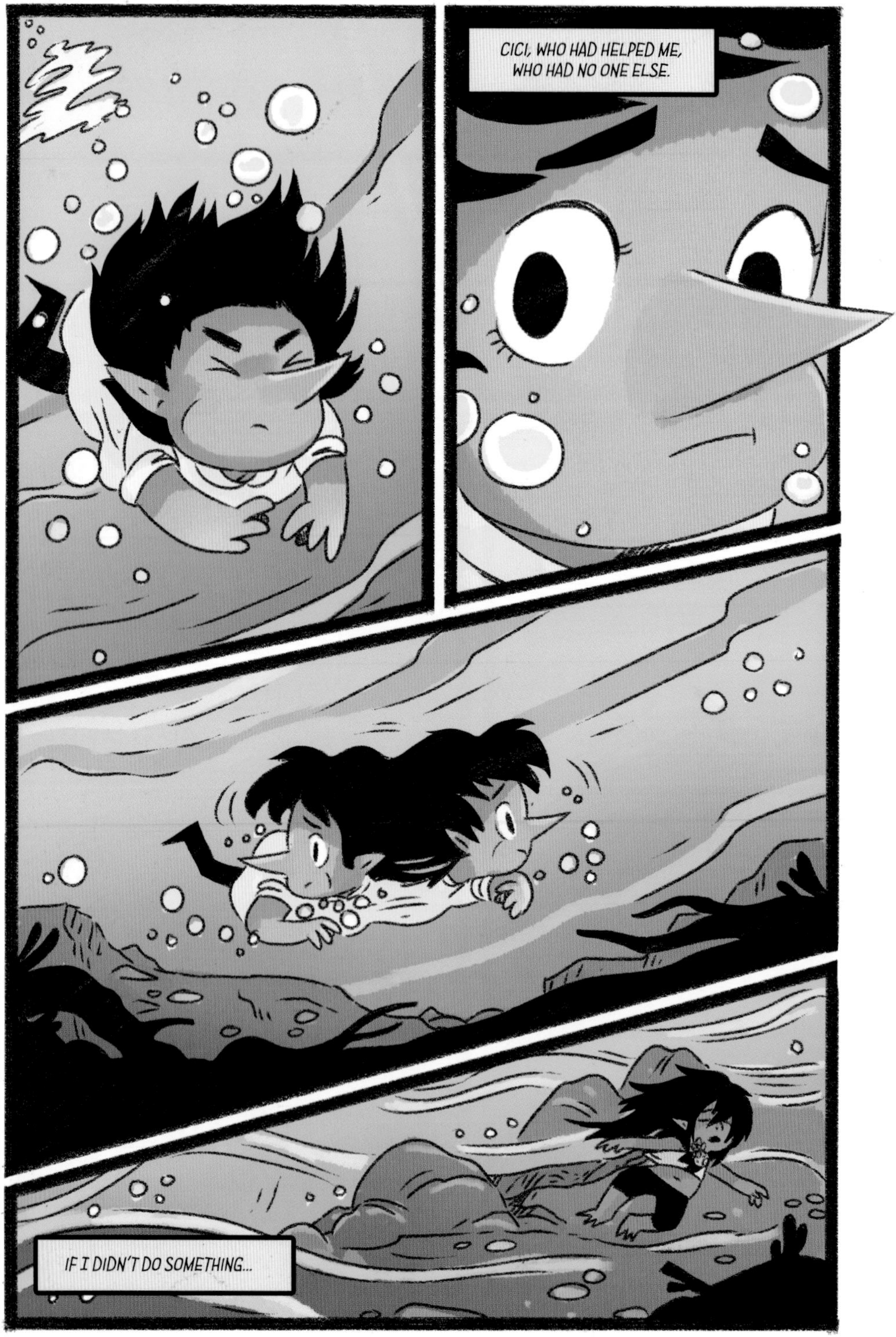

CICI, WHO HAD HELPED ME, WHO HAD NO ONE ELSE.
IF I DIDN'T DO SOMETHING...

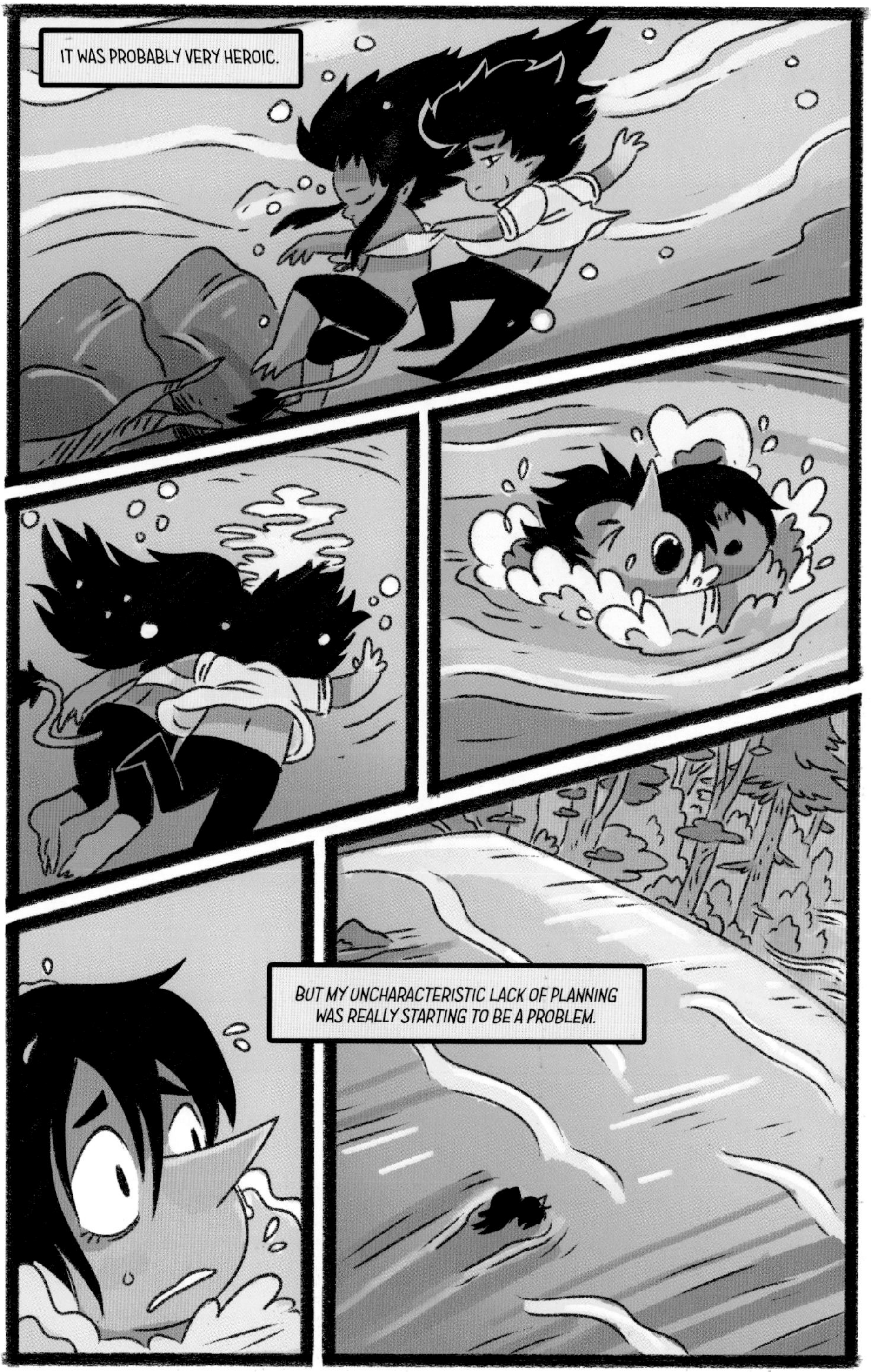
IT WAS PROBABLY VERY HEROIC.
BUT MY UNCHARACTERISTIC LACK OF PLANNING WAS REALLY STARTING TO BE A PROBLEM.

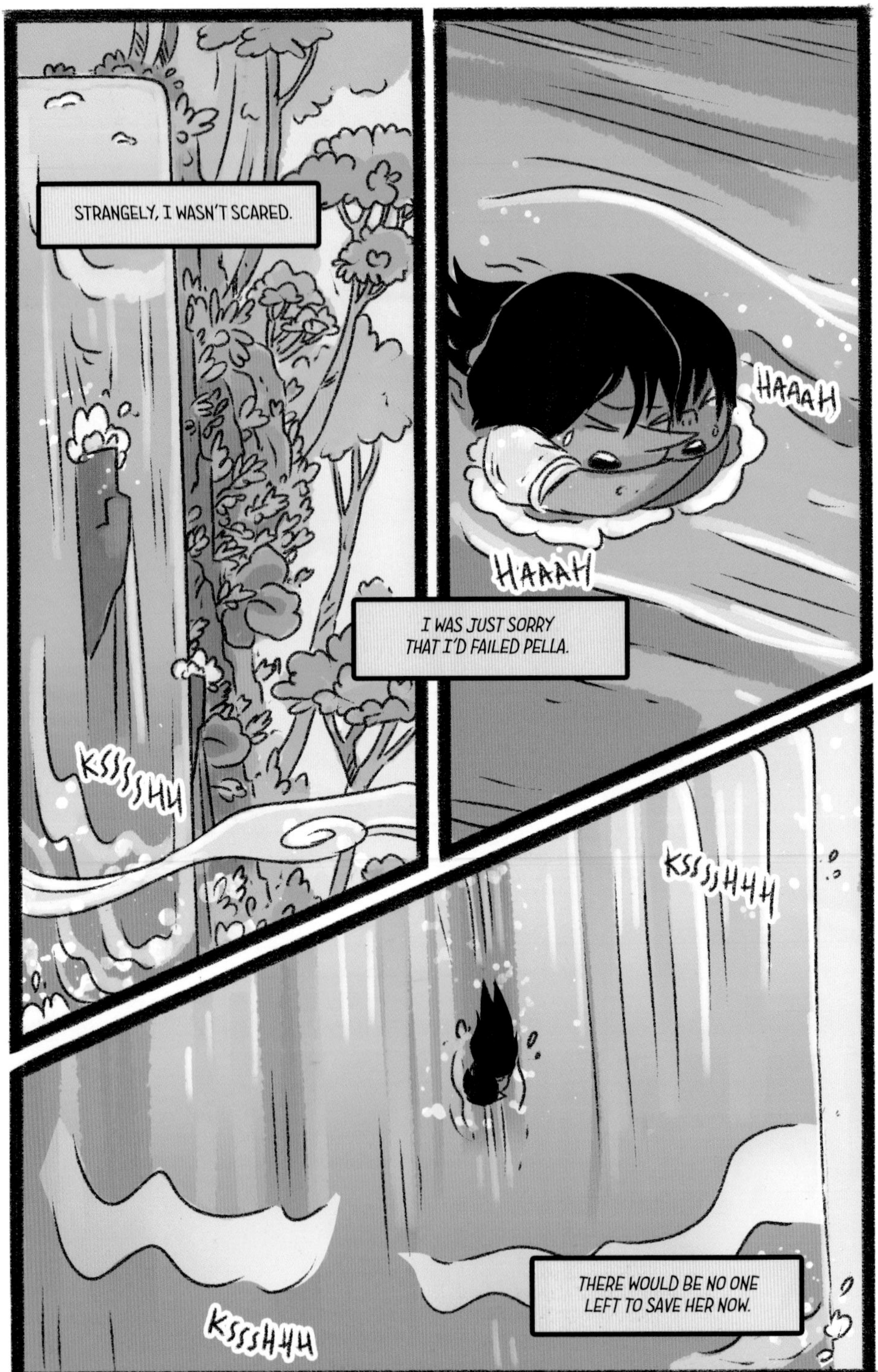
STRANGELY, I WASN'T SCARED.
KSSSSHH
HAAAH
HAAAH
I WAS JUST SORRY THAT I'D FAILED PELLA.
KSSSSHHH
KSSSHHH
THERE WOULD BE NO ONE LEFT TO SAVE HER NOW.

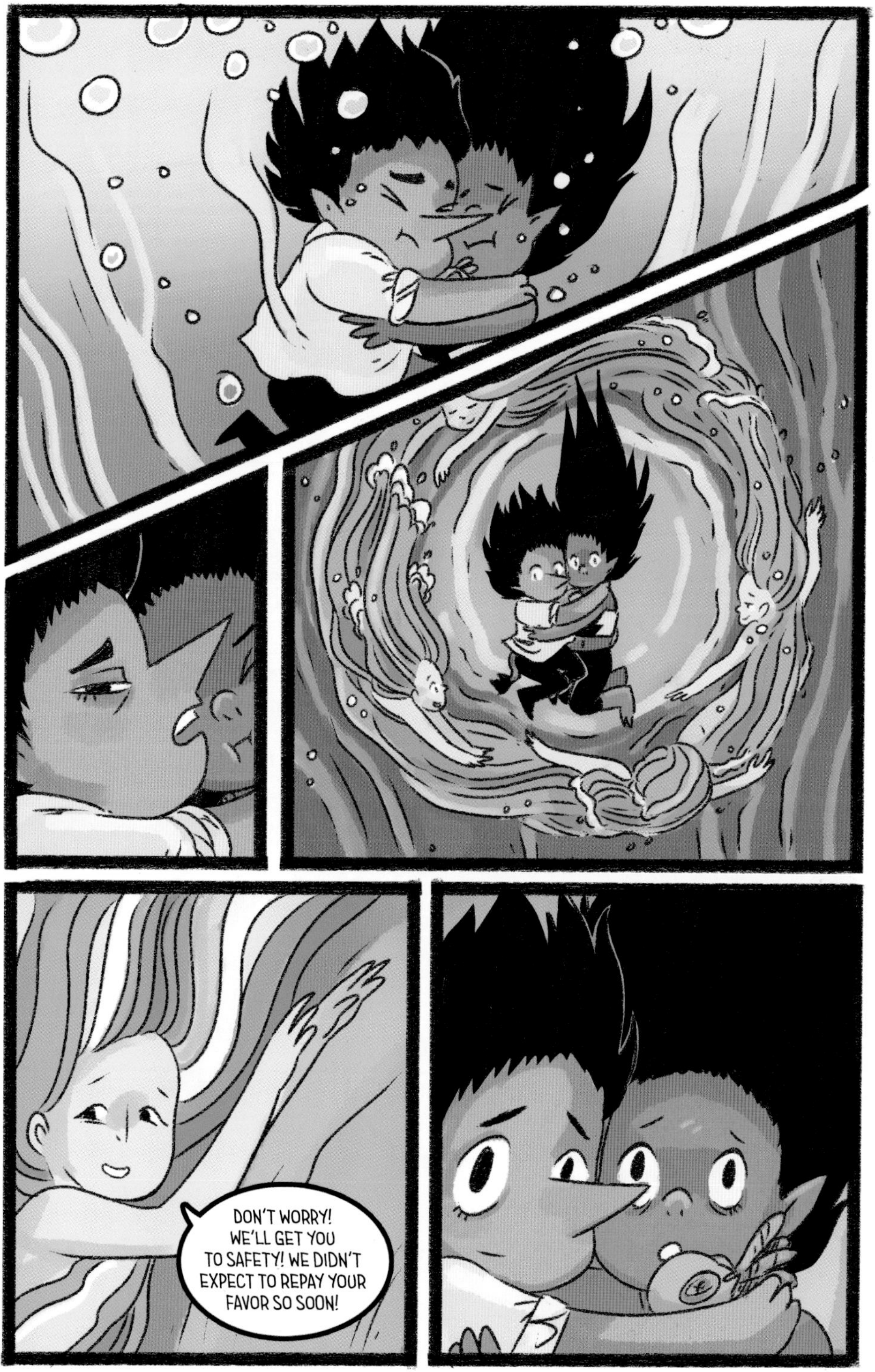
DON'T WORRY! WE'LL GET YOU TO SAFETY! WE DIDN'T EXPECT TO REPAY YOUR FAVOR SO SOON!

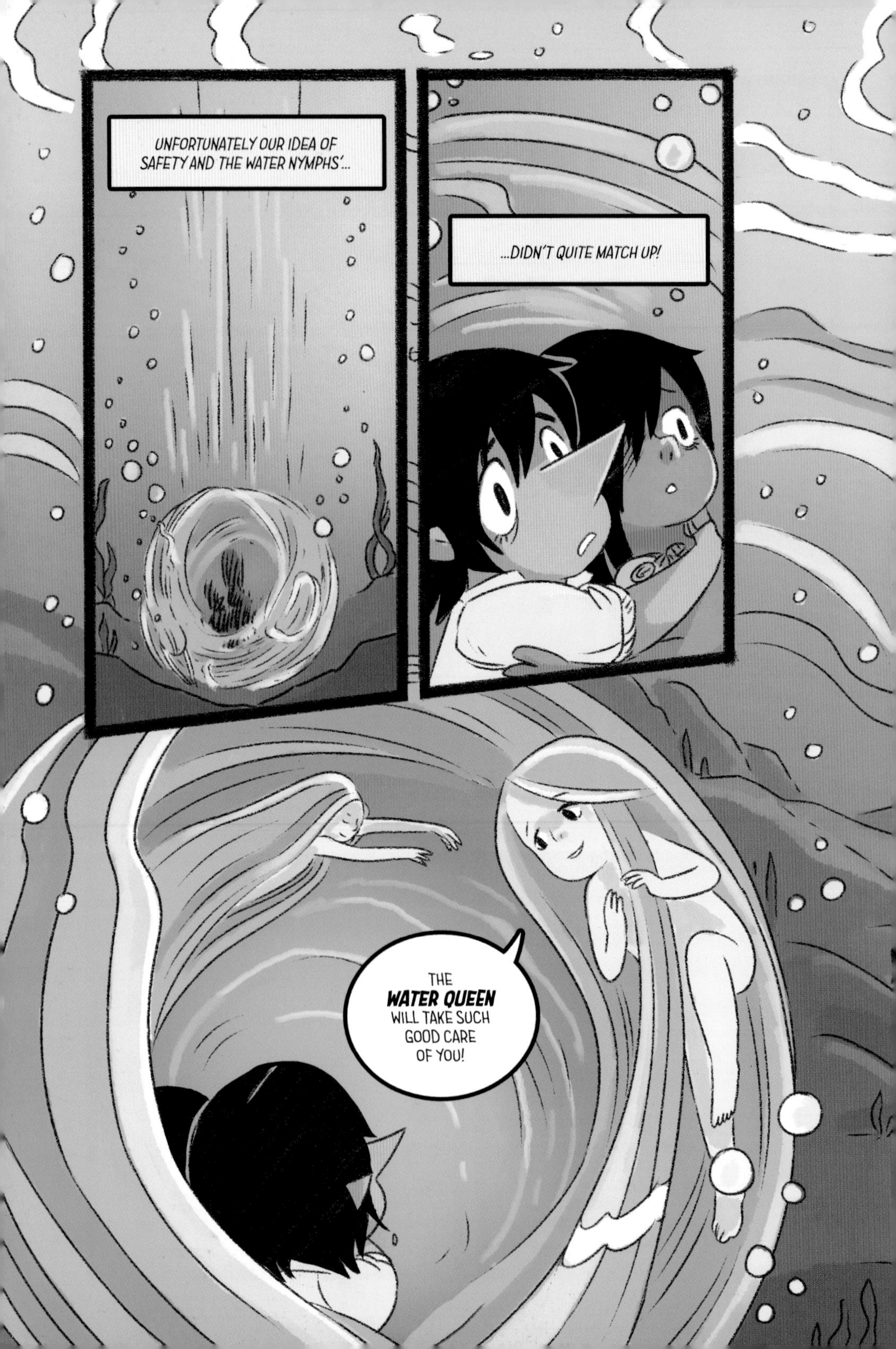
UNFORTUNATELY OUR IDEA OF SAFETY AND THE WATER NYMPHS'...
...DIDN'T QUITE MATCH UP!
THE WATER QUEEN WILL TAKE SUCH GOOD CARE OF YOU!

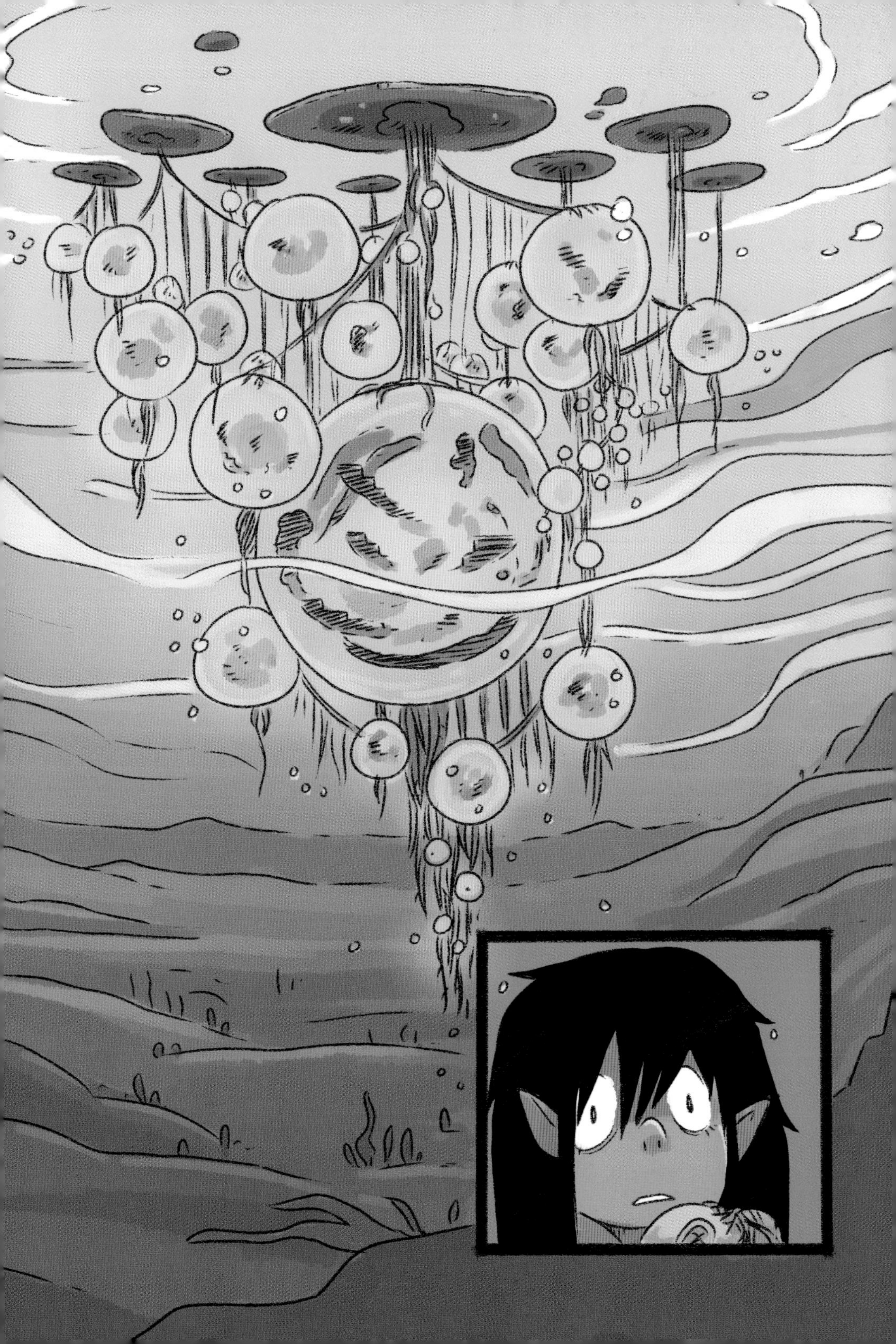

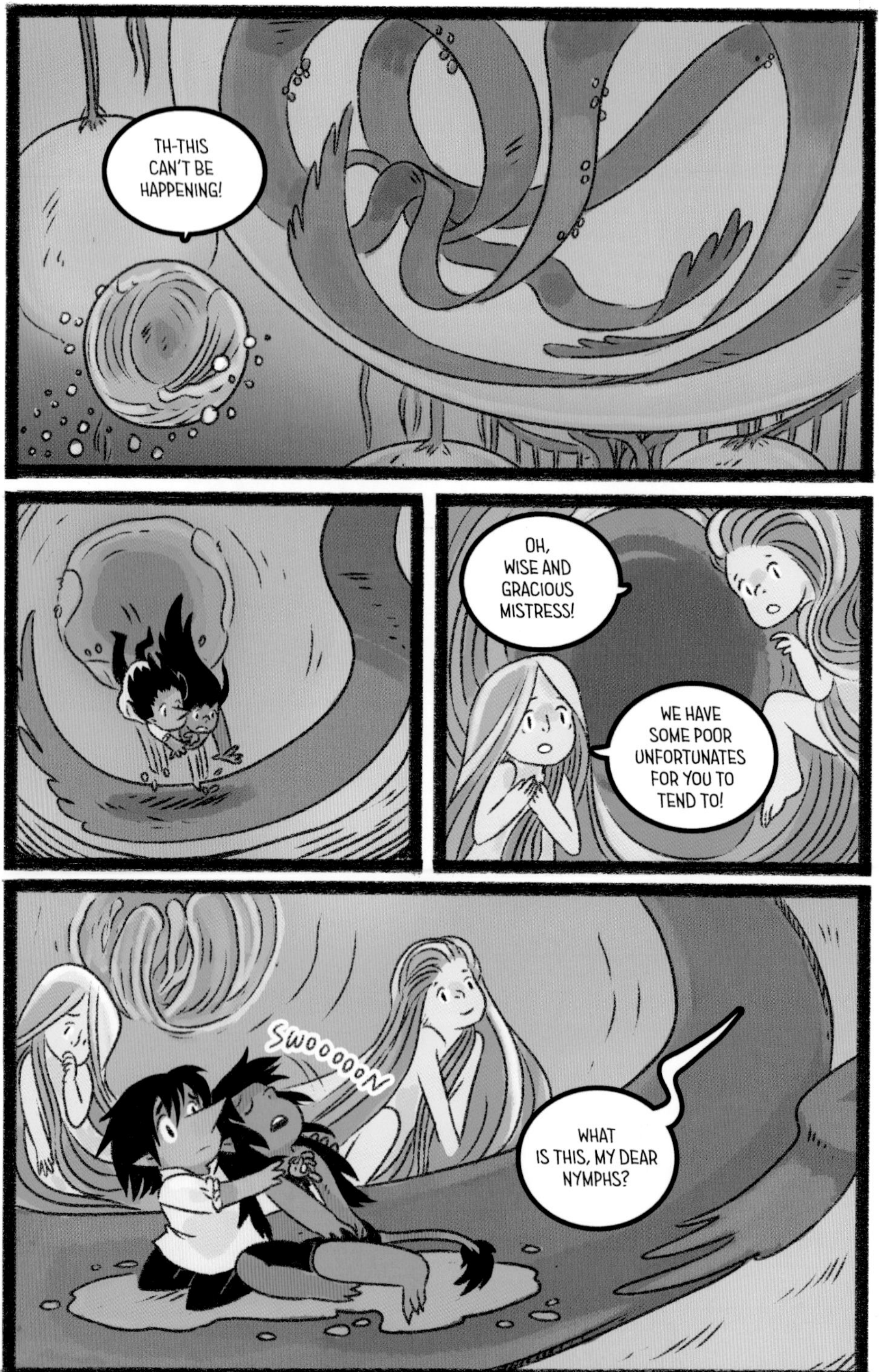
TH-THIS CAN'T BE HAPPENING!
OH, WISE AND GRACIOUS MISTRESS!
WE HAVE SOME POOR UNFORTUNATES FOR YOU TO TEND TO!
SWOOOOOON
WHAT IS THIS, MY DEAR NYMPHS?

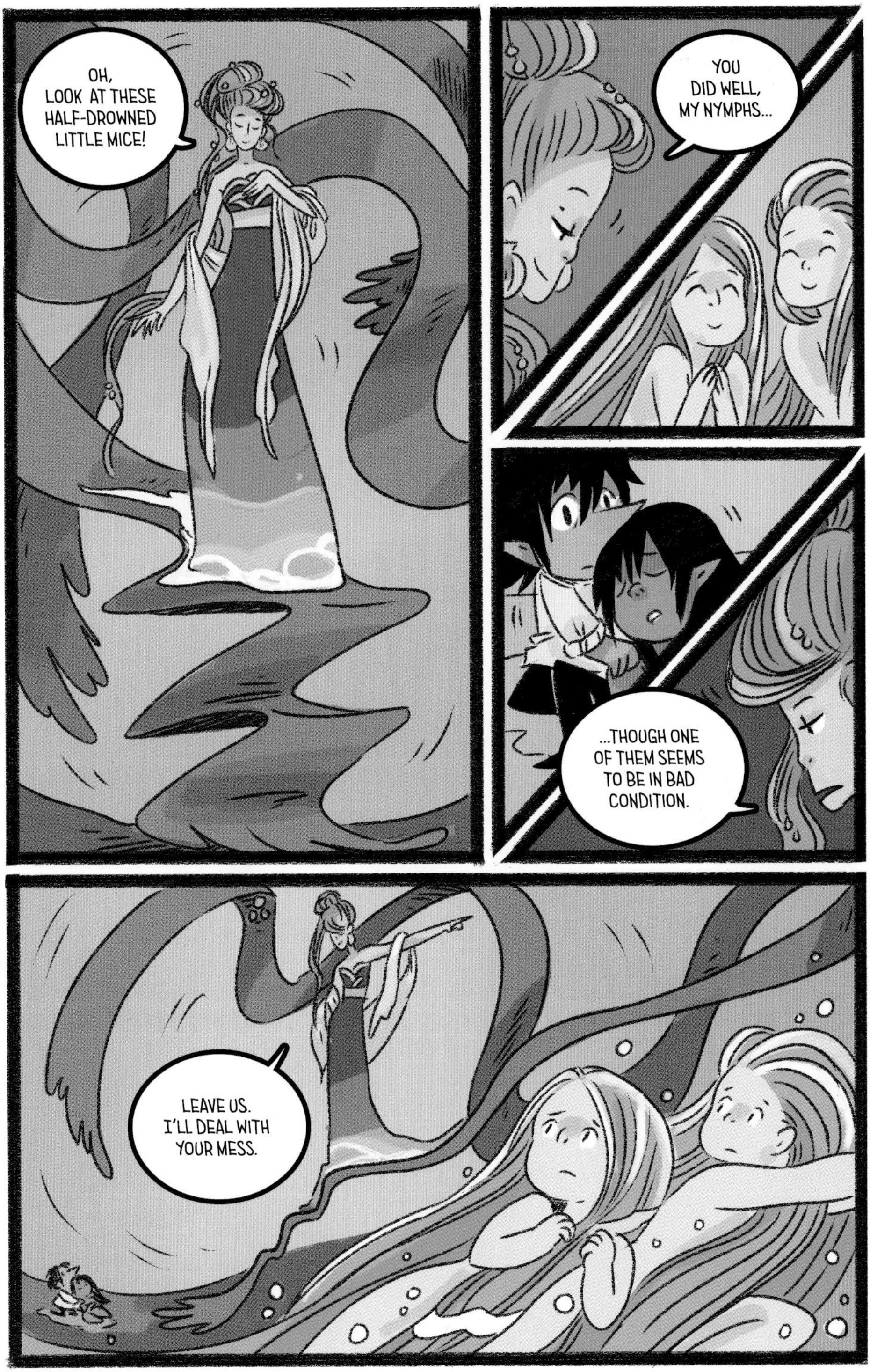
OH, LOOK AT THESE HALF-DROWNED LITTLE MICE!
YOU DID WELL, MY NYMPHS...
...THOUGH ONE OF THEM SEEMS TO BE IN BAD CONDITION.
LEAVE US. I'LL DEAL WITH YOUR MESS.

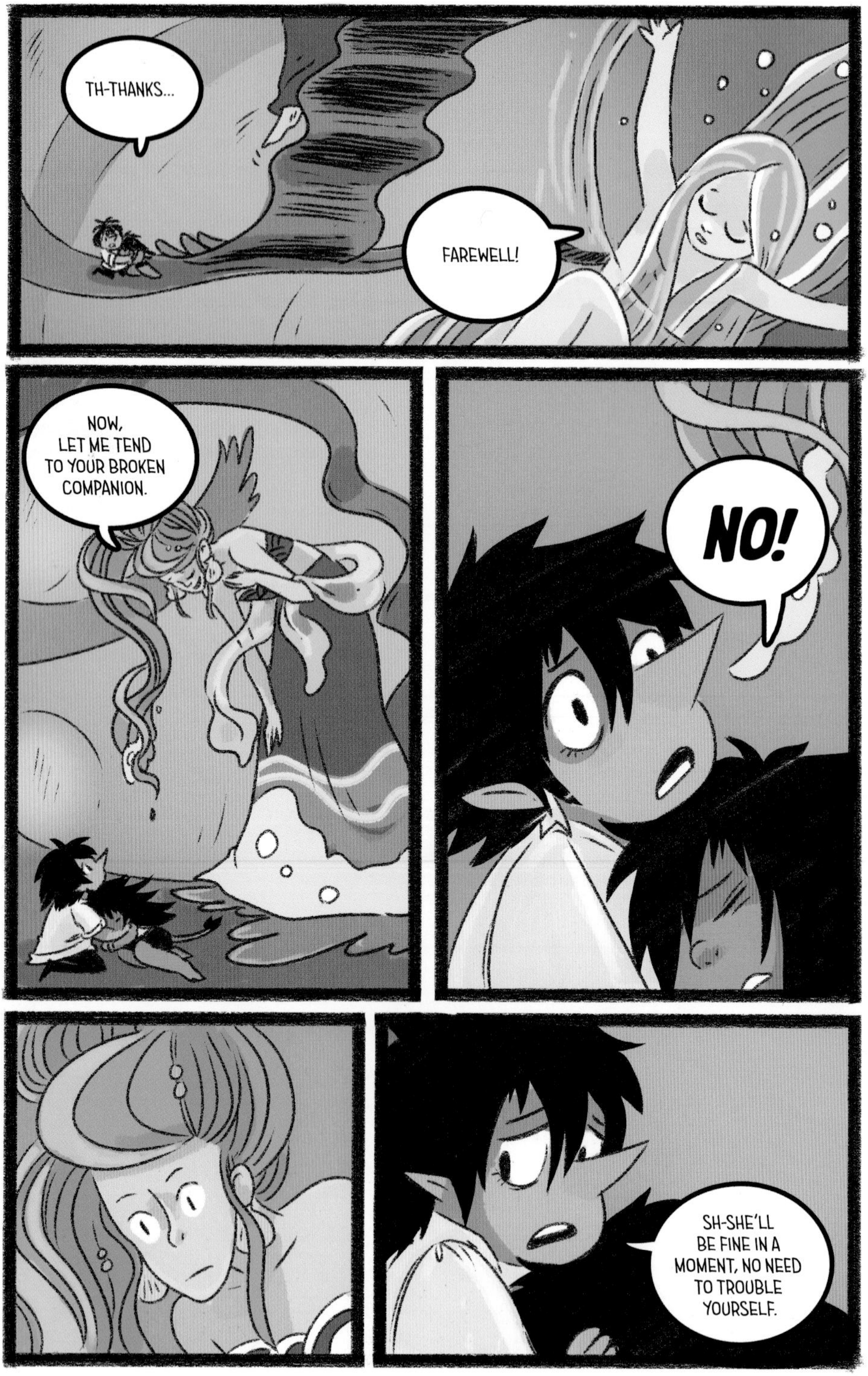
TH-THANKS...
FAREWELL!
NOW, LET ME TEND TO YOUR BROKEN COMPANION.
NO!
SH-SHE'LL BE FINE IN A MOMENT, NO NEED TO TROUBLE YOURSELF.

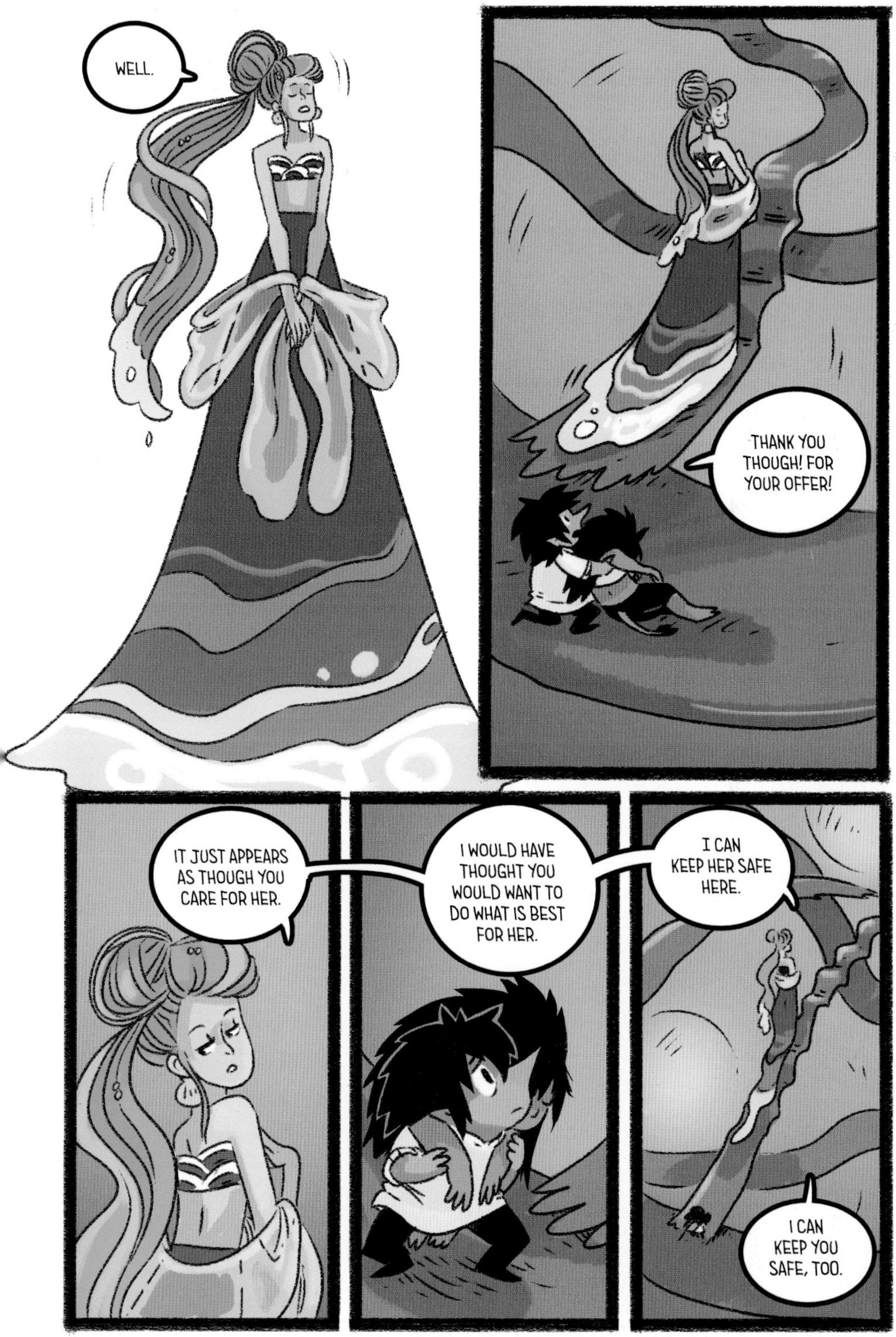
WELL.
THANK YOU THOUGH! FOR YOUR OFFER!
IT JUST APPEARS AS THOUGH YOU CARE FOR HER.
I WOULD HAVE THOUGHT YOU WOULD WANT TO DO WHAT IS BEST FOR HER.
I CAN KEEP HER SAFE HERE.
I CAN KEEP YOU SAFE, TOO.

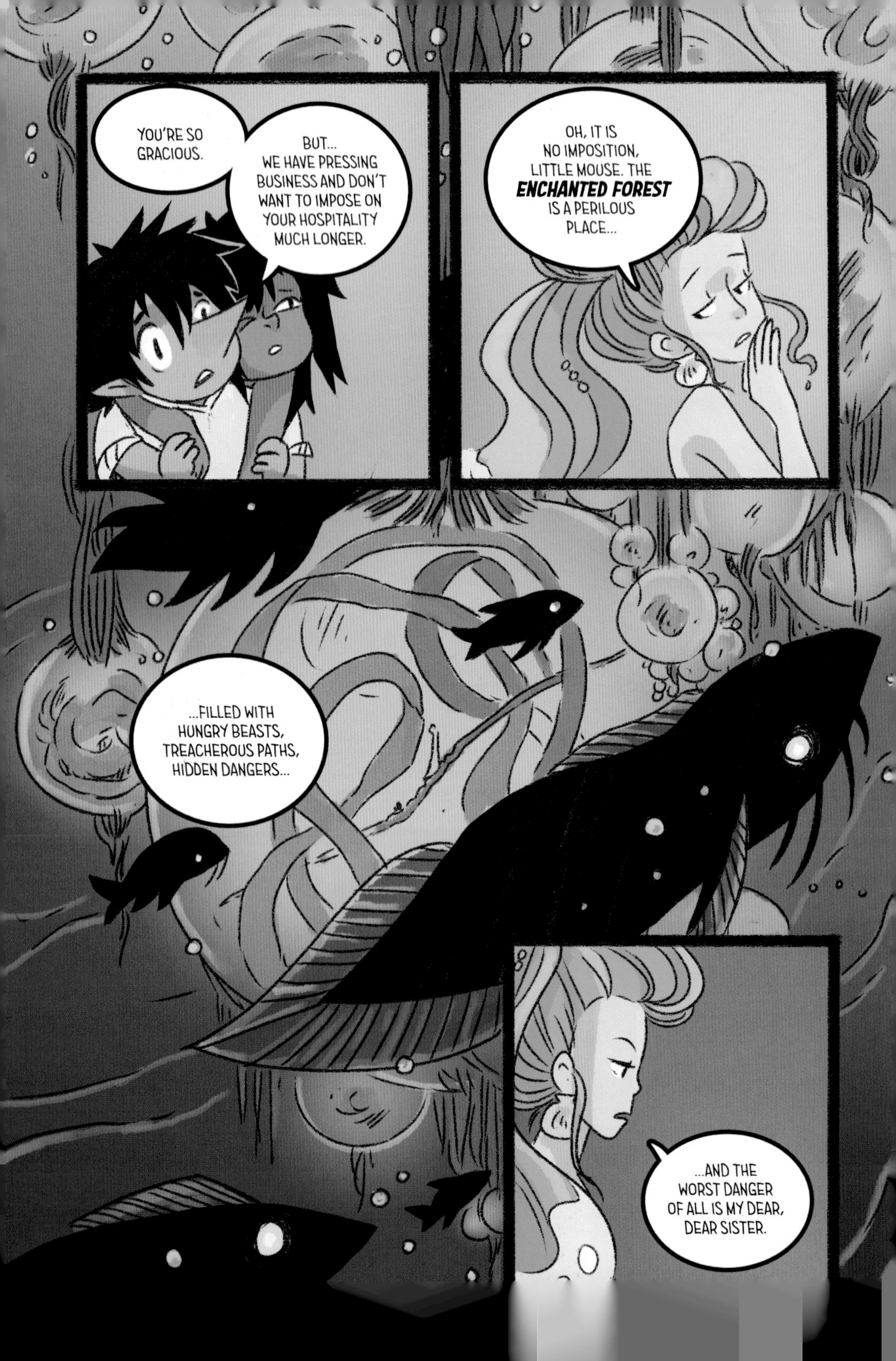
YOU'RE SO GRACIOUS.
BUT... WE HAVE PRESSING BUSINESS AND DON'T WANT TO IMPOSE ON YOUR HOSPITALITY MUCH LONGER.
OH, IT IS NO IMPOSITION, LITTLE MOUSE. THE ENCHANTED FOREST IS A PERILOUS PLACE...
...FILLED WITH HUNGRY BEASTS, TREACHEROUS PATHS, HIDDEN DANGERS...
...AND THE WORST DANGER OF ALL IS MY DEAR, DEAR SISTER.

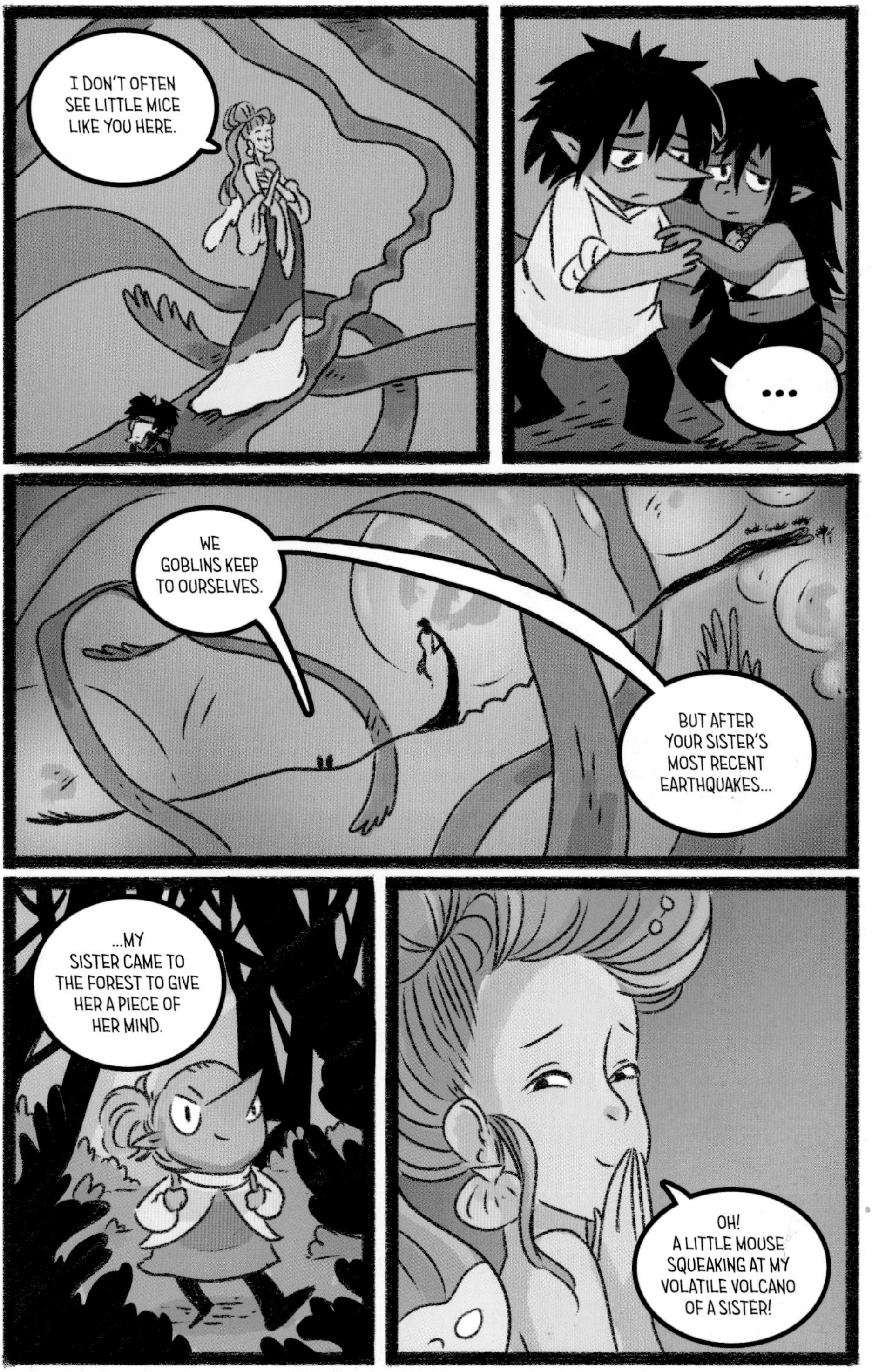
I DON'T OFTEN SEE LITTLE MICE LIKE YOU HERE.
...
WE GOBLINS KEEP TO OURSELVES.
BUT AFTER YOUR SISTER'S MOST RECENT EARTHQUAKES...
...MY SISTER CAME TO THE FOREST TO GIVE HER A PIECE OF HER MIND.
OH! A LITTLE MOUSE SQUEAKING AT MY VOLATILE VOLCANO OF A SISTER!

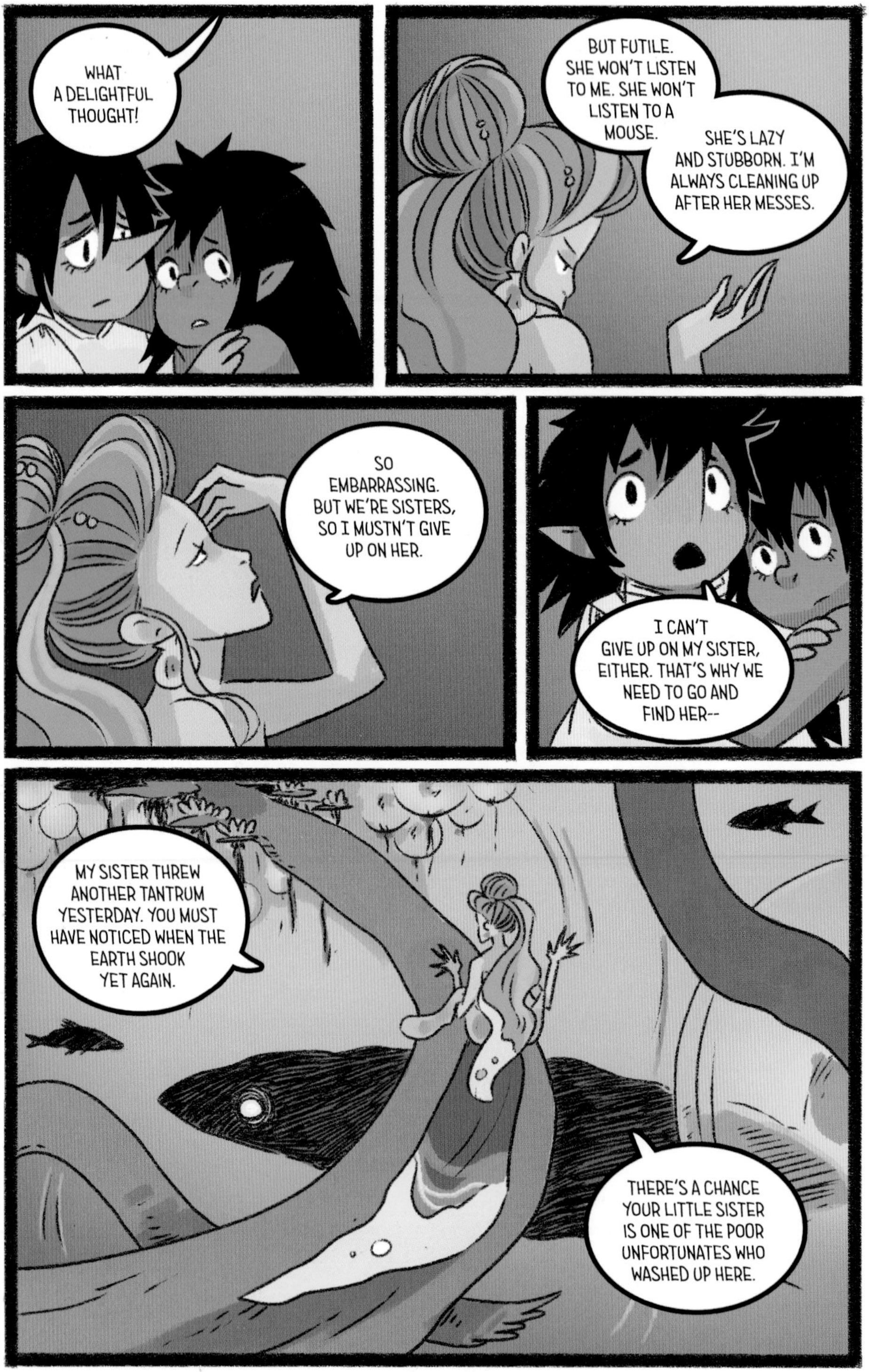
WHAT A DELIGHTFUL THOUGHT!
BUT FUTILE. SHE WON'T LISTEN TO ME. SHE WON'T LISTEN TO A MOUSE.
SHE'S LAZY AND STUBBORN. I'M ALWAYS CLEANING UP AFTER HER MESSES.
SO EMBARRASSING. BUT WE'RE SISTERS, SO I MUSTN'T GIVE UP ON HER.
I CAN'T GIVE UP ON MY SISTER, EITHER. THAT'S WHY WE NEED TO GO AND FIND HER--
MY SISTER THREW ANOTHER TANTRUM YESTERDAY. YOU MUST HAVE NOTICED WHEN THE EARTH SHOOK YET AGAIN.
THERE'S A CHANCE YOUR LITTLE SISTER IS ONE OF THE POOR UNFORTUNATES WHO WASHED UP HERE.

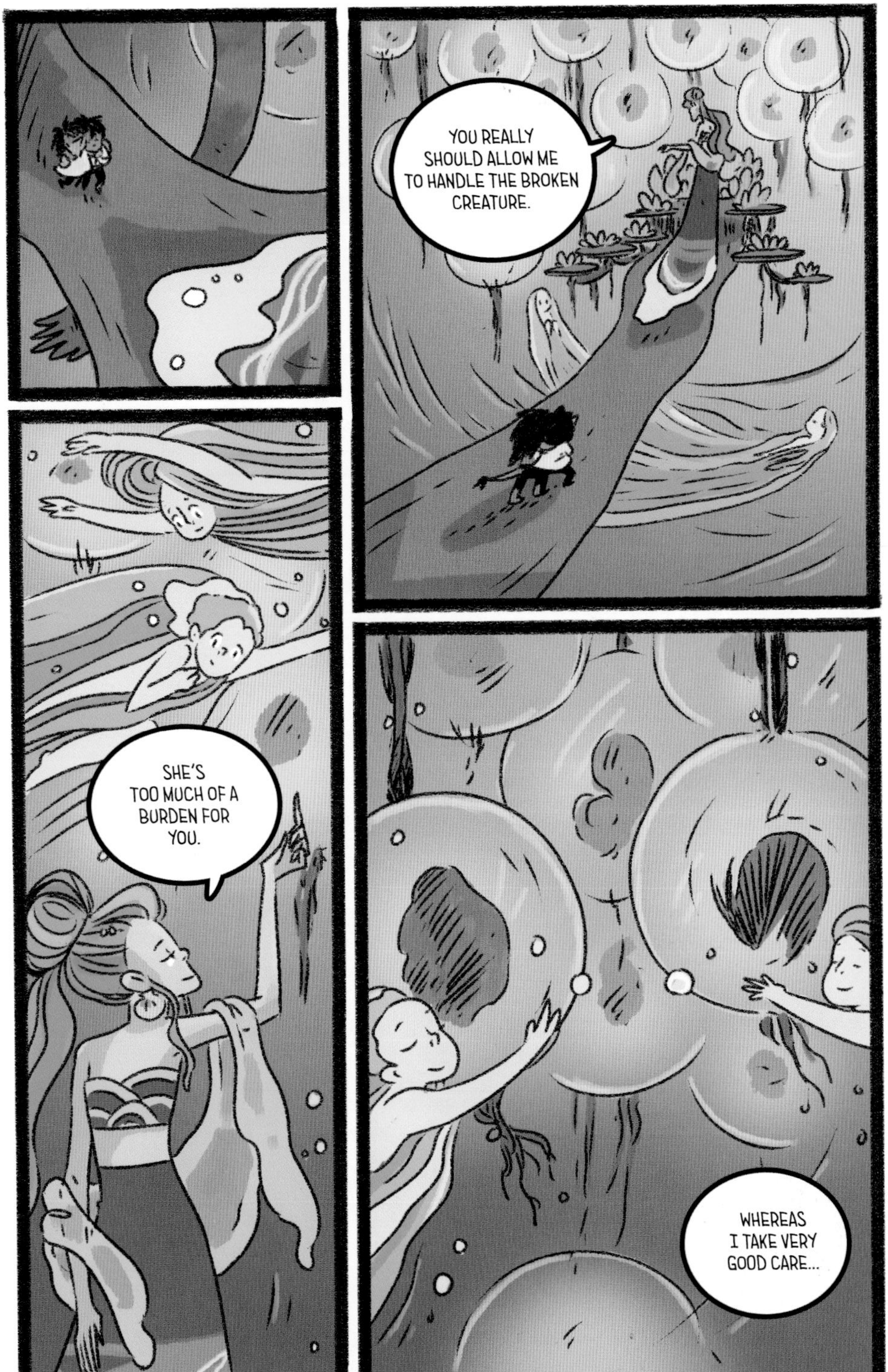
YOU REALLY SHOULD ALLOW ME TO HANDLE THE BROKEN CREATURE.
SHE'S TOO MUCH OF A BURDEN FOR YOU.
WHEREAS I TAKE VERY GOOD CARE...

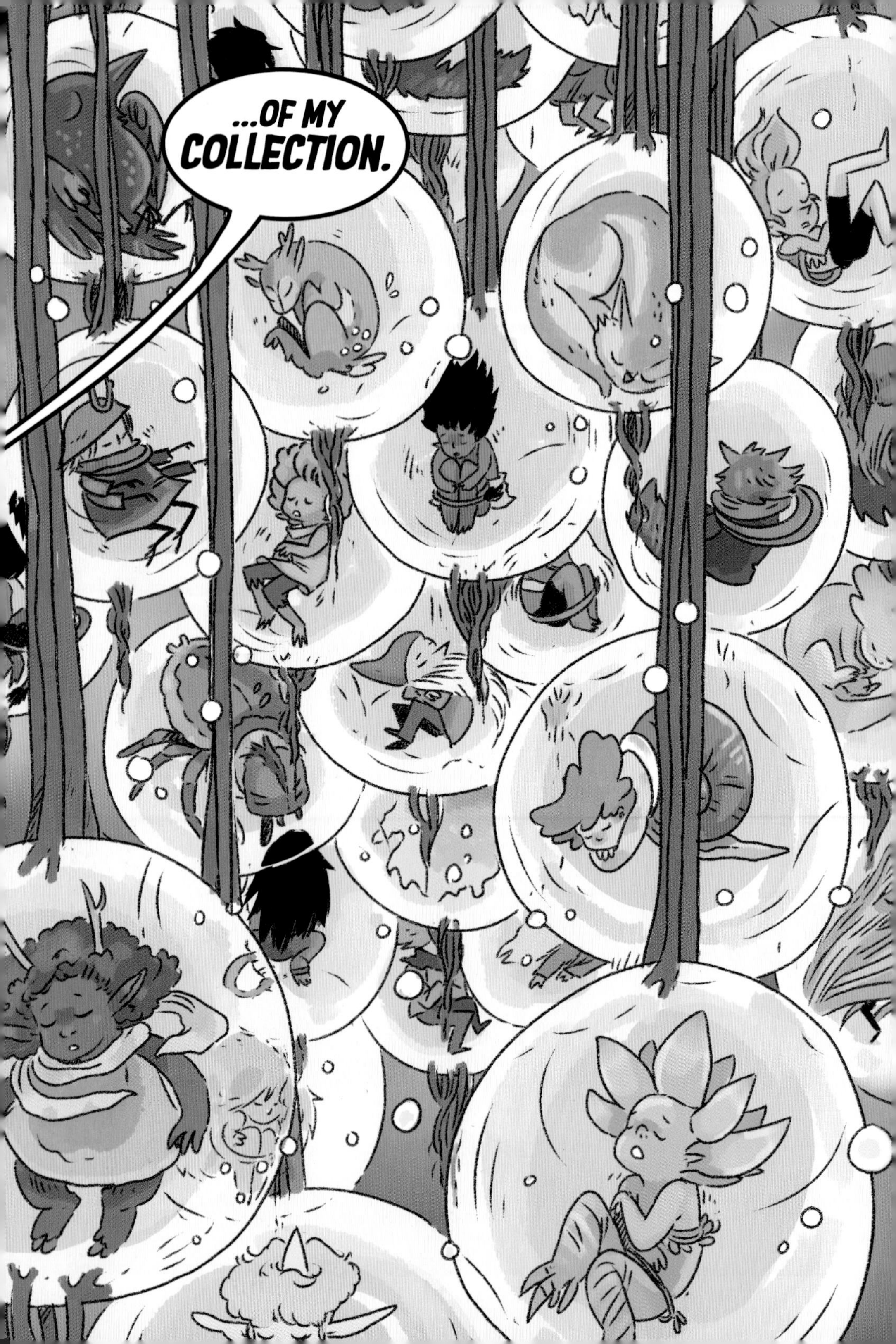
...OF MY COLLECTION.

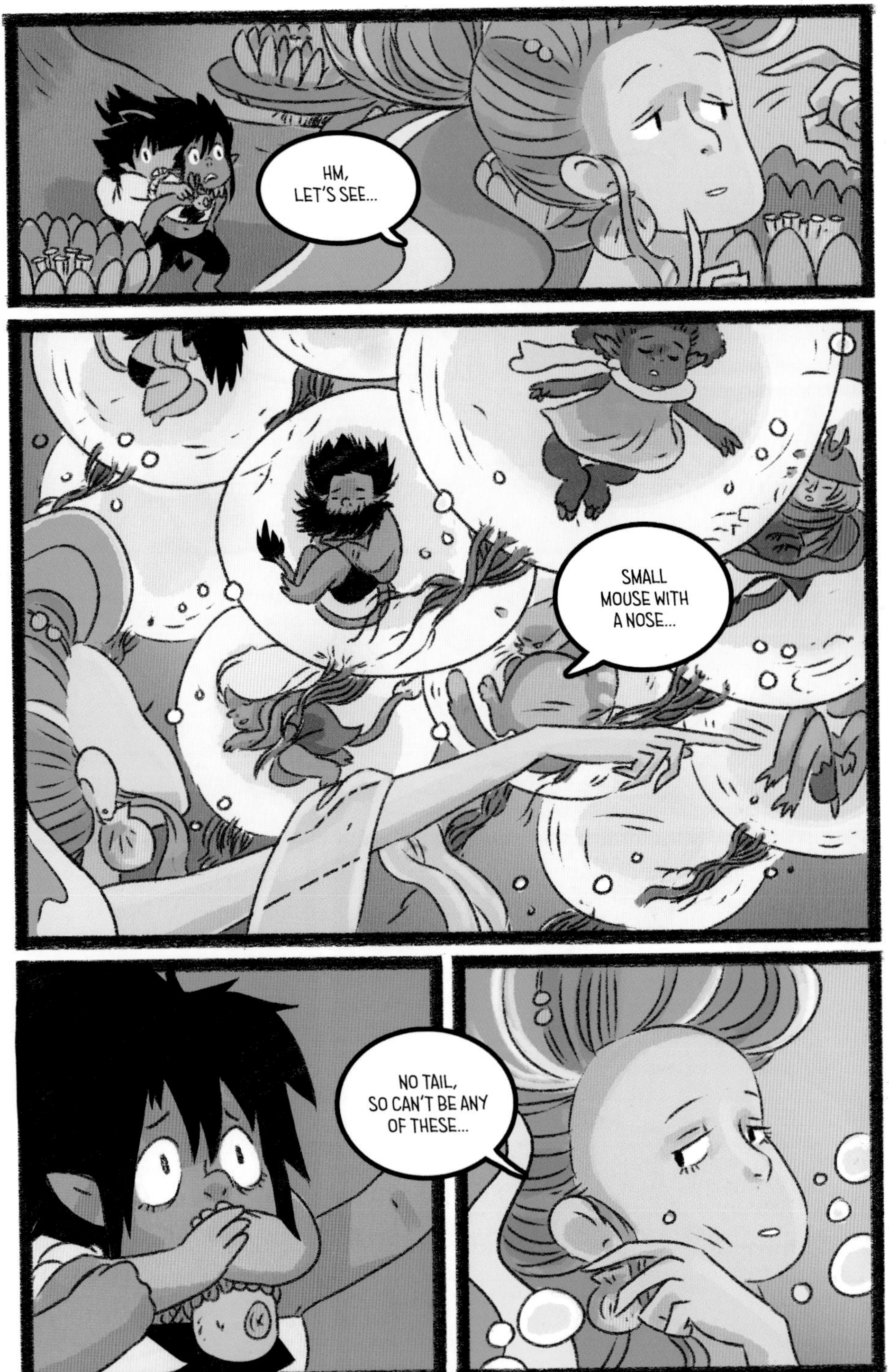
HM, LET'S SEE...
SMALL MOUSE WITH A NOSE...
NO TAIL, SO CAN'T BE ANY OF THESE...

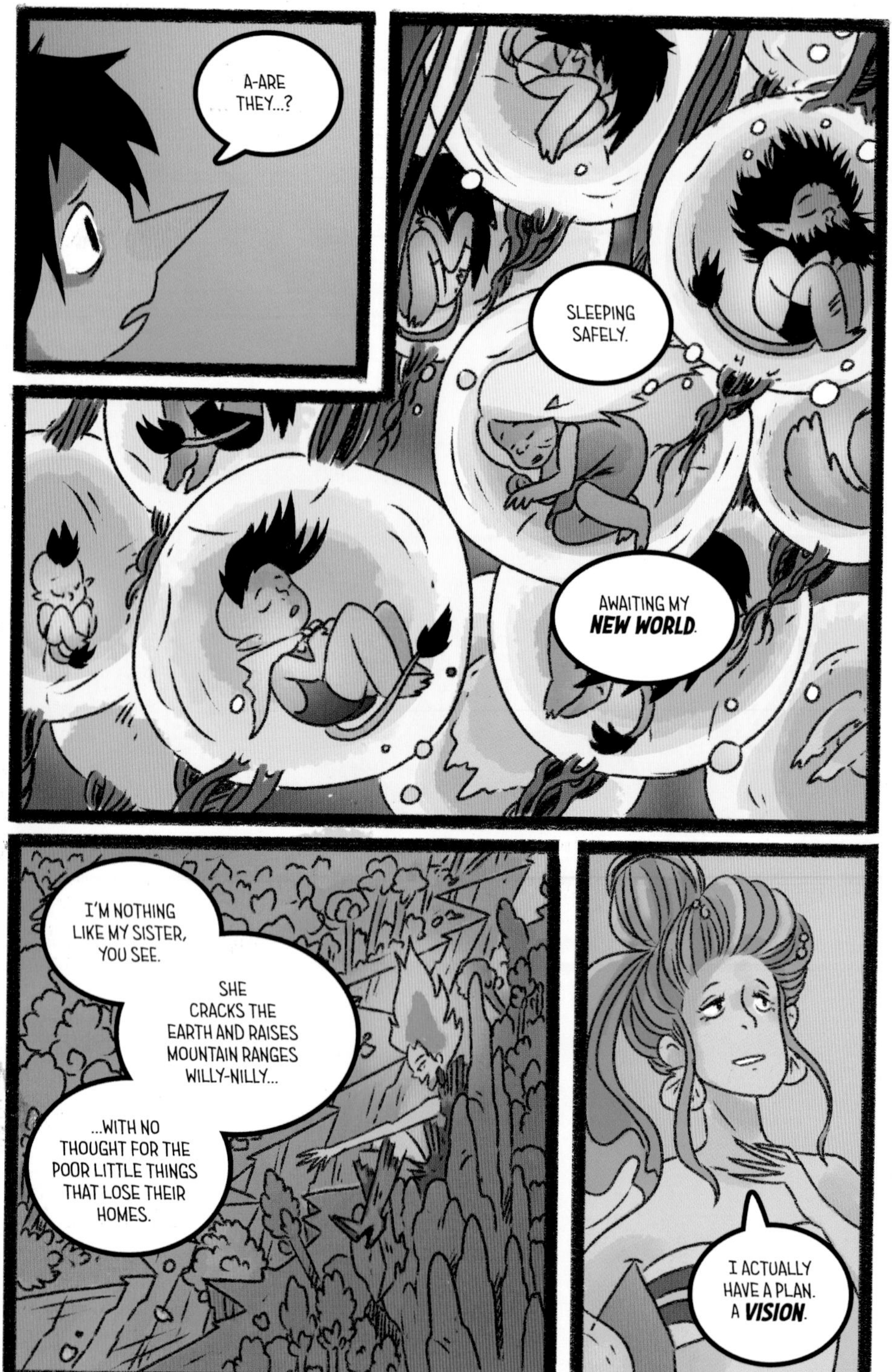
A-ARE THEY...?
SLEEPING SAFELY.
AWAITING MY **NEW WORLD**.
I'M NOTHING LIKE MY SISTER, YOU SEE.
SHE CRACKS THE EARTH AND RAISES MOUNTAIN RANGES WILLY-NILLY...
...WITH NO THOUGHT FOR THE POOR LITTLE THINGS THAT LOSE THEIR HOMES.
I ACTUALLY HAVE A PLAN. A **VISION**.

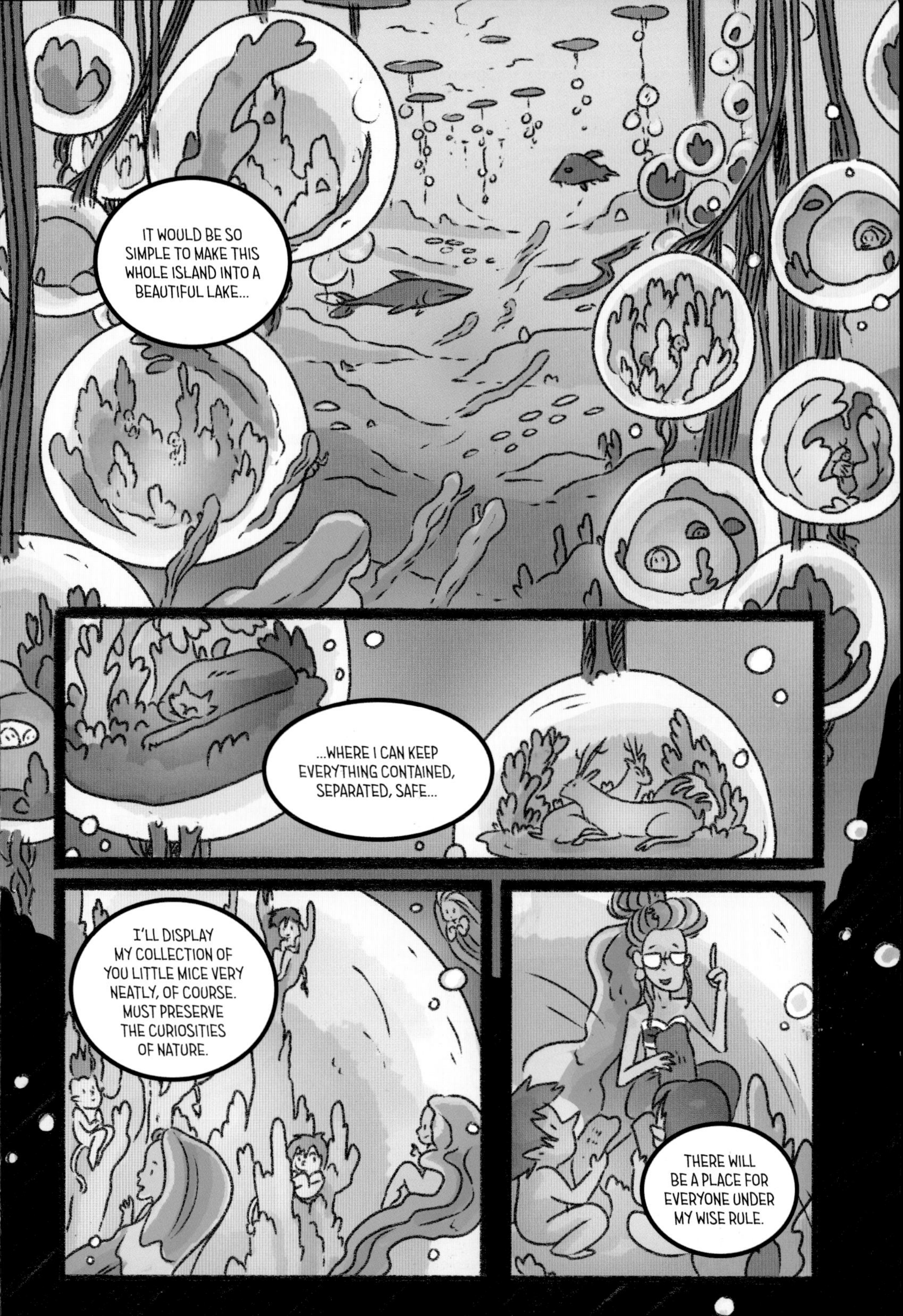
IT WOULD BE SO SIMPLE TO MAKE THIS WHOLE ISLAND INTO A BEAUTIFUL LAKE...
...WHERE I CAN KEEP EVERYTHING CONTAINED, SEPARATED, SAFE...
I'LL DISPLAY MY COLLECTION OF YOU LITTLE MICE VERY NEATLY, OF COURSE. MUST PRESERVE THE CURIOSITIES OF NATURE.
THERE WILL BE A PLACE FOR EVERYONE UNDER MY WISE RULE.

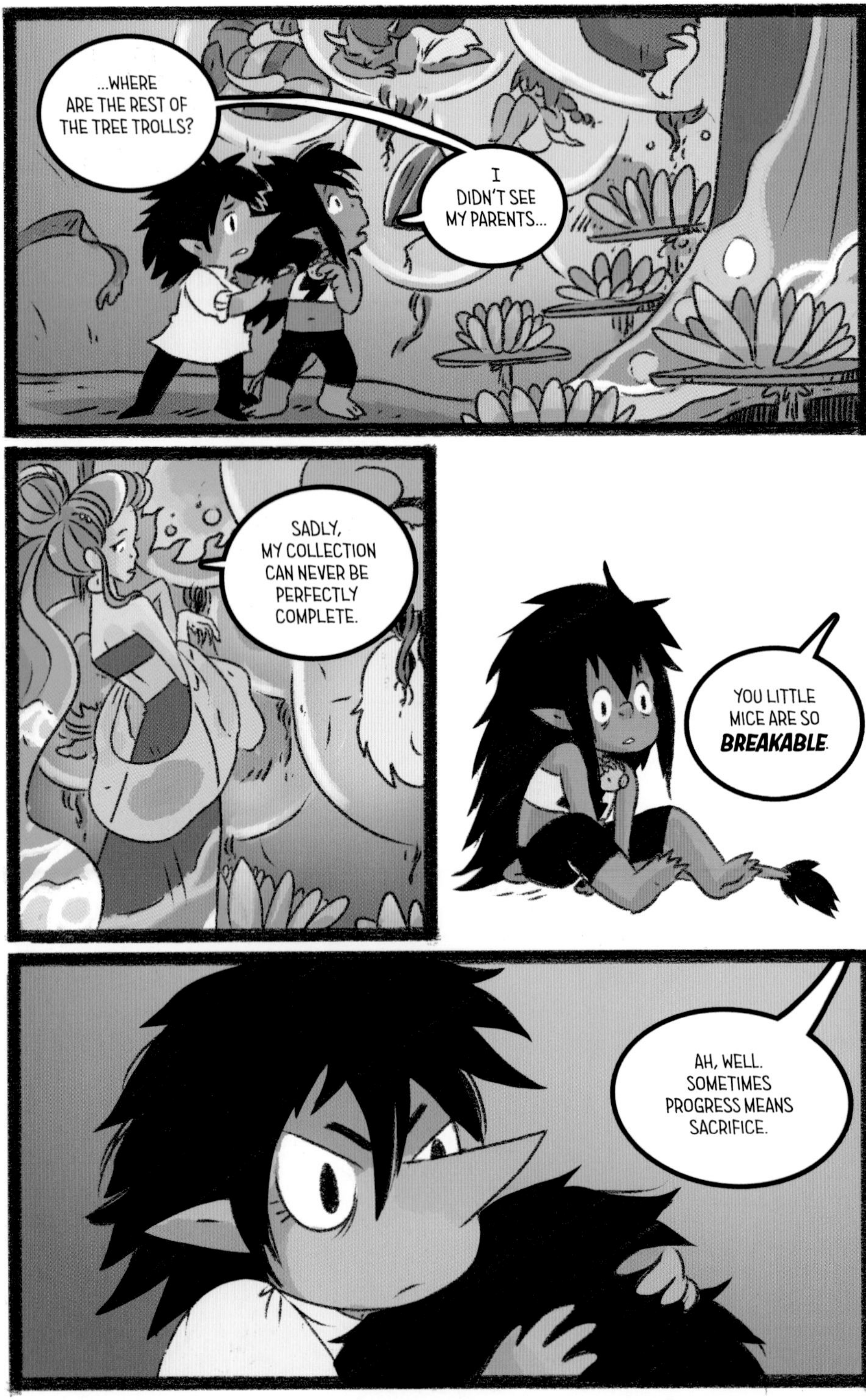
...WHERE ARE THE REST OF THE TREE TROLLS?
I DIDN'T SEE MY PARENTS...
SADLY, MY COLLECTION CAN NEVER BE PERFECTLY COMPLETE.
YOU LITTLE MICE ARE SO **BREAKABLE**.
AH, WELL. SOMETIMES PROGRESS MEANS SACRIFICE.

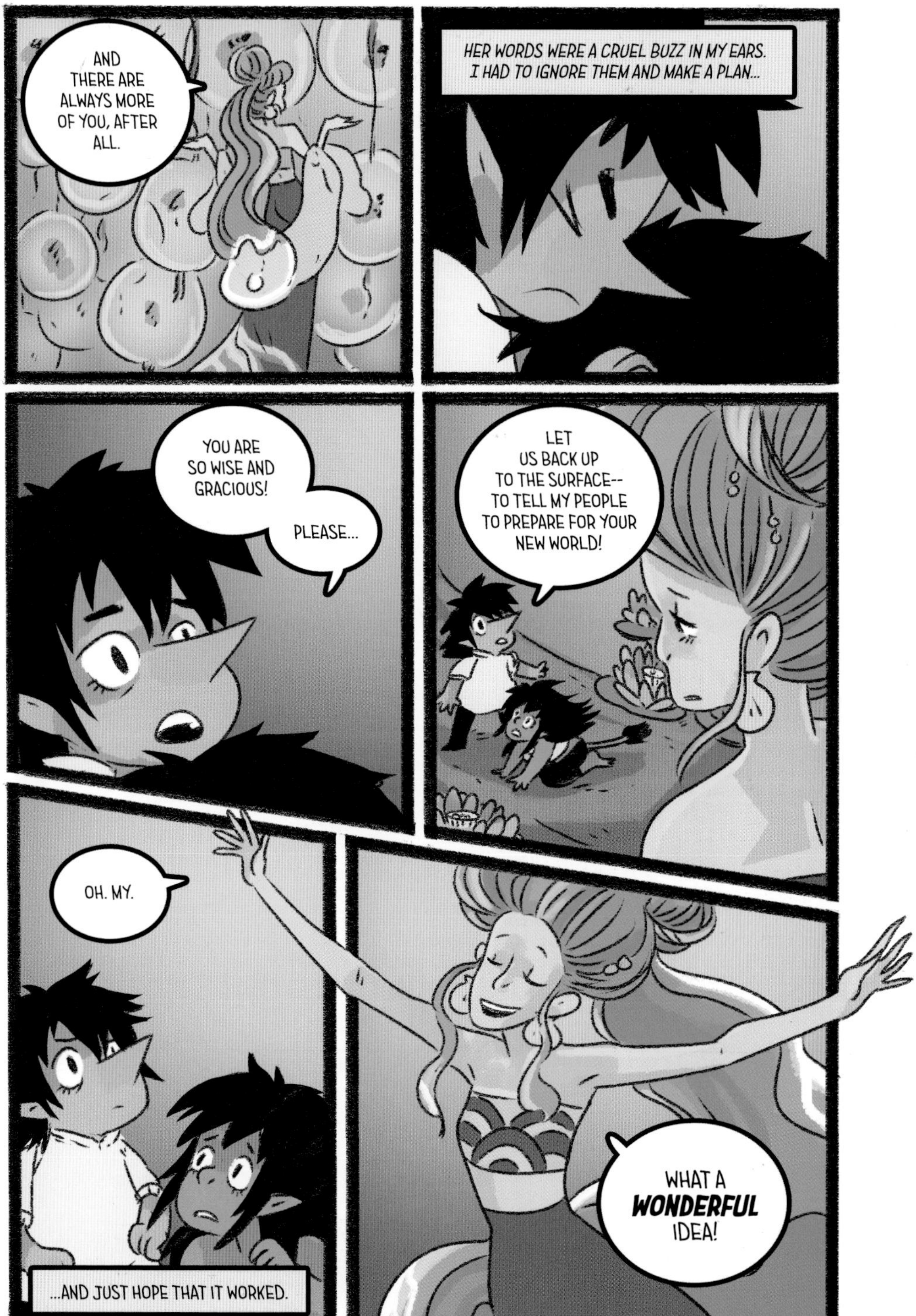
AND THERE ARE ALWAYS MORE OF YOU, AFTER ALL.
HER WORDS WERE A CRUEL BUZZ IN MY EARS. I HAD TO IGNORE THEM AND MAKE A PLAN...
YOU ARE SO WISE AND GRACIOUS!
PLEASE...
LET US BACK UP TO THE SURFACE-- TO TELL MY PEOPLE TO PREPARE FOR YOUR NEW WORLD!
OH. MY.
...AND JUST HOPE THAT IT WORKED.
WHAT A **WONDERFUL** IDEA!

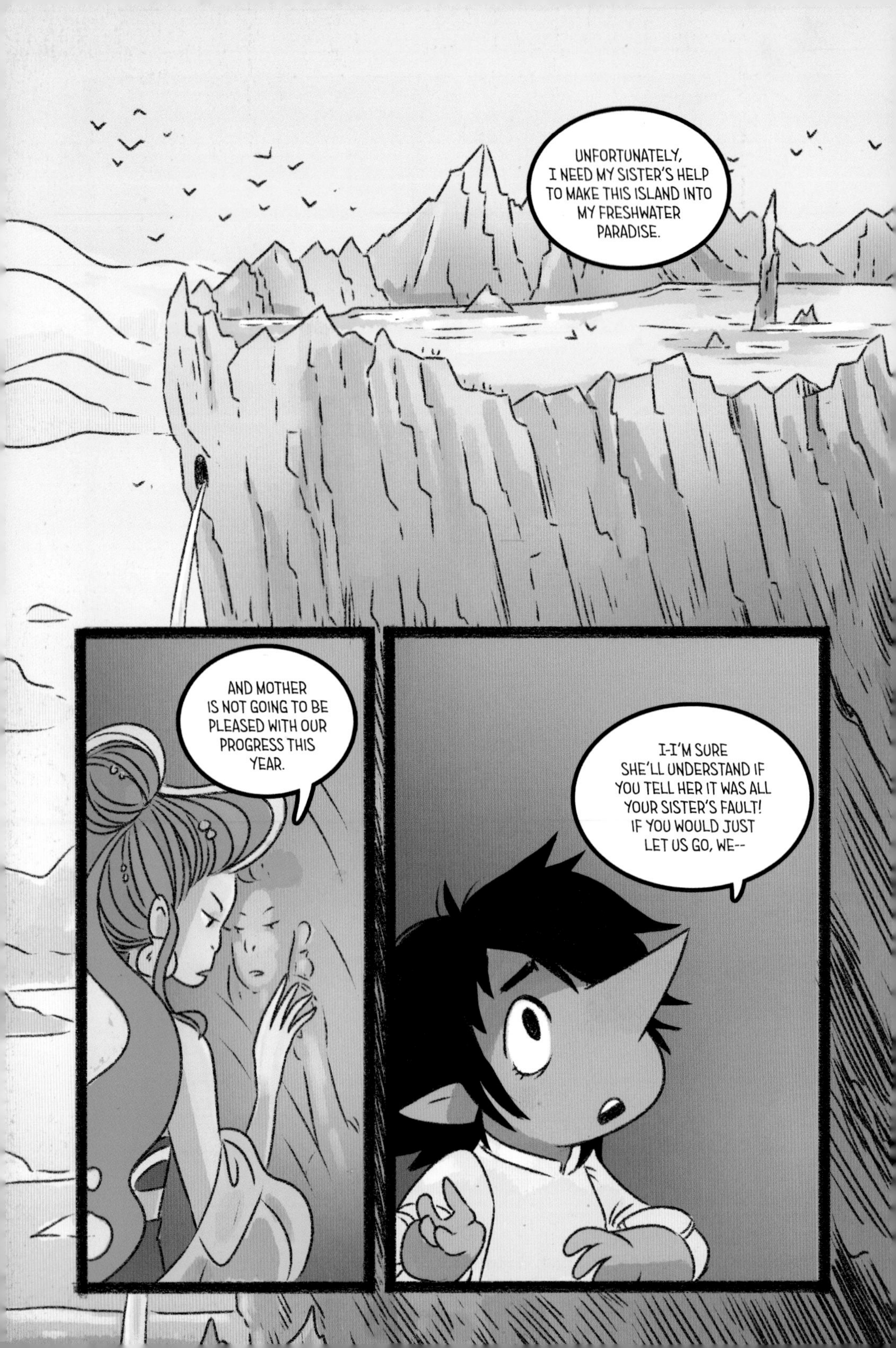
UNFORTUNATELY, I NEED MY SISTER'S HELP TO MAKE THIS ISLAND INTO MY FRESHWATER PARADISE.
AND MOTHER IS NOT GOING TO BE PLEASED WITH OUR PROGRESS THIS YEAR.
I-I'M SURE SHE'LL UNDERSTAND IF YOU TELL HER IT WAS ALL YOUR SISTER'S FAULT! IF YOU WOULD JUST LET US GO, WE--

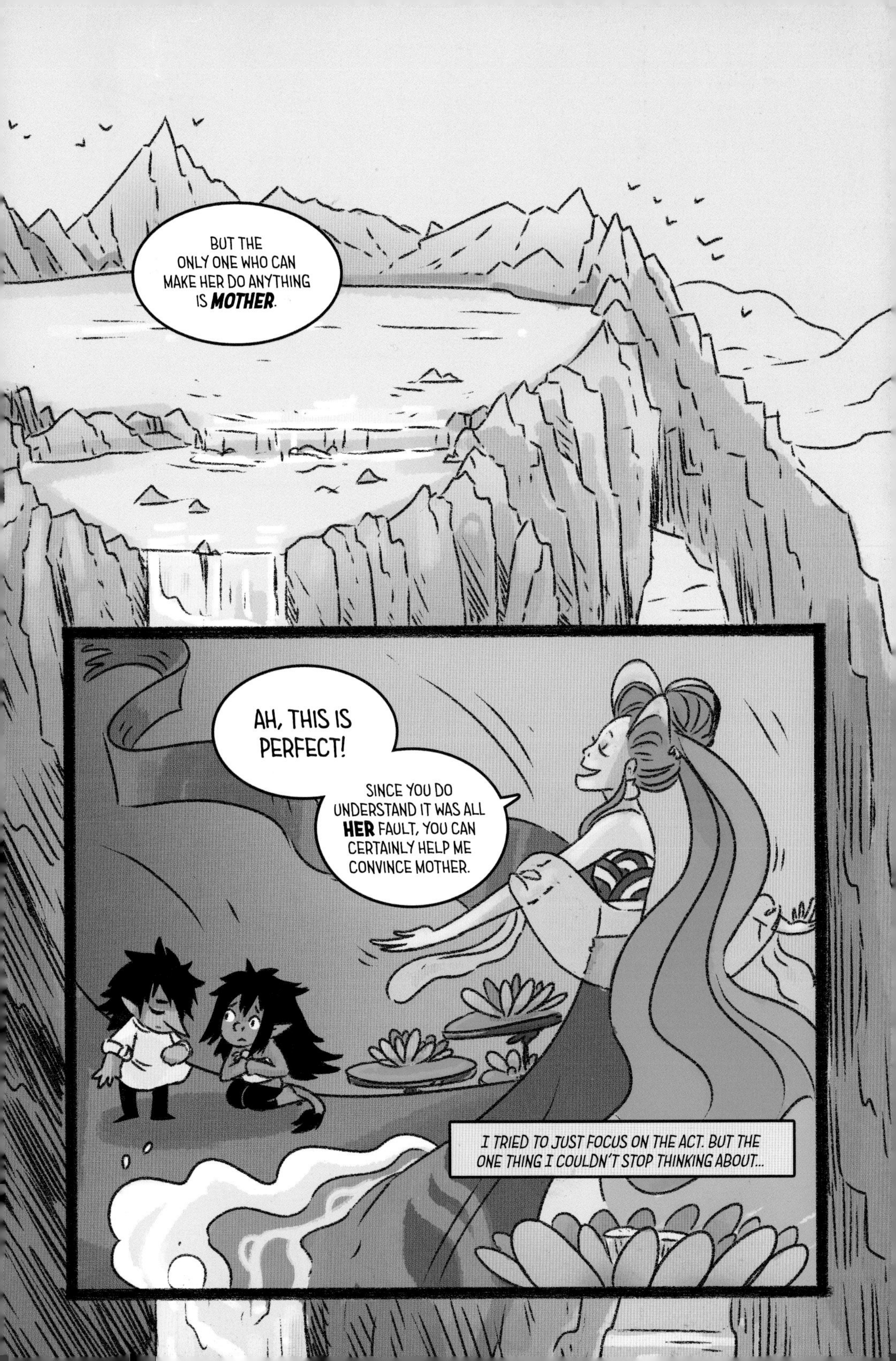
BUT THE ONLY ONE WHO CAN MAKE HER DO ANYTHING IS **MOTHER**.
AH, THIS IS PERFECT!
SINCE YOU DO UNDERSTAND IT WAS ALL **HER** FAULT, YOU CAN CERTAINLY HELP ME CONVINCE MOTHER.
I TRIED TO JUST FOCUS ON THE ACT. BUT THE ONE THING I COULDN'T STOP THINKING ABOUT...

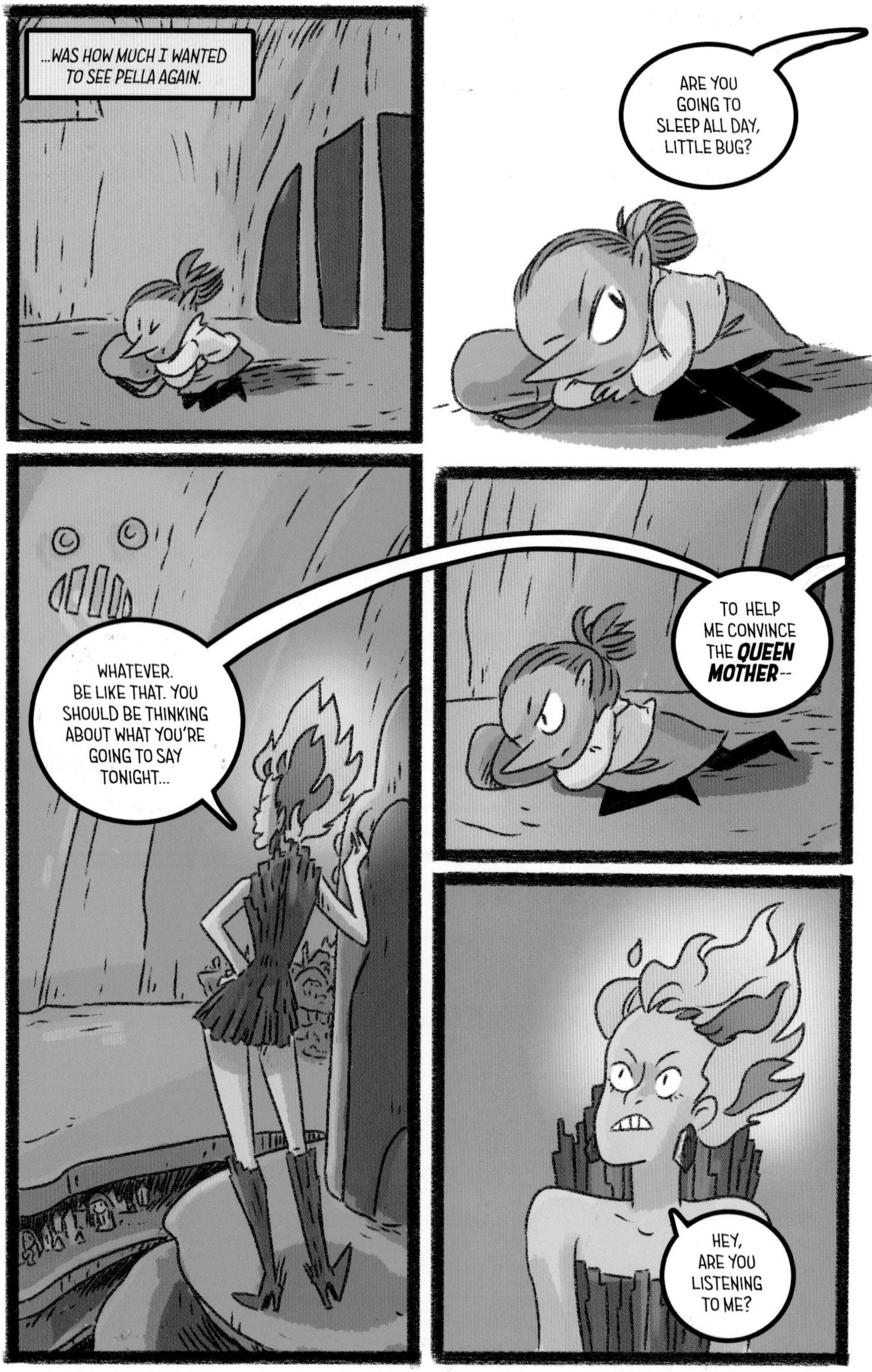
...WAS HOW MUCH I WANTED TO SEE PELLA AGAIN.
ARE YOU GOING TO SLEEP ALL DAY, LITTLE BUG?
WHATEVER. BE LIKE THAT. YOU SHOULD BE THINKING ABOUT WHAT YOU'RE GOING TO SAY TONIGHT...
TO HELP ME CONVINCE THE ***QUEEN MOTHER***--
HEY, ARE YOU LISTENING TO ME?

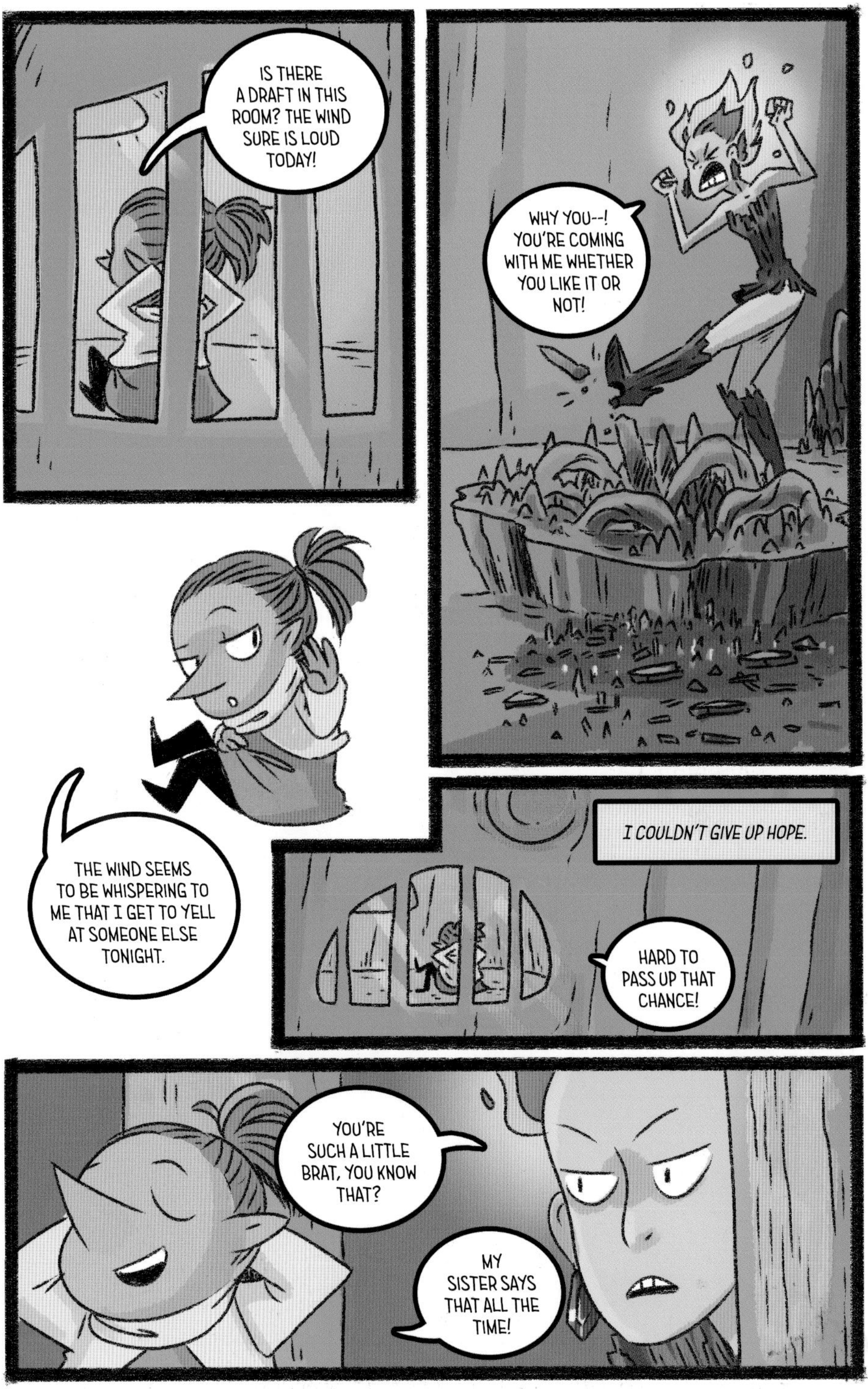
IS THERE A DRAFT IN THIS ROOM? THE WIND SURE IS LOUD TODAY!
WHY YOU--! YOU'RE COMING WITH ME WHETHER YOU LIKE IT OR NOT!
THE WIND SEEMS TO BE WHISPERING TO ME THAT I GET TO YELL AT SOMEONE ELSE TONIGHT.
I COULDN'T GIVE UP HOPE.
HARD TO PASS UP THAT CHANCE!
YOU'RE SUCH A LITTLE BRAT, YOU KNOW THAT?
MY SISTER SAYS THAT ALL THE TIME!

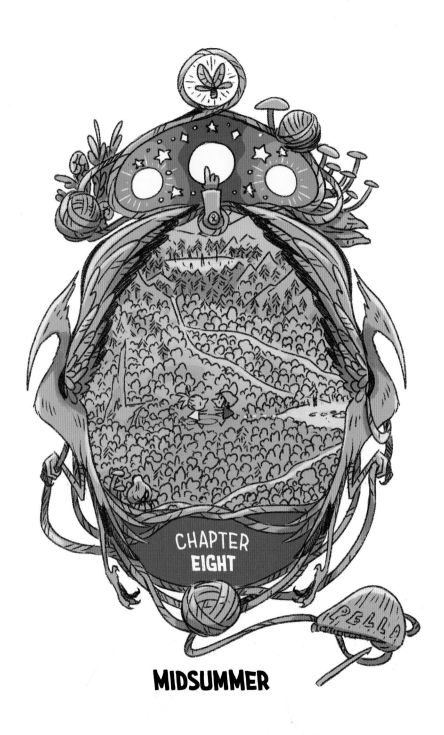

CHAPTER
EIGHT

MIDSUMMER

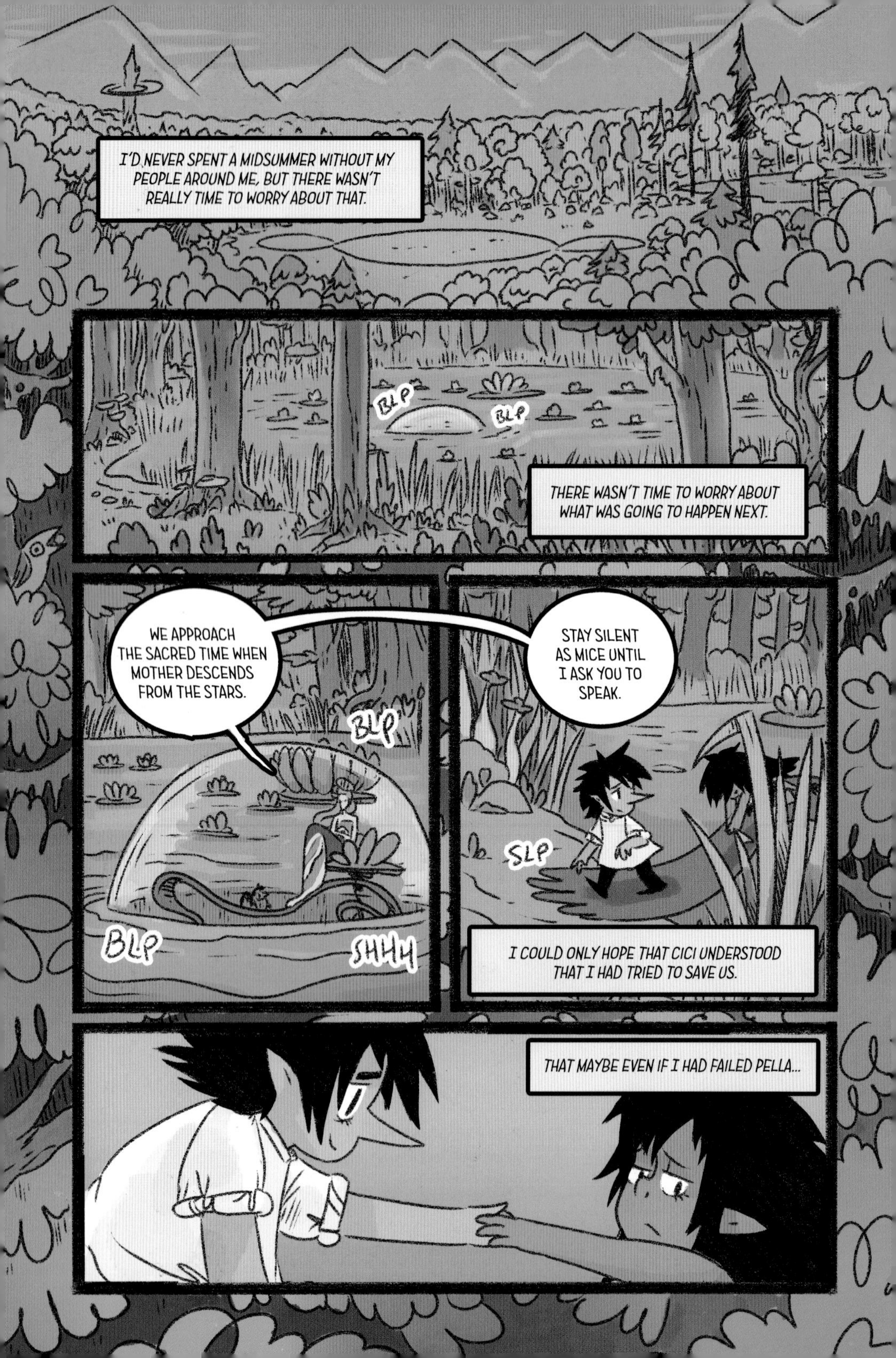
I'D NEVER SPENT A MIDSUMMER WITHOUT MY PEOPLE AROUND ME, BUT THERE WASN'T REALLY TIME TO WORRY ABOUT THAT.
BLP
BLP
THERE WASN'T TIME TO WORRY ABOUT WHAT WAS GOING TO HAPPEN NEXT.
WE APPROACH THE SACRED TIME WHEN MOTHER DESCENDS FROM THE STARS.
BLP
BLP
SHHH
STAY SILENT AS MICE UNTIL I ASK YOU TO SPEAK.
SLP
I COULD ONLY HOPE THAT CICI UNDERSTOOD THAT I HAD TRIED TO SAVE US.
THAT MAYBE EVEN IF I HAD FAILED PELLA...

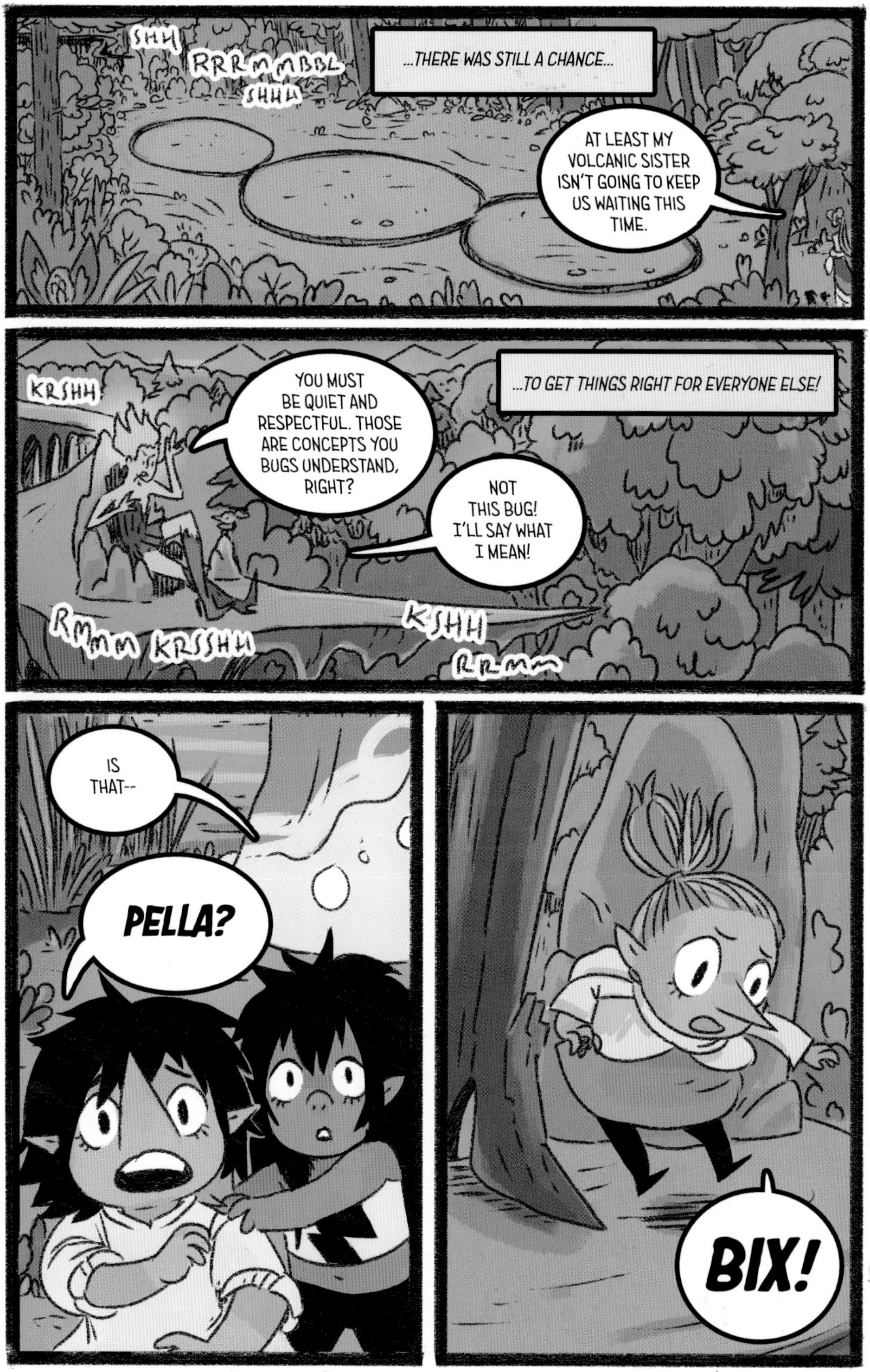
SHH
RRRMMBBL
SHHH
...THERE WAS STILL A CHANCE...
AT LEAST MY VOLCANIC SISTER ISN'T GOING TO KEEP US WAITING THIS TIME.
KRSHH
...TO GET THINGS RIGHT FOR EVERYONE ELSE!
YOU MUST BE QUIET AND RESPECTFUL. THOSE ARE CONCEPTS YOU BUGS UNDERSTAND, RIGHT?
NOT THIS BUG! I'LL SAY WHAT I MEAN!
RMMM KRSSHH
KSHH
RRMM
IS THAT--
PELLA?
BIX!

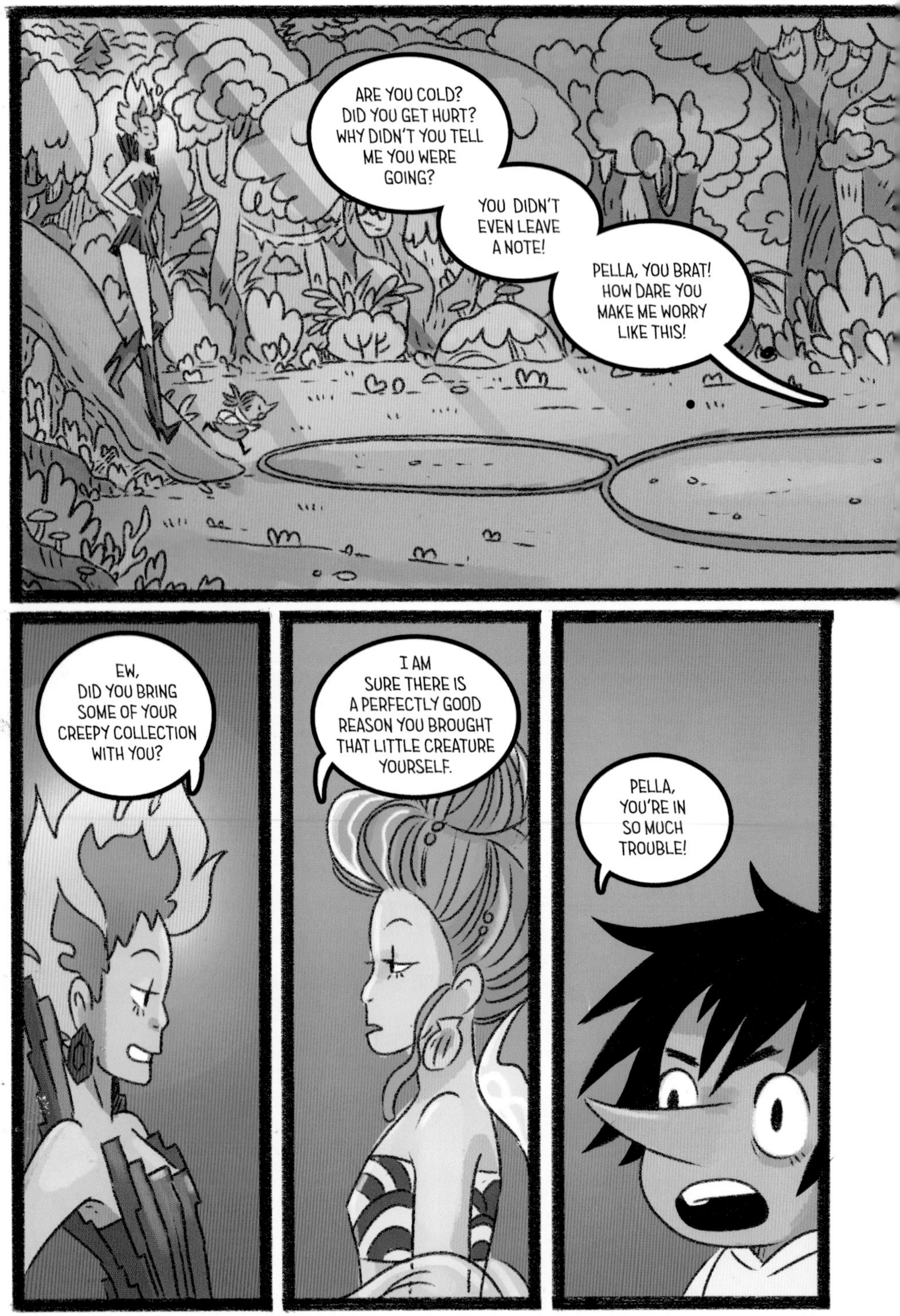
ARE YOU COLD? DID YOU GET HURT? WHY DIDN'T YOU TELL ME YOU WERE GOING?
YOU DIDN'T EVEN LEAVE A NOTE!
PELLA, YOU BRAT! HOW DARE YOU MAKE ME WORRY LIKE THIS!
EW, DID YOU BRING SOME OF YOUR CREEPY COLLECTION WITH YOU?
I AM SURE THERE IS A PERFECTLY GOOD REASON YOU BROUGHT THAT LITTLE CREATURE YOURSELF.
PELLA, YOU'RE IN SO MUCH TROUBLE!

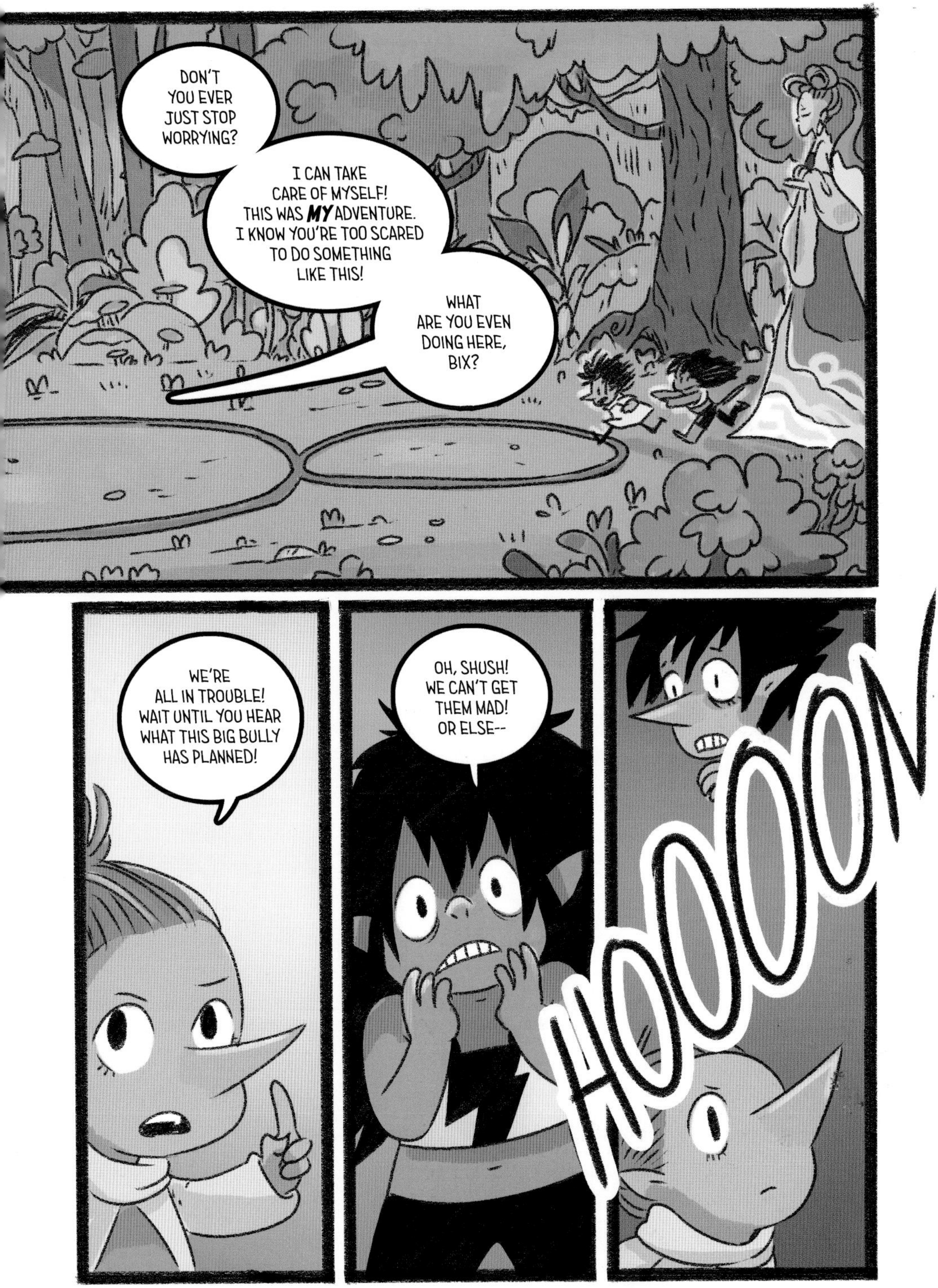
DON'T YOU EVER JUST STOP WORRYING?
I CAN TAKE CARE OF MYSELF! THIS WAS MY ADVENTURE. I KNOW YOU'RE TOO SCARED TO DO SOMETHING LIKE THIS!
WHAT ARE YOU EVEN DOING HERE, BIX?
WE'RE ALL IN TROUBLE! WAIT UNTIL YOU HEAR WHAT THIS BIG BULLY HAS PLANNED!
OH, SHUSH! WE CAN'T GET THEM MAD! OR ELSE--
HOOOOO

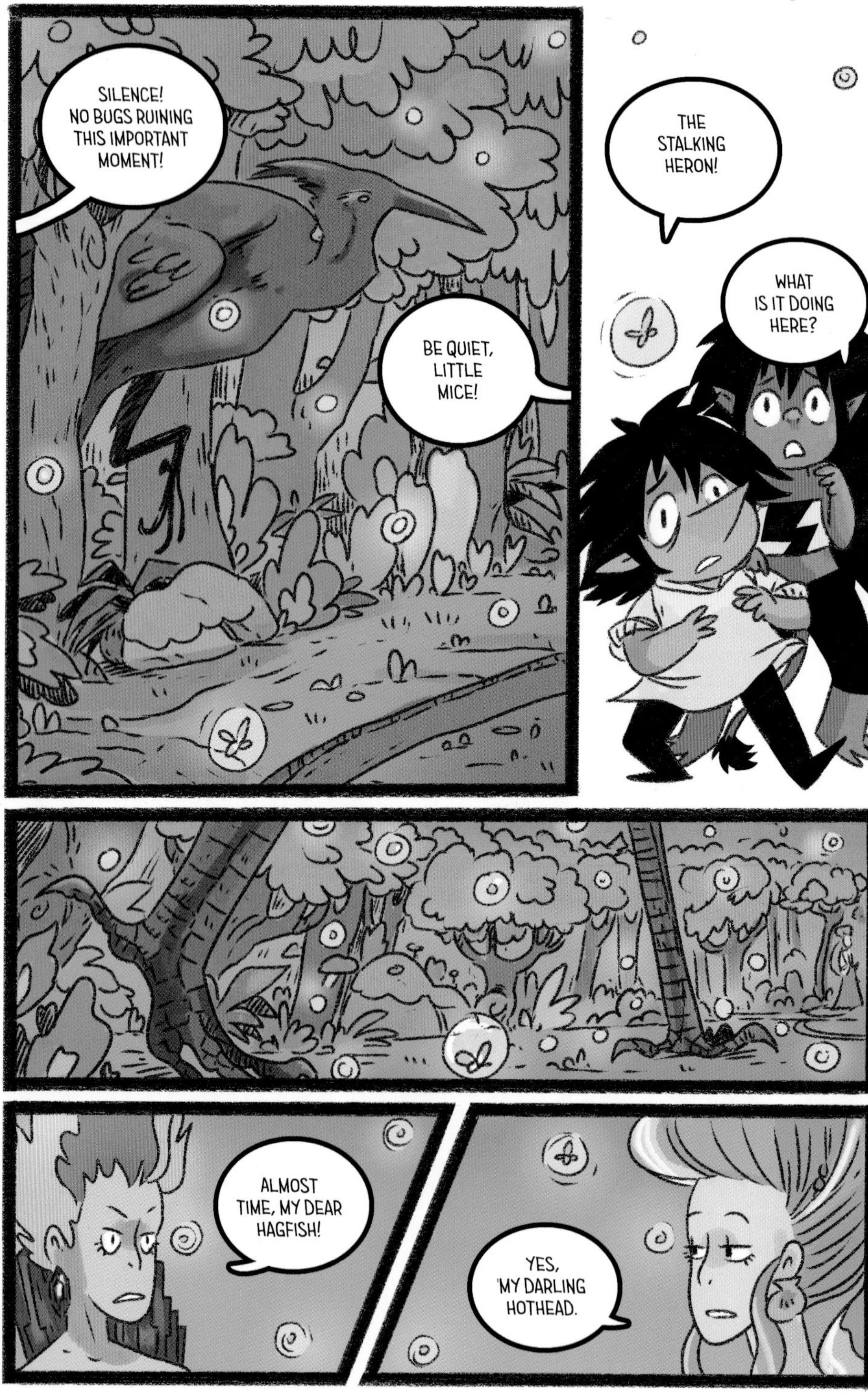
SILENCE! NO BUGS RUINING THIS IMPORTANT MOMENT!
BE QUIET, LITTLE MICE!
THE STALKING HERON!
WHAT IS IT DOING HERE?
ALMOST TIME, MY DEAR HAGFISH!
YES, MY DARLING HOTHEAD.

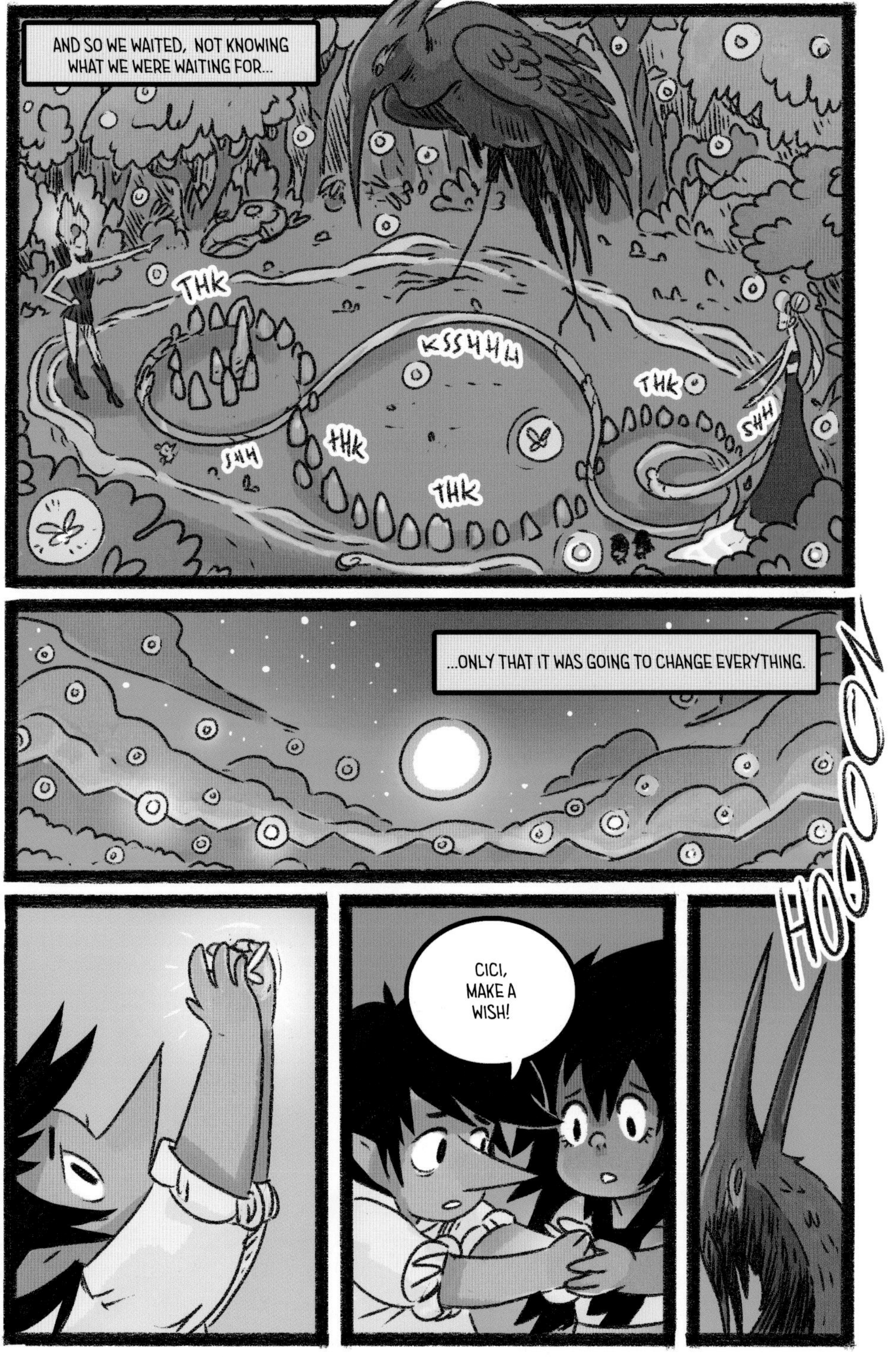

AND SO WE WAITED, NOT KNOWING WHAT WE WERE WAITING FOR...
THK
KSSHHH
THK
SHH
THK
SHH
THK
...ONLY THAT IT WAS GOING TO CHANGE EVERYTHING.
HOOOOZ
CICI, MAKE A WISH!

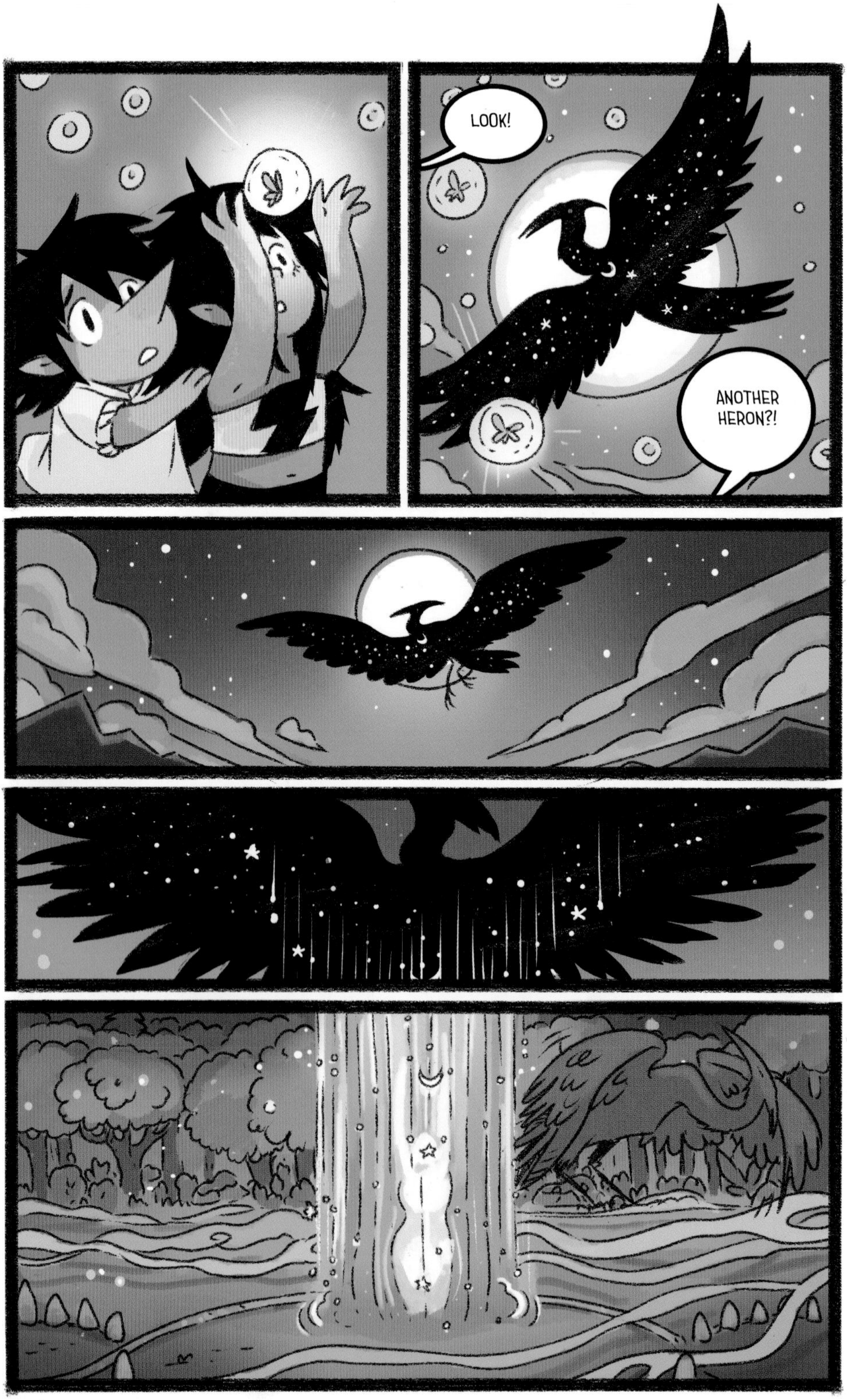
LOOK!
ANOTHER HERON?!

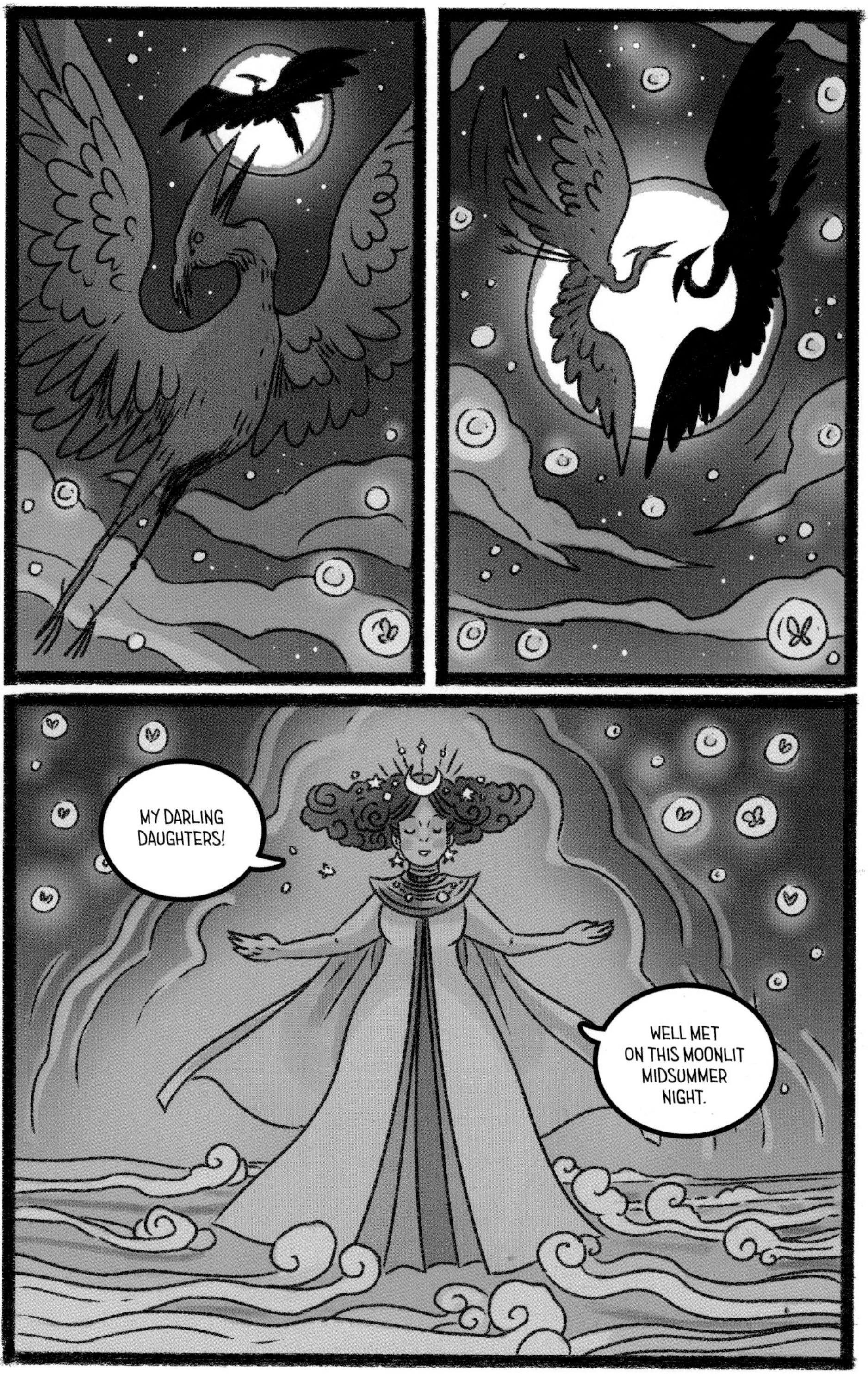
MY DARLING DAUGHTERS!
WELL MET ON THIS MOONLIT MIDSUMMER NIGHT.

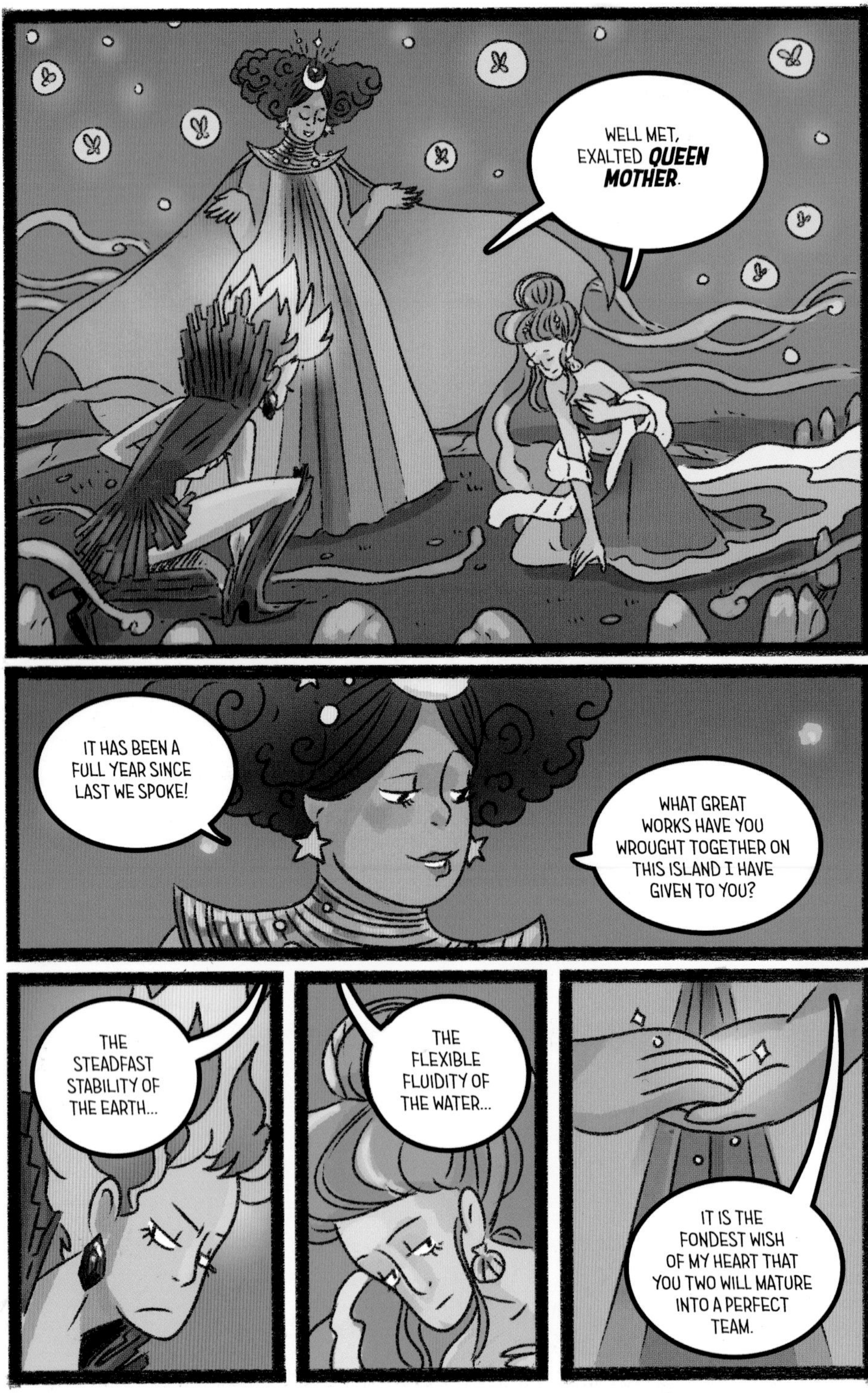

WELL MET, EXALTED **QUEEN MOTHER**.
IT HAS BEEN A FULL YEAR SINCE LAST WE SPOKE!
WHAT GREAT WORKS HAVE YOU WROUGHT TOGETHER ON THIS ISLAND I HAVE GIVEN TO YOU?
THE STEADFAST STABILITY OF THE EARTH...
THE FLEXIBLE FLUIDITY OF THE WATER...
IT IS THE FONDEST WISH OF MY HEART THAT YOU TWO WILL MATURE INTO A PERFECT TEAM.

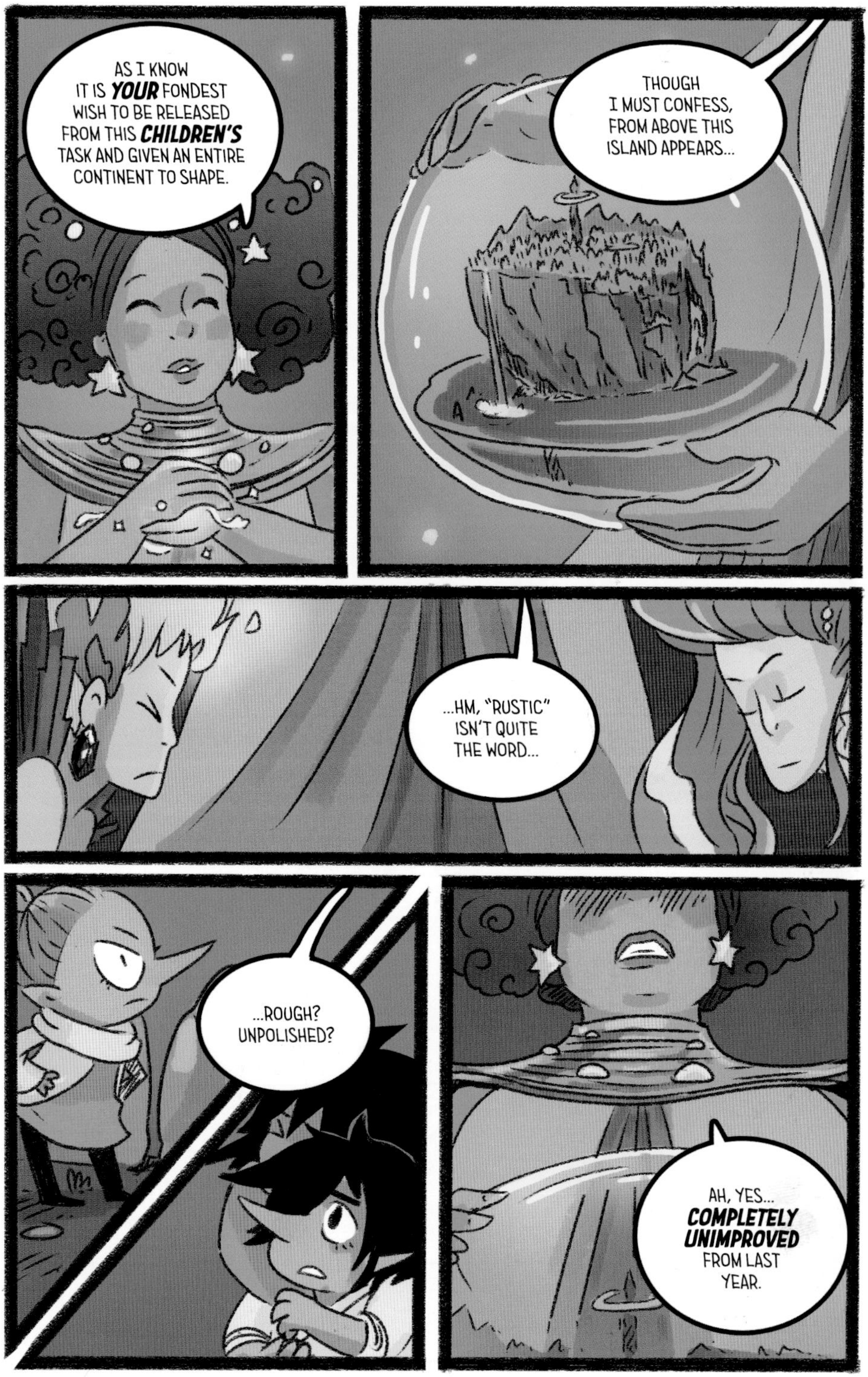
AS I KNOW IT IS **YOUR** FONDEST WISH TO BE RELEASED FROM THIS **CHILDREN'S** TASK AND GIVEN AN ENTIRE CONTINENT TO SHAPE.
THOUGH I MUST CONFESS, FROM ABOVE THIS ISLAND APPEARS...
...HM, "RUSTIC" ISN'T QUITE THE WORD...
...ROUGH? UNPOLISHED?
AH, YES... **COMPLETELY UNIMPROVED** FROM LAST YEAR.

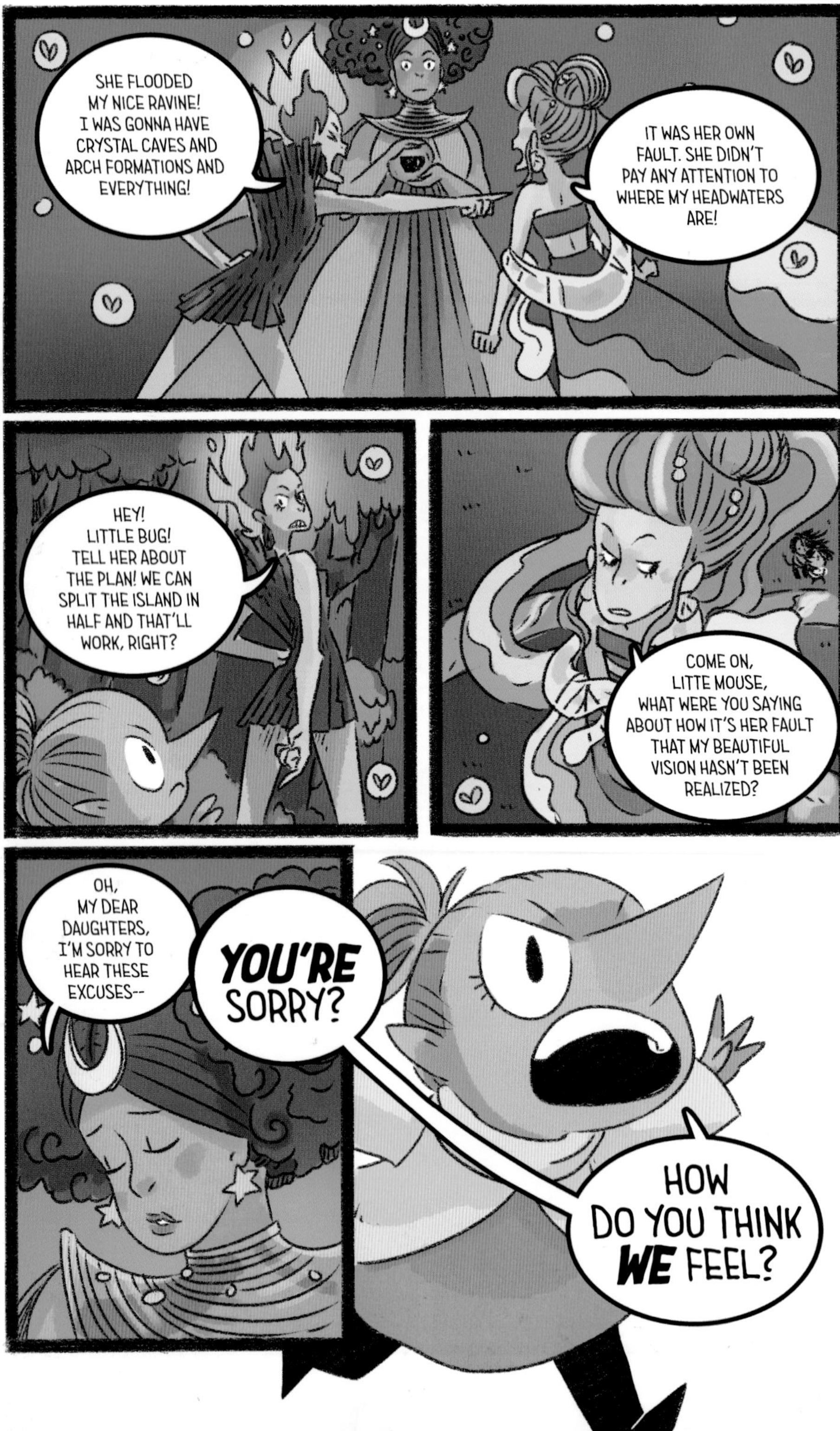
SHE FLOODED MY NICE RAVINE! I WAS GONNA HAVE CRYSTAL CAVES AND ARCH FORMATIONS AND EVERYTHING!
IT WAS HER OWN FAULT. SHE DIDN'T PAY ANY ATTENTION TO WHERE MY HEADWATERS ARE!
HEY! LITTLE BUG! TELL HER ABOUT THE PLAN! WE CAN SPLIT THE ISLAND IN HALF AND THAT'LL WORK, RIGHT?
COME ON, LITTE MOUSE, WHAT WERE YOU SAYING ABOUT HOW IT'S HER FAULT THAT MY BEAUTIFUL VISION HASN'T BEEN REALIZED?
OH, MY DEAR DAUGHTERS, I'M SORRY TO HEAR THESE EXCUSES--
YOU'RE SORRY?
HOW DO YOU THINK ***WE*** FEEL?

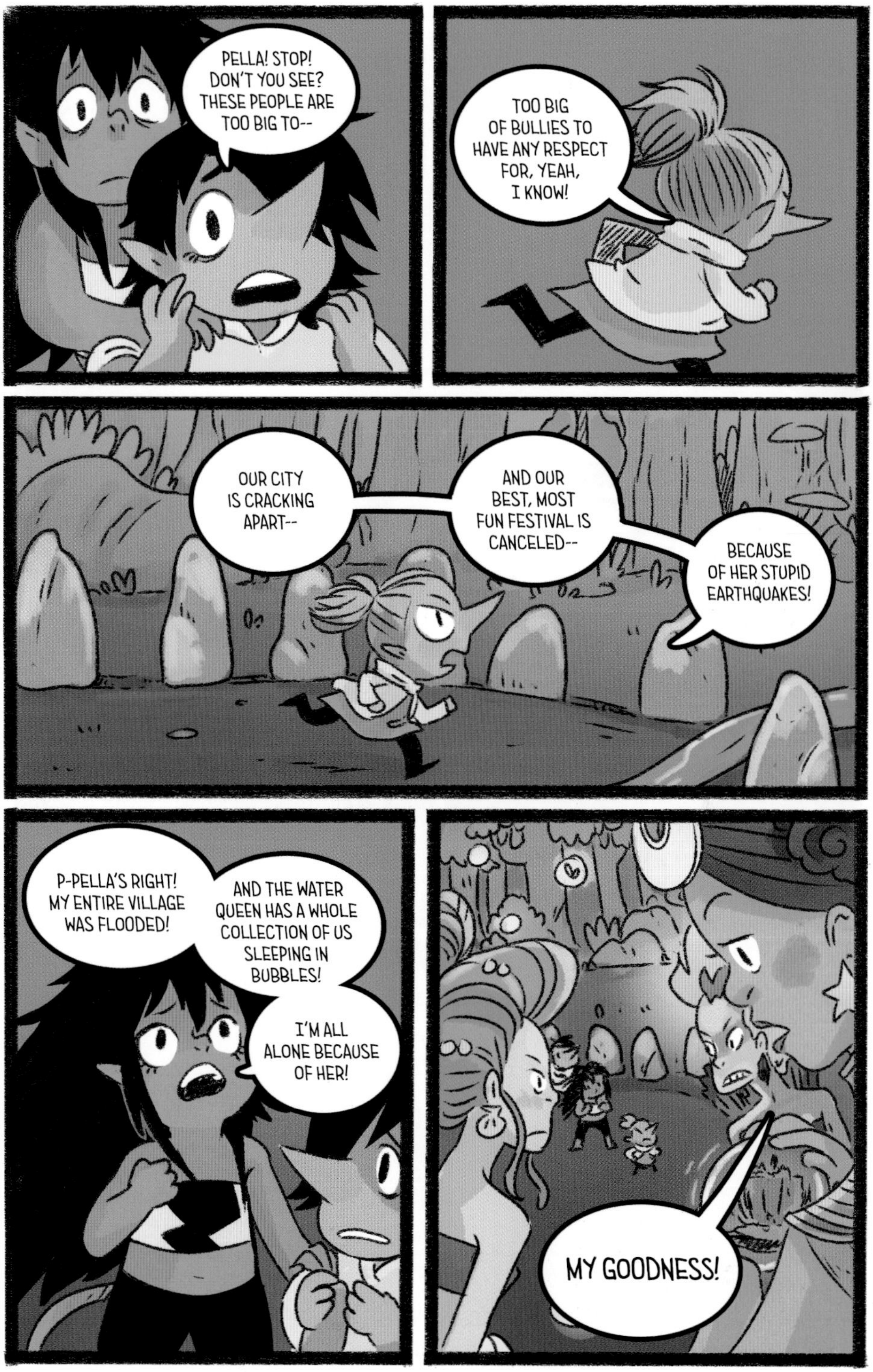

PELLA! STOP! DON'T YOU SEE? THESE PEOPLE ARE TOO BIG TO--
TOO BIG OF BULLIES TO HAVE ANY RESPECT FOR, YEAH, I KNOW!
OUR CITY IS CRACKING APART--
AND OUR BEST, MOST FUN FESTIVAL IS CANCELED--
BECAUSE OF HER STUPID EARTHQUAKES!
P-PELLA'S RIGHT! MY ENTIRE VILLAGE WAS FLOODED!
AND THE WATER QUEEN HAS A WHOLE COLLECTION OF US SLEEPING IN BUBBLES!
I'M ALL ALONE BECAUSE OF HER!
MY GOODNESS!

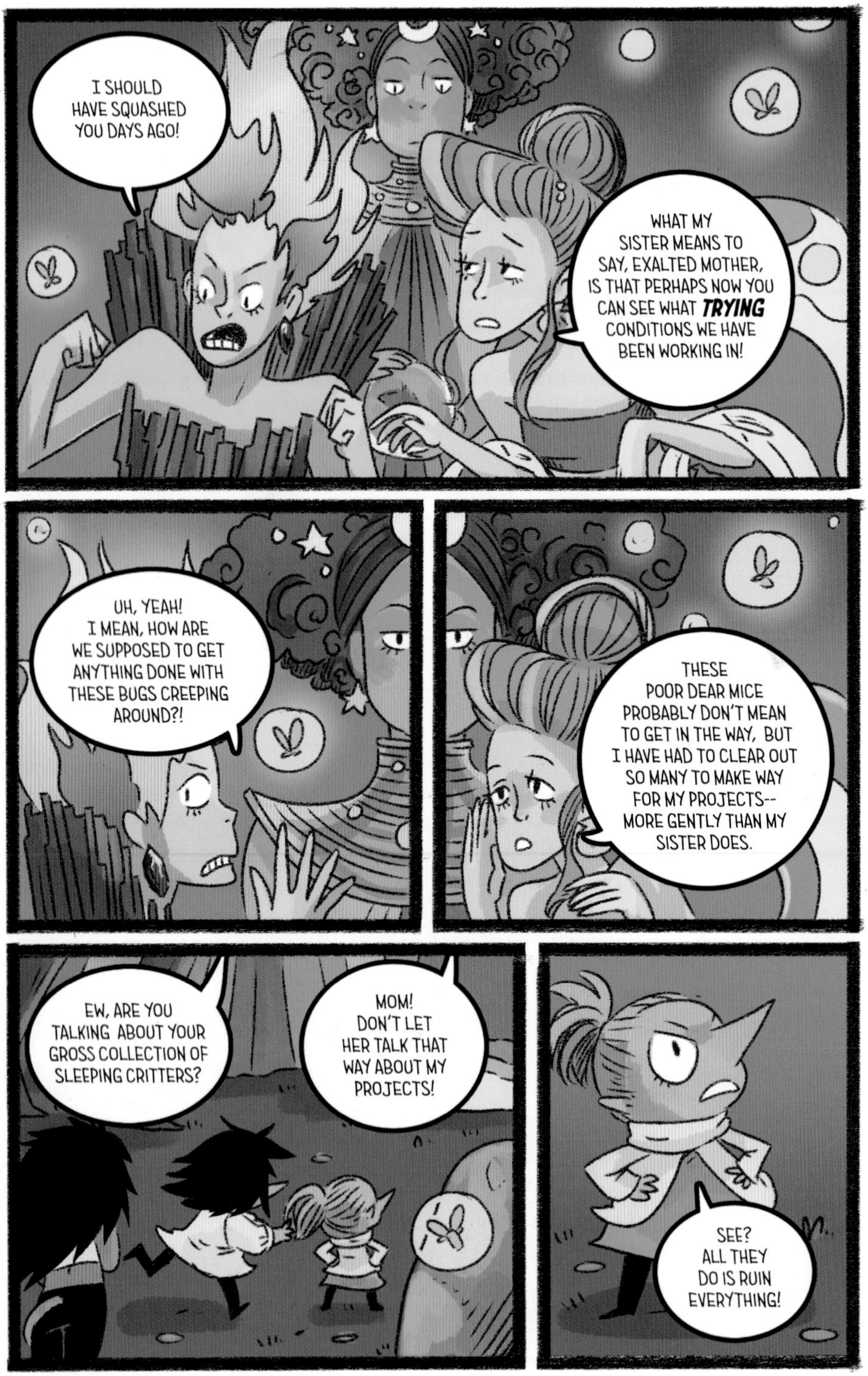
I SHOULD HAVE SQUASHED YOU DAYS AGO!
WHAT MY SISTER MEANS TO SAY, EXALTED MOTHER, IS THAT PERHAPS NOW YOU CAN SEE WHAT **TRYING** CONDITIONS WE HAVE BEEN WORKING IN!
UH, YEAH! I MEAN, HOW ARE WE SUPPOSED TO GET ANYTHING DONE WITH THESE BUGS CREEPING AROUND?!
THESE POOR DEAR MICE PROBABLY DON'T MEAN TO GET IN THE WAY, BUT I HAVE HAD TO CLEAR OUT SO MANY TO MAKE WAY FOR MY PROJECTS-- MORE GENTLY THAN MY SISTER DOES.
EW, ARE YOU TALKING ABOUT YOUR GROSS COLLECTION OF SLEEPING CRITTERS?
MOM! DON'T LET HER TALK THAT WAY ABOUT MY PROJECTS!
SEE? ALL THEY DO IS RUIN EVERYTHING!

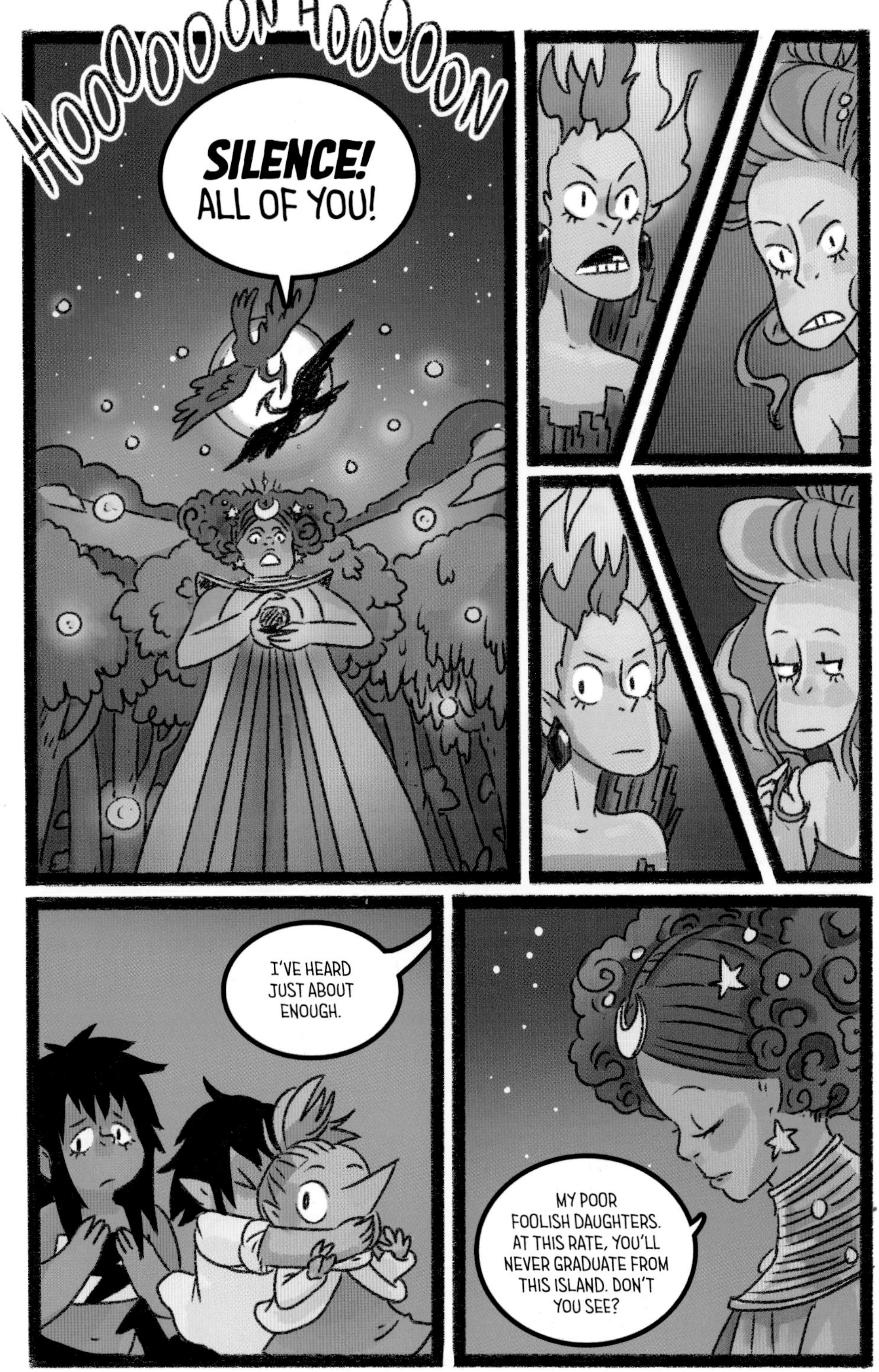
HOOOOOON HOOOOOON
SILENCE! ALL OF YOU!
I'VE HEARD JUST ABOUT ENOUGH.
MY POOR FOOLISH DAUGHTERS. AT THIS RATE, YOU'LL NEVER GRADUATE FROM THIS ISLAND. DON'T YOU SEE?

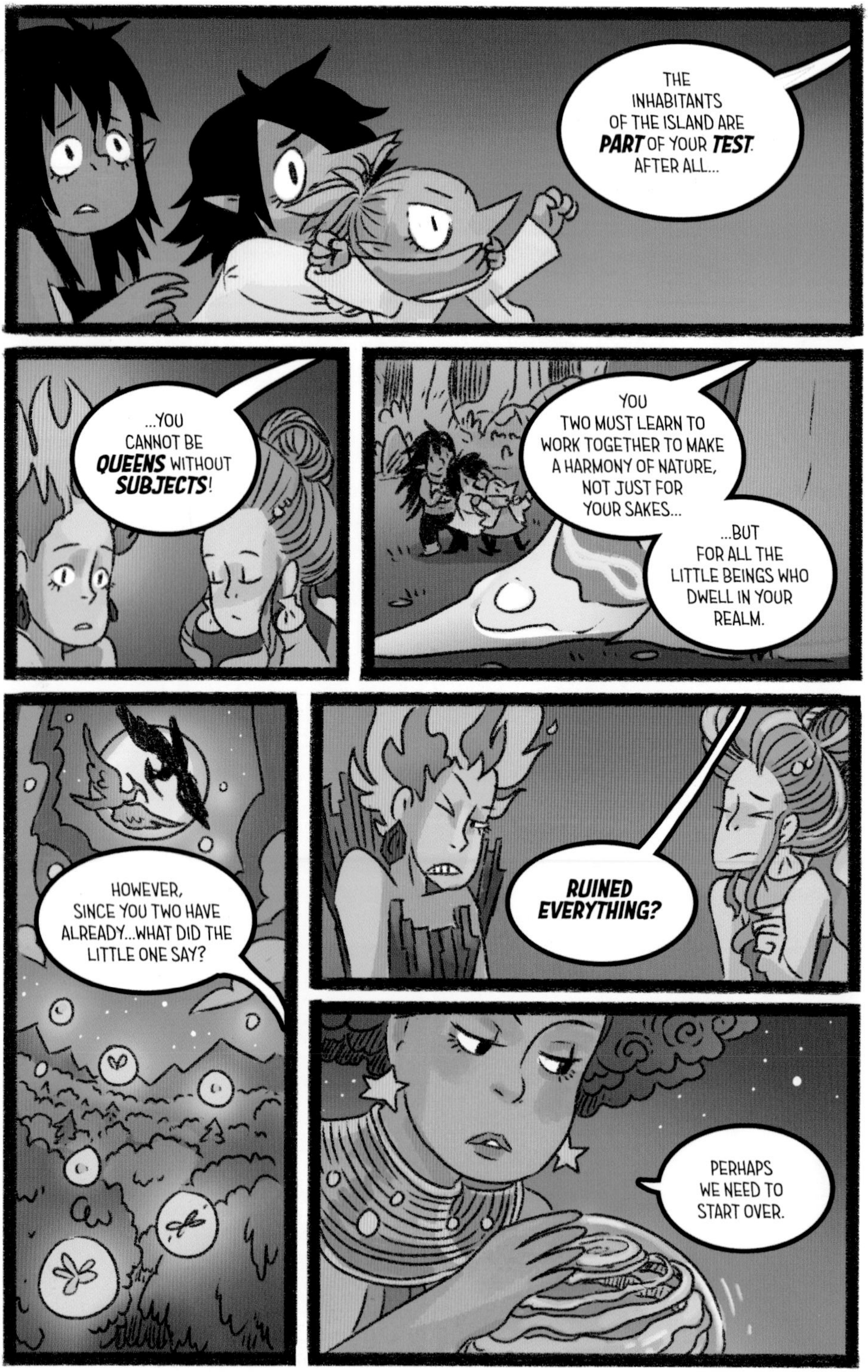
THE INHABITANTS OF THE ISLAND ARE **PART** OF YOUR **TEST**. AFTER ALL...
...YOU CANNOT BE **QUEENS** WITHOUT **SUBJECTS**!
YOU TWO MUST LEARN TO WORK TOGETHER TO MAKE A HARMONY OF NATURE, NOT JUST FOR YOUR SAKES...
...BUT FOR ALL THE LITTLE BEINGS WHO DWELL IN YOUR REALM.
HOWEVER, SINCE YOU TWO HAVE ALREADY...WHAT DID THE LITTLE ONE SAY?
RUINED EVERYTHING?
PERHAPS WE NEED TO START OVER.

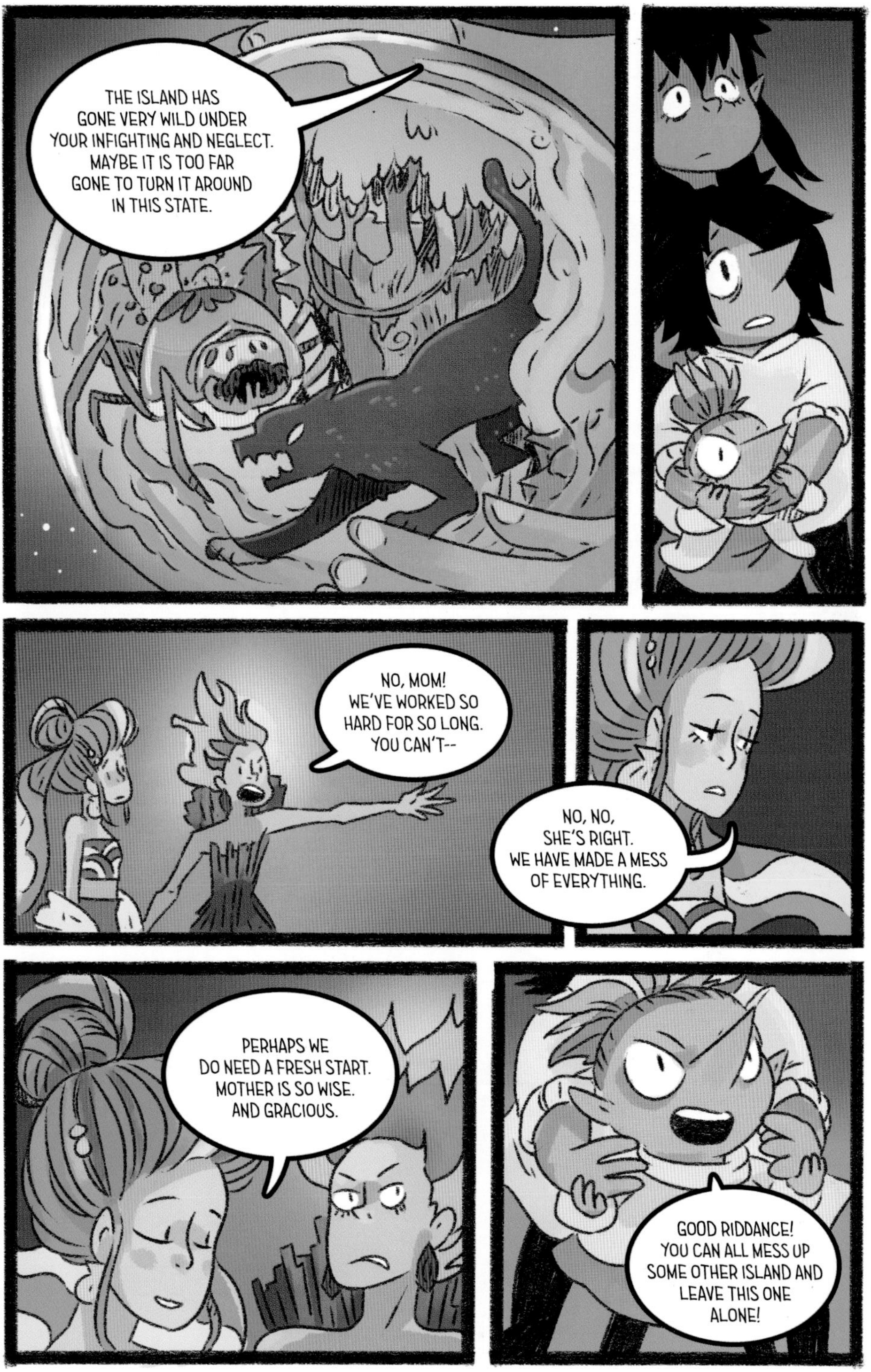
THE ISLAND HAS GONE VERY WILD UNDER YOUR INFIGHTING AND NEGLECT. MAYBE IT IS TOO FAR GONE TO TURN IT AROUND IN THIS STATE.
NO, MOM! WE'VE WORKED SO HARD FOR SO LONG. YOU CAN'T--
NO, NO, SHE'S RIGHT. WE HAVE MADE A MESS OF EVERYTHING.
PERHAPS WE DO NEED A FRESH START. MOTHER IS SO WISE. AND GRACIOUS.
GOOD RIDDANCE! YOU CAN ALL MESS UP SOME OTHER ISLAND AND LEAVE THIS ONE ALONE!

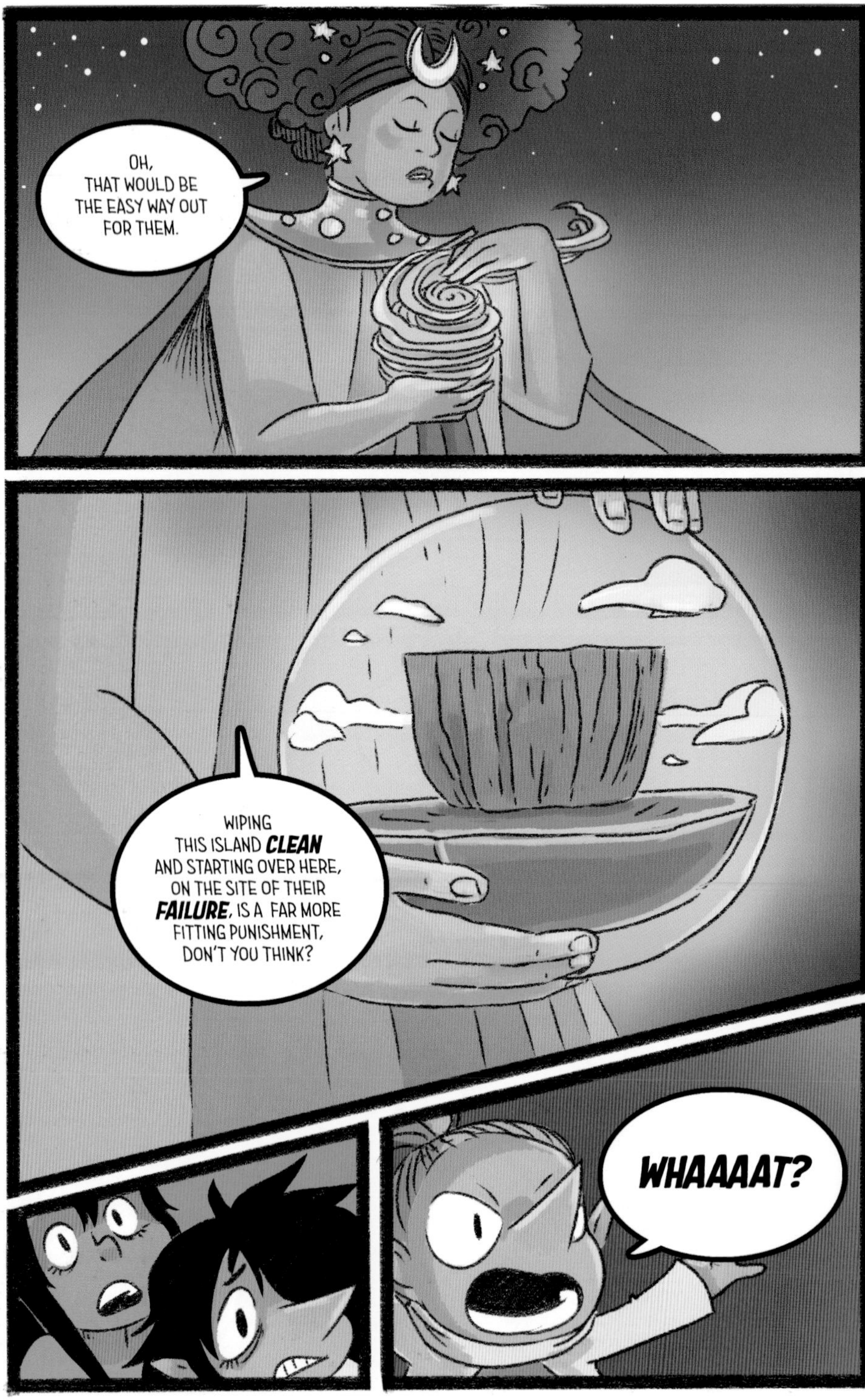
OH, THAT WOULD BE THE EASY WAY OUT FOR THEM.
WIPING THIS ISLAND **CLEAN** AND STARTING OVER HERE, ON THE SITE OF THEIR **FAILURE**, IS A FAR MORE FITTING PUNISHMENT, DON'T YOU THINK?
WHAAAAT?

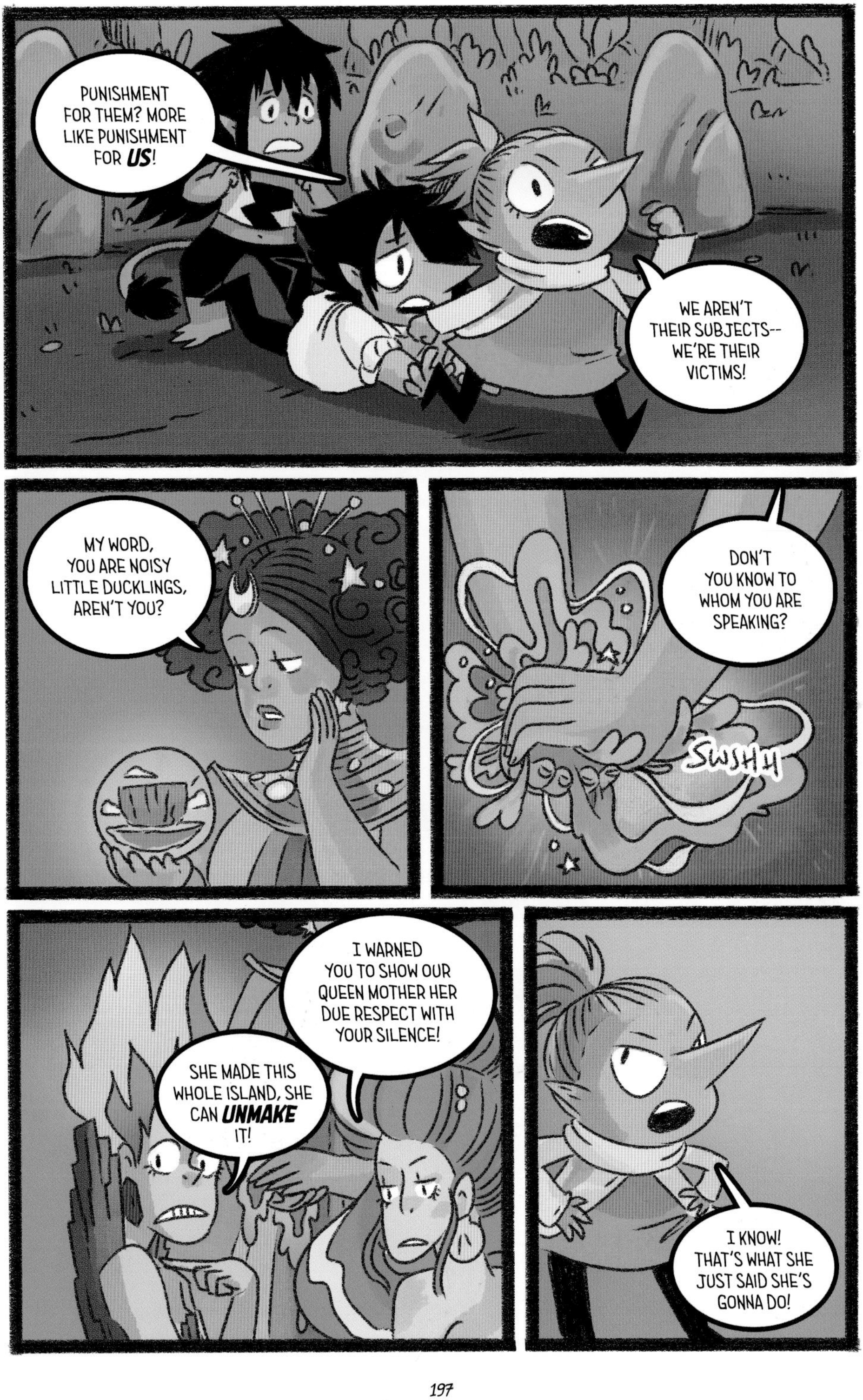
PUNISHMENT FOR THEM? MORE LIKE PUNISHMENT FOR **US**!
WE AREN'T THEIR SUBJECTS-- WE'RE THEIR VICTIMS!
MY WORD, YOU ARE NOISY LITTLE DUCKLINGS, AREN'T YOU?
DON'T YOU KNOW TO WHOM YOU ARE SPEAKING?
SWSHH
I WARNED YOU TO SHOW OUR QUEEN MOTHER HER DUE RESPECT WITH YOUR SILENCE!
SHE MADE THIS WHOLE ISLAND, SHE CAN **UNMAKE** IT!
I KNOW! THAT'S WHAT SHE JUST SAID SHE'S GONNA DO!

MY DAUGHTERS NEED TO LEARN TO BE GOOD QUEENS OF NATURE, TO LEAD THEIR NYMPHS AND CREATE IN HARMONY WITH EACH OTHER...

...AND I KNOW NO BETTER TEACHER THAN **EXPERIENCE** TO TEMPER THEM.

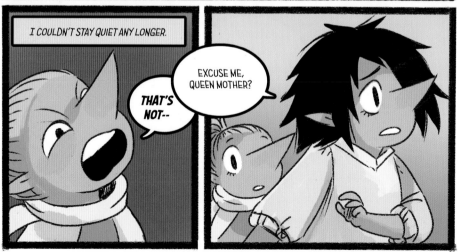

I COULDN'T STAY QUIET ANY LONGER.

EXCUSE ME, QUEEN MOTHER?

THAT'S NOT--

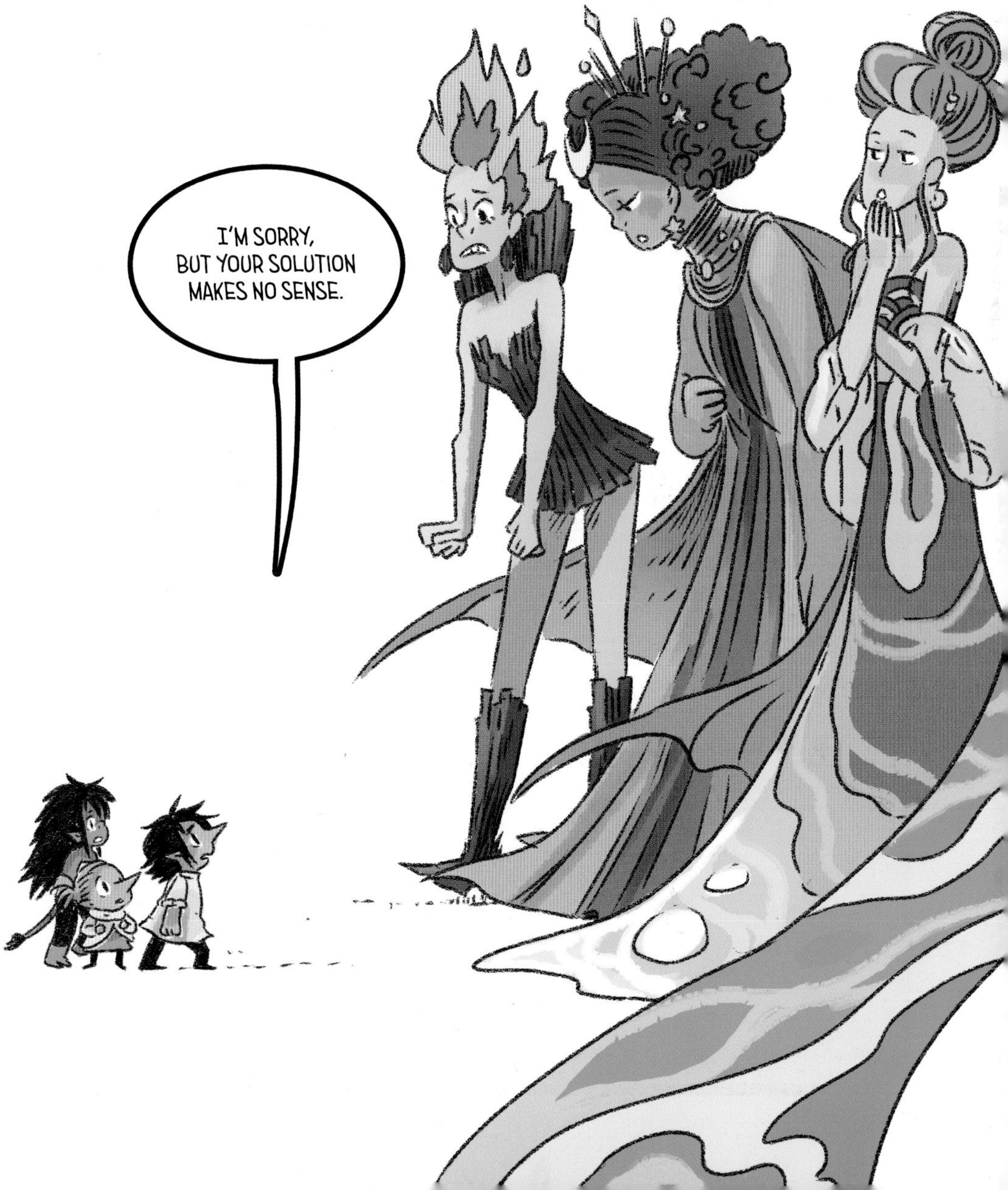
I'M SORRY, BUT YOUR SOLUTION MAKES NO SENSE.

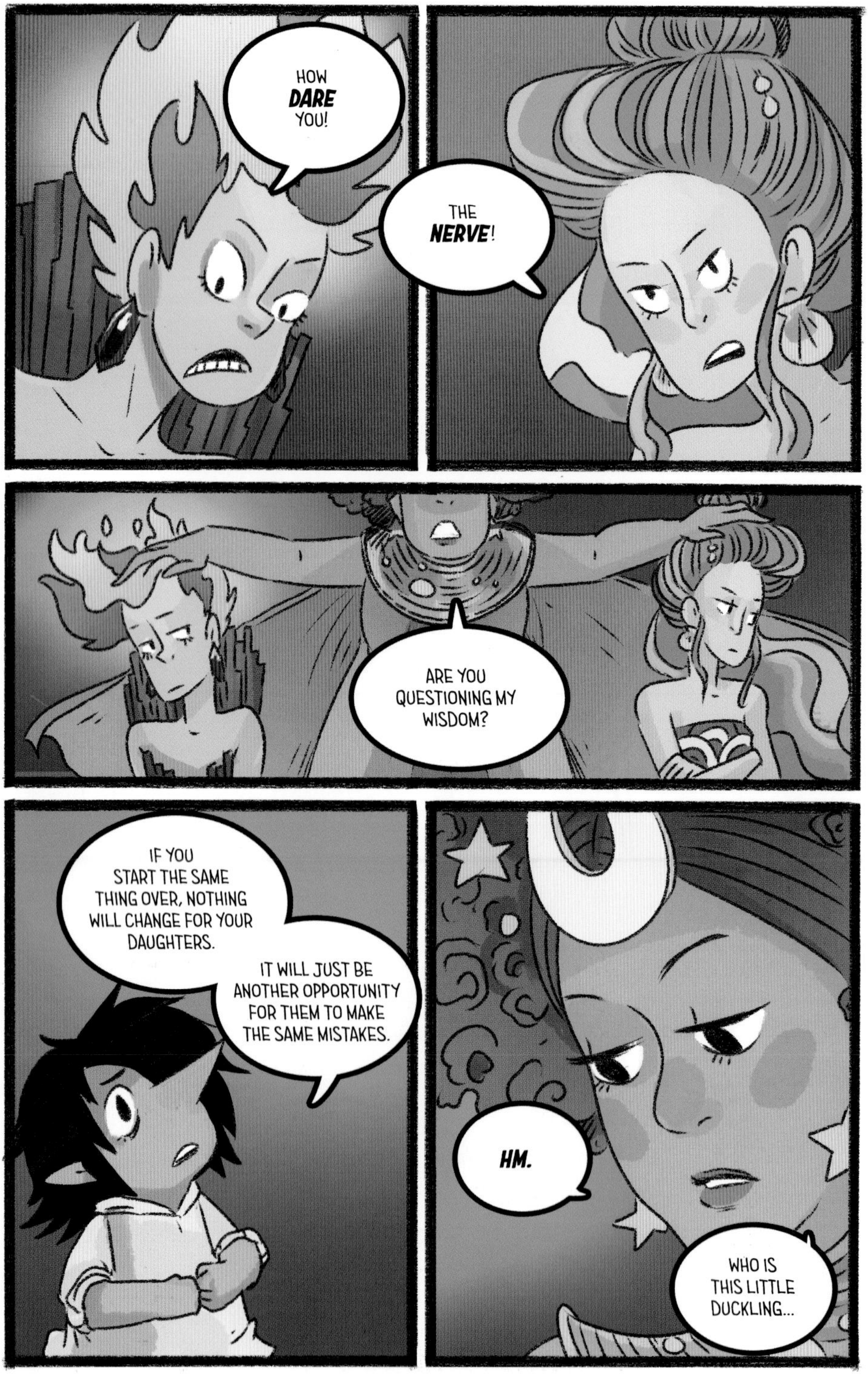
HOW **DARE** YOU!
THE ***NERVE***!
ARE YOU QUESTIONING MY WISDOM?
IF YOU START THE SAME THING OVER, NOTHING WILL CHANGE FOR YOUR DAUGHTERS.
IT WILL JUST BE ANOTHER OPPORTUNITY FOR THEM TO MAKE THE SAME MISTAKES.
HM.
WHO IS THIS LITTLE DUCKLING...

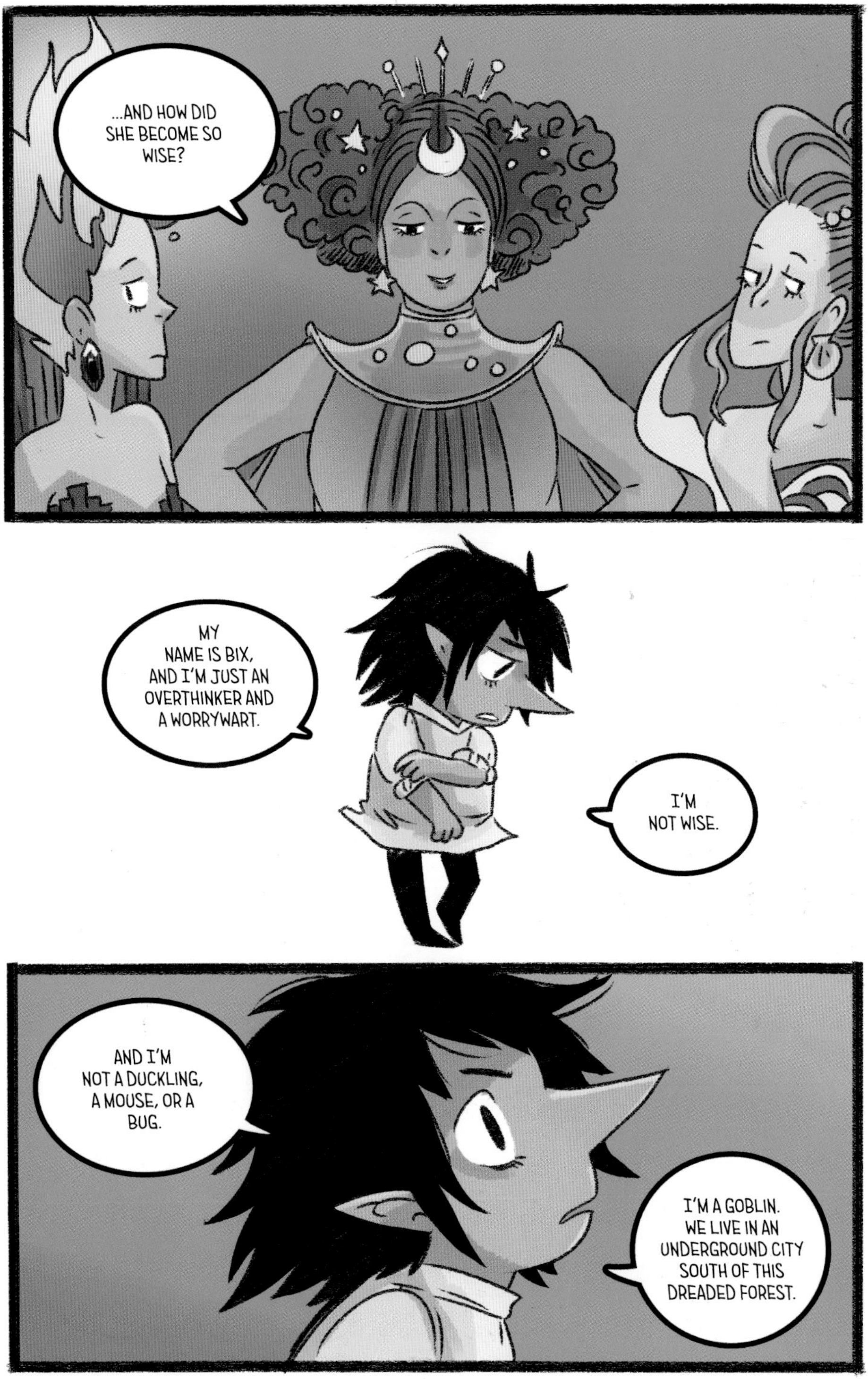
...AND HOW DID SHE BECOME SO WISE?
MY NAME IS BIX, AND I'M JUST AN OVERTHINKER AND A WORRYWART.
I'M NOT WISE.
AND I'M NOT A DUCKLING, A MOUSE, OR A BUG.
I'M A GOBLIN. WE LIVE IN AN UNDERGROUND CITY SOUTH OF THIS DREADED FOREST.

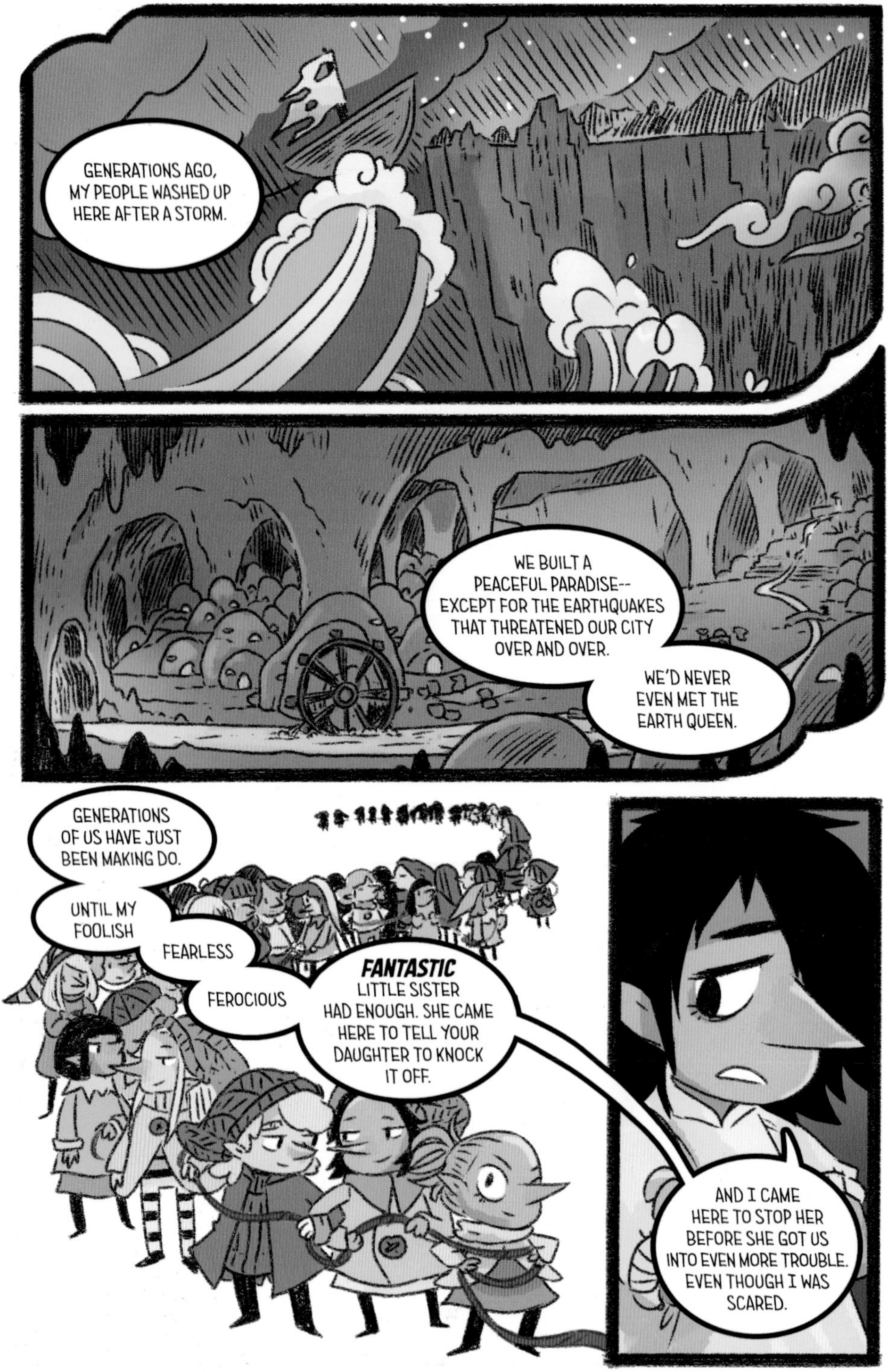
GENERATIONS AGO, MY PEOPLE WASHED UP HERE AFTER A STORM.
WE BUILT A PEACEFUL PARADISE-- EXCEPT FOR THE EARTHQUAKES THAT THREATENED OUR CITY OVER AND OVER.
WE'D NEVER EVEN MET THE EARTH QUEEN.
GENERATIONS OF US HAVE JUST BEEN MAKING DO.
UNTIL MY FOOLISH
FEARLESS
FEROCIOUS
FANTASTIC LITTLE SISTER HAD ENOUGH. SHE CAME HERE TO TELL YOUR DAUGHTER TO KNOCK IT OFF.
AND I CAME HERE TO STOP HER BEFORE SHE GOT US INTO EVEN MORE TROUBLE. EVEN THOUGH I WAS SCARED.

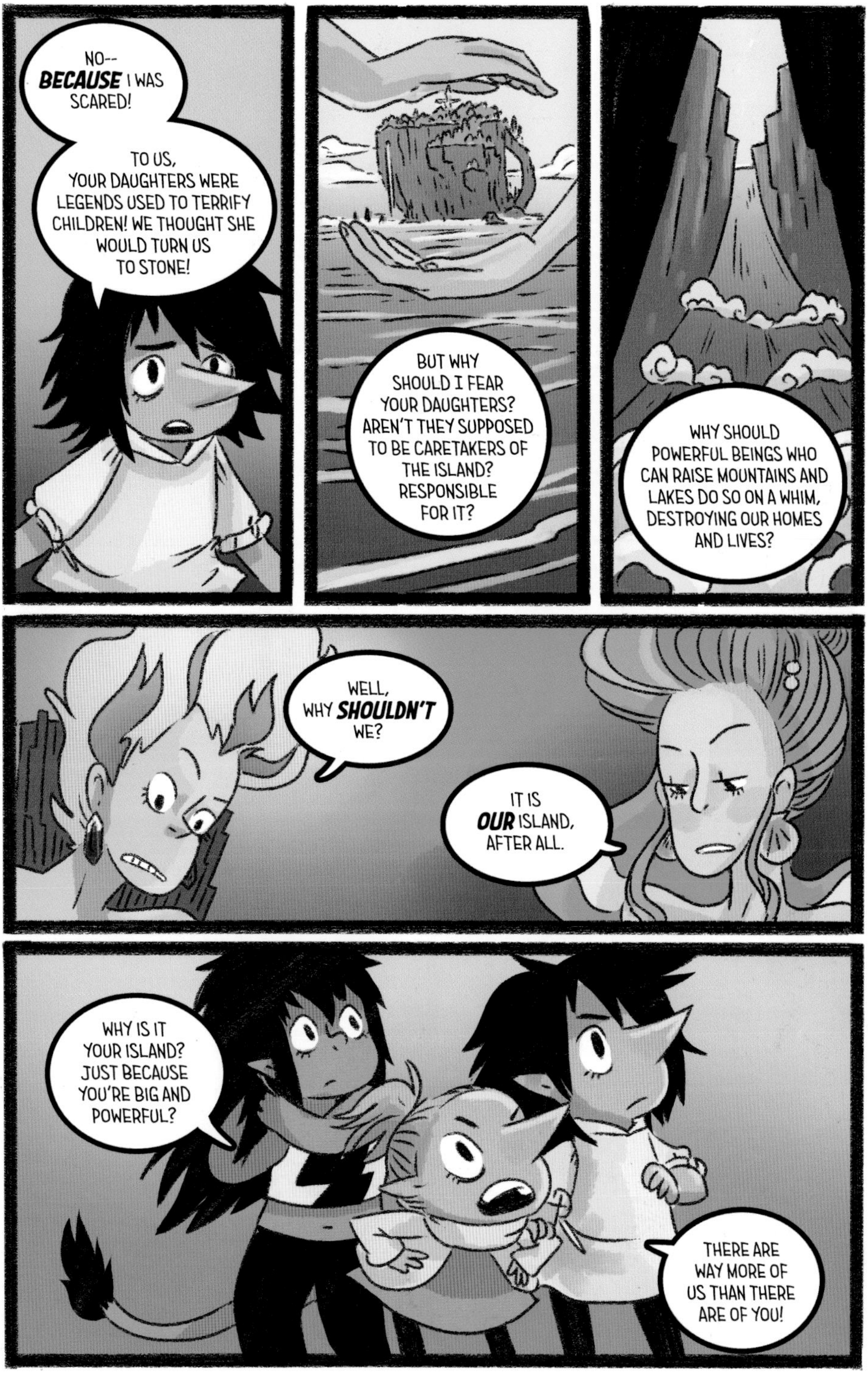
NO-- **BECAUSE** I WAS SCARED!
TO US, YOUR DAUGHTERS WERE LEGENDS USED TO TERRIFY CHILDREN! WE THOUGHT SHE WOULD TURN US TO STONE!
BUT WHY SHOULD I FEAR YOUR DAUGHTERS? AREN'T THEY SUPPOSED TO BE CARETAKERS OF THE ISLAND? RESPONSIBLE FOR IT?
WHY SHOULD POWERFUL BEINGS WHO CAN RAISE MOUNTAINS AND LAKES DO SO ON A WHIM, DESTROYING OUR HOMES AND LIVES?
WELL, WHY **SHOULDN'T** WE?
IT IS **OUR** ISLAND, AFTER ALL.
WHY IS IT YOUR ISLAND? JUST BECAUSE YOU'RE BIG AND POWERFUL?
THERE ARE WAY MORE OF US THAN THERE ARE OF YOU!

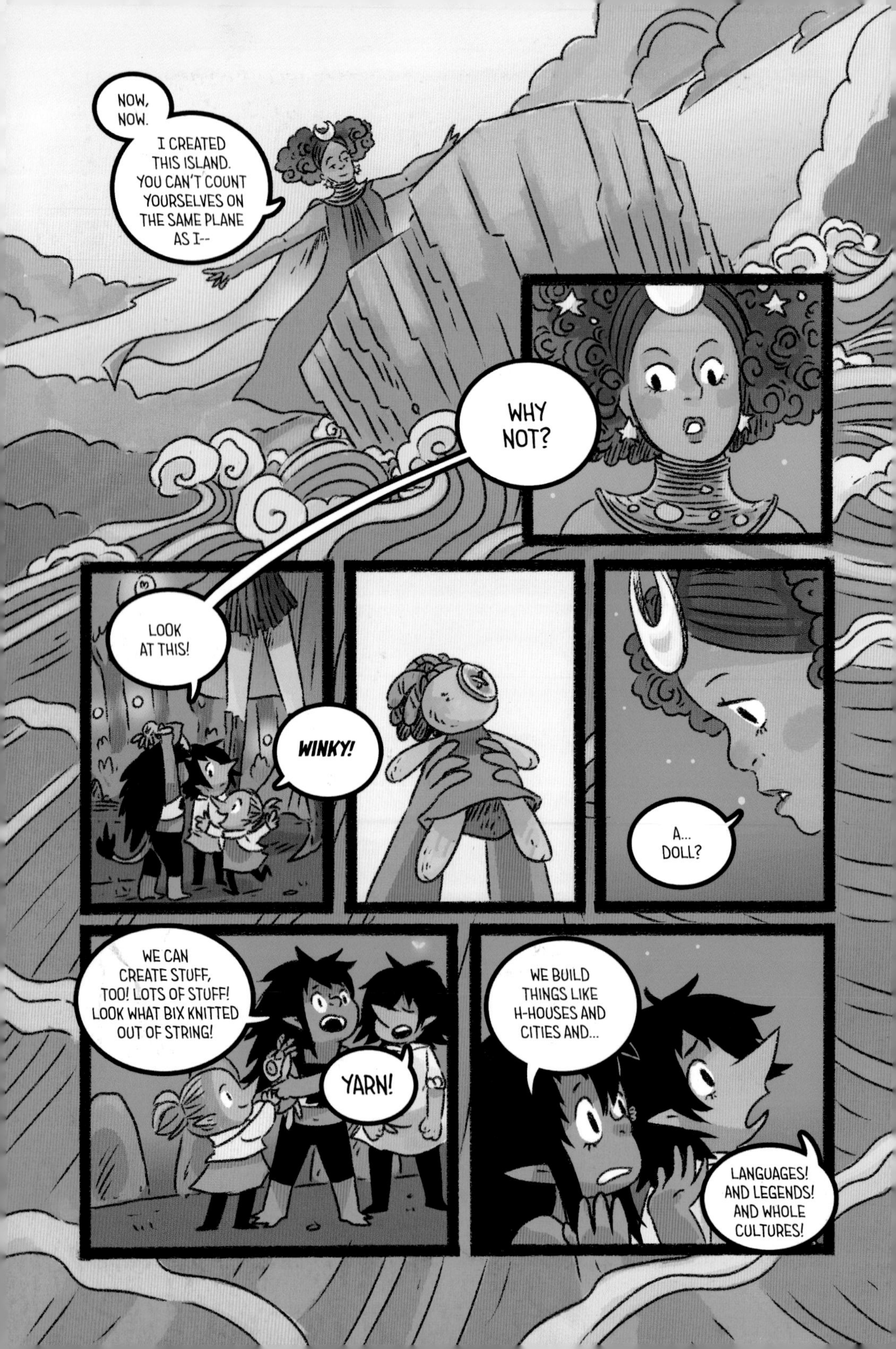
NOW, NOW.
I CREATED THIS ISLAND. YOU CAN'T COUNT YOURSELVES ON THE SAME PLANE AS I--
WHY NOT?
LOOK AT THIS!
WINKY!
A... DOLL?
WE CAN CREATE STUFF, TOO! LOTS OF STUFF! LOOK WHAT BIX KNITTED OUT OF STRING!
YARN!
WE BUILD THINGS LIKE H-HOUSES AND CITIES AND...
LANGUAGES! AND LEGENDS! AND WHOLE CULTURES!

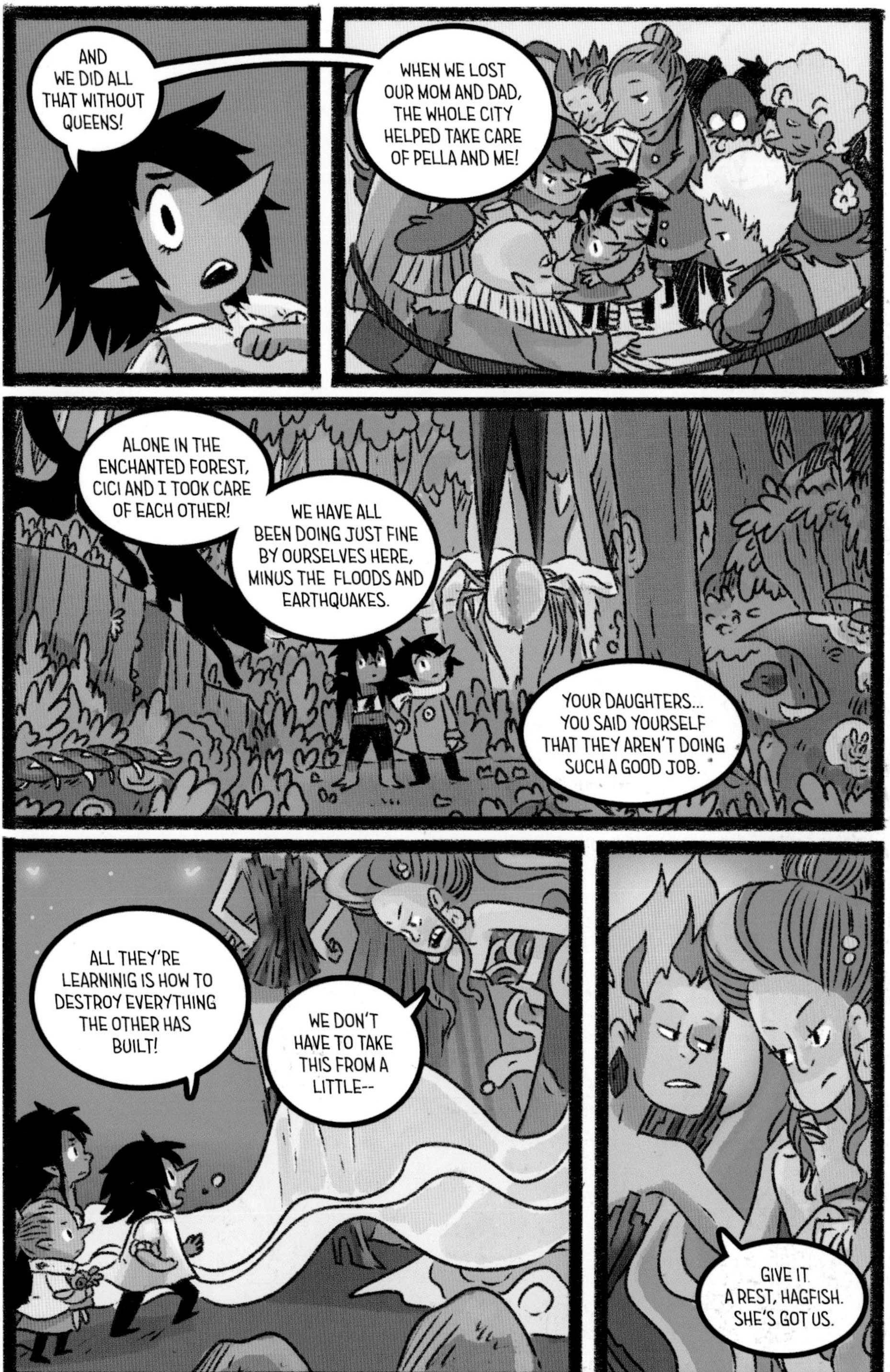
AND WE DID ALL THAT WITHOUT QUEENS!
WHEN WE LOST OUR MOM AND DAD, THE WHOLE CITY HELPED TAKE CARE OF PELLA AND ME!
ALONE IN THE ENCHANTED FOREST, CICI AND I TOOK CARE OF EACH OTHER!
WE HAVE ALL BEEN DOING JUST FINE BY OURSELVES HERE, MINUS THE FLOODS AND EARTHQUAKES.
YOUR DAUGHTERS... YOU SAID YOURSELF THAT THEY AREN'T DOING SUCH A GOOD JOB.
ALL THEY'RE LEARNINIG IS HOW TO DESTROY EVERYTHING THE OTHER HAS BUILT!
WE DON'T HAVE TO TAKE THIS FROM A LITTLE--
GIVE IT A REST, HAGFISH. SHE'S GOT US.

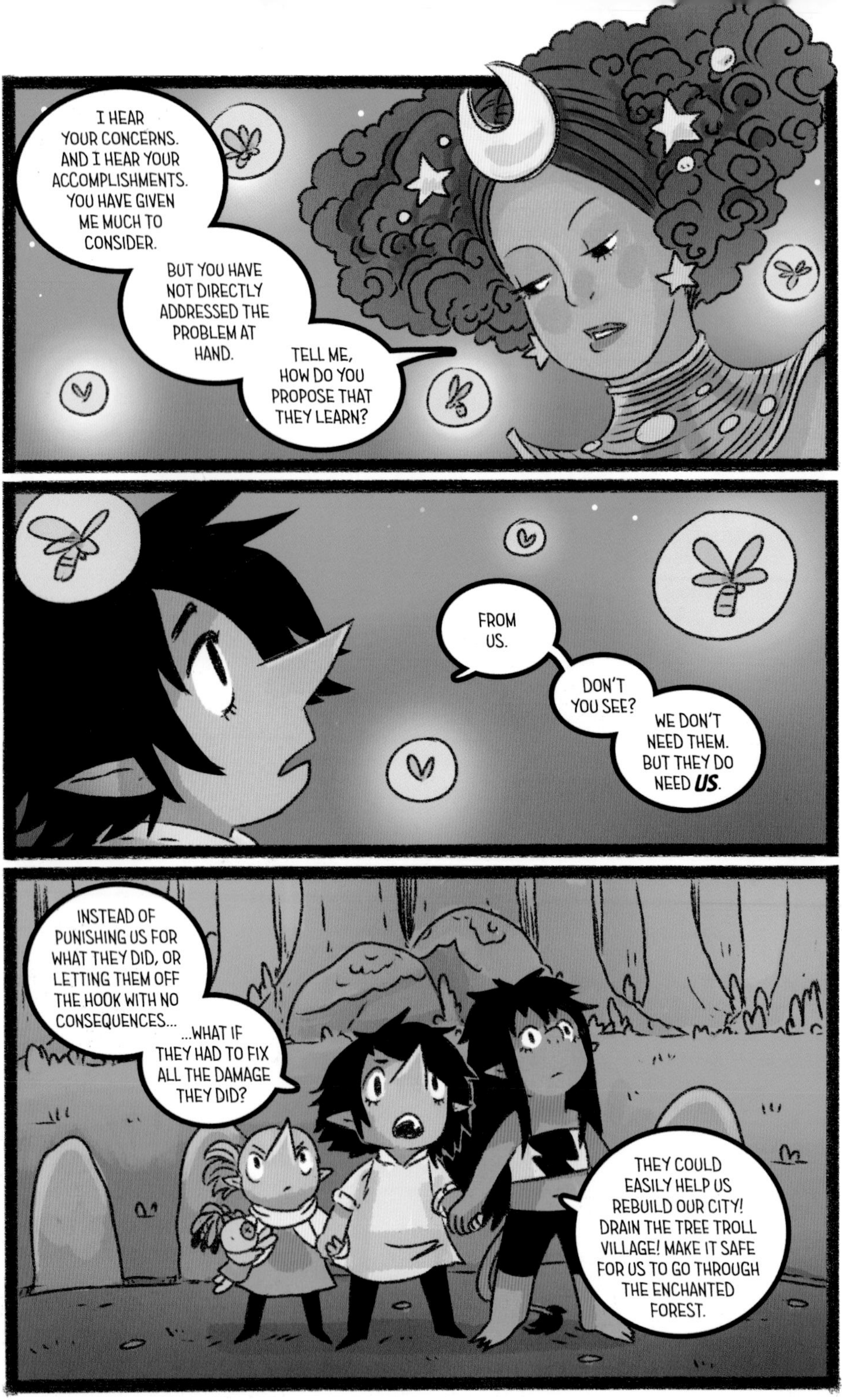
I HEAR YOUR CONCERNS. AND I HEAR YOUR ACCOMPLISHMENTS. YOU HAVE GIVEN ME MUCH TO CONSIDER.
BUT YOU HAVE NOT DIRECTLY ADDRESSED THE PROBLEM AT HAND.
TELL ME, HOW DO YOU PROPOSE THAT THEY LEARN?
FROM US.
DON'T YOU SEE?
WE DON'T NEED THEM. BUT THEY DO NEED ***US***.
INSTEAD OF PUNISHING US FOR WHAT THEY DID, OR LETTING THEM OFF THE HOOK WITH NO CONSEQUENCES...
...WHAT IF THEY HAD TO FIX ALL THE DAMAGE THEY DID?
THEY COULD EASILY HELP US REBUILD OUR CITY! DRAIN THE TREE TROLL VILLAGE! MAKE IT SAFE FOR US TO GO THROUGH THE ENCHANTED FOREST.

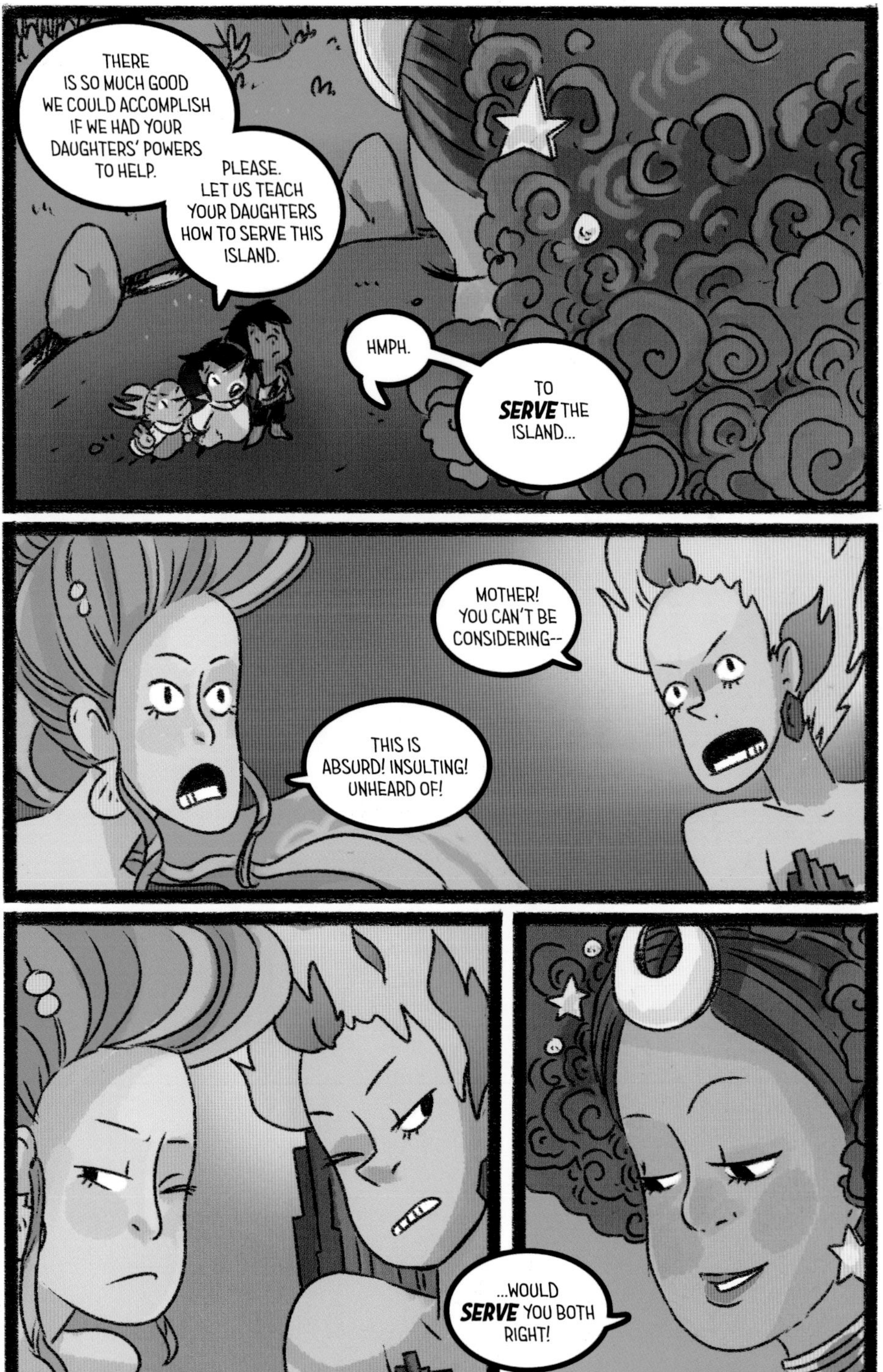
THERE IS SO MUCH GOOD WE COULD ACCOMPLISH IF WE HAD YOUR DAUGHTERS' POWERS TO HELP.
PLEASE. LET US TEACH YOUR DAUGHTERS HOW TO SERVE THIS ISLAND.
HMPH.
TO **SERVE** THE ISLAND...
MOTHER! YOU CAN'T BE CONSIDERING--
THIS IS ABSURD! INSULTING! UNHEARD OF!
...WOULD **SERVE** YOU BOTH RIGHT!

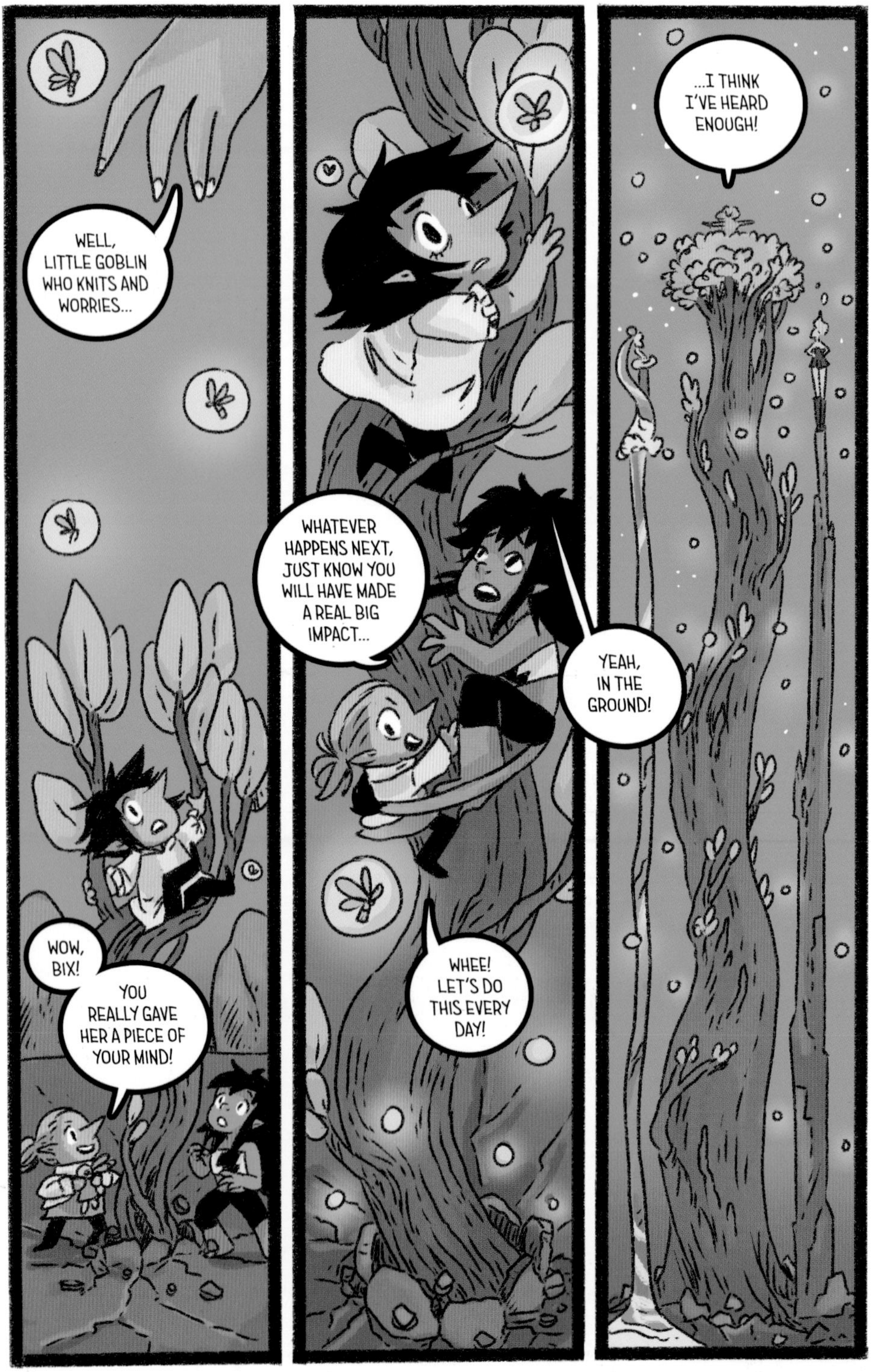
WELL, LITTLE GOBLIN WHO KNITS AND WORRIES...
WOW, BIX!
YOU REALLY GAVE HER A PIECE OF YOUR MIND!
WHATEVER HAPPENS NEXT, JUST KNOW YOU WILL HAVE MADE A REAL BIG IMPACT...
YEAH, IN THE GROUND!
WHEE! LET'S DO THIS EVERY DAY!
...I THINK I'VE HEARD ENOUGH!

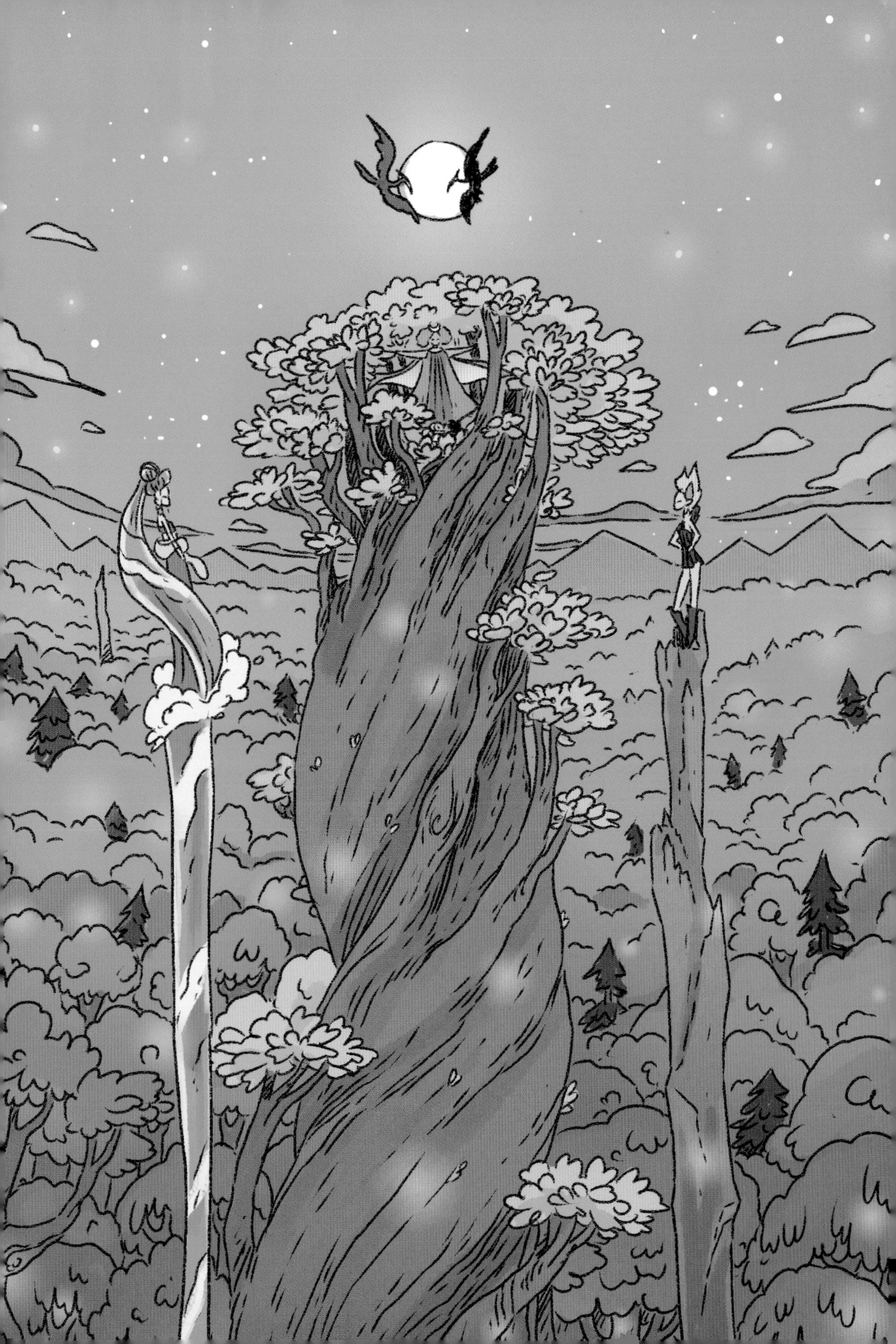

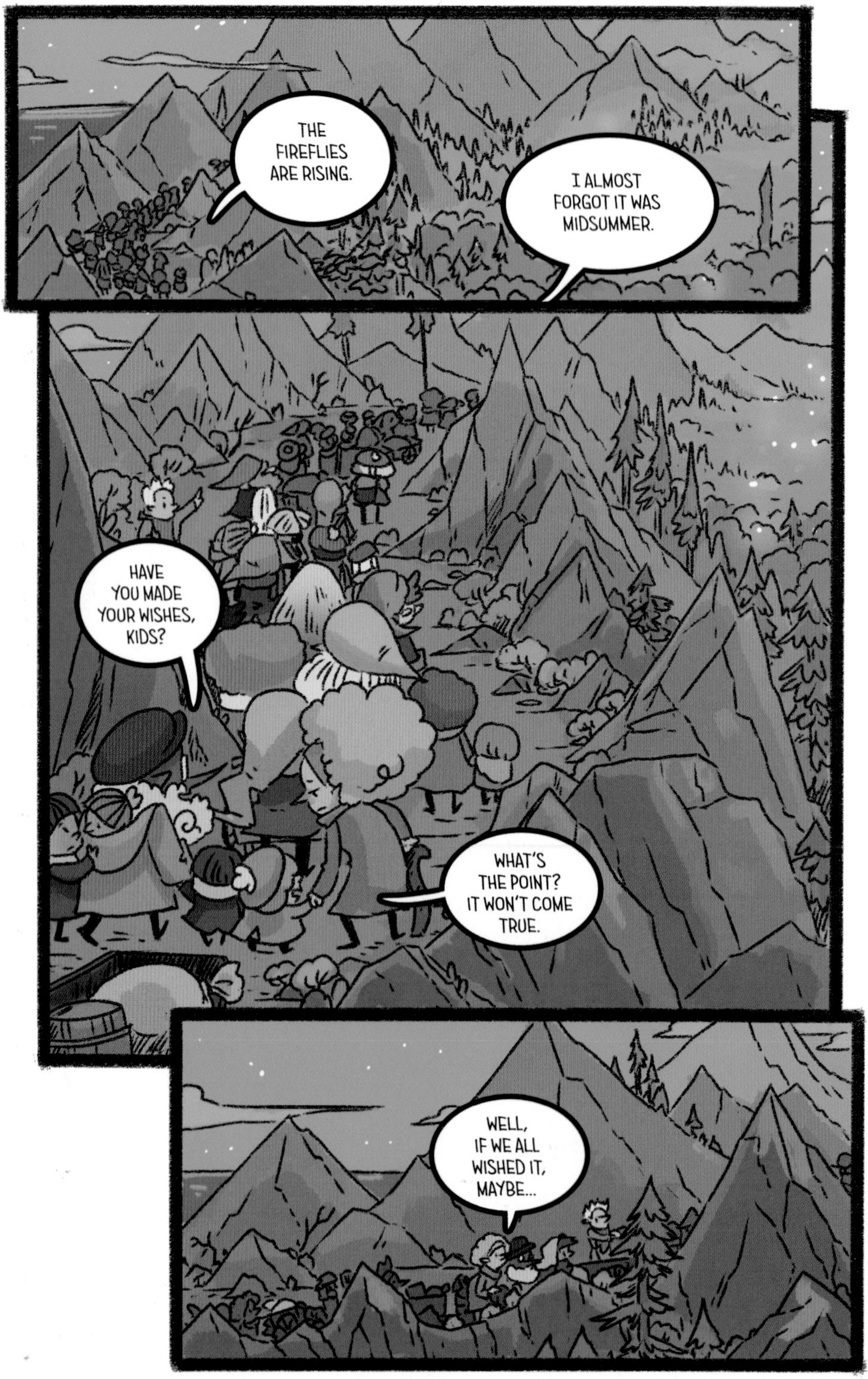
THE FIREFLIES ARE RISING.
I ALMOST FORGOT IT WAS MIDSUMMER.
HAVE YOU MADE YOUR WISHES, KIDS?
WHAT'S THE POINT? IT WON'T COME TRUE.
WELL, IF WE ALL WISHED IT, MAYBE...

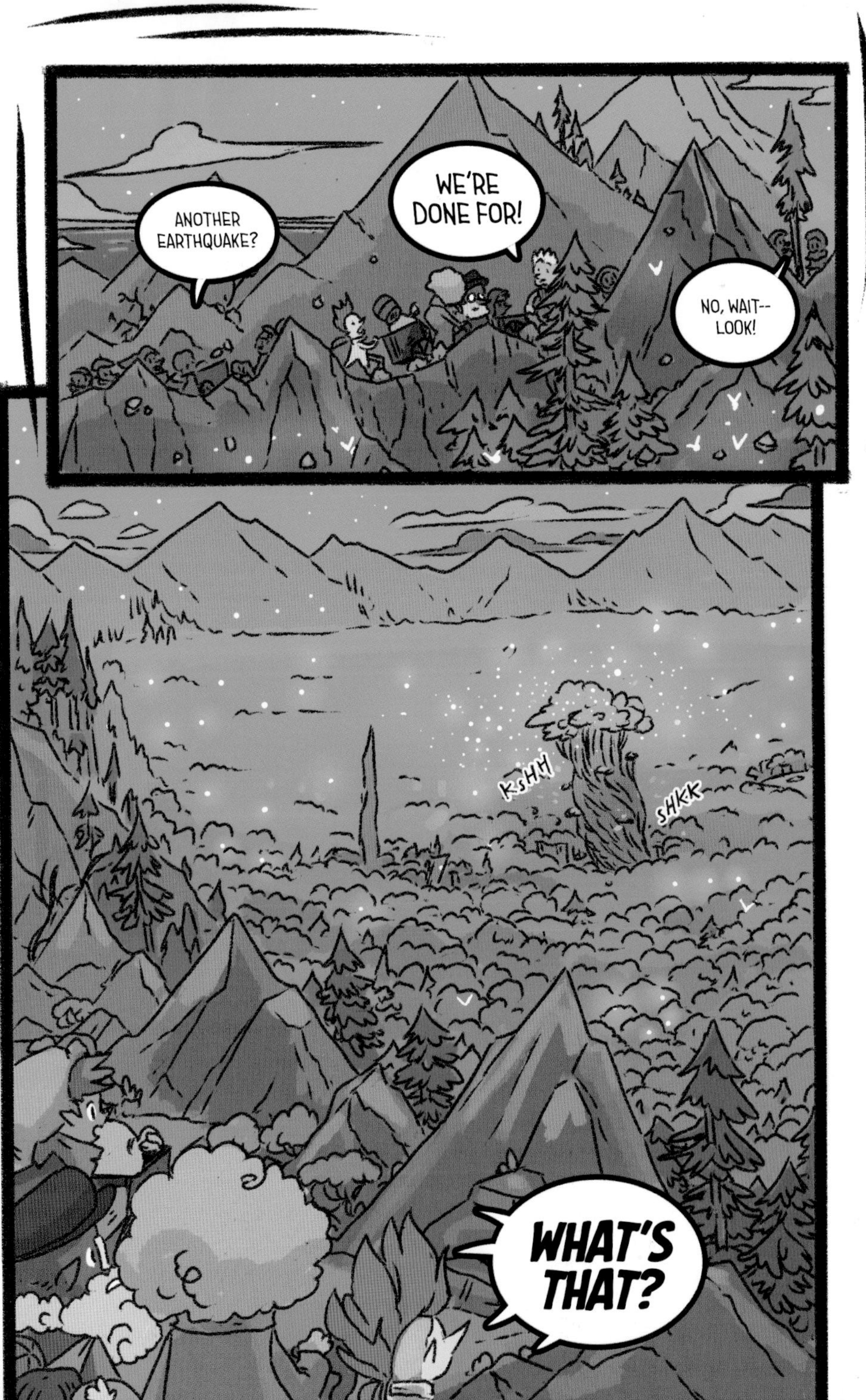
ANOTHER EARTHQUAKE?
WE'RE DONE FOR!
NO, WAIT-- LOOK!
KSHH
SHKK
WHAT'S THAT?

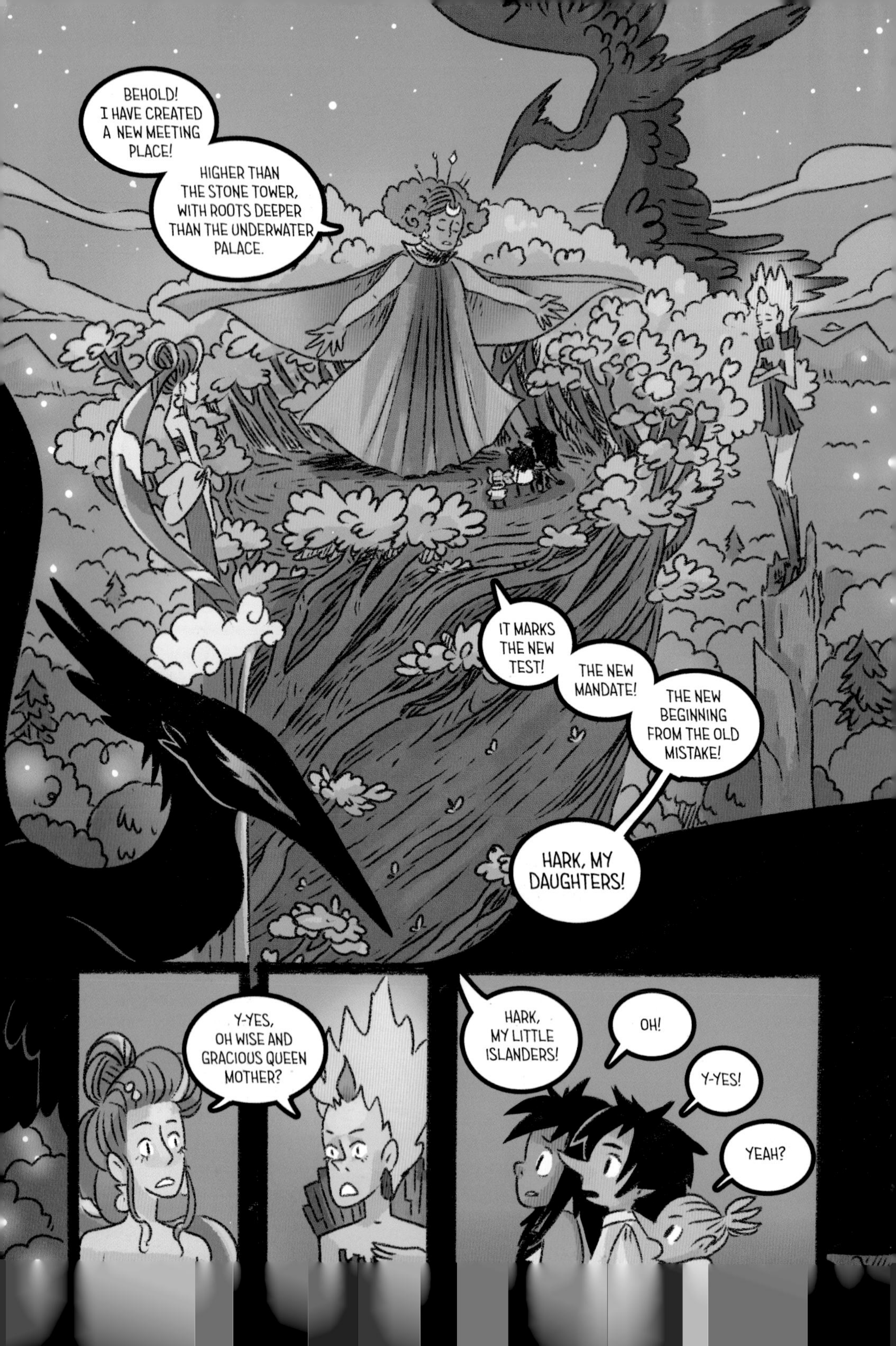
BEHOLD! I HAVE CREATED A NEW MEETING PLACE!
HIGHER THAN THE STONE TOWER, WITH ROOTS DEEPER THAN THE UNDERWATER PALACE.
IT MARKS THE NEW TEST!
THE NEW MANDATE!
THE NEW BEGINNING FROM THE OLD MISTAKE!
HARK, MY DAUGHTERS!
Y-YES, OH WISE AND GRACIOUS QUEEN MOTHER?
HARK, MY LITTLE ISLANDERS!
OH!
Y-YES!
YEAH?

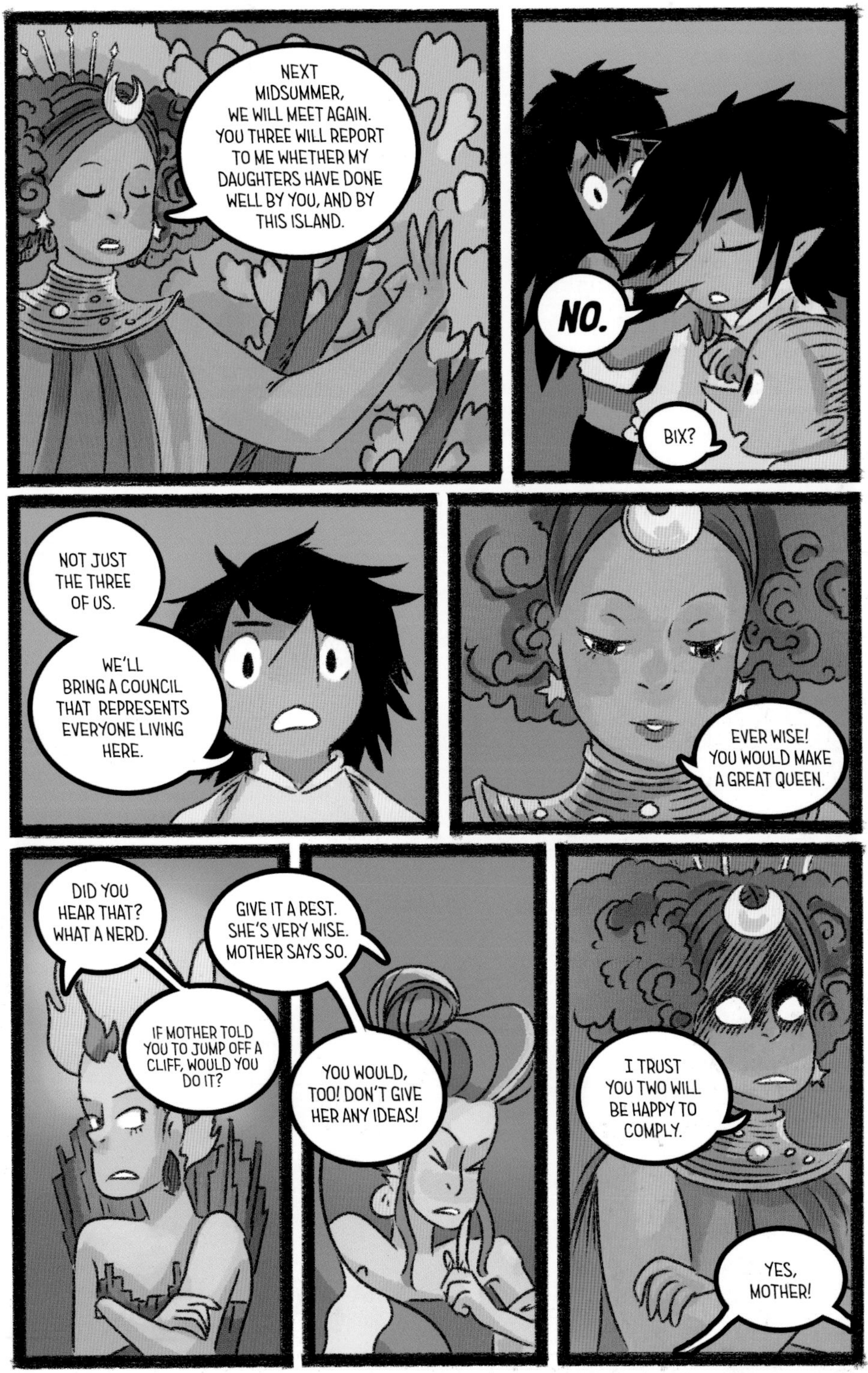
NEXT MIDSUMMER, WE WILL MEET AGAIN. YOU THREE WILL REPORT TO ME WHETHER MY DAUGHTERS HAVE DONE WELL BY YOU, AND BY THIS ISLAND.
NO.
BIX?
NOT JUST THE THREE OF US.
WE'LL BRING A COUNCIL THAT REPRESENTS EVERYONE LIVING HERE.
EVER WISE! YOU WOULD MAKE A GREAT QUEEN.
DID YOU HEAR THAT? WHAT A NERD.
GIVE IT A REST. SHE'S VERY WISE. MOTHER SAYS SO.
IF MOTHER TOLD YOU TO JUMP OFF A CLIFF, WOULD YOU DO IT?
YOU WOULD, TOO! DON'T GIVE HER ANY IDEAS!
I TRUST YOU TWO WILL BE HAPPY TO COMPLY.
YES, MOTHER!

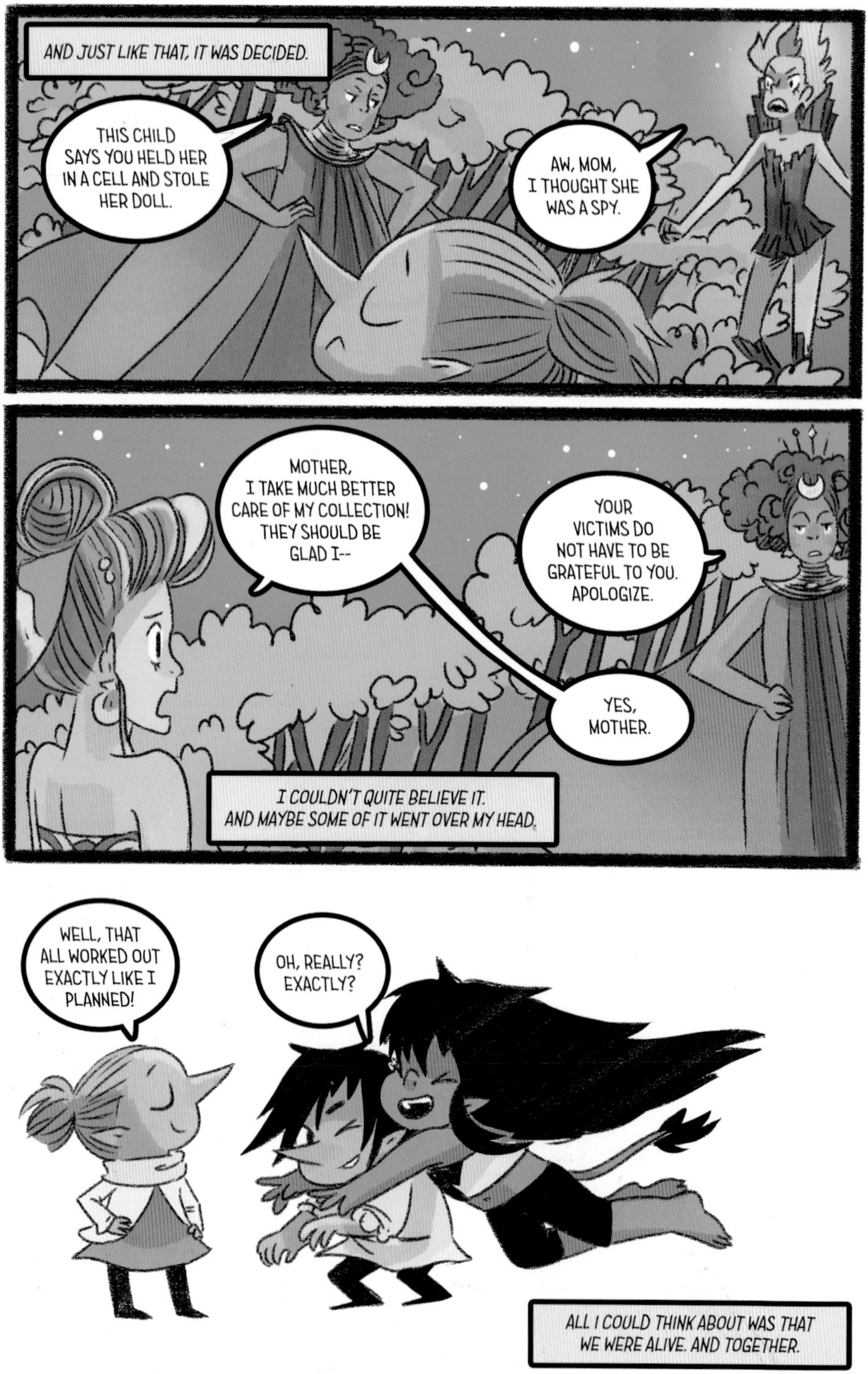
AND JUST LIKE THAT, IT WAS DECIDED.
THIS CHILD SAYS YOU HELD HER IN A CELL AND STOLE HER DOLL.
AW, MOM, I THOUGHT SHE WAS A SPY.
MOTHER, I TAKE MUCH BETTER CARE OF MY COLLECTION! THEY SHOULD BE GLAD I--
YOUR VICTIMS DO NOT HAVE TO BE GRATEFUL TO YOU. APOLOGIZE.
YES, MOTHER.
I COULDN'T QUITE BELIEVE IT. AND MAYBE SOME OF IT WENT OVER MY HEAD.
WELL, THAT ALL WORKED OUT EXACTLY LIKE I PLANNED!
OH, REALLY? EXACTLY?
ALL I COULD THINK ABOUT WAS THAT WE WERE ALIVE. AND TOGETHER.

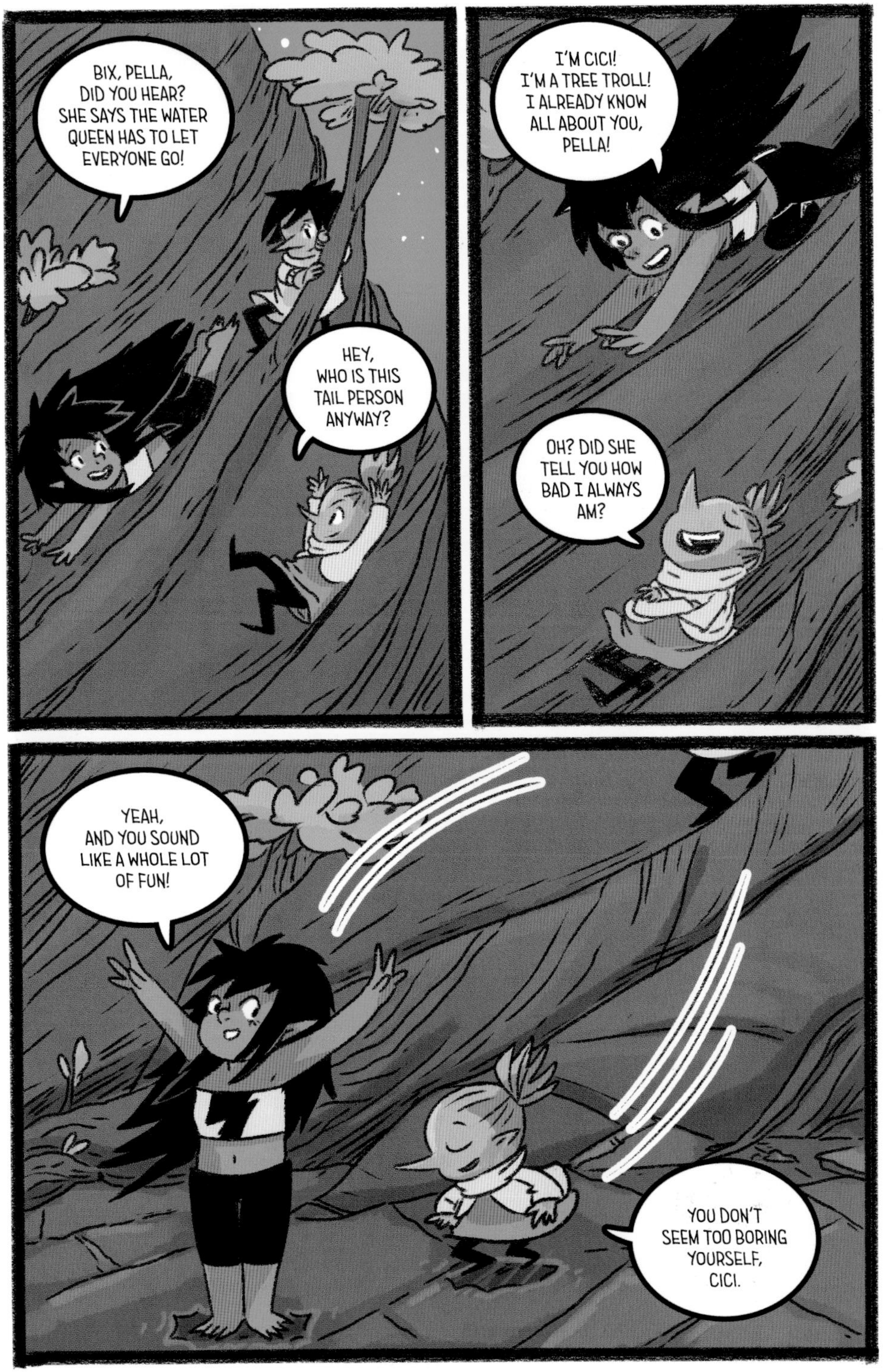
BIX, PELLA, DID YOU HEAR? SHE SAYS THE WATER QUEEN HAS TO LET EVERYONE GO!
HEY, WHO IS THIS TAIL PERSON ANYWAY?
I'M CICI! I'M A TREE TROLL! I ALREADY KNOW ALL ABOUT YOU, PELLA!
OH? DID SHE TELL YOU HOW BAD I ALWAYS AM?
YEAH, AND YOU SOUND LIKE A WHOLE LOT OF FUN!
YOU DON'T SEEM TOO BORING YOURSELF, CICI.

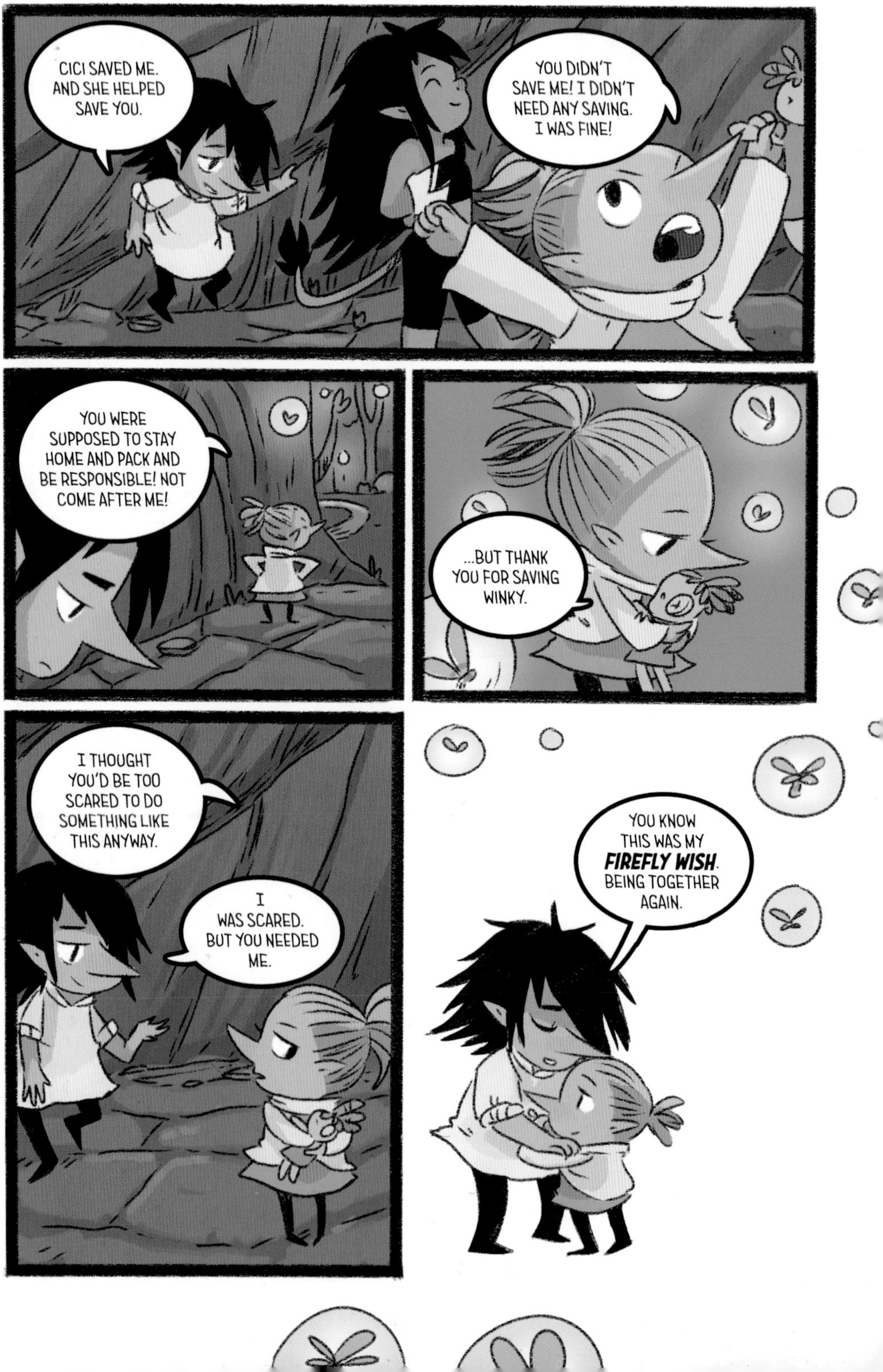
CICI SAVED ME. AND SHE HELPED SAVE YOU.
YOU DIDN'T SAVE ME! I DIDN'T NEED ANY SAVING. I WAS FINE!
YOU WERE SUPPOSED TO STAY HOME AND PACK AND BE RESPONSIBLE! NOT COME AFTER ME!
...BUT THANK YOU FOR SAVING WINKY.
I THOUGHT YOU'D BE TOO SCARED TO DO SOMETHING LIKE THIS ANYWAY.
I WAS SCARED. BUT YOU NEEDED ME.
YOU KNOW THIS WAS MY **FIREFLY WISH**. BEING TOGETHER AGAIN.

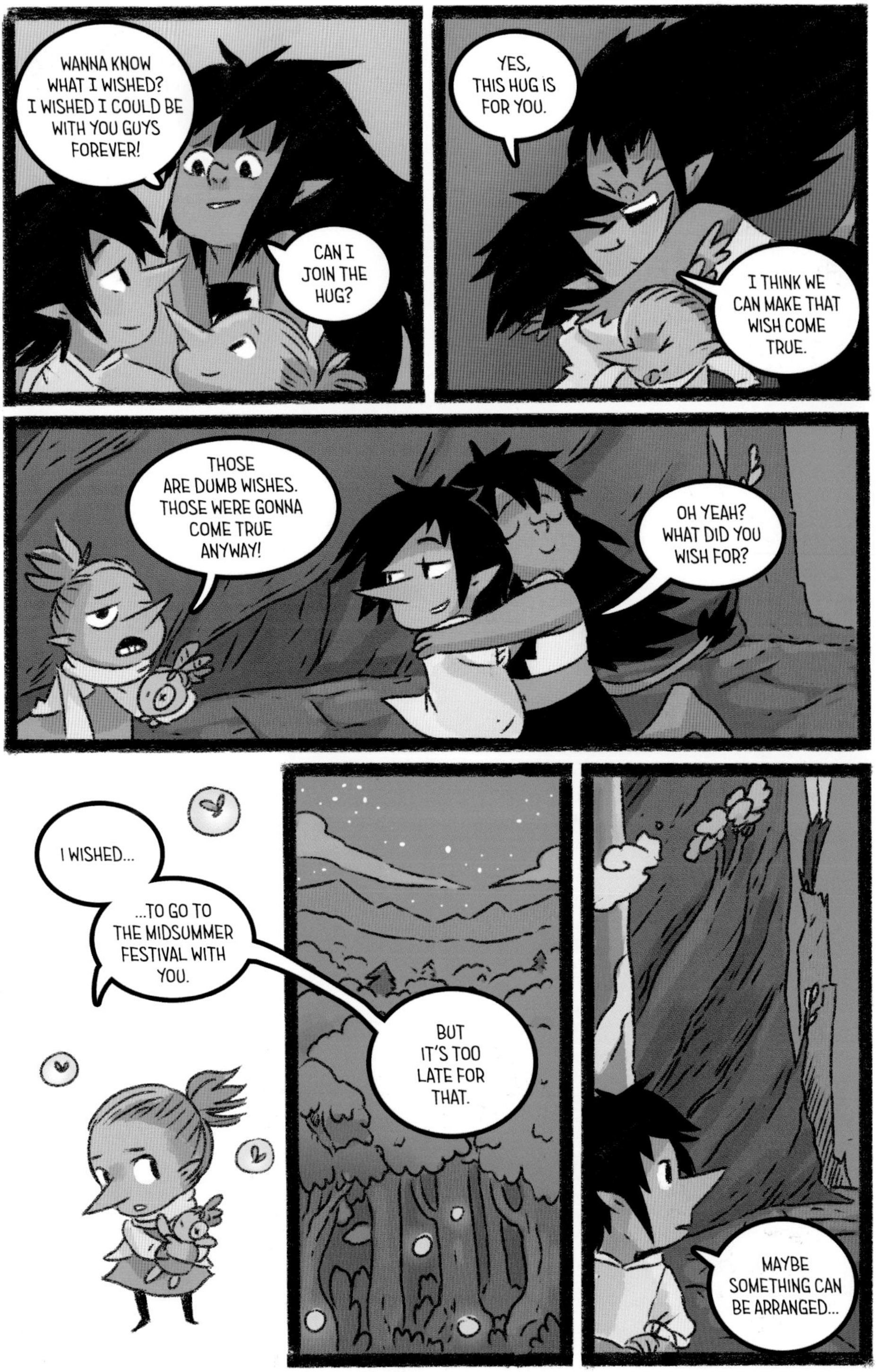
WANNA KNOW WHAT I WISHED? I WISHED I COULD BE WITH YOU GUYS FOREVER!
CAN I JOIN THE HUG?
YES, THIS HUG IS FOR YOU.
I THINK WE CAN MAKE THAT WISH COME TRUE.
THOSE ARE DUMB WISHES. THOSE WERE GONNA COME TRUE ANYWAY!
OH YEAH? WHAT DID YOU WISH FOR?
I WISHED...
...TO GO TO THE MIDSUMMER FESTIVAL WITH YOU.
BUT IT'S TOO LATE FOR THAT.
MAYBE SOMETHING CAN BE ARRANGED...

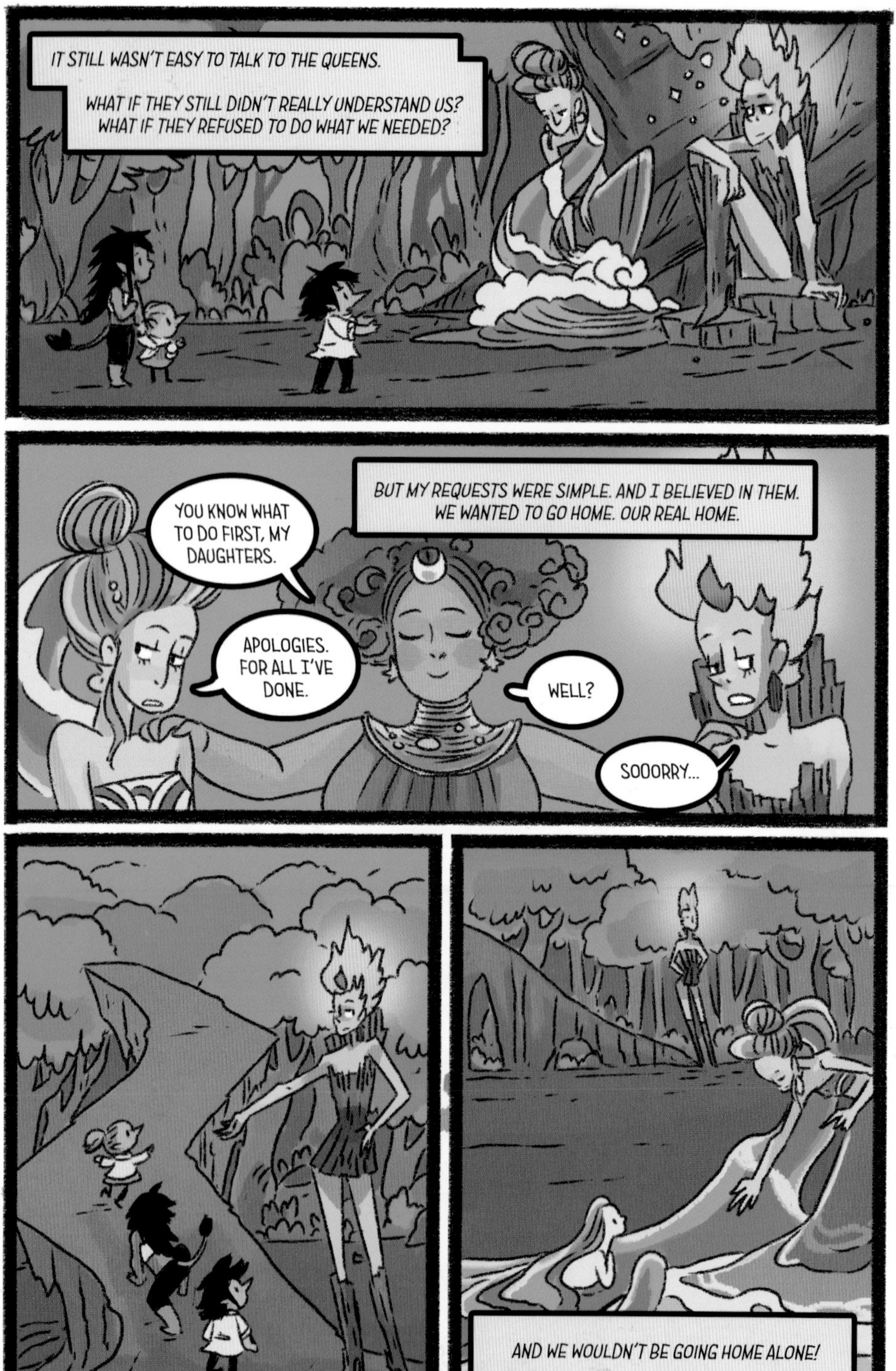
IT STILL WASN'T EASY TO TALK TO THE QUEENS.
WHAT IF THEY STILL DIDN'T REALLY UNDERSTAND US? WHAT IF THEY REFUSED TO DO WHAT WE NEEDED?
BUT MY REQUESTS WERE SIMPLE. AND I BELIEVED IN THEM. WE WANTED TO GO HOME. OUR REAL HOME.
YOU KNOW WHAT TO DO FIRST, MY DAUGHTERS.
APOLOGIES. FOR ALL I'VE DONE.
WELL?
SOOORRY...
AND WE WOULDN'T BE GOING HOME ALONE!

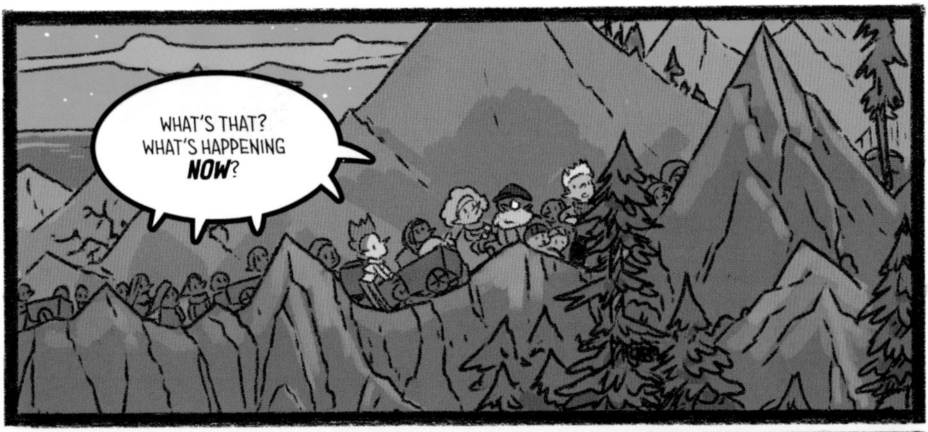
WHAT'S THAT? WHAT'S HAPPENING **NOW**?

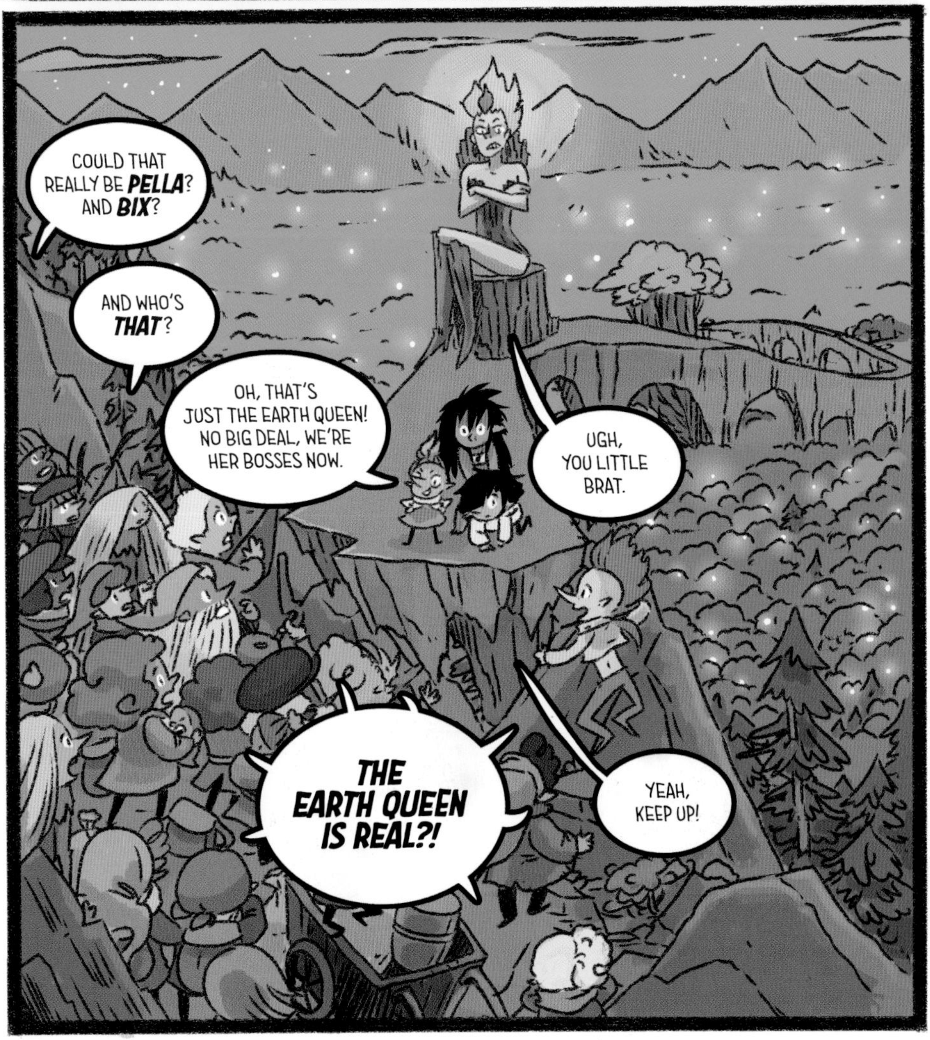
COULD THAT REALLY BE **PELLA**? AND **BIX**?
AND WHO'S **THAT**?
OH, THAT'S JUST THE EARTH QUEEN! NO BIG DEAL, WE'RE HER BOSSES NOW.
UGH, YOU LITTLE BRAT.
THE EARTH QUEEN IS REAL?!
YEAH, KEEP UP!

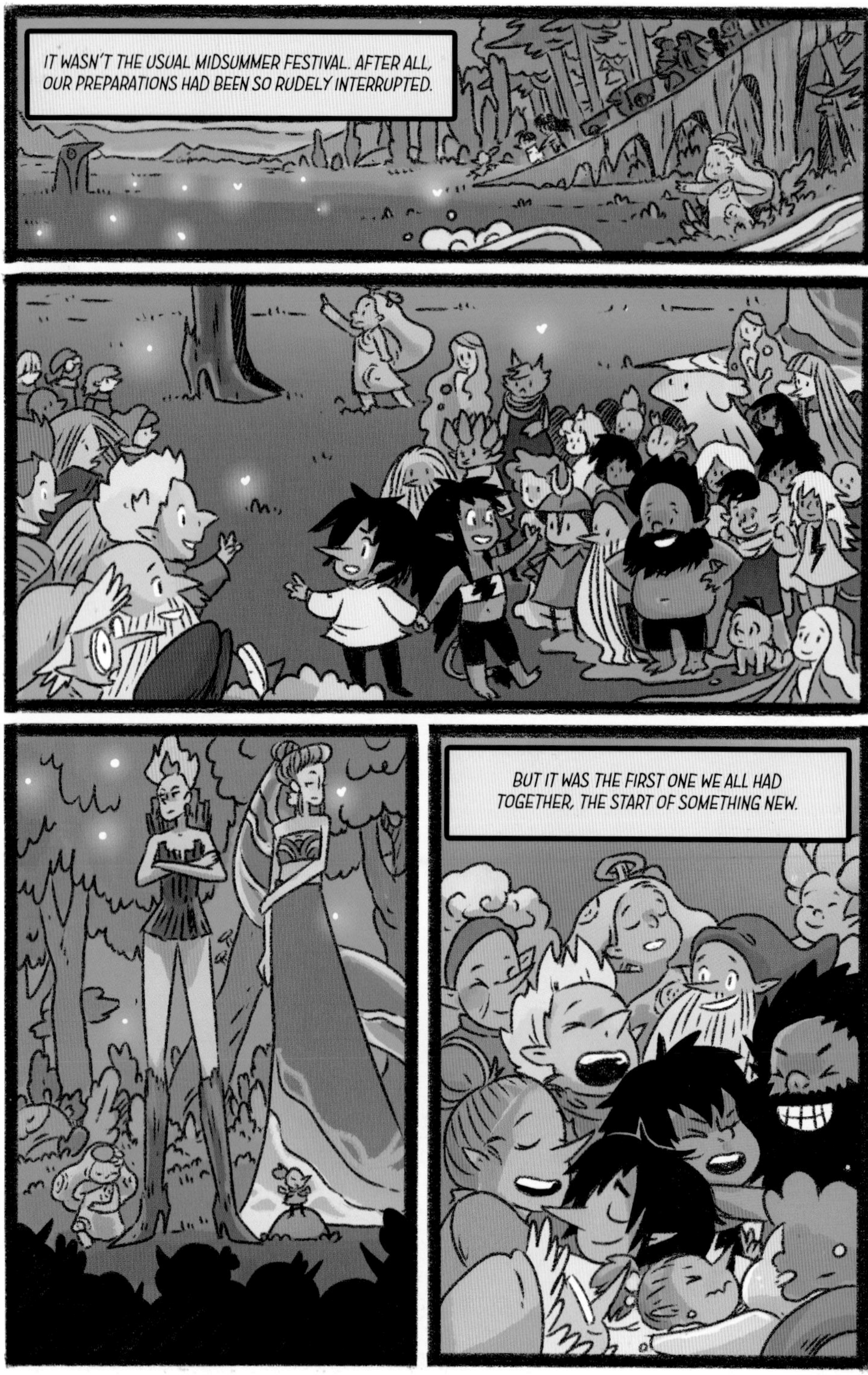
IT WASN'T THE USUAL MIDSUMMER FESTIVAL. AFTER ALL, OUR PREPARATIONS HAD BEEN SO RUDELY INTERRUPTED.
BUT IT WAS THE FIRST ONE WE ALL HAD TOGETHER, THE START OF SOMETHING NEW.

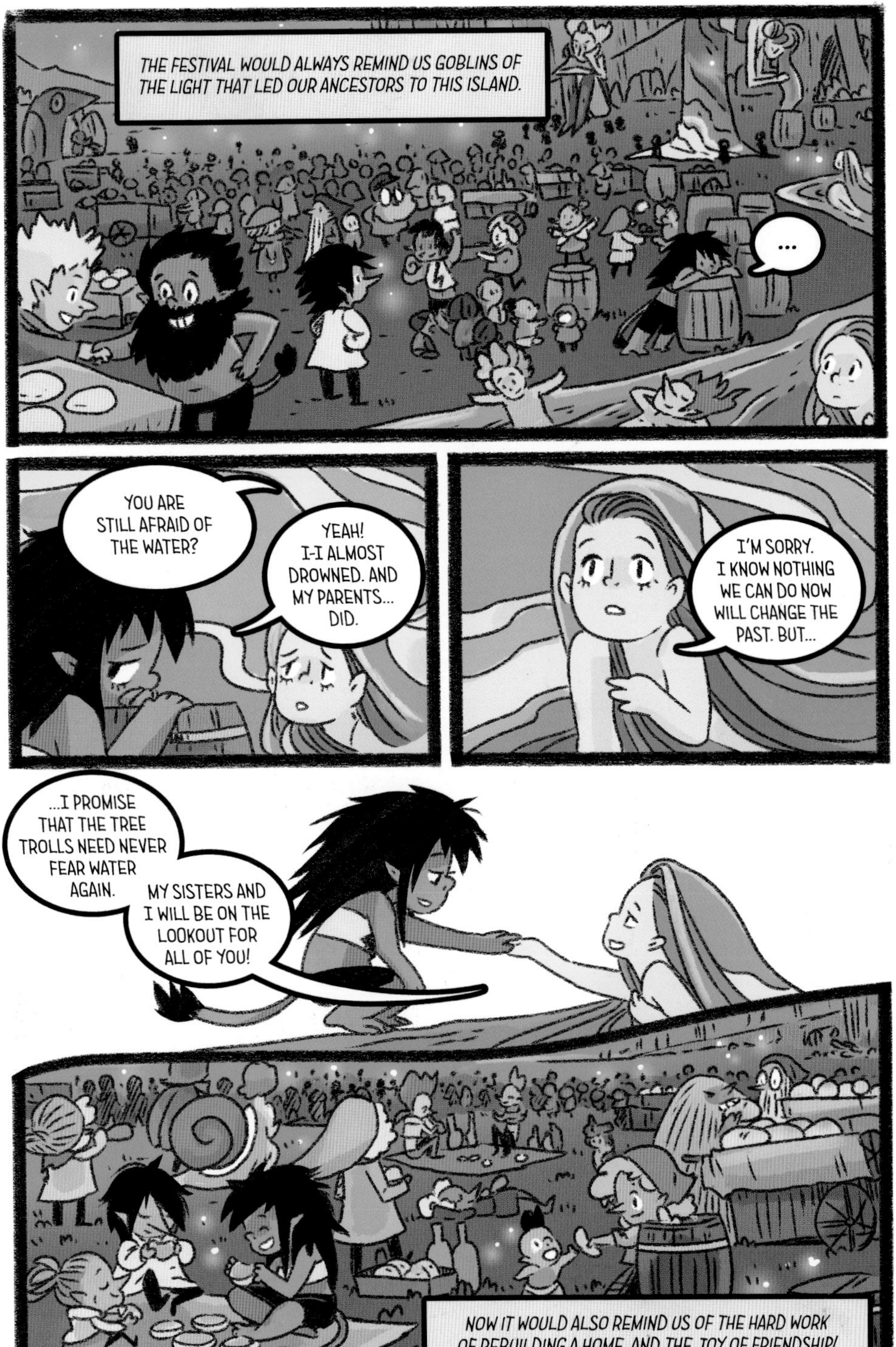
THE FESTIVAL WOULD ALWAYS REMIND US GOBLINS OF THE LIGHT THAT LED OUR ANCESTORS TO THIS ISLAND.
...
YOU ARE STILL AFRAID OF THE WATER?
YEAH! I-I ALMOST DROWNED. AND MY PARENTS... DID.
I'M SORRY. I KNOW NOTHING WE CAN DO NOW WILL CHANGE THE PAST. BUT...
...I PROMISE THAT THE TREE TROLLS NEED NEVER FEAR WATER AGAIN.
MY SISTERS AND I WILL BE ON THE LOOKOUT FOR ALL OF YOU!
NOW IT WOULD ALSO REMIND US OF THE HARD WORK OF REBUILDING A HOME. AND THE JOY OF FRIENDSHIP!

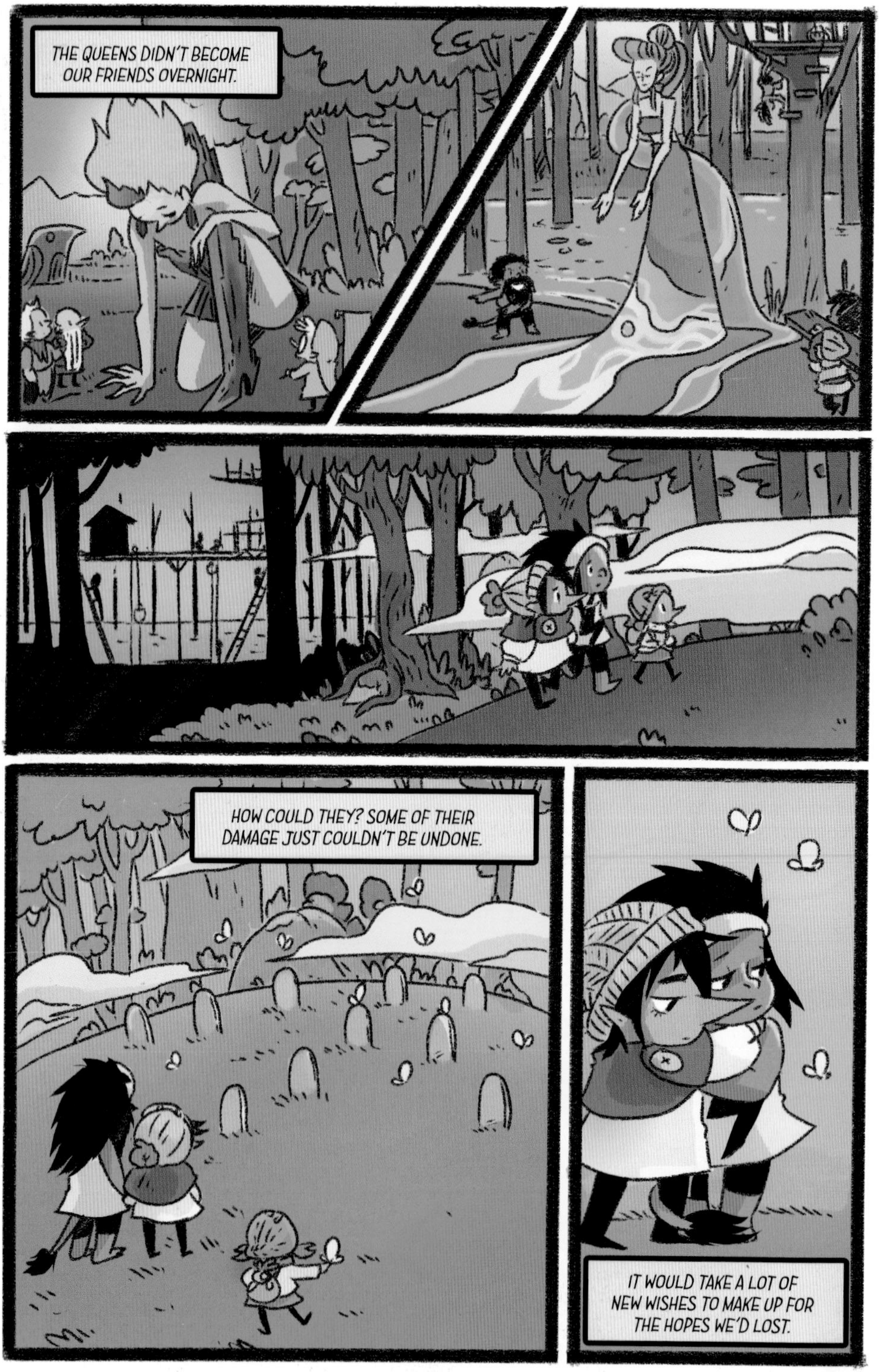
THE QUEENS DIDN'T BECOME OUR FRIENDS OVERNIGHT.
HOW COULD THEY? SOME OF THEIR DAMAGE JUST COULDN'T BE UNDONE.
IT WOULD TAKE A LOT OF NEW WISHES TO MAKE UP FOR THE HOPES WE'D LOST.

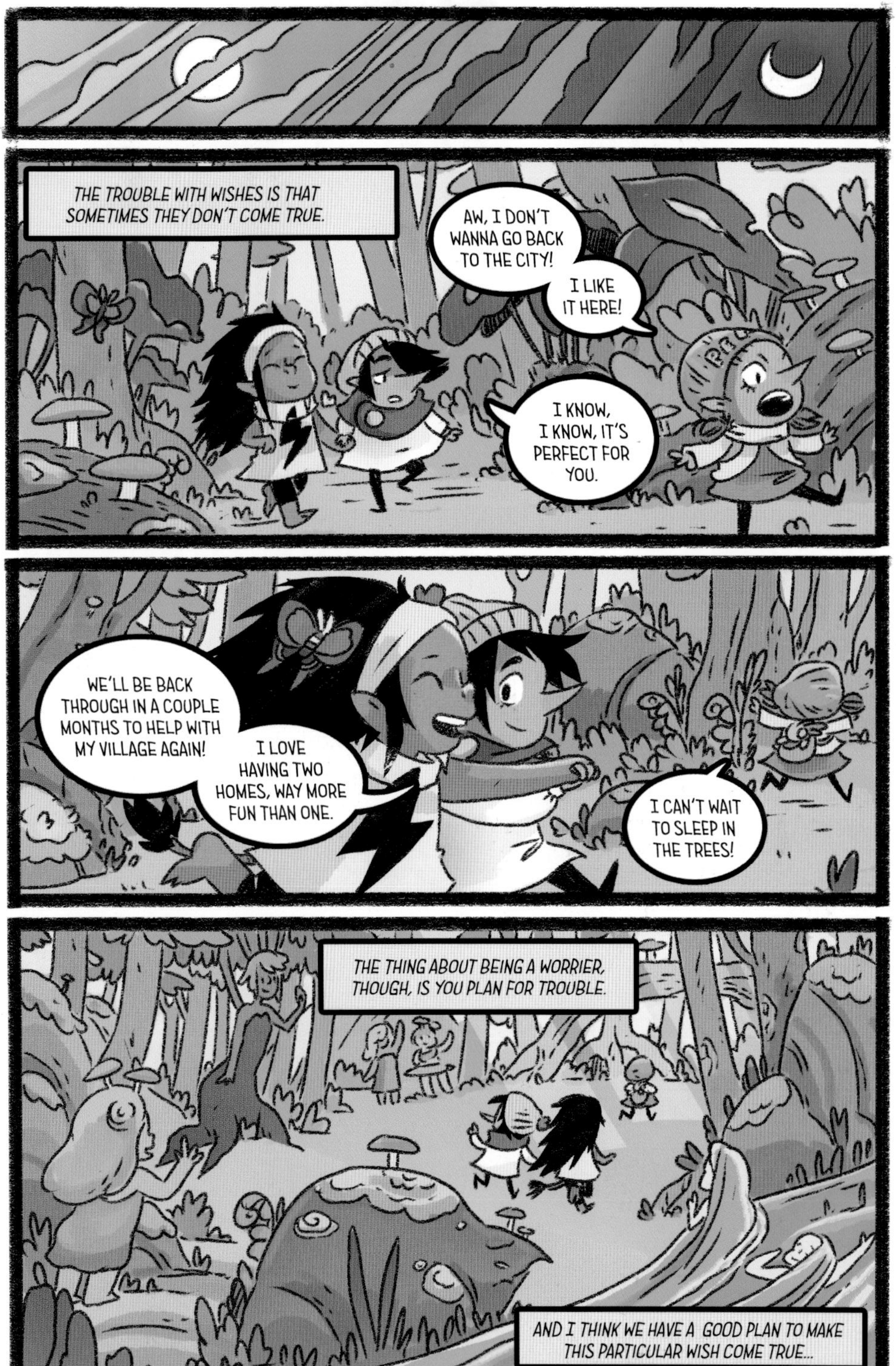
THE TROUBLE WITH WISHES IS THAT SOMETIMES THEY DON'T COME TRUE.
AW, I DON'T WANNA GO BACK TO THE CITY!
I LIKE IT HERE!
I KNOW, I KNOW, IT'S PERFECT FOR YOU.
WE'LL BE BACK THROUGH IN A COUPLE MONTHS TO HELP WITH MY VILLAGE AGAIN!
I LOVE HAVING TWO HOMES, WAY MORE FUN THAN ONE.
I CAN'T WAIT TO SLEEP IN THE TREES!
THE THING ABOUT BEING A WORRIER, THOUGH, IS YOU PLAN FOR TROUBLE.
AND I THINK WE HAVE A GOOD PLAN TO MAKE THIS PARTICULAR WISH COME TRUE...

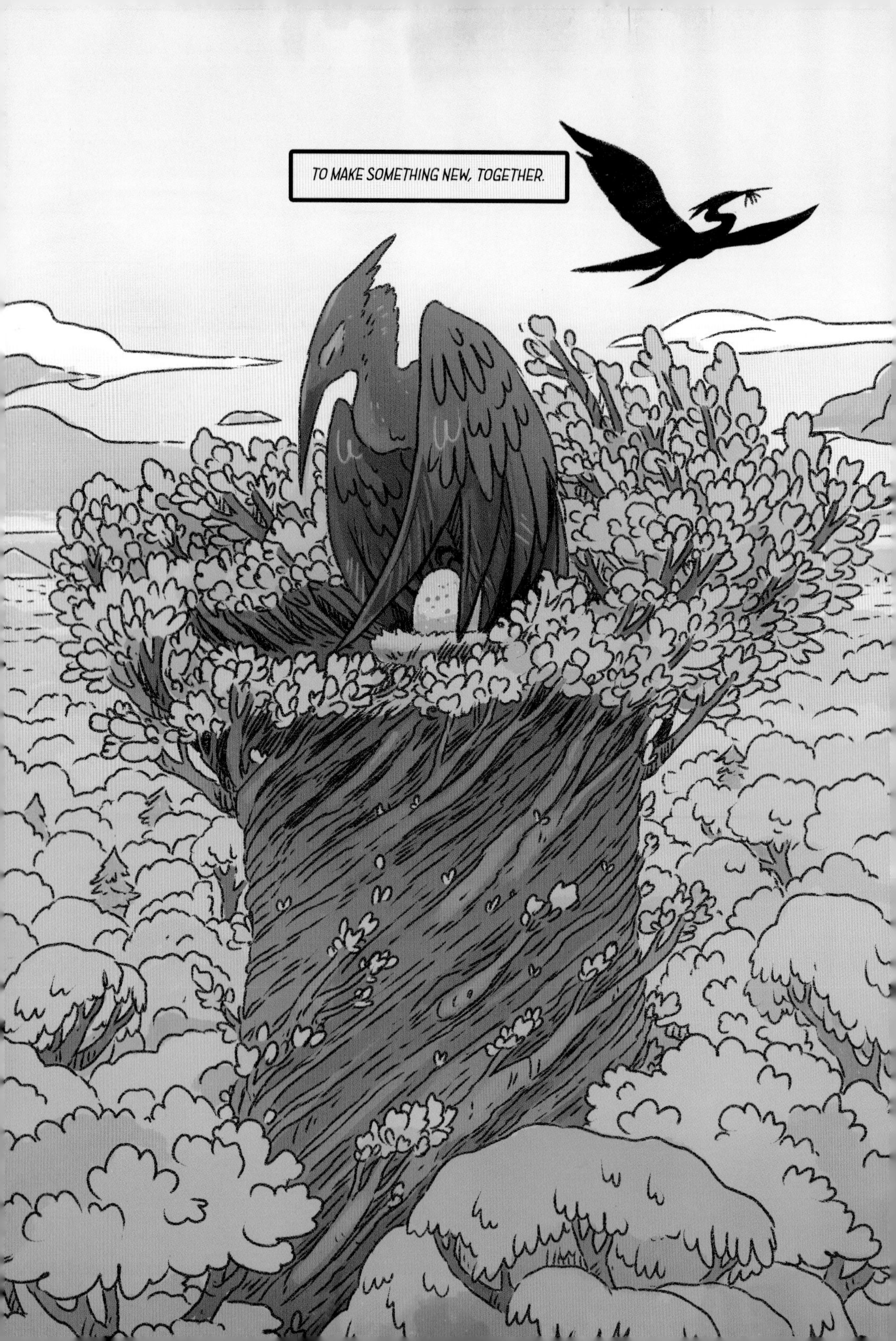
TO MAKE SOMETHING NEW, TOGETHER.

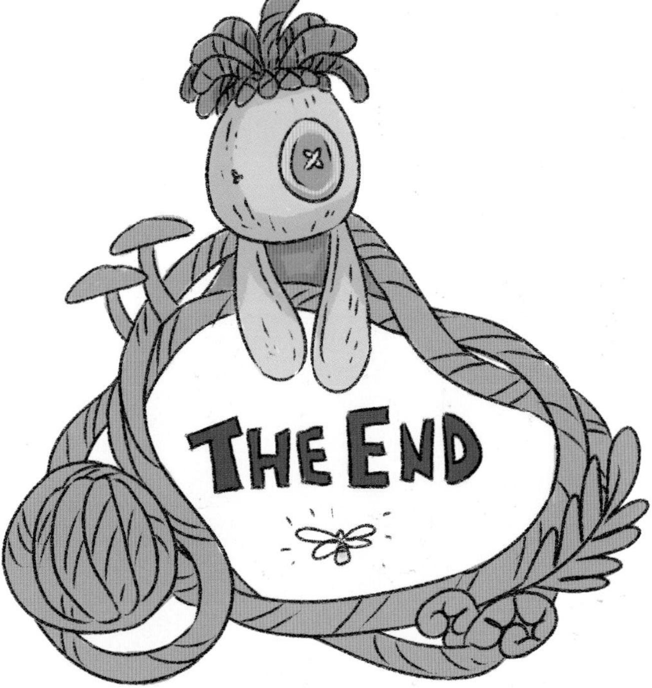
THE END

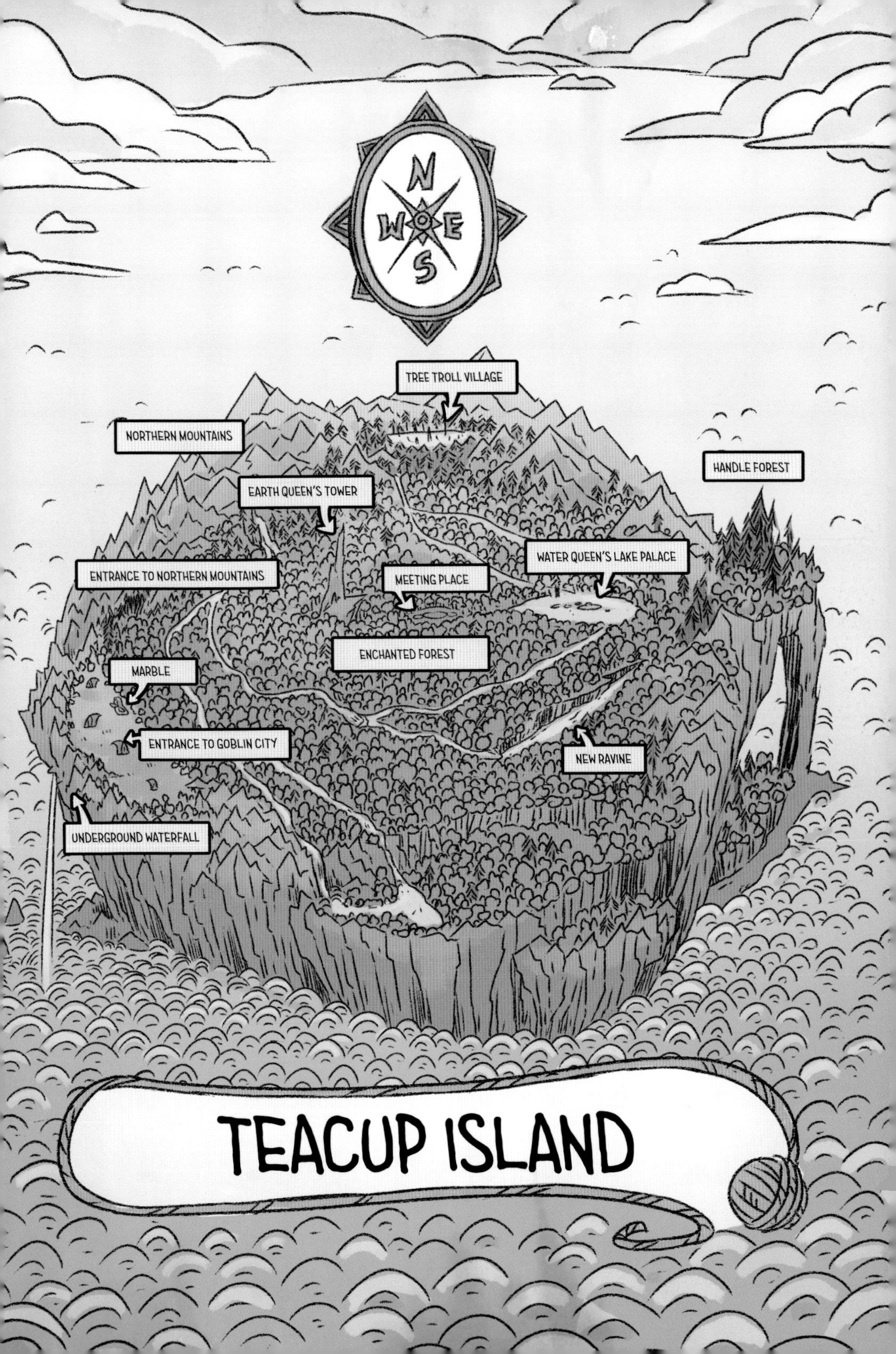
N
W
E
S
TREE TROLL VILLAGE
NORTHERN MOUNTAINS
HANDLE FOREST
EARTH QUEEN'S TOWER
WATER QUEEN'S LAKE PALACE
ENTRANCE TO NORTHERN MOUNTAINS
MEETING PLACE
ENCHANTED FOREST
MARBLE
ENTRANCE TO GOBLIN CITY
NEW RAVINE
UNDERGROUND WATERFALL
TEACUP ISLAND

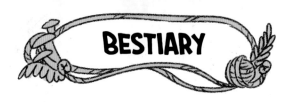

BESTIARY

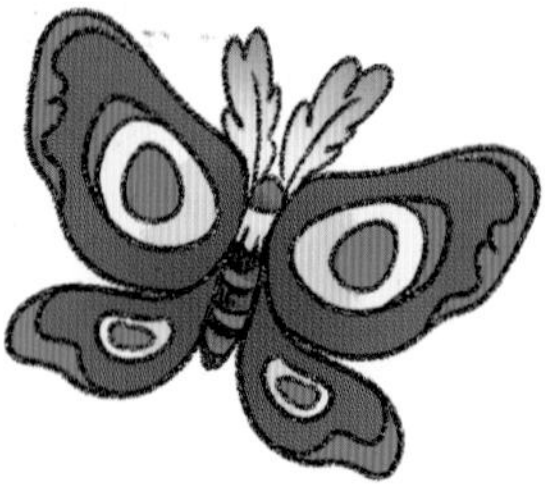

EYEWING MOTH

IT'S NOT POISONOUS OR CANNIBALISTIC. THESE MOTHS HELP POLLINATE THE FLOWERS WHOSE NECTAR THEY DRINK.

FYGBORE

A SMALL ARTHROPOD THAT LAYS ITS EGGS IN UNRIPE FYGS, THEN EATS THE RIPE INSIDES OF THE FRUIT SO THE PEEL BECOMES CAMOUFLAGE FOR ITS OWN SOFT BODY.

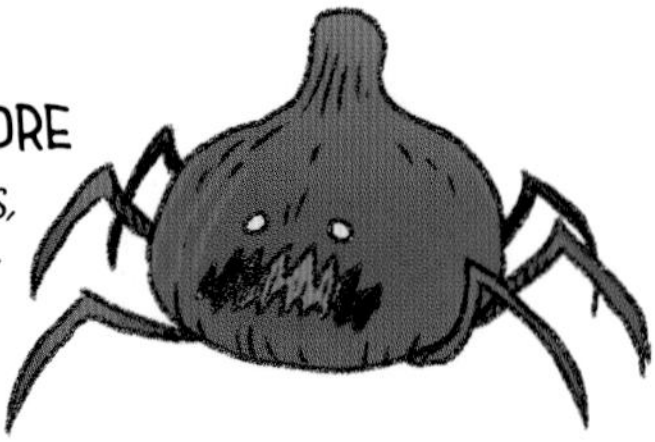

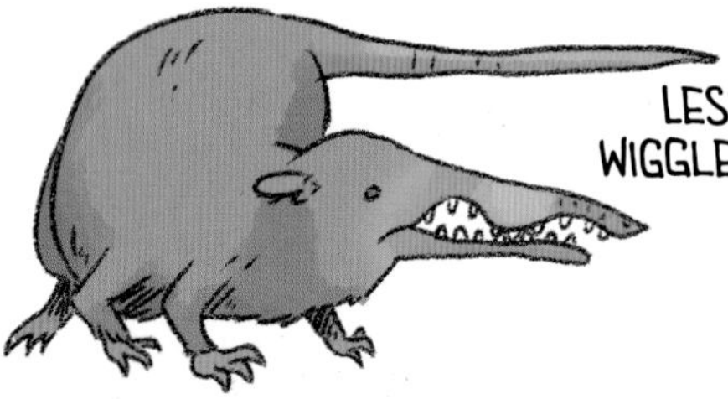

LESSER WIGGLESNOOT

A PRIMITIVE SIX-LEGGED MAMMALOID THAT IS EXTINCT ON THE MAINLAND BUT ENJOYS EATING THE NUTRITIOUS BUGS OF THE ENCHANTED FOREST.

PLIDER

THIS PACK-HUNTING ARTHROPOD WITH A SOFT BODY AND SWIFT LEGS CAN SHOOT STICKY WEBBING TO ENSNARE ITS PREY.

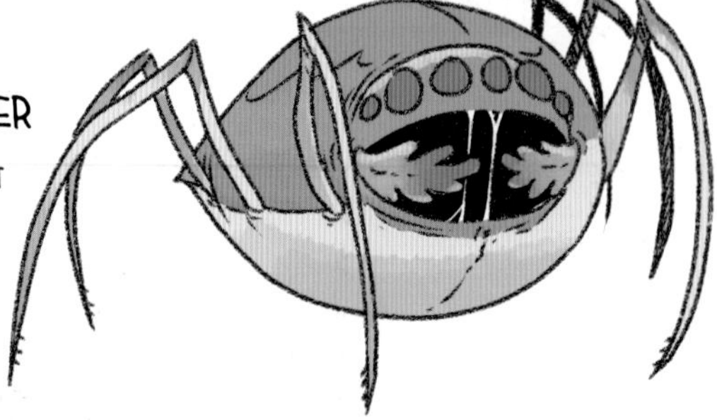

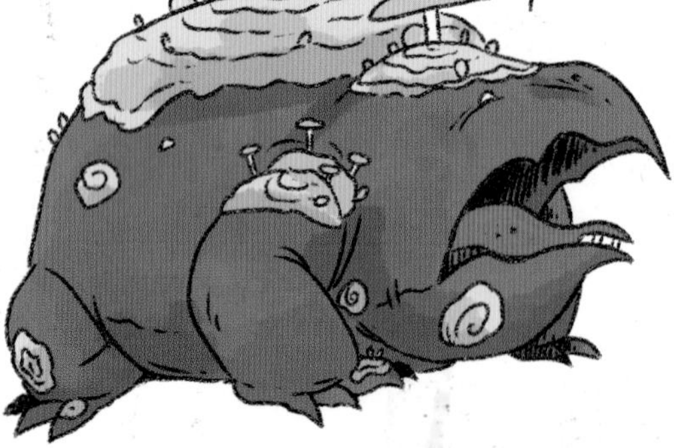

BOGGET

MOSTLY STATIONARY AMPHIBIAN PREDATOR WHO RELIES ON CAMOUFLAGE TO HIDE FROM BIGGER PREDATORS AND AMBUSH PREY.

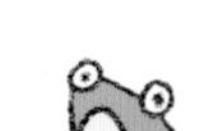

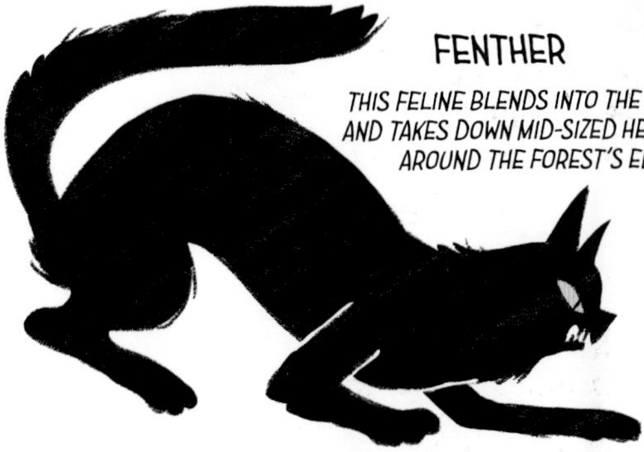

FENTHER

THIS FELINE BLENDS INTO THE SHADOWS AND TAKES DOWN MID-SIZED HERBIVORES AROUND THE FOREST'S EDGE.

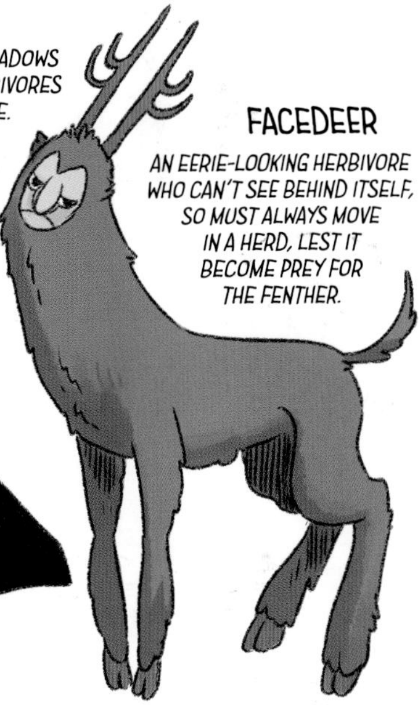

FACEDEER

AN EERIE-LOOKING HERBIVORE WHO CAN'T SEE BEHIND ITSELF, SO MUST ALWAYS MOVE IN A HERD, LEST IT BECOME PREY FOR THE FENTHER.

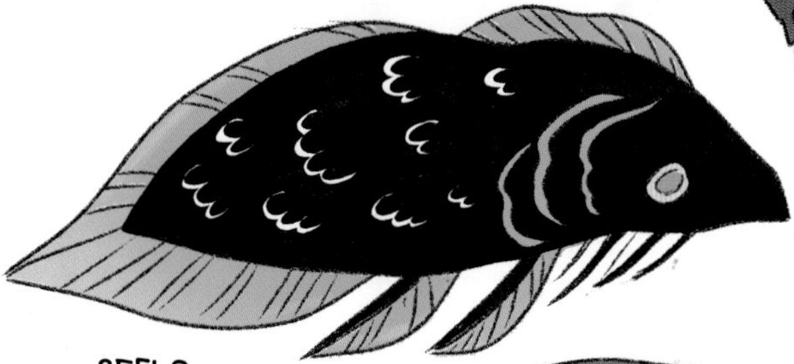

SEELO

A LARGE AND MYSTERIOUS FRESHWATER FISH THAT FEEDS ON THE SMALLER FISH ATTRACTED TO THE GLOWING PODS OF THE WATER QUEEN'S PALACE.

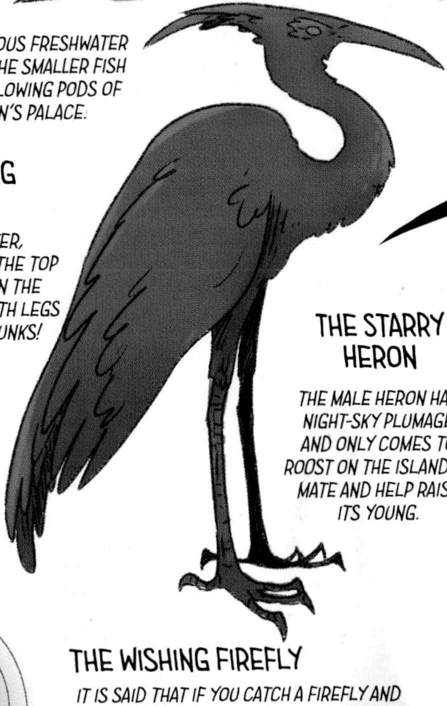

THE STALKING HERON

A VORACIOUS HUNTER, THE FEMALE HERON IS THE TOP OF THE FOOD CHAIN IN THE ENCHANTED FOREST, WITH LEGS THE SIZE OF TREE TRUNKS!

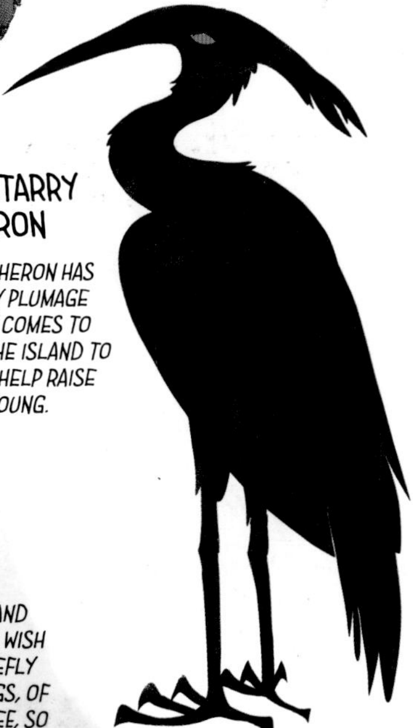

THE STARRY HERON

THE MALE HERON HAS NIGHT-SKY PLUMAGE AND ONLY COMES TO ROOST ON THE ISLAND TO MATE AND HELP RAISE ITS YOUNG.

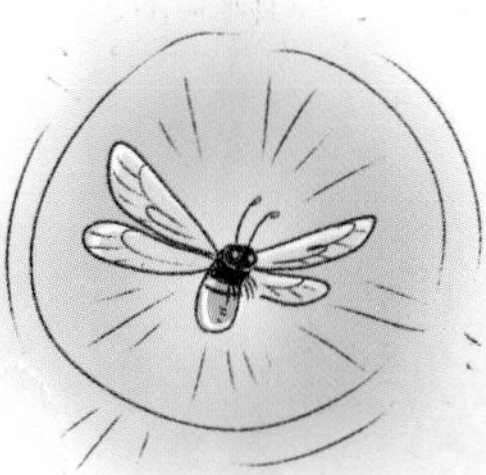

THE WISHING FIREFLY

IT IS SAID THAT IF YOU CATCH A FIREFLY AND MAKE A WISH, WHEN YOU RELEASE IT, YOUR WISH WILL RISE UP TO THE STARS WITH THE FIREFLY AND SOMEDAY IT WILL COME TRUE. THE BUGS, OF COURSE, ALWAYS JUST WISH TO BE SET FREE, SO THE LEGEND HELPS ENSURE THAT, AT LEAST!

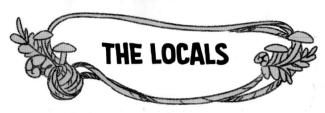

THE LOCALS

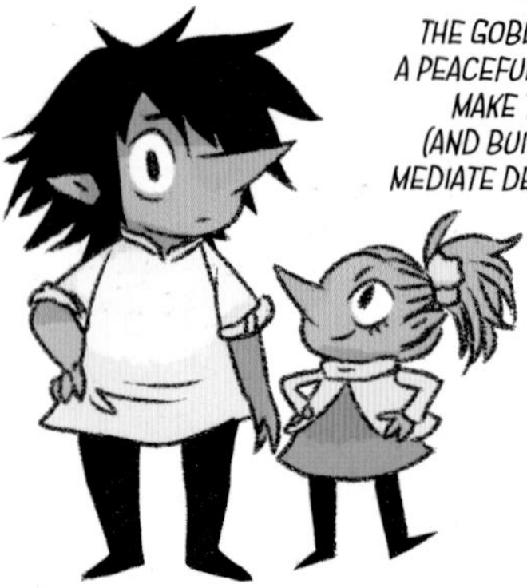

GOBLINS

THE GOBLINS OF TEACUP ISLAND ESCAPED WAR ON THE MAINLAND TO SET UP A PEACEFUL CITY ON THE ISLAND. THEY LOVE TO BUILD AND DESIGN THINGS THAT MAKE THEIR LIVES EASIER AND GIVE THEM MORE TIME TO TELL STORIES (AND BUILD AND DESIGN NEW THINGS!). THEIR THREE COUNCIL ELDERS HELP MEDIATE DECISIONS THAT THE PEOPLE BRING TO REGULAR MEETINGS IN THE CITY CIRCLE, AS WELL AS TEACH CLASSES FOR ALL AGES.

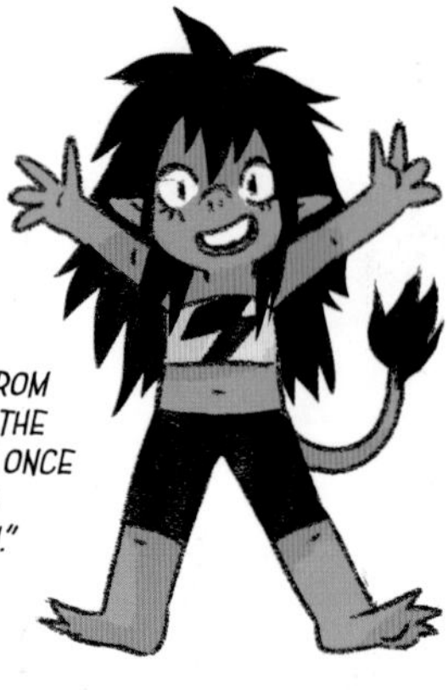

TREE TROLLS

THE TREE TROLLS ALSO CAME FROM THE MAINLAND, DESCENDED FROM A SHIPWRECKED PIRATE CREW. THEY USED THEIR SKILLS CLIMBING THE MASTS OF SHIPS TO MOVE INTO THE TREES AS THEIR ANCESTORS HAD ONCE DONE, AND A FEW GENERATIONS LATER, THEY BECAME SKILLED ARCHITECTS. THEY STILL CALL THEIR ELECTED LEADER "CAPTAIN."

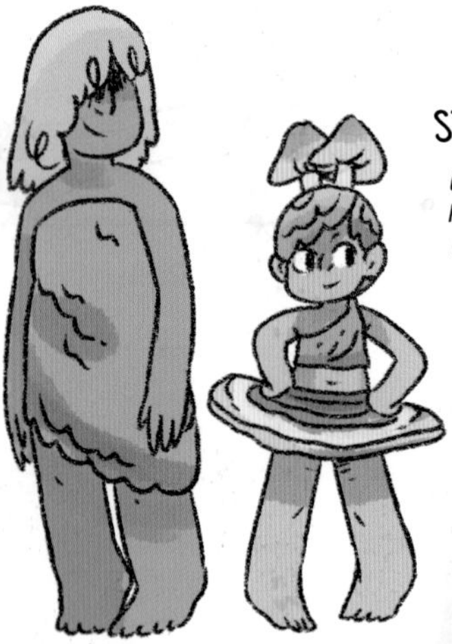

STONE NYMPHS

CREATED BY THE EARTH QUEEN OUT OF THE NATIVE STONE OF TEACUP ISLAND. IF THEY STRAY TOO FAR FROM HER THEY LOSE THE ABILITY TO MOVE UNTIL SHE COMES CLOSER. THEY ARE TOUGH AND STRONG AND DURABLE ENOUGH TO DEAL WITH HER TEMPER TANTRUMS, BUT THEY NEED A BREAK!

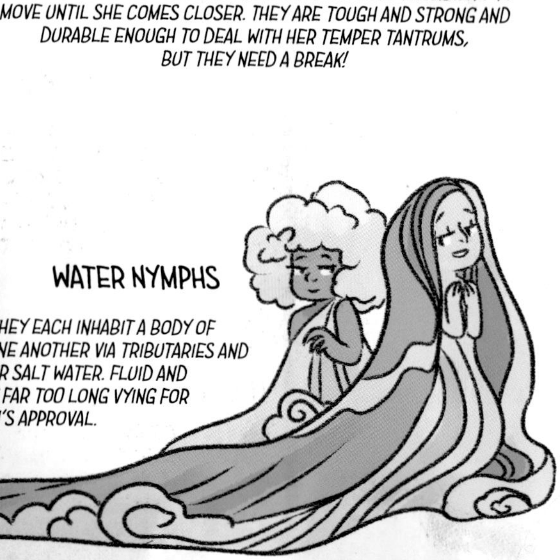

WATER NYMPHS

CREATED BY THE WATER QUEEN, THEY EACH INHABIT A BODY OF WATER, BUT ARE ALL CONNECTED TO ONE ANOTHER VIA TRIBUTARIES AND AQUIFERS. THEY CANNOT ENTER SALT WATER. FLUID AND ADAPTABLE, THEY HAVE SPENT FAR TOO LONG VYING FOR THE WATER QUEEN'S APPROVAL.

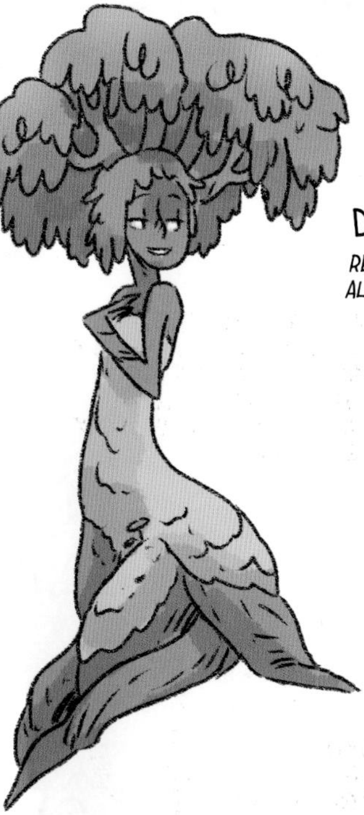

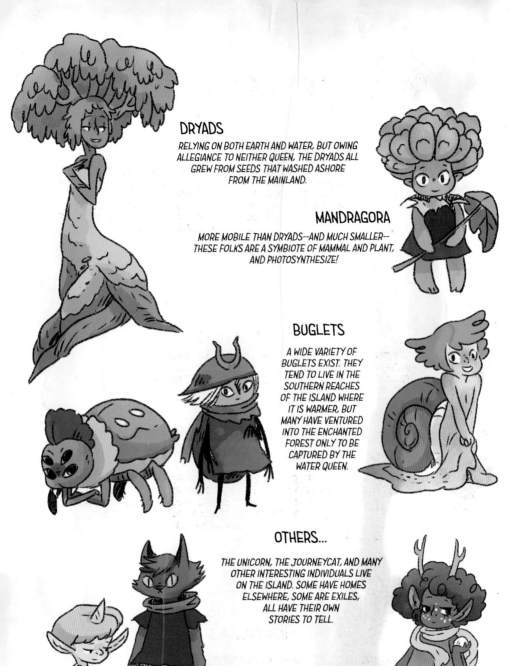

DRYADS

RELYING ON BOTH EARTH AND WATER, BUT OWING ALLEGIANCE TO NEITHER QUEEN, THE DRYADS ALL GREW FROM SEEDS THAT WASHED ASHORE FROM THE MAINLAND.

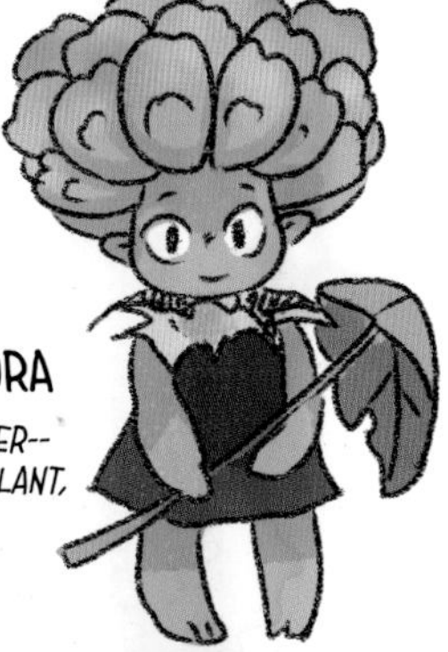

MANDRAGORA

MORE MOBILE THAN DRYADS--AND MUCH SMALLER-- THESE FOLKS ARE A SYMBIOTE OF MAMMAL AND PLANT, AND PHOTOSYNTHESIZE!

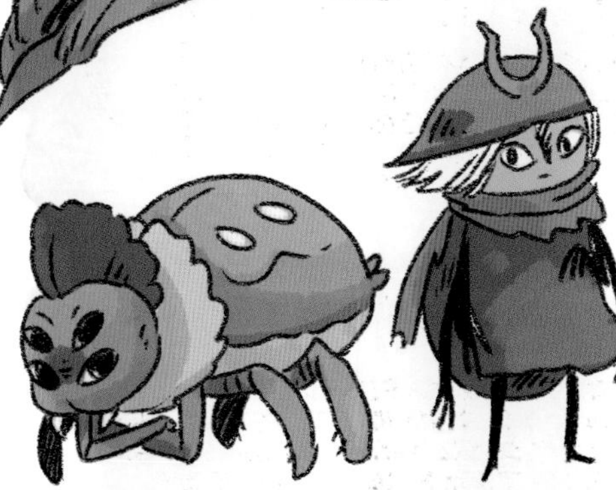

BUGLETS

A WIDE VARIETY OF BUGLETS EXIST. THEY TEND TO LIVE IN THE SOUTHERN REACHES OF THE ISLAND WHERE IT IS WARMER, BUT MANY HAVE VENTURED INTO THE ENCHANTED FOREST ONLY TO BE CAPTURED BY THE WATER QUEEN.

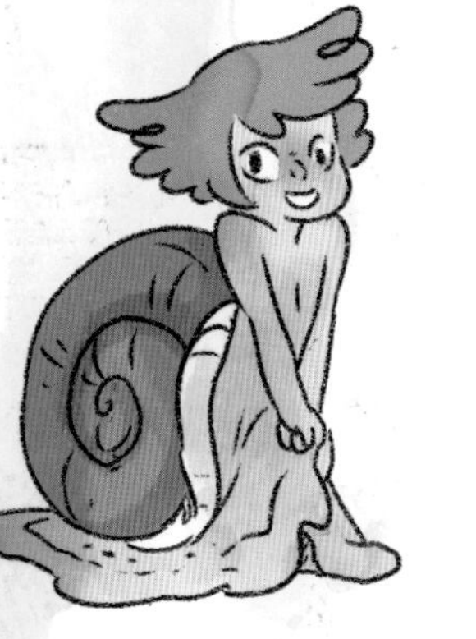

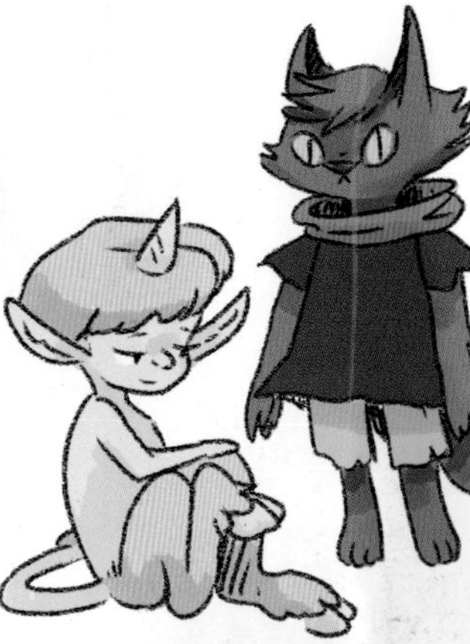

OTHERS...

THE UNICORN, THE JOURNEYCAT, AND MANY OTHER INTERESTING INDIVIDUALS LIVE ON THE ISLAND. SOME HAVE HOMES ELSEWHERE, SOME ARE EXILES, ALL HAVE THEIR OWN STORIES TO TELL.

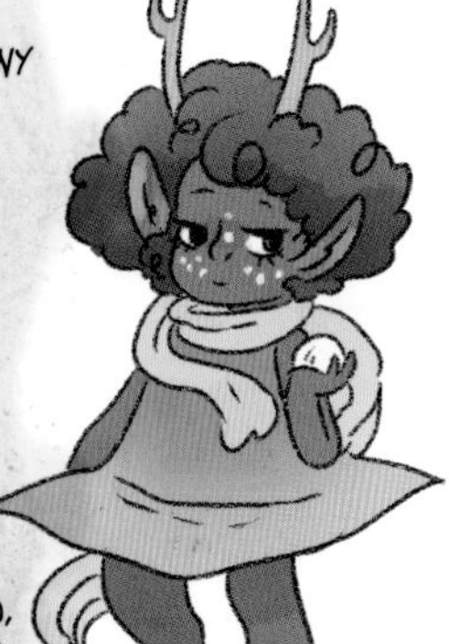

THE DEW FAIRY

THE MOST BEAUTIFUL AND MYSTERIOUS INHABITANT OF THE ISLAND, SHE'S UNIQUE AMONG THE LOCALS, AND NOW THAT SHE'S FREE, NEW MAGIC MAY BEGIN TO WORK ON THE ISLAND...

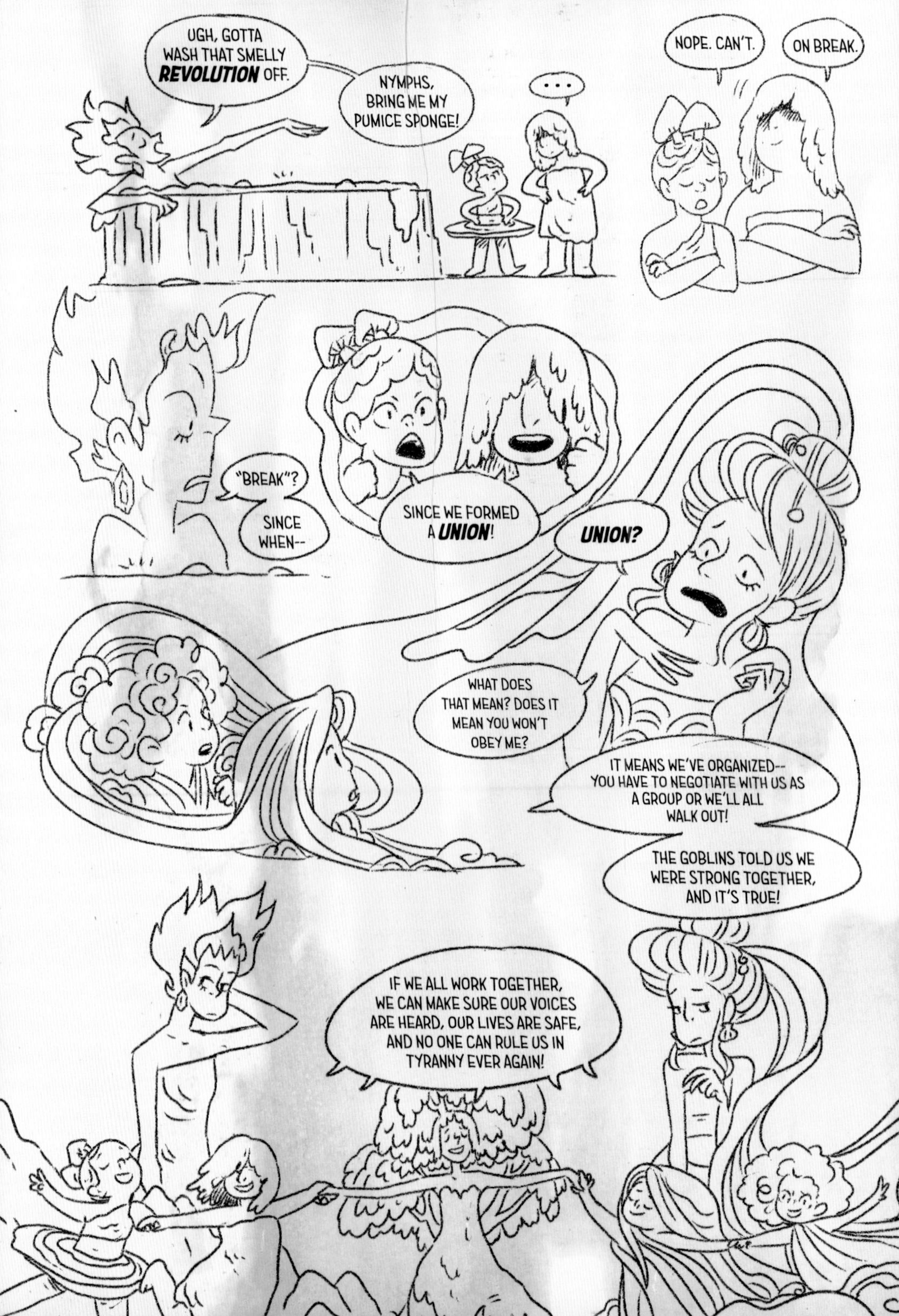
UGH, GOTTA WASH THAT SMELLY **REVOLUTION** OFF.
NYMPHS, BRING ME MY PUMICE SPONGE!
...
NOPE. CAN'T.
ON BREAK.
"BREAK"?
SINCE WHEN--
SINCE WE FORMED A **UNION**!
UNION?
WHAT DOES THAT MEAN? DOES IT MEAN YOU WON'T OBEY ME?
IT MEANS WE'VE ORGANIZED-- YOU HAVE TO NEGOTIATE WITH US AS A GROUP OR WE'LL ALL WALK OUT!
THE GOBLINS TOLD US WE WERE STRONG TOGETHER, AND IT'S TRUE!
IF WE ALL WORK TOGETHER, WE CAN MAKE SURE OUR VOICES ARE HEARD, OUR LIVES ARE SAFE, AND NO ONE CAN RULE US IN TYRANNY EVER AGAIN!

TIME FOR A THANK-YOU PILE!

This is my first author-illustrator book to roam the wild, and while it was a very personal
achievement, it also took so much help from other people to make it happen.
You can't do something this big alone!

Thank you to the team at First Second for all your hard work,
and thanks to my agent, Amy Stern, for everything behind the scenes.
Without the kindness and generosity of my friends and family,
I could never have completed this book, let alone to my satisfaction.
Elle, you counseled me through many bouts of impostor syndrome.
Steph, you inspire me to write better so I can catch up with you!
Rachel, you make me feel like a star.
Jamie, you make me want to work hard!
Caitlin, thank you for luring me out of hermitage with bubble tea.
Hannako, you challenged me to grow and helped me do it.
Stephie and Nike, you believed in me when we were just artist alley kids!
Lucy and MaryEllen, you brightened every week!
Betsey, I will never capture the energy you have, but I'll try!
CJ, you keep me going.
Nathan worked hard to color every character in this book,
and Will fed me breakfast that powered me through dozens of pages.
And of course I owe a special debt to Alan and Jesse,
who taught me how to be a big sister.
Also, Alan taught me how to letter comics, and encouraged me to make better
comics than I knew I could, so that's a lot of lessons from one little brother.
Thank you both for the musical inspiration as well. You are incredible.
There's room in this world for every person to be themselves and make an impact.
Never forget that.

DISCOVER NEW WORLDS WITH :01

First Second
firstsecondbooks.com

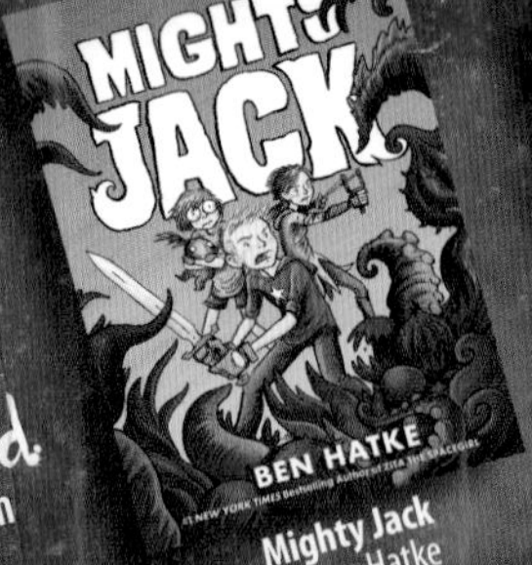
MIGHTY JACK
BEN HATKE
Mighty Jack
by Ben Hatke

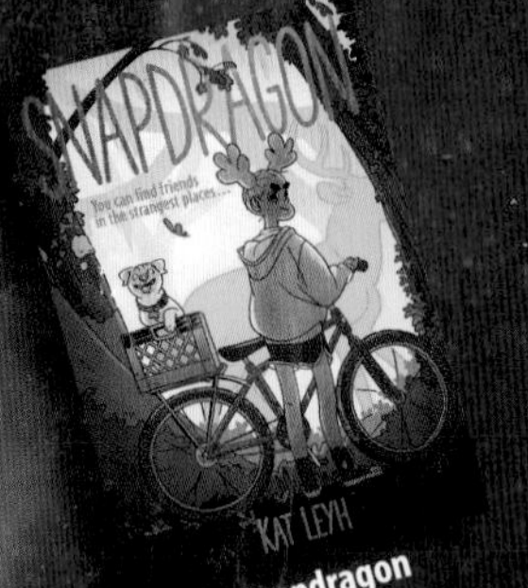
SNAPDRAGON
You can find friends in the strangest places...
KAT LEYH
Snapdragon
by Kat Leyh

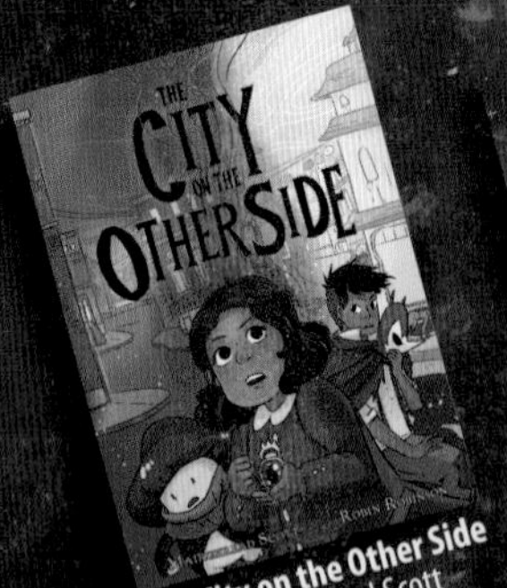
THE CITY ON THE OTHER SIDE
The City on the Other Side
by Mairghread Scott
and Robin Robinson

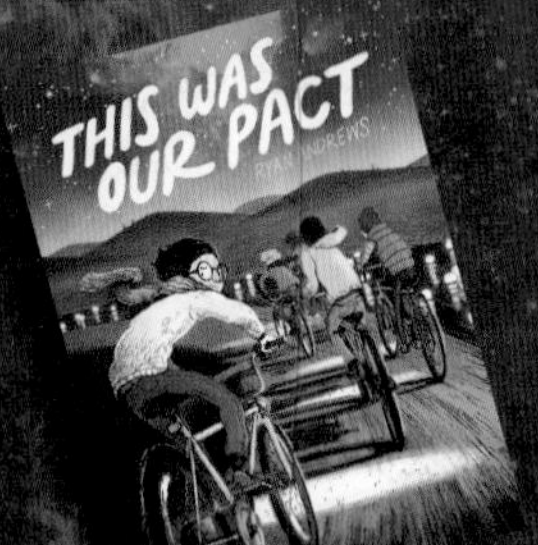
THIS WAS OUR PACT
This Was Our Pact
by Ryan Andrews

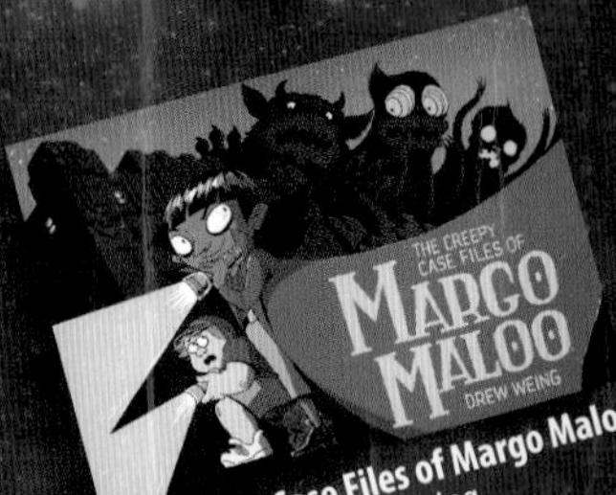
THE CREEPY CASE FILES OF
MARGO MALOO
DREW WEING
The Creepy Case Files of Margo Maloo
by Drew Weing

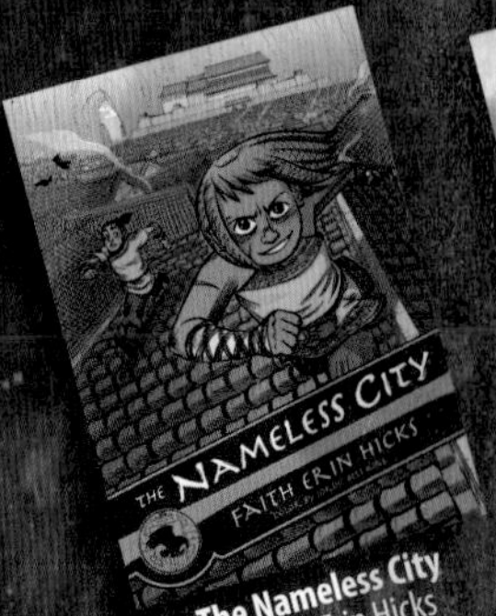
THE NAMELESS CITY
FAITH ERIN HICKS
The Nameless City
by Faith Erin Hicks

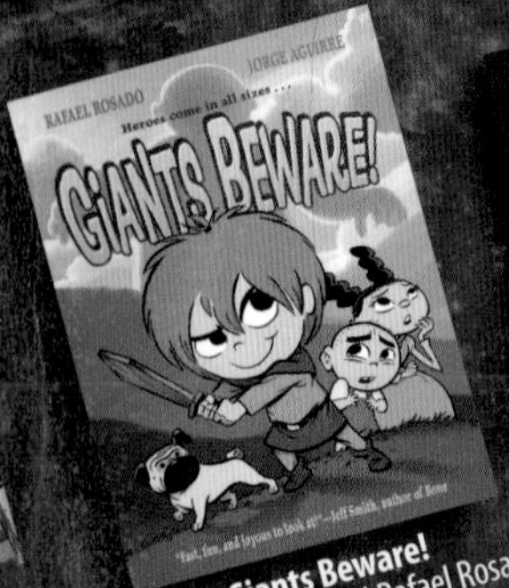
RAFAEL ROSADO
JORGE AGUIRRE
Heroes come in all sizes . . .
GIANTS BEWARE!
Giants Beware!
by Jorge Aguirre and Rafael Rosado

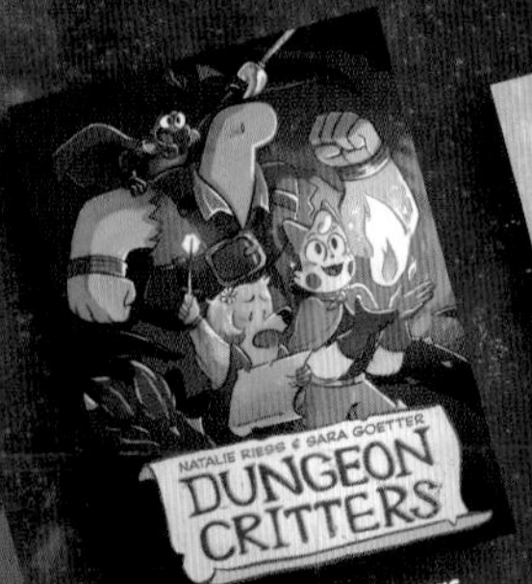
NATALIE RIESS & SARA GOETTER
DUNGEON CRITTERS
Dungeon Critters
by Natalie Riess and Sara Goetter

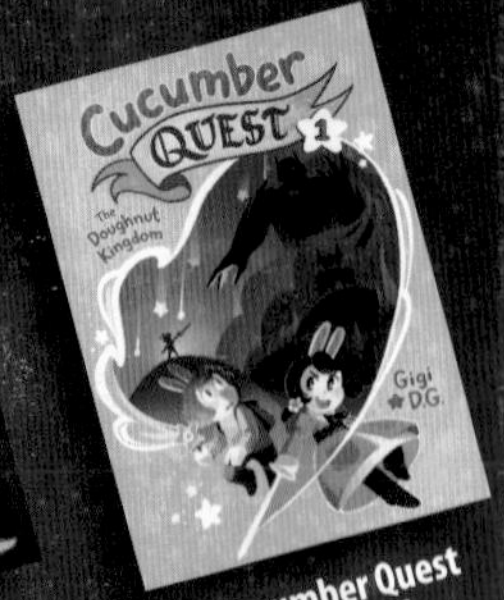
CUCUMBER QUEST 1
The Doughnut Kingdom
GIGI D.G.
Cucumber Quest
by Gigi D.G.

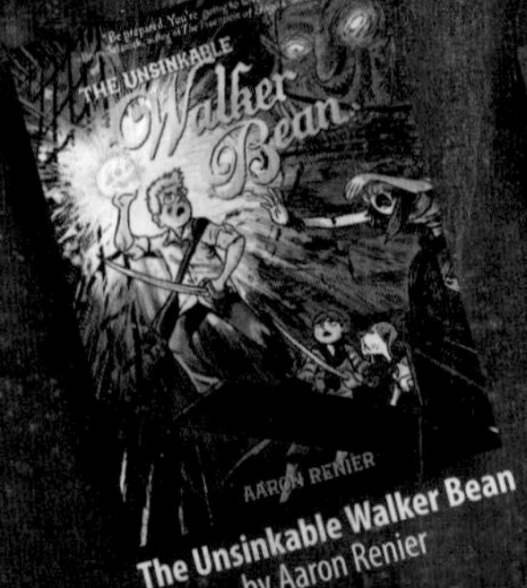
THE UNSINKABLE Walker Bean
AARON RENIER
The Unsinkable Walker Bean
by Aaron Renier

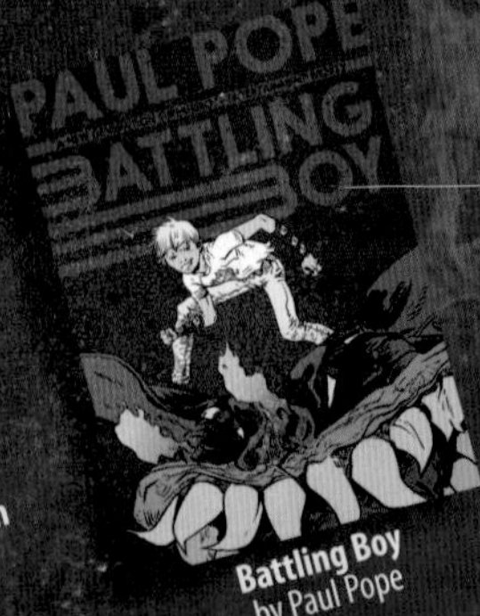
PAUL POPE
BATTLING BOY
Battling Boy
by Paul Pope

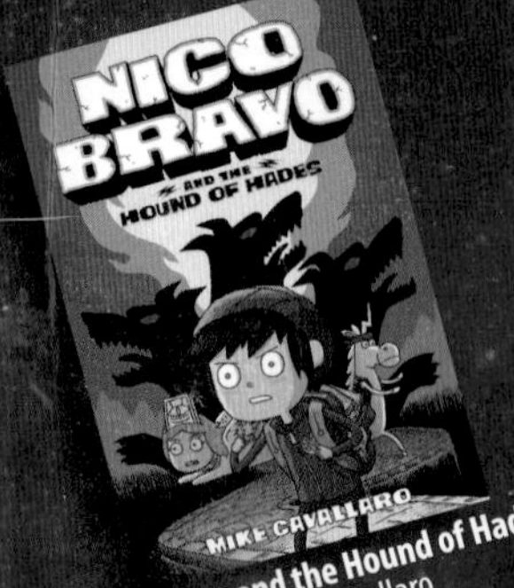
NICO BRAVO
AND THE HOUND OF HADES
MIKE CAVALLARO
Nico Bravo and the Hound of Hades
by Mike Cavallaro

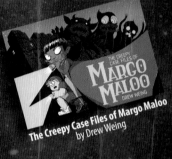